DEFIANT

SONGS OF CHAOS
BOOK 3

MICHAEL R. MILLER

CONTENTS

Foreword   v
The Story So Far Recap   vii

Prologue – Drops of Blood   1
1. Cold Words   9
2. Scrambled Eggs   14
3. A Calling   26
4. The Five   43
5. Rake's Test   60
6. Unknown Songs   73
7. A Dance of Champions   88
8. The Split   96
9. Foundlings and Floundering's   106
10. As Things Were Meant To Be   118
11. Spiritual Studies   129
12. Promises   146
13. The Bard and the Smith   159
14. Rites of Passage   176
15. A Soldier for Hire   196
16. A Check of Will   210
17. Mired in the Morass   219
18. Creepers and Crawlers   232
19. Even Unto Death   245
20. Dark Tunnels, Darker Tidings   253
21. Remembrance   263
22. The Council of Four   278
23. No Choice At All   292
24. In Search of Answers   311
25. Freya's Tale   321
26. Unity or Strife   338
27. Dying Light   356
28. The Outcast   367
29. Lessons in Humility   377
30. The King of Fire   390
31. The White Ape   399
32. Leader of the Pack   417
33. An Old Swine and the Silver Sow   436
34. Blood and Beer   453

35. A Tug of Puppeteers   469
36. To the Edge of the World   486
37. One of a Kind   506
38. A Last Chance   519
39. Disenchantment and Disappointment   525
40. A New Home   545
41. Outlandish Dragon Alchemy   564
42. A Sea of Black and Gold   575
43. Repentance   583
44. Friends of Fire   598
45. Progress, Insight, and Advancement   609
46. The Want to Forgive   626
47. The Great Chasm   644
48. The War Begins   655
49. Healing Truths   669
50. Defiant   682
51. Monsters   689
52. Consequences   705
53. The Fall   718
54. Here to Help   729
55. Letting Go   740
56. To Dream Beyond the Dream   748
57. The Most Useful Servant   758
   Epilogue – Defining Destiny   766

   Afterword   771
   Acknowledgments   773
   Also by Michael R. Miller   775
   Songs of Chaos DnD 5E   777

FOREWORD

Hi everyone! Before you dive into *Defiant*, I'd like to cover a few quick topics.

First, I want to say a big thank you to everyone who has reached *Defiant*. Your support of the series is what enables me to keep writing it.

I'll also get the usual disclaimer out of the way that I'm a UK author writing these books in US English. This is due to Amazon only allowing one file to be uploaded, and with the US being the larger market, it makes the most sense. I hope my UK readers will understand. There may be some phrases or words remaining which aren't commonly used in US English, so I hope my US readers will also be understanding if they come across them.

I've had a lot of requests for a series Wiki or appendices with added information. Developing a full Wiki is too great a task for me to do on top of writing the books and would be a major distraction, but I've now written a glossary that covers the magic system used in the series with specific details on Holt's magical abilities.

There's also now a world map for the *Songs of Chaos* series, created by the wonderful cartographer Soraya Corcoran. You can find both the map and the glossary on my website.

In *Defiant*, the chapters shift between different character

POVs, and the chapters don't run in strictly chronological order. While I do try to keep things chronological as much as I can, sometimes pacing takes precedence.

Since *Unbound* was released, I've also noticed some confusion among listeners and readers as to the length of *Songs of Chaos*. Right now, I envision the series will be five books in total. This means that after *Defiant*, we have two more to go. This could change, of course, but that doesn't seem likely. If it does change, it will be to make the series longer, but my gut tells me that five books will be the right length.

These books do take me quite a while to get right, so if you want to stay up to date on my progress, there are multiple places you can do so. I keep a progress update on my website, on my Discord server, on my subreddit, on Facebook, and via my mailing list. If you want to be sure of getting updates, I'd suggest joining my mailing list or Discord server, as they're the most reliable. If you join either of those, you'll receive a link to a free novella about Brode and Erdra, as well as a bonus story from the world of my first series, *The Dragon's Blade*.

Lastly, many readers have emailed me asking about hardback editions and signed editions. Right now, the best way to get ahold of signed hardback editions of *Songs of Chaos* is by visiting The Broken Binding's bookstore online. I'm sure many of you have bought special editions from them already.

You can find links to all of these channels and to the signed hardbacks on my website at www.michaelrmiller.co.uk.

THE STORY SO FAR RECAP

If you recently read or re-read *Ascendant* and *Unbound*, you can probably skip this recap and jump right into *Defiant*. For everyone else, this is a very brief – I repeat, VERY brief – recap of the story so far, especially of *Unbound*. By its nature, it cannot cover every nuance, but hopefully it can jog your memory if it's been a while.

Holt Cook and his blind dragon Ash helped to save the Kingdom of Feorlen against impossible odds, but despite their efforts Holt was still banished from society as a 'role breaker.' Judged harshly by the Order of dragon riders, Holt and Ash also refused to swear the oath to join the Order. Tasked by the Life Elder to find the Elder Dragons and convince them to join the fight against the scourge, Holt and Ash were beset by dangers in the wild from agents of the dragon Thrall and members of the Order itself.

After scattering Brode's ashes to rest alongside his dragon, Holt and Ash were reunited with the half-dragon Rake, who came to recruit them for a dangerous mission. That mission was to kill Thrall, end the threat he posed, and save the dragon eggs now in his possession.

Along the way, they recruited more companions to join them in this daring mission. Aberanth, a stunted brown emerald dragon with an unusual interest in human scientific techniques. Eidolan, a seven-hundred-year-old mystic dragon who can cast illusions and was formerly part of the Order. And the powerful Wind Champions Farsa and Hava.

As part of the preparations for this mission, Rake locked Holt and Ash in a network of scourge tunnels under the lands of Ahar, where they endured weeks of hunger and battle but managed to grow their bond to the level of Champion.

Holt also worked alongside Aberanth to develop jerky that can enhance the magical powers of those who eat it, similar to the cycling elixirs that Aberanth had previously created.

On their way to Thrall's stronghold at Windshear, the team argued over the objective and priority of the mission, leading Rake to strike out on his own to try and kill Thrall. When Holt and the others reached the fortress, they found Rake had been taken captive and decided to try to rescue him. Only help from Talia Agravain managed to distract and panic Thrall enough to abandon the fortress during the rescue, but Holt and the team remained hard-pressed, and sadly they could only save one of the new hatchlings and a single unhatched egg.

Eidolan took the surviving mystic egg with him back to his flight. Osric Agravain – who had been under Thrall's control – broke free of his bond in order to save the small black dragon from death at the hands of Thrall's zealous cultists. Rake wished to kill Osric to make sure he would no longer be a threat, but Holt stopped him on the grounds that he had already bonded with the little black dragon. With nowhere else to go, Osric reluctantly joined the group, who returned to Aberanth's underground grotto in the Fae Forest, while Farsa and Hava (who reached the rank of Lord during the battle) left to return to their posting at Oak Hall.

Holt, Ash, Osric, the black dragon, and Rake decided to stay with Aberanth at his grotto over winter while they recovered, trained, and thought on what their next steps would be. Rake revealed that he and his dragon fused together during an attempt to reach a new rank of power beyond even Lord, wherein the rider would form their own core. Rake hopes that Holt and Ash can succeed where he failed, and once Rake understands the error, he hopes to fix what happened to him.

Talia Agravain was a princess, second in line to the throne of Feorlen. As such, she should never have been allowed to join the dragon riders, and after joining, she should never have been allowed to become Queen of Feorlen. But in the aftermath of the great scourge incursion into her kingdom, orchestrated by Thrall, she faced a terrible choice: to keep her oath as a rider and allow her kingdom to fall into war and ruin as it searched for a new monarch, or break her oath, take the crown, and spare Feorlen further bloodshed.

Talia chose to accept the crown but, in so doing, angered not only the dragon riders but also other great powers of the world. Political opponents in the realms of Risalia and Athra started forming alliances against her, while Paragon Adaskar, the Fire Paragon and leader of the dragon riders, demanded she renounce her crown and submit to having her bond broken. Desperate to seek stability and security for her kingdom, Talia formed a marriage pact with Prince Fynn Skadison, the third son of Empress Skadi of the northern Skarl Empire. This alliance staved off an invasion from her enemies, if only for a while.

Meanwhile, Talia and Pyra also worked alongside the Life Elder and the Emerald Flight to combat the scourge in new ways. After heading to the Withering Woods, they led an expedition down into the network of scourge tunnels freshly opened from the recent incursion. Underground, they suffered great casualties due in part to Pyra and Talia's hot-headedness. Despite the losses, the mission was ultimately successful. Talia discovered a chamber deep underground with a strange orb that, once destroyed, turned the remaining scourge in Feorlen wild and feral, causing them to attack each other and scatter.

Concluding that these orbs were vital for the scourge to hold any cohesion, they set about trying to discover other possible locations. Talia also thought they owed it to the riders to take this new discovery to them, and so she flew to Falcaer Fortress to tell the Paragons directly. Talia hoped this news might spur the Order into locating more of these control orbs and assist her rather than oppose her. However, Paragon Adaskar refused to help her, claiming her actions were incredibly dangerous. By opening up scourge tunnels long since sealed, she threatened the world. Adaskar gave Talia a chance to submit and have her bond broken, but Talia refused. Instead, she gave an impassioned speech to the gathered riders of Falcaer about her plan to take the fight to the scourge rather than fight a strategy of containment. A small number of riders joined her, but sadly no Lord or Lady.

When another chamber location was found on Feorlen's southern coast, Talia led a better-prepared force of soldiers and riders into the depths, where they fought inside another great chamber with a control orb. This time, a powerful entity spoke to Talia through one of her guards, revealing itself as the controlling mind of the whole scourge. This 'Hive Mind' asked her to keep destroying the control orbs so that Thrall's control over the scourge would be weakened. It was clear that the Hive Mind was not yet so dominated by Thrall as to not have some agency of its own. These events distracted Thrall enough to allow Holt to rescue Rake at Windshear Hold.

Talia returned to the surface to find Paragon Adaskar and a group of Lords waiting for her. Adaskar revealed he and the other Paragons had long known of a dark creature in the depths but decided the best policy was to contain it rather than try to locate and destroy it. Too many riders had lost their minds in the attempt or become puppets of the Hive Mind.

Adaskar was prepared to break Talia's bond right there in order to prevent her continuing to open tunnels, threatening a greater scourge incursion, but the presence of the West Warden and many dragons of the Emerald Flight made the Paragon think twice. Breaking Talia at that moment would have required fighting a Wild Flight, which would have violated the terms of the Pact the dragon riders have with all the Elder dragons.

Ultimately, Adaskar left rather than fight, but he views Talia and her 'New Order' as a genuine threat to the entire world, believing that their actions will have grave unintended consequences.

Storm Peaks

Reaving River

Northern Tear

◇ Smidgar

SKARL EMPIRE

Skipta

Roaring
Fjord

◇ Groef

Claw
Point

Brekka

◇ Upsar

FORNHEIM

FJARRHAF

Bitter
Bay

Vardguard ◇

S
Sp

Stroef ◇

Haldask River

RISALIA

Drakburg

Port
Bolca

Wismar

Azure

The Crag

WITHERING
WOODS

Red

Toll Pass

Red Rush

Midbell ◇

Sidastra

Sunset Sea

Howling Hills

FEORLEN

Range

Sable
Spire

Mort Morass

BRENIN

Versand River

Ruin
Ald

Laone ◇

The Stretched S

S

Scalding Sea

JADE

LAKARA

JUNGLE

Songs of Chaos

WHITE WILDERNESS

hite
atch

Dead Lands

FALLOW
FRONTIER

pine

rost Fangs

Windshear
Hold

Oak Hall

Brown Wash

COEDHEN

Bright Wash

FAE FOREST

Grim Gorge

IRA

Red Rock

Loch Awe

DISPUTED
LANDS

The Serpentine

Ruins of
Freiz

caer
tress

eat Chasm

MITHRAS

Alamut

Squall
Rock

ING SANDS

Negine
Sabra

AHAR

een Way

The Caged
Sea

gkor

PROLOGUE – DROPS OF BLOOD

Paragon Adaskar and his dragon Azarin flew north from Falcaer Fortress. Between rider headquarters and the city-state of Athra lay tracts of once fertile farmland, abandoned in the seven centuries since the Great Chasm's eruption laid waste to Aldunei. The only remnant of that great civilization was the Vectigalia, a wide, well-maintained highway built on the deep foundations of the old republic's northern road.

From on high, Adaskar passed over dozens of supply caravans. These carried the tithes of goods and materials from across the western and northern world to Falcaer. Long trains of cattle, sheep, and other beasts were also being herded along. All tithes flowed into Athra and from there down to Falcaer, save for those tributes from Mithras, Ahar, and Lakara, which were brought up from the coast of the Stretched Sea.

Athra's control over the flow of tithes granted the city special prominence in the calculations of the Paragons. When the Archon of Athra spoke his mind, even Adaskar found himself forced to listen. Today, at least, it had been Adaskar who summoned the Archon to a meeting.

They flew onward, veering off into wilder country where crumbling ruins were the norm and tall weeds stood in place of wheat fields. A thin layer of early season snow turned to ice completed the desolation.

After a time, they came upon the site of an old villa. It would have been grand in its heyday, a senatorial estate with walls to defend the farmers who tilled the land. No longer. The roof was missing, and the countryside rose in vines and thorns to pull the house back to the earth. Today, however, life had returned to the villa, and men and horses could be seen in and around the old estate in great numbers.

Azarin's bulk forced him to land outside the walls, out of sight of the Athrans and their steeds. His presence melted the nearby ice at once and caused the horses to whinny in high-pitched fright.

"Let us be swift," Azarin said.

Adaskar intended to be. He wore a black gambeson under his full brigandine, a burning red to match Azarin's molten scales, replete with golden studs and golden thread, and, striking a powerful image, he strode into the estate.

A heavy smell of horse met him, though it was clean, like the tang of salt air or freshly cut wood. Servants, senators, and high-ranking cavalrymen alike withdrew from him, their heads bowed beneath winter cloaks. The horses, however, tried to keep him in their vision, assessing the threat. Many of them wore cloth or armor more expensive than the people, and the Archon's steed – a palomino stallion of great stature, armored head to flank in a chaffron, crinet, and crupper of white steel with blue etchings – stood out as the most resplendent.

Ahead, the villa's entrance was marked by a standard bearer who alone of the Athrans stood firm, though he also lowered his gaze as Adaskar approached. Atop the flagpole was the city's banner, a palomino's head with its neck wreathed in a laurel crown upon a red field. Presently, the flag hung limp in the still air.

Adaskar crossed the threshold of the villa to find the delegation in a flurry of activity. When a servant rushed to meet him, she fell to her knees and raised a bowl so fast that water sloshed over its rim. Adaskar washed his hands and dried them with a casual use of his power. As the steam left his skin, the servant bobbed away, and several high-ranking Athrans scurried out to meet him. They wore dark riding jackets, cream jodhpurs, and tall black boots flecked with mud.

At the head of their string was the Archon himself. He too wore the formal equestrian fashion of the city, though his colors alone matched the city's flag. His tan velvet riding jacket covered a crisp red shirt, the cuffs of which were large and stiff around his wrists, while his jodhpurs were wine red and descended into tawny boots.

A man in his fiftieth year, the Archon was lean of frame, with shrewd eyes and pale brows. His white-gold hair once matched the mane of his palomino stallion but had since receded to leave him with an appropriate horseshoe of hair. Most importantly, upon his head, he wore the city's civic crown – a chaplet of woven hay, seasonal flowers, and branches bearing red currants.

Adaskar drew close to him and said in a low voice, "Let's dispense with the ceremonies."

"As you will."

The Archon pronounced every word with the same precision with which he rode. It was said the Athrans had a neutral accent, yet they claimed their voice to be the true voice of Aldunei, the origins of all, and any difference from them was the fault of those who broke away. That the Skarls and Adaskar's own people in Ahar never fell under the sway of the old republic did not affect this assertion.

"Leave us," the Archon said to his officials, before gesturing for Adaskar to follow him into an inner courtyard, where brick dust salted every drawn breath. A battered and color-worn mosaic lay in the ground between six decaying columns and makeshift tables of flat-cut hay bales had been arranged. The bales were covered with fine cloth and laden with food and drink.

Adaskar took a seat on one of the smaller bales, and the Archon gestured at the table, saying, "Khosh amadi" to welcome Adaskar in his own language.

Adaskar nodded appreciatively. A glance at the food on offer confirmed much of it had been specially made for a fire rider, including peppers that were so large they had the appearance of whole fish and such a dark green they might have been black. These were the hottest, finest chilies from the Jade Jungle. It must have been expensive to haul them all the way to Athra.

From across the bond, Adaskar felt Azarin's pleasure as he tore into a haunch of beef, roasted for hours in a blend too hot for human consumption.

Adaskar accepted a goblet of red wine and drew in a deep sniff of its deeply spiced scent; it tickled pleasingly at the back of his throat.

"Dastet dard nakone," Adaskar said to thank him.

In reply, the Archon presented his palms to show they were unharmed. Such a gesture was usually only made by Aharis speaking to each other. Translated literally, the Ahari, 'Thank you' came out as 'May your hands not hurt.' A display of clean, uninjured hands signaled, 'It was no trouble at all.'

The simple efficiency of 'Thank you' and 'You're welcome' in Alduneian Common was much more to Adaskar's liking, though he arranged his expression to look more pleased than he was. Better to let the Archon think he was being softened up.

The Archon poured a regular red into his own goblet, raised it, and said, "Noosh."

Adaskar raised his goblet in return. "Noosh."

Then he drank of the wine. Thickened from slow simmering, it was closer to syrup, and its intense heat satisfied even his cravings and warded off the winter chill.

"Feel free to speak in our common tongue," Adaskar said.

The Archon smiled and inclined his head. He reached for a piece of thick, heavily oiled bread coated in chopped olives and sundried tomatoes.

Adaskar set his goblet down, then selected one of the huge dark chilies. He cycled fire to the tips of his middle and index fingers, then ran them over the chili to blister its skin. He charred the stalk too, then ate the smoking pepper whole, stalk and all.

Looking pleased, the Archon swallowed his bread, sipped at his own drink, then leaned forward, eagerness clear in his eyes.

"Has a decision been reached?"

"No," Adaskar said bluntly.

The Archon hesitated, expecting more. "Have you called a vote yet?"

"No."

The Archon frowned. "Why not?"

"The matter is not so out of hand. I have not recalled the Paragons."

"Have not? Or will not?"

Across the bond, Azarin's fires stirred. *"Warn him that I shall feast on his horse next if he cannot show respect."*

Adaskar dispersed his dragon's anger with well-practiced cycling.

"I *have not*," he emphasized, his voice crackling as a wisp of smoke escaped his throat. "And I would prefer not to resort to it. But I will. If you fail."

The fact he was unsure if Vald would vote in the affirmative was information the Archon did not need to know.

The Archon placed a hand on his chest and made a breathy laugh. "If I fail?

This time, Adaskar allowed a flicker of Azarin's rage to flow upward to his head. It gathered behind his eyes, causing them to flash red. That cooled the Archon like a bucket of ice water.

The Archon of Athra straightened his expression as though he were smoothing wrinkles from a coat. "Forgive my tone, Paragon. I am only anxious to remove the girl. To set the world straight."

Adaskar growled.

Still holding his gaze, the Archon sipped more of his wine, swirled his goblet, then looked at Adaskar's goblet sitting on the hay table and asked, "Is the wine not to your satisfaction?"

"It is not the custom of Ahari to drink while eating."

To the Archon's credit, if he was fazed by this oversight, he did not show it. Instead, he sipped his own wine again, holding Adaskar's eye while he did so.

Adaskar reached for a second great chili. As he gently cooked its skin with one finger, he said, "The withdrawal of my riders has strained her resources and alliances as predicted. It will break her in time, but I see no harm in increasing the pressure."

The Archon smacked his lips. "Where would such pressure come from?"

"It would be a shame for her if pirates harassed the ships keeping the Brenin-Skarl trade flowing. Jarls in the western empire still bear sore wounds from the civil war. Were they to be stoked and supplied, there would be a chance of rebellion. In Brenin, her uncle is reluctant to split his barons in two. If King Roland faced increasing raids by bandits, highwaymen, perhaps a free company or two turned to looting—"

"It would be ill luck in the extreme," the Archon interrupted, "for so many misfortunes to befall the girl at once." He nodded heavily and picked at some more of the olive bread. "My senators have no love for her, but even they would be shocked to learn of such misfortunes."

"Of course," Adaskar replied, his breath billowing as a cloud of steam.

The Archon smiled. "Revered Paragon, for one who claims he has no part in politics, you have a keen... theoretical grasp of its workings." The Archon's smile became knowing, something Adaskar did not appreciate.

Does he think me a hypocrite?

"It's a coincidence you should mention such tragedies," the Archon went on, "for I too have thought them possible in such a time of chaos. Pirates and rebels may spring of their own accord, of course, though Free Companies are not known to seek any danger without proper backing.

"Should any company begin ravaging Brenin, let me assure you that Athra would investigate any occurrence thoroughly. Though such investigations can become... expensive. I could not guarantee Athra would fund it, never mind Mithras and Coedhen."

And so they came, in their meandering way, to Adaskar's offer. He was glad the mincing of words had not dragged on any longer. The Paragon of Fire had thought long and hard on this, hated the necessity of it, but recognized the long-term benefits.

Victuals and gold could be gained again, but without order, they had nothing.

"With the world suffering such hardships, Falcaer would be honored to relieve the city-states of their burdens for two years."

"The Senate would appreciate this generosity," said the Archon. He pulled his hay bale chair forward by an inch. "Although, given the expenses I foresee, would the noble riders be willing to assuage seven years of tithes?"

"Seven?" Adaskar said brusquely, forgetting for a moment the dance they were in. Seven was ridiculous.

"Only of gold. Food and other such victuals will be maintained."

"Do such investigations truly command so high a bill?"

The Archon made a non-committal gesture. "Dealing with mercenaries has its dangers."

"Three."

"The Senate will feel most comfortable with seven."

Adaskar blew fresh smoke. He ought not to have let his ire toward Talia show in their previous meetings. The Archon understood how much he wanted this.

"Five," Adaskar offered. Five held power and significance. Five Paragons, five true types of magic. Five years of lost tithes from three city-states seemed a small price to pay to end this mess with minimum damage to the world and the riders.

The Archon feigned being pushed to his limits, then said, "Five it is." He smiled again and returned to his wine. "Can we be sure such unfortunate measures will break her?"

"Nothing is certain except that the scourge will rise again."

"Only," the Archon said, carrying on as though Adaskar had not spoken, "you were sure before that the girl would take the option of breaking her bond rather than face a war."

"War was *thankfully* avoided all the same."

"Oh, of course. Do not mistake me, the Senate was delighted that war was averted."

No thanks to the regiment of heavy horse you lent to the Risalians.

"Still," the Archon said, "a rider in the saddle of any kingdom is of great concern. The Senate yearns for a peaceful resolution, but we must prepare ourselves for the worst."

Azarin scoffed across their bond and outwardly rumbled loud enough that the sound reached them in the courtyard. Horses whinnied again, and calls filled the air as Athrans tried to subdue them. Adaskar shared his dragon's sentiment, and his patience with the Archon's word games ran out.

"I regret every drop of blood that will be spilled as it is," Adaskar said. "Must you dream of turning droplets into rivers?"

The Archon gave him a sour look. "Should Talia fall, Feorlen will be thrown into utter chaos. Her alliances will shatter. Nothing will be certain then. Athra is willing to step in and restore order in such an event. And," he added, a sly smile spreading from cheek to cheek, "isn't restoring order the most important thing of all, Paragon?"

Despite his irritations, despite his disgust at such dealings, Adaskar couldn't help but agree.

1

COLD WORDS

The Life Elder breathed deeply. The air tasted of pine and fresh dew. Beneath his feet, the grass was lush, and snowdrops and pansies showed the first stirring of spring. For the first time in half a year, the mountains felt clean.

Another change came upon the air. The chill from the far north had abated, and its end heralded a deeper shift. Victory might be closer to hand than he'd dared to hope for.

The Life Elder faced north and took off. Over the northern reaches of the Spine he flew, and in his spiritual sight, he beheld the fruits of his flight's labor. Great swathes of the mountains now shone like bright islands amidst a shadowed sea. Much of his and his Wardens' power, as well as the lives of many fine emeralds, had been spent on rolling back the blight to this extent. Given the cost, he could only hope the gamble would be worth it.

Flying north, he fast approached the White Wilderness. Although the frigid northern winds had subsided, his sister was not to be taken lightly. Traveling to the borders of her territory – or that of any of his siblings, for that matter – alone, these days, would be foolhardy, so he summoned his three Wardens to his side.

And so, as he glided high over the world, his Wardens of East, North, and South rose to join him. They entered his slipstream, adding their will to his own. With their aid, he combined his spiritual will with power from his core and crested forth toward the wilderness. The barrier obscuring those lands had indeed fallen, and, sure enough, as the endless white came into view, he found the great blizzard gone and the skies clear once more.

The Life Elder suppressed a roar of triumph.

Not yet. Not until the work is done.

He touched down, and his Wardens flanked him, their presence comforting and reassuring him, and he let them know it.

The South Warden, the most bullish of the three, addressed him privately. *"Take heart, Honored Elder,"* she said. *"Our progress has been greater than ever before. Do not let the words of the white ape distract you."*

If only it were just a distraction. That recent meeting had rocked the Life Elder to the foundations of his soul. Was it even right or just to think of himself as an 'Elder' at all?

Worse, his Warden's arrogance was a vexing reminder of how ignorant dragons had become, and in his frustration, he rounded on her.

"He was no ape. Such an intelligent creature deserves more respect from you."

The Warden's scales were a muted green, browned like the cacti of the southern deserts, and seemed a world apart from these freezing lands. She had flown far and fought hard. Perhaps he should have summoned them all to the fight in Feorlen, for even the West Warden's stubbornness had tempered there, if only a little.

Chided, the South Warden pressed her neck low to the snowy ground.

The Elder softened. What right did he have to claim others to be ignorant? He bade her rise and ordered his Wardens to steel themselves. There were greater fights to be had now, and he swept his gaze back to the endless north.

He didn't have to wait for long.

Across the vastness between them, the Ice Elder said, *"You waste no time, brother."*

It wasn't that his sister's voice was cold; rather, it was *the* cold. To hear it was to court turning blood to ice, and it felt weighted by a heavy, hidden power, as the tip of an iceberg alludes to its greater mass beneath.

From where she spoke, the Life Elder could not say. Out beyond the horizon of the White Wilderness lay another horizon, and then another, until the true domain of ice unfolded at the roof of the world. To communicate across such distances drained even an Elder's power.

"You have felt the retreat of the sickness?" he asked.

"Naturally, and I am relieved to know my flight and domain are once again safe from its encroachment."

A ripple of spiritual power surged from her voice and into the Life Elder's soul, affirming that the terms of their oath were being rightfully fulfilled. Relief flooded him, nearly causing his legs to buckle, but he suppressed his emotions and remained firm.

"The time for our attack draws sooner than expected," he said.

"Does it?"

A painful sliver of a moment passed. He feared hesitation or reluctance from his sister, although her promise to aid him had been sworn on her soul and thus was binding.

"How can you be sure?" the Ice Elder asked, her voice unchanged.

"I have learned much of late. Much that we ought to have known, or perhaps that we forgot. There may be a way to deal a death blow to the scourge."

"This sounds promising, brother, if… vague. I'm afraid I do not fully understand. You speak as if the scourge is a single entity to topple, but crush one bug and a thousand more will surely scuttle out of the depths."

"Crushing one bug does little, you are right to say, as the loss of one hatchling will not ruin a flight. But what if an Elder should fall?"

"I'm not sure I follow."

It was the Life Elder's turn to hesitate. A rapid and silent battle waged within him. Everything would come out in the end, of course, but what should be revealed in the here and now?

The Elder again considered that cold, bitter, faraway presence. His tail curled inward of its own accord, and he decided his sister required only as much detail as it took to secure her assistance. Once matters were settled, there would be time enough to untangle all else. All wrongs could be brought forth, all ills put right.

"I believe there is a dragon out there, a mystic of great power, who has taken hold of a considerable measure of the scourge."

Something changed upon the icy winds. There was a quickening, a tightening, a hurrying. Whether it was excitement or tension was hard to say.

"That is an alarming claim, brother. How could that be? Who is this dragon?"

"He goes by the name of Sovereign. His magic allows him sway over the minds of others, and there is one great mind that he has gained control of."

"You believe the scourge has a guiding mind?"

The Life Elder was pleased his sister was quick on the uptake. He would not expect his brothers of Fire and Storm to understand so readily.

"Some manner of mind, yes." It was a Hive Mind, or so his loyal West Warden had described it, though that report came via Pyra and hers via Talia. There could be errors in such translation. Whatever Talia had encountered had been intelligent and held a strength of will, telepathic power, and clarity of thought and goals at odds with everything they understood of the scourge. *"We hope to learn where and how we might strike it soon."*

"We?" his sister asked, as though relishing some riddle. *"Who is this 'we'?"*

The Life Elder cursed himself. He'd lost strength from his core, but not his wits. On this matter, though, he knew he must hold his tongue. His sister had not pushed for the Pact – that had been their brothers of Fire and Storm – but they had all sworn to obey it. Working closely with one lowly Fire Ascendant in Feorlen would raise little ire, but working with a Paragon of Falcaer certainly would.

He knew his response was taking too long to muster, and he sensed his sister was enjoying it. Snow appeared from nowhere to blow around and tickle his snout. A few flakes blew into his mouth, wetting his tongue.

"Could it be our long-silent sister?" the Ice Elder asked. *"No... For she would be able to tell you all you wished to know."*

"Our sister's foresight is imperfect. She failed to see the consequences of our great mistake."

"Be that as it may, will she join this endeavor?"

"To my disappointment, she won't."

"And our brothers?"

"I have not sought them. They will not look past the measures taken to achieve all that we have."

"We?" Ice asked with a bite. *"Dearest brother, your actions are your own."*

"Which of us can claim innocence?" he said, frustration entering his voice for the first time. *"Our blight scarred the world, but we can undo it."*

"Again with the 'we,' the 'our' – as I recall, the blight was your idea."

The Elder's legs almost buckled again, except this time from crippling shame.

Yes, his idea. His fault and failure. Something in their designs had gone terribly wrong. The original blight could not raise the dead, nor morph creatures into monstrous forms, but the scourge were something else entirely – a magical enhancement to the disease none of them understood, leading to the infection of dragons as well as humans.

He, of all of them, should have known better than to meddle with the natural songs of the world.

"I've met hatchlings with better sense than we had in those spiteful days, sister." The Life Elder drew upon his spiritual will to reinforce his next words. *"You swore to aid me in the coming conflict. Let that be enough for now. Can I be assured of your assistance?"*

"But of course, dear brother. When the time times, Ice will aid you."

2

SCRAMBLED EGGS

Holt watched with apprehension as Osric crouched over the black pot. Wielding the wooden spoon in a reverse grip, the former general stirred eggs as though meaning to crush them.

"Steady on," Holt said. "Fold them gently."

Osric slowed, but barely. Worse, Holt could smell the pot getting too hot for their purposes.

"Take it off the heat."

"Allow me to try," Osric growled. Over the winter, his gray-speckled brown hair and beard had grown out, giving him a beastly look.

Holt watched the eggs drying out before his eyes and bit his lip. Seeing some of their precious supply treated like this made him anxious to wrest the spoon from Osric, though the damage was already done. Eggs could not be saved after the fact.

He continued watching with a heavy heart as Osric spooned his lumpy, rubbery eggs into a bowl and cradled it in the crook of his maimed right arm. He returned to his spot by the fire, his folded gray cloak on one side and his dragon on the other.

The little black dragon – who Holt referred to as Soot – raised her head from the forest floor and sniffed furtively. Osric lowered a spoonful of the eggs under her snout, but after one sniff, she gagged and pulled away.

"Suit yourself," Osric said, then continued to eat.

He didn't even add salt, Holt thought, weeping a little on the inside.

All the same, despite Osric's amateur attempt, it gave him a craving to make eggs of his own. It must have been weeks since he'd last indulged, and their poor hen could only produce one every few days.

Bringing the chicken back from a bartering expedition to Red Rock had been a huge win. The only issue had been Soot. She had assumed it was a meal for her, and Holt had resorted to taking the poor hen underground into Aberanth's care.

He counted the remaining eggs in the basket and decided there was enough for a luxurious breakfast. Well, luxurious by the standards of camping in the Fae Forest.

Ash still slept. Holt wanted to let him rest while they had the chance, for Rake's training regime was relentless, but Rake had left two days ago to check in on the emeralds in the Eastern Grove and had yet to return.

Deciding to take advantage of the time and surprise Ash when he woke, Holt got to work on his own version of scrambled eggs. First, he cleaned the dregs out of the black pot, filled it one-third of the way with water, and set it at a medium height over the fire. For the very best results, he ideally needed a glass bowl. Leaving the water to warm, Holt dashed down into the grotto to grab something suitable. When he returned, the water in the pot was beginning to bubble.

Holt set the glass bowl over the water – secure against the rim of the pot – and threw in a large knob of butter brought from Red Rock. As it melted, he cracked in as many eggs as the pot could comfortably hold, pierced the yolks with his spoon, then stirred gently so that the whites flowed in long ribbons and slowly mixed with the oozing yolks.

It felt like a treat to take his time over something, especially without Rake's frequent asides. Osric and Soot weren't the greatest company, but at least they were quiet.

As he folded the eggs, Holt considered it fortunate that dragons required less food as they aged, or else he'd never be able to feed Ash properly. Rake was centuries old and barely ate, and there were dragons far older than him. Eidolan had eaten little during their time together. He stirred and stirred and wondered whether the Elders ever ate at all.

Within the glass bowl, the eggs turned velvety, and the gentler cooking made them smooth as cream. He took them off the heat and salted them.

As if on cue, Ash's nostrils twitched. He sniffed heavily, then stirred from his slumber.

"Did someone scorch eggs?" Ash asked across their bond.

"Osric insisted on making his own breakfast," Holt said. *"He was acting a bit odd."*

"What's unusual about that?" Ash yawned deep, stretched his wings, then sat upright and tucked his feet under him like a cat in repose. He licked his lips. *"Smells good, boy."*

"You say that a lot."

"Because it always does!"

"You don't say that about mushrooms."

Ash shivered at the thought. *"They stink. They're not for me."*

Chuckling, Holt doled out a good portion into a bowl and took it to Ash.

Ash's scoffing sounded more like inhaling. By the time Holt returned the pot, Ash had already licked his bowl clean.

Holt sighed. *"Would it kill you to savor your food just once?"*

Ash licked his lips, and a warm glow of pleasure crossed their bond.

Holt took a small spoonful to Osric. "Want to taste it?"

Osric grunted. "It's not right that you should hunt as well as cook." He looked despondently at the stump of his right wrist.

"You've repaid that debt a hundred times over in the training ring." Holt pushed the spoon into Osric's hand. The general accepted it with a grunt, placed the spoon into his mouth, then grunted again, though this time in satisfaction.

Feeling pleased with himself, Holt took a bowl of his own to his spot by the campfire and began to eat. His tongue and jaw tingled as if they were coming back to life. It had been too long since he'd enjoyed something so rich and creamy.

Soot looked forlornly between them all, then turned her

enormous eyes on Holt. She cooed lightly, which was about as bold as she got. None of them, so far as Holt knew, had ever heard her speak, and if Osric had, he kept it to himself.

Even Holt's nickname for her was only used between himself, Ash, Aberanth, and Rake. She hadn't responded well to the name when he'd suggested it, but she hadn't offered any alternatives either. Osric insisted she be left free to choose her own.

Soot cooed again. Then, looking quickly between Holt, Osric, and the black pot, she yapped – a high, whining sound.

"Do you want some?" Holt asked tentatively.

She scrutinized Holt's bowl, then gave Osric a skeptical look.

"Be certain," Osric said. "It's a sin to waste food, though I assure you they're much better than mine."

Soot's eyes went wide at that assertion, then she yapped and rustled her wings and tail.

"I'll take that as a yes," Holt said. There was a small amount left in his own bowl, so he set it down for her to try.

Soot waited until he'd backed off, then she took a daring lick of the bowl with the very tips of her forked tongue. After two more, she'd licked it clean. She stared in disappointment at her empty bowl, then daintily nosed it toward Holt. Her tail beat on the ground, and her flapping wings struck Osric.

"Careful," he said, rapping her on the snout with his spoon and sending flakes of egg flying.

"Don't fret," Holt told her as he collected her bowl. "When have we ever let you starve?"

During their months together, he had learned that, despite acting as though she were ravenous, Soot mostly ate like a small bird. He gave her a very modest scoop from the pot, and what remained, he gave to Ash.

Both dragons finished at the same time. Ash stretched his long neck high and growled. Soot chirruped in imitation, and a blob of egg slipped down her chin.

Although Holt still thought of Soot as little, she had grown. Rake reckoned she was the size of a young female black bear with a tail as long as her body. But she was slender even for a female dragon, and she couldn't yet support Osric on her back.

Osric gathered the dishes, adding them to a basin along with the cooking utensils to clean later in the lab.

The light in the glade shifted as morning rays found their way through budding leaves, and for the first time in months, Holt felt a measure of heat in the sun. He noticed his breath no longer steamed upon the air either.

After a long winter, spring had come at last.

A sudden restlessness overcame him, and his mind began to wander beyond the trees. A change of season seemed ripe for a change in circumstance.

Ash sensed his thoughts. *"With luck, Master Rake will bring back good news."*

"Feels like we've stayed long enough," Holt said. *"Thrall won't have been hibernating this whole time."*

"We've made the best of Master Rake's tutelage, at least."

Holt agreed. Their efforts had yielded good results.

As a window to the core, their bond now had broad edges of solid light, giving Holt the impression of building a grander house upon strong foundations. His human mind still interpreted Ash's core as a nightscape filled with a bright moon and glimmering stars, but now, months into their training as Champions, the moon was larger and sharper, its surface less craggy and shadowy than before.

The trap door to the grotto rattled, quivered, then flew up and open. Aberanth, pony-sized and mud-brown, with wings knobbled like bark, scurried out of the opening, a small basket dangling between his teeth.

"Sorry I'm late," Aberanth said in a hurry. *"I lost track of time studying the new fungi colonies. Quite fascinating actually – the mycelium patterns alone—"*

"Is it time already?" Osric asked.

Ash growled, looked quickly between the pair, then snaked his neck around to peer down at Aberanth.

Quite at a loss as to what was happening, Holt took a moment to collect himself. He frowned. Ash's side of the bond had suddenly gone dark and dim – deliberately keeping Holt out.

The two dragons were having what seemed a private discussion, but in his frazzled haste, Aberanth let a few things slip.

"—no idea when Rake... tomorrow, a moon's turn, it's Rake – who's to say... but I thought it was today – it won't last, you know!"

Ash's growls turned angry.

Aberanth backed up a pace, basket swinging, and looked to Holt in alarm. His already large eyes seemed to widen as though behind spectacles. *"Oh, rot, I'm sorry. I'm no good at keeping secrets. Gives me a stomachache."*

Holt found his voice. "What's going on?"

Ash groaned, then slunk down and hung his head, seemingly defeated.

"The mission isn't a failure," Osric said, as close to friendly and encouraging as Holt had ever heard him. "Holt's clearly surprised. Just tell him."

Thoroughly perplexed, Holt furrowed his brow and waited for an explanation.

Ash took a few moments to compose himself. He seemed physically excited as he built up to it. *"Holt, it's your hatching day!"*

"What? My birthday?"

Holt ran some mental calculations and raised his fingers to tick off months, then weeks and days, but he had long since lost his sense of time when it came to the exact date.

"I can recall the cycles of the moon. It has been exactly one year since you spoke to Talia about it in that cave."

Memories of that night flooded back to Holt, of the dragons sleeping while he and Talia talked late into the night. He was surprised he remembered it so clearly, given all that had happened. It was just after he had met Rake and the West Warden for the first time, after Brode had been killed by Silas, and before he had become an Ascendant.

But something nagged at him. The timing wasn't right. He had missed his birthday back then, for it had really fallen while they'd been in the Withering Woods.

"That night wasn't my birthday."

"What?" Ash's voice faltered.

"It was earlier. I'd missed it and only realized that night in the cave, but it was close."

Ash dipped his snout and drooped his wings. *"I wanted to surprise you."*

Holt's love for Ash rang like a gong across their bond. He went to hug Ash around the neck, an increasingly difficult feat. The dragon was now the size of two great warhorses in body, twice as tall if he stretched his neck to his full height, and his tail could loop four times around Holt.

"I'd all but forgotten, and it's close enough!" Guilt twisted inside him. "And I feel terrible for us not doing something special for your own hatching day. That must have been over a month ago."

"That's okay, we were training."

"But it's fine to stop on my behalf?"

"You need to take a rest sometime. You work as if we're still trapped in those tunnels."

A shiver crept up Holt's spine, remembering the freezing cave by the underground lake. Their time trapped in the scourge tunnels had been effective, but he did not wish to repeat it. Rake's training – relentless, ruthless, and regimented – was a picnic by comparison.

"Osric brought back a cake," Ash said, delighted.

Holt did a double take. Three days ago, Osric had volunteered to make the supply run into Red Rock despite it not being his turn.

Holt met the ex-general's pale eyes, wondering what to make of it all.

"It was no trouble," Osric said stiffly. "Seemed the least I could do," he added more softly. Soot looked adoringly up at him, as though Osric was the most thoughtful man in the world.

While one human act did not transform the beast – did not wash out murder – Holt was nonetheless touched. Winter had cooled his previous hatred, and though the words felt partly wrong and insufficient, he said, "Thank you."

Osric gave a curt nod.

"So, where is this cake?" Holt said more brightly, his mouth watering.

Aberanth trotted over, a basket swinging between his teeth. Holt took it and lifted the cloth covering. The cake was plain, lacking frosting or other decorations, save for a coating of chopped almonds. He picked it up. The sponge felt a little stale, but he hardly cared; he'd have been grateful even if it had been brick hard.

"Thank you, all of you." He stood there, painfully aware he was holding a whole cake between his hands, and immediately felt awkward and somewhat selfish. "But it feels like you're giving me special treatment. It hardly seems fair."

"Perish the thought, Master Cook," Aberanth said. *"Dragons don't track the date of our hatching. It would become monotonous after a century or two. Besides, we can't eat cake."*

Tentatively, Holt glanced at Osric.

"I don't care for birthdays."

Holt blinked. "Do you care for dessert? Have a piece. I can't eat it all."

"I've not earned it."

Holt tore off a small chunk. Layers of jam lined the inside of the sponge like mortar in a wall. He tossed the piece to Osric, who caught it. Holding it in his one good hand, Osric almost looked sad as he inspected the food. Rather than eat it, Osric placed the cake atop his bundled cloak, then stood with purpose.

"Excuse me."

Without waiting for a reply, he found a clear spot of ground and fell into a set of one-armed pushups. Soot slinked after him and slipped into the shadow of a tall tree.

Feeling less awkward now everyone else was distracted by Osric, Holt ripped off another chunk of his late birthday treat and ate. The jam turned out to be a sour raspberry preserve, barely sweetened, but to Holt's palette – adjusted to living in the wilds for so long – it might as well have been honeycomb. Holt took another large bite, then thought he would save the rest for later.

Osric continued rising and falling.

Aberanth padded over to Holt and picked up the cake's basket between his teeth. *"Well, if that's us done, I'll head back below. Lots to do, you know. Merry hatching day, Holt,"* he added awkwardly as he disappeared into the tunnel.

Ash stretched out luxuriously and yawned again. *"Let's not train today. Let's go into the woods instead."*

"That sounds great. I'll do the rest of my chores first, then we'll go, I promise. Rake might not be here, but Aberanth still needs help."

After heading down the winding passages and past the inviting glow of the fireflies, Holt reached the laboratory. The central beech tree blended root and branch into the floor and ceiling, so it was hard to tell where the tree ended and the earth began. All those roots, spindly branches, and the fine fossil-like imprint of leaves within the walls emitted soft white and yellow light. As far as winter hideaways in the woods went, Aberanth's grotto surely ranked among the best.

Holt started by feeding their chicken. She lived in an alcove off the main lab Aberanth had been using to store books and scrolls. The fireflies and roots mimicked the light of the day outside, allowing the hen and anyone else sleeping below ground a chance for a natural rhythm. This morning she bobbed around as usual, pecking at the ground in the hope of a worm or other small bug. Holt scattered seeds and a few mushroom stalks for her before getting on with the rest of his duties.

In the shroomery he made precise cuttings and planted fresh spawn, in the storerooms he counted their latest batch of elixirs and packed them safely, and in the lab he attempted to clean up after Aberanth. Stacks of books, piles of bark notes, and crates of scrolls made the space feel a lot smaller, and having so many guests flustered and distracted Aberanth further. The perfect order and neatness Holt had beheld on his first visit were but distant memories now.

Aberanth bustled around, tending to several small fires and experiments at the same time, seemingly not aware of Holt's presence as he rumbled to himself.

Once he'd completed his chores, Holt went to fully dress and arm himself before heading into the woods with Ash. While he wasn't afraid, it was better to be safe than sorry.

His chainmail shirt was now tight across his shoulders and chest, and his trousers were slightly short. With Aberanth's aid, he had made several improvements to his gear, turning his belt into a veritable potion rack, complete with several pouches and an attachment for his cooking knife. Leather bags hung from his hips and were secured just above his knees.

The baldric that carried Brode's sword was already strong enough to hold a rider's blade, and he'd modified this as well. Loops ran in close intervals up the baldric like a bandoleer, and each could be tightened or loosened depending on whether Holt slotted a vial or piece of jerky into them.

Armed and ready, Holt was on his way out when he found Osric in the corner of the lab, tackling the basin of dirty dishes. Knowing full well how tricky it would be to do it one-handed, Holt went to assist him, and they completed the task in companionable silence. Holt didn't fail to miss the cake crumbs in Osric's beard. He smirked but left it at that.

At last, Holt headed for the exit.

"Just a moment, Holt," Aberanth said. *"If you don't mind, I need more hog weed. Can you keep an eye out for me?"*

"Of course," Holt said, and he went to grab his satchel. Aberanth was experimenting with new herbs to form the base mixture of elixirs, but that was where Holt's understanding ended.

Back on the surface, he grabbed Ash, and they strolled out into the wider Fae Forest. As they wandered, Holt covered his eyes with his blindfold and shared his senses with Ash. This blurred his promise not to train, for he would often blind himself in sparring sessions with Rake and Osric, yet blending his senses with Ash brought them closer.

Without a fight to worry about, they went at a leisurely pace, stopping only to harvest hog weed for Aberanth, and played guessing games for subtle sounds, feelings, and smells around them. Holt was certain he only won on occasion because Ash let him. But he didn't mind.

When night fell, they decided to seek unfiltered moonlight. It had been much too long since they had taken to the open skies under the stars. At first, they circled close to Aberanth's glade, then risked going higher and higher, circling ever upward until they breached the clouds.

"Hold on," Ash said, before he tucked in his wings and descended steeply and swiftly. They pulled up sharply to glide along the top of a cloud, close enough for Ash to run his knuckles through it.

The clouds reflected the moon, becoming a silver sea. Ash's scales glowed, and across the bond, Holt felt a pleasant tingling all over Ash's body. Lunar motes cascaded through the orbit of Ash's core, but Holt allowed himself to enjoy the moment and not worry about Forging. He spread his arms out, whooping with glee as they soared under the perfect half-moon.

"Night is our time," Ash said, and Holt recalled powerful memories in the old mucker's hut when they'd only had the stars and each other for company. Now stars also twinkled in the nightscape of Ash's core. Even as Holt observed them, some rearranged themselves, growing bold and bright to form a constellation. Silver lines joined the starry points together, leaving Holt with the distinct impression of a hut with a broken roof.

Holt laughed with joy. His mind raced, marveling at what other constellations might crystalize in the nightscape. And in their happiness and closeness, Ash's dragon song played as clear as ever, drowning out the wind and warding off the cold.

The flute sounded rich and mellow now. It spoke of confidence and security. Compared to the frightened loneliness of Ash's early song, this made Holt's heart swell with relief and pride. What had once been delicate harp notes had aged as well, still otherworldly in their origin, yet now filled with a power of their own. It was the song of a young stag from a kingly line stepping comfortably through his domain at night, a song to rouse lost souls in the dark and give them the courage to find their way home.

Holt felt more at ease than he had since saving Ash's egg. Awash with the dragon song, hours passed blissfully by. How wonderful it would be to fly like this forever.

Alas, came a thought from the back of his mind, they could not.

Something white blazed across the night sky.

Whether consciously or not, Ash changed course toward it and picked up speed.

"We don't know what it is," Holt said.

"It must be a falling star," Ash said, sounding surer than Holt thought the situation warranted. Whatever it was left a trail of sparkling dust for miles behind it.

"Can't you hear it?" Ash asked.

"Hear it?"

Even through Ash, Holt heard nothing new, and once the dragon song quietened, there was only the wind and the cold. Once again, he wished his human senses were more closely attuned to the magic of the world.

The streak of white fire fell out of sight, passing over the tree line far to the south. Ash flew harder as though he meant to catch it, as sure as ever he'd been, and Holt trusted him. So they raced high above the Fae Forest, chasing the glistening trail of a falling star to wherever it might lead them.

3

A CALLING

They chased the falling star until dawn. Somewhere on the southern border of the Fae Forest they came upon its crash site, and Ash touched down amidst splintered trees. A deep crater exposed thick, scorched roots, and while a charred smell of earth and bark remained, the white fire was extinguished.

Holt jumped down, took a step over the crater's rim, then gasped. A swell of ethereal music filled his mind, a melody akin to Ash's song, though more ancient, woven with a note from every night which had come before. A voice sang in a lyrical tongue he could not comprehend. It stirred his dragon bond. No, not his bond. It was his whole soul that thrummed.

"It's beautiful," Ash said.

Holt gulped. A tear ran down his face, not from pain or sorrow but from incomprehensible splendor, as though everything they had ever suffered or worked for had been leading to this: to a message from beyond the night.

"Do you think it's safe?"

Ash rumbled and nudged him into the crater.

Holt half-staggered, half-slid down the bank to the fallen star. On closer inspection, its metallic surface was more white than black and flecked with rusted silver veins, all rough and grainy save for an exposed pearl-smooth opal embedded in the ore.

Light rippled through the gem as though a rainbow were caged inside it.

Holt picked the lump of ore up. For something small enough to fit inside his black pot, it felt dense and heavy. Although the opal protruded out of the ore, it was stuck fast and would not budge.

"We have to take it with us."

"I should like to have it close just to hear it."

Holt ran a finger over its surface again, wondering as to its nature. He climbed back out of the crater and held the white ore under Ash's nose.

"It definitely has a tang like metal, though unlike any I have smelled before."

Wordless excitement passed between them.

"Aberanth or Master Rake will know."

Ash's demeanor then shifted from awestruck to tense. He snarled. A moment later, Holt felt it too.

Another core.

Holt dashed out between the broken trees to survey the lands to the south. Here the wilderness sloped away to flatter plains below, where little grew above the height of a thorn bush. The dawn sky was streaked with pale orange, the approaching morning's hazy glow bleeding through foamy clouds against which the silhouette of a dragon clearly stood out.

"There's no rider."

"Do we stay?"

Holt's stomach lurched. Avoiding detection had been one of their top priorities for months. Now, their curiosity might have cost them dearly.

"If we try to run, we'd lead it straight to Aberanth's grotto."

"Is it a storm drake?"

Holt squinted, trying to make out its coloring.

"I think it's green."

"Emeralds are more likely to be friendl—" Ash fell quiet. Holt raised a hand to the hilt of Brode's sword, then Ash growled in shock. *"He knows our names. Talia sent him!"*

Relief surged across their bond and gave Holt such a strong kick he might have drunk ten of Aberanth's elixirs. Ash's delight mixed with his, but then, thankfully, cooler thoughts buttressed the surge of joy. Rake's brutal reality checks, Aberanth's methodical nature, and Osric's cynicism had all rubbed off on Holt in their own ways.

Any of their enemies might claim to have been sent by Talia, especially an agent of Thrall.

Holt drew Brode's sword and cycled motes, ready for anything.

Ash went quiet again. At length, he announced, *"Talia gave him a message to pass on. A servant out of his depth once told her that if you love with your eyes, death is forever. If you love with your heart, there is no such thing as parting."*

Something squirmed through Holt. He could not name the feeling. His father had taught him those words, and he'd been comforted by them during some of the worst moments of his life. Why, then, was there something like longing in him? He did not wish to return to how things had been, especially to when he and Ash were as vulnerable as two lambs.

Whatever it was, the sensation wormed its way through him and left him uneasy.

Talia was alive. And that was wonderful.

Maybe, just maybe, this meant he was to be pardoned and could return home without bringing the stain of 'chaos-bringer' with him.

Holt sheathed his weapon. He and Ash moved out beyond the edge of the forest to meet the emerald in the open. The emerald's scales were the shades of dark apples, and it was small, roughly the same size as Ash. When it landed, to Holt's surprise, it pressed its neck and wings low to the ground – honoring their superiority in power.

That felt strange to Holt. Unnatural. He'd always been the one to bow. He supposed if they continued down their path with Rake and pushed at boundaries even Lords feared, he had better get used to it.

"I am honored to be the one to find you, Sons of Night. My name is Turro of the Emerald Flight. I come bearing word from the West Warden and the Red Queen."

"You are most welcome, Turro," Ash said. *"Though there is no need to bow before us."*

"You are gracious." Turro rose to all fours and tucked in his wings. He then relayed his message. When he was done, they asked him to repeat it three times. Though Turro spoke the words, Holt could almost feel Talia's desperation behind them.

"And she can find no one else to do this for her?" Holt asked eventually, his voice stiff. "With all her power and resources?"

"The Red Queen has exhausted all other options."

A heaviness fell over Holt's heart. It seemed like pressure from Falcaer had been behind her decision.

Holt looked warily to the skies and cast out his sixth sense as far as he could, expecting a rider at any moment. He sensed no other cores, but he wasn't entirely reassured.

As Holt mulled the request over, Ash's thoughts bubbled to join his own.

"We can't forget our mission from the Elder. The reason we stayed was to train with Master Rake and gather our strength. We must still seek the Elders of Fire, Storm, and Ice."

Holt bit his lip. They couldn't just abandon Talia, could they? Hope – cautious hope – had sparked within him, and he was loath to snuff it out.

"If Talia is asking us to return," Holt said tentatively, *"surely this means we are no longer banished?"*

"Does that matter?"

Ash's casual dismissal took Holt by surprise. Somehow it hurt. He couldn't hide it, but even as remorse swept over from Ash, Holt deflected by answering Turro.

"We must consider this carefully. Your own Elder provided us with a mission. We would not abandon it lightly."

Turro gave a rumble of approval. *"I should trust not. But know the Red Queen works closely with my Elder, and her trials are now woven into his own. Great strides have been made against our enemies, and your aid would push us closer to victory. I believe you would be doing the Elder's work in this, but to which task you fly is yours to decide."*

Holt now felt a bout of guilt. Had Talia and the emeralds been fighting Thrall and the scourge while they skulked in the woods?

Ash sensed his concern and said privately, *"We couldn't have known, boy. Now… now, if we do go to help, we'll be that much more capable."* His tone was bright but forced, trying to make up for the hurt he'd inadvertently caused.

"What's done is done," Holt said, chewing everything over.

"Might I have an answer to return with?" Turro asked.

Holt's attention snapped back to the emerald. "We have friends we must talk this through with. I'm afraid we can't take you with us without permission. Will you wait here for our answer?"

Holt was certain he and Ash would be able to find the crater of the falling star again. Haunting notes from the white ore echoed all around the area.

Turro bowed. *"I shall await your answer here."*

Holt and Ash made their way back to the glade in low spirits. The thrill of the fallen star had been overshadowed by Turro's news from Feorlen and the new task set before them.

Holt could just refuse it. Ash had made a good point, but if going to Talia's aid would help the Life Elder in the immediate future, that seemed more pressing, or so Holt reasoned.

They found everyone in the clearing, including Rake. He must have returned sometime in the night. Presently, he was sitting on his favorite stump, the hood of his cloak down and his polearm planted in the ground beside him.

"Ah, they deign to return," Rake said. "I suppose when the cat's away, the mice will slack off. I'll be sure to rectify that, but first I have important news to…" Rake fell quiet as his gaze came to rest on Holt's lumpy satchel, sapphire eyes flashing. "What have you got there?"

Holt jumped down from Ash, unslung his bag, and opened it.

"A bunch of hog weed for Aberanth," he said, pulling out the curly, pig-tail grass. "And this," he added anticlimactically. He held up the ore for all to see. "We think it's a fallen star."

All eyes focused on the ore. Even Soot dragged herself out of the shadow she was hiding in to get a better look.

Aberanth stepped lightly toward Holt, eyes drawn to the white ore like a moth to a flame. *"A meteorite? What is that... Ahhh, yes, there is a music, faint to me, of course – oh, put it down, Holt!"* Aberanth rushed forward, boisterous as a puppy.

"Take it easy," Holt said before placing the ore on the grass.

Aberanth sniffed the ore, then, to Holt's surprise, he licked it. His eyes popped. *"Steel – gracious but this is intriguing!"*

"Steel does not fall from the sky," Osric said. "It must be iron."

Holt looked at him, puzzled. "It's something different. Can't you sense it?"

"Sense what?"

"Lunar magic. I know it's not Soot's type, but surely you can feel... something?"

Osric shrugged his shoulders and looked sour.

Holt was surprised. If Osric could not even sense the latent energy in the star, his sixth sense was truly lacking.

Rake cleared his throat pointedly. "Pardon me, General Grumps, but perchance this is a sign that you should train—"

"I won't embrace such chaos again. Nor do I need it."

That had been Osric's position all winter. Rake rolled his eyes.

"Do you think I could forge a sword out of it?" Holt asked.

"Don't see why you think I would know," Rake said. "Aberanth?"

Aberanth clawed at the lump, turned to examine it from a fresh angle, then snorted. *"Hmph. Hmph! What secrets lie within you..."*

Rake turned back to Holt and shrugged. "You can only try."

Holt noticed Osric staring at him. His pale eyes were piercing and all-seeing. "What else happened? You're not so hard to read," he added in answer to Holt's questioning look.

Holt told them of Turro and the message from Talia. Rake looked pensive, leaning forward with an elbow on his knee and his chin upon his fist. Osric's expression remained stern. He clenched his remaining fist and beckoned Soot closer. She trotted over to him and nuzzled her snout into his side, and they seemed to engage in a silent conversation. Aberanth was still too busy circling and prodding the meteorite to notice anything else.

"Any thoughts?" Holt asked, looking pointedly at Rake.

Remaining in his pose, Rake said, "Let's be clear. The Life Elder and Talia are still working together. She wishes us to delve into another scourge chamber, destroy a control orb, and help flush Thrall out into the open?"

Turro's message hadn't mentioned Rake at all, but Holt saw no point in correcting the record on that. Rake would go where Rake wanted to go.

"That sounds about right," Holt said.

Rake smiled. "Sounds like fun! And a lot more information than I managed to weasel out of the emeralds in the Eastern Grove."

At last, Aberanth stopped his circling of the white ore and fell quiet. *"The grove was occupied again?"*

"Emeralds have indeed returned to the Eastern Grove," Rake said, as though beginning a bard's epic. "They were recovering from injuries or drained cores. A bad whiff of the blight clung to their scales like Osric's smallclothes." He allowed a moment to enjoy the reaction. Osric folded his arms, his expression remaining stone. Rake shrugged and carried on. "But the East Warden has not returned. He remains with the Life Elder, although the emeralds would not deign to tell me where they are."

"Why would they be so secretive about it?" Ash asked.

"Because I'm a filthy soul-cursed half-breed, and no respectable dragon wants to indulge me for long."

Holt gave him a reproachful look. "Don't say that."

"It is what it is. None of you are exactly *respectable*, hence why you indulge me. In any case, I suspect the Elder bound the emeralds to hold their tongues. Reading between their growls, this lot had only begrudgingly left the front lines recently. Safety in numbers. Typical, though," he added with a low laugh. "I take some time to rest, and the Life Elder finally stretches his wings and takes up the fight. Such things feel like a natural law."

Aberanth rumbled, and his tail swished quick and agitated across the forest floor. *"This doesn't quite add up to me. Why would Thrall be drawn out so easily? There must be a great quantity of these orbs all over the world. It could take a lifetime to hunt them all down, if it's even possible to do so. What results can you realistically hope for by destroying one?"*

"The Elder must think it's possible," Ash said, as though that settled the matter.

Aberanth made a sound somewhere between a hiss and a snarl. *"My Elder is not always right... nor are the Wardens."*

Remorse welled in Ash from his lack of tact. Holt felt it across the bond, but before either of them could say anything, Rake cut in.

"I wonder..." he started loudly, scratching his scaly chin before snapping his fingers. "Osric, you mentioned you thought Thrall's control of the scourge might be slipping."

"I never got a clear answer on it."

"Maybe the Elder has found out more. That is to say, Ash, that drawing Thrall out may not be so hard. Maybe he just needs another good poke."

"And then what?" Ash asked. *"The Elder and his Wardens ambush him?"*

"Oh, I'm sorry, Ash," Rake said. "Would you like to do it instead?"

"That's not what I meant."

Aberanth puffed up his chest. *"I agree with Ash. We're wildly speculating at best."*

"They'll underestimate Thrall at their peril," Osric said.

"You've been quiet, Holt," Rake said. "What say you on the matter?"

Holt had been trying to weigh things up as rationally as he

could, but his gut seemed set on what he should do. "I wouldn't want to rush into another scourge tunnel, but if Talia thinks removing these orbs is important and it helps whatever the Life Elder is doing, then it seems to me that we ought to try."

"Sounds like you've made up your mind," Rake said wryly.

Ash squirmed and swished his tail like Aberanth. *"Master Rake, should we not seek the Elders of Storm and Fire? If we convince them to join the fight against Thrall, there would be no need to draw him out. They could all fight him head-on."*

"A fine point," Rake said, then he leaned forward and grinned mischievously. "Nothing quite like sibling solidarity, is there, Grumps?"

Osric's upper lip twitched, but he remained startlingly still.

Rake's grin fell away, his manner becoming suddenly serious. "You make a good case, Ash. Naturally you wish to return to your quest, but to visit either of those distant flights, we'll need to head west anyway. The Storm Peaks lie far beyond the north-western boundary of the Skarl Empire. The Fire Elder's domain is on a volcanic island in the deep south, over the Stretched Sea and the Scalding Sea. Unless you can suddenly carry both Holt and me on your back, we'll need a ship. Feorlen isn't the jewel of civilization, but it's got ships. Perhaps my favor from Talia could be a pleasure barge? In any case, making you stronger won't do us any harm in our attempt to charm the Elders of Storm and Fire. Seeking out and destroying another one of these chambers can only benefit you two in that regard."

"Or get you killed," Aberanth said helpfully.

"At least that would free us of making more agonizing decisions," Rake said. He clapped his hands. "Let's put it to a vote. All in favor of assisting Talia – which will also help the Life Elder?"

Rake and Holt raised their hands.

"And those in favor of ignoring our friend's plea for help?"

Ash growled. *"That's not fair,"* he said, though he remained resolute and raised one wing.

Everyone's attention then turned to Aberanth.

"Don't look at me. Last year was quite enough excitement to be getting on with."

An unexpected heaviness descended over Holt. "You'd really not come?"

Aberanth looked his way but did not quite meet his eye. *"My place is here… my work…"*

"Well, that's two to one so far," Rake said. "Osric, would you and our youngest friend like to share your thoughts?"

Without answering, Osric sought the comfort of the dying fire. He stoked it with fresh wood, and the flickering light danced across his face.

"Still waiting," Rake said.

"It doesn't matter what I think."

"If we're to return to Feorlen, you should have a say," Holt said.

Osric's expression hardened. "Go where you will. But I cannot go back. Not yet."

Soot squawked in agreement and glared at Holt and Rake as though they were cruel. Rake made a sudden movement toward her. Her squawk turned into a squeak, and she slid into Osric's shadow, half-melding with it so that only her head remained visible.

Rake chortled.

Osric thumbed the beard of his blood-red axe, the one he called Vengeance.

The pair of them stared each other down.

Holt felt a tapping at his leg again. He looked down to find Aberanth staring at him with imploring yellow eyes.

"H-he can't very well stay here," he said privately to Holt and Ash. *"If he thinks he will, then he has another thing coming, hmph."*

Aberanth's threat might have been more convincing if his wings hadn't been trembling.

"Don't worry," Holt said. *"We'll take him with us."*

Having reassured Aberanth, he discovered Rake and Osric were still staring at each other as though they were in the midst of a blinking contest.

Holt huffed. "Enough. Let's make a decision."

Without blinking, Rake raised two fingers in one hand. "Two votes for Feorlen. And as Osric has exercised his right to abstain"—he raised one finger on his other hand—"that leaves one for the Elders. Apologies, Ash. But fair is fair."

Ash bowed his neck low.

"Hop to it then. That includes you, Grumps."

But Osric was already on his feet and heading for the entrance to the grotto.

Holt's heart picked up. After so long in the forest, it was high time they rejoined the fight against Thrall. He and Ash might get to fight alongside Talia and Pyra again. That gave him another jolt of excitement, and then he noticed Rake was staring at him. Holt looked away in shame, unable to fully suppress the blush that warmed his cheeks.

He became aware that Aberanth was no longer beside him.

"Aberanth?" he said, looking around, but the little emerald didn't answer. Holt only caught sight of a brown tail sliding down into the tunnel to the grotto.

Ash padded over, rumbling low in his throat.

"I know it wasn't what you wanted," Holt said across their bond. *"But we're still working toward the same goal."*

Ash scoffed but allowed Holt to stroke his nose.

"We should return to Turro to let him know," Ash said.

Holt agreed, then told Rake what they were going to do.

"I'll come with you," Rake said.

"We'll be quicker if we fly."

Rake gave them both an appraising look, then reluctantly nodded. "You've had an easy time of it here. Don't let that sway your good sense—well, it's you, Holt, so maybe not *good* sense —but—"

"You've made your point," Holt said, already climbing onto Ash and blending senses with him. "We'll be fast. We promise."

Ash growled in agreement before he took off, leaving the glade behind. They kept their promise and flew as fast as Ash's wings could propel him back to where the white star had crashed.

By the time they arrived, night was quickly gathering. Yet Turro was not there, and despite using the full range of their perceptions, neither of them could sense any core.

Ash sniffed deeply. He crept forward, stretching his neck first one way and then the other. Whatever he picked up on only reached Holt dimly across the bond.

Maintaining the sensory connection, Holt jumped down from Ash and lowered his blindfold. After months of practice, it only took a few moments for Holt to adjust and enhance his smell, touch, and hearing.

Aided by Ash's impressive senses, Holt heard the low hoot of a distant owl, the light vibrations of a burrowing creature, and the fresh scent of flowers and berry bushes carried on the breeze. He breathed deep through his nose, sifting earth, bark, plant, and beast from each other until he detected what Ash was most interested in.

"Another dragon was here."

Holt squatted amid the long grass and carefully felt the ground. He traced the edges of a dragon's footprint, larger than Ash's and too big to be Turro's. The temperature in the ground subtly shifted, and his sensitive skin registered a single sputtering spark of static.

Something new caught in his nose. The oiliness of hair. Holt followed it, and between the cool blades of grass, he found something fine and coarse – a long strand of hair.

Ash came to sniff it. *"Human."*

"Must have been a rider."

"Riders don't attack wild dragons."

"Unless they're working for Thrall, though it would be risky, surely? It might reveal their true loyalties to the Order."

The back of Holt's neck tingled with unease. All that reassured him was a lack of blood. If Turro had been attacked, he seemed to have escaped in one piece. As to what happened next, the trail of evidence ran cold.

"We should go, boy."

Holt wholeheartedly agreed.

After arriving back in the glade and reporting what they'd found to Rake, Holt descended underground to begin packing at once. Down in the lab, he found Aberanth on the opposite side of a workbench, tending to a large alembic. Various herbs – the hog weed included – bubbled in the alembic's chamber.

"How's it coming along?"

Aberanth started as though Holt had jumped out of the shadows. *"We'll see, we'll see. Early days yet. More data needed."* He leaned his snout closer to the alembic, and through the curved glass, his eyes widened to the size of saucers. *"You'll be eager to pack, of course. Call me if you need any help."*

"Oh," Holt said, taken aback. He hesitated, unsure what he wanted to say, before shaking the feeling aside. "I'll do that."

He passed Osric, who was carrying a crate of elixirs, and they exchanged a curt nod before Holt entered his earthy quarters. The roots within the alcove wall awoke with a soft orange glow at his movement, making the cramped space seem even smaller.

His sleeping roll lay crinkled and unmade. He rolled it up first, then gathered and packed the rest of his possessions. After taking a full account of his supply of venison jerky in all flavorings, he restocked his pouches and filled the loops on his belt and baldric with potions.

Fully packed, he began taking his possessions up to the surface. On each trip, he threw Aberanth a glance, but the alchemist was too preoccupied with his work to look up. Indeed, Aberanth grew increasingly flustered until Holt caught him clanking around the lab and growling to himself, lifting boxes, books, and equipment.

"Looking for something?"

"A stirring rod. A clean one. I'm sure I had one."

Holt knew exactly where to look. He shifted two boxes on the opposite side of the lab to where Aberanth was thumping around, then found the one containing clean beakers and glass stirring rods, one of which he brought to Aberanth.

"Here you go."

Aberanth's grumblings settled at once in a long groan. *"Thanks, Holt. How will I work without you?"*

"You'll get the place clean and back under control in no time," Holt said.

"Hmph," Aberanth grunted noncommittally. *"I've appreciated having an assistant, you know. You've been of great help."* With that, he bustled back to his workbench.

Holt felt that was an insufficient farewell, but he didn't want to intrude any more.

He hoisted his packed cooking equipment, and the contents clanged. "This is the last of them."

Aberanth twisted his neck around. *"The last?"* he asked, but then some idea seemed to distract him, and he trotted off to a back room.

"Bye, then. For now," Holt said quietly.

He left the lab.

Up in the glade, Rake, Osric, and Soot were ready. As Rake couldn't fly and Osric didn't yet fly upon Soot, they would travel on foot. Each carried their fair share of supplies and equipment, including Ash and Soot, who had bags, sacks, and boxes lashed to their backs. Holt tied his cooking equipment onto Ash, and with that, they were ready.

Rake cast his gaze about, then looked perturbed. "Where is our fastidious host?"

"I'm not sure he's coming," Holt said.

Ash rumbled. *"But I haven't said farewell."*

"I wouldn't take it personally," Rake said. "He's not the type to wear his heart on his wing. Alright then," he added with an air of great portent, pointing north with his polearm. "Let's be on our way."

They'd barely made it to the edge of the glade when the trap door burst open behind them and Aberanth scurried out.

"Wait! Wait, I've got something for you!" He carried a tiny cloth wrap between his teeth.

"Surely not more things?" Rake said, sounding as though he dared any of them to tell him to carry this latest imposition.

"It's for Holt," Aberanth said brusquely. *"Though I dare say he'll*

do something special with it that you can all appreciate." He dropped the cloth wrapping at Holt's feet, then, a little breathless, he stepped reverently back.

Ash sniffed. *"Ohhhh, you'll like this."*

Holt flicked the folds of cloth down.

A truffle?!

He had to catch his breath. It was no bigger than a chestnut with knobbly onyx skin. Holt took it lightly in his hand and sniffed its rich perfume of fresh leather, roasted garlic in browned butter, and autumn leaves, which set his mouth to watering and his mind racing as to how he might use it.

Momentarily, he was lost for words.

He got down on one knee to be closer to eye level with Aberanth. "Thanks, Aberanth. This must have taken years to grow."

Aberanth averted his eyes and seemed preoccupied with itching his tail. *"Oh, it's nothing. You'll put it to better use than I would."*

A mad urge came over Holt to take the little emerald in a bear hug. One part of him felt it somehow right, and the other screamed it to be disrespect. Aberanth was not Ash. Caught between the two forces, Holt leaned in and half opened his arms, causing Aberanth to yap and squirm away.

"Don't give him a heart attack," Rake said.

Holt pulled back.

Aberanth shook his head, muttering, insofar as a dragon can mutter, meaning Holt caught snippets of Aberanth's rushing thoughts.

"Humans… sentimental…"

Ash hummed high in his throat. *"Goodbye, Aberanth. Thank you for taking good care of us."*

Aberanth cast Osric a wary look, then returned his gaze to Holt. *"Yes, hmph, well, you're both welcome to visit any time."*

In his peripheral vision, Holt caught Rake winding up to some comically over-the-top cry of ill-treatment, but Aberanth headed it off by saying, *"You too, you thick-skulled show-off. Try not to go on any more suicide missions. I can't be there to save you every time."*

Rake laughed, a genuine full belly laugh. Recovering, he said, "Aww, Aberanth. It's good to know you care. Stay safe, my finicky little friend."

"Oh, I intend to. Well then," he added, somewhat lamely, *"goodbye."*

He began to back away, deliberately avoiding Osric, but the ex-general stepped forward, causing Aberanth to speed up until Osric hastened to block the dragon's path.

"I know you have your reservations about me," Osric said, "but I cannot leave without offering my gratitude for sheltering us. You have a kind and generous soul, and I hope I can repay it one day." Before Aberanth had a chance to respond, Osric gestured for Soot to join him. "Come along, say thanks."

Hesitant as ever, Soot crept toward Aberanth on the balls of her feet. It was almost comical, seeing Soot advance so cautiously toward a dragon who was smaller than her.

Aberanth looked apprehensive, staring between Holt, Ash, and Rake in turn, begging silently for one of them to intervene. But no one did, and Soot stretched her neck out, straining so as not to get an inch closer than she had to. She shut her eyes – while Aberanth's popped in alarm – then delicately pressed the tip of her snout to his. A second later, she scurried behind Osric and half-melded into his shadow.

Ash hummed in amusement, and Rake raised his scaly brows as though waiting for the next part of the show.

Holt tried to ease the situation by saying, "That was very nice of her, wasn't it, Aberanth?"

Under Osric's glare, Aberanth nodded vigorously. *"Oh yes, erm, really very nice. Wonderful, even. Well, farewell to you both. It's been a pl— well, it's— you've both been— polite."*

Osric growled but appeared satisfied and stepped aside.

Aberanth padded past, then, just before he headed back down into his tunnel, he turned and looked at Soot. *"I do wish you all the luck in the world, young one. Be good."*

With that, he trotted down the tunnel, and the trap door closed behind him.

The group allowed the bang of the door to ring out into nothingness. After a moment or two, Rake broke the stillness.

"Partings are always so sad, especially when they seem to drag out forever." He spun his polearm with great aplomb, ending in a pose in which he pointed the tip of the glassy orange blade to the north. "So, for the second time, we're moving out!"

4

THE FIVE

Paragon Kalanta closed her eyes, pressed her hand into the mountain, and listened to the stones.

The world wept. Of late, its cries had become whimpers. What progress she and the emeralds had made was only surface-level, barely skin deep. She didn't need to stretch her perceptions far to find death and decay.

Deeper and deeper Kalanta pressed her perceptions, down to the roots of the mountain, where even the stone began to rot. A tear bubbled and rolled, streaming hotly down her cheek.

She whipped her hand from the rock as though scalded. The pain. The grief. Even with all her might and that of her dragon Tanyksha, she couldn't bear it for long.

None had heeded her warnings. They only saw the surface world, where the wounds were shallow and few and the lushness of life masked the festering beneath.

Tanyksha drew in close and wrapped her limestone wings around Kalanta. Inside this cocoon, Kalanta felt safe, but before she could find solace in the embrace, a voice reached out to her. One she had hoped not to hear.

"The Paragons are recalled to the council." The voice was ethereal and feminine, the voice of Wynedd, mystic dragon of Paragon Eso.

Kalanta fought a flare of anger. To fly now would mean returning empty-handed. Again.

Wordlessly, Tanyksha added her spirit to Kalanta's own, filling her soul with a will of granite to buttress her doubts. Kalanta's soul steadied. There was no need to return immediately. They had time yet. Kalanta sent her love over the dragon bond and braced herself to listen to the world. They had to keep trying.

This time, Kalanta bent low and pushed her hand a few inches down into the dirt and earth. Its rich brown scent gave her momentary pleasure before the sound of weeping filled her mind.

She searched through the sorrow, hearing the thrumming feet of the enemy, and then, at last, came a beat from the heart of the sickness. It roiled like a stomach in insatiable hunger – always starving. Kalanta strained, trying to lock onto its location.

She found it. She would inform the Elder at once.

Then, for the first time, the hunger noticed her.

The Emerald Paragon screamed.

On the blustery fringes of the Storm Peaks, Paragon Vald forced the surrounding motes to rise and form black clouds. He continued until the gathering storm stretched to each horizon and swallowed the sun. When he released them, the relief of pressure upon his mote channels felt as rewarding as sinking into a hot bath. The work was strenuous, but advancement never came from meager efforts, whether a Novice or a Paragon.

His soul space reverberated.

He was close now.

He could feel it.

Yet the final revelation eluded him. Together, he and Raiden'ra knew their purpose – to breach the last boundary. It had taken them to Lordship long ago. What further insight could be necessary? It seemed cruel, as though a sheet of glass separated him from the treasure on the other side.

Vald gathered himself, sinking his mote channels to focus the flow of energy inward around his soul and dragon bond. Doing so made drawing magic across the bond more efficient, and such was the power of his cycling that the wind on the valley floor was pulled to gust around him. Were he not careful, he would create a tornado, but Vald had mastered storms before Adaskar could light candles. He summoned another storm cloud, held it until the horizon, then released and enjoyed the relief again.

As he did so, Raiden'ra – out of sight, sitting high upon the nearest peak – spoke across their bond. *"Will you continue?"*

Without even scrutinizing his mote channels, Vald snapped, *"Of course!"*

"I meant no offense. You are still only human."

Vald continued his meditations and training in silence.

Soon. It would surely be soon. Once he achieved the impossible – once the others felt his new core – they would ask to be led along the path. Defeating the scourge would be within reach. The deep places would be traversed and cleansed once and for all.

His thoughts mixed with Raiden'ra's.

The dragon saw them leading the Order from the front, saw storm heralded as the true bane of the scourge, saw even Elders treating them as brothers.

"Fire has led since the beginning," Vald said.

"They are stubborn. They will break themselves before bending."

"Once we ascend, the others will follow. Our might will be unquestionable. Even to Rostam and Azarin."

He was about to generate another storm cloud when Raiden'ra bellowed from the mountaintop. Irritation flashed across their dragon bond like a bolt of power, then it dissipated as Raiden'ra collected himself and passed along the message from Wynedd.

Adaskar was demanding they return, just as Vald was so close to breaking through the last and greatest boundary. Typical. Yet duty called, and they would not delay. If they were quick, they might be able to sneak in some additional training before Kalanta and Neveh arrived.

Paragon Neveh drew in a deep breath and felt icy tendrils bloom in her chest. In her homeland of Lakara, people enjoyed inhaling scented, flavored smoke and other fumes to alter the mind. She could not abide direct heat inside her lungs, but breathing in this pristine cold gave her an appreciation of her countrymen's habits. The air was thin and light, tasting dry and cleansed – as pure as anything in this world could taste.

While she waited for Nilak to return, she scooped up handfuls of soft snow from the tundra, white against her ebony skin. Neveh had been born a contradiction, a cold girl in a hot land, and bonding with the lone ice dragon at Angkor had confirmed that.

Despite the oppressive sun of the Jade Jungle, she and Nilak had grown strong. Faced with the impossible, their understanding of the motes Nilak craved had deepened and propelled them through their advancement. All the same, this land of cold blue light where the sun hung low like a great white star – this was where they belonged.

Would it that she could stay here north of the White Wilderness where no mortals could tread, but alas, return she must: once she had answers.

There was no longer the luxury of time. The facts were clear. Even the White Wilderness had an element of decay to it these days. While passing through the unnatural blizzard which had gripped the wilderness for months, Neveh found the frigid airs tinged with a deathly damp as revolting to her as hot smoke. The Elder's will and power had fueled those blizzards, a drastic measure, but if the blight penetrated even the most inhospitable places, then drastic measures were required. Adaskar was right to worry about the state of the world, but Neveh feared his rigidity would be the death of them.

Neveh sought results. She was prepared to accept Adaskar's methods to be true – however much it pained her – but she needed to understand what lay beneath it all. No longer would she blindly follow.

Why had the Pact been devised? Why limit the interactions between the Wild Flights and the riders? Why not reach out, join forces, and tackle the scourge once and for all? The Order was shrouded in ritual and symbols, but they had all, Adaskar included, forgotten the *why*. Surely matters from thousands of years ago could not apply to the present?

Freezing winds swept from the north again, carrying a call to all who held ice in their hearts. Upon those winds, she also felt Nilak's presence returning to her.

Neveh stood to greet him. As she beheld her dragon and his crystal-bright wings, a strained voice crossed her dragon bond, though it was not Nilak's. Wynedd's voice sounded like a whisper from a deathbed. Neveh attributed this to the sheer distance they were from Falcaer. From anywhere. Even the Paragons had their limits. Still, she could not claim to have not received the message or to have misunderstood it. Adaskar wished her to return.

Not now, she thought on impulse, but unless she had good reason, she could not abstain from such a council.

As Nilak drew close, Neveh stepped upon the air to reach him, freezing what little moisture there was to create a short-lived stairway. At the top of the steps, she reached up to his snout and asked aloud, "Tell me, is it time?"

Nilak hummed high in his throat. *"The Elder will grant you an audience."*

Paragon Eso began to withdraw his spirit from Wynedd's own. Magical power flowed one way, from dragon to human, but the human might lend vigor from their own soul in times of need. To call it draining would be like calling a hatchling ill-prepared to face a scourge queen, for rather than tapping into a store of magic, the human was giving of their very spirit, will, and life force. However, it served its purpose in special circumstances, such as aiding Wynedd to stretch her mind across the world in search of the Paragons.

As Eso's spirit returned to him, Wynedd tried to hide the pain in her mote channels, but he felt the aftershocks regardless.

"He asks too much of you," Eso said. Her recovery would be long after such an effort.

"No task in service to Falcaer is too great. It would be far worse to fail... to falter."

Out in the grounds, she curled up in her nest. Eso felt her shudder.

His own mote channels throbbed, especially those serving his mind, causing a headache even Vald would flinch at.

"Whatever you must endure," Eso said, *"I shall suffer it with you."*

Wynedd did not respond. Only an ache for sleep crossed the bond, and Eso's worry for his dragon mounted higher.

He opened his heavy eyes, and it took him a while to recognize his own quarters. It was a simple abode that smelled musty from the adjacent library and was crammed with tall shelves laden with books, scrolls, ghost orbs, and strategically placed amethysts and rose quartzes. When riders wrote or studied in the library or chatted in the mess hall below, the mystic motes from their thoughts would tether between his perfectly aligned crystals.

Eso got to his feet too fast. Blood rushed from his head, and he swayed, threw out a hand to steady himself, and knocked several books to the floor.

Across the bond, Wynedd bristled at her sleepiness but soon succumbed to slumber.

Eso groaned. With Wynedd asleep, he would have to hurry before sleep also took him. He stepped awkwardly through the room, his body not yet fully responsive after being yanked out of its deep meditation.

Groping, he found his staff, then the door handle. Somehow, he made it out of the mystic barracks and headed for the sanctum at the heart of Falcaer. His indigo robes fluttered as he forced his legs to move in swift, fluid strides so that none would second-guess his vitality.

Throughout this short journey, he examined the impressions he'd received of the Paragons. Of Vald, irritation. Doubtless there would be tensions upon his return. Conflict against the scourge had to be borne, but Eso couldn't stand conflict between his comrades. Then there had been Nilak and Neveh's silence. It had been almost impossible to reach her in the first place, and Neveh's recalcitrance would only lead to a stand-off as well. Kalanta had been closed off, which was not unusual for one of the earth. All the same, Eso had wished to hear her voice. He hoped she was safe.

Turning all of it over, he saw nothing positive to latch onto. His thoughts darkened, congealing into a dead weight inside him.

"Is it done?" a voice crackled.

Again, it took Eso a second to realize where he was. He'd entered the inner sanctum. He looked around, lingering on each empty alcove, trying to recall better memories. In his bleariness, he mistook the man upon the coals to be Aodhan, the previous Paragon of Fire. A yearning swelled then died in him. Those had been better days.

Adaskar sat as Aodhan had, legs crossed on his patch of burning coals, half hidden in a haze of smoke and heat.

"Is it done?" Adaskar repeated.

"They've been informed."

No sooner had the words left Eso's lips than his vision burst into a rainbow of light. All of time stretched out before and behind him, and at every step, branching pathways flowed out infinitely. A web of all that was and that could be, changing faster than he could perceive.

Paragon Adaskar moved to catch Eso before he hit the floor. The fall wouldn't have harmed a Paragon, but it seemed callous to let the old man topple.

Wynedd's dreams took a heavier toll on Eso with each passing year. He'd already been half in a trance upon entering the sanctum, muttering under his breath and staring vacantly before his eyes rolled to the whites.

Adaskar lifted Eso's limp frame and took him to his alcove within the pentagon of the sanctum. The amethysts there could aid him, and when he placed Eso in their vicinity, a violet light began to flow in long floating strands between the crystals.

"Perhaps we should use this council to seek his replacement," Azarin said.

"You know we cannot."

Paragons, once named, served for life, or until their spirits were broken under the weight of their own power. Some were forced to resign due to the death of their dragon or crippling damage to their dragon's core, but neither of these yet applied to Eso and Wynedd. The very notion that custom should be thrown out rankled Adaskar.

Flames lashed across his dragon bond, but Adaskar was a master at ensuring his head remained his own. Azarin meant nothing by it. It was simply his nature.

"Eso is loyal to Falcaer most of all," Adaskar said. *"He will lend his voice to ours."*

Adaskar longed to return to his coals, but there was now a pressing issue to attend to. He made sure Eso's staff was firmly in his grasp, then left him to sleep.

"Our guests must be dealt with before Vald and Raiden'ra return," Azarin said.

Adaskar was already on his way, steam rising from where his bare feet touched the marble floor, willing her from afar to cooperate this time. One Lady of Storms could solve everything by testifying before the Paragons, but her resistance caused him to despair.

Trust. Loyalty. Were these made of motes, the world would be perilously short of their power.

He had been apprehensive about recalling the Paragons at all, for the last thing the Order needed was to witness disharmony between its leaders. Any rider harboring deceitful thoughts may be pushed over the edge should they demand the Paragons return and come up wanting. However, while the Archon's efforts had applied further pressure, Talia still refused to break. The time had come for more decisive action.

If a unanimous agreement between the Paragons could be reached, then the splinter Order in the west would be undone. Any consequences would be softer in the long term than allowing Talia to continue her schism.

The world would thank him in the end.

Adaskar was halfway to the storm barracks when Azarin said, *"Reports on the emeralds have come in."*

"And?"

Some time passed in which Adaskar waited for Azarin to collect word from the other dragons.

"They're flying all over the east but are concentrating on the Fae Forest. A few have flown as far as the ruins of Freiz and others north into the Frontier. There have been engagements."

"Engagements?" Though he spoke telepathically, a wisp of black smoke escaped his nose. *"Their orders were to watch and learn. Gather those who did this. Examples must be made of them."*

"Agreed," Azarin said, and his voice bloomed as though oil had been poured onto his inner fires. Azarin's presence in Adaskar's mind dimmed as his dragon focused elsewhere.

Adaskar longed for his coals. In these uncertain times, he found it harder to empty his mind anywhere else. As it was, his patience was already straining as he strode into the storm barracks.

An Exalted Champion in gray brigandine met him on one knee, proffering a bowl of lemon water. He dipped his hands in, washing off flakes of soot between his fingers.

"Revered Paragon, how may I assist you?"

Adaskar saw the ends of the Champion's hair were singed from a permanent coiling static. A shame. A flaw must have formed within her mote channels or soul that she had failed to correct. Advancing may only make matters worse for her – if she was able to advance at all.

"Where is she?"

"Meditating in the windcatcher courtyard. Allow me to—"

"There's no need."

He dried his hands with a cycle of fire, then blazed by the

Champion. Aside from the urgency of the situation, he disliked the cool air within the barracks.

In haste, he entered the windcatcher courtyard. Here the storm riders of old had constructed towers to funnel prevailing winds down into the open yard, increasing the volume and strength of the motes many times over. Today there was only a light breeze, but the windcatchers still did their work, creating a gust of wind on the courtyard floor. Adaskar Floated his mote channels, cycling magic to the surface of his skin to create a layer of magical protection. At once the ill effect of the wind ceased and he felt warm, as though enveloped in a thick blanket.

Eight storm riders were meditating in the courtyard. All gasped or flinched from his overwhelming spiritual pressure – all but one. A single Lady remained still, sitting with legs crossed and eyes shut. Her sheets of long black hair fell straight, unaltered by the blowing wind. Maintaining such composure in his presence must have strained her, for she had advanced only recently. Compared to him, she was as distant as a new Ascendant is to Lordship.

"Leave us."

The smoke that trailed from his mouth caught in an updraft and spiraled out of the courtyard. The lesser riders scurried off, and with them gone, the Lady opened her dark eyes, stood, and drank him in.

If she felt any fear, she did not show it. Her features were steel-cut. Dressed in silver silks, her body could have been a shard of metal. After a moment, she steepled her fingers and bowed her head.

"Sobh bekheir, Paragon," Farsa said.

Good morning? He almost smiled at her gall. It could still be a good morning, and he told her as much.

"Hanoz ham mishe."

Now it was just the two of them, they continued in their native tongue.

"How may I be of assistance?"

"Are you prepared to tell the truth?"

"I already have, though if my account lacked the clarity desired by a Paragon, please allow me to do better."

Once again, she went over the misadventure at Windshear Hold and her discovery of a conspiracy to steal and hatch dragon eggs, in which Champions Dahaka of Alamut and Orvel of Sable Spire had been involved.

This much Adaskar believed, and then Farsa prattled into lies again. A mystic dragon called Sovereign had orchestrated everything, she claimed. Orvel's dragon, an emerald called Gea, had come clean to her after the battle, and then she had let Gea go.

This was the first sticking point.

"That was not for you to decide."

Farsa bowed lower. "Forgive my poor judgment in this matter. With Orvel dead, what greater punishment could we have placed upon her?"

Little enough, Adaskar knew, but Gea would have been a fount of knowledge on this murky mess. He said nothing, however, knowing it would be better to let Farsa try to over-explain herself.

"Gea wished to seek a new purpose and redemption in her Flight. Hava bound Gea to a soul oath to this end."

In saner times, when the Wild Flights could be trusted to uphold the Pact, a dragon of the Order had low prospects of making a new life among their wild kin. But in this present madness, Adaskar was unsurprised. If the emeralds already worked with rogue riders in Feorlen, why not take in a disgraced dragon from the Order too?

All these matters seemed bound to Talia. Whether the girl was the true orchestrator or not, all roads led to her splinter sect. Despite the obvious links, and despite Adaskar's repeated questioning, Farsa claimed to have no knowledge of Talia's involvement.

She was hiding something from him, but there was enough truth in the tale to make teasing out the falsehoods difficult. Her version of events at Alamut, of Dahaka's departure and a missing egg, corroborated Flight Commander Umbra's report. And then, somehow, alone and upon her own initiative, Farsa had tracked

Dahaka down, defeated her, and uncovered a conspiracy to gather stolen eggs at Windshear Hold.

Eggs had been disappearing from Order Halls across the world, some even from Falcaer itself. The theft of eggs was no new thing. Sometimes rogues fancied they could raise dragons loyal to themselves. Dahaka and Orvel couldn't have been the only members in such a wide conspiracy, and it seemed more likely that Talia and those who had flown to join her insurgency were part of this larger plot. The cook boy and the blind dragon had also been sighted in the east.

Farsa claimed to have resolved the entire operation at a stroke.

It was so neat as to be laughable.

In fact, it was insulting. The very thought of it aroused Adaskar's inner fires, boiling his blood and piquing his anger. How he longed to unleash it... but she was a Lady of Storms. Until guilt could be proven beyond doubt, she would have the respect her rank demanded. Holding her at Falcaer, not quite as a prisoner but nonetheless chiefly confined to the storm barracks, was already a stretch Vald would take issue with on principle.

"You requested your seasonal transfer be to Oak Hall," Adaskar said calmly. "Why?"

"The Fallow Frontier is a drain for brigands, traitors, and chaos-bringers. Windshear Hold has been residence to rogues in the past as well. Of all the Order Halls, I saw Oak Hall as my best chance to come across rumors of Dahaka. That she and Zahak acted so brazenly around Windshear shows how unhinged they had become."

"Within a week of arriving, and upon your first patrol, you encountered Dahaka. That seems a great coincidence for such a wide world."

"I was as shocked as you are, Master Adaskar. What can I call it but good fortune?"

Adaskar snorted. Such a clear evasion fatally hurt her account. Luck, she claimed. Luck. More likely, she had known where her quarry would be. The real question was how? Had she been part of the conspiracy and gained cold feet? Had a disagreement led to death? Such violence was common among oath-breakers and chaos-bringers.

"Why not report your suspicions to Commander Umbra?"

"I had no proof, only hearsay. If it turned out to be true, I'd hoped to be able to bring Dahaka to her senses and bring her home before her honor was befouled forever. I wish with all my heart that that had been the way things had gone."

This, he felt, was genuine. Adaskar had watched many friends, peers, and old mentors wither or stray under the burden of service. He'd wished for them all to come to their senses too, wished for them not to pursue reckless deeds, wished for them to know their limits and serve as their capabilities allowed, not as their desires yearned.

"To my grief," Farsa said, unprompted, "she was too far gone. Dahaka's views became increasingly radical over the years, but one always hopes..."

Adaskar thought of Vald, of Neveh, and of Kalanta.

"One hopes." More smoke spilled from his mouth. He huffed and cleared his head. Sentiment would be the ruin of him, of the Order, if he let it. Returning to his line of inquiry, his tone was coarse. "Why such a concern for Dahaka's honor?"

"I felt... I felt partly responsible for what she had become."

There was truth in this too, Adaskar sensed. A pain from old wounds inflicted by the burdens of riderhood. Of choosing who would live and who would die.

A pain he recognized.

Naturally, he'd investigated her record. Both Farsa and Dahaka had served during the desert swarm of twenty-nine years ago. During that rising, Farsa had been forced to make a choice, to save one settlement or the other.

She'd made her choice.

Dahaka's family perished because of it.

"It is the first lesson," Adaskar said.

"She hated me for it. I've wondered whether... whether I ought—"

Adaskar stepped forward, hunger rising in his voice. "Yes?"

Farsa spoke to her toes. "I wonder whether I ought to have

taken her feelings into account. The town I saved was the right one, strategically speaking, but Dahaka's broken heart led to consequences I did not consider. Had she not been stopped, who knows what horrors she may have committed."

Adaskar slumped. He had thought she was about to admit to something serious.

"Dahaka swore her oath," he said. "She had no family but the Order."

"If the Order is our family, should we not treat our family well? Would less danger and less harm have come about if I had treated Farsa as a true sister and saved those she loved?"

Despite himself, Adaskar found her words touched a sore spot in his soul. A tender spot with a conscience. Yet as far as Adaskar was concerned, in this matter at least, Farsa had nothing to be sorry for. She had made the correct decision and saved the town that could be saved. Dahaka's pain was understandable, but her acting upon it was inexcusable. The Oath meant nothing if one did not hold to it in the hardest of times.

Farsa seemed to regret her words. Her rigid expression broke, and she blushed. "Forgive my idle musings, Paragon. I am ashamed."

Farsa was about to speak again, but Adaskar raised a hand to cut her off. They had deviated from the real issue.

"The only shame here is in lying to a Paragon." Hoping to catch her off-guard, he added quickly, "Tell me what you know of Holt Cook."

Without missing a beat, Farsa frowned. "Who?"

Adaskar began to pace. Black soot flaked across the stones where he walked.

"My apologies, Master Adaskar, but I cannot speak of things I do not know."

"Gea and Orvel encountered Holt Cook. Did she fail to mention that?"

"Gea only spoke to me of a dragon called Thrall. This is where your attention should lie. Other riders in the Order will still be in service to this enemy."

"Thrall?" he said, suspicious. Talia had bleated on about a

dragon called Sovereign. What was this new ploy? So many distractions, so much smoke, but he could not see the fires. "A moment ago, it was Sovereign, and now you say 'Thrall'. Which is it?"

"Sovereign and Thrall are one and the same. Thrall is his true name."

More like the story has just changed in the telling.

"Thrall was once a dragon in the Order," Farsa beseeched. "His rider was a Mystic Lord – there must be records of him."

"None have been found."

That Farsa could not conjure the name of this rider did not help.

Fast losing patience, Adaskar began pacing again. The wind nipped at his skin like a pestering fly. He drew upon the spiritual energy of his soul and pressed Farsa with it. As a check of her will, he asked, in the wordless tongue of spirit, 'Is this your full account?'

She met his eyes, and somehow, despite everything, her expression became steel-cut again. Her own spirit checked his. 'I have nothing more to tell you.'

Against his better judgment, Adaskar was impressed with her resolve. They were cousins of a kind, though how distantly he did not know. It mattered not once the oath was sworn. Such bravery and courage were not uncommon to the proud families of Ahar, where every day was a struggle against nature. Perhaps that accounted for her obstinance.

"I am not unreasonable, Lady Farsa. Provide irrefutable evidence, and the Paragons will investigate the matter." He pulled a small, purple orb from a pouch at his belt. "Place in here any evidence you have of this dragon," he said, holding the ghost orb out to her. "For the record."

"I don't... I don't have direct memories of Thrall himself. I never encountered him at Windshear, else I would not be here now."

"So, there is no proof," he said, throwing her words back at her. "Only hearsay."

"There is the word of a Lady."

"Words are not enough these days. Not when so many seem willing to break them." Adaskar stepped closer and thrust the ghost orb out for her to take. "I want Gea's confession in full, as well as your fight with Dahaka and Orvel."

The use of a ghost orb for a Lady was a severe break with convention, showing a lack of trust and respect for one of the Order's most powerful assets. But he *had* to know the truth. Even half-truths and blank spaces in the narrative she provided would be informative.

Wordlessly, Farsa took the orb, closed her eyes, and began infusing her memories into it.

Ghost orbs were not perfect solutions. Unless you were a blood relation of the memory giver, the only way to view the contents of an orb was to spill them by smashing it. Picking up on all the details within in a single viewing was not ideal. Besides, memories were complex things. Ghost orbs could only contain a few minutes at most, and anyone seeking information was wise to ask for memories the person had already admitted to having – in this case, Gea's confession and the duels. The final irksome issue was in looking for signs of tampering. Those with sufficiently strong will could do it, and while most who attempted did so in clumsy ways, Farsa had already proven herself in that regard.

Still, it was better than nothing.

Farsa's eyelids fluttered as though in a waking dream. Uttering a sigh of exertion, she pulled her hand back from the orb and took a moment to collect herself, then steepled her fingers and bowed.

"I hope these prove useful to the Paragons."

Azarin's presence crossed the bond. *"What shall we do with her?"*

Adaskar considered. Sending Farsa back to Ahar was out of the question. It was her home territory and too easy a place for her to scheme. Angkor to the deep south was as far away as he could send her, but it was always better to keep worrisome riders close. But he didn't wish her to be at Falcaer when Vald arrived either. Nor were the Skarl Empire and Brenin possible, for he had emptied those lands of riders until the business with Talia was concluded.

Adaskar made his decision, shared it with Azarin, and his dragon agreed. Azarin added a suggestion to ensure she fulfilled it, and Adaskar agreed with this in turn before directing his attention back to the Lady.

"Lady Farsa, you will report back to Oak Hall. You will leave at dawn tomorrow along with five Champions being redeployed to the Fae Forest."

"Understood. I will be glad to escort these Champions to their new post. A sudden change from the Roaring Fjord or Sable Spire will be a hard transition for them."

"They will be glad for your presence and guidance in these uncertain times," Adaskar said. And then to Azarin, he said privately, *"And see to it that these Champions understand their purpose."*

"Consider it done."

Two Exalted Champions and three High Champions ought to be sufficient to keep a newly minted Lady in check.

As a parting to Farsa, he said, "A time will come when loyalties will be tested. Fly safe, Lady Farsa."

5
———

RAKE'S TEST

Holt sat with his back against a beech tree and his cookbook propped open in his lap. By campfire light, he flicked through the pages, searching for recipes containing truffles. His single earthy treasure would not stay fresh for long, so he intended to cook it tonight.

Being a collection of recipes with dragons in mind, he was unsurprised that most dishes calling for truffles were pork ones for emerald dragons with an earth affinity. Besides those, he found a few designed for human consumption. Truffles could make a simple pot of bacon, onion, carrots, and beans more decadent, infuse a woodiness into a Mithran risotto, or ground the tangy soured cream sauces from the Province of Fornheim.

He lacked bacon and carrots, but they had bartered dried white beans and onion from Red Rock. Rake had also returned with a brace of rabbits, and Holt had some salted venison to spare. A stash of wild thyme and parsley wouldn't hurt either.

His decision made, Holt closed his book and set to work. As he dressed the rabbits, he found his trusty cook's knife blunter than usual, and he thought he ought to pick up a new one if he could. Lacking a skinning knife, he'd been using his cook's one for all purposes, and the iron was looking worn.

As the aroma of simmering onions, beans, rabbit, venison, herbs, and truffle filled the air, even Osric perked up. When it was ready, even Rake asked for some. It seemed his stomach could tolerate beans well enough.

With stomachs full of hot delicious food, the group sunk into a languid slumber around the campfire.

Ash lay in a prime position by the fire, resting his snout upon his front talons. Osric and Soot crouched in the shadows, of which there were plenty. Away from Aberanth's spacious glade, the Fae Forest was densely wooded. Many species of trees grew in proximity at odds with nature. Oak, spruce, birch, pine, and a peculiar strand of beech tree whose leaves bloomed a coppery red in early spring. Green, blue, and indigo mosses clung to bark or draped over fallen logs, creating homes for exotic fungi even Aberanth wouldn't contemplate eating.

Holt returned to reading his recipe book out of habit, but eventually, his instincts picked up that Rake was staring at him, his eyes seemingly boring holes through the leather cover.

"You can read when you're dead," Rake said, standing with his polearm gripped in both hands. "Up you get."

Closing his book with a gentle thud, Holt tucked it safely away, then got up, stretched, rolled his shoulders, and shook out his legs. With a puff of breath, he drew Brode's sword from its scabbard, which was resting on his packs, but did not strap on his belt or bandoleer. Careless accidents would cost him in smashed vials or jerky covered in dirt.

Ash yawned.

"You think you're getting off?" Rake said.

Ash rose to all fours, though he struggled to stretch the full length of his neck and tail between the packed, oppressive trees.

"You as well, Grumps."

Ash rumbled in surprise.

Holt raised his eyebrows. "You want to fight all three of us?"

"All *four* of you, if our anxious girl is willing to take part?"

Soot yapped and hid her snout behind her wing.

Rake shrugged. "Three versus one, then. You might still have a chance."

Wordlessly, Osric got to his feet and lowered the hood of his gray cloak. Soot babbled and pressed her snout into his leg by way of encouragement. Osric ran his hand down her head, then brought a finger to his lips and made a hushing sound, and she settled at once.

A tense moment passed, then Osric pulled Vengeance from his belt. Without its connection to Thrall, the oxblood steel had lost its luster, no longer radiating a black hatred. That left the gray patterns across the steel easier to discern, even in the dim firelight. They were almost Skarl in nature, interweaving yet rigid.

Osric stepped into position, his pale eyes locked onto Rake. Though still an imposing figure, he was undeniably diminished without his right hand and second axe. A Lord reduced to a Novice; from bonded to Thrall to a mute hatchling; from a raging berserker to a simple soldier.

Without the experience of wintering with the man at Aberanth's grotto, Holt might have felt confident against him, but Holt did have such experience, and he still sported the bruises to prove it.

"One moment, please," Rake said. He ran a hand over his orange blade and blunted its edge with mystic energy.

Holt gulped. Blunting meant Rake intended to land real blows. This would hurt.

He had tried and failed to blunt Brode's sword many times. As the steel wasn't attuned to Ash's lunar motes, their magic never took to it. Osric couldn't have infused Soot's magic into his axe for the same reason. Rake, however, seemed able to get around this impairment through brute force or skill.

Rake took their weapons to blunt them.

Holt took the chance to lower his blindfold and meld his senses with Ash. As he did so, an overpowering smell of dead leaves from the forest floor mingled with his and Osric's sweat, the gentle heat of the campfire burned upon his skin, Rake's breaths rang like sirens through a fog, and four more hearts drummed in his ears.

With Ash's assistance, ghostly outlines of his surroundings sketched in his mind, forming the trees, the contours of the root-filled earth, each of the combatants, and the movements of cold steel through the air.

Rake handed back their now blunted weapons.

"I've spent a lot of time, energy, and patience training you." Though he spoke to no one in particular, Holt had a suspicion this was directed at him. "We're about to enter the wide world again, and out of professional pride, I need to know you've got a chance of surviving on your own."

Holt set his jaw. Rake wasn't going to hold back this time. Instinctively, he turned toward his jerky, following the strong scents of ginger, vinegar, and wine.

Rake wagged a finger. "No elixirs or food. Three strikes to yield. And remember," he added in a wry tone, "try to have fun."

Rake swung his polearm in an arc, sucking in air around it, as though the world were drawing a short, sharp breath. Condensed mystic power formed, mirroring the movement of Rake's swing, and a moment later, the Soul Blade rushed forward.

As Holt dropped to avoid the sweeping attack, he heard Osric step forward and met the mystic projection with his axe. A screech rang. Magic flared brightly in Holt's sixth sense, and the Soul Blade shattered into crumbs of ill-defined motes.

Ash crunched through the undergrowth, sending an intention to flank Rake.

Holt rose, only to be confronted with a pulse of mystic power. One of Rake's Arcane Blasts. Holt deflected it with Brode's sword; Rake launched more. His attacks were so numerous it was all Holt could do to block or avoid them, and Holt Floated his mote channels in case he failed, cycling the flow of energy to project a layer of magical armor like a second skin.

Osric rushed forward, using Vengeance to chop through the Blasts Rake sent his way as Ash slowly negotiated his way through the trees.

Holt risked a step, then misjudged one of his blocks. A mystic pulse flew under his arms and hit him square in the chest, driving the wind clean out of him. Hacking, he managed to remain upright. At least Floating had done its job.

Osric closed the gap, forcing the half-dragon to counter. Wielding his polearm in just one hand, Rake thrust with maddening speed.

Despite being one-handed, Osric remained a ferocious warrior. He had been a Lord, of course, and seemed to have maintained a good measure of his former strength. Both he and Rake fought aggressively, but without a second weapon, Osric struggled to overcome Rake as he had before.

As Holt rushed to join the fight again, he felt elation spike over his bond. Ash had found a clear line of sight. He opened his jaws and let loose a dense beam of moonlight.

Rake extended his free arm and conjured his Barrier ability. Mystic power swirled to shield Rake, and Ash's moonbeam crashed into it. A small explosion erupted on the magical landscape.

Osric stepped past the tip of Rake's polearm and used his maimed right arm to pin the polearm's shaft against his body. Just for a moment, it seemed Rake was trapped. All Holt had to do was close the distance and score a strike, but Holt knew what Rake could do and, anticipating Rake's move, he slowed.

A force *shifted* in the vicinity. It was hard to quantify yet perceptible to his heightened instincts; part hearing, part magical, part primal, as though his soul could register a distortion.

Rake disappeared.

The hairs on the back of Holt's neck quivered.

There was a soft whoomph, then a swish of steel from behind.

Holt spun and blocked Rake's swing. Backing off, he switched cycling techniques to Grounding, boosting the flow of energy to his limbs to help with his strength and agility. Despite this boost to his body, Holt still struggled to defend himself.

Rake was a powerhouse in melee combat. His seven-foot frame granted him a much longer reach than Holt, even without the use of his polearm. His agility belied his size, and his tail acted as both weapon and limb, granting further coverage.

"Attack," Rake growled, even as he forced Holt onto the back foot.

Osric was moments from joining the fight when Rake gathered mystic power at his feet.

Holt disengaged, jumping back.

Osric skidded to a halt, coming up short.

Rake stamped his foot, unleashing his Kickback ability. Where his foot touched the ground, magic blasted out in a pulse, and he sprang up into a soaring backflip before landing in a graceful crouch.

Rake's abilities made him hard to pin down. However, he could not use them in quick succession, and now was the moment to swarm him before he could safely use Blink or Kickback again.

Ash sprang his trap. With his wings tucked in, he barreled forward, snapping branches and scraping bark from trunks, and managed to bowl Rake over.

"One," Ash called in triumph, *"Master Rake,"* he added apologetically.

"You shouldn't have stopped," Rake said, leaping to his feet and striking one, two, three blows into Ash, knocking him out of the fight.

Ash staggered. Blunt pain flared across their bond.

Without a moment's pause, Rake charged Holt and Osric, pressing the attack again.

Holt still Grounded his body, but he needed a greater boost if they had a hope of winning. He channeled magic to his legs, then pressed a firm foot into the earth, laying down a Consecration. He could feel the silver power expand through the soil, creating a haven of warm, friendly power that compounded the benefits of his Grounding, sending his strength to new heights and sharpening his reflexes.

Quite unexpectedly, Osric howled and backed off the lunar-infused ground. Rake leaped off the Consecration after him and swung his polearm with full force. The reinforced wood slammed into Osric's side. Dazed, Osric took the blow and buckled but, through a screaming effort, managed to parry Rake's next attack.

Rake clenched his free fist and swung at Osric's right side.

Out of instinct, Osric raised his stump to block the blow, but lacking a weapon or a shield, Rake's punch drove Osric's forearm into his face, followed by Rake's fist. Osric crumpled.

"Yield," Rake demanded.

Part of Rake's training over winter had included basic lessons in the use of spirit, and they had started with a method of surrender. A ribbon of spiritual energy now emanated from Rake and wove its way to Soot, an invitation to surrender.

Bent on all fours, Osric spat blood. "I yield."

Soot squeaked in agreement, and the spiritual power connecting her to Rake went taut, then tied tight.

Holt cursed himself, though he'd had no idea Osric would be affected like that. Their spars over winter had all been without magic.

With Osric out of the fight, Holt at least had no qualms about laying down another Consecration. He did so and maintained his Grounding. Rake sent another barrage of Arcane Blasts, but upon his lunar ground, Holt dodged or deflected them all.

"Good," Rake cried, then he Blinked, reappearing on Holt's right. Holt whirled just in time to clash steel.

"Blind him," Ash suggested.

It was all Holt could hope to do. Flare wouldn't work. Rake was fast enough to take measures to avoid it. Eclipse would be the better option, but for that he needed to get as far from the campfire as he could.

Holt pulled back, hoping to use Rake's aggression against him. As Rake pursued him, Holt performed the delicate dance of staying inside Rake's 'dead zone' between the polearm's tip and the reach of Rake's arm – a cheap trick to play for time, but that was all he needed.

Deeper into the night of the forest he dragged Rake, back and back, until the crackle of the fire faded and its heat vanished from his sensitive skin.

Holt switched cycling from Grounding to Sinking. His energy flow turned inward to his center, pulling ambient lunar motes into his body, into his soul, which he funneled over the bond to

Ash. The sudden disappearance of scant moonlight would turn him into a wraith-like figure cloaked in pure darkness.

Rake went still. He ceased breathing and even lowered his heart rate, but Holt could still smell him, could still hear the polearm swinging. He side-stepped, and Rake cut into the empty blackness.

Holt seized his chance. If he managed two strikes, he would win.

But at the very last moment, Rake's tail whipped around. Holt heard every movement of the half-dragon's muscles and bones, but he was too slow to react. The tail clobbered into his belly, bending him over double, then a scaly hand shoved him into the dirt.

"Yield," Rake said. The invitation flowed out to Ash.

"I yield."

"We yield," Ash confirmed, and like Soot, the ribbons of spiritual power flowing between Rake and Ash knitted into a knot. As the yield took effect, Holt's dim thoughts to keep fighting were met with a crushing resistance.

Dragons could commit each other to soul oaths, and something about this method of surrender had a similar effect, though it was less binding. With time, the effect would wear off. Aberanth theorized this may have mattered more in ages past and in the forming of the flights, where power coalesced around the Elders.

Annoyed and breathing hard, Holt allowed his channels to return to an even flow of energy. He lifted his blindfold. In the scant moonlight, the dark figure of Rake stood above him, flexing and punching at the air.

Holt returned to sit by the campfire. Osric was already there, holding his right arm like a broken wing. Soot sat beside him, unusually fully corporeal.

Ash picked his way over to join him, sat down, and placed the tip of his snout onto Holt's lap. *"That could have been worse."*

"Could have been a lot worse," Holt agreed, stroking Ash's nose. He quickly replayed the fight in his mind and couldn't help but think he'd made a big mistake at the end. Catching Rake's eye, he asked, "Did you fake that thrust at me when I used Eclipse?"

"No," he said in a long drawl. "I couldn't see you at first. But as you were the center of the darkness, when you moved, the darkness shifted with you. I could track that, but I had to work for it," he admitted.

"I'll keep working on making the area bigger."

"Oh, it's much larger than before. Keep practicing your Sinking technique, and with a little food or elixir in a pinch, you'll be good and concealed."

"I'm not sure I got the Floating right. That Blast of yours hurt something fierce."

"I put more oomph into it than usual. In fact, I held back less than I usually do throughout the whole fight. You did well."

Despite his throbbing chest, sides, and everywhere really, Holt smiled.

"But—"

Holt's smile drooped.

"—you still fight too defensively."

Holt considered. "Should I not have guarded against your Arcane Blasts?"

"For the first barrage, you stood your ground and Floated. The second time you were Grounding, I assume, and standing on your Consecration. Both times you relinquished the fight to me, allowing me to send attack after attack, meaning the odds were always on my side. One Blast will always make it through in time, do you see?"

Holt nodded. That made plenty of sense, as it had every time Rake explained it, but it was tough to fight his natural instincts.

"But still much better," Rake said proudly. "I'm having to try to get through your defenses now."

Holt's dragon bond burned with satisfaction.

"How would you rank Holt now, Master Rake?"

At once, Holt felt Rake's presence brush against his bond, gauging its strength and Ash's core. Rake crossed his arms, frowned theatrically, then raised one eyebrow as he scrutinized them. He exclaimed in surprise, growled, frowned again, and finally said, "Not sure I can say until I've seen you fight for real."

"What?" Holt spluttered. "That's not how it works."

"So says the pot boy. I forgot you were the expert. If you're so sure, rate yourselves. You know your own strength."

"We don't have much to compare it to."

Another presence inspected his soul bond, this one much rougher. The spiritual touch had all the finesse of a boot crushing a bug.

"I'd say they're almost High Champions," Osric said.

"Well, if you say so, Grumps," Rake said. "You *were* a Lord, after all."

Osric gave Rake a blank expression. "Why must you always jape? Sometimes a direct question deserves a direct answer."

"Yes, but where's the fun in that? A bit of verbal sparring adds a zest to life. You might try it if you can spare the time from brooding."

"If you say so."

Rake scoffed. "You're hard to like, you know, but despite myself, I might be starting to. I trust you learned something from that short bout?"

"Avoid Ash's magic."

Rake folded his arms. "That is hardly a winning attitude."

"You mean for me to be hurt by it instead?"

"I'd rather see you not be harmed by it at all," Rake said. "They are light, you are shadow, but if your own magic was stronger—"

"I will not touch such chaos again."

Rake sighed and gave a mocking, defeatist shrug. "What are you going to do, wander around just as you are? Two lambs in a world of wolves?"

Soot yapped and stood on all fours, scowling. Rake hissed at her, and while she shrank back, it was only by a pace. Rake raised one eyebrow as if impressed.

"Why do you care?" Osric asked.

Rake's eyebrow descended as his face took on a deep frown. "You know what? I don't care about you. Do what you will, but I do care about the little one. She's a new power in this world, just like Ash. Who knows what she might be able to do? Everyone will either want her for their own or try to kill her to make sure she doesn't become a threat. Doesn't that bother you?"

"My only objective is to keep her safe."

"Then *advance!*"

"She's not bloodthirsty like the rest of us," Osric said. "She's good at hiding. We can hide together. Power would only invite challengers. Build an impregnable fortress and someone will dream of toppling it. Let us be."

"He's really given up, hasn't he?" Holt said to Ash.

"I think he's afraid. It's harder to interpret his voice and heart, but it's there, I'm sure."

"You're being a coward," Rake said. "You're too afraid of your own shadow, and yes, that is ironic."

Osric snorted like a branded bull, and his maimed hand reached for an axe that was no longer there. That seemed to catch him by surprise, and he stared at his stump as though waking from a bad dream. When he glanced at the group again, his pale eyes seemed stricken and lost.

"I can't be trusted with power," he said, his voice hoarse. "Call me a coward if you will, but I know the monster I can be."

Perhaps, Holt considered, it would be best if Osric crawled off into a shadowy corner of the world and remained there, but Rake had the right of it.

Holt shuffled forward tentatively, as though approaching a wounded bear. "Things are different now. She isn't a monster. I don't think you'll ever become what you once were, not while you're with her."

Soot gave Holt a look of deepest appreciation, then she turned her dark, wet eyes to her rider and cooed so softly and sweetly it almost broke Holt's heart.

Rake cleared his throat. "The pot boy is right. This isn't about you, Agravain. Don't let fear make you selfish. In a bond, there is no room for that."

Osric's lower lip shook. It was the closest Holt had come to seeing the man break into an emotion that wasn't anger.

However, Osric did not break. Instead, he composed himself. He filled his chest, raised his chin, and ushered Soot closer to him.

"If you're willing to help, I am willing to work."

Holt smiled. Ash rumbled, swished his tail, and vibrated his wings.

Rake almost purred with pleasure. "Finally," he said, thrusting his polearm high in triumph. "Let's see what these shadows can conjur—"

His voice cut off, descending into a fit of painful coughs. He groaned, dropped his polearm to his side, and clutched at his chest with his free hand.

Holt's smile vanished. "What's wrong?"

He got up, but Rake threw up a hand to stay him. "It's nothing," he said through gritted teeth.

"What happened to having 'no more secrets'?" Holt asked.

"It's strange," Ash said. *"His heart has slowed, but when it beats, it rings too loud, as though trying to burst."*

"Is it Elya?" Holt asked, not giving up. Rake had spoken little on the matter over winter, but as Holt understood it, he had lost all feeling from her completely. Anything, even pain, would be better than nothing.

"It's not her," Rake said. He rubbed his chest and seemed to ease from the discomfort. "I think it's the mote channels around my core. They're still recovering."

"I trust we did not strain you?" Osric asked.

"Hardly," Rake sneered, then descended into coughing again.

Holt and Ash shared an anxious flutter over their bond.

"I know it's no use saying it," Holt began, "but I hope you aren't pushing yourself too hard."

"Me? Push myself? Perish the thought."

"You were so weak after Windshear, Master Rake. A broken wing cannot be flown on too soon."

"Listen," Rake said, bracing himself on his polearm. "I've gone through many ups and downs. I'm in good enough shape to deal with most anything we come across, though maybe not multiples of most anything. Just you wait. One day I'll be back as fighting fit the day I stormed Windshear Hold."

"Your display at the fortress was impressive," Osric admitted. "If only you'd thrust six inches lower."

Rake gave Osric a mocking, overly elaborate bow with much hand waving. "Touché, Grumps. Though it wouldn't have given you the wonderful opportunity to hack off a piece of yourself. Now, if we're all quite done fretting over me, we should move on."

They gathered their things and set out again, heading north, and Holt cast silver light from his palm to guide them.

Heading north had seemed strange to Holt at first, but they could not go directly west, for that would have led them through Athra's territory. Rake said he wanted to reach the Brown Wash, then turn west and skirt the southern mountains of the Spine. Having consulted his maps, Holt still thought this presented an issue.

"I get we're trying to avoid Athran territory," Holt said. "But won't we end up in eastern Risalia if we go around the Spine?"

"At some point," Rake said. "But there are few settlements in those hinterlands, so there's less chance we'll bump into anyone. At least anyone civilized. Riders patrol the area infrequently. It might make sense to cross the Brown Wash and dip our toes into the Fallow Frontier for the same reason."

Osric came to a halt.

"Something wrong?" Rake asked over his shoulder irritably.

Osric shook his head, adjusted his packs, and rejoined the march. "The Frontier is a region of ill repute."

Rake laughed. "Well then, we'll fit right in."

6

UNKNOWN SONGS

As they headed north through the Fae Forest, Holt noticed two changes come over the group. The first was that Soot seemed much more eager to walk alongside Ash. She was still not talking, but she was eagle-eyed and observant of his every action. If Ash jumped over a fallen tree, she would too, and when Ash gathered light to his mouth to practice his moonbeam, she opened her jaws to mimic him. For the most part, this resulted in her breathing heavily and gathering little more than saliva, but at least she was trying.

"Better late than never," Rake remarked.

Soot's newfound enthusiasm arrived right alongside Osric's efforts to train in magic. Turning his single-minded focus to the task, Osric Cleansed and Forged whenever he found a moment to spare. It wasn't darkness Soot was linked to, not a lack of light, but shadows. Osric even found motes present in the pale shade of passing clouds. Forests, craggy mountains, and urban environments would be ideal for them.

Given his experience, Holt assumed the basics would come easily, yet despite almost three days of attempting to gather swirling shadows in his hand, Osric had yet to achieve anything solid.

When they reached the border of the forest, they rested. Osric tried again, and veins on his temple and neck swelled from the effort. Darkness roiled at his wrist, and shadowy strands flaked almost lazily between his fingers as he tried to form it into a ball.

While Soot's magic looked like Thrall's black light at a glance, Holt sensed a material difference. Thrall's light had been just that – dark in color yet still radiant, something which pushed power and will outward. Soot's shadows were like rips in the fabric of the world: dense and dark, illuminating nothing.

Osric still struggled; his face turned beet red, and sweat gathered on his brow. His arm shook, then his hand. The shadows flared into a small spinning ball, then snapped and dissipated into weak motes.

"Again," Rake said without sympathy.

Soot chirruped encouragement. Osric huffed and gave her a strained smile, then he gathered himself and tried again. And again. Until, on the tenth attempt, his whole body spasmed.

"Almost," he spat, then the shadow ball crumbled into smoke on the wind. He gasped, groaned, and cradled his hand against his chest.

Holt, who well remembered the difficulties of his early training, felt he was in no position to criticize.

Soot looked from Ash to Osric and back again, her eyes imploring.

"She seems to think I can do something to help," Ash said privately.

"Well, you're the only other dragon here, and while you're young, you're older than she is. Seems she's looking up to you."

While Holt and Ash wrestled over whether they should say anything, Rake tutted.

"You must keep going."

Osric drew a shuddering breath and lowered himself to the forest floor. "I'm not sure that I can." Admitting this seemed to deepen the lines around his eyes and further hollow out his face. He placed his hand over his sternum. "It aches."

Holt couldn't hold back any longer. "This can't be normal, Rake."

"How astute. Not even Aberanth could have worked that one out."

Holt ignored him. "Isn't there anything we can do?"

"I have no experience in re-bonding. It almost never happens."

Something niggled at the back of Holt's mind. He was sure he knew of at least one story.

"It happened for Hild the Humble, or it did for her dragon, I suppose. She bonded to her husband's dragon after he died in battle."

"Well, I'm afraid I did not know Hild the Humble," Rake said. "I might be old, but she was around many centuries before me, as was her 'husband.' Riders still married on occasion in her time, and in the version of the tale I was taught, she was not quite so humble. Point being, I've not dealt with anyone who has bonded for a second time, whether human or dragon."

"You must have hunches?" Ash said.

"A few."

Osric had curled up into himself as though his abdomen was unable to support his torso.

"What does it feel like?" Holt asked. "Aside from being painful," he added quickly.

"Sometimes…" Osric croaked, "sometimes… it feels like the only thing holding me together is her presence." He braced, hands on his knees, then pushed himself upright. "Were it not for her, I doubt I could push through it. And for her sake, I will."

Soot cooed and brushed her tail over the earth. With a burst of energy, she braced herself, planting her four feet firmly into the ground, and opened her jaws wide. Her short pink tongue dangled for a moment before she retracted it and began gathering shadows. A ball of pure darkness shuddered into life, swelling to the size of a melon.

They were all taken aback, but it was Ash who recovered first.

"You can do it," he urged.

Yet rather than encourage her, his words seemed to spook her into self-consciousness. Soot's snout dropped, the shadow ball seemingly suddenly weighing her down. She growled as the shadows flickered in and out of existence, and then they collapsed into nothingness. Soot stepped backward, gnashing her teeth and dry heaving as though a bug had flown down her throat.

Rake pursed his lips, then turned away to contemplate the world beyond the forest.

Osric went to his dragon. Ash padded over next, but she shrank away from him, melding into Osric's shadow like a shy pup. Only her head remained visible.

Ash hesitated, then said kindly, *"The first time I managed to use my breath properly, I accidentally drained my entire core."*

Soot made a squeak of surprise, then furtively moved an inch out of her shadow and closer to Ash.

"It's true," Ash said. *"Knocked me out. Knocked Holt out. The swell of power rushed up unchecked and frayed our bond too. We were lucky not to get killed."*

Soot's eyes widened to two purple globes. She cheeped, then emerged from her shadow and gave the group a sweeping, embarrassed look before lifting a wing over her head.

Feeling he ought to say something, Holt said, "It just takes practice. We're still trying to improve all the time."

"Quiet," Rake growled, an edge of worry to his voice.

In response to the warning, Holt reached for the hilt above his shoulder, Osric drew his axe, Ash lifted his ears, and Soot disappeared into Osric's shadow, though it was a bit pointless. When she fully submerged herself, her core became unde-tectable, but that would help little with Ash still around.

Rake stepped out between the trees, his head held high and tilted up, scanning the skies. Gripping his polearm, he turned his gaze this way and that.

"Ash," he said, beckoning the dragon to his side. "Can you hear anything?"

Ash moved out of the forest to join Rake. He twisted his head back and forth, sniffing deeply. When he faced west, his ears stood up, keen as a cat caught in fright.

Holt drew Brode's sword. "What do you hear?"

"The wind is blowing from the east, so it's hard to tell. A fight... maybe."

"Do you sense any cores?" Holt asked.

"No…" Rake said hesitantly. "Truth is, though, my reach isn't what it was. I just feel the faintest of echoes of magic as Ash might sniff a scent upon the wind." He tittered. "Look at how on edge I've become. Aberanth must have worn off on me."

Holt sheathed his weapon and breathed easy. Even Osric let out a sigh.

"Better to be careful," Ash said.

"Indeed," said Rake. "We should be on our guard every step of the way, and if I ever tell you to run, give me a good slap – that ought to bring me to my senses. Then we'll make a fight of it."

Rake led them out of the forest, declaring they should reach the banks of the Brown Wash by the following afternoon. Holt kept his belt bags and bandoleer stocked in case of trouble, but given Rake still had far-reaching senses, he didn't stay on heightened alert himself. Instead, he settled into a comfortable pace and drank in the rolling countryside.

The forest had been beautiful at times over winter, especially when snow covered everything like powdered sugar, but the scenery had grown stale. Out here, the wind blew unimpeded, no canopy blocked the sky, and the spring sun fell upon his face.

He had trained, grown stronger.

He was ready.

Rake's prediction proved correct, and they arrived at the Brown Wash the next day while the sun was still high and took a break there for some food. Holt sat on the riverbank, gnawing at some plain jerky. Having consulted his maps, he knew these waters originated from as far away as the edge of the Grim Gorge, where wild mystics made their nests.

His thoughts turned to Eidolan. Had the old illusionist made it back to his nesting grounds? Had his fellow mystics welcomed him or reviled him? And what had become of the egg he'd retrieved from Windshear?

With no way of answering his idle wanderings, his attention turned to the remarkable and unmistakable sight further north on the other side of the river. It was a colossus of a mountain formed out of jagged slopes as though many smaller mountains had grown one on top of the other, uniting to pierce the heavens. Snow lay so thick upon its slopes that one could be forgiven for thinking that clouds had laid down there to rest. From where Holt stood, the mountain looked conquerable, but it was easily the largest thing he had ever beheld. Even the mountains around Windshear Hold paled in comparison to this.

It could only be one of the Frost Fangs. The eastern one, to be precise. The Spine split the northern world in two, and the fangs were no exception. To the west, the second fang rose monstrously high in the Province of Fornheim on the other side of the range. Depending on their route, perhaps he would glimpse it as well.

Holt finished his strips of jerky and checked on the others. Ash had stretched his neck out over the river. Water lapped at the banks, driven on by a swift current. Giving a little attention to the bond, Holt sensed Ash's pleasure in the cooler air above the water and the soothing sound of the running river.

Osric and Soot had finished their food and were huddled together under Osric's gray cloak to shield them from the sun. Holt felt a stab of pity for them. The forest had been an ideal retreat for them, a land of shadows Osric and Soot had become accustomed to.

Rake stood rooted to the spot, gazing west with a fierce intensity. Holt moved to stand by him and followed his gaze to find a trio of green dragons. They were well out of Holt's magical detection, and even Rake's at his best, but in the clear sky they were visible and might have been mistaken for three birds were it not for the great span of their wings. They were moving fast, already shrinking to specks as they hurried west.

"It's a shame we missed them," Holt said. "We could have asked after Turro."

"I'm happier to avoid the risk of discovering whether they are friend or foe."

Leaving Holt to stew on that, Rake rounded on the others to cajole them into movement. There was a ford further downstream that they could cross.

Although the sunlight was gentle, Soot kept her head down and held one wing awkwardly over herself. Ash trotted to her side. She trilled at him, but as he raised and spread his wing, she settled and relaxed inside the larger shadow. She even took a step closer to him so that white and black, light and shadow, walked together as they followed the course of the Brown Wash.

As the sun began to dip into a watery, golden haze, they drew within sight of a settlement upon the opposite bank defended by earthen rises, ditches, and thick palisades. Had it not been spread across several hillocks, it might have been a fort. Rake said it was called Silt Grave.

Below Silt Grave lay the ford. Holt wondered if Rake had forgotten they were traveling with two dragons. Rake, Holt, and Osric might draw up their hoods and pass at a distance without remark, but they could not conceal Ash or Soot, and anyone from the vantage point of the town would spot them.

As if sensing Holt's concerns, Rake said, "Let them have a tale to gnaw over in their taverns and ale houses. The next crossing is a two-day journey further west, which brings us too close to the edge of Athran-controlled territory for my liking."

As though the world was on their side for once, the sky darkened as they approached the ford, and it began to rain. Not a downpour, but enough to veil them in a blur of raindrops. Ash raised both wings, and Holt took shelter under one and Osric and Soot the other. Rake trudged on ahead, letting the rain soak his cloak.

When they were within a mile of Silt Grave, Ash spoke to the group with concern.

"I don't hear anything from the town. Not a laugh, not a voice, no barking dog or closing door. Were this before dawn or the middle of the night, it might not seem so strange, but even then, I think I'd hear something."

"Would you hear anything over the rain?" Holt asked.

"The rain is constant, so it fades into the background if I focus. I can

still hear all your hearts, your lungs fill and empty of air, and how the rain hits different things in the town – soft on thatch, pinging hard onto cobbles, and pattering into rain barrels."

They reached the ford. Crossed it. With squelching steps, Holt climbed onto the northern bank, then he froze.

"You sense it too?" Rake asked.

Holt nodded. Magic. Imprints of power, hard to define, like an untidy palette where all the colors bled into one.

One color he managed to discern. His skin prickled, and Ash both felt and smelled it at the same time. Their joint revulsion gripped their bond and wrung it taut, ready for a fight.

Holt drew Brode's sword and charged for the track leading up the first hill.

"Wait," Rake called.

Holt turned but didn't stop moving, continuing to backstep up the slope. "The scourge has been here. There might be people we can help. Come on!"

He turned back up the hill, running through the rain. Ash followed him as his feet splashed over the wet dirt track, their equipment rattling on his back.

Predictably, horribly, the town gates were broken. Great chunks lay strewn about on the approach, including one of the large metal hinges, seemingly ripped free of the gatehouse. Gouge marks in the stone confirmed this.

The rain continued to fall as Ash joined Holt before the broken gates.

"It must have been a team of juggernauts that caused this."

Ash sniffed deeply. *"I don't smell any bodies. But there's blood... there's blood everywhere."*

Together they stepped into the desolation.

Though braced for the worst, all they found in the settlement was churned earth, smashed glass, splintered wood, and dropped possessions. Ash was right. There were no bodies. Nothing. Not even a stray limb or severed hand, though most ominous of all was what Ash had got wrong – frighteningly wrong.

There was no blood. Anywhere. Not a drop mixed in the muddy pools or streaked across wood or stone. Were it not for the obvious signs of disturbance, the inhabitants might have vanished into thin air.

The town had been picked clean.

Running feet splashed behind them.

"This must have been what I sensed," Rake said forlornly. "We were too far away to have offered help even if I— well, it's no good thinking about it."

"Something isn't right," Holt said mechanically.

"Is it?" Rake asked, his tone serious, not mocking. "We know why the scourge would gather the dead."

"They don't clean a site of all blood."

"I'll admit that is worrisome." Rake bent and righted an over-turned wagon with a single hand. Beneath it, the soil was drier, and the footprint of an abomination was evident.

Ahead of them looked like an area for the town's market with a central well that had seen better days; its stone arch covering had collapsed on one side, and its pulley system hung uselessly. Ash padded over to the broken well on the trail of some scent.

"Two carriers were here," he gestured with his snout. *"A third over there. I can still smell blood everywhere,"* he said, his tone pleading, as though the others had called him a liar. *"It's in the air, and there are other strange smells too, but I don't recognize them."*

"Did you see this?" Osric called. He was at the gatehouse, running his hand over the damaged gate hinge still holding onto the wall. "These were forced open from the inside."

Holt thought he should have noticed this, for how else could pieces of the doors be strewn over the road leading up to the town?

It only raised more questions.

"How could juggernauts get inside the walls?"

"Perhaps they were carried," Rake offered. "A blighted dragon could probably lift one."

"One juggernaut couldn't have managed this," Holt said.

"Maybe Osric can offer insight?" Ash asked. *"Did you ever see such a thing when bonded to Thrall?"*

"No." Osric seemed to be only half paying attention and was drifting away as if following his own invisible trail.

It was then that Holt noticed where Soot was. She stood where the second of the great metal hinges lay in the mud, peering up at where it had been gouged from the wall. Three ragged lines trailed through the stone. Like Ash, she sniffed at the area and the hinge itself, then started whining before Osric could reach her.

"What's the matter?" he asked.

Soot continued to whine while she stared intently into Osric's eyes.

"Are you sure?" he asked her.

"Is she speaking to you?" Holt asked. Despite the situation, he was excited by that prospect.

"No. It's more feelings. Impressions."

The downpour did not abate. Osric's untamed hair was now plastered over his face, and water ran from his beard in a single long stream. He pushed hair out of his eyes, then fixated on the same spot as Soot.

Then, without warning, he drew his axe and jumped. Sinking his axe into the gatehouse wall, he hung by one arm and braced his legs against the wall to inspect the marks close up.

"She's right," he called down. "These were made by talons."

"Then there was a scourge risen dragon," Holt said.

Rake narrowed his eyes. "The markings look too narrow to be the talons of a mature dragon."

Osric pushed off the wall, pulling his axe free as he dropped down. Mud splashed up his boots and trousers.

"We know of one young dragon who could do it."

"We?" Rake said, looking at Soot.

Soot growled, and, whether due to the cold rain or some dark memory, she shivered.

"One of the hatchlings Thrall favored," Osric said. "Ginger scales and bulging muscles. Thrall said his physical affinity could turn him into a fortress breaker. She recognizes his scent."

Soot yapped and extended her neck to point further into the town.

"More of the same or different?" Rake asked.

"Different," Osric grunted.

Ash went to the talon marks left by this powerhouse of a dragon and got a feel for its scent. Then they all moved further into Silt Grave, allowing Soot to guide them. As Ash started to isolate the scents she was chasing, he was able to take the lead in looking for evidence of more dragons.

Beyond the market square with the broken well, they came across a long line of sharp, shining crystals rising between the cobblestones like weeds.

Rake dislodged a crystal with his foot, then picked it up. Rolling it between finger and thumb, he announced, "This is no mineral, but pure energy made solid."

"There was an amethyst hatchling," Osric said. "Its scales were crystalline."

"Was it a mystic?" Holt asked.

Rake turned the crystal over and frowned. "Not mystic. Its power feels disconnected... as though it's not part of the world at all."

Even as Rake spoke, the crystal dissolved in his hand, and those in the ground followed suit.

The rain began to abate then, and as it lessened, another form of magic became clear enough to register. Not far from where the purple crystals had been, they found what looked like scorch marks across the walls of a ruined tavern. On closer inspection – and with the help of more light leaking through the dissipating clouds – Holt saw that the blackened trail on the remaining wood was flecked with orange and gold.

Something beat in his magical senses, almost familiar, something which drew him and repelled him in equal measure. He held his hand over the markings. Closed his eyes.

Music reached his mind, strong, fiery, bombastic at heart yet muffled, as though several walls stood between him and the source. As he listened, Holt couldn't help but recognize a pattern deep in the song.

"It's light magic."

"We'll take your expert word for it," Rake said.

His hand still over the scars of light, Holt felt an instinctual pull west to face the lowering sun. He raised a hand against the golden hue, and it took on a different meaning in his mind. A source of unimaginable radiant power, a huge cosmic core: undrainable, unfathomable. Of course, Ash could only absorb its soft reflections like a pup scrounging for scraps. Sunlight was hot where moonlight was cold, revealing instead of merely guiding – denser, purer, superior.

The moment passed, Holt's head cleared, and the sun continued its dip to the horizon.

Something moved at his feet. Holt jumped back, but it was only Soot, and she seemed drawn to the light-scorched wall.

"Careful," Holt said. If Ash's moonlight could sting her, this solar power would surely burn her. But after inspecting it, she growled in excitement and wiggled her tail.

"Her brother," Osric said.

Ash rumbled, looking between Rake and Osric and Soot. *"Dragons do not have family in that way. Master Rake said so."*

A desperation tinged his voice that wrenched Holt's heart. There was a lonely quality in Ash's dragon song, being the only one of his kind. Holt had not heard those notes in some time, but it had been too much to hope they had simply vanished.

"Not strictly as humans do," Rake said. "But my guess is this is different."

Osric nodded. "They hatched from the same egg. The very egg I carried from the Grim Gorge. They're twins."

Soot bounded off, apparently hoping to find her brother up an alley.

"He won't be here," Osric called after her, but she did not listen and roamed around, uncaring whether she stepped into sunlight or shadow.

"You said Thrall took five hatchlings?" Holt said. "We've only found evidence of three."

"Is the absence of blood not a clue?" Rake said. "Ash can smell it, and yet there is none. I'll cut the end of my tail off if that isn't some form of magic."

"There was a crooked, rust-colored hatchling," Osric said. "Its eyes looked painful, bloodshot to the point of being fully red."

"Blood magic?" Ash said, a tremor in his voice.

Holt gulped.

"Well, this is a nasty business," Rake said. "Who wants a drink?"

With that, he strode into the tavern by means of a collapsed section of the wall and went to rummage behind the bar.

"And the fifth?" Holt asked Osric.

"Sea-green, no wings, but it had webbed talons and a strange structure of scales along its neck. Not sure that one was here, though. She hasn't picked up any more scents," he added with a nod to Soot, who was still searching in vain for her twin.

Ash sniffed heartily at the drying air. *"I don't smell a fifth one."*

From behind the bar came the loud pop of a pulled cork.

Still sniffing, Ash grumbled, stuck out his tongue, and backed away as though offended. *"That smells like it could burn my scales off."*

"Good, isn't it?" Rake called. He stood triumphantly holding a dark brown bottle, then drank straight from it. Drops of rich amber liquid dripped down his chin. Wiping his mouth, he said, "A shame it would take about five of these to take the edge off. There's beer and ale back. It would rot my stomach, but the pair of you are still human."

"I don't like magic in my body," Osric said. "Never mind drink."

"You are consistent, Grumps, I'll give you that. As consistent as stale porridge."

Holt entered the tavern, and glass crunched underfoot. "I feel like we should keep clear heads."

Rake rolled his eyes. "You'd need to drink a lot for it to affect you. It's okay to live a little, I promise."

Holt joined Rake behind the bar. The floor was sodden from the contents of three broken kegs. Beer still dripped from one, pit-patting onto the pooling liquid below. A malty, hoppy smell was in the air. Holt's past experiences with ale had always been with weaker, watered-down versions, and he hadn't loved the taste even then. But why not. One keg remained intact, as did tankards under the bar. He filled the cup and appreciated the strong head of froth that foamed on top. He took a sip. Then a second.

"Mmm," he said, rolling the crisp, smooth liquid around his mouth. "That's actually pretty nice." Perhaps it was a sign of changing tastes or a result of sparse dining in the wilds, but there was something deeply pleasant about the drink. He drained half the cup before remembering the circumstances they were in, and he found his appetite for the ale quickly diminished.

Rake drained the last glug of his bottle, placed a hand against his chest, and shuddered. Then he reached for another.

Holt set his cup down on the counter. "You know, Rake, if it hurts that much, then Osric is right. Sometimes talking plainly is all we need. Might be the cure you seek is not best served by constant wise-cracking and thrill-seeking."

Rake locked eyes with him, raised his new bottle to his mouth, pulled the cork out with his teeth, spat it out, and drank.

"Maybe," Holt soldiered on, "restraint and reflection would be the best thing for figuring out how you messed up advancing beyond Lord."

The liquid glugged as Rake held the bottle over his open mouth until it too was empty, and he licked the last drops with his forked tongue. Smacking his lips, he lowered the bottle slowly. He hadn't taken his eyes off Holt the whole time.

"Our bond was solid. Of that I'm certain. What went awry was a technical error." Rake threw his newly emptied bottle across the room, where it shattered. "Hundreds of years of reflection haven't helped thus far." He smirked, picked up a third bottle, then traipsed out of the tavern.

Holt followed.

A silent understanding came over the group that it was time to leave.

There was nothing to be gained here.

Osric called Soot to his side, and reluctantly she scurried back, clearly crestfallen. Ash raised a wing again to shield them from the setting sun, and Holt fell in beside them. Rake splattered mud with each heavy step.

Back near the broken well, with the gatehouse in sight, Rake stopped again to raise the bottle to his lips. He bit on the cork, pulled it out by a hair, then froze. He turned to face the rest of the group, eyes wide and teeth still sunk into the cork.

Holt drew his sword, Osric his axe. Slowly, very slowly, Rake yanked out the cork, then spat it out high over the adjacent buildings.

"Riders."

Rake took a sip and raised three fingers.

Holt began cycling motes in preparation for a fight. If they'd been sensed magically, the riders would have to investigate, and the scourge's presence in the ravaged town would draw them, if nothing else. Osric and Soot couldn't yet fly together, and Rake looked eager to hit something.

It was unfortunate the riders wouldn't be able to sense Rake's strength. They would probably assume he was weak or had no core at all.

"What do we think?" Rake asked. "Will they be from Falcaer or Thrall? Shall we make a bet?"

Not wishing to encourage him, Holt didn't respond.

"Let's hope it's Falcaer," Osric said. "Thrall's loyalists will attack us on sight."

The riders descended below the edge of the passing rain clouds and entered the range of Holt's magical senses. Hazy rays of the evening sun glinted off the scales of the three dragons.

One emerald, one fire, one ice.

One Low, one High, and one Exalted Champion.

7

A DANCE OF CHAMPIONS

Three riders headed right for them. Holt and Osric set their burdens down, but there was no time to take everything off Ash's back.

Rake rummaged in an inner pocket of his cloak and withdrew a handful of clear Grounding elixirs. He drank them all, alternating with more sips of whiskey.

Holt ran a hand over his belt rack and bandoleer. As none of the approaching riders were mystics, he discounted Lifting jerky and potions.

The High Fire Champion landed close to Holt and Ash. An imprinted memory of burning pain ached at Holt's side. Dahaka's lashing fires had been horrible to withstand, so he ate a strip of gingered jerky to improve his Floating and readied an elixir of the same type in case he needed it.

The Low Emerald Champion landed by Osric and Soot, while the Exalted Ice Champion and his cobalt dragon confronted Rake. His red hair and beard clashed against his pale blue brigandine, and his wide frame was not typical for an ice rider. Holt recognized him as one of the Champions who had tried to force him to join the Order before he left Feorlen.

"What a glorious day this has turned out to be," Champion Sigfrid said in thick Skarl. "We began by tailing emeralds and ended up catching the most wanted of rogues. You should have come with me the first time, cook boy."

Rake took a swig from his bottle and wiped his mouth. "This a friend of yours, Holt?"

"An unfortunate acquaintance." Then, in a carrying voice, Holt said, "I didn't come with you then, and I won't now. You should leave before..." his voice caught for a moment while he formed the threat, "before you get into a real mess."

Rake made a so-so gesture with his hand. "Needs work." He suppressed a belch, then pointed a finger toward Sigfrid. "Are you loyal to Adaskar or to Sovereign?"

"What are you talking about, beast? Our loyalty is to no individual but unquestioningly to the Order of Falcaer."

"Unlucky, Holt," Rake said. "Looks like you lost our wager."

Holt gave him a sideways glance. "We didn't make a bet," he said in an undertone.

"I suppose we shouldn't kill them then," Rake said, also in an undertone. "If you want them to flee, take out the rider, not the dragon."

Sigfrid was taking in the devastation with a grave expression. "What horrors have you wrought here?"

"You can't think we did this?" Holt said, but his heart sank. Sigfrid had proven himself stubborn and dull-witted before.

"This seems like the work of chaos to me," Sigfrid said. Both the fire and emerald dragons snarled. Beneath the feet of the emerald, the ground quaked. Its affinity must lie in the earth, Holt realized.

Sigfrid's furrowed brow then trained onto Osric. "And who are you, cripple?"

Soot bared her teeth and – impressively, given the circumstances – stood her ground.

"I am Osric Agravain."

"An Agravain? Yes, small wonder to find one of your family amid this business. You'll return with us as a prisoner to pressure your oath-breaking queen. Kill the others," Sigfrid snapped.

"I don't think they're going to listen, Holt," Rake said. From beneath his cloak, he raised his polearm. "You and Ash can take that one," he said, thrusting his bottle to indicate the fire rider.

It wasn't a question. Rake believed them capable of taking on the High Champion.

Both the High Fire and the Low Emerald Champions jumped down from their dragons. The earth rider drew a heavy mace in each hand while Osric readied Vengeance and shifted the weight on the balls of his feet.

The fire rider advanced on Holt with a swagger, performing flourishes with his red sword. He had a long tail of blond hair streaked with a thick band of orange, and gold loops hung from both ears.

Holt drank his Floating elixir. Its woody heat nipped the back of his throat, and with both food and potion aiding him, he began to cycle. With the dual boost, his mote channels turned visible, lighting his skin.

Sigfrid remained mounted. He drew his long blade, which gleamed to a jagged, frosted tip, and pointed it down at Rake.

"Now look," Rake said. "We've had a hard day. I'm tired. I promise I'll take it easy on you if—"

Sigfrid shot a lance of ice.

Rake dodged it, but the shard struck and shattered his bottle. Whiskey sloshed to the cobblestones, and Rake was left holding its broken top. He dropped it with a worn sigh, and mystic power began gathering around his glassy orange blade.

"I wish you hadn't done that."

Then he thrust hard with his polearm. A pointed Soul Blade formed and hurtled forward, rushing toward the leg of Sigfrid's dragon.

Before seeing the outcome, Holt faced his own opponent. The Fire Champion hurled a flaming clenched fist and, expecting Holt to dodge the attack, stepped into a position to catch him. With Rake's advice to be more aggressive fresh in his mind, Holt chose another, riskier option. With his magical defenses as strong as he could make them, he raised Brode's sword and ran right into the flaming fist.

The ability was part force and part fire, much like his own

Lunar Shocks were part force and part light. Brode's sword took the brunt of the fiery punch, then Holt took the rest. Protected as he was, the heat was no worse than holding his hand over a steaming pot for too long; the blunt impact hit true, nearly staggering him, but he powered on, rushing at the fire rider where he'd been least expecting it.

He caught a glimpse of the shock on the fire dragon's face before a thick moonbeam struck the dragon full in the snout.

The fire rider's side was exposed. Holt seized his chance and made a clean cut at his opponent's unarmored leg. He struck, cutting the rider's upper calf. As the rider buckled, Holt kicked hard, bringing the man crashing down onto his remaining good knee.

"Yield," Holt cried, then fire bathed his left side. The dragon's breath was hastily made, dispersed and weak. Holt's empowered Floating allowed him to withstand it, but sweat poured into his eye.

He brought Brode's sword across to block the flames and slid aside, and while Holt had the dragon distracted, Ash sent another moonbeam into its neck. It swayed into a nearby building, then Holt and Ash pummeled the dragon with the concussive power of their lunar light, shock after shock, beam after beam, none at full strength but enough to batter the dragon's head as though with a hail of stones. Roaring, the fire dragon took flight, and Holt's next shock missed.

He saw the rider coming out of the corner of his eye, unsteady on his injured leg. Holt spun and parried the overhead strike, then pushed through, forcing the fire rider to keep his weapon high and his body exposed.

Holt could have slashed down across his chest, but the aim was to force a retreat, not to kill. He let go of the hilt, brought his palms together, and produced a full-fledged, double-powered Lunar Shock. The bolt of light blasted the rider clean off his feet, and as the man skidded along the mud, Holt snatched Brode's sword back out of the air.

He could feel the fire dragon bearing down on him, so he moved to stand above the enemy rider and brought his sword to the man's throat. Looking up at the fire dragon, he cried, "Yield!"

Ash sent out a ribbon of spiritual power for them to accept. The dragon roared, but the fire at its mouth dissipated.

Below, the High Fire Champion hacked for breath. "I yield," he said. Above, his dragon bellowed in fury, but it reached out telepathically to confirm and then tied the spiritual ribbon into a knot to seal the surrender.

Holt withdrew the edge of Brode's sword from the man's throat. He backed away, then turned and rushed to help the others.

Osric was fighting beneath the gatehouse. His back was against the wall, but the way he'd positioned himself meant the emerald dragon couldn't directly interfere with the fight. She was perched atop the gatehouse, waiting to strike. Soot must have been hiding.

To Holt's surprise, Rake was still fighting Sigfrid near the well. Ice spread underfoot, causing Rake to half-skate with every move he made.

As Rake was closest, Holt ran in his direction, but a sheer, thick barrier of ice rose to block him. Ash swung his tail hard into the ice, and though the cold wall creaked and cracked, it showed no sign of breaking.

Over their bond, they decided to split up.

Holt jumped onto Ash's back, ran up his neck, then leaped high over the ice wall. When he was gone, Ash headed to help Osric instead.

As Holt landed, the Fire Champion flew in to hover overhead and began attacking Rake with lancing flames. They hadn't surrendered to him.

Rake must have started Floating, for the fire bounced off him. He turned, showing Sigfrid his back, then used Kickback and soared up and over Sigfrid, whose frosted sword swiped at the air where Rake had been. At the peak of his backflip, Rake looked up at the fire rider and used Blink. A split second later, he appeared at eye level with the rider and yanked him off his dragon.

The Champion hit the ground with a rending crack. A broken bone emerged from his already injured shin in a burst of dark blood, then he collapsed and struck his head on the ice. Rake landed a second later, brought the edge of his polearm to the man's throat, and raised a Barrier to block the fire raining upon him.

"Yield!"

The fire ceased.

Sigfrid, however, continued readying some swirling storm of ice.

Holt reached Rake's side then and stood firm beside him. A chill snapped in the air, but his continued Floating protected his body from any severe drop in temperature.

The ice dragon stamped, breaking more ice underfoot.

"Both of you," Rake called. "Or I'll kill him."

Holt tensed. Blood gushed from the fire rider's wounds.

A few painful heartbeats passed as Sigfrid and his dragon weighed the problem.

Out by the gatehouse, Osric's duel with the earth rider carried on amid the debris. Hard pressed, Osric ducked down, looped his stump through the open slot of the metal gate hinge, then, with a roaring, superhuman effort, raised it like a shield to block the earth rider's next hammering blow. The clang set Holt's teeth on edge, and he felt Ash's stab of pain as it rattled his sensitive ears.

Sigfrid had now focused on the gatehouse fight as well, as though waiting to see whether his comrade would win and free herself to come and outnumber Rake and Holt.

She appeared to be channeling an ability to her legs, but before she could unleash it, a ball of pure darkness collided with her face. She spat and waved her hand as though swatting a cloud of flies, but the distraction had cut off her ability.

Atop the gatehouse, the emerald dragon pounced in the direction the ball of shadow had come from. Ash roared and leaped too. He hit the Low Emerald side-on, knocking her aside from her intended target. Wood snapped and splintered, and a torrent of mud thrashed as the dragons writhed with tooth and talon.

Holt wanted nothing more than to go to Ash.

"Yield!" Rake shouted. He pressed his blade just enough to draw blood from the fire rider's neck.

Sigfrid dropped his sword and threw out his hands. "So be it!" he yelled in disgust. "We yield to you, half-breed."

His dragon yielded, and so did the fire dragon. Ribbons of spirit flowed up from the emerald dragon as well. Once the agreements were settled, Rake took his polearm away.

"Take him and begone," Rake said.

Holt sheathed Brode's sword, then dashed down the road. Ash's blindfold was mud-splattered and askew, leaving one of his crystal-blue eyes visible.

"I'm not hurt. Is Soot okay?"

Holt looked for her and found Osric crouching in the shadow of a pile of rubble. An oily black snout protruded seemingly from thin air.

"I think she's alright," Holt said. He sagged with relief and allowed the energy flow in his mote channels to return to normal. With it, the glow on his skin faded as well.

The earth rider stalked past and spat in their direction for good measure before running to join her comrades.

Deciding it would be better to stand by Rake, Holt and Ash made their way back to the well. The remainder of its arched covering had been blown off during the fight, and the opening was now clogged with ice.

Sigfrid knelt by their fallen squad member. He realigned the man's broken bone and held a splint of wood he'd picked up from the wreckage. The earth rider brought a wineskin to the fire dragon, who touched it with his snout, then she poured the contents over her friend's injured leg. Hot wine steamed in the twilight, smelling rich and sweet, and to the man's credit, he did not scream and remained still as Sigfrid secured the splint.

Holt opened one of the belt bags on his upper leg and withdrew a small jar of Aberanth's lurid green healing paste.

"Use some of this," he said. Sigfrid looked at him, bewildered, and Holt tossed him the jar. Sigfrid caught it and opened it, releasing a pungent, herby bitterness from the mixture. He applied some of the paste to the wound, and the fire rider's shin bubbled as muscle and skin reknit, undoing the worst of the damage.

Sigfrid threw the paste back to Holt, who caught it.

"This changes nothing," Sigfrid said.

"If you insist," Holt said. "I'm sure Paragon Adaskar thinks he's doing the right thing, but he needs to realize that we're all on the same side. In the end, what we fight is the scourge."

"Then why does your rogue queen open tunnels to the deep places? All she does is let the enemy out onto the surface."

Holt almost started to explain why Talia would open scourge tunnels, but the mere thought of it exhausted him. Not physically, but mentally. From Sigfrid to Adaskar, all in the Order who were bent on destroying them weren't prepared to listen.

"If we were so terrible, why wouldn't we just kill you?" Holt said. "You wouldn't have held back. What does that make you?"

No one answered him. Instead, Sigfrid and the earth rider bundled the fire rider onto his dragon's back, then went to their own dragons. With much snarling, they took off to the south, leaving Holt, Ash, Rake, Osric, and Soot in the ghostly shell of Silt Grave and the gathering night.

"Well, well, well," Rake said as though the silence had been unbearably awkward. "We stumbled across some mysteries tonight, but after that fight, I'm sure of one thing. Thanks to me, Holt Cook, you're equal to a High Champion now. You're very welcome."

8

THE SPLIT

Holt only allowed himself to relax once the three Champions left the range of his sixth sense. He and Rake wasted no time grabbing their bags and equipment. Ice had to be chipped off a sack or two and some elixir vials had smashed when their crate overturned, but otherwise, their supplies had pulled through intact. Nothing had been burned.

When Osric rejoined them by the frozen well, he still carried the hinge of the town gates upon his stump. A massive dent in the metal showed where the earth rider had struck it. Holt staring at this makeshift shield seemed to make Osric realize he still held it, and he discarded it with a groan of relief.

They left Silt Grave as night fell. Rather than head directly west, Rake wished to march north, deep into the fringes of Fallow Frontier. Sigfrid might return with more riders, or else riders within the Order loyal to Thrall might be alerted to their presence and converge on the area. Following the Brown Wash would make them easy prey.

Enhanced as they all were, they managed to cover thirty miles before sunrise and would have pushed on farther, but Soot appeared to be on her last legs. Panting and growling under rays from the rising sun, she lay down for a breather but would not get up again.

"She's had a right shock," Rake remarked. "Though severe

stress can speed up their development, as it did for Ash. Perhaps she'll be speaking by lunchtime."

"She managed to produce a Shadow Ball," Osric said like a proud father. He laid a hand on her belly, and her breathing visibly calmed.

"My point exactly," said Rake. He planted his polearm into the grass, then rubbed his hands together. "So, what have we got for breakfast, Master Cook?"

Rake rarely ate, so he must really be hungry, Holt thought. He dug out biscuits bartered from Red Rock for himself and Osric. Oven-blasted until brick hard, the biscuits might have been tooth-breakingly tough, but Holt softened them in warm water and added butter and honey to help them go down.

For the dragons and Rake, he used portions of well-salted game he'd gathered over winter. They had venison, rabbit, hare, wood pigeon, and even some wild boar. Given they had just encountered a strong group of riders and come away unscathed, Holt chose the boar for Rake and Soot by way of celebration. Ash, of course, wanted the venison.

While they ate, Holt wondered aloud why Thrall's hatchlings would have attacked a town. Given the state of the place, no bodies, no blood, nothing at all, it seemed painfully clear that the operation had been to harvest materials for the scourge.

"Might also be for him," Osric said. "For mystic motes."

Holt's stomach turned at the thought. Osric had told them how Thrall could break people's minds until the mystic energy within spilled out like a soup for him to feast on. Worse was how brutally efficient it all seemed. Break minds, then raise the corpses as fresh ghouls, or else perhaps send them deep underground to be thrown into the acid vats that fed the grotesque chamber orbs and the miles of connective tissue beneath the earth.

"Whatever he's doing," Holt said, "he's using his new dragons to do it." His gut clenched, though that might have been from the effort of digesting the biscuits.

Ash rumbled sadly. He'd only eaten half his food, and currently he was nosing it back and forth across the ground.

"They must be monsters."

Soot made a peep of protest but shuddered without elucidating.

"The hatchlings revered Thrall," Osric said, sounding as kind as Holt had ever heard him. "I do not think it their nature, at least none but the ginger menace."

"All the more reason we have to do everything we can to stop him," Holt said. "At least we can take this information back to Talia. She has gathered riders to her now, or so Turro said. And if the five dragons are near here, then Thrall can't be far off either. Might be we can come back in force and face him."

No one seemed especially enthusiastic about that. Osric sat quiet as the grave. Ash nibbled at his food. Rake placed his hand, whether consciously or not, over his chest. Soot had fallen asleep.

Holt took the time to Cleanse Ash's core of impurities. He was pleased to find the moon still bright and solid after their fight with the High Champion, and the constellation he'd interpreted as the mucker's hut where they'd first met was still visible. He thought a second rough constellation was also taking shape – a dragon seemed to be flying over the vague outline of treetops, though the thick mist of impurities in the nightscape made it difficult to discern. There were more impurities than usual, perhaps as a result of encountering the aftermath of the new dragons and their new magics.

Whatever the case, Holt found it harder to remove them. Each time he pulled some of that dust across the bond, it felt like gravel in his mote channels. Controlling his breath to raise them gently up then out of his body caused every exhale to rattle until such a lump formed at the back of his throat that the coughing required to expel it would have made any onlooker assume he had a fever.

Osric, however, sounded like he was in far more pain as he Cleansed, hacking and beating his chest as though to dislodge a bone. Yet he didn't remark on the difficulty. In fact, he didn't speak at all until they were standing again, packed and ready to press on.

"This is where we part ways."

Though Holt had been expecting it before reaching Feorlen, somehow it still took him by surprise.

"Where will you go?"

Osric pointed his thumb over his shoulder, indicating the vagueness of the Fallow Frontier. "She needs to find her brother."

Holt spoke without thinking it through. "That's crazy. Thrall can't be too far away. There are scourge on the loose, probably the Wyrm Cloaks too, and you want to go into the middle of all that?"

He had almost added, 'You're only a Novice,' but managed to stop himself. Countless people had told him he was too weak, too lowly, or too young to do the things he and Ash had to do. Osric was not some teenage Novice getting used to the grip of a training sword. He was more seasoned than Holt by leaps and more dangerous by bounds. And yet, Holt couldn't help but feel worried for Soot.

"What if he catches you?"

"Out there? I'll blend in. Just another stranger fallen on hard times." Osric raised his stump to underline the point. "And no one hides better than she does."

Soot nodded, though a little sheepishly.

Holt looked to Ash and Rake, hoping one of them might spring forth with a solution to keep them together, to keep Soot safe. Ash felt his yearning but said, *"She has a flight that calls to her. She must find him… whatever that may mean."*

A flutter of the lonely flute drifted out of Ash's dragon song and across their bond. Holt understood then, though he didn't like it.

He had grown accustomed to Osric and Soot's presence. When he put his blindfold on, they had been two extra hearts beating in the dark. Though far from family and not quite friends, and – given Osric's history – Holt wasn't sure he could ever feel warm toward him, they were on the same team now, and that wasn't nothing. He was sure of one thing though: Osric would die before rejoining Thrall. The question wasn't whether he would help in the fights to come, only how much.

He went to Osric with his hand outstretched. Osric accepted it in a firm shake. The ex-general opened then closed his mouth, unable to find the words. Holt didn't linger on the moment. He withdrew his hand and was about to turn to Soot when he paused, then asked, "What shall I tell Talia?"

Before, when they'd returned to Aberanth's grotto after Windshear, Holt had promised darkly to tell Talia everything and not to spare any foul detail. As Holt's passions had cooled over winter, so had his urge to further twist this knife. Doing so would only burden Talia and hurt Osric for nothing. Yet he must tell her something.

Osric's eyebrows knitted into a strong line. "Tell her whatever she wishes to know. If you hold back, do it to spare her, not me. Tell her… tell her I'm sorry."

Holt nodded, then he dropped down to be level with Soot's giant purple eyes. For once, she sat calm and collected, allowing him close.

"I know you don't like it when I call you Soot." Predictably, she bristled and flashed a tooth, but more playfully than she might have before. "So when we next meet, I look forward to hearing your real name. I hope you find it, and what you're looking for."

He lowered his palm beneath her snout. She blinked several times. Holt expected her to push her snout into his palm by way of affection, but instead she licked him with her bright pink tongue, coarse as bark. One flick, then she retracted it as though he were food past its prime. She cooed and flapped her wings.

"She's picturing how you blocked Rake from killing me," Osric said in a choked voice. "She wants you to know she's grateful." He cleared his throat. "We both are. Thank you, Holt. I never thought I'd owe my life to a servant."

Holt did not relish holding people to ransom via favors and life debts as Rake did, but nor did he wish to dismiss the gesture. Such things were not lightly offered, especially where dragons, souls, and cores were concerned.

Holt stood. "Repay us by helping her grow strong." Then he stepped back to let Ash say his goodbyes.

Osric presented a clenched fist to the dragon. Ash hesitated, then pressed his snout briefly against it. He spent longer with Soot. There was some rumbling, some growling, then Ash raised one wing and extended it to her. Soot looked alarmed and almost backed away, then allowed it. Once in the embrace, she pressed her head into Ash.

"She wishes she'd spent more time learning from you," Osric said. "And she's grateful for you saving her from the emerald yesterday."

"That's what friends do."

Ash's willingness to call them friends without reservation made Holt reflective. Was he right, or was Ash that much softer than him? *No, not soft*, he decided. *He's just the better of the two of us.*

The dragons broke apart, then lowered themselves to the ground, vibrated their wings, and waved their tails in the ingrained manner of parting dragons.

"Become the hunter," Ash advised. *"Not the prey."*

He too backed off, coming to join Holt.

"That was nice," Holt said over their bond.

"I just hope they make it out there."

Holt gave a firm nod to Osric and Soot, then hoisted his packs. He assumed they would be on their way now. Rake would give them a wave and a cutting remark if they were lucky.

"You two go on," Rake said to Holt. "I won't be a moment." He wiped his hand on his cloak, thrust it out, and stepped forward.

Osric's shock was nothing on Holt's, but he took the half-dragon's hand, and they shook convivially. Rake threw a look over his shoulder and flicked his free hand to shoo Holt and Ash on.

"Go on, I'll be quick."

Still with his hand in Osric's, Rake pulled the man in closer and began a hushed conversation. A fuzz of magic emanated around the pair like a cloud of flies.

"*Rake's muffling his words,*" Ash said. Unperturbed, the dragon moved off, giving Holt a knock with one wing to encourage him to follow.

Holt lingered, wondering what was so secret, then hurried to catch up to Ash.

~

Now the time to part had come, Osric wondered if he would miss the boy and his blind dragon. They could be as irritating as a hard-to-reach rash, but such good natures were hard to find in such a crushing world.

The black dragon held mixed feelings too. Her gratitude for what Holt and Ash had done for them was as genuine as his own, but, like himself, she harbored a longing for solitude: for a cool shadow to lay down in.

Osric shook his head a touch to either side and blinked hard. It amazed him how many of her thoughts and desires so easily mixed with his own. Other than when Thrall was enraged, every modicum of magic, every thought and feeling had been carefully rationed. She flowed into him like a running river.

"*Become the hunter,*" Ash told her. "*Not the prey.*" Even in this, the dragon sounded young and hopeful.

Once, Osric would have thoroughly agreed with the sentiment. Better, much better, to be dangerous than weak. A man incapable of wickedness and hard deeds could not truly be good. A mouse was not moral. A mouse was just a mouse.

Though, as a small voice at the back of his head well warned, he should be careful. Growing her power would develop his own, and when he had been dangerous before, he had also been weak. Too weak to show restraint, feral beneath a veneer of discipline.

Holt and Ash stood back and gave them a last nod and an appraising look.

"You two go on," Rake said. "I won't be a moment."

Taken aback, Osric stood rooted in surprise and apprehension as the half-dragon stepped forward with his hand outstretched.

Expecting some trick, Osric took the hand. Rake squeezed needlessly hard.

Osric resisted showing that on his face, keeping a neutral expression as he squeezed back with as much strength as his left hand could produce. The corner of Rake's mouth twitched up in a crooked smile, then he glanced over his shoulder.

"Go on, I'll be quick," he told the boy before pulling on Osric's arm. Unable to resist, Osric was yanked forward and found himself right up against the half-dragon.

From his impressive height, Rake tilted his head down and spoke low. "I'd like a quick word before we part. Don't worry, not even Ash can hear this."

"Consider me enraptured."

Rake hissed a laugh. "We have our differences, Grumps. You're right to thank the boy. I'd have ended you, and I think you would have been happy with that were it not for her. I'll admit, you've proven true and faithful so far, but you wouldn't be the first to crawl back to an abusive partnership. Maybe you think it's all you deserve?"

Osric held his breath, giving Rake nothing.

"If I come across one hint of you returning to him or betraying Holt's kindness in any way, I won't hesitate. Next time, I won't be drained of all my power." Quick as a flash, Rake's manner softened, and his grip on Osric's hand eased. "Of course, I dearly hope that never happens. Deep down, I'm fond of you, Grumps, and of her."

"I'll never go back."

"See that you don't. As a parting gift, allow me to offer some advice."

Osric nodded and waited.

"This pain you feel while using magic, I have a theory. There are ways in which a soul can be so damaged as to leave open wounds."

Osric recalled it like a nightmare, the searing through his soul when his bond with Thrall ripped apart. Pain unlike any he had felt. Neither physical nor emotional, but as though the fibers of his spirit had been hacked at with a rusted hatchet.

"Breaking my bond with him damaged me?" Osric asked.

"You said you felt pain even when connected to Thrall. I suspect your soul was damaged even before he came along, but breaking the bond in the violent manner you did no doubt exacerbated things. You can't lift a great weight using a broken arm, and you can't support a strong bond upon cracked foundations."

Osric glanced at Soot. She looked up to him – so supportive, so innocent, so good.

"What are you saying?" he asked, letting fear tinge his voice. "A broken arm is easy to mend. How can I heal a wound I cannot see?"

"I might be magnificent, but I'm not omnipotent. You and the boy don't fit the usual trends. Forming a second soul bond is so rare I could count the occasions on one hand. That you managed to bond immediately after tearing out your first makes you a complete exception. That alone speaks volumes as to its purity. I can only give you my best guess, but I'd say your potential is near limitless, so long as you can heal the open sores you stalk around with. What those are, only you can know."

Rake let Osric's hand go.

The ex-general stood there unsure, his stump and arm hanging limp as he pondered.

Wounds in my soul?

Killing Godric was an obvious one, yet when he thought of his brother, the ache felt dull. Scar tissue covered that now. He'd already faced the truth of it. Older then. There had been damage even before Thrall.

Wounds in my soul?

Like a starved animal rushing for food, he turned immediately to Esfir, even as her silhouette turned away from him upon the dunes.

Wounds, he thought. They were multiple. Open, never given the chance to heal. His father had been no comfort to him, but Osric had been there when he died, skin and eyes gone yellow and belly swollen. That was long settled. Next came Talia's look of disgust in the throne room, but that had been recent, not prior to Thrall, and as he lingered on it, he found it didn't sting as much anymore. She would hear the truth when Holt returned to her, and the truth could heal.

His mother.

Osric's breath quickened. He shifted his gaze to the expanse of the Fallow Frontier and to all who might dwell within it. Ever since Rake had told them they would pass through the frontier, he'd felt the tug of old rumors. He was not a man to believe in luck, never mind such fanciful notions as fate or destiny, yet this felt like some cosmic power was drawing him. Magic, he thought grimly. Magic, a power that cared not for the whims of men. Could it be that there was some order within the chaos?

He became so lost in thought he all but forgot Rake.

"Dare I say you have a hunch?" Rake asked.

Osric twisted back and met Rake's sapphire eyes. He took the half-dragon's taloned hand again, and this time it was he who pulled Rake down and closer to him.

"You have my thanks. Train hard as well. When next we meet, I plan on thrashing you."

"I look forward to it."

They broke apart, and Rake hastened after Holt and Ash. The foothills of the Spine were on their right and the Brown Wash on their left. A long road lay ahead of them to reach Feorlen.

Osric about turned and faced his own road. The river on his right, the shadow of the eastern fang on his left. Ahead lay naught but hardship and toil.

Yet for the first time he could remember, he felt a spark light the way and chart the course. It tasted like hope.

9

FOUNDLINGS AND FLOUNDERING'S

Clanks, scrapes, and the sound of breaking wood carried across the West Quarter as masons and carpenters chiseled, hammered, and sawed. Gulls screeched, dry salt air carried the scent of fish from shore markets beyond the island walls, and strung out down the freshly paved road before Talia was a huddled column of children, all orphans from the incursion the year before. Their clothes were at least clean, if too small, too large, or too tattered on many.

Most of the children watched Pyra carefully. They pointed at her and conferred in hushed conversations. Pyra held her head high, and their dragon bond burned warm. Talia smirked. Pyra was so enamored with the attention that she'd not growled once at Fynn since they'd touched down, which was always a plus.

Eadwulf, garbed in crimson, strode up the column of orphans as a thin-framed rolekeeper in baggy robes struggled to keep up with him. Eadwulf reached Talia first, saluted, and reported.

"All are accounted for, my queen." A ghostly twitch of a side glance to look for his lost brother remained. Perhaps it always would.

The rolekeeper arrived breathlessly but managed to nod to confer with Eadwulf.

"Then we'll begin," Talia said. Stepping forward, she pulled fire across her dragon bond and cycled it to her head. The purple circlet of dragon steel flickered to life with naked flames. Even without her brigandine – instead, she wore a wine-colored tunic, trousers, and soft boots – the flaming crown and her blade struck a look none could mistake.

One little girl with uneven pigtails and a red dragon toy clutched close to her chest caught Talia's attention. Her cheeks were pinched, and Talia felt fresh guilt at the provisions set aside for the wedding. She would have stripped the feast further back, but she feared Lady Ida would resign in protest rather than offer poorer fare to the Skarls.

Holding the child's eyes, Talia said, "It lightens my heart to see you standing tall and smiling. Last year, we all suffered, but you worst of all. Whether your parents were cruelly taken by the blight or laid down their lives to defend the living, their sacrifice will not be forgotten, and nor shall you. The care of Foundlings is of the highest priority to the crown. Prince Fynn and I hope you will find a safe home here until your new roles are found."

She moved to join Fynn and the matron on the threshold of the orphanage. Were Talia a stickler for the minutiae of tradition, there would have been more pomp, a ritual in granting the matron the key to the building, and a small chest of silver to demonstrate the crown's promised patronage. But Talia had little enough time, and Lady Elvina would handle the silver. Besides, the children looked hungry.

"Step forth and receive blessing and bounty."

The first child – a boy no older than nine – scampered to her and bowed. The harassed rolekeeper checked his papers and called out the lad's name.

"Master Alwin, formerly a Ferrier."

"Health and honor to you, Alwin Foundling," Talia said. One of her Queen's Guard placed a linen bundle into her open hand. "Rise and live well."

She presented the bundle to the boy, who took it with a silent smile. He all but ignored Fynn as he crossed the threshold, busying himself with untying the strings.

The bundle contained a wedge of strong cheese, a round loaf, and a yellow slice of honeyed cake. A pittance rather than a bounty. By rights and law, Foundlings should be given more, but an incursion followed by a year of restricted grain from Athra and recent attacks on merchant ships had stretched resources thin.

The Foundlings came to her one by one, each receiving their alms and their new name. They weren't nameless, role-less, for such horrors awaited only the illegitimate or the banished. People like Brode or Holt. In time, the Foundlings would be granted new names wherever roles needed filling.

Prince Fynn was quieter than usual, and his smile was enigmatic as ever. Rather than remain at her side like a handmaid, he set off with his lute and played a song every Feorlen child knew well. Rousing and light, it encouraged them to dance in simple moves to an infectious rhythm.

An ingrained response to the music sent signals to Talia's legs, though she resisted the urge. Some of the older children folded their arms or rolled their eyes, but not the youngest and, wiggling merrily, they danced around their elders and tried to drag them in.

Eadwulf groaned and ventured out to try and restore his carefully ordered line.

Eventually, the little girl with the pigtails and the red dragon skipped forward to Talia. She could not have seen her sixth winter.

"I'm Edyth," she announced before the rolekeeper could draw breath.

Talia raised a hand to calm him, then gave Edyth her new name and alms and bade her live well. "And I like your dragon," Talia added. "I used to have one like that when I was your age."

Gingerly, Edyth looked at Pyra, then averted her eyes and looked to her toes.

"You can look," Talia encouraged. "Pyra only wants the best for you, as do I."

Across the bond, Talia urged Pyra to lower her head so the children could see her eyes rather than her neck. Pyra snorted, but she obliged, albeit slowly.

Edyth shook with an excitement hard to contain. With

childish clumsiness, she extended an arm, opening and closing her hand, and took half a step before Pyra growled. Talia gently pulled the girl back.

"I wouldn't advise approaching a cat on the street like that, and definitely not a dragon."

The matron looked horrified and came to usher Edyth away. "A thousand pardons, yer majesty."

"This was always the danger of being informal around your kind," Pyra said. *"My good behavior has led them to think of me as some pet."*

Between presenting alms, Talia replied over their bond. *"Would you rather they fear you?"*

"There is space to fly between fear and impertinence."

Talia had to resist a snort of her own. *"Perhaps if you spoke to them occasionally, they would understand you're a thinking being, not a beast as they see you. And before you get all indignant, you've made exceptions in speaking with non-riders before."*

Pyra huffed and clacked a talon against the spotless cobblestones. Then, to Talia's astonishment, Pyra beat a heavy step down the street and surveyed the Foundlings with the same stern look she'd once given Ash.

Her rumbling brought the children to silence.

Fynn ceased playing.

"Little hatchlings, we dragons defend our flights with tooth and claw. My rider is my flight, and my rider is your elder. So long as I, Pyra, Daughter of Fire, have strength in my wings, I shall raise them over you."

Along the street, spirals of flames erupted like firecrackers, wheeling in short-lived spins safely out of reach. Those children not too stunned from hearing a dragon's voice inside their heads whooped and cheered at the display of magic.

Eadwulf gave up trying to maintain the line.

Fynn doffed his feathered cap.

Pyra's chest swelled.

"Perhaps adoration is better than fear?" Talia suggested.

Fynn strummed his lute again, and the ceremony went on. With the last Foundling safely inside the new orphanage, Talia thanked the matron, assured her the crown would not forget its duties, even in dire times, then took her leave. She dismissed the rolekeeper, then called for her Queen's Guard to fall in.

"Prince Fynn and I will inspect the reconstruction efforts."

Fynn, seemingly miles away, took a few moments to acknowledge her. Public or semi-public spaces were the only times they might have a chance to talk openly. Anything private would be inappropriate.

"Are you going to tell him?" Pyra asked.

"I will. Fly around if you like but stick near the island."

"Don't let him bring you down." Pyra took off without causing more fuss, and Talia felt her dragon's pleasure unfurl with her wings.

"Shall we?" Talia said.

Fynn gestured ahead. "Lead the way."

As they walked, Eadwulf and the rest of her Queen's Guard followed at a distance.

At the end of the street, they met the main road where passing trains of workers and horses hauled in the endless supply of wood and stone. To their right, the road ran toward the repaired bridge connecting the West Quarter to the city's inner ring, rising in a bright arch over blue-green waters. They turned left instead, shadowing the trundling wagon train.

Soon, the well-paved road regressed to a dirt track within a jungle of wooden scaffolding, cranes, pulleys, hanging ropes, and treadwheels in which men walked to hoist burdensome loads. Shells of buildings were still blackened from the flames, and the tang of fish was exchanged here for one of dust, clay, cut wood, and musty mortar. On every side, the canticle of construction rang loud and clear.

"There's still so much to do," Talia said.

Fynn's expression was blank. Several steps later, he seemed to realize a response was expected of him. "No worthy poem is composed in a single sitting." He frowned, then seemed to emerge from his reverie. "I'm sorry. I was distracted. The Foundlings…"

Talia nodded. She'd worried taking Fynn to see the orphans would heat already simmering emotions. Given the delicacy of her news, what she wanted was a more private setting, or at least a quieter one.

She spotted a new horseshoe tower that looked complete. Its top would be free of the noise of the street. She gestured toward it.

At the base of the tower, she told the masons the Queen and Prince had come to inspect it, and they dutifully emptied it.

As they climbed, Talia brooded on Fynn's burden. The matter had been brewing since the new year brought ill news of a revolt in the Fjarrhaf region of the empire, placing Fynn's true love in danger. The girl's name was Freya, and when Skadi had forcibly parted her and Fynn, the empress had sent her to marry Jarl Sigmar Olafson of Stroef – almost as far from Smidgar as could be managed.

During a chilly walk around the palace gardens, out of the earshot of guards and courtiers, Fynn had confided his fears to Talia. She'd tried to reassure him. With luck, the rebels would realize their folly and quit before a war really began. Alas, the rebellious jarls – inexplicably well-armed and supplied – seemed determined to fight.

Speaking furtively when they could, during court dinners or laying foundation stones in the West Quarter, Fynn revealed more of Freya than he'd allowed before. He described how Freya's parents had been thralls freed at the end of the civil war, how they'd made the brutal journey to Smidgar and perished from the effort, leaving little Freya as a Foundling. Eventually, he made his first real request of Talia, asking for help to get Freya out. Not to be brought here to be with him – not for his own sake – just to make sure she was safe.

Skadi was open to suggestions, Ambassador Oddvar had said, providing Talia aided in subduing the rebellion. If troops could not be spared, then Skadi suggested riders might quell the rising.

Talia had refused in no uncertain terms.

"I ought to be shocked at such a demand," Fynn had said. "But perhaps now you see the measure of my loving mother?"

After that, his songs grew more somber.

Today, fresh tidings had reached Talia. She hated being the one to deliver the news to Fynn, but she knew him well enough to know he'd rather hear it now than wait until his Skarl handlers deemed it appropriate.

Finishing the ascent of the tower, Talia stepped out onto the summit. Bricks were piled near missing gaps in the crenellations. The old siege platforms had been taller but made of wood, as much of the island had been. Burning had always been a contingency against swarms, but Talia had a mind to rebuild in stone, to think in the long term, beyond just preparing for the next attack. Besides, there would still be space enough here for two ballistae and their crews.

From this vantage, the islands of the west central and inner rings seemed to float upon the glassy waters of Lake Luriel. In the distance, Pyra dove down and skimmed across the water's surface.

Fynn caught up, emerging onto the tower top with labored breath. Talia allowed him to gather himself.

He took off his cap and wiped his brow. "I've braced myself. Give me the bad news."

Without preamble, she got right to the point.

"Word reached me today on the progress of your mother's forces."

Fynn's smile pressed into a fine line.

"They've crossed the Skipta," Talia continued. "It seems the rebels intend to meet them in the open field."

A crease rippled across Fynn's forehead.

Talia tried to comfort him. "Stroef is far from the front."

He seemed to consider something, then said, "Early in the civil war, when Jarl Sigmar was young and fierce, he led the armies of Fjarrhaf to great victories, defeating superior forces. Did you know that?"

Talia shook her head. Intricacies of the civil war were hard to come by outside the Empire's borders, and what little the world knew of the long conflict came from the victors – namely Skadi. The most pertinent issue was the ending of thralldom in the Empire.

She made a mental note to ask Ida to prepare her a dossier.

"Sigmar wasn't a genius," Fynn said, "but he was brutal and reckless where the northern forces were not. He might have won the war for Fjarhaff, but illness struck him down and confined him to his bed. He had to watch as his cause unraveled, and he was one of the last to surrender to my mother. I think that's why she pushed Freya onto him," and here his voice shook, "as an added punishment."

"What is it you fear?" Talia asked. "You can tell me."

Fynn almost looked ashamed to unveil the weight of it and add it to her already burdened shoulders.

"Both my mother and Sigmar would be pleased to see her gone. She fears poison in her mead as much as an axe in the back should Stroef be sacked."

Talia wondered whether Fynn's penchant for the romantic and poetic might be getting ahead of him, though she well understood fearing for a loved one from afar, being capable of acting yet forced to do nothing.

"Not that I know how she feels," he added quickly. "It's just my fear."

"Fear can be more crippling than reality. I feared the scourge a lot more until I slayed my first ghoul. I'm sorry, Fynn... I wish there was more we could do."

His blue eyes were far away again. "This isn't your burden. Risalia, Athra, and Adaskar are throwing enough at you. Is there any news from Brenin?"

"The Stricken Souls broke camp days ago. They're moving south, skirting the Morass, completely unchecked. No word on the Frayed Banners, though last we heard, the company was heading west, sacking towns along the Red Rush."

Adaskar's abandonment of order halls would be her undoing. Her uncle, King Roland, was struggling to hold Brenin together in the face of a remnant swarm, pressure from Athra, and now these marauding Free Companies. His barons were split or else entrenched in their strongholds to defend against the unchecked scourge from the Mort Morass. Talia didn't have the riders to cover Feorlen and Brenin, never mind the whole empire, nor could she afford to send more troops and still garrison the Red Range forts against Risalia. Skadi had men to spare, but she'd become single-mindedly focused on her rebellious jarls.

"There isn't a clear way out," she huffed. "If Uncle Roland falters, so might the Skarls, and the whole thing will crash down. If I could just help Ethel clear out the Morass, I'd feel better. Feel like I was doing something. But no. I'm stuck here plodding toward this blighted weddin—"

She stopped herself, for her ire was stirring her dragon bond, causing Pyra to distantly roar in anger, risking a feedback loop as her anger fueled Talia's again in turn. They made efforts not to let things spin out of control like that anymore, but it was like asking a fire not to burn, and a lance of wayward flame still crossed the bond and shot through Talia like triple-brewed nairn-root tea. She subdued it by cycling the fire to her head to catch and burn off on her circlet. She pinched the bridge of her nose, sighed, then cleared her throat.

"Sorry, you must have heard this rant half a hundred times already."

"At least two hundred," he chuckled.

She still felt the heat on her neck and cheeks. "About the wedding – I didn't mean it like—"

Fynn waved her down, still chortling. "Compared to your old temper, that was the guttering flame at the end of the wick. You've been doing well lately."

"We've been trying."

Fynn rummaged in one of his pouches and produced a handful of dark-crusted almonds. "Are you hungry?"

She wasn't, but she graciously accepted the nuts anyway. As she ate, she felt Pyra purr from the echoing taste, and she did feel a bit calmer. Spice to her was as butter and honey to others.

"Thank you, Fynn. I keep forgetting to bring some with me."

"I know."

He handed her some more, but she turned them down.

"They're running out. I'd rather make them last."

"As you wish." He pocketed the almonds, then strode over to the edge of the tower top and peered over the crenellations.

"The Skarls could learn a thing or two about construction from you southerners."

"You're joking, right? I've seen Smidgar – it's breathtaking." She went to join him in peering over the wall, half-expecting to see something wondrous to have evoked such a comment, but all was normal. More cranes, pulleys, and winches.

"Smidgar has its beauty," Fynn said, "but most of it is hewn from the living rock. It took generations of workers to cut and chisel it. Countless hands. My people relied on thralls for so long that we had little thought to build machines to replace muscle and bone. The thralls are gone, but we have not yet adapted to their absence."

"Jarl Sigmar and his ilk most of all."

Fynn grunted. "My mother took their harp and snapped the strings, then offered no replacement."

"What do you mean?"

"The thralls were just... set free. Told to do as they pleased."

"What?" Talia said, taken aback. "But surely those people needed roles?"

"We do not have your rolekeepers. The jarls used to determine roles for their lands, but few thralls wanted to remain where they'd been. They fled into the northern empire, seeking new work, moving as long as they had the means and demanding better."

It sounded wild to Talia. It sounded like pure chaos. It sounded... like exactly what Holt had done. What she had done.

Looking at the workers crawling along the rooftops below them, she asked, "They can just choose to do whatever they want?"

"It was madness for a while," Fynn said. "Even as a tot, I remember some of it, but it turned out those former thralls worked a lot harder once they found means to do as they wished. Or at least they got to make their pick of poor options. Better than no choice at all. They worked harder, they worked better. Even the most stubborn of the old guard might see what a benefit it was in time, albeit that was not mother's intention when freeing them."

"What was her intention?"

"To win the war. Once it became about ending that practice, the southern jarls lost their grip on their workforce."

Talia still couldn't quite shake a feeling of unease at such anarchy. Thralls had no rights and were treated no better than cattle, but to just let people do as they pleased? What if no one wanted to fletch arrows or grow wheat?

"To fight the scourge, we need cohesion, organization. We need to know who is where, what they can do, and how much food they need."

"What about a world without the scourge?" Fynn said, slipping into his enigmatic persona of the bard like an old glove. "Your pot boy is on his way to help. You speak of defeating the scourge, but what comes after that? Is all to remain the same?"

A workman below bellowed for others to watch out. Others echoed the sentiment, and creaking wood and a distinct sound of twisting rope drew Talia's attention. A crane upon a rooftop shuddered under a load of slate tiles pulling the whole frame toward the edge.

Talia dropped from the tower top onto the half-built roof. She pulled magic from Pyra's core and channeled it down her arm to form her burgeoning Champion ability. A whip of fire formed in her hand, its handle solid as any other, and she swung it toward the upper beam of the crane. The tip of the whip caught and wrapped around the beam, and she pulled, managing to hold the frame above the precipice.

As the weight of the crane's load pulled on her, Talia slid forward an inch before she Grounded her body and braced. With her free hand, she formed a compact Fireball and sent it searing through the hanging rope, freeing both her and the crane from the tiles. With a hard yank on her whip, she brought the crane back onto firm footing even as the slate shattered beneath.

Talia unfurled her whip, then approached the cavity's edge. Workmen were coming to inspect the damage. No one seemed hurt. Indeed, many were laughing, perhaps at their near escape, though they fell silent when they noticed Talia peering at them.

"I trust no one is harmed?"

Those with caps removed them, and there was a deal of bobbing, bowing, and mumbled majesties.

"Have a care," Talia said down to them. "Feorlen can't afford one needless lost life."

"Humans," Pyra sighed.

"You can come and pick this human up."

Their bond burned.

Talia glanced back at the tower top. Fynn waved at her.

Jumping down was one thing, but getting back up was quite another. She called to him that she would see him back at the palace. Eadwulf and her Queen's Guard would escort him back.

By the time he'd acknowledged her with another wave, Talia felt Pyra's hurtling presence overhead. She turned and leaped from the roof with no fear of missing her mark. She landed on Pyra's back and swung herself into place.

All talk of thralls, roles, and new worlds faded from her mind. Brenin was her real issue right now. Brenin, the Mort Morass, and her inability to strike at the next orb. She hoped Holt and Ash had been found, for she feared the fate of Feorlen would once again be placed unfairly upon their shoulders.

10

AS THINGS WERE MEANT TO BE

High above the ruins of Aldunei, where the Great Chasm stretched east as a gash in the world, Adaskar and Azarin hovered and waited. Far below, on the north-western outskirts of the wasteland, Falcaer Fortress looked perilously small against the yawning maw of death.

Four legionary bases of the old republic had been sewn together with centuries of brick and timber, making Falcaer the largest military base in the world. There were no high walls and no towers, for every soldier inside was a dragon rider and would live or die in the sky.

Adaskar could not recall when he'd last surveyed the city ruins, the chasm, or the fortress from such a height. Too often, his duties confined him to the sanctum, especially as his fellow Paragons rarely felt compelled to linger at headquarters. It would behoove him to leave the fortress more than he did to meet with riders from Angkor in the south to White Watch in the north and from the Roaring Fjord in the west to Alamut in the east.

Azarin thoroughly agreed. *"When these matters are settled, and the world put to rights, then we shall go."*

The end would begin today.

Eso, through Wynedd, had foreseen Vald's return. While his visions of the distant future were haphazard, those of the immediate future were far more accurate, and so Adaskar intended to greet Vald in the open air.

Eso's prediction came true.

Vald and Raiden'ra emerged directly from the northwest as though following the needle of a compass to an exacting degree. Adaskar felt a fire burn in his stomach, his equivalent of nerves. Though he knew himself to be in the right, this would be no simple task. It was vital Vald side with him.

From a distance, Vald was but a speck on his dragon's back. Raiden'ra was the smallest of the Paragon dragons yet also the eldest and magically superior.

Gray as hard iron, his body was sleek in all ways to cut through the air, from his pointed snout, flat ears, and fin-like bone ridges to his short tail, which reduced drag. He was so suited to being a storm dragon that one could have made the mistake of thinking he'd been made as such by design. The worst of it was that Raiden'ra's true affinity lay in the destructive power of lightning.

Even Azarin could not help but be impressed. *"I should like to fight by his side again."*

"If good sense prevails, then we shall."

Adaskar turned his focus to the magical and the spiritual. Even at a distance, Vald's spirit radiated more power than it had when the Paragons last convened.

"He will not stop," Azarin said, his tone lacking the reverence held for Raiden'ra.

"I fear you're right."

Azarin bellowed in greeting, then beat his heavy wings and flew in an intercept course. When they met above Falcaer, the dragons twisted around each other, rising and falling in a display of grace that was as much to best the other as it was to welcome them. Raiden'ra could outpace Azarin with ease, so Azarin turned his bulk to his advantage, becoming the pillar around which Raiden'ra had to weave, and thus, in a manner of speaking, he led the dance.

Adaskar's pride for his dragon burned deeply.

At length they broke apart, and Azarin descended to the ruins of Aldunei, landing inside the hollowed-out remnants of a once grand colosseum. Here they were close to the tip of the chasm, where the sky began to divide between living blue and a void of sickness. Vald and Raiden'ra joined them within the vestiges of the arena. Both dismounted.

"I am glad to have you back," Adaskar said. "I thought we might meet in private first."

Vald's expression was cool. Indeed, he seemed hardly to have changed since last they met. Still clean-shaven, his brow locked into a furrowed crease, his nose and mouth hard set and resolute. His power had long ago blackened his fingertips, and they remained so.

Even as he met Adaskar's eye, a spark of cleansed magic bloomed from his back like a cape. Vald deplored wasting even a second. There was a tradition that the Paragons should never be seen to be at rest, but Vald had internalized that even as a Novice. Tirelessly, he had mastered the art of Cleansing and Forging even while performing any mundane task, and if it had been possible to do so while sleeping, Vald would have found a way.

"These matters must be grave," Vald said, "if you saw fit to summon the full council."

Vald's accent, like his power, was strong. Hailing from Risalia, he still spoke the common tongue with a staccato style of speech, emphasizing his consonants and issuing words from the back of his throat.

Adaskar studied his old master's face for signs of judgment, but he saw none there.

"Have you any knowledge of our revered sisters?"

"Neveh traveled to the White Wilderness," Vald said. "To train, I should think. Of Kalanta, I know nothing." He cast an eye back through the crumbling ruins to where Falcaer stood in the distance. "Does Eso sleep?"

"His turns take him more often."

"A pity." Another streak of lightning, edged with black light, burst from Vald's shoulders. Without missing a beat, he continued, "Perhaps it is time to consider—"

"We cannot replace him."

"If we can no longer rely on his strength—"

"Raw power is not what Falcaer needs. Victory can only be achieved if we stand together."

"And if one of us is on our knees?" Vald asked. "The humans do not allow cripples into their shield walls. Each man must stand, or all will fall."

Such words troubled Adaskar. Vald had been a rider for so long that he must have all but forgotten his days as a regular nobleman, as an adult forgets their memories of infancy. Still, the casual comparison to humans, as though they were different, as though he were not still one himself, spoke of how far down the path he'd gone.

Will I lose even him before the end?

It would be the cruelest twist of fate to have to check one of his mentors against waywardness and chaos.

"Paragons serve for life," Adaskar said. "It is tradition."

"Let us pass the matter by until our sisters are here to discuss it. Eso was not the reason you summoned us."

"No," Adaskar said. He gestured with an open palm. "Shall we walk?"

Vald inclined his head and followed. They left the dragons in the colosseum and walked under old archways into a once great boulevard of the grand republic, where the earth glowed a livid green between shattered paving stones. The presence of the scourge seeped from everything into everything here, but for two Paragons, it was less consequential than a spittle of rain.

Adaskar recalled walking this path with his predecessor, Paragon Aodhan. No matter who walked this path after them, the chasm would remain as an abyss at the end of the road. The threat remained. The work remained. Why could the Order – the world – not focus solely on that?

Another burst of cleansed power peeled from Vald's shoulders, but his sparking eyes were fixed ahead.

"How has the chasm been?"

Adaskar wanted to tell him that he'd know if he'd been present. Instead, he said, "Much as it's been for years. Things should be stable for a time, for we just conducted a thorough purge of the western half."

"I'm glad the riders of the Empire and Brenin were put to good use."

Adaskar sensed no hint of judgment in Vald's tone, though he suspected it was there. They walked along the stricken road.

"I trust you know of events?"

"Tell me your view of them," said Vald. "And I shall know in full."

Adaskar explained the troubles at hand. He began with a complete account of the rising in Feorlen as best as he understood it, leading to the brainwashed riders leaving to join Talia. He spoke of the rogues at large in the eastern wilds, the theft of dragon eggs, and the political powers teetering on the brink of a great war.

Adaskar finished the tale. And he waited.

"To refuse three times to give in," Vald said. "The girl is bold."

Adaskar disliked his admiring tone. The memory of Talia not accepting the only way out still angered him.

"I could not have seized her."

"Of course not."

"I should have punished Denna when I had the chance," Adaskar added darkly. Denna had taken Talia on without permission, hoping to bridge the growing divide between the nobility and the riders in her region. Given how things had turned out, she'd succeeded too well.

"The question is," Vald said, "what shall we do now the unthinkable has occurred?"

His tone was leading, and Adaskar braced himself for the critique.

"I worry you may have acted in anger," Vald continued. "By withdrawing riders, you essentially ceded territory to her."

"Her paltry numbers cannot possibly cover it. Most are young. She lacks even a single Lord or Lady. Fear of the scourge from the Skarls and Brenish will destabilize her alliances. The cleanest solution would be if she crumbled from within."

"But that has not worked."

"Not yet." Adaskar's voice crackled like woodfire. He almost said, 'Perhaps I made a mistake' but restrained himself. He had not.

"You should have waited," Vald said. "All storms break."

Adaskar balked at that. "Doing nothing was not an option."

Vald moved off the road toward a colonnaded building, its function long-forgotten. Closer to the chasm, the air grew thick and foul. A darkness both physical and mental pressed in on all sides.

"I know you, Rostam," Vald said. "This sort of thing will lead you into obsession, to mistakes. You cannot let it."

That's rich of you to speak of obsession.

Vald did not let up. "Confining one of my Ladies to barracks for so long already troubles me."

How Vald knew of Farsa before having had a chance to return to the storm barracks was beyond Adaskar. Each of the types had its own inner workings, and he'd not expected to be able to keep Farsa from him for long, but even so, this was most unwelcome.

"What did you hope you achieve by it?"

In response, Adaskar drew out the ghost orb. "I asked for the truth. She confessed to the killing of Champions Dahaka of Alamut and Orvel of Sable Spire. Both were believed to have gone rogue, being involved with the theft of eggs." Vald narrowed his eyes, but Adaskar continued before he could interrupt. "At my request, she placed the pertinent memories in this orb. I surrender it to you now."

He extended his arm, the purple orb balanced perfectly in his cupped hand.

Vald lifted it delicately with his fingertips. He held it to eye level, then his demeanor relaxed.

"We shall observe it together."

Vald flicked his wrist, sending the orb to shatter against the decaying stones. Smoky figures emerged, ghostly puppets without strings, replaying the memories from Farsa's perspective.

She demanded Dahaka surrender, entered a fight, battled an

emerald dragon fighting alongside Dahaka and Zahak, stood over Orvel's fallen body, and then came Gea's confession. All of it truncated to fit inside the limits of the orb.

Farsa had been clever.

"I detect no tampering," Vald said.

Adaskar could not disagree. There were no signs at all. The memories shown were pure.

"We did not see her fight Orvel directly," Adaskar said.

"His dragon was in the fight. He would have been riding her."

"He lay sprawled on the ground, clearly from a high fall."

"Farsa is gifted with the wind. Most likely, she hurled him from Gea's back."

Adaskar breathed hard. Smoke billowed from his nose. "All convenient."

"It's debatable at worst," Vald said. With another flick of his wrist, he sent a puff of air to disperse the shapeless smoke that lingered from the orb. "I am satisfied." And then, with more bite than before, he said, "In such trying circumstances, I can understand your zeal, but do not take one of my Ladies from their duties again without consulting me."

Though he had been expecting it, Adaskar bristled. This was Falcaer's saving grace and its greatest flaw. The Paragons ruled together, and though the Fire Paragon led from the front, Adaskar was, in effect, the first among equals. It kept the Order free from tyranny and the crisis of ill rule, but when a crisis arose from within, it could prove hard to resolve. If the world understood how hard, no one would sleep soundly.

"Do not let one rogue girl color your judgment of every rider," Vald said, attempting a conciliatory tone. This time it was he who gestured back to the ancient road.

A little farther on their walk, as they drew ever closer to the chasm, Vald made fresh appeals.

"Agravain must be handled. No one will disagree with you on that, yet if the Emerald Flight works with her, does their Elder too?"

Neither Adaskar nor Azarin liked where Vald was heading with this.

"We have no information on the Life Elder's whereabouts. He was in Feorlen for a time, so he must be working with the girl on some level."

"Riders, dragons, armies, and nations all working together," Vald mused, and it was clear he was impressed.

A flash of lightning erupted from his back and stretched to strike a column. More of its stone crumbled, throwing up black dust.

Still musing, Vald gave a wan smile. "It won't last. It's too unstable."

"It's already been too long."

Vald waved a dismissive hand. "It's been months. Let us wait a little longer. Let us watch. Let us learn."

Across their dragon bond, Azarin growled. The golden bridge that connected their souls began to glow from the heat.

Adaskar frowned. He reached forth with his magical senses to inspect Vald's soul and bond again. The Storm Paragon's bond was strong as dragon steel, the most robust Adaskar had ever felt. Being honest, it was stronger even than his own bond with Azarin. Yet where Vald felt materially different was in the size of his soul. Vald had grown the space to new heights, and Adaskar's fears magnified accordingly.

"You never had a subtle touch," Vald said.

Adaskar withdrew, but before he could voice his objections, Vald's face lit up, as if with his very power. Shadowed with etched blues and blacks, his being seemed to swell.

"If an Elder is aiding the girl, think of what new opportunities this presents. Think of the power we might discover."

"Power?" Adaskar grunted.

"Power. Power against the scourge." Vald clenched both fists. "Yes. Then we take it for ourselves and deal with their treachery."

Adaskar wondered whether Vald believed his own excuses or whether his lust truly blinded him, but they had argued this point too many times and never to a fruitful end.

Adaskar would have to try a different approach.

"The girl is opening scourge tunnels."

For the first time, a shadow of fear creased Vald's face. "How much does she know?"

'Voices hissing in the deep, whispers even while you sleep.' When Aodhan had told Adaskar why the tunnels were sealed, he hadn't slept for a week.

"Enough that she should be terrified."

'The endless depths are never done; thousands, thousands into one.'

Adaskar pushed the horrors aside. "You see why we cannot just sit idle."

Vald's fear passed from his face, and Adaskar knew his thoughts were already returning to Elders, to souls and cores, and to power never hitherto achieved by any rider in history. The tensions tying Adaskar in knots quickly returned to choke him.

He tried another route.

"The Pact has been broken. Should the other Elders act, a war between the Wild Flights will inflict more damage than reprimanding a score of riders and one queen ever could."

"Will they act?" Adaskar was shocked to hear the question, and it must have shown on his face, for Vald added, "I'm serious, Rostam. Neither of us can know the mind of an Elder."

Adaskar knew that was true of himself, and he deeply hoped it was still true of Vald.

"Perhaps this is…" Vald continued, but he hesitated and gave the slightest of frowns.

"Say it."

"Perhaps this is the next stage of the fight. A horror lurks in the deep places, and it seeks our destruction. We contain it but never strive to destroy it."

"Efforts were made—"

"And they failed, I know. Do not forget who I trained under. I would not wish the Order splintered, nor would I see turmoil on the surface advantage the scourge, but riders and a Wild Flight working together is a new sort of power."

And there it was. Vald's insatiable desire for advancement.

Vald stepped closer and placed a hand on Adaskar's shoulder. "I know what you fear."

Across their bond, Azarin assured him, *"Fire shall never be supplanted."*

In truth, that was not Adaskar's fear. Vald's respect for the laws of the Order was second only to his own. He did not fear for his position. He feared for Vald. Too many had died in the attempt to jump beyond Lord, so why would Vald be different? Some things did not change – some things could not be changed – but Vald would try anyway. Adaskar feared losing him. He was one of the few people in the world who could understand him, who could share his burdens.

Who could be called a friend.

But to admit such things to a former master was unbearable. Instead, Adaskar said, "If the living escalate, who knows where that will lead? When the Athrans breed a heavier warhorse, the Risalians extend the length of their pikes. When the Brenish thicken their armor, the fletchers in Coedhen harden their arrows. Containing the scourge is not perfect, but it is the only safe and balanced measure we have."

Some of the color and energy drained from Vald's face. The currents of power faded, making him seem mortal again. He took his hand from Adaskar's shoulder. "You speak of us as though we were common firefighters."

"Is that not a noble role? We never presume to stop all fires from starting. The scourge are part of the world. To conceive of removing it is folly. Shall we stop all illness, the chill of winter, and the frailty of age? These things simply are. Will always be. We risk consequences we cannot dream of if we allow drastic change to occur."

Vald pressed his lips into a fine line but said nothing. Taking this for his consideration, a measure of relief washed through Adaskar.

He'll come around.

"When our sisters return," Adaskar continued, "I will call a vote to move on the girl on the grounds of global emergency. I'd prefer it if the vote is unanimous."

A simple majority would pass the motion, but if Vald lent his voice to Adaskar's, there would be no more debate. They both knew it.

"If we act as one with the utmost authority, no other loyal rider can dare question the validity of what we must do."

Those actions went unsaid.

The civilized world would quietly thank them, even if they feigned outrage at the Order's overreach in harming a monarch.

Order would be restored.

A sweet, sickly, humid air curled up from the chasm. Something rumbled and shook deep below, though that was nothing unusual when walking in the ruins of Aldunei.

Vald remained grim as the chasm.

"Please, M— Vald." He had almost called him 'master.' "Let us come together, end this chaos, and return things to how they're meant to be."

"You ask a high price of the Paragons."

"It is my burden as the leader of the Riders of Falcaer."

Vald's cheek twitched, but he inclined his head. "It is your burden and your right."

Movement flashed in Adaskar's peripheral vision. He turned and saw the first leg crest over the chasm's edge. A stinger scrambled up, its wings twisted and still.

Adaskar cycled fire and acted. Flames and lightning met the bug, obliterating the creature before it placed another foot down.

He sighed. The release was welcome.

Azarin and Raiden'ra roared. Adaskar felt Azarin take flight, intending to join them.

Vald drew his sword. "Let us set matters of rogues and traitors aside for now. Will you join me in a hunt?"

Adaskar drew his own blade. "I'd be honored to."

In that moment, things felt just as they always had and as they always should.

11

SPIRITUAL STUDIES

For months, Holt and Ash had been part of a group of six living in the woods. A team of sorts, hiding from the world and training to return to it. Now, in what seemed no time at all, they had gone from six to five and from five to three.

The first day after parting from Osric and Soot passed quietly. Heading west, they traversed sparse countryside with the southern mountains of the Spine on their right like a curtain of sheer gray rock guarding the northern world. Growing up, Holt had always heard of the Spine as a place of scourge activity. Given what he now knew about the network of tunnels running beneath the earth like roadways, he could well imagine why such a large mountain range would harbor a lot of scourge. Thankfully they encountered no trouble as they traveled, and he put that down to Thrall.

That first night was also peaceful. Rake did not insist on training, perhaps because of their recent fight with Sigfrid and the Champions. Holt Cleansed and Forged under the blooming stars and was pleased that the nausea he'd suffered during his last session was absent. Distance from the echoes left by Thrall's five hatchlings meant no trace of their motes remained in the orbit of Ash's core, and he was well used to regular impurities by now.

In the morning, Holt and Ash woke before Rake. While Holt packed and made ready for another day, Rake continued sleeping, his torso rising and falling softly beneath his black cloak.

Ash listened closely, then said, *"He isn't injured as far as I can tell."*

"Not physically anyway," Holt muttered. Though their fight back at Silt Grave had been brief, it must have taken a greater toll on Rake than he let on.

Quiet as they could, Holt and Ash left Rake to sleep and went to the nearby stream. Holt started to fill their waterskins.

"I wonder how Osric and Soot are getting on."

While drinking from the stream, Ash said, *"I think they'll have managed one day. We got along fine on our own."*

Holt laughed. "Sure, if you count almost getting killed by Orvel as fine." He lowered a second waterskin, gasping as his hand touched the frigid waters. "But we're Champions now. High Champions, even. We can stand up to a lot more than we could hope to before."

"You're definitely not as squishy as you once were." Ash raised his head and shook the water off his snout. *"You were as soft as an old apple when I first hatched."*

"Ouch," Holt said in a teasing voice. He raised the second waterskin and stoppered it. "Still tougher than you, I reckon. Take that," he added with a laugh, playfully lobbing one of the filled waterskins at Ash. It thumped dully off Ash's back before flopping to the ground.

Ash staggered theatrically. *"Oooh, my scales shall chafe from the pain, oooh, how shall I take another hit so fierce?"*

"Wow, you're *hilarious*." He started filling a third waterskin. "How's that wonky aim of yours doing these days?" He picked up a large pebble from the riverbank with his free hand and carelessly threw it up. A second later, Ash's moonbeam blasted the rock clean out of the air, and he stood comically braced, white vapor steaming from his mouth, though his excitable tail and wings made him look anything but threatening.

"Eh," Holt said nonchalantly. "Everyone gets lucky, I guess."

Ash approached. *"My aim is better than your clumsy footwork."* As he finished, he turned and made a playful swipe with his tail along the ground toward Holt's legs.

"Hey," Holt called, jumping to avoid the tail. In the process, the water from the third canister sloshed up and all over his face.

Ash tried to growl but ended up laughing high in his throat. Holt tried to keep a straight face, but the water dripped from his nose, and he failed hard in the attempt.

"Alright, we're both tough now, how's that?"

"Er, I think I'm still a little tougher. I'm a dragon, after all."

"Best one I know." Holt scooped up the fallen waterskin, filled it, then retrieved the one by Ash's feet and gave the dragon a one-armed hug along the way. "You did well back at Silt Grave, probably knocked a tooth out of that fire dragon."

"They'll think twice before attacking us again."

"We can only hope so."

Privately, though, he didn't count on it.

Sigfrid had ordered they be killed, meaning the noble riders of Falcaer were long past trying to arrest them, and Holt doubted they would cease such efforts after one skirmish. As strong as they were now, they would have to keep on improving if they were going to survive. The first step would be for Holt to create his own weapon, one attuned to Ash's magic. His imagination burst at wondering whether the white steel of the fallen star could be forged.

Together, they made their way back to camp and found Rake sitting up and rubbing at his eyes.

"What time do you call this?" Holt said. He threw him one of the waterskins. Like with Ash, the canister thumped dully off Rake before sliding to the ground. It took Rake a moment to register what had happened, then he reached for the skin and took a long drink from it.

"Thanks," Rake said, his voice almost hoarse.

No jibe. No smart remark or lithe overabundance of energy. Holt began to feel seriously concerned.

"How are you feeling?"

Rake shrugged. "Been better but also a lot worse. I'd say don't worry about me, but you worry about everything."

"I'm just trying to help."

"I know," Rake said, sounding a little sad. "But for now, there isn't much you can do." He cleared his throat and seemed to drag more of his usual bouncy self out. "Let's not tarry here."

The trio set out, maintaining their westward route toward the hinterlands of eastern Risalia. A rolling land of verdant grass speared with towering cones of dark needles and dotted with rocks as though scattered by a giant's hand. Spring flitted through the air, a fresh, floral scent moistened by the dew. When Holt lowered his bandanna to sense beyond sight, he discovered a clean, almost minty taste of pine sap upon the breeze.

On occasion, Ash sniffed out and followed hints of the blight. What infections they found were minor – a root here, a bush or flower there, or in the mosses under rocks or fallen logs. A gentle touch with lunar light banished the blight from bark or foliage, leaving streaks of white or purple-silver bruises in their wake. And while striking a casual pace for their capabilities, they still traveled with a speed and agility to shrink the landscape.

Small cliffs were climbed or dropped down from without issue, streams were leaped, and steep hillocks were negotiated with ease, all while lugging the weight of their luggage.

Holt watched Rake carefully during each physical feat and saw no sign that he was less capable. It affirmed that the half-dragon's woes were deeper than his scales and bones, haunting him at the level of his soul. That would affect his mote channels, and that was why the battle with the Champions had left him unusually wearied. The simple fact that Rake hadn't taken care of Sigfrid in moments was worrying enough.

As strong as Sigfrid was, he was only an Exalted Champion. What was that compared to Rake? Rake, who claimed to have been stronger than any Lord at the height of his power. Rake, who had almost skewered Thrall with one thrust of his blade.

As these thoughts filled his head, Holt broke their silence. "Back at Silt Grave," he began tentatively, "when you threatened to kill that fire rider…"

Rake faced resolutely ahead but grunted to acknowledge he was listening.

"Would you really have killed him?"

Rake did not answer at first, taking several more great strides, using his polearm as a walking stick, before he said firmly, "No. Not like that, at any rate." Holt waited for Ash to weigh in, but Rake was ahead of him. "How did I do, Ash?"

"He's telling the truth."

"Don't I always? I know I can be callous, but we agreed to no killing. Not unless we must. I intend to honor that."

Though he'd been optimistic this was the case, Holt still felt relieved to hear Rake confirm it. The memory of him hurling Orvel from the mystic tower at Windshear Hold and Gea's broken sobs over his body gave him no joy at all.

"For a moment back there, I worried they wouldn't yield."

"That's because you know you wouldn't follow through with your threats," Rake said. "But *they* don't know that. To them, we are rogues and chaos-bringers. What have we left to lose? Though I fear the more encounters we have with riders, the more they'll start to question our metal if we force a score of them to yield and nothing worse."

"Well, so be it. I'm not going to kill one of them just to prove I can. Not unless we have no other choice. They aren't going to stop coming for us either way."

"True enough. And if they don't yield the first time around, we'll just have to beat them senseless until they do."

The glibness of Rake's remark aside, Holt was pleased. "I'm glad we're in agreement."

Rake turned to him and nodded. "Of course. We're a team, aren't we? I help you advance, and you help me in return."

Holt decided not to bring up the three bottles of whiskey Rake had gulped without so much as a thought. No one drank three bottles for the taste alone.

"I suppose," Rake said in a long drawl, "I should discuss the next steps in your journey."

Holt perked up at that, and Ash raised his ears. All thoughts of Rake's deeper issues were temporarily wiped clean from their minds.

"You've obtained the early strength of a High Champion now," Rake said. "But reaching Exalted Champion is more than just sheer power. It's the staging ground between Champion and Lord and requires subtler developments. If you were to advance to Lord before you're ready, your souls would be damaged under the weight of the connection. Think of the bond like a bridge and your souls as riverbanks. Without proper foundations and supports on both sides, the bridge will collapse."

Holt followed so far. Rake had gone over most of these concepts in passing already during their winter training.

"Until now, you've enjoyed the benefits of a uniquely strong bond. Ash's early reliance on you, Holt, was unlike the average dragon. And you, in turn, only wished to save and help Ash, not use his power in any way for your own end, noble or otherwise. A rare sort of purity. You both dug deep foundations in each other's souls, allowing you to build your Novice, Ascendant, and even your initial Champion bridge quicker and safer than most.

"But I'm afraid those early advantages peter out here. The burden will be more on your end now. Ash is a dragon, and magic is as much a part of them as their blood and bones. For a human to cope with increasing amounts of magic, your soul, your spiritual strength, must also expand."

Holt blinked in astonishment. "I have to grow my... my soul?" He placed a hand against his chest as though he might feel his soul as he could his heartbeat. He'd had no concept of his soul at all before he'd bonded with Ash, and it was the bond rather than his soul that he felt inside him.

"I'm afraid it's difficult," Rake said.

Holt sighed. "I'm sure it is."

"There are practical benefits beyond preparing for advancement. As your spirit develops along with your mote channels, you'll find you can better manipulate magic beyond the techniques you practice endlessly for combat. Layering a little spiritual strength over motes imbues them with your will and allows you to affect the world."

"Affect the world?"

"Remember how Farsa would manipulate the air to keep her afloat or lift her?"

Holt did. Farsa sometimes stepped down from Hava as though on invisible stairs or lifted small items toward her on updrafts of her own creation.

Rake must have read the knowing look on Holt's face, for he continued, "That was her exerting spiritual force to command the air to bend to her will. The combination of spiritual will and magic forms the material difference between Exalted Champions and Lords."

"Can you do this?" Holt asked. He tried to think of occasions where Rake had manipulated the world or performed some feat outside his regular abilities but came up wanting.

"I can, a little," Rake said, clearly uncomfortable in admitting he wasn't a prodigy. "When I opened the seal on that scourge tunnel in Ahar, that took a bit of spirit."

"It did? I assumed that was just magic."

"If it was only magic, then any low-ranking member of the Order might open them. When I muffle my feet or otherwise," he added, conjuring the hazy orange slippers which softened his footsteps to a whisper, "it takes spirit. Not a lot, thankfully. It's a small thing." He canceled the muffling. "My Soul Blades are stronger when I weave spirit into the ability, for that helps me to *will* them in the direction I want. But..." He hesitated again, then seemed to decide upon something and halted, looking serious. "My soul has... issues right now."

Holt and Ash stopped alongside their beleaguered mentor. Between them, they couldn't help but wonder just how much trouble Rake was in. The Rake of a year ago would rather have died than admitted to fault. His time at Windshear had rattled him.

"I do not understand, Master Rake," Ash said. *"You've said before that you were stronger than a Lord, and now you're saying you're weaker in some way?"*

"I'm both stronger and weaker. When Elya's soul and mine collided, so too did her core with the burgeoning one I was attempting to build. When I'm at my peak, I have a far deeper pool of magic to draw on than almost any rider, save perhaps a Paragon. I could brute force my way through most situations with sheer magical power, and that was good enough to almost kill Thrall," he added defensively. "But since Elya went silent on me... I can hardly call upon my spirit at all." He placed a hand over his chest. "Sometimes I think it's there again, though when I reach for it, it's like my hand passes through a ghost."

"I'm so sorry, Rake, but I'm pleased you've told us. Thank you."

Rake grunted. "No point in hiding it. You've seen how it's affecting me."

"Is that why you had to strain when fighting Sigfrid?" Holt asked. "If he's Exalted, he must already have some of this spiritual power."

Rake looked disgusted at the memory. "Yes and no. He's quite tough for his rank, my reserves aren't what they once were, and I'm... well, I'm not used to pulling my punches. It's easier just to be lethal. But the truth is that if a Lord or Lady fell upon us, I wouldn't feel confident in fending them off anymore. An Exalted Lord is out of the question, and if a Paragon gets us, it would be over in seconds. I'm not the same creature who could attack Silas Silverstrike and Clesh for sport."

"We appreciate your honesty," Ash said. "But you don't have to fight alone, not so long as we're together."

"That's right," Holt said. "We're here to help each other. Besides, you can keep refilling your core. In time you'll be as strong as you were, right?" he added, the words catching a little in his throat.

"I'll be better than I am."

Taking his cue, Holt said, "I'm sure you will. Besides, you keep saying how a challenge is good for your development."

"Ha," Rake barked. "You have me there, Master Cook. But we were discussing your own advancement." He resumed their march again, taking great strides, which Holt had to move quickly to keep up with. "Spiritual strength has another critical benefit, at least for those of us who believe there to be a rank beyond Lord. If a human is to develop their own core, then strengthening and expanding one's soul is a practical prerequisite. A core must go somewhere."

This sounded like common sense to Holt – as far as common sense applied to these matters, anyway.

"So, what should I do? Some new meditation?"

"Ah, if only it were as easy as Cleansing or Forging. Strengthening your soul requires several things, but first and foremost, it means being and acting true to yourself. But I warn you, this is not simple. Our minds are strange things. Full of doubts and indecisions. There is something that separates our minds from our souls. We can trick ourselves into thinking something we don't truly believe and tell ourselves lies to rationalize it. Fortunately, you stand up for what you believe in almost to a fault, so there are no worries there, but in this matter, you should know that every small act or belief counts. Discover your own truths and think and act in accordance with them. Catch even the small lies you tell yourself, correct them, and your soul shall be stronger for it."

Holt's grip on the concept began to slip. If he ever tricked or lied to himself, then how would he know? That, he assumed, was what separated Exalted Champions from all others below them.

"I think I know myself," he said, and he was struck by how contradictory such a phrase was. He had to *know* himself, not think that he did. That wrinkle in his thought stirred Ash to come to his aid.

"You held on when Thrall tried to dominate you. Hold onto whatever did that."

Rake coughed. "With a little help from the barrier I placed inside his head too, but yes, a fine point, Ash."

Holt thought back to that moment at Windshear when Thrall had tried to seize him. His father's dying words had anchored him. *'Help the others.'* Holt did want to help those in need, to make good use of the power he'd acquired through his rashness.

As he lingered on this, he swore he felt a stirring in his chest, a light, butterfly sensation around his bond.

The beginnings of a grin spread across his face, and he half-opened his mouth to tell Rake, but as quickly as they came on, the butterflies vanished, and he twisted his features to try and cover his exuberance.

Perhaps he had imagined it.

Rake seemed about to question his odd behavior, so Holt spoke quickly to spare himself the embarrassment. "Alright then, so as long as I strengthen my soul sufficiently, we'll be able to develop a Lord-level bond safely?"

"If you're ready, then the weight of a Lord's bond won't damage you."

"And if we keep training, fighting, and growing together, it will just happen when the time is right?"

Rake seemed to consider something deeply. "Something like that," he said anticlimactically.

Holt felt that hesitation had lasted much too long to go without remark.

"You know something more, don't you?"

"One or two things."

"Are you going to share them?"

"I don't think so," Rake said cheerfully. "Not because I wish to hinder you, quite the reverse. Even if I'm right, I believe every pair is best served by reaching each stage of their connection naturally. Even if that takes kicking them down a scourge tunnel with naught but a cryptic clue to go on," he added wryly.

"Wouldn't it help just a little to know?"

Rake shook his head. "It must arise genuinely or not at all."

A silence fell over the trio as they marched on. Holt and Ash were absorbed in unpacking the meaning of this. Holt couldn't envision how he and Ash could be better connected than they were already, yet he had thought the same before their bond strengthened to Champion levels.

"Master Rake might be right to say nothing," Ash said. *"If he told us, we'd obsess over it."*

Holt knew that to be true. And, knowing that, he tried an

experiment. He focused inward, trying to perceive only the bond and the vague space surrounding it. *I will obsess over learning how to become a Lord because I want the power to help others.* Something and nothing occurred at once, as though he'd struck a match but failed to light it.

Accepting that expanding his soul wouldn't be easy, Holt returned his full attention to the present and the world ahead. These rocky foothills felt as good a place as any to feel both safe and free, and he was determined to enjoy the view while he could.

Completely determined.

He certainly tried to take in the scenery, and yet… and yet… something about all Rake had just explained nagged at him.

"I have a question."

Rake threw him a sideways glance. "When do you not?"

"If you need a strong soul to support a Lord bond, how did Osric ever reach Lord while bonded to Thrall? I don't think we would honestly describe Osric as especially, uhm, spiritually whole."

Rake hummed as though happy Holt had picked up on this niggling issue. "Far from being whole, I reckon he has spiritual holes." He chuckled. "But you raise a pertinent question. How indeed was he able to make it to Lord without a strong and stable soul?"

"You once said that Thrall and Osric had a bond of hate," Ash said. *"Is such a thing possible?"*

"Maybe? Though that was my first crude guess, and since then, I've come to understand Thrall's powers of domination a lot better. I think any rider under Thrall's influence loses so much of their agency and self that they don't become a living, breathing member of the partnership; they're more like a vessel, or an awkward puppet. There are things about advancement I can't tell you, so you'll just have to take my word for it that these parts of the process would be greatly aided were you so dominated."

Holt screwed his face in thought, but no matter how he turned it over, that explanation was barely better than no explanation. He wished Rake would just tell him what these critical pieces of advancement were.

"It sounds like Thrall cheats to me," Ash said.

"That's a perfect way of considering it," Rake said. "And do cheaters ever prosper? Yes, at first, but not in the long run. I believe that Thrall can push his riders through the advancement process at rapid speed, but in doing so, he creates a connection too strong for their weak souls to handle, meaning they always get crushed by the weight of a Lord bond in time. Some will last longer than others, I'm sure, but they'll always fail when trying to bear a spiritual weight they are unable to bear. Such a bond cannot last."

"Huh," Holt said. "Osric must be even tougher than he looks to have lasted as long as he did."

"Especially tough," said Rake, "considering he was already running around with cracks in his soul to begin with, although I also suspect that's what helped him break his bond with Thrall in the end. An unstable connection built on unstable foundations, and then enough will on his part to sever it forever. In short, I wouldn't recommend Thrall's methods to anyone interested in forming an unbreakable bond for life."

"No, I shouldn't think so," Holt said, with a nervous laugh, for he was at once consumed by phantom images of all of Thrall's riders – who knew how many there had been – he had taken, used, then discarded one by one over the centuries. "It would have been better for everyone had Thrall's rider lived instead, even if he was cruel enough to turn his own dragon's powers against him in the first place."

"Harsh," Rake said, "but fair. A cruel rider who's lost their dragon might remain heartless, but they aren't so much of a threat."

Ash rumbled lowly. *"Do you think Osric can overcome the damage to his soul?"*

"I like to think everyone is capable of anything if they work hard enough. I certainly hope he does, Ash. For Soot's sake, I hope so."

Ash nodded and puffed white smoke.

"Does that answer your question, Holt?"

"Well enough."

Rake smirked. "I know my withholding things from you makes you mad. You get such an irritable look on your face it's almost cute," he said, tousling Holt's hair. Holt pushed him off, now definitely irritated, and Rake carried on, "I swear it's really for your own good this time. I swear that once you and Ash advance, I'll tell you the theory behind each stage of advancement. Will that placate you?"

He offered his hand to Holt to shake.

"Not a soul oath?" Holt joked, though he had no desire to create an oath to advance and then fail in it. He took Rake's giant, scaly hand and shook it. "I look forward to hearing all about it."

"I look forward to that day as well, Master Cook, even more than you."

Two days later, Rake announced they had crossed into Risalia, though nothing in the landscape changed until they turned south. Descending out of the foothills of the Spine, they began to move in haste. Rake ran, and Holt and Ash flew close by overhead, blazing as quick a trail as they could across the narrow strip of eastern Risalia to reach the border with Brenin, hoping with every breath to avoid riders from the region's Order Hall of Drakburg.

Rake pushed himself so hard he had to stop every so often to hack a breath, spit, and heave in gulping breaths before starting again. This they did through the day, then through the night, then the day again, until, whether by luck or some unknown intervention, they made it unscathed and unchallenged to the Red Rush.

Bridges across this river were too well guarded for Rake to cross, but they managed to find a barge crossing. Holt and Ash waited on the Brenin side while Rake heaved at the chain connecting the barge between the banks.

As Rake reached the halfway point, the irate bargeman came

out of his lodgings, lantern bobbing and fist shaking. It took Rake just one menacing look to send the bargeman to squeal in fright, slip, and fall flat on his back, legs kicking like a bug before he scrambled onto all fours and crawled back inside.

Despite his evident tiredness, Rake was still guffawing when he reached Holt and Ash at the opposite shore. He just about managed to secure the barge onto the dock pilings before he doubled over, fighting for his breath between raucous heaves of laughter.

"Oh, I needed that," Rake said, a tear forming in one eye. He wiped it away with a long finger, then, with good grace, untethered the barge and pulled on the chain to send it back to the Risalian bank. With Holt's help, they soon returned it.

Trusting they would be unmolested inside Brenin, they slowed their pace, though still headed west with a single focus, crossing the lands of northern Brenin that Holt and Ash had traversed the year before.

At a distance, they passed an army bivouacking in orderly rows of yellow tents.

"The Frayed Banners?" Rake said with intrigue. "Now that's a surprise."

"Who are they?" Holt asked.

"A Free Company," Rake said. "No doubt Osric would have a thing or two to say about them. Look." He pointed toward a torn gold flag flying over the camp. "They were once the Golden Banners, then they stood against a swarm unaided for so long even their bannermen fought. Though the flags were torn, the company did not fall. Or so the story goes."

"*Is it true?*" Ash asked.

"Could be. I wasn't there."

"I wonder what they're doing here," Holt said. Far beyond the company's campsite, smoke rose, though too far away for Ash to be able to smell. An ill feeling came over him. "Turro said Talia's alliance was facing attacks. Maybe this company is part of it?"

"We can ask her when we reach Sidastra," Rake said, turning

Holt around by the shoulders. Holt shrugged him off, a little irritated. Rake had been the one to stop and look.

They moved on.

For five days, they encountered no emerald dragon nor any other rider until they came within sight of the Red Range, whereupon they spied dragons patrolling above the mountaintops. As they reached the forested foothills, a group of emeralds flew out as if to challenge them, but upon seeing Ash, they hailed them, told them to continue west, then dispersed to relay news of their presence.

Over the Red Range they trudged until they crossed the invisible line back into Feorlen. Once they were firmly on Feorlen soil, some instinct came over Holt to bend down and take some of the earth into his grasp. An anticipation of coming home had been building, yet the ground felt the same as any other, and, unmoved, he let the dirt fall through his fingers.

An approaching dragon roared, and Holt tilted his head sharply upward, his heart hammering. Part of him hoped to see Pyra blazing toward them, but it wasn't her. It wasn't even a rider. In fact, it turned out to be Turro. A weight lifted from Holt, and his disappointment at not seeing Pyra and Talia was banished.

Turro landed, and he and Ash greeted each other in the draconic fashion. When they settled, Holt noticed Turro's body was scarred by lesions resembling fern leaves. The dark scars reached one wing joint, where a small piece of the wing's membrane seemed to have been burnt away.

Turro sensed Holt's gaze. *"I can perform my duties."*

"Who attacked you?" Holt asked.

"A pair of riders. A young Storm Ascendant with a more experienced partner. I did not imagine myself in true danger, but the younger rider was nervous and struck whilst I parlayed with the elder. Others of my flight have been hounded closely, observed, and followed, but direct confrontation has been rare."

"We were attacked as well," Ash said.

"Then I am glad to see you prevailed, Sons of Night. Come with me

now. *The Red Queen has allowed me the honor of escorting you to the city.*"

"Talia sent you?" Holt asked, disappointment rearing inside him once more. Ash felt his sadness and tried to buttress it.

"She and Pyra must have many pressing duties."

Holt agreed with that and chided himself. It had been foolish and selfish to think Talia would be able to drop everything just to come and meet them here.

"I asked to come," Turro said, answering Holt's question. He seemed to notice Rake for the first time and cocked his head and sniffed lightly, doubtless trying to gauge his core. When he inevitably sensed nothing, Turro's eyes widened.

"No need for alarm, young emerald. My name is Rake. You might have heard of me."

"I was warned of you, Soul-Cursed. My Warden says you are not to be trusted."

Rake sighed.

"Rake is our Master," Holt said defensively. "And Talia knows we're with him. If she wanted us to return, then she must have known Rake would come as well."

Turro straightened out and ruffled his body as though drying himself. *"My Warden and the Red Queen do not agree on every matter. I was ordered to tell your Master to wait on the lake's northeastern shore. Transport will be arranged for him there. You two may fly directly back with me."*

Holt was ready to argue this, but Rake shook his head.

"Just go," he said. "I know you're eager to return."

Holt thought he detected judgment in Rake's tone, but he couldn't help but be excited. They'd see Talia and Pyra again. Soon his name would be cleared, and Ash would be treated as the hero who'd helped save the city from annihilation.

With this joy in mind, he melded senses with Ash and settled onto the dragon's back. Meeting Rake's eye, he said, "We'll see you in the city then?"

Rake inclined his head and set off at a run as Ash launched himself into the air and followed Turro.

The flight was a long one, longer than their first fearful flight to the capital while evading the gathering swarm. And yet, as they passed over the hill upon which Holt had first defied Sigfrid and finally came within sight of the city of a hundred isles, Holt began to feel the stirring that had eluded him until now.

He was coming home.

12

PROMISES

Holt and Ash followed Turro over Lake Luriel and were soon flying over the eastern islands of the outer ring. Only now did other riders fly to meet them, two Ascendants, one mystic and one fire, falling in on either side as an honor guard.

Damage from the siege of Sidastra was still evident, even to the palace at the heart of the central ring. Sections of its white walls remained tarnished, its statues and turrets toppled. A dragon-sized portion of the red-tiled roof from where Clesh had crashed to his death was still missing.

In the palace grounds, a purple dragon lay curled up on the grass. Holt's excitement peaked, then Turro and their Ascendant escorts banked right, turning north.

"You are to land on the rider's isle," Turro told them.

Holt's back went up at that. He glanced at the Ascendants on either side. Their proximity struck him now as too close. Surely Talia wouldn't care if they went straight to them?

He and Ash followed Turro to this northern island, where a new tower was under construction. It was currently seven stories and climbing, though it had nothing like the grandness he associated with an Order Hall. The Crag had been ancient and wind-worn, like an obelisk summoned by old magic, and Alamut had been a dazzling castle of white stone atop a cascading town upon a golden hill.

Sidastra's new tower, instead, was plain and functional. Around its base were other hastily erected buildings, though dragons had been taken into consideration, for there was space enough for two dragons to walk abreast up every street.

Their escorts peeled off as Holt and Ash descended, their mission seemingly complete. Turro landed, and they touched down beside him.

"Someone will come and show you to your quarters," Turro said, then he looked to the skies. *"There is much work to be done. Until next we meet."*

And with that, he took off again, heading west over open waters.

"I can hear people," Ash said, *"but they're moving away from us."*

With his own sixth sense, Holt could feel the presence of several bonded riders within the tower. None seemed in a hurry to come and greet them.

He jumped down from Ash and took off some of their packs. "Not exactly the welcome I'd hoped for."

An Exalted Ascendant in vibrant green brigandine eventually emerged from the tower. He was a young man, no older than his early twenties, his skin a deep umber-brown. He must have come from the lands around Lakara, beyond the desert of the Searing Sands.

"Hail, Champions," the Ascendant said, his Alduneian Common richly accented. He dipped his head, not quite the full reverence a Champion like Holt might expect to receive. "Please follow me. Your rooms and nest have been made ready."

The Ascendant turned and marched down a street leading west, away from the tower. Finding the interaction slightly odd, Holt shouldered his pack and followed. The Ascendant led them as far as the outer wall of the island, where there was a clearing of unused land covered in straw instead of grass and covered by an open timber structure with a thatched roof. There were also three huts with freshly woven wattle and daub roofs, presumably not built to last.

A pang of disappointment rang through Holt. Sensing this, Ash said, *"Were you hoping for a room in the palace?"*

"*No*," Holt said, a little defensively. Perhaps he had been.

The bare-bone conditions did not bother him – though he would have wished for a nicer bedding space for Ash. No, he was deflated because they were clearly to be kept apart from the other riders.

As if they were still tainted.

As if nothing had changed.

"Thank you," Holt told their escort without a hint of complaint. "As soon as I unburden Ash, we can report to the tower."

The Ascendant grew tense. Holt recognized a man searching for the right, carefully calibrated words, seeking to make himself clear – or his orders – while not causing offense to someone of higher rank.

Or someone he was afraid of.

"The Flight Commander wishes you to rest after such a long journey and to await the Red Queen here."

He backed off, clearly wishing to leave. Holt let him.

The sun was still high, though it was already past midday. Holt set about taking down the remainder of their baggage, then lugged it inside one of the huts. Though small, the roof's cruck frame made the space feel larger than it was. There were no furnishings save a roughly carved table, a single chair, and a bedframe. The tiny grate lacked firewood.

Holt dug out his recipe book, which he set on the table. Grief flared, though it was duller now after time and distance. His father had died in this city, along with countless others. When his mother had passed, his father took him out to one of her favorite spots along the cliffs. They'd scattered her ashes there so she would become part of the vista she loved so much, but there was no private place to mark the passing of Jonah Cook, just the bleary memory of a large pyre, weeping tears, and an internal burning drive growing hotter than the bonfire of the dead.

Next, he withdrew the fallen star. The hum of lunar energy locked within the white steel seemed stronger than ever, perhaps because his chance to harness it seemed tantalizingly close.

Holt ventured back outside to find Ash bedding down. The dragon looked even smaller in so large a space. While Ash rested, Holt took the opportunity to Cleanse. Not long after, servants arrived outside his hut with an assortment of food, firewood, and a haunch of roasted venison for Ash. When Holt tried to thank them, they averted their eyes, fumbled their words, and retreated so fast he might as well have had the blight.

The departure of the servants left Holt under no illusion that something was wrong.

Vowing to ignore it, he riffled through the food for things he'd missed in the wilds; soft cheeses, seasonal apples, and freshly baked bread with crusty tops felt like treats after an endless parade of teeth-breaking biscuits.

When he finished, he looked to the skies, hoping to see Talia and Pyra gliding toward them, but there was nothing up there save for squawking seagulls.

Holt returned to his meditations, and as day turned to night, he switched to Forging. The moon was waxing, almost three-quarters full that night, hanging in a clear sky near bursting with starlight. Perfect conditions by all accounts, yet it felt like one of the toughest Forging sessions of his life. He struggled to match his heartbeat to the rhythm of the bond, and when he did, the raw motes barely budged, no matter how relentlessly he pressed them. Every additional mote he fused into the moon core felt hard-earned.

Stubbornly he kept at it, determined to make headway, and he stayed up all night and well into the morning until the rivers of lunar energy reduced to spurting trickles. When he raised his bandanna, the harshness of the sun caused his eyes to water. He raised an arm, turned to avert his gaze from the east, and again felt that same sense of submission he'd perceived when comprehending the solar magic of Soot's twin brother.

It was a visceral, physical reaction, a shiver and shake through his nervous system, causing his muscles to clench as though his whole being bowed before this greater entity.

Setting his jaw against it, Holt was about to go in search of some breakfast when, at long last, he heard Pyra's voice enter his mind.

"We are coming, little ones."

Ash jerked awake. Holt lowered his arm and forced his watery eyes to look south, where a purple dragon was diving toward them.

Pyra landed just outside of Ash's nest. Both dragons rumbled and hummed, happiness high in their throats. They pressed their heads together and vibrated their wings. In their excitement, they shimmied around in a circle, which, given their size, required a wide berth. Talia leaped from Pyra's back and landed in a hard crouch before Holt.

Garbed in cherry red from head to toe, Talia wore a light tunic and soft boots. A circlet of flaming purple steel sat on her head, holding her hair in place. Glowing strands of her power seemed to run through her golden-red locks. Even her lips seemed unnaturally red.

Against all this crimson, her green eyes were like two jade stones. She was not as Holt remembered her. She seemed much older, though she had not suffered for it, as though reaching her full potential.

Talia the princess, Talia the girl, had transformed into a Queen and Champion.

Amid the rumbling of the dragons, Holt managed to say, "Hello."

Talia beamed. "Hello, pot boy." She hugged him. Her whole body was warm.

When they parted, he cleared his throat and said in a rush, "You made it through that tunnel then? And you stole riders from Falcaer? And you made it to Champion?"

"Not all in that order, and I didn't *steal* anyone," she added with mock pride. "I announced what I intended to do, that we would fight the real enemy, and they came. If they hadn't, then... well, it doesn't matter now. You haven't been waiting long, have you?"

"Not too long," Holt said quickly. Now Talia was here, his

previous irritations melted away. Talia was a Queen and headed a faction of riders; of course she was busy.

"Good," she said, absent-minded. Then, suddenly business-like, she asked, "How much did Turro tell you?"

Holt explained that, as he understood it, Talia had wished for them to return to help her with a mission for the Life Elder.

"You found more tunnel openings then?" Holt asked.

"We've used old supply requisitions from the riders to odd locations to map as many locations in Feorlen as we can, but Feorlen isn't really the problem. You remember me telling you that another swarm was building under Brenin?"

Holt nodded. He remembered everything about their reunion in the ruins of Freiz last year.

"Well, even after we took out the orb under the Red Range, a remnant of the growing swarm remained strong. We assumed there had to be another orb somewhere under Brenin. Sable Spire had been sealed, so we couldn't check the records there. Uncle Roland sent us the old requisition requests from Sable Spire, but nothing suggested a major operation. If there is one under Brenin, we can't find it."

Her struggles poured out of her now, her newfound maturity cracking at the edges, and a glimmer of the overwhelmed girl peeked through. She seemed to sense this and collected herself.

"We don't have the luxury of looking any longer. The Mort Morass teems with the scourge, and we barely have enough riders to keep them penned in, never mind root them all out. We're stretched too thin. A few more riders have come, but we've lost people too, and we can't afford a single death."

Holt braced himself, ready to lend his aid as soon as she asked. Given the extent of her difficulties, however, he couldn't envision how he and Ash could tip the balance on their own, even if Rake agreed to help as well.

"We're fairly certain of one location," Talia continued. "From what we've gathered, it seems like the riders of the Crag, Sable Spire, and Drakburg once came together for a huge joint opera-tion in western Risalia. However, I don't have jurisdiction there, so even if we weren't bogged down everywhere else, my hands would still be tied."

She seemed almost apologetic, and Holt sensed she was coming to her point.

"So, if we're to strike there, I need riders and dragons who aren't officially affiliated with the New Order."

Holt's heart seized.

"Who, if caught," Talia went on, "I can... deny ever sending."

Holt couldn't quite find the words to respond. Ash and Pyra ceased their happy greetings. Ash growled, backing away, and Pyra, crestfallen, tried to nip at him playfully, but he wasn't having it.

Talia looked grave but resolute. "Do you understand what I mean?"

Holt swallowed hard. "Yes, you need outcasts."

And, by implication, they would remain outcasts. They were not to be welcomed back into society, never mind hailed as heroes. Talia's promise to clear their names seemed hollow now.

"I'm so sorry, Holt. Really, I am."

Holt pressed his lips together and nodded.

"This island has been declared independent of the kingdom," Talia said. "So, you can be here, although some of the other riders, well, they had concerns—"

"Concerns?" Holt said, his voice cold. He couldn't help it. "About a role-breaker? About a chaos-bringer? What are they all if not those things too?"

"Most don't want to think of themselves like that," Talia said, her tone diplomatic. "Leaving Falcaer took a lot of courage. They see taking the fight to the scourge as *upholding* their oath, not breaking it."

Holt scowled.

Ash came to his side. *"I know this isn't fair, but it's not their fault. Pyra has explained it to me."* He tried to soothe Holt over their bond, but a darkness had fallen over him that not even Ash's light could currently alleviate.

No choice, he thought bitterly. He distinctly recalled Brode telling them they always had a choice.

"I'm sorry," Talia said again, "but I promise, once this is all over—"

"You promised before."

Her cheeks flared scarlet, hot enough to let off steam. Shame stung Holt, but he felt hurt. He felt used.

"Can we even manage this alone?" he asked. "Thrall must have placed stronger defenses around the orbs now. Our magic is effective against the scourge, but we can't fight a whole swarm, especially underground."

"Rake is with you, isn't he?" Talia asked.

"He's making his way to the northeastern shore of the lake. Just as you ordered."

The flames on Talia's circlet dimmed. "Holt, I couldn't let him… Look, the truth is, I don't know if you can do it on your own. I thought you might still have the others with you…" She trailed off, gesturing to the additional huts and the far larger nesting space than Ash alone required.

Holt enjoyed a moment of imagining that the whole team had stayed together and come with him to Sidastra.

"Farsa and Hava had to return to Oak Hall," he explained. "Eidolan took the only egg we rescued back to his flight. Aberanth didn't want to leave his grotto again. Rake's not what he was. And Osric—"

Her uncle's name slipped out before he realized what he was saying.

"Osric?" Talia said, her voice high and her queenly demeanor gone. Pyra rushed to place a reassuring wing at Talia's back. "He… he's alive?"

Holt hesitated on what to tell her.

"I know you're hurting," Ash said privately, *"but be kind, boy."*

Holt felt ashamed that Ash felt the need to remind him. *"I will be."* And aloud, he said, "He's alive. He even broke free of Thrall and bonded with a new dragon."

"He did?" Talia's voice was at once both disbelieving and delighted, and before Holt could react, she seized him again in a crushing hug.

Despite his woe, he squeezed back.

"Thank you, Holt. That's the best news I've had in months."

"You're welcome," Holt said softly. For a wild, insane moment, a moment in which his oversized heart made itself heard, he wanted to tell her to leave everything, to fly away so they could save the world together, as they had saved a kingdom.

Thankfully, his head prevailed. Brode would have been proud. She would refuse, and she should refuse. Putting her on the spot would have been unkind, for he could no more ask her to abandon everything than she could ask him to break his bond with Ash.

It felt like a long time before they parted, and though Talia's embrace had been hot, Holt felt cooler and calmer than before. She stepped back but kept a firm grip on his shoulders.

"Look… I didn't think you'd be on your own. And if Rake is injured, we can find some other way."

"There isn't another way, is there?"

"We would not ask this of you if there was," Pyra said.

Ash rumbled and clawed at the earth. *"What of our quest?"* he asked them all. *"We came to find out what you needed of us and because Turro said you were working with the Life Elder. Did the Elder ask that we aid you?"*

Talia looked crestfallen. "Not specifically."

Holt appreciated the honesty.

"Truth is, I haven't seen the Elder since he opened the tunnel under the Red Range. What word we get from him comes through messengers sent to the West Warden, and they've become infrequent. I don't know exactly where he is, only that he's pushing back against the scourge in the north and wants us – wants me – to keep pressing here as well. Force Thrall to focus on two fronts. The West Warden was delighted the last time I saw him. I think the Elder is about to make a major play, maybe even move against the Hive Mind."

"What's the Hive Mind?"

Talia explained in full her encounter with the creature in the depths. It sounded horrifying, but it made some sense of the orbs and why they were so important, even if it raised new questions.

Whatever the creature was, Thrall's control of it granted him power over all the scourge. So, if the Elder was able to destroy it...

"It might all be over," he said to Ash as an end to their shared, swirling thoughts.

Ash considered. *"The Life Elder sent us out to find his siblings and unite them against the scourge. If he could do it alone—"*

"We've learned a lot since then," Holt said. *"As the Elder must have too. Maybe he's found allies on his own. Osric said the Ice Flight might have turned against Thrall."*

"He said the ice dragons at Windshear acted funny, that's all."

"He said they left."

"But he didn't know why."

"We know so little for sure, but we have to make a choice anyway," Holt said, and then, speaking aloud, he asked Talia, "One mission?"

She bit her lip. "Just one," she resolved. "No one can expect you to delve into every tunnel we cannot. But if it works..."

Her excitement was palpable, though she didn't seem bold enough to say it aloud, so Pyra roared and said it for her.

"If it works, then either Thrall or the Hive will be slain. Either death would herald the end. Without Thrall's influence, the scourge will weaken. Should the Hive Mind fall, then Thrall will have his talons pulled."

Talia nodded earnestly. "It could all be over."

"And Adaskar will leave you alone?"

"Your guess is as good as mine. If the scourge are destroyed, then how can he claim I'm a threat to the living's ability to fight back? I know we're asking a lot of the pair of you," she added imploringly, "but this could be it. Will you help us?"

Holt had not forgotten his hurt from before, but how could he refuse?

Ash's reservations had dampened too. *"It has to be us."*

Across their bond, they shared a spiritual smile.

"Of course we'll help," Holt said. Ash nodded and flapped his wings.

Talia beamed. "Thank you."

Holt enjoyed seeing the relief on her face. He and Ash had lifted some of the weight that had been crushing her.

"You can stay here until we're ready," she said, speaking in a giddy rush. "I'll coordinate with the Warden to let the Elder know we're making a move, and I'll make sure a boat is ready for Rake as soon as he arrives. In the meantime, I'm sure there's something we can do for you. You haven't got brigandine yet, have you? I'll give my smith your measurements – no one will begrudge me a set of armor. And a blade? You should create one while you're here. Oh, damn, the furnace is set up in the palace grounds... Actually, that might not be a problem," she said, positively luminous. "The wedding will be soon, and everyone will be too distracted. You can do it then!"

Holt's brief elation withered and died. His insides turned to jelly.

She'd had to marry to secure her alliance. He recalled everything about their reunion in the ruins, but somehow he'd all but forgotten that fact.

No, if he had an ounce of honesty with himself, he'd repressed it. Being reminded of it now in so excitable and blunt a fashion felt as though the news had been screamed deafeningly into his ears by an irate dragon.

He drew in light from Ash's core and cycled it broadly through his channels to stiffen himself.

"That sounds like a great idea." A part of him yearned to tell her about the fallen star, but despite having been so desperate to see her, he now found himself wishing she'd leave him alone. In a wooden voice, he said, "Well, you must have so many other duties to attend to. We won't keep you."

"Oh. We do. Thank you, Holt. Ash. Thank you so much. We'll come to see you again, I promise."

Holt nodded, not trusting himself to say anything further. He realized he hadn't greeted Pyra properly, so he went to the fire dragon and raised his hand. She accommodated him by lowering her snout, and he gave her a good rub along the nose.

"*Victory is within our reach,*" she told them. When Pyra pulled back, she actually bowed to them and pressed her neck to the earth before Ash.

Holt was too shocked to react.

They were now stronger than Talia and Pyra. A quick and careful inspection of their bond was sufficient to learn Talia was nowhere close to being a High Champion. Doubtless all her burdens kept her from training with Pyra every hour of the day and night, the one luxury he and Ash enjoyed.

"There's no need for that," Ash said.

But Pyra kept her neck low. *"There is every need to recognize greatness. You have earned it, little one."*

Ash's heart thundered so loud that Holt marveled that it didn't burst from his chest. He roared long and deep, and satisfaction swelled and spilled over their bond so that Holt too felt the burn of pleasure, of friendship, of acceptance.

"Same goes for me," Talia said, giving Holt a dip of her head. "I'd love to learn all about those elixirs you spoke of last time. And this magical food you've made. We'll need all the help we can get."

Holt nodded. He could teach them how to make jerky easily enough, though he doubted he could brew elixirs without Aberanth.

Talia withdrew. She gave them both a wide smile, then took off on Pyra, racing back to the central ring.

Holt tore his gaze from them and found himself awash with emotions he had no hope of untangling. Despite a long night of meditation, his mind was a cluttered, chaotic mess. He slumped down on the grass, lowered his blindfold against the sun, and melded his senses with Ash. Bathing in Ash's presence soothed him some, but it took a deal of effort to empty his mind and center himself.

As he delved deeper to focus on his bond, on his soul, a rogue thought emerged that he didn't immediately set aside. When it kept returning to the front of his mind, he decided to linger on it. As unhealthy as it might be, he thought it must be true.

I don't have a home anymore.

He waited.

Nothing.

When he'd tried to expand his soul before, there had at least been a quiver, but if this thought wasn't true, why did it consume him? He was beginning to understand Rake's warnings that this would be no simple thing. Brute force and hard work weren't going to advance him this time.

13

THE BARD AND THE SMITH

Despite her promise, after three days, Talia was yet to return. Stuck in his little hut at the edge of the rider's isle, Holt felt claustrophobic. Even in Aberanth's underground laboratory he hadn't felt hemmed in like this. He'd tried to show Talia's riders the elixirs and jerky but was met with stiff responses. They wouldn't even take a message to Talia for him, and Rake was nowhere to be seen.

On the morning of the fourth day, willowy wind-blown notes drifted into Holt's ears. He stirred, then woke. Sitting up in bed, he found pale pink light seeping in through the cracks in the shutters.

Ash sensed him waking and said, *"There's a music man out here."*

"A musician."

"He woke me up," Ash huffed. *"And just laughed when I growled at him."*

The music grew louder. Curious, Holt pulled on his shirt and trousers, then opened the door.

A slender man with a short dirty-blond beard was leaning against one of the timber posts of Ash's shelter and playing a panpipe. Though his clothes were simple, the materials were of high quality – a feathered cap, an open white shirt tucked into faded red trousers, and high boots of the same color. A satchel hung to one side, and the neck of a lute protruded over his shoulder like a rider's sword.

Whoever he was, the bard was perfectly at ease. His eyes were shut, and he was playing his instrument as though performing beside a blind dragon was commonplace.

Ash raised his wing to cover his ears. *"It's early."*

Holt blinked. The world was not awake yet, so why was this bard?

He stepped outside.

"Can we help you?"

The bard opened his eyes. He smiled, whistled a flurry of quick notes, then cut his song and doffed his cap to reveal a knot of blond hair.

"I am humbled by your offer, Honored Rider." Holt thought he detected a Skarl accent. The bard dipped into a bow, then rose and replaced his cap. "Perchance you may be of help, though not before I have earned some right to it."

With fluid movements, the bard let the panpipe fall to hang around his neck, pulled his satchel around to his front, opened it, and removed two scrolls with leather covers.

"Maps from the Red Queen," he said, holding them out to Holt.

Holt went to snatch the scrolls out of the bard's hand. Inside the leather covers, each tightly rolled piece of parchment had been sealed by plain wax.

He broke the seals and unfurled the maps. One was of western Risalia with a neat circle drawn over an area not far beyond the border with Feorlen. The other parchment mapped out that circled area in greater detail, marking the rough location of the tunnel.

"I trust all is clear, pot boy?"

Holt glanced up, meeting the visitor's vibrant and absorbing eyes, which drank in every detail they saw.

"Who are you?"

"To Talia Agravain, I am but a bard in her service. Music eases the stress of the throne." He brought his lute around and began to strum and sing.

"'Ere Mithras was raised, there was a bull of great rage, and it roamed day and night 'cross the land. Washed on the shores, the waves did bear, a child with no voice but a song. And the sailors, they say, as the bull rushed her way, her sweet song softened its soul."

The bard played lightly, and he looked at Holt as though hoping for an invitation to continue.

"I'm afraid I don't know that song."

"Did you like it? I always love hearing new songs."

"I'm not sure I understood it. I'd sooner hear of food from your lands."

From under his wing, Ash rustled. *"I actually liked that one."*

The bard made a fingertip kiss into the air. "Ah, my pale friend. You have an artist's heart."

The bard took up his lute again and began to play the same song, though this time without the lyrics. Ash lifted his wing. The material of Brode's cloak struggled to cover his eyes, revealing a hint of his striking icy blues. He rumbled and swished his tail happily.

"You're too easy," Holt told him privately.

Holt's general ill mood had not eased with the bard's arrival, which only seemed to reinforce how desperate all the other riders were to ignore them.

"Aren't you afraid my role-breaking will rub off onto you?"

Fingers strumming lightly at his lute, the bard said, "I don't think we need to get so close as to rub anything. Besides, I have thick skin. Boar skin, my family claims. Had I not, I would be a poor musician."

The mention of a boar triggered something in Holt's memory. There was something about the Skarls and boars he couldn't quite put his finger on, but his distracted mind put the Skarl tongue and the moniker of "pot boy" only a few had ever called him together.

Holt felt like an idiot for not realizing it sooner, but then he would never have conceived of a Skarl princeling as a bard.

"You're Fynn, aren't you?"

"Prince Fynn Skadison," he said, still playing.

Holt's mouth went dry. His immediate reaction was one of dislike. The sly words, the evasion of the truth – why play such games?

"Why lie and say you're only a bard?"

"Because it is so," Fynn said. "To Talia, I am a bard. To the Red Queen, well, I'll soon be the King Consort. An uncomfortable title, is it not?"

"That's a trickery of words. I thought Skarls were direct?"

"And I thought all pot boys worked in kitchens?" His mouth dropped in some sudden inspiration, then he tilted his lute and began playing some new tune. He sang a few words, though they were in Skarl and Holt didn't understand them. After maybe a verse, Fynn stopped again and looked pensive.

"There's something to that, I'm sure. I shall work on it." With a flourish, he pushed his lute onto his back. "I like to observe and hear what people truly think and feel. I take it that Talia told you little of me?"

"Didn't mention you."

"But of course, you both have concerns far greater than I. She has told me much and more about you, though."

Holt stood straighter. "We've been through a lot together."

"A fine song your adventures would make. You both matter a great deal to her and that haughty dragon of hers."

"And they to us," Ash said.

Fynn nodded sagely. "I'm impressed you managed to make such an impression. They can be… guarded."

"She's a fire rider." The fact Holt knew Talia wasn't as fierce inside as she let on was something he kept to himself. Let Fynn discover that in his own time. Talia's worries were hers alone to tell.

Fynn pushed off the timber post and, for a wondrous second, Holt thought he would leave. "I hope you don't begrudge me for being the one to deliver these maps. Talia would have done it, but I volunteered myself. No, I insisted. Do not hold any of the riders here to blame."

"I don't blame her riders."

"Not *her* riders," Fynn said carefully. "They're not at her beck and call like guardsmen. A rider called Ethel is the Flight Commander here."

Caught off-guard by the rebuke, Holt mumbled in a fluster, searching for the right words, but Fynn raised a hand.

"I'm sure you meant nothing by it. You've been away from civilization for a long time. Don't forget we don't all have the luxury of being as direct as we'd like, Skarl or otherwise. Just take care while you're staying here. Not all of them are comfortable with the idea of harboring you."

"Talia mentioned…" Holt started, but he trailed off, unsure where he wanted to take it.

Ash huffed, blowing up dust from the dry road. *"If they got to know us, they would realize we are not to be feared."*

"In time, perhaps they will," Fynn said, then his tone became more serious, more like an adult speaking to a child. "But please, try to understand the situation from Talia's perspective. Some of the riders here have doubts now they've seen the insurmountable task ahead. Talia and Ethel can't afford dissent to foment, and I'm sorry, Holt, but you and Ash could become a reason for it. You are our guest, not a prisoner, but keeping a low profile is better for everyone. We'd hate for spies to become aware of your presence too easily. Let's make them work for it, shall we? Is it ideal? No. Talia did not want to put you in this position, but there was no choice."

Holt was ashamed into a stunned silence. In his disappointment and frustration, he hadn't even considered half of that. Fynn watched him for a response, and all Holt managed was to swallow hard.

Though Holt was the rider – stronger in every measurable way – he felt a lot smaller than the prince before him.

Ash recovered first. *"Thank you, Prince Fynn, for these insights. We can appreciate the situation better now."*

Holt nodded. His mouth and throat dry, he said, "Yes. Much better."

Fynn's smile was gratifying. "I knew you would." A jovial tone returned to his voice as he continued. "Now, if you feel I've earned that help you offered, I should like to ask you something.

My request to deliver your maps was not purely out of curiosity."

Bemused, Holt gestured with an open palm. "Please, go ahead."

Fynn reached for his lute again. His eyes lost some of their intensity, turning glassy as he absentmindedly strummed his instrument. "All those rash choices you made, all the bold decisions – what made you sure you should choose them?"

Taken aback, Holt thought about it. Other people had asked him this before, though usually, they did so accusingly.

"It's hard to say, really," Holt said. "Truth is, I didn't think a lot of it through very well. Like taking Ash's egg. I just acted on my conscience. I felt... compelled."

"Compelled," Fynn echoed. "Not all the consequences were happy ones. Do you regret anything?"

Holt looked at Ash and the icy blue of his partially visible eyes.

Mad as it seemed, Feorlen would not be standing now if he'd never saved Ash's egg. Talia and Pyra probably wouldn't have made it. Despite their failure to save more hatchlings from Thrall, their actions had at least hindered his plans and saved Soot. She'd otherwise either be enslaved to Thrall or dead.

His gaze lingering on Ash, Holt said, "Nothing has gone perfectly, but I'd have more regrets, I think, if I'd done nothing. More good than harm has come about so far."

Saying it aloud reaffirmed it for him.

Fynn nodded slowly. He played several more rising and falling chords, hummed to himself, then cut the music short with a firm palm against the strings.

"Thank you for your insight, Holt Cook."

Holt turned back to face him, puzzled. "Is that all?"

"That's all," Fynn said cheerfully. He headed toward the dirt track, clearly intending to leave this time. On the road, he turned on his heel. "The wedding begins tomorrow—"

Holt's stomach twisted.

"—so you'll be invited to the palace isle tonight to make your weapon. May it serve you well on your mission."

"We hope so!"

"If songs and fables are anything to go by, I'd say there is hope yet." Fynn doffed his cap. "I am glad to have met the infamous role-breaker, chaos-bringer, lunar rider, and pot boy. Always good to put a face to a name."

"Same here."

Fynn spun and strolled off, whistling some new song on his panpipe.

Holt stood rooted to the spot, feeling embarrassed, as though he'd been stripped bare somehow and left exposed.

"Wait!" he called.

Fynn stopped moving but did not stop playing.

"Please, let me give you something to take back." Holt ran into his hut, opened his recipe book, searched for the page of his notes on jerky, then ripped it out. He brought it out and handed it to Fynn. "Please, take this back to Talia. It's my notes on special food that can help her and every other rider too."

Unfazed, Fynn took the sheet. "Are you sure you don't need it?"

Holt shook his head. He had it memorized and could easily make more notes. "Think of it as a wedding present."

Fynn smiled. "Thank you, from both of us." He placed the notes neatly inside his satchel, picked up his pipe, and began playing again as he headed off.

Holt watched him shrink into the distance until he disappeared around a corner and was lost from view.

With a modicum of reflection, he was surprised at how he'd reacted to the treatment from the other riders and Talia. Egotism had got the better of him. He vowed to put an end to that.

That night, just as Fynn had promised, Holt and Ash were invited to fly to the palace grounds under the cover of night. Holt left everything behind save for the fallen star.

They touched down behind the storehouses and servant quarters. Prior to the battle, they had sat meditating and preparing in these grounds, but even cloaked in darkness, it was clear much had changed. Most of the neat hedgerows were still missing, and only small sections of the once pristine gardens remained.

The biggest change was the wide space given over to an open-air smithy, complete with a modified furnace to support dragon-sized bellows. Every tool of the smith's trade hung in long racks, clanking as they swayed in the breeze. Fierce heat from the furnace kept the chill of the night well at bay.

To Holt's delight, Talia and Pyra were present to meet them at the forge.

"I wasn't expecting to see you!"

"I make do with less sleep these days," Talia said without enthusiasm. "I can't stay for long, but I thought I'd see you make a start, and my blacksmith should be joining us soon to take your measurements. Ah, here he comes."

Sure enough, an experienced-looking smith with thinning black hair and a heavy leather apron approached out of the night. He had thick arms somewhat gone to seed and carried a notebook, ink, a quill, and a ball of marked twine.

"Talia," he said, inclining his head. Holt wondered why he wasn't giving her the full title she deserved, but Talia did not seem fazed. The smith inspected Holt with tired eyes. He yawned deeply. "It will take at least a week, maybe more. Will that be an issue... sir?" he spoke politely enough, though he failed to meet Holt's eye.

Assuming this had something to do with being a role-breaker, Holt let it slide this time. "Take your time. I'm grateful for the service."

The blacksmith grunted.

"Thank you also for your discretion in this matter, Mr. Smith," Talia said. "The crown owes you a boon."

The blacksmith went red in the face and scratched nervously at his neck. "Shall we start?"

After taking Holt's measurements and confirming he wanted the armor in white, the smith bowed to Talia, nodded to Holt, then scurried off like a thief in the night.

Talia smiled. "Shall we make a start? Rake should be here soon—"

"He's close? Where?" Holt stretched his sixth sense to its limit in a fruitless search, expecting to hear Rake's rebuking voice at any moment.

"I had word he was running along the eastern shore. I've sent transport for him."

"That's well," Ash said. *"We'll need Master Rake's help if Holt is to work the star."*

"The star?"

"We didn't have a chance to mention it before," Holt said. He went to Ash and withdrew the lump of white steel from a sack. He returned to the forge, and against the heat of the furnace, the fallen star felt cool and rejuvenating in his hands. The exposed opal shimmered in its many colors.

When Talia beheld it, all queenly strength dropped from her face. Talia the enthusiastic student of rider lore shone through, happy and eager above the orange hue of the oven's fire.

"Oh, how intriguing! May I?" she asked, holding out her hands. Holt handed her the star. "I've heard of meteorites being forged before, but they're usually lumps of poor-quality iron."

"Aberanth said it was already steel."

"Huh," Talia said, turning the star around and gazing at it. "Well, you get to skip a stage of the process then. No need to make steel first if you already have some." She squinted. "There's something else in it too."

"Lunar magic. It was a lot stronger when it first fell, but it's in there."

"Huh," Talia said again. She shook the star as though it might be coaxed into revealing its secrets. "Could it be some form of natural dragon steel? Huh. If it is, then it's likely already pure as can be. I can see why you'd want to use this, but I have no idea if the furnace will be hot enough to melt it. Dragon steel is usually impervious to damage once it's made, but who knows with this stuff…"

She trailed off, deep in the moment, whatever other matters required her attention quite forgotten.

Pyra cut into the silence that had fallen. *"It won't get hot at all if you don't place it in the furnace."*

Talia emerged from her reverie. "That's true enough." She handed it back to Holt. "Stick it in the oven, then. What's the worst that can happen?"

"It could explode and sink the island."

Talia laughed again and punched him hard on the shoulder. "When have you ever been a pessimist?!"

Grinning, Holt set the star down on an anvil, then pulled on a pair of thick leather gloves that covered his forearms and, using a large pair of tongs, he lifted the star and placed it in the furnace.

"You're up, Ash," Talia called, and Ash eagerly came forth. "You need to keep the furnace as hot as possible, much hotter than humans can on their own. Holt will pull on the bellows, and you can blow a lot of air into it on your side."

It took Ash a little while to negotiate with his set of bellows, but once he got his mouth around them and began to blow, the effect was immediate. New levels of heat bloomed out of the furnace, and Holt's sweating increased in earnest. As he took up the rider bellows on the opposite side of the furnace, he looked to Talia to check that he was doing it right.

"That's it," she encouraged.

Holt huffed as he pulled on the bellows. "I should never have complained about washing dishes."

Talia chuckled appreciatively, and to Holt's delight, she didn't hurry off back to queenly duties. For a moment, he became lost in the firelight dancing off her hair.

"Boy," Ash said between heaving puffs, *"don't stop."* Holt only realized then he'd let his rhythm on the bellows slack. Redoubling his efforts, he tried to act naturally.

"How are you feeling?" he asked. "About tomorrow?"

Some of the natural glow on her face dimmed. "It will be good to finally seal the alliance. Empress Skadi will have no excuses to avoid sending military aid once her own issues have been dealt with."

She spoke in terms of statecraft and business, which Holt supposed a royal marriage was.

"What did you think of Fynn?" she asked, perfectly innocently.

Holt pulled on the bellows, unsure of what to say.

"We liked him," Ash said.

Holt nodded. "He seems like a good ally for you."

"He's made it clear he's prepared to stand up to his mother, which is reassuring. And he's got a beautiful singing voice."

Holt pulled a bit too hard, and something in the mechanism of the bellows creaked. He winced, as if that would undo the damage. Luckily nothing seemed to be broken, so he carried on.

"It's the right decision," Talia went on. "For the good of Feorlen."

Holt forced a smile. Silently, Ash sent him comfort over their bond, as though the dragon were giving his soul a hug. There was no judgment in it. He loved Ash for that more than he felt words would ever convey.

"I got your notes on drying meat," Talia said. "Seems promising. That's amazing that you and Aberanth discovered it."

Holt feigned nonchalance. "Beef dries nicely. We're just sorry that's the only wedding present we could bring."

"Are you joking? This discovery is worth a fortune alone! But if you'd like to get me more, bring me that scourge orb, and I'll consider it the greatest present in the world."

"That we can do."

Talia looked off into the distant night. "Rake's landed. My people will escort him in through a postern gate. He won't be long."

"Oh good," Holt said, though, if he were being honest, he'd blissfully forgotten that Rake was on his way.

As though he could read Holt's mind from afar, Rake reached out to him. *"I hope I'm not interrupting?"*

Holt didn't dignify that with a response and kept pulling on the bellows. For a while, no one spoke, though Pyra made an unusual squirming growl and began fidgeting with her wings and licking her talons.

Eventually, Talia caught his eye and gave him a soft smile. "I ought to get going. Rake's hands will be more capable than mine, I'm sure."

Holt swallowed hard to prevent himself saying something he'd regret. "Thanks for getting me started."

"I really want to know what happens with that meteor. Pyra will stay up with you. She usually sleeps here by the heat of the furnaces."

Happiness rushed across his dragon bond from Ash. *"We'll be glad for the company."*

Pyra lifted her head and went suddenly still as though caught naked. After a moment, she rumbled and said, in a regal, threatening manner. *"We'll get the steel hot one way or another."*

"That we will," Holt said. Then, a little lamely, he added to Talia, "Good luck tomorrow."

"Tomorrow is the easy part. A day in a hot sweat lodge sounds like a dream."

"Well, good luck with the sword rites, then. And the hearth rites – don't burn the bread," he added with forced humor.

"Don't put ideas like that in my head, or I'll definitely worry about it." She took a step back. "Goodbye for now, Holt. I'll see you again before you leave." And before he could do more than utter a feeble farewell, Talia vanished into the darkness.

Holt and the dragons entered an amicable silence. The crackle from the furnace and the whoomph of air from the bellows all retreated into background noise.

Rake's arrival put an end to that.

Covered in his great cloak, the big half-dragon sauntered toward them as though this were another evening in Aberanth's glade.

"Having fun, are we?" Rake asked.

Holt ignored the question. "What took you so long?"

Rake lowered his hood, his grin unfaltering. "Nice to see you as well. Some would consider such a journey made on foot so fast to be a marvel."

Holt frowned. "What kept you? Are you feeling alright?"

Rake rolled his eyes. "If you must know, I took a nap."

"A nap?"

"Quite a long one, but I feel much better for it." He narrowed his blue eyes to slits, studying Holt. "Might be you'd benefit from one too. You seem to have your britches in a bunch."

"Don't mind, Holt," Ash said. *"Things haven't been how he hoped."*

Rake raised a scaly brow. "Have they ever?"

Pyra rustled and shuffled closer to Rake along the grass, her amber eyes as round as two large dinner plates. *"It is good to see you again, Master Rake."* She extended her neck, as though Rake were a proper dragon to touch snouts with.

"Nice to see you too," Rake said, meeting her snout with his great orange hand. Then, pointedly, he added, "Now this is a proper welcome. Holt, take notes." With that, he took up a seat at the edge of the smithy and put his feet up onto one of the workbenches, leaving Pyra with her neck and snout still extended. With a snort, she curled up on the grass.

Holt and Ash worked until Rake advised they check on the start. Holt drew the white steel from the furnace and placed it on an anvil. The meteorite was warm, but it was still a single solid lump without any hint of becoming hot enough to work.

"No glow," Rake said. "That's not encouraging."

Holt sighed. "Now what?"

Pyra got up and braced as though for battle. *"Place it back in. I shall push the oven further."*

Holt placed the star back into the furnace, refueled the fire, then he and Ash returned to work the bellows. They tried again and again. Hours passed, then dawn broke, and the morning wore on.

They kept going until Rake had had enough. "This is dreadfully dull. Is it working at all, Pyra?"

"It is, but barely."

Holt withdrew the star and set it on the anvil. As before, it seemed little affected by its time in the blistering heat.

Pyra came to inspect the ore. Eyes shut, she held her snout over it, as if listening to instructions from what little heat was in the metal. She rumbled and shook out her whole body in irritation.

"Let us see if it can withstand core-forged flames."

She gathered fire at her open mouth, then narrowed her lips until the flames became a focused cone. Holt and Rake backed away just before she began to breathe a searing stream of fire onto the metal. When she stopped, she sniffed the steel, then growled.

"I will not be defeated by this lump of rock. Return it to the flames. Together we will triumph."

"I don't want this to take up too much of your magic," Holt said.

"I have come to terms with the fact that your light is superior against the enemy. If my fire can serve to create a great weapon against the scourge, I will empty my core, if needs be."

Ash stamped his feet and rumbled in appreciation.

"Third time serves for all," Rake said.

"Let's try," Holt said, finding fresh enthusiasm as he returned the star to the furnace. This time, as he and Ash worked, Pyra urged the fires to greater heights. Periodically they brought the steel out for Pyra to douse with her concentrated breath, so hot the fire emerged blue and jagged.

Pyra's focus was unwavering. The first time she broke concentration was to inform them that Talia was now in the sweat lodge with her mother and maids.

"Will you go to her?" Ash asked.

"As delightful as hot steam sounds, I can hardly fit inside the lodge. Right now, this is more important. We go on."

And so, they did. Again and again, Holt removed the steel, Pyra bathed it in flames, then they returned it to the forge, all three of them working doubly hard to ensure the oven was kept at its peak capacity. Rake enjoyed supervising with his feet up.

Working so closely with Pyra gave Ash endless satisfaction. Holt enjoyed the opportunity too. The way she tensed her wings while she concentrated, tapped the ground with her tail as she worked herself up, and growled under her breath when frustrated, almost nattering to herself, were subtleties Holt had never noticed before.

Although Pyra wasn't much of a conversationalist, they

learned more of her and Talia's adventures through snippets of chatter. Holt attempted to get Pyra's opinion on Prince Fynn, but all she said on the topic was, *"I've made it clear what his place is."*

"Have the Skarls been informed of this?" Rake jested. "Perhaps someone ought to change their oaths for tomorrow."

"Were it that I could influence such things. I can always glare at him. That seems to leave him unsettled."

"I see no reason to worry," Ash said, continuing to heave great breaths into his bellows. *"Talia is your rider. Nothing can be closer, and no one will change that."*

Holt thought this rather insightful of Ash. He had wondered why Pyra held a low level of animosity toward Fynn, but it made sense she was concerned about Talia's affections being diverted. More sense – much more, in fact – than his own misgivings about the skinny bard and his dainty lute.

Pyra grumbled. *"You are right, Ash, of course. But still…"*

"The ceremonies sound fun, at least," Ash said. *"So much food,"* he added dreamily. *"And this dancing. I've never been around humans dancing. It sounds funny. I can imagine their hearts beating too fast."*

"The rites sound so drawn out to me," Rake said. "In Freiz, we would shove the clasps onto each other's cloaks, say some words, then get to the good stuff."

"It would be nice to be at the wedding all the same," Holt said.

"Really?" Rake asked skeptically.

"Of course, I'd have liked to be there. Talia's our friend, and everyone would see that she trusts us."

Pyra stepped back from the furnace and blew plumes of smoke from her nostrils. *"Talia trusts you more than anyone,"* she said in a low and very serious tone. *"Take it out,"* she added with a nod toward the oven.

Twilight was giving way to true night. A full day of heating the ore had almost passed. Surely this would be the final round.

"You don't need to spare my feelings," Holt said as he pulled on his leather gloves. "There's clearly a lot more going on than she's telling us. I'd want to help in more ways if I could, but that's her choice."

He grabbed the tongs, retrieved the ore from the fire, and took it to the anvil, where he found a snarling Pyra waiting for him.

"*Holt Cook,*" she said with well-practiced disdain. "*Do you think I would sweeten my words just to please you? Talia doesn't burden you with everything that assails her because what she asks of you is already so much. Worse in some ways than what she must face, for she at least will not be so alone. I assure you, there is no one else in the world she would trust to face this mission. Such strength between two humans might as well be a dragon bond.*"

Wordless and thoroughly rebuked for the second time in two days, Holt placed the star upon the anvil. No one moved or said anything, not even Rake.

"I'm sorry," Holt said at last. "I didn't think—"

"*How could you think otherwise?*" Pyra interrupted. She shook her head, clawed at the earth, and thumped her tail. After snorting fresh puffs of thick smoke, she calmed down and turned her amber eyes upon the white steel.

Holt scrambled aside just in time before Pyra unleashed her power as never before. Anvil and star were lost in an inferno, and when she relented, Pyra panted from the effort.

But the star remained insolently intact.

Though heat radiated from it like any dark stone under a punishing sun, it did not glow with transformative heat. At best, after all their efforts, it had turned reddish.

It could not be worked.

Pyra snarled louder and stomped off and slammed her tail over and over, throwing up clumps of earth and grass. While venting her rage did nothing to melt the meteorite, it did aid in dislodging the opal. The heat must have been just enough to loosen it, and Pyra's thundering tail did the rest.

As Pyra fought to settle herself, Holt placed the opal into one of his leg pouches and tied it in place. Perhaps he could find a use for it in the future.

Rake came over to Holt and placed a scaly hand on his shoulder.

"It's a great shame," Rake said. "But we can't waste any more time. You have just over two days now."

"I know." Holt pulled off his gloves and pinched hard between his eyes. He wasn't physically drained, not yet, but disappointment had its own wearying effect. Ash came to him, and they sought solace in each other.

"We'll still make the best sword we can," Holt said across their bond.

"I know we will."

Holt would have to start from scratch after all, as all riders must, creating pure plain steel.

"Remind me how to begin, Rake?"

"Pot, sand, glass, iron, charcoal."

"Right," Holt said. "Right," he repeated, more determined.

He got to work while the fallen star sat cooling upon the anvil.

14

RITES OF PASSAGE

Before joining the Order, Talia had never cared for sweat lodges. Now she wondered if she would ever find the strength to leave. She kept asking for the temperature to be raised, and after her mother and maids fled, she enjoyed a rare moment of solitude.

Alone in the hot dark, she stripped naked. Velvet steam caressed every inch of her skin, sinking the heat into her very soul. If the aim had been to purify herself prior to the wedding, she must have sweated out every wrong or ill thought she'd ever had.

The next morning, she prepared for the sword rites by dressing in plain garments adorned only with a simple necklace and a ring of flowers woven with myrtle. Even her dragon steel circlet was left behind so that her hair hung loose. With her wedding party, she took a boat east across the lake, and from there, they made the short journey to the rites mound, a hillock covered with tall wild grass and fragrant flowers.

As Talia climbed the mound, Pyra landed by her side. She stroked her dragon's snout, and Pyra closed her eyes and leaned into her touch.

"This ritual takes too long," Pyra said.

Talia pointed down and said, "Look here." She bent to show Pyra the heavy stone sunk into the hilltop. Carved in the stone were oblong grooves for two sets of feet to stand opposite each other. "This stone is more ancient than the whole kingdom. No one knows its true origins."

Pyra cocked her head and sniffed. *"Meaning what? It's just a stone."*

"It means humans have been doing this for so long we can't remember how it began or why. Dragons have songs and blood memories, and we have ceremonies."

As she finished, the last of her wedding party reached the hilltop. Ealdor Hubbard, the Master of Roles, came trudging at the rear with the help of a cane.

The Skarls weren't far behind. They came blowing horns and rattling their shields and took to the hillock with long strides as though it were second nature.

Prince Aren looked broader than ever. His shoulders and chest strained his fine clothes. Even the boar tattoo on one side of his forehead seemed stretched. His beard was longer now, but his braid was little more than a knot, like Fynn's. After his actions in the scourge tunnel, Aren had cut his hair as a mark of atonement, although his entourage of housecarls and fair maidens had swelled in the run-up to the wedding.

Ambassador Oddvar stood out, being neither a burly warrior nor young and pretty. The poor man also suffered from summer fever, leaving his eyes red and watering amongst so many flowers.

Fynn was as plainly dressed as Talia, without his cap and clothed in simple white garments. Instead of his instruments, he wore an axe and a set of tinkling keys at his belt. He carried himself well, though his pale skin seemed gray, and a hollowness lay under his eyes.

Before joining Talia upon the ancient rock, Fynn respectfully stopped short, and, alone of all the members of the bridal party, he focused his attention on Pyra. Nothing was said, but a silent request for permission was made. Pyra puffed smoke, narrowed her eyes, then assented with a nod. Fynn gave her a bow before stepping onto the stone and placing his feet into the grooves.

He met Talia's eyes and did not let go.

The Master of Roles shuffled in to officiate. "We give thanks that the blight has not taken this site. Today we are gathered to witness the sword rites between Talia of House Agravain, Red Queen of Feorlen, and Prince Fynn Skadison of the line of the Silver Boar." Hubbard turned to Fynn. "Do you have the bride gift that you oathed to bring?"

"I have."

Three of the Skarl maidens came forth with silverware etched in black patterns. Felice stepped forth to receive it in lieu of Talia's father, and it was to her Fynn spoke.

"Though this treasure cannot balance that which you gift to me, I offer this to your kin, the bride gift, as I oathed to do."

"My kin are honored to receive your gift," said Felice. She took each basket and handed them to her own maids, who bowed and trotted back to the Feorlen side.

Talia eyed the glinting silver as it passed and made a mental note to have Lady Elvina sell it and claw back a few coins into the Treasury.

The Master of Roles wheezed, then carried on. "The bride gift has been given. Now vows and swords shall be exchanged. Prince Fynn, take one knee."

Fynn knelt and pulled the axe free from his belt. In two open hands, he raised it up in offering. "I give you this axe, which has defended my line, for our sons to have and to use."

Talia accepted it and handed it to one of her maids to sit with the bride gift. Then it was her turn. Her mother passed her a short broadsword in an ornate scabbard bound in yellow and gray leather. Not red, for this new blade represented the family, not her alone. The pommel had been shaped into the Feorlen crest of crossed swords and encircling crown.

She placed it into Fynn's open hands and said, "With this sword, keep safe our home."

Fynn got to his feet. Taking the keys from his belt, he looped the oversized keyring over the hilt of his new sword and presented it to Talia, hilt first. As the keeper of his new household, Talia took it, wondering whether the keys opened anything or whether they were just for show.

As the Master of Roles led them through the next stage of

the rites, a rider entered the outer reaches of Talia's detection. Pyra twisted her neck and looked skyward to where dark wings appeared from the east. Talia lost track of Ealdor Hubbard's words as the dragon's voice entered her mind.

"Your pardon, Red Queen," a young male said. *"We bring urgent news from Commander Ethel. A greater threat has been found in the Morass. Immediate assistance is demanded."*

"I'll respond," Pyra told Talia. *"End this."*

Hubbard's words returned hazily to Talia, and she lowered her gaze from the distant dragon to Fynn. He must have read the truth on her face. Frowning, he turned to address the Master of Roles.

"Apologies, Ealdor. I believe we'll need to adjourn our rites here."

He let go of her hands.

"Adjourn?" Hubbard said, bewildered.

"There is urgent news from the Flight Commander," Talia said. "I must address it."

"What of the vows?"

Talia met Lady Ida's gaze. The Mistress of Embassy nodded wearily, as did Oddvar, one eye covered by a kerchief.

"I believe the vows have been agreed by both parties. Let them be entered on the charter."

Regular citizens would need to say them aloud for the benefit of the rolekeepers in writing them down. However, Talia and Fynn's vows had been carefully negotiated over recent months. And they were long. Saying them aloud was just a formality.

Ealdor Hubbard bristled. Talia anticipated a grumbling 'most improper' from him, but sagely he let this one go.

"We shall gather again tomorrow for the hearth rites," he said, then pressed his cane hard into the earth and stalked off.

Talia climbed onto Pyra's back, and they set off at once. As they flew, the wind caught Talia's ring of flowers and tore it from her neck.

They met the rider near a copse bordering a cattle pasture. The herd beat their hooves and headed as far from the dragons as they could. It was a mark of the situation that Pyra did not eye them beadily.

The wind rider was an Ascendant called Lucia, and she was originally from Athra. As with many from that melting pot of a city, everything from her skin tone to her heritage was hard to place. However, even before she spoke, it was plain to see she was from the equestrian class of Athra from how at ease she looked riding her dragon, Amon, his scales dark as iron.

"What's happened?" Talia asked.

Lucia inclined her head, though it was to acknowledge her superiority as a rider, not as a queen. "Honored Champion, the fight to contain the scourge within the Morass has turned ill. A smaller, half-formed queen lends cohesion to the swarm. Commander Ethel and the vanguard were ambushed."

Talia clenched her jaw. Years back, the thought of scourge organizing a coherent trap for riders would have been absurd. No longer.

Pyra snarled.

"Were there losses?"

"One pair dead. Champion Galasso's dragon has been grounded."

Fire rushed over their bond, burning out the jolt of panic on Talia's side, though she wished she had her circlet to help release the heat. Their first joint instinct was to fly at once to seek offer battle and flame, and it was a struggle to contain it.

"What does Ethel require?"

"She summons all the reserves from Sidastra, even the Novices."

"We must do more," Pyra said.

Talia clenched her fist and nodded. This wasn't just hot-blooded talk; if the New Order failed to contain a remnant swarm in Brenin, then Adaskar would prove his point. The barons would turn on her uncle, her alliances would break, and, when weakened, war would follow. She and Pyra would then have to watch her kingdom burn or else burn men, women, and horses in trying to save it.

Either path seemed monstrous.

"I'll ensure all riders are supplied for the mission. In two days, I'll join you myself."

Talia wanted to say they would fly tonight, but little less than the Toll Pass crumbling to the beat of Risalian drums could allow her to leave the wedding incomplete.

Lucia looked surprised.

"Go," Talia beckoned.

"Yes, Honored Champion." She and Amon took off, making straight for the rider's isle on the northern outer ring.

Pyra scratched at the earth.

"We aren't being reckless in going, are we, girl?"

"Ethel and Strang wanted every rider to fly – perhaps we should get Holt, Ash, and Rake to help as well?"

Talia dearly wanted to say yes, but instead she said, "For all we know, it's an orb under Risalia keeping these forces in play. It needs to be removed. Hopefully they won't hold it against us."

"They won't – I am certain of that. But if not them, then I shall beseech the West Warden for aid."

The West Warden and many of his drakes were making a new grove amongst the reclaimed trees of the Withering Wood. If she flew day and night, Pyra should be able to make the journey there and back and return sometime after the mead rites, the final stage of the wedding.

"I'll miss you tomorrow."

"You'll have Fynn for company."

"Are you warming to him?"

Pyra snorted, then took off with such force Talia was rocked from side to side before they settled into a course back to the palace.

Sweat streamed down Holt's face, stinging his eyes, salting his lips. Wiping his brow, he went to find the chisel. He disliked this part, always fearing he would cut through the red-hot steel.

Raising the hammer over the chisel, he was about to strike

when he felt Pyra's return to the island. He looked up at the palace but saw nothing.

"She's on the other side," Ash said. *"I think Talia just stepped off onto a stone ledge and went inside."*

Holt thought that odd. Would she really return from the sword rites on her own?

A moment later, he sensed Pyra was on the move again. Purple flashed in the corner of his eye, and he twisted to see a smoking trail heading west as Pyra used her core to fuel her flight. Why would she go alone?

Another bead of sweat ran into Holt's open mouth. He swallowed the unpleasantness, then said, "Something's wrong."

From his lounging position, Rake snapped his long fingers. "Focus."

Holt's heart, already lively from the long labor, twinged painfully. Then he returned to his latest attempt and cut a groove into the steel with the chisel, then began to fold. Under heat and hammer, he attempted to fuse the layers of steel while cycling Ash's light around the hammerhead.

Despite himself, his mind still wandered.

Where was Pyra going? Had something happened during the ceremony? Why would Talia return alone without her wedding party or Fynn?

Had it been called off?

"Holt!"

Too late. His arm fell heavily, there came a white flash and a snap of metal, and the steel lay cloven in two upon the anvil. Only now did Holt feel the surge of motes down his right arm. He'd been pressing magic in too fast.

Rake stood. "You're too distracted."

"I know," Holt said, sounding breathless. He gulped. "I'll start again."

As he did so, he felt angry with himself. Pyra had already put him in his place last night. If Talia wasn't telling him something, she must have good reasons, but why was it so hard to accept and let go?

"Remember in the tunnels," Ash said, *"when I asked you to trust me and let me guide the way?"*

"I'll never forget."

"I was grown and strong, but you still thought of me like the helpless hatchling I'd been. Maybe you're still clinging onto something here which is holding you back as well."

Holt met Ash's gaze across their bond. They stared deeply into one another and, not for the first time, Holt marveled at how Ash seemed to know him better than he knew himself.

In the real world, Holt set his jaw, sealed the new crucible with soft clay, and turned Ash's words over in his mind.

He was holding onto something. Something outdated. Something no longer real. Had it ever been?

A tremor ran through his soul. It passed in a moment, but Holt followed its feeling like a lone star through a cloudy night.

He placed a hand over his chest.

Rake flicked his tail. "Ah, progress?"

Holt nodded. "Maybe. Thanks, Ash."

Their bond brightened and warmed. *"Let's finish this."*

Following the sword rites, tradition dictated that the bride spend her evening with family. No-nonsense food would be served and fond stories of her shared.

Talia had never thought she would go through these rites, but now she was, she felt the loss of her father and brother worse than ever. Osric too. Perhaps, in another strand of fate, they would all be here with her, whole and well, smiling and laughing, each sharing increasingly embarrassing stories about her. Nor was Pyra here, nor even could Talia feel her dragon's presence across lake and land and woods.

She only had her mother, but for tonight, that was enough. They supped quietly on a plain, unfussy meal. At first, there were musicians and singers, though Talia found it a distasteful indulgence while so many still suffered, so she dismissed them.

Besides, none were quite as good as Fynn. After that, they returned to work.

Late in the night, Talia spared a moment to peer out to the forges. From on high, Holt appeared the size of a thimble. Talia could almost feel the hammer as his arm rose and fell.

Her heart felt heavy. There was every chance Holt and Ash would not return from striking at this next tunnel. They stood to gain little and risked everything, yet they were willing to delve into the abyss for her anyway.

Talia had already made decisions that had cost lives, and she knew she would make many more. Deploying troops and hearing of the losses was part of her role. She'd built layers around herself to guard against it; even hearing of Ethel's losses in the Morass today had barely touched that armor.

But Holt and Ash were different. They shouldn't be, not to the Red Queen, but to Talia they were – and they always would be.

If she had been stronger, she would not have gone to them at all. Distancing herself would have been the best protection; it would have made her numb, just as her soul felt now with Pyra so far away. Were she numb, the rage could never take her.

It was a strange thing to find herself on the eve of the hearth rites and feel deeply that love was not a strength but a weakness.

A chill entered her soul.

The next day, Talia found herself standing in a no man's land between two great tables running the length of the throne room. No longer in the plain garments of the sword rites, she wore a crimson gown and her hair in an elaborate style, held in place by her circlet. Wafts of lavender rose from an ointment at the nape of her neck. She held a ceremonial bowl filled with pieces of bread and only her mother and an iron brazier for company.

Beyond the ealdors, jarls, guild masters, and leading merchants at the long tables, there were standing guests made up of citizens drawn by lot. The packed mass of bodies on both sides of the hall appeared like two armies ready to clash.

Fynn came alone from his side. Rather than a bowl of bread, he carried an ornate fire poker. His strides were perfectly balanced, not too quick to be eager, not too slow to betray regrets, just right, as though he were savoring the moment. He played his part well.

Felice placed Talia's hand into Fynn's, then, voice brimming with emotion, she said for the hall to hear, "May your love bring order, may your love bring life, may all you sow be free of strife." She squeezed their hands together.

Talia caught her mother's eye and saw the strained repression of tears. Seeing her mother so moved would have overwhelmed her were her soul not so cold and dull.

Felice left them. Talia and Fynn had rehearsed the next steps so many times it felt strange to be doing it at last. They let their holding hands fall as they turned to face the lit brazier. Talia passed the bread bowl over the top of the flames, then handed it to Fynn, who skewered two crusty pieces onto the end of the poker and passed them through the hottest part of the fire. They each took a piece in hand, entwined their arms at the elbow, and ate.

Feorlens applauded and banged their fists upon the table. The Skarls followed suit on a slight delay, taking their cue from their hosts.

Two larger bowls piled with pieces of bread were rushed out by servants. Talia passed her bowl quickly through the fire, Fynn did the same, and then they split, Talia heading to serve each member of Fynn's table and he to hers. Some Skarls looked bemused as she handed them kernels of bread, and some seemed alarmed, perhaps fearing this would be the extent of the feast.

They needn't have worried. As soon as Fynn and Talia reunited in the center of the hall and displayed their emptied bowls, doors at the back of the hall were opened and the true feast was hauled in, dish by dish. The crusted smell of pastry from the pie tops seemed boldest to Talia, though there was a roasted boar too and heaps of root vegetables shining in butter. Though the occasion was extravagant and needed to be, Talia was heartened that many would benefit from it.

A form of organized chaos ensued. Following Feorlen custom, each wedding party would serve the other food, and the hosts took the lead. Ealdor Hubbard had a small plate carried for him to the Skarl table. Soon after, he made a dignified exit before the ale really started flowing. By the time desserts arrived, the Skarl custom to earn one's meal had asserted itself. The music and toasting and cheering and laughing became a din.

Ealdor Horndown, the Master of State, arm wrestled with Prince Aren over a portion of stewed apples. Horndown had let his beard grow over the winter and had yet to trim it, making him more bearlike than ever. The outcome of the match seemed far from certain.

Lady Elvina enjoyed the rivalry of two young jarls vying for her affection – each with hair as golden as her own. Lady Ida's stern face had been exchanged for the drunken grin of a far younger woman. She danced without shame or care with Ambassador Oddvar, he several more tankards to the wind than she.

With her bond hanging as a dead weight in her chest, Talia did her best to endure it all with a smile. More than once she looked around the hall for Drefan, but her Master of War remained in the Toll Pass, bracing for an attack they feared could come at any moment.

Night rolled in, and even royal weddings had their end. As the revelry quietened and guests departed or slumped in ale dreams, the calls arose for the bedding procession. Those still capable of climbing the stairs followed Fynn and Talia, slurring bawdy jokes to raucous laughter.

Once over the threshold of Talia's chambers, the Feorlens departed. Rowdy Skarls attempted to enter, pushing on the door as Talia tried to close it. Bangs and thuds against the wood ran up her arm, then guards and Skarls with their wits about them entered a scuffle to haul them away.

"You Skarls have some odd ways."

"It's a big place, the Empire," Fynn said in an ever so tipsy voice. "In some places, they don't consider the marriage true unless witnessed."

Talia was glad this wasn't the case in Feorlen. Here, as in

most lands of the old republic, the rolekeepers needed no public witnessing of a royal bedding. If a marriage was in their books and all was in order, then it was so.

The fracas in the hallway died down. Talia locked the door.

Fynn slumped onto a long couch under a window with his lute. He looked even paler now in the moonlight, his skin paper thin. A dim light burned from low candles placed artfully around the four-poster bed.

Far from the stifling heat of the throne room, Talia found the chamber frighteningly dark and bitter cold. Ice gathered at her soul. She shivered and rubbed her chest.

"I'm... s-sorry," Fynn said.

"For what?"

"For the pain. It must hurt when you're apart like a piece of you has been... t-torn away."

Talia sighed. Still clutching her chest, she went to sit on the edge of the bed.

Fynn set his lute down, then went to tend to the fireplace. Talia reached out her hand and extended her fingers instinctively, and it took a moment to realize what was wrong.

With a huff, she brought her hand down so hard the whole bedframe shook and a slat under the mattress snapped. She bit her lip and brought her hand slowly back to her chest. Maybe her temper wasn't entirely Pyra's fault.

Unperturbed, Fynn lit the fire, then returned to lie on the couch and clutched his lute.

Talia shifted along the bed to be closer to the fireplace.

They sat for a time in silence until Fynn played gentle strings to fill the void. It struck her then that they were alone – completely, privately alone – for the first time since their official engagement.

"I thought you couldn't play music for a maiden?"

"We are wed."

"Not until the mead rites in the morning."

"Oh," Fynn said, distracted. "Well, it can't do any harm now."

The ice in Talia's chest eased by a fraction.

"I'm sorry I can't be here to help show you your new duties, but Mother will walk you through it all."

Fynn continued playing, though his fingers slowed. "Don't worry for me."

Talia opened her mouth, hesitated, then asked, "Do you think it reckless if I go?"

"Some may think so, but it doesn't matter what they think."

"I'm asking what you think, Fynn."

He tilted his head to his other shoulder to look at her. "Why do you doubt yourself?"

The question took her aback. "Isn't it right for a leader to wonder if they're making the right decisions?"

"It is, but you only have that issue when it comes to what you will do."

Talia stared into the flames.

"I find it hard to talk about these things to anyone. Even Pyra, sometimes."

"I've noticed." Head still resting on his shoulder, he gave a faint smile. "I'm also not one to talk."

"You told me of Freya."

"Because I had to."

"Well, maybe I have to. I held back from Pyra at times because I feared she would think me weak, then regret her choice to bond with me. But we've grown by sharing our fears and pains. You're to be my... *husband*... That too is a bond for life."

Fynn's fingers grew slack, and his music lulled. The lids of his eyes grew heavy. Talia wondered whether the ale was catching up with him.

"The best artists do not... judge," he said. "We seek to understand."

She patted the mattress. "Sit with me."

Fynn blinked blearily, then managed to get up and make his way over, using the bedpost to support his short journey. He swayed forward as he sat down, then recovered and continued playing. Notes from both lute and fire blended into one song.

Talia took a few moments to gather herself, fighting back the frosty ache in her chest. Then, with a deep breath, she began.

"During the war, I wondered every day whether I should have gone to help my father. I wanted to."

"Of course you did."

"But I was a rider."

"No words can strip your feelings from you. No words... no distance..." He trailed off and, with a nod, signaled she should continue.

"I could have saved my father if I'd gone. I didn't. Same with my brother." She found it easier now she had started, and there was always a chance Fynn may not remember how frail she sounded come the morning. "I didn't know he was in danger until it was too late, and there wouldn't have been much I could have done, but—"

"But you don't know for certain..."

"I had all this power. Even as an Ascendant, I had magic, a dragon, strength. All that, but I didn't... I *couldn't* help them."

Fynn sat up straight. Any effect of the drink seemed suddenly dispelled.

"You wonder what the point of it all is if you cannot save those you love?"

He understood. Of course Fynn understood. Why was she only now piecing that together?

Words caught in her throat. She nodded.

"May I ask you something?"

Talia nodded again.

Fynn strummed a final set of notes, the strings reverberated softly, then he placed the instrument on the bed between them and met her gaze fully.

"Do you regret not going?"

Talia answered reflexively. "I did my duty." Her soul twisted painfully; the cold sank deeper. She gasped and bent over. Fynn's hand fell gently on her back. Perhaps it was due to the burst of pain, but the truth asserted itself. "Sometimes. Sometimes I regret it. I wonder what might have been."

The frigid fist inside her relaxed. Her throbbing soul ebbed. Groaning, she sat upright.

"Are you okay?" Fynn asked.

"I'll be fine once Pyra returns."

His fingers twitched against her back, then withdrew. "Thank you for being honest with me."

Talia stared into the fire again. "Seems easier to tell the truth than remember lies. As for my father and my brother, all I can do is try to honor them by making the best job of this that I can. A rider was never supposed to rule, and there are good reasons for that, not least my long life. Assuming I don't fall in battle, I could live another hundred years and still be firm of mind. The best I can do is try to make things better if I can."

"That's why you build in stone."

"That's why I build in stone."

She wished to help him in turn, but words were not her natural strength. She took after Osric in that regard. All the same, she tried.

"I realize I don't know the whole story, but it sounds like you did everything you could for Freya."

Still looking at the fire, she felt him shrink into himself, hunching and closing off his body.

"Three times we tried to run away. Each time farther, each time believing we'd made it. Each time they found us. I'm sure if we'd fled to the edge of Ahar or even to the hanging gardens in Lakara, they still would have found us. If I'd been able to let go, she would not have paid this price. But I was selfish."

Talia discovered a lump in her throat. She swallowed it.

"If your love for her is anything like a dragon bond, I'm not sure it can be called selfish. Is it selfish to want to breathe?"

At once, she felt embarrassed. What word pottage was this?

"Sorry. I'm not great at this."

"You're better than you think."

Fynn yawned and rubbed his eyes.

Talia could not recall yawning as a Champion, but she did feel weary.

"We should get some rest," she said.

"Yes, there's a big day ahead. We shall go down the stairs, drink some mead, and kiss for your rolekeepers."

Talia laughed from nerves. "It'd be nice if they didn't need *that* to be so public."

"You've faced worse horrors, no?"

"I've had training with sword and magic to handle those horrors. This one not so—"

Fynn's lips met hers. He'd moved so lithely one might have thought him a rider. Taken aback, she froze, feeling his beard against her cheek, his fingertips brushing her neck.

Her eyes closed.

Even with ice in her chest, something rose within her, but the wasteland of her bond was too great a distance for the force to cover.

It ended. Fynn pulled away and his enigmatic smile returned, the first evidence she'd seen of it in days. It seemed to say, 'That wasn't so bad, was it?'

"I thought it best not to let you overthink it. Now it won't be so strange tomorrow." He rose and picked up his lute. "Get some sleep, Talia."

He pulled the hangings around her four posters. She heard him slump onto the couch beneath the window, and his shoes had hit the floor before she found her voice.

"Fynn?" she said, concerned by how delicate she sounded. "Will you play that song? The one I like?" Then, recalling the origins of the song, she said, "If it's not too painful."

"Music cannot cause pain. That, we do to ourselves."

And he played. The haunting song she'd first heard drifting through the corridors of the Silver Hall and then again in her encampment on the edge of Brenin. Soft, ethereal, yet able to penetrate flesh and blood and bone.

Safe behind the heavy curtains, Talia undressed, slipped into her nightgown, then got under the covers.

Just before sleep took her, she swore she heard Fynn sniff.

∾

Their third night at the forge wore on. Twice, now, Holt had reached the folding stage. Twice the steel had snapped.

The moon was just shy of being full. Perhaps that hurt his chances, but he couldn't wait. As he worked on his third attempt, he lost track of the number of folds, struck molten steel until he no longer heard it clang.

Sweat dripping from his brow, he tried pushing lunar motes into the steel, but they wouldn't take. So, on he went, folding and hammering, till the red dawn pushed back the darkness and his time was all but spent.

Not long from now, Talia and Prince Fynn would emerge together and drink mead before witnesses. The marriage would be considered, at last, complete. He carried on, yet the image of the royal couple standing arm in arm did not leave his mind.

This has to end.

When next he struck the whitening steel, something in his arm gave. He let it fall limp while the metallic ring wavered into nothingness.

"What's wrong?" Rake asked.

"Just need a moment," Holt said, his breath heavy.

Now he'd stopped, he noticed the morning light had arrived in full. He could hear the servants in the grounds bustling with the work of a new day, sailors calling from the lake, yet nothing from the palace.

A quiet gripped the throne room. A collectively held breath.

Holt looked up to the still shattered stained window and found himself unable to look away.

Ash stirred, both physically and spiritually. Soothing coolness crossed the bond, and Holt let out a shuddering sigh.

"I'm sorry, boy."

Holt's lower lip dropped by a finger's breadth, then stiffened. Words felt useless. It was hard enough trying to understand how he felt, never mind trying to convey them.

Months ago, he had reacted defensively to every side remark Rake had made about his feelings for Talia. Too defensively. He knew, logically, at the conscious, rational level, that nothing would develop between them, that nothing *could* develop between them.

He knew that. He was not so delusional.

She had not been the one admiring him from afar for years, nor incorporating him into daydreams about becoming the rider she could never be. That had been Holt.

Years back, he'd fantasized about becoming a rider, slaying countless scourge, winning the hearts of the people he saved and perhaps that of a noble girl.

When had that noble girl acquired flowing crimson hair? Probably when Talia arrived at the Crag because she suited that role perfectly. But it hadn't really been her. Just an image, a phantom, as if conjured by Eidolan.

He studied that phantom now. The noble girl had Talia's face, but that was all. The girl in his dreams had no flaws, no worries, nothing but wide-eyed admiration for him, and certainly no demands of him.

She was not Talia, and she was not real.

Reality had turned out far from those old dreams. The dragon he'd envisioned had never been blind, his father had never died, and the world had not teetered on the brink of ruin. What then remained of his fantasies? Just a kernel deep down inside, a kernel of the Holt who did not understand the world as he did now, who thought all his woes would be solved if he were a rider and had magic powers. The part of him that still dreamed that possibly, maybe, if Talia had not been made queen, if she had come with him after they saved the city, then, just maybe…

Thunderous applause erupted from the throne room.

Colors danced off the shards of stained glass, and Holt swallowed hard.

May your love bring order, he thought. *May your love bring life, may all you sow be free of strife.*

The illusion of Talia appeared in his mind's eye, looking crestfallen and confused. *Farewell,* he said to her, and as she departed and his mind cleared, he allowed himself a wistful smile. A single tear ran down his cheek and fell to sizzle on the shining steel. With it, the last piece of his fantasies melted away.

He let his gaze fall from the throne room to the hammer, to his advancement, to his mission, to reality.

Not long after this, when he pushed lunar motes into the blade, the magic held. The dragon steel was ready. And perhaps it was a sympathetic sign from the world, but on that morning, of all mornings, the moon was still visible, hanging low in the sky with a red hue. Its reflection shimmered on the water in the quenching tank, which had sat all night under its silver rays. When Holt plunged his new sword deep, he cleaved the image of the red moon in two. The steam that rose was bright silver and carried with it an echo of the night song.

A weariness came over him as he beheld his creation. Holt had lost something in making it. Well, he'd let something go.

The body of the blade was pristine white. Every fold he'd struggled to make shone in rippling layers of silver. Thinner than Brode's broad blade, yet thicker than Ethel's icy point. Solid. Sturdy. Dependable. His own.

Ash couldn't help himself. He bellowed in jubilation, drowning out all noise coming from the palace.

Rake looked genuinely proud. "Congratulations, Holt, but it's time to go."

Back at their meager lodgings on the rider's isle, there was but one task left. Only a scale from the dragon whose magic created the metal could sharpen and polish the finished steel. Ash kindly flecked off a loose scale, and Holt sat on the grass and straw with his dragon curled up around him. Under the spring sun, he sharpened his new blade, and once it gleamed, he finally set it down.

He felt exhausted, much more so than at any time since breaking into Windshear Hold. Far more than when they'd fought Sigfrid and the Champions at Silt Grave. Yet it was a good ache, a tiredness that had been earned. Ash lifted a wing to cover him, and the world became peacefully dark and cool.

A tug at the back of his mind called to him. This time, he attended to it.

I am not a child anymore.

His soul shook.

He had let go of being a rider in the Order. He'd dulled the loss of his father by running right into Rake's arms, only to find Rake was deeply flawed. He'd let go of Talia too.

I am not a child anymore.

Like a knotted muscle massaged to peace, his soul smoothed out. It bloomed, and Holt Cook took his first taste of a new flavor.

Spirit.

15

A SOLDIER FOR HIRE

In his long career, Osric had traveled from the snowy wastes at the fringes of the Skarl Empire to the scrubland at the edge of Ahar, where the dunes of the Searing Sands blocked the southern world to all on foot. The Fallow Frontier was its own unique sort of desert, a wild expanse of rugged land reclaimed by nature.

They traveled east between the Brown Wash and the looming presence of the Eastern Frost Fang, following a road crumbled into disrepair, now little more than a dirt path cutting through tall grass and thorny tickets. Osric considered it ancient, for some cracked and worn paving stones remained dotted at the side of the track, and it was straight in a way only the roads of Aldunei had been.

During the day, the black dragon took shelter from the sun within Osric's shadow, emerging only when a clouded sky stole his shadow from him and then at dusk. He was glad to have her visible as the light faded, for the wilderness seemed to come to life with rustling in the undergrowth, deep hooting, and swift-running foxes, bigger than any Osric had seen. But with a dragon beside him, even one as small as she, nothing dared to trouble them.

Those first days and nights were quiet, and their progress slow. There seemed little need for haste, and Osric required far longer than normal to Cleanse and Forge her shadowy core. Years of forcibly attending to Thrall's black chains meant he'd grown accustomed to performing the breathing techniques through pain.

Her quiet anxiety was ever-present within him, for her emotions continued spilling into him, raw and unfiltered. He sensed the deepest sense of loss. He'd lost a hand; she'd lost something too – there was a hollow space within her that should have been filled. To her, her golden twin was still a bright star far away, something which guided her through her darkest thoughts.

And on they trudged.

Such a journey as this grated at him, for its aims were ill-defined, its end unknown, his path aimless. Wanting any sort of lead, Osric allowed the dirt track road to lead him to tiny hamlets with next to no defenses to enquire whether anyone knew of a woman called Petrissa Vogt. Asking directly seemed his only option. He couldn't just amble around the Frontier hoping to spot her one day.

As a rule, folk were guarded in the Frontier, and they seemed especially so now. Osric found the flimsy gates of two small settlements shut to keep out clusters of refugees from Silt Grave, appearing half-starved, manic, and covered in dirt – some in blood. They cried their tale of dragons, men in rough cloaks, and scourge all working together, and from the jumbled reports, Osric discerned that only four of the hatchlings had taken part in the attack. The wingless, webbed-footed dragon was not accounted for. However, while it made sense to him, such wild talk only made the townsfolk surer of their madness.

"You've all been too much at the marrow," a weasel-faced man with a loaded crossbow shouted from his post. "Away with you!"

Osric attempted to reason with him. "May I enter? I only seek information."

The weasely man trained his crossbow on Osric and frowned. Osric hoped his calmer demeanor would count for something.

"And what information would that be?"

"I'm looking for a woman. Petrissa Vogt is her name."

"None such 'ere that I know of," he said, too quickly for him to have really considered the matter, Osric thought. "And just what sort of role is a *Vogt* anyways?"

"A Risalian family name."

Osric didn't mind a direct approach. The name Agravain might risk attention, but he reckoned Petrissa would have abandoned that name – as she had the family.

The weaselly man gave a rather nasty laugh. "You've gone a long ways to be lookin' for some fancy Risalian lady 'ere." He raised his crossbow, his laughter cut off at once. "Makes me think you're up to summin' no good. One o' the Vulture's or the Jackal's boys, are ya?"

"No," Osric said, opting for calm again. "I only seek a woman named Petrissa."

"Well, I told ya, there's none called Petrissa here. Now get goin' before mi' finger slips."

From experience and a growing willingness to make use of his dragon's magic, Osric sensed the beginnings of the blight taking hold in a few of the refugees from Silt Grave. He pitied them. They would find no help now.

Osric returned to the road, and after putting some distance between himself and the refugees, he tightened his travel bags and started to run, intending to reach the next settlement long before news of blight-ridden people barred every gate.

The dragon remained hidden in his shadow as he ran, feeling like a lumpy weight dragging behind him, though while submerged, she weighed far less than her physical self. After miles of this, he came to a stop and squatted down to search for her in his shadow. Two purple eyes stared back at him.

"I can't keep this up."

She blinked back at him.

"Come out. It won't be long until dusk, and there's a little cloud cover."

Her eyes vanished, then one of her feet emerged, followed like oil by the rest of her body. The moment she fully materialized, she averted her head from the sun and uttered a croaked cry.

Osric feared he'd been too soft on her until now.

"There will be worse to come."

She mewled.

"Look at me."

She did.

"You want to get stronger like Ash?"

She rumbled, flicked out her little pink tongue, and nodded.

"Then you ought to get used to hardship. Nothing will become more bearable unless you face it."

She chirruped, then gently touched his stump with the wet tip of her snout. A rush of her shadowy magic crossed the bond, pushed from her side to his. Out of instinct, Osric tried to cycle it around his body to disperse it, but his network of mote channels had collapsed to that of a Novice, and the best he could do was send the magic down his arms. It was only a little and fizzled out before reaching his stump, but it still burned fiercely. He snatched his maimed arm away from her and cradled it. The dragon cooed and blinked at him.

Sucking in a winced breath between his teeth, Osric said, "Point taken." He got up and started walking again at once. Sensing she wasn't following, he called, "Keep up."

When she scampered up beside him, he allowed himself the slightest of smiles.

That evening, they took shelter in the ruins of a farmhouse overgrown with ivy, and only in the morning did Osric notice the rusted plow that had been left to rot in its barren field. Such was the Fallow Frontier, and this was but the western edge of it.

Ever in the presence of the Eastern Fang, their journey brought them back within sight of the Fae Forest, and Osric followed its winding border as it meandered north and east. The land descended and turned muddy, then, at last, they came upon the first settlement of any real size on the outskirts of the forest. High palisade walls were bolstered by a stone gatehouse and at least four siege platforms with small ballistae.

You might hold this against an initial wave, but four ballistae hardly cover enough of the air.

Pigs snorted and wallowed in fenced pens just in front of the walls, and ravens perched upon the gatehouse like so many black-cloaked guards.

Osric placed a hand on his dragon. "Stay in my shadow for this if you like. No need to draw any more attention than a one-handed vagabond already might."

And with her melded into his shadow, a crippled vagabond was all Osric appeared to be as he approached the gates. He knocked once. Then he knocked a second time, harder.

A hatch opened in the door, but no one challenged him.

"I'm looking for a hot meal," Osric said, which was true enough.

Someone on the other side grunted. "Payments in Faywallow can be made in coin or leaf. No bartering, no mercenary work. Any breakers o' the peace will be punished. Understand?"

"Perfectly."

The guard sniffed heavily, hawked, then spat. "In you come."

The gate hinges creaked, and the heavy door yawned open.

"*Craa-craa,*" the ravens cried as he passed beneath the gatehouse.

The dirt streets of Faywallow were only marginally drier than the hog pens outside, and they were quiet. And they were wide and flat.

Not a single choke point, Osric thought, ever in the habit of sizing up fortifications.

He stalked up the widest road until he came across what passed for a tavern. A tall signpost outside depicted a crudely carved hog's head with a piece of tattered cloth covering its eyes.

"*I wonder if it's a lunar pig?*" he asked his dragon.

Her amusement came over the bond like a tickle in his chest. At least speaking telepathically to her stirred no ache in him.

A low hum of quiet chatter could be heard from the tavern's patrons inside. Some might already have had too much of a good time, for several people lay languidly outside the premises, wearing vacant smiles and staring glassy-eyed at their mud-caked shoes.

But on closer inspection of the layabouts, Osric changed his mind. He'd been in enough military camps to recognize those under the effects of marrow. The substance came from the Frontier, though physicians always called it by its proper name, Kosora's Tears. Osric had never taken it himself. He barely allowed alcohol to pass his lips, never mind a toxin like marrow.

He put one foot upon the threshold of the Blind Pig, then paused, wondering if the dragon would be able to stay inside his shadow. So long as he cast even a small one, she should be alright, but he'd never had to give thought to doing so inside until now. The tavern had few windows, and half of those were shuttered. Taking her in ran too great a risk of discovery.

He searched for a solution and found it in the shadow cast by the signpost.

"Can you wait for me in there?"

Over their bond, she peeped and pipped, so Osric positioned himself such that his and the signpost's shadows met. Her weight left him, and the post's long shadow bulged in one spot.

"I won't be long," he told her, then he entered the Bling Pig.

Ever vigilant, Osric noted the other exit at the far back of the common room, how many people were huddled in their groups, and the fact that a trio of grizzled men were eying him. They appeared no better than ruffians, and perhaps they thought of him as an easy mark with his one hand, though he imagined he'd be safe enough while he remained inside the town.

Having assessed the threats, he took in the rest of his surroundings. The Blind Pig was like any darkened tavern in any other unsavory location, with pipe smoke and the stale smells of sweat and ale thick in the warm, damp air. The only notable feature was a curious door mounted on the wall behind the bar, its wood splintered and red paint worn away.

Osric approached the bar.

"What'll it be?" asked the barman gruffly. He appeared to be cleaning a tankard out with an already dirty cloth.

"Information."

The barman seemed to perk up. He was a piggy sort of man, short, thick-set, with a round, maroon-hued face.

"Information, is it? Jus' what could you need to know from 'ere, I wonder?" He seemed more excited than the situation warranted. The tankard and the dirty cloth were entirely forgotten.

"I'm looking for a woman. Her name is—"

"Hold up. Will you be payin' in coin or leaf?"

"That will depend on whether I get what I'm looking for."

The barmen narrowed his piggy eyes. "Coin? Or leaf?"

Osric rolled his shoulders. "I have neither, but as your local laws prevent bartering, perhaps you'll give it to me out of charity."

The barman frowned so hard that his brows and eyes seemed to merge into one. Then, all of a sudden, he gave a laugh somewhere between a bark and an oink and began tapping his fingers jovially upon the countertop.

"That's clever, that is, sir. Oh yes. I should be pleased to be given what I seek by way of charity." He leaned forward, his wide face all anticipation. "Go on then, fella, ask away."

"Petrissa, or she may go by Petrissa Vogt. She'd be two and sixty at most. Know of anyone by that name?"

The barman considered it, then shook his head, wobbling his jowls. "Oh no, sir, I don't rightly do. Never met anyone on any world with that name."

With that, he picked up his dirty tankard again and moved to the far end of the counter, leaving Osric perplexed.

What strange phrasing, he thought. He wondered if marrow accounted for the man's odd manner, then decided not, all things considered. Marrow numbed users from both physical and emotional ailments, and while some found it a pleasant sensation, it wasn't known to create eccentricities.

He also got the distinct, skin-crawling feeling of being watched by many eyes. He turned and found more than a few in the tavern staring at him none too subtly. It saved him from having to ask them one by one, he supposed.

"Petrissa Vogt?" Osric asked the tavern at large.

Some of the onlookers averted their gaze at once, returning to their huddles as though he'd revealed something grotesque. Others looked startled.

Feeling he'd struck upon a nerve of inquiry, Osric walked among them.

"Well? Speak up and I'll leave you to your drinks."

A man in a faded red jacket spoke into his mug of ale. "What's it to you, stranger?"

Osric went to him. "She's my mother." Out of the corner of his eye, he saw the grizzled trio pick up and leave.

The man in the red coat met his eye over the rim of his mug, then scoffed, drank more of his ale, and said no more. Everyone else turned their backs or closed ranks against him.

Osric left the Blind Pig and once more allowed his shadow to cross with that of the tavern post. Her weight re-entered his shadow, and he found it comforting.

With little to go on, he took to walking the streets. His foray into the tavern hadn't been entirely fruitless, for the reactions of the patrons had told him he was onto something. Unless, of course, they thought him delirious.

Maybe he was being a fool.

"Should I give up this hopeless hunt?" he asked his dragon. *"We've a better chance of finding evidence of your brother than of one old woman."*

Her sympathy touched him, and Osric resolved to leave. On his way back to the gatehouse, he came across a man curled up on a street corner, lethargically eating a steaming bread roll. Osric recognized him as one of the patrons who'd been slumped outside the Blind Pig. Given how the man seemed unfazed by the heat of the bread in his hands, Osric was left in no doubt that he'd taken marrow.

Hideous substance, Osric thought, then he caught himself. He could hardly judge anyone for anything anymore. Some men were weak and wished to numb out the horrors of the world, and some like him were strong, capable, but monstrous. He'd inflicted more harm than ten thousand marrow users ever could.

Something else flickered deep inside him, like the phantom

pain of his missing hand. A noble soul had given this man fresh bread, and a piece of goodwill given even here was touching to witness. No one in wet and muddy Faywallow could have much to spare.

"Oi!"

The gruff call came from behind.

Osric turned slowly to find the grizzly trio from the tavern swaggering toward him. One was tall and sinewy, one short and heavy with muscle, one of medium height with a wiry, agile frame and a long scar down his temple. Each had a short sword at their waist and carried a club, and they all wore dark cloaks with black hoods.

The scarred one called out again, "Hold it right there."

"Is there a problem?" Osric asked.

"You were askin' some right unusual questions back at the Pig."

"Is asking questions a crime in this town as well?"

The squat one dragged his club through the mud. "Who d'you work for?" he demanded in a nasally voice that took Osric aback.

"Myself."

"Ooo, come now, don't lie," said the lanky one, his voice as high as he was tall. "You one of the Jackal's pups?"

"No, but listen closely. I was just about to leave, and I advise you allow me to do so unhindered."

The muscular one snorted like a bull while his tall companion gawped, as though no one had dared defy him before.

Out of sight, a conspiracy of ravens croaked, and their cawing carried through the muddy streets.

It was the scarred thug who recovered first. "Who's that behind ya?" he asked, leering to get a look at the man with the bread roll. "Oi! Hand that over. We don't take kindly to thieving 'round 'ere."

"Use your sense," Osric said. "The man is clearly numb on marrow. Someone must have given him the food. Now, surely you all have better things to do."

The scarred thug sniffed, flared his nostrils, and took a measured step closer. "That's a nice cloak, that is."

"Yes," said the tall one. "Well-woven. Should fetch a fine penny."

The squat one breathed heavily and moved from foot to foot. "Hand it over then."

"My cloak?"

His gray cloak. The cloak he'd worn to make his name. The one he'd wrapped Esfir in to keep her warm on a freezing desert night.

"Never."

To make sure they understood him, he pulled back the fold of his cloak to reveal Vengeance at his hip and placed his hand upon the axe head.

The marrow user remained behind him, possibly blissfully unaware of what was happening. A nudge came from across his bond, and he agreed with his dragon.

A soldier defends, he thought as he positioned himself between the beggar and the thugs.

The trio laughed hard. One might have thought nothing so funny had ever occurred in Faywallow.

"Whatcha gonna do?" asked the squat one. "Fight us all?"

The lanky thug fell quiet and bent to grab his associate's arm.

"What?"

"That's dragon steel, that is. I seen them patterns on rider weapons."

"What you on about?"

"I's tellin' ya. That's rider steel."

The scarred thug shouldered the pair aside, beating his club into one hand. "Well, I don't see no dragon here. Just a cripple with a nice cloak."

A part of Osric wished that his right hand remained with him. He doubted anyone in the world, even in a backwater such as Faywallow, would look at a man with the Gunvaldr's Horn tattoo and think him easy prey.

But it was only a small part of him. For one, that hand had

deserved to go. For another, he had something more threatening now.

"I think you should give them a fright."

She emerged from his shadow – head, neck, one foot, and a dark wing – then hissed.

The eyes of each thug popped from their sockets.

"I told yous," the lanky one said, pointing at her. "I told yous!"

"Run!" the muscled thug cried, and he did.

The scarred one bobbed and bowed as he backed off. "Beggin' yer pardon, Master Rider, a thousand pardons."

"Leave."

They scarpered, but when Osric turned to check on the marrow user, he found the beggar hobbling away in the opposite direction. Osric couldn't blame him. The sight of a dragon appearing out of thin air would be shock enough to break through the mental fog of the drug.

"Best hide again," he told her. *"Time to leave."*

She slipped back into his shadow. Osric turned to continue down the route he'd been traveling before the incident when he saw a man in a red jacket sitting on a low wall. The same man from the Blind Pig. He must have witnessed his dragon's appearance, if not the whole encounter with the thugs.

Osric approached him slowly, and the man did not move from his perch. He had a full head of wavy, if unwashed, black hair, a rough beard flecked with gray, and the bearing of a soldier, even if he no longer was one.

"I trust you can hold your tongue?" Osric asked.

"Certainly. All I ask for is a quiet word in return." The man spoke far better than the thugs or even the barman, meaning he could not have been raised in the Frontier, though there was a roughening of his tone that made him hard to place.

"I have no time for intrigues. If you have something to say to me, then say it."

The man eased himself off the wall and seemed intent on leading Osric off. "Might we do so somewhere more secluded?"

Osric feared no one as incompetent as the ruffians, though a competent Wyrm Cloak armed with blood elixirs would prove dangerous.

"You'll tell me here or never," Osric said.

The man threw a wary glance to either side, then stepped closer and dropped his voice conspiratorially. "I recognized the name you gave at the Pig."

Osric's suspicions were immediately aroused, yet for want of any other lead, he had to listen.

"Do you know where she is?"

"I believe so, and I'd be happy to divulge that to you—"

"I have no coins."

"I'm aware of that, yet payment can come by other means."

"Not in this town, I'm told."

"Our business can be completed far from Faywallow. You're clearly a tough fellow, and this is a land where that is of more value than gold. If you and your dragon escort me safely to my destination, you'll have your information."

"That doesn't seem like a lot to go on."

The man dipped his head. "Of course, you're a rider, of sorts, and you know best, I'm sure. If it be that you do need me, you can meet me on the road after dusk."

"After dusk?" Osric asked, his suspicions growing ever more. Travel by night was ill-advised even in the best-governed realms.

"Just so," said the man, straightening and adjusting his red coat. "Crows don't see well in the dark."

After leaving Faywallow, Osric sought the relative safety of the wilds just off the road and contemplated his options. He could carry on flitting from hamlet to shanty settlement until he'd walked the whole Frontier and could easily obtain nothing for his efforts. Or he could escort the man with the red coat.

Whoever he was, Osric thought him shrewd. He'd figured Osric out at least; a man in want of something and with nothing else to give but his strength. And while he could never be sure, he didn't sense the man to be a secret Wyrm Cloak. There was a certain madness behind the eyes of the true believers that he hadn't detected.

So it was that Osric crouched in the undergrowth just off the road from Faywallow. Dusk fell, and as the last light began to fade and the shadows on the ground grew thin and watery, the man in the red coat approached from down the road, traveling in the driver's seat of a horse-drawn wagon, heavily laden. Osric stepped out to meet him.

"Ah, Honored Rider, good evening."

"If I'm to undertake this assignment, I need to know more about it. What are you transporting, and where to?"

"Selling trotters across the eastern settlements."

Osric's suspicions once again stirred. "May I?" he said, gesturing to the back of the wagon. The red-coated man pulled back a corner of the tarp, revealing baskets of pig trotters packed in salt.

"You require one of my talents to protect trotters?"

"I could not afford such talents with gold, sir, but you haven't asked for that."

Osric grunted. "Are you expecting to be attacked?"

"It's the Frontier, sir. Better safe than sorry."

"Be evasive if you wish, but if I'm not briefed on all the parameters, I may not succeed in the objective."

The man waved him down. "There's nothing out there that can hurt you."

That's where you're wrong.

"At least tell me your name," Osric said.

"You strike me as the type to know the value of a name. Tell you what, you can call me Merchant, for that is what I am. And I shall call you Rider, if that satisfies."

"I'm no rider. Call me Soldier, if you will."

"I shall indeed, Soldier. Do we have a deal?"

"We do."

Merchant scooted along the driver's seat to make room.

"I can walk," Osric said. "Come, we're losing the light."

Merchant clucked, jostled the reins, and his horse started forward.

"I told you; night isn't the worry, Soldier."

"An attack isn't my concern."

Thankfully, they were well out of sight of Faywallow by the time darkness fell and the dragon was forced to leave Osric's non-existent shadow. Her sudden appearance spooked Merchant's horse, though he spoke to her in a soothing, expert manner, stroking her neck and withers, and she soon settled.

The black dragon crept to the back of the wagon, sniffing furtively at its cargo.

"Not now," Osric said, dragging her back. "You'll only get some if offered. We're here to guard it."

She rumbled at him, licked her lips, but reluctantly allowed herself to be led away.

With his horse calmed, Merchant climbed back onto the driver's seat.

"You have a way with horses, Mr. Merchant," Osric said.

"And you with strange dragons."

With that, they were moving again, following the distant border of the Fae Forest north and east, heading deeper into the Frontier.

16

A CHECK OF WILL

Holt checked the map Ethel had given him three times, then gave it to Rake to check again. The gully they'd come upon looked like an old scourge tunnel, not least due to its width and descent. Even the largest scourge could have traversed it, perhaps even a queen. When Holt and Ash scouted the landscape from on high, they could see woodland to the east, which was clearly marked on the map. Going past it would be going too far.

"I'll take a look," Rake said, handing the map back to Holt, then he set off down the gully in search of a seal in the rock.

Evening drew in. A muggy gray day ended with drizzling rain, marking the ninth day since leaving Sidastra. Before leaving, Rake had managed to scare up some leather cord – Holt had not asked how – and they had lined the mouth of Brode's scabbard during their trip to adjust it for Holt's new, narrower blade. It wasn't a perfect solution, but it would do until he could get a custom sheath made. Brode's sword was now wrapped in heavy cloth and kept amongst the rest of their gear. Holt intended to lay it to rest properly once the mission was complete.

He checked the map for a fourth time, turning it in his hands to appreciate it from all angles. They were still a good way from the Risalian capital of Wismar and very far from Drakburg in the east. With luck, they would go unnoticed.

While they waited for Rake to return, Holt performed exercises with his new sword. He felt more balanced using it than he had when wielding Brode's sword, although there had been something comforting in the weight of the thick green blade on his back. His own sword felt light by comparison, and though it felt more natural in his grip, he was still putting too much strength behind his movements out of habit.

In terms of using his magic with it, there was no comparison. His new sword was as superior in that regard as dragon steel was over bronze, although Holt's initial experiments had yielded mixed results.

When he pushed magic into the blade, light dispersed up the length of the steel quite fast, making it hard to gather with enough concentration for something like a Lunar Shock. If he brute forced it and sent more magic into the sword, it would blast out much like a Shock, though with such force as to cause a physical blowback that rattled his arm, Champion's body and all.

Beyond this, he found it hard to manipulate the magic once it left his body. Still, he knew other riders could create abilities through their sword, like Rake and his Soul Blades, so he would keep trying.

Unfortunately, there was one significant downside. Whenever Holt practiced Sinking his channels to create an Eclipse, some of the moonlight being pulled toward his soul would stick in the dragon steel as though caught in a magical web. With a shimmering sword, enemies would be able to track him, defeating the purpose of the ability. A part of him hoped it was a kink that would smooth out, like a new shoe, stiff and unyielding until worked in.

After performing his drills, Holt sheathed his sword and returned to where Ash sheltered from the rain under a lip of rock in the ravine. He considered digging into their supply of dry wood to start a fire when Rake reached out to them.

"I've found it, but there's a small snag."

"What's wrong?" Holt asked.

"Best you see for yourself. We can use it as a lesson for you."

Deciding it would be best to stick together, Holt and Ash

wound their way down the gully on foot. Through the gathering dark and haze of misty rain, he saw the seal on the rockface quite clearly. It was a runic symbol similar to the letters Aberanth scratched out on his bark, lavender, bright yet wan, as though drawn in luminous paint long ago.

Holt thought back to the seal on the tunnel in Ahar but could not recall it glowing, only its vague outline, as though the rock were misshapen. Stranger still was that the glow revealed nothing of the ravine floor or even Rake right beside. Somehow, its light – if that's what it was – touched upon nothing. It was as if it wasn't there at all.

"Can you see it?" Rake asked.

"I think so," Holt said. "I couldn't in Ahar."

"That's because you've got a pinch of spiritual power now," Rake said. He rapped the seal with his polearm. "You're not really *seeing* it with your eyes so much as you are sensing the will behind the seal. This one was made by a mystic rider, hence the coloring. And a whopping powerful one at that, maybe a High Lord. Can you sense its strength?"

Holt squinted as though the lavender rune would twist itself and spell it out for him.

"Not really," Holt said, disappointed.

"Try a little harder. It isn't magical, so you won't feel it in the usual manner. Spiritual power is born from truth, from will, from authenticity. It carries a commanding feel, a certain authority. It challenges and questions you rather than moving you as magic might. Listen closer," he added softly, and he laid an orange hand on the lavender rune.

Holt followed suit, pressing his hand against the rock.

He listened, waited.

A subtle force, unlike any he'd experienced before, touched his very soul. It asked a question of him in a wordless language of its own.

'Do you have the strength to pass this point?'

Holt tried to answer it, but the force was unyielding. His soul buckled and bowed, and he stepped away, staring dumbly at his hand as though the rune had burned him.

He rubbed the tips of his fingers together and said, "That was strange."

Ash growled and stepped closer. *"It felt as though the wind were blowing against me."*

"But it didn't push you back?" Holt asked.

Ash shook his head.

"Dragons have a different relationship with their spirit," Rake said. "It's a deeper part of them, and they instinctively use it alongside their magic. It actually makes it harder for them to actively develop it; like their wings, they don't need to train to grow them. Higher control is what separates Wardens from other strong wild dragons, and the Elders... well, they're Elders."

"We've felt that," Holt said, vividly recalling the sense of being overwhelmed while in the presence of both the Life and Mystic Elders. That must have been the exertion of their spirit on his, of an authority that could impact the world around them.

"It's eerie," he said. "It felt a little like Thrall's mind control."

"Thankfully it's far from that. You just backed away due to your own natural reaction. Ash wasn't moved, and nor was I. Come, stand in front of me, and I'll demonstrate."

Holt did as instructed.

Another quiet force breached Holt's mind and body. A mental pressure pushed down on him, and this time it was commanding.

'Pinch your nose and hop on one foot.'

Holt dismissed it with barely a conscious effort. The pressure lifted.

"You see?" Rake said.

"Was that you?" Holt asked, shocked. "I barely had to put any effort into that."

"Forcing people to do something is hard. Most people, even non-riders, have wills strong enough not to simply be made to do something they are not inclined to do. And all I tried was to make you do something silly. If I tried to make you slit your throat, your will to live would repel it in an instant. However, subtler uses, questions, and challenges work far better. Observe. I shall provide you with two similar checks of will."

Once more, the mental weight pressed on Holt.

'Turn back.'

Holt did not wish to turn around, so he met the check head-on and stood his ground.

Then a question was asked of him.

'Are you prepared for what lies ahead?'

Holt found himself less sure. He did not know what lay ahead of him, nor whether he would ever be ready for the worst. Heading into a scourge tunnel alone was madness, but it was what he had to do. He could leave, of course, but no, he'd promised.

The mental pressure increased. Holt winced and turned away from Rake.

"How do you feel?" Rake asked.

Holt shivered, though he told himself that was the rain. "I feel a lot less enthused about this mission now. Thanks."

"Well, that just means you're sane."

"Do riders use spirit in battle?"

"For the most part, they use it as a check of willpower or morale, similar to what I just did on you. A spiritual attack won't harm you physically, but if it succeeds, your morale will weaken, you'll be on the back foot, and your opponent will feel emboldened. And isn't that true enough? If you're not fighting with your whole self and full belief, you'll likely lose to those who are. I know this will seem vague and overwhelming now," he added, "but don't let it distract you. Right now, your chief aim in growing your spirit is to support your growing bond."

Holt ran a hand distractedly through his wet hair and reached out to Ash over their bond. *"Always seems like there's more ahead than behind, no matter how far we come."*

"I like long flights better than short ones," Ash said brightly.

Holt laughed, then returned to consider the runic seal. With some trepidation, he asked, "If it was made by a High Lord, can you open it?"

"Eventually," Rake grunted. "I hope," he added gravely. Holt appreciated his honesty. Rake sighed and traced the rune softly with the tip of his nail. He drew a sharp breath, held it, then released it in a hard huff. "Bear with me. This may take a while."

Holt and Ash found shelter and decided to bear the cold rather than use their precious dry wood, which might be needed in the depths.

When a full day had passed and night gathered again, Holt feared they would be forced to retreat and seek the assistance of the West Warden to open the tunnel. His presence would almost certainly alert Drakburg to their whereabouts, and every hour they spent here increased that risk already.

Thus, come morning, rather than complete his drills and exercises, Holt approached the lavender seal again and pressed his hand against the rock. Ignoring Rake's sideways glance, he tried to summon his burgeoning spirit to answer the seal's check of will but soon found himself backing away to Ash without conscious thought.

"Nice try," Rake said, breathing heavily. He spat on the earth, then heaved and pulled back from the rock, his eyes screwed shut as though Holt had unleashed a Flare. When Rake recovered, his eyes were watery, but he grinned through the pain. "Don't worry. I'm getting close."

"It's okay if you can't," Holt said. "We're risking a lot by being here. Talia knew that. She can find some other way to help the Elder."

"That's a change of tune," Rake said. "You'd be fine with it if we just walked away from helping her?"

Holt pressed his lips together, then met Rake's eye and nodded solemnly. "That's over now, Rake. I'm done with it. I'm not a child anymore."

"Bold words, but if your soul expanded because of it, then it must be true."

Holt grunted. "Seems an odd thing to be a deep truth. Wouldn't every rider go through something like that?"

"Everyone is unique." Rake wrung his hands, then rubbed them together, clearly suppressing something. "What truths define you today may not be the same tomorrow," he continued stiffly. "Riders live a long time. Fifty years from now, who knows what will underpin you. It requires constant self-reflection and realignment."

"Does that mean riders can go backward?" Holt said. "I mean, backward in their advancement? If they don't succeed in realigning themselves."

"Not exactly, but also, yes. Remember, the dragon bond, your dragon's core, and your own spiritual power are distinct. A full regression of a dragon bond is almost unheard of, but a powerful Exalted Lord, tipped to become the next Paragon, may lose their spiritual strength if things go wrong. They could be reduced to the power of a Low Lord if things got severe, but their bond would remain at Lord, and their dragon's core would be unaffected, although any rot in the rider is bound to negatively affect their dragon in some way."

Holt could not decide whether this was reassuring or not. On the one hand, it meant no one had the luxury of resting on their laurels, and even the strongest riders could take nothing for granted. On the other hand, it meant he too would need to stay vigilant his whole life. Everything he and Ash had gained felt hard-won. To undo it through his own lack of self-awareness in the future would be tragic.

"Are you always realigning yourself?"

Bent over double, Rake steadied his breathing. Drool fell from his mouth like an animal, and he wiped it away with the sleeve of his cloak. "My troubles are distinct and mine alone," he managed to say.

"But it couldn't hurt, could it? I know you had difficulties drawing on your spirit in this form, but—"

"Do you not think I've tried everything I can already?" Rake asked, a little curtly. "Do you think I like being like this?"

"Seeing as something went wrong, I only thought it worth considering. You said yourself you can't hear Elya ever since Windshear."

"Precisely," Rake said, angry now. "Since Windshear. Since Thrall invaded my mind over and over and over, day after day after day. I think that would cause anyone issues." Rake twisted his head suddenly skyward and snarled. With Champion reflexes, Holt drew his sword, turned, and began cycling magic.

Ash lifted his head and ears. *"Two dragons."*

"Riders?" Holt asked.

"Yes," Rake growled painfully. Snorting like a bull, he rose to his full height, spat at the gully floor, and lunged again for the seal on the rock.

Holt steadied his breathing, then sensed the approaching riders himself. One Low Champion and, terrifyingly, one Lord.

Miraculously, the rock wall of the gully started to groan. Rake staggered to his knees while the mystic rune melted away and, with it, the stone, revealing a tunnel of deepest darkness.

Shuddering, Rake said, "Amazing what necessity facilitates." He rose to one knee, then collapsed again.

With a Lord descending on them and Rake so weak, Holt only saw one viable option. Wordless, he shared his thoughts with Ash, and Ash agreed.

Holt sheathed his sword, pulled out a piece of Floating jerky, and chewed fast as he went to Rake. With ginger burning the back of his throat, Holt bent down, threw Rake's arm around his shoulder, and pushed him upright. Given the difference in size, Rake slumped to one side, but then Ash arrived and Rake wrapped his other arm around him.

The seal of the tunnel continued to widen, and together, Holt and Ash half carried Rake across the threshold. Once ensconced in darkness, Holt allowed himself a glimmer of hope. He swallowed the meat, washed it down with a Floating elixir in one great gulp, dropped the vial, and turned his cycling efforts to Floating. Against a Lord's magic, even his peak defense may not matter, but it would be better than no defense at all.

A crash sounded from behind, which he took to be a rider landing in the gully.

"Keep going," he said, then he ducked out from under Rake's arm and turned to face back up the tunnel.

Two dark figures appeared against the haze of sunlight, one male, one female. Judging from their radiating power, Holt realized the Lord was actually a Lady. The riders hesitated at the mouth of the tunnel, unwilling to enter, as Holt had hoped. Their dragons weren't behind them; perhaps they were too large to land in the gully.

The roving magical reach of the Lady swept over Holt's soul, inspecting his bond. Another power swiftly followed, this one carrying a heavy spiritual weight.

'Is it wise to fight?'

Right now, Holt could not honestly say that it was. Fighting a Lady on his own was most certainly unwise, and though he tried, his pitiful spiritual power utterly failed to meet the Lady's check of will. His heart sank, and it took a great effort to maintain his Floating even as he instinctively backed away.

As the Lady raised her hand, Holt braced himself, then the mouth of the tunnel began to re-seal, the stone swirling back in on itself, closing off the daylight until it slammed shut and trapped them in darkness.

17

MIRED IN THE MORASS

Scourge forces swarmed around a high, flat-topped hill rising from the endless bog. Bursts of power flashed and crashed on all sides as the New Order fought to hold the high ground.

Talia and Pyra flew at the head of the reserves along with five emeralds sent by the West Warden, Turro among them. Talia drew her sword, Pyra bellowed, and they dove hard upon the enemy flank, where the shallow, waterlogged land on the hill's west side made an ideal hunting ground.

Their bond thrummed, Pyra's fire poured into Talia, and the dragon song roared at its riotous—

Pyra spotted an abomination carrying a tree trunk like a mace. She would dust its bones, rip them with her teeth...

—Talia Lifted the fires within her to soak into her circlet, regaining her senses. As Pyra flew low, Talia leaped down, landing in a crouch and splattering mud and foul water over her brigandine. Cycling power to her sword, she took a moment to drink the battlefield in.

Icicle stakes speared ghouls; patches of the bog still burned; juggernauts were distracted and confused by mystic energy, leading them to ram into their ghoulish kindred; and flayers were crushed by emeralds' breaths, heavy as stone.

The New Order fought well, but the enemy just kept coming.

Closer by, ghouls charged at Talia in their hastened shamble.

Their jaws opened unhinged as though to swallow her, spilling black drool and revealing brown teeth in green gums.

Her sword aflame, Talia cut two of them open. With a whirling twist, she cut down three more, pivoted, turned, and faced another advancing group. Cycling magic to her legs, she pressed her foot down and her Flamewave ability rose, crested, then rushed forth to meet them. Flame met rotting flesh, then their charred husks splashed into muddy waters, and invisible spouts of marsh gas ignited with loud pops into winnowing yellow flames.

With wet whoomphs and heavy thuds, stingers fell dead, throwing up mud to fall like a brown rain. Where the bog stench began and the scourge stink ended was hard to tell. Everything was muggy, close, sticky. The Mort Morass was as oppressive as a scourge tunnel.

Through her bond, she caught a fleeting impression from Pyra: the dragon had swerved to avoid a screaming bolt of black magic, then dove after a stinger.

Talia searched for more foes, but the scourge were running back for the cover of the dense, skeletal trees.

"Do not pursue," came the high, crisp voice of Ethel's dragon, Strang. *"Dragons, close ranks around the hill. Riders, take to high ground. Champions, to the Flight Commander."*

Talia waited to make sure the Ascendants on this side made it back, thumping their backs as they passed her: Yax, Alvah, Einar. So far, they'd all made it through unscathed.

Pyra touched down, splashing more mud, and Talia went to meet her head-to-snout.

"Three stingers."

"Twelve ghouls for me."

Pyra rumbled. *"A stinger counts for more."*

"There will be more."

Pyra purred as they pressed closer into each other, and Talia patted her dragon's head. Then they parted, and Talia took to the hill.

The Novices were already on the hilltop, each looking flushed but fresh. Under normal conditions, they would not be called to fight, for they lacked the enhanced body of an Ascendant. The three of them had set out eagerly with Talia from Sidastra all the same. *Too eager*, she'd thought.

They huddled around one of their Low Ascendants, a young man called Hugon; long-limbed and long-nosed, he had a gangling nature that made him appear younger than he was. His dragon, Enhadyr, held unique mystic powers so valuable to the fledgling New Order that Ethel had taken them with the Champions in the vanguard. Enhadyr's music could raise morale, and Hugon helped to amplify and weave the power through his channels for humans to understand – they called it the Battle Chant.

The only other dragon Talia found on the hilltop was the injured Liliane, an ice dragon with teal scales and ragged rips and burnt holes in the membrane of one wing. Her rider, a Low Champion from Mithras called Galasso, caught Talia's eye and approached at a run. His olive skin was pale from blood loss and a bond hanging by a thread.

"Thank you, Red Queen," Galasso said. He wanted to bow but stopped himself. "We would not have lasted without you."

"Commander Ethel summoned all reserves from the New Order. I am but one of those reserves. I'm just glad we arrived in time."

Galasso nodded, his eyes distant and void of energy.

"And do not bow to me. I am only a Low Champion like you."

Despite this, he stood to attention, though he was looking over Talia's shoulder.

"Your arrival was timely, Champion Talia."

Talia turned to find Ethel striding toward her. Like everyone else, her brigandine was drenched in muddy water and green grime, and the braid of her golden hair was now disheveled beyond recognition.

Still, her smile was bright, and Talia had to strain to remember Ethel's actual age. She had fought with Brode during the last world-threatening incursion at Athra yet still looked no older than her own mother.

Talia stood upright, arms at her sides, and inclined her head. "Commander."

"Come, the Champions are gathering for a council," Ethel said, indicating a spot across the hilltop. Talia could make out the turned backs of the other huddled Champions, Ensel's presence among them evident due to the prominence of his spear.

Galasso moved off. Talia intended to follow, but Ethel stayed her with a light touch.

"Thank you for correcting him," she said in a hushed voice.

"Of course."

Ethel gave a curt nod, then shot off at a brisk walk, and Talia hastened to follow.

"I trust Lucia and Einar informed you of the situation?"

"They did."

Einar, their second Wind Ascendant, had met them on the borders of the Morass and led them to the fighting. The vanguard had been ambushed close to Sable Spire. Ramos and Onistrasa had been slain and Liliane badly wounded. The retreat had faltered when Liliane's injury forced her to land. Grounded on the hill, the vanguard fell in to defend her, and more and more scourge followed until it became something of a siege, which Talia and the reserves had seemed to break.

"Do we have a plan?" Talia asked.

"All will be explained. I should not show favoritism."

Embarrassed, Talia asked no more.

There was a good vantage over the Morass here, and the great dark tower of Sable Spire could be glimpsed to the north. The air was marginally fresher as well.

Aside from those patrolling their wider territory, the entire Order was present. Nineteen they were, including Talia. Six Champions. Ten Ascendants. Three Novices. Not a single Lord or Lady, and only one Exalted Champion amongst them.

Ethel gathered the Champions to her. Talia joined them, standing shoulder to shoulder with them like any other rider. The only difference was the fire burning around her head.

"The enemy will return soon," Ethel said. "With this little queen out there, and us defending this hill, I'm treating it like the defense of any city. We need to wear the assault down and goad the queen into showing herself."

Though the shortest among them, Ethel had a commanding presence Talia envied. It seemed effortless for the Exalted Champion, but then she'd been leading squadrons and fighting scourge since before Talia's father had been born.

Ethel continued. "Once she's in the open, we cut off her head and avenge Ramos and Onistrasa."

The Champions echoed the sentiment, and Talia joined them. "For Ramos and Onistrasa."

"I'll strike down that little queen myself," said Druss, their High Champion of Storms. Though from Athra, he had a husky voice possibly altered by his lightning affinity.

Ensel clenched his fist. "This queen may be small, but we cannot take it lightly." His Risalian tongue was strong. "It has enough cunning to lure us into an ambush, and I don't think it was a coincidence that our fire rider was targeted first."

"Its magical power was not that remarkable," Druss said. "We weren't expecting it, that's all. That little thing will fall fast once its minions are wiped out."

Oline, their Emerald Champion, spoke next. "Pardon, Druss, but I do not think raw power is meant to be its purpose." Hailing from Fornheim, her affinity for the earth seemed fitting, and there was something deep and assured as stone in her voice. "Even I felt its spirit, as I've never felt from the scourge before. As a High Champion, surely you did as well?"

Druss looked uneasy. "I'm not sure what I felt."

"Point being," Oline said, "that Ensel is right. We cannot underestimate it. Don't take it on alone."

"Wise words," Ethel said. "And a clear sign you ought to reflect more on your spiritual progress, Champion Druss. Time for that after we've cleansed the Morass. For now, rally your will; stand strong. Hugon's abilities should prevent the Ascendants from wavering too quickly."

Around the base of the hill, the dragons roared in unison.

Below them, the marsh trees shook, and shrill shrieks rang upon all sides.

"They are coming," Pyra told Talia a moment before Strang also sent the warning out.

Ethel drew her sword. "Oline, cover the west. Ensel, the east. I'll take the north. Talia, the south. Druss, reinforce where needed. Galasso, Liliane cannot fly but she can stand. You and the Novices will guard the hilltop in case carriers or stingers make it through."

Though he looked as ragged as his bond felt, Galasso gave a grim nod. "We'll fight on our knees if needed."

The Champions confirmed their orders, then broke apart and headed for their positions. Talia descended to the south side, where the scourge presence was thin. Pyra joined her, growling at the deployment, but they agreed to save it for the scourge. Save it for this little queen.

"Earning that kill would be a worthy honor," Pyra said.

Two of the wild emeralds came to join them, as did Alvah upon Nani.

The battle began. Powers scorched and thundered.

Talia went to work with fire, sword, and whip. She found a new use for the whip in slowing rampaging juggernauts; a lash to their heads turned them aside, breaking the momentum of their charge, though it also drew their attention onto her.

One, two, three, four waves they threw back.

Then a new cry reverberated across the swamp. It came from the north, most unlike the queen that had attacked Sidastra. The sound was lighter, crueler, filled with frustration.

"To me!" Strang called. *"To me! Fall back for the counterattack!"*

Cresting the hill again, Talia found evidence of carriers that had managed to touch down. Strewn ghouls surrounded their broken bodies, and two dragons and two Ascendants were wounded. The Novices were tending to them as best they could while the remaining riders gathered into a tight wedge and the dragons kept the skies clear. Pyra engaged what had to be the last of the stingers.

Talia joined the forming wedge, fearing for the failing bonds of her fellow Champions. They'd fought for so long, and as sparing with magic as one could be, no core was infinite and none of their bonds were yet unbreakable. Galasso's had now frayed, though he still stood in the wedge, blood running from his nose.

Out from the marsh trees stepped the new queen. It was far smaller than even the incubating one Talia had found under the Red Range, though still larger than an abomination. Hooded under a thick carapace, its head remained shrouded in an unnatural dark save for swirling red eyes. Its pincer remained overly large and man-splitting, yet the fingers on its other hand seemed more proportionate and included a thumb, and strangest of all, it strode out on two tall legs.

An invisible force began pressuring Talia. It started in her head, a heaviness as though her skull had turned to lead, then squeezed her soul. Her chest tightened; she felt an urge to gasp and give into despair.

"Hold!" Ethel called, even as the Ascendants wobbled under the attack.

The queen advanced, its long legs making easy work of the boggy ground.

Talia's soul felt restrained as though shackles had been placed on it. She focused inward; such things were a test of will.

"Hugon! Enhadyr!" Ethel cried.

A rousing music stirred Talia, unintrusive but there within her soul and bond and mind. A new confidence filled her. She was fire – the Red Queen – her people needed her – the world needed her – this tiny queen was nothing to that. Her soul shook, then swelled and burst free of its shackles.

The pressure lifted.

"Don't you kill it before I get a bite in," Pyra told her.

Hugon shook as he worked the Battle Chant. Formerly of Laone, the young man bellowed, blowing out his voice as he did so, "For Brenin!"

Perhaps it was the Battle Chant, but that felt good enough for Talia. She screamed the same, and the others did too. Ethel's voice – who had long guarded these lands – carried loudest of all.

As the New Order rushed down the hill, Oline and the wild emeralds flattened and dried the earth to ease their charge. The queen sent a volley of black bolts, but Ensel raised violet barriers, and any bolts that made it through were deflected by Ascendants with their swords. Carriers dove in suicidal drops, and Druss unleashed lightning at them. His cry of effort carried upon the strike that hit the first carrier, then jumped to a second, a third, a fourth. The fourth carrier withstood the reduced power, but Einar and Lucia harnessed the wind and blew it spinning off course. Druss gasped and stumbled, but Galasso helped him upright.

Knowing she was the freshest of the Champions, Talia cycled motes to Ground her body and pushed to the front with Ethel. Red steel blazing, Talia was the second to hit the swarm after their commander.

Driven by the Battle Chant, the New Order carved through the scourge until Ethel enjoyed the first strike on the little queen. The queen's pincers were strong enough to turn that blow, but in between keeping the rest of the bugs at bay, each Champion took their swing, drawing blood but nothing fatal.

The queen backed up to the dense marsh-forest of deadened trees, blackened as though burned in a wildfire. As their foe entered the cover of the branches, another great cry shook across the shallow waters and another force poured forth to flank the New Order.

Ethel, Ensel, and Oline were locked into fighting the queen.

Galasso and Druss were spent.

Their wedge broke.

Pyra was furious. She could not unleash her fire with impunity, not now the riders were so embroiled in the melee.

Hoping three Champions could handle the queen, Talia turned to face the new threat, rallying those Ascendants she could to her while the dragons began to land to fight on foot. Her morale took a knock. She must have left the range of Hugon's Battle Chant, wherever he was. The press was tight and the fight bloody.

She watched helplessly as a flayer ripped a Novice to red ribbons. A wild emerald fell dead with a long gash across its chest. She fought an abomination, and it took far more effort than before to hack through its leg joints.

Is it a stronger version?

A worse thought skittered through her mind.

Am I weaker?

She was a Champion now, but somehow her blows lacked a punch she'd had as an Ascendant, lacked a fury.

Out of the corner of her eye, another abomination wielding a thick, shining black sword bore down on an Ascendant. Isak. Talia twisted around to aid him, readying her whip and running to close the gap. Fire coursed down her arm, and water sloshed up and over the rim of her high boots.

For a moment, she froze—

What she had taken to be an abomination was nothing of the kind. While its limbs were in human proportion, its body was armored in a thick exoskeleton and a helmet of hard chitin from which two horns curved up like antlers. Its hideous face comprised a mouth with oversized teeth, eyes shrouded like its queen with solid red pupils. Now she looked at it more closely, its black weapon seemed more like the scythe of a flayer's arm with an added hilt, which the hybrid gripped with two fully functioning hands.

None of these features were the most alarming.

A hum of magic emanated from it with a density that could only mean one thing.

This hybrid had a core.

—the fire of battle unfroze her.

Talia released her whip, aiming for the hybrid's wrist. She struck; the fall of the whip latched and tightened, and Talia heaved. The hybrid stumbled, swiping at Isak, but it missed. Furious, it turned on her.

Talia found herself staring the hybrid down. She tried to get a read on its core strength but found it hazy and amorphous.

Her whip still gripped its forearm. She heaved again, but it resisted her, then dug in, sinking deeper into the bog. Taking hold of her whip, it yanked her. Standing only in water, Talia was pulled off her feet. She let go of the whip's handle, letting it fizzle out, and landed ungracefully in the sticky mud.

Her bond flared hot. She saw a fleeting image through Pyra's eyes, scanning the bog for the hybrid, then Talia cycled the fires to her head, enjoyed the burn of her crown, met the hybrid in a level stare, and charged.

Expecting the brute to lumber forward, it instead waited for her, holding its sword up in a distinct guard. She got within its reach, let it swing, swerved, dodged—

Something within her registered the danger before she could knowingly think.

Talia twisted back and clashed her red steel against the black blade.

The force behind the creature's attack sent her to her back. She hit soft moss, bounced, rolled, and was up again in a second, dazed, shocked but gathering fire in her hand and cycling fresh power through her channels. Only then did she realize she had never stopped Grounding her body, yet she'd been bowled over like a Novice.

The hybrid was *that* fast and *that* strong.

She hurled a Fireball at its armored head as it charged her, and though it struck, it had no effect. Talia sent a wordless plea over her bond. The connection to Pyra began to shake and grow taut; the great bonfire core was now half its size, though how much Talia had personally drawn upon in the fight she couldn't say.

Talia pulled on more magic and stamped out a Flamewave, only to see the hybrid meet it with a black-green power of its own. Magic wasn't going to win this one, she realized, so she met the creature sword to sword. Three times in the exchange her training failed her, and only natural aptitude scraped her through it.

She lost all sense of the wider battle, even Pyra. Only that black blade and the placement of those red eyes mattered.

The ground shook: water, moss, and mud erupted around her. A purple dragon unleashed a torrent of fire at the hybrid, freeing Talia enough to lash its weapon with her whip and pull it aside. Under constant assault, the hybrid's magical defense weakened, and Pyra's fire engulfed it.

Even smoldering and face down in the bog, its hands grasped around for its sword.

Talia leaped onto its back, pressed its head into the filthy water, and drove her sword through its neck. Its hands went still.

She remained on the hybrid's back for a moment, breathing hard, then, recovering, she searched for Isak and found him lying in the bog. A juggernaut's body lay over him with two feet of blue steel sticking through its head.

Her heart sank, but the air began to lighten. The scourge were either dead or running wild, and as they ran, the dragons pursued from above.

Strang announced that the queen was slain.

Pyra came to her side. *"What was that thing?"* she asked in disgust.

"I don't know. But either it was strong, or I'm... weak? Maybe I'm rusty?"

She had filled the role of Red Queen solely for many months now.

"Hmm," Pyra grunted. *"I did not feel myself either."*

There would be time enough to ponder why, just not now amid the blood and marshes.

Talia lifted Isak's body free of the monstrous beetle, then cleaned his sword on the moss and placed it in his sheathe. Vasuk, his dragon, had arrived by then and slumped over his rider, weeping silent tears. Talia left Vasuk to grieve in peace and checked on a fallen wild emerald nearby her. It wasn't Turro. A pang of relief shot through her. He had proven a staunch and capable ally over and again. Losing him would hurt more than some of the New Order.

All the survivors gathered amid the blood and mud before the hill. Bonds had been frayed and cores emptied. All in the vanguard were ragged, and having fought for so long, Talia thought it a miracle they remained upright. Even Ethel seemed on her last legs.

"Burn the dead," the Flight Commander ordered. "Ensel,

Einar, escort Alvah to find and burn Ramos and Onistrasa, then return to Sidastra."

Those remaining gathered the weapons from the fallen. When they piled the riders together, Pyra had the unenviable task of ensuring they were reduced to ash. A fallen dragon of the New Order was too large to move, so they burned the body where it lay. Ensel and Druss had to physically restrain the Ascendant from leaping into the flames to join her dragon, and her broken wails and pleas to be let go chilled the fire left in Talia's veins. Every rider feared such a loss, but hearing someone tear their throat, seeing the life leave their eyes, seeing them kick, stamp, and bite, wild as an animal; well, it turned fear into terror.

As the riders readied to leave, Talia and Pyra went with the surviving four emeralds, led by Turro, to pay respects to their fallen flight member.

Turro's dark apple scales were barely visible beneath caked mud, and he bled from a cut on his head.

"From the world song we come, and to the world we return." Turro had sounded young and wet behind the ears when they'd first met. He was anything but that now. *"May we hear your notes in the song of another one day. Be at rest."*

His fellow emeralds bent her necks in respect. While they did so, Turro spoke privately to Pyra and Talia.

"You may begin the burning."

"It is good of you to allow it," Pyra said.

The Emerald Flight liked to bury their kindred using magic, or so the West Warden had explained when his flight had removed their bodies from Sidastra. The Warden had assured them that their buried kin could not rise again, though he avoided the specifics as to how.

"We are spent and cannot move her," Turro said. *"Nor is this a place fit for burial. The land aches. If it must be fire, then flames from the Red Bane of the scourge are the worthiest there are."*

"You honor us," Pyra said. *"I promise it shall be quick."*

Pyra bathed the emerald in fire, and Talia stood sentinel.

When the emeralds grew agitated, she feared they had

changed their minds on the burning or some disastrous misunderstanding had taken place. Turro must have read this in her face, for he assured her, *"We sense tremors in the ground, coming from the north."*

Talia's first thought was of the Life Elder, then of Holt and Ash.

"Can you tell where from? How strong are they?"

"Strong," Turro said, unhelpfully. *"They roam wide and deep."* He closed his eyes and pressed his talons deeper into the earth, though here that meant sinking to his knees in water and mud. He snuffled and snarled, his head twitching as he listened to the tremors.

Talia looked north, but the only thing on the horizon was the dark shard of Sable Spire. Could it be from Risalia? Victory in the Morass and underground at once seemed too much to hope for, but short of another answer, Talia allowed herself to smile.

They'd managed the impossible twice before.

Why not a third time?

18

CREEPERS AND CRAWLERS

Being sealed inside a scourge tunnel would have panicked most people. Most riders, too. Fortunately – or perhaps unfortunately - Holt had experience in such matters, so he took some small comfort in knowing he and Ash would fare better than their would-be trappers could conceive. Memories of his time in Ahar were grim, but he clung to the euphoria he'd enjoyed upon surviving that ordeal, and they were stronger now.

Anger in the present also helped to burn away fear. Sealing them inside was a decision with clear intention. The Lady meant for them to die. Perhaps she assumed she was dealing with a tunnel breach and two dangerous rogues in a single stroke.

The first thing Holt did was to cease Floating, returning his cycling to an even flow. Next, he lowered his bandanna before joining senses with Ash. In the utter dark, he didn't strictly need to cover his eyes, but Rake would need some light to see by, and Holt preferred the option to use Flare in a fight and not blind himself.

"Everyone okay?" he asked into the darkness.

Ash let him know over their bond.

Rake groaned and said, "Could be worse." He was still supporting himself against Ash. His breathing sounded heavier than ever to Holt's enhanced ears. Each exhale seemed to rattle his ribcage, his heartbeat was erratic, and the muscles in his tail sounded stiff, like twisting leather.

"It's not as bad as you think," Rake said.

"Feels pretty bad," Holt said. "Sounds even worse."

"Let's cross our talons I don't have to break more Lord-level seals."

Holt focused his senses on where the mouth of the tunnel had been. Vibrations reverberated from the wall there; movement, raised voices, perhaps growling from the dragons outside. Given Rake's state, they couldn't have reopened the seal to leave even if they wanted to, but their enemies were making sure of it.

"Only one way to go," Ash said.

"Down," said Holt. He drew his sword and began channeling lunar motes to the blade. A small amount would do the trick in such total blackness. "Is that enough, Rake?"

"Dim it a little. No point in standing out more than we already will. Just don't go charging on ahead."

"Afraid we'll abandon you?" Holt said, keeping his tone light. "Don't worry. The head cook always has need of his kitchenhands."

Rake snorted. "I really did prefer it when you two were in awe of me."

With another grunt of pain, he pushed himself off Ash to support himself on his own two feet. He braced himself and twisted his polearm in his grip, his scales grating coarsely against the wooden shaft.

"Lead the way, Master Cook."

Down they journeyed. Down and down.

Luckily for Ash, the passage was spacious, which suggested why riders from three Order Halls had once united here in a joint operation. Holt's suspicions were confirmed when the descent leveled out and they found themselves in a massive tunnel of swarm-sized proportions. Try as he might, even with Ash's help, he couldn't hear where the tunnel ended. Every slight sound dwindled into the rocky distance.

"Quite large, this," Rake remarked.

"It's as large as the passage we found in Ahar. Maybe bigger."

"The enemy will be patrolling it."

Holt reminded Rake of the convoys of carrier bugs and ghouls that traveled around collecting dead material to take to the control orb chambers.

"You two keep your ears open," Rake said. "I'll let you know when I sense this orb."

On they went, their route running straight east under Risalia, yet the longer they went without encountering resistance, the more Holt's fears grew of finding substantial defensives around the chamber.

However, not only did they encounter no scourge, but they saw little evidence of them either. The floor of the highway lay bare, with no fallen scraps from a passing convoy and no shed carapaces from juggernauts, flayers, or carriers. The tunnel had been swept clean, but Holt wasn't naïve enough to think that meant the enemy wasn't present.

As in Ahar, time was of little consequence below ground. Now he was a Champion, Holt could go even longer without sleep, meaning he lacked even a regular pattern of rest to help keep track of the time. They stopped only once to nibble on some hard rations before moving on. Holt's biggest concern was not being able to feed Ash if they were stuck down here for long enough.

Using his best judgment, he thought they walked for a day and a half before anything of note occurred. It was a distant splat and patter that broke the silence of the tunnel, unlike any noise made by the scourge: not the dashing pace of agile flayers, nor the pounding of juggernauts, nor the lumbering scrape of a carrier's belly upon the ground. Abominations would take greater strides, and no pack of ghouls would move with such uniformity.

Something new then.

Perhaps something worse.

The creature, whatever it was, half-scuttled, half-slid down a winding passage ahead. Ash couldn't fully count its many hundreds of legs.

"No light," Ash said, and Holt cut the gentle flow of motes to his blade.

Rake moved in closer and placed a hand on Holt's shoulder.

"Would you like me to hold your hand?" Holt asked.

Rake squeezed, and it was evident his physical strength was unaffected by his spiritual pains. Holt clenched a fist to stop himself groaning.

"*Quiet,*" Ash hissed.

They fell silent, went as rigid as the rock around them.

Far ahead, the creature emerged into the highway. Luckily it turned east and moved away from them, its long body swaying grotesquely as it slithered along. More and more of the foul thing kept emerging out of the passage it had been in, making Holt's skin crawl.

"*What's out there?*" Rake asked telepathically. "*I can't hear what you two can.*"

"*I don't think you want to know,*" Ash said.

"*It sounds like…*" Holt began, searching for the right comparison. "*Like an enormous centipede.*"

Rake made no physical sound, but telepathically he made a gag of revulsion.

"*I can't shake the feeling of its legs crawling over my scales,*" Ash told them. "*I hope never to see it as you will.*"

Once the crawler had left Ash's hearing, they started moving again. Ash maintained the lead, and Holt kept his sword dark with Rake close by him.

As they approached the passage from which the crawler had emerged, a pop and sizzle like frying bacon reached Holt's ears. Alas, there was no salty, meaty, mouth-watering smell, but instead a scent akin to rotten eggs seasoned with hot vinegar, pungent and choking.

Ash slowed his pace, sniffing cautiously. He hacked and spat before taking them to the far side of the highway and as far away from the sizzling as possible.

"*That's the most revolting thing I've ever smelled,*" Ash complained. "*It's everywhere that creature moved.*"

The smell wasn't quite so bad on the far side of the tunnel, though it remained a light threat to their noses as they passed it.

Mercifully, the trail soon ran cold, and the sizzling fell silent a few hundred yards down the highway.

"It didn't leave," Ash said. *"It carried on, but it must have stopped releasing whatever caused the smell."*

"I'm not sure what's worse," Holt said. *"That the crawler thing can leave that smell or that it can do it on purpose."*

"I wonder what it's for?"

"Sounds like it's eating the rock to me," Rake said. *"Aberanth has acids strong enough to do that, so why not a big ugly scourge bug too?"*

Because that would be horrific, Holt thought.

Sometime later, though how much Holt could not say, Rake came to a halt.

"What's wrong, Master Rake?" Ash asked.

"I see a green light," he whispered.

Holt reached as far as he could with his sixth sense but found nothing. Whatever it was, it wasn't caused by magic.

"The orb we found cast a greenish light," Holt said.

"Seems high up," Rake said, "and I don't think it's coming from a single source."

Holt tightened his grip on his sword.

As they drew closer, Rake claimed that the green light focused into a pattern, and soon after that, Ash could make out an archway and a tunnel descending deeper.

Holt crested out with his magical senses and thought he at last tasted a whiff of the orb's presence. Scourge and yet not scourge, dead and yet not dead. This time, though, perhaps due to his advancement, he felt something both human and dragon within it. Thin strands of each, just as Aberanth had concluded from his examinations of the orb he'd dissected.

"You might want to see it," Rake said.

Holt lifted his bandanna.

His first thought was that the archway had been too well made, as though carved by the hands of masons from Fornheim. Above it, green resin had been arranged into patterns bearing an eerie resemblance to the runic symbols of rider seals, or of Aberanth's notes. As they were still sense-sharing, Ash was able to view the resin through Holt's eyes.

"*They aren't right,*" Ash said.

"What do you mean?" Holt asked.

"They don't make any sense," Rake said. "The symbols Aberanth uses aren't always easy for me to interpret at the best of times. They're ways to convey feelings, sounds, and images, and only dragons truly understand them, but these... They look draconic in origin, but it's like someone wrote a sentence mixing three languages together, then threw in a few letters of their own invention."

Rake stepped forward, his cloak rustling against the tunnel floor. "I can almost understand pieces of it. It's like hearing a word you know amid the babble of a foreign tongue."

Holt blew out his breath. He wanted nothing more right now than to sever this orb and find a way out. He lowered his bandanna again.

Together, they passed through the archway and followed the tunnel's descent. Here, the sickly sweet smell of the scourge became plain, and at last they heard the enemy. Bodies moving, mandibles clacking, and heavy feet shifting. No breathing, though, for the dead had no need for air.

Holt extinguished the dull light on his sword, then listened carefully with Ash to assess the defenses. Once their count of abominations ran over ten, Holt's nerves began to strain.

The chamber was larger than the one they'd found under Ahar, providing enough space for a small army to squeeze inside. Besides the abominations, they counted eight juggernauts, nine flayers, six stingers clinging to the ceiling, and ghouls packed tight between them all: a force they'd never faced alone, never mind in cramped conditions. Lunar magic would only take them so far.

Yet here they were – and going back wasn't an option.

Two things gave Holt comfort. The first was that the scourge were plainly at rest, almost in a state of sleep, given their lack of activity. In attacking, the trio would have the element of surprise. The second was that the giant crawler wasn't here.

The chamber had three other passages leading off from it. Assuming they were approaching from the chamber's western side, then the three others bore north, east, and south, each as large as the highway they were in right now.

Their target, the orb, hung from stiff tendrils of muscle and tendon high above the ground in the center of the chamber.

Quiet as they could, they crept down until the hazy aura of the orb granted enough light for Rake to see into the chamber. Holt was alerted to it by the sudden hammering of Rake's heart, which he found bizarrely comforting. Rake could be afraid just like anyone. Perhaps Windshear had affected him in more ways than one.

Assuming Rake would be listening for telepathy, Holt said, *"We need to take out the orb as a priority. If Talia is right, that should sever the connection to this Hive Mind and to Thrall."*

"Then we just have to deal with a chamber filled with rabid, wild scourge," Rake said.

"Thanks for pointing that out."

"You're most welcome."

Holt inwardly sighed. *"Last time, I used Flares to throw them into chaos. I'd say that's our best bet to stop them swarming us. Think you can shield your eyes in time?"*

"Holt, I'm not in my prime, but I'm not infirm. I'll go for the orb. I'm the most mobile of us. You two keep them busy."

They formed a plan, such as it was. Shock and awe, quick and decisive.

"Exciting," Rake said sardonically.

Holt handed Rake a Grounding elixir to push his physicality. He prepared himself by eating a piece of Sinking jerky and washed it down with another Grounding elixir.

Vinegar stung the back of his throat as he started cycling, and the energy flow around his soul intensified. Magic would flow easier and quicker over the bond, allowing him to form Flares faster.

"On the count of three, then," Rake said. He raised three fingers. *"One... two..."*

He skipped three and hurtled down the tunnel.

Caught off-guard, Holt scrambled after him, Ash pounding down behind.

"Not funny!" Holt yelled in his head, hoping Rake was still paying attention.

Rake laughed as he swiped his polearm in a wide arc and pushed out a Soul Blade. Ghouls fell in silence and without reaction, but the moment the first corpse hit the floor, the chamber roared into life. Every head of every bug snapped around to face them. The screeching hit Holt like a tidal wave, so suddenly and so strong that he almost dropped his sense-sharing.

Ash let loose, and his moonbeams carved through the scourge. Holt leaped and landed in front of Rake, pushing an inordinate amount of magic through his legs into the ground. A Consecration spread beneath him, searing the scourge standing upon it.

Still Sinking his mote channels, Holt drew a lot of power over the bond. A thin shadow crept over the moon of the core, and as their bond blazed furiously, Holt sent a warning to Rake, then released his Flare.

Dazed, blinded, and standing on burning ground, the closest scourge crumpled or scattered. Others further back howled, then ran into each other; flayers sliced ghouls apart as they flailed around, while an abomination fell right into the path of a charging juggernaut.

Ash maintained a solid moonbeam on their right flank, visibly draining his core with each passing moment, but ghouls foolish enough to run into it were cut in half.

Rake turned so his back was to the orb and used Kickback.

As Rake flipped up high, Holt met a juggernaut muscling its way through the carnage with his new sword. Lunar-infused dragon steel cut through its armored chitin like paper.

Meanwhile, overhead, Rake twisted in mid-air, faced the orb, and Blinked. Two stingers collided in mid-air where Rake had been, then he reappeared before the hanging orb and cut the bloody tendons holding it in place.

The chamber went still.

The shrieking ceased.

Only the stingers' buzzing wings made any sound at all.

Then the weighty orb hit the ground, and a crack of stone

rent the air.

Rake landed a moment later, one knee bent.

It seemed they had succeeded.

Yet if that were true, the scourge would be going wild. Frozen in place as they were, that meant they were still under some form of control.

"Rake!" Holt called. "Destroy it!"

Rake stood to his full height, raised his polearm—

A scream filled his mind, and Holt staggered and clutched his head. He cried out, but he couldn't hear himself.

In the chamber under Ahar, he'd heard a shriek as he tried to take the orb, shocked, frightened. This was one of loathing, of a hungering desire to consume. So many layers to the voice. Endless. Half a world was screaming at him, and he knew his ears would burst.

Then the screeching stopped.

Holt went deaf.

Something hot ran from his ears and nose. Wiping his face with the back of his hand, he could smell the blood. He felt the leather on the grip of his sword, the clothes against his skin, the slipperiness underfoot, but with the loss of his ears and his eyes still covered, Holt found himself truly blind. Only his bond granted him a sense of where Ash was. The dragon had his neck pressed flat to the floor, his snout twitching.

Then Holt's hearing began to return. Muffled sounds reached him as if through water, and he began to rebuild a mental picture of the chamber.

Scourge were all around like a foul, unmoving fog. He could feel the stare of every ghoul, the leer of juggernaut and flayer, every one of the stingers' compound eyes, and the empty sockets of the abominations.

In his mind, he heard a new voice. A terrifying voice. A thousand voices layered into one.

"We hoped thou wouldst be sent."

He knew it to be the Hive Mind, but no warning could have prepared him for such a voice. It made every inch of his skin itch to be ripped off – to get as far from the voice as possible.

"I know what you are," Holt said, fighting to maintain the strength of his own mental voice. *"Talia said you wanted these orbs destroyed."*

"We thank thee for thy work here. The dragon's reach withers."

"Let us go, and we'll destroy more."

"We think not."

The floor shook. A stalactite fell halfway across the chamber, skewering a stinger on its way down before it smashed apart on the floor, but the creature's words still rang loudly between Holt's ears.

"You wanted this," he said.

"Thou speakest true, but others can continue thy work."

The floor's shaking became worse. Holt's Champion reflexes helped him regain balance without conscious effort, but across the chamber, a piece of the gut-like structure that had held the orb collapsed, wet and heavy.

"Thou art too much of a threat. Thou shalt not leave."

The Hive Mind's presence left him.

The scourge shrieked again, this time manic and wild. There were more heavy crashes as debris fell in earnest, and the whole chamber shuddered.

Holt shared his intent with Ash, who agreed at once. A sense of the southern tunnel was firm in their minds.

Holt fell in behind Ash, who used his greater bulk to bowl ghouls and thin-framed flayers aside. Another stalactite fell, its sharp tip hurtling down toward Ash's back. Instinct brought Holt's hands together for a dual Lunar Shock, and he rushed power to his hands before recalling he held his new sword. Lunar magic filled the sword to its tip, then burst out in an empowered Shock. The ability caused a blowback, staggering him and punching the wind from his chest, but it struck the stalactite and blew it apart. Ash roared and pushed on.

Scourge were already running into the southern passage. Ash rammed his way into the mouth of the tunnel and under the archway, lashing with his talons to clear the way. Before joining, Holt turned back for Rake.

He opened his mouth only to inhale dust and debris, and he

coughed violently. Were he using his eyes, it might have been impossible to pick Rake out, but even through the din, he heard Rake growl and his polearm cut the air.

Rake burst upward, having used a Kickback, but an abomination reached a long, skeletal hand up, caught Rake's cloak, and dragged him down. More rocks and guts crashed down. Rake wasn't far away, but he was bogged down amid the scourge and blocked by a mound of rubble.

Rake's voice entered Holt's mind, loud and insistent.

"Go!"

A pang of need surged from Ash. At once, Holt wheeled around, entered the southern tunnel, and cut down several ghouls clawing at Ash's side. There came a crash and thunderous shake as though the world were falling apart, then, after killing the last ghoul, Holt turned back for Rake.

The archway had collapsed. Now blocked, he couldn't hear or smell anything inside the chamber.

"Rake?" he yelled, then he fell quiet, expecting to hear Rake's voice in his head any moment to let him know he was fine.

Nothing came.

It's just the rocks, Holt told himself. It was just the rocks blocking Rake's telepathy.

Rake couldn't be dead. Not like this.

"Ash," Holt said, his voice cracking. "Tell me you hear him?"

"I can't hear anything."

"No," Holt said loudly, uselessly. "No!"

The floor of the tunnel still shuddered as he half-stumbled in dismay to the debris. He dropped his sword and pressed on the stones as though they might crumble at his touch to reveal a grinning Rake on the other side.

"No, no, no…"

Holt's cries descended into incoherence. He scrambled at the rocks, clawed at them, trying to find purchase. He managed to heave out a few small pieces, but they were mere pebbles in the larger problem.

The chamber had completely caved in. Anything inside it would have been crushed.

"Rake!" Holt called, banging his fists against the rocks. He called over and over until he'd emptied his lungs and even his Champion's throat had grown sore.

Taking rasping breaths, he slid slowly to his knees, hands dragging down the rock. Dirt and dust coated the back of his mouth. He hawked and spat, hesitated, then he doubled over, clutched his stomach, and retched violently.

Rake was dead.

He retched again. And again. His guts turned rigid, yet still he dry heaved. Blood rushed to his head. A pressure formed behind his eyes, threatening to burst them from his skull.

The cloth of his bandanna was damp now. Hot tears flowed so thick that the water slipped out from under the material to stream down his cheeks and salt his lips. He gasped for air all the while, one arm clutching his chest and another his belly.

Holt didn't hear Ash backing down the tunnel toward him. He only felt some of his grief drawn from him like poison from a wound, out of his soul and over the bond. Then he felt a dry snout nuzzle him softly, softer than anything its size should be capable of.

Holt uttered a low wail and pushed himself onto Ash, wrapping his arms around his dragon's snout. Ash didn't say a word. He didn't have to. More of the venomous anguish was drawn out of Holt, enough that he found strength in his body again and allowed himself to be slowly lifted to his feet.

"Master Rake will have f-found a way," Ash said, his voice straining not to crack. *"I can't believe he's... gone. I w-won't believe it."*

Holt gasped again and, at last, managed to refill his aching lungs. Standing, though still half-cradled by Ash, he wheezed.

"Come on, boy. Rake would tell you to straighten out. Right now." His tone was not unkind, just firm, because Holt needed him to be. *"We've got to get out of here."*

Holt wiped his nose with his sleeve, which only served to rub more grime onto his face. Slowly, he stood on his own two feet. With everything he had left, he steadied himself.

Because Ash needed him too.

"Okay," Holt croaked. "Okay."

"Good, just give me a moment."

Then Ash sagged and dropped to his knees.

Holt checked him for wounds. Ash had a gash on his side; the stabbing pain of it crossed their bond. A deep ache throbbed from Ash's back as well. Holt climbed up to feel the damage. He had blasted apart one stalactite, but clearly others had hit Ash with blunt force.

Under the scales, he could hear and feel the heat of pooling blood. Ash's spine was inflamed in places but thankfully not severely damaged. The dragon had suffered many other small cuts, scrapes, and bites besides, but whether through luck or lunar magic, none had the blight in them.

Holt slid back to the tunnel floor. The back of his own left shoulder flared with sharp pain, though he couldn't recall taking a hit. His head rang, and he felt small cuts all over himself, including on his hands, where he'd probably cut himself hammering on the rocks. The damage to his supplies totaled nine elixirs lost or smashed and three pouches of jerky ripped in the chaos.

All things considered, they weren't in as bad a shape as they might be.

Tremors still ran throughout the passage. Whatever the Hive had done must have affected more than just the chamber.

"We should get up into the highway," Ash said, stretching his neck up the ascending passage. With a groan, he got back to his feet. *"Some enemies fled up this way."*

As though he'd been temporarily deaf to them, the gargling, skittering, clanking, shrill cries of the scourge finally reached Holt. He picked up his sword, his fingers feeling numb around the grip. When he tightened them, sticky blood oozed from the wounds on his hands. But the thought of more scourge helped to push the pain away. In fact, it pleased him. He needed the distraction.

Seething, he said, "What are we waiting for?"

Sword held forth, he broke into a run.

19

EVEN UNTO DEATH

For weeks, the Life Elder had tried to rest. He needed to rest to heal, to recover his strength, yet there was no true rest anymore. Where his conscious mind helped to shut out the sickening moans of the world, in sleep he heard it all – every last gasp for breath, every last weak thump of a heart, a constant dirge that made his every effort seem futile.

Death was certain. The scourge were certain.

It could not be fought. It could not be undone.

Whispers reached him. He could not understand their words, but he could understand their tone. They sneered and hissed, relishing his failures, though in the rare moments of his success, they would fall quiet for a time.

Of late, they had grown louder. They tittered and mocked him, growing bolder, more confident. Now they were jubilant. Victorious. Euphoric to the point of incoherence until, with no warning, with no slow decline, the whispers ceased. A tense sputter of garbled words, then a shrill scream. Millions of voices rolled into one, ringing into a shuddering echo, not of pain but of fury.

The Life Elder awoke.

Within the northern grove, all was well, yet the ringing continued from deep beneath the earth. From the south and west it came, as a tremor running through the earth. Something had drawn the dark presence of the deep and caused it to surge with hateful power.

The Elder listened closely but couldn't hear the whispers anymore. Had the great beast withered? Retreated? Whatever had happened, the world's suffering had lessened for the first time in years.

His first thought was of Paragon Kalanta. She must have delved deep and struck this blow, though the location of the surge placed it closer to Feorlen. Could Talia, Pyra, and his West Warden have worked with her? Whether Paragon or otherwise, the children were once again proving themselves more tenacious than the Elders.

The Life Elder got to his feet. As he stirred, his emeralds roused with him. They sniffed the air, pressed their talons into the earth, and must have felt, as he had, the relief radiating out from the world's soul. He rumbled with delight, and as hope bloomed within him, so did a field of flowers at his feet.

He closed his eyes. Extended his great wings. Swayed with the soft mountain breeze.

The Life Elder allowed himself this moment, which heralded the beginning of the end. He knew what the consequence could be, but, for just this moment, he kept that fear at bay. When it passed, he began to prepare.

First, and most importantly, he drew on his spirit, his will, his core, and sent word to his sister in the far north. A conversation was impossible at this distance, but there was no time now to fly to the borders of the tundra. Only something short had a hope of crossing the distance.

'It is time,' he willed her to hear.

Such was the uproar and quickening of his blood, the Elder did not immediately notice the cold wind that rippled through the glade in response.

'Ice is on its way,' it assured him.

He spent three days gathering his flight from all over the Spine to the Northern Grove, intending to strike the moment his sister arrived. Before she could join him, though, his North

Warden, scouting from afar, announced from as far away as his telepathy would allow, *"The controller has come forth."*

So, Sovereign, you offer battle freely?

A desperate move. A fatal move. The Life Elder did not hesitate to respond, roaring for battle. The emeralds in the grove with him gnashed tooth and talon, beat wings, and growled in anticipation.

He would have preferred to wait for his sister, but with Sovereign on the move, he did not have the luxury of waiting. If he trapped Sovereign in battle, she would be able to sweep in and finish him off.

The Life Elder launched himself high and climbed above the peaks, above the clouds. Every emerald fit to fight rose to join him and they soared onward, guided by the North Warden's instruction.

By the time the Life Elder sensed the enemy, they were deep into lands he and his flight had purified over months of toil. How fitting that it would be these valleys in which Sovereign would fall.

The Elder's only fear now was for the other members of his flight, though each, he knew, would rather rot than be left behind. Two of his Wardens flew with him, the stewards of the North and East, who had fought the longest and hardest. The North Warden's scales were a dark mix of browns and greens, as if mosses grew upon him. The East Warden was a lithe male, his scales hard and shiny as the very emeralds from which their flight took its name. There were scores of veteran dragons as well, gathered from every grove, brimming with youthful wroth of their own.

Into the great valley they descended, and soon the battle roars reverberated between the peaks. The two flights approached each other. On the one side, Sovereign and his treacherous brood; on the other, the Elder and his emeralds.

Sovereign's flight – a mix of fire, storm, mystic, and even rogue emeralds – seemed a new type, a chromatic one, bound together in treachery, in hate, in lies. Sorrow gripped the Elder's heart as he wondered how many flying against him were doing so of their own accord. He found it hard to believe, especially of his own kind, that so many could be swayed to such a bloody, apocalyptic cause. At least the enemy counted no ice dragons amongst their number. That gave the Elder some small comfort.

While the chromatic flight could not match the emeralds, Sovereign bulked up his forces with scourge-risen dragons, whose scales were so warped from the sickness it was impossible to tell what they had been in life. Some even had exposed bones yet still flew. There were so many scourge dragons that Sovereign's forces outnumbered the Elder's own.

Sovereign's power was second only to the Life Elder's own. When the Elder sent a spiritual check against the enemy flight, he found his authority buffeted by a strong will buttressed with raw, coarse power. It should not have been possible, but of all the remarkable discoveries of late, this was the least of them. And while mighty, Sovereign's power felt unnatural and ill-gained. A core too big for his spirit to truly lift. An aura of endless resentment with equal amounts of hunger, the same ravenous force the Elder had felt from the deep places.

Were it not for his power, Sovereign might have been mistaken for an old fire dragon. His dark, black-blood scales held no luster, his bone ridges were a tarnished ivory, and his wings were crumpled and leathery. The coward also flew behind his minions, whereas the Life Elder spearheaded his attack.

It began with a barrage of breaths from each side. Above the pine trees and teal mountain rivers, jets of core-forged magic collided. Green and brown hues exploded as they met fire, storm, arcane, and dark scourge powers. The Elder channeled the might of summer to his snout and reinforced it with his spirit. Great leaves of verdant light spun outward before him, taking the brunt of the attacks and shielding the center of his formation.

When the two flights met, the enemy parted to avoid the shield, diving down or climbing up, yet they reconverged on him the moment they could. It became apparent he was their ultimate target. Kill the Elder, and the flight would fall.

Under immense assault, the Elder drew upon the power of

the earth to toughen his scales, but his wings, like those of all dragons, remained a weak spot, and that was where the enemy struck. Clawing attacks tore small rips at the outer edges of his membrane, forcing him to draw his wings in close and limit his range of movement. The enemy swarmed around him like so many stingers, and he lost sight of Sovereign as his emeralds hurtled into the mid-air melee.

Up close, it became a fight of tooth and claw, and in such a crush, the emeralds held an advantage, with many able to reinforce their scales like their Elder could. Blood fell as red rain.

Then a new pressure exerted itself on the Elder's mind. Sovereign was testing his defenses, but while the Elder was cycling his immense power around his mind, only his mystic sister could have broken through. He cast out his spirit and will to shield his dragons, but Sovereign redoubled his mental assault and probed for weak points.

When an emerald battling close to his back foot turned and clamped its jaws into him, the Elder roared and shook the dominated drake free. He pushed more spiritual power into his shield, but others soon followed, their minds taken by Sovereign.

It was then that the Elder understood his folly. Sovereign's powers did not depend upon spirit. His technique was as basic as a young dragon might adopt, yet it was fueled by a magical strength such as only an Elder could wield.

Four emeralds turned on their own before he could recalibrate his defenses, and blood splattered him from all sides. A flash of lightning heralded a bolt he could not avoid. It struck his back even as he blasted one of his own enslaved dragons from the skies.

Enemy storm dragons began to work the air to their advantage, channeling wind to throw emeralds off course and speed the momentum of their allies.

The Elder called for a descent. He poured a torrent of green flames to clear a path, and the emeralds dove for the safety of land. On the ground, on earth and rock, they would hold the advantage.

Touching down, the Elder could focus his defenses overhead.

His Wardens added their power to his own, creating a dome of light, woven like a nettled thorn bush, which the breath of their enemy could not penetrate.

Aid would come. Ice would come. The Elder only had to hold.

Scourge dragons landed and charged in on foot.

No technique was spared, nor magic conserved.

The ground awoke to clamp enemies in place. Trees walked upon their roots and pounded foes with their branches and trunks. Yet what the scourge dragons lacked in magic, they made up for with a lack of fear and feeling. On broken limbs they continued crawling forth, spewing vile breaths and biting at anything in reach.

Assaults were made. Assaults were repelled.

Above, storm dragons worked together, summoning a black cloud that blotted the sky. Their bolts were beyond the sum of the emeralds' individual powers, and the strikes began to shake the integrity of the Elder's shielding dome.

His core began to wane. Inch by inch, the dome shrank, and the enemy grew bolder. Sovereign's dominating techniques slipped through cracks and claimed more noble emeralds.

One by one, the bodies piled higher. Blood soaked the soil. Darkness swallowed the sky whole until the only sources of light were the flashes of lightning and magic and the burning trees of the valley.

Besieged on all sides, the emeralds held throughout the night.

And then, a Warden fell.

The guardian of the north, beleaguered after a long campaign, exhausted his core. He collapsed, too weak to resist Sovereign's mental assault. When he stirred again, he was not himself. His spent core did not make him a real threat, but the blow to morale caused by slaying such a mighty emerald came as the worst wound to the flight.

Rage overpowered any grief. In that moment, the Life Elder matched the fury of his fiery brother. Roaring mournfully, he redoubled his efforts, pouring forth more of his reserves to maintain the shield even as Sovereign renewed his assault.

The distant dawn beyond the rim of black clouds brought little relief. And when he was forced to put down another of his kin, something in the Elder gave out.

Enough slaughter. Enough of having others fight his battles. These evils in the world could be traced back to him.

"Let us settle this between us," he demanded of Sovereign. He offered an oath, sworn on his soul and thus binding. Their forces would leave. No more bloodshed, save for their own. It took Sovereign a long time to respond, but he agreed to the terms.

A charge of spirit entwined them, creating unbreakable terms.

The assault on the dome lifted, and Sovereign's forces – all of them, even the scourge dragons – flew away.

"Go," the Life Elder ordered of his kin.

His surviving Warden, the East Warden, stood firm. *"Elder, I won't leave you alone."* Despite being wounded and worn, the serenity of his voice remained.

"Do as I say. Protect your grove. We will fly together again."

The East Warden hesitated, clawed up earth in fear and anger, but ultimately relented and followed his orders. When the last emerald passed beyond the reach of his senses and was safe, the Life Elder felt reassured he'd done the right thing.

Smoke curled up from the valley. The corpses lay in mounds upon the battlefield, a tragic loss such as no flight had endured since the primal times.

Amid the smoke and cold morning light, Sovereign touched down half a mile from the Elder. He snarled, and it was plain the battle had taken its toll on him as well. Such a pointless, needless struggle. So much death, and for what?

"Why do this?" the Life Elder asked. *"With control of the scourge, you could have ended it."*

"Once the humans are gone, I will," Sovereign said. *"I do not understand why you fight me. Isn't this what the Elders wanted?"*

His last question was the angriest of all, asked in a tone of utter dismay.

Because there was a terrible truth in it. He, the Elder of Life, had once desired it. He feared some of his siblings still desired it, and so they did nothing but retreat and tend to their own.

But not him. Not anymore.

In the primal days, when he'd first awoken and found himself strong, he'd assumed stewardship of all life in the world. Humans were as much a part of it as any other creature. Their own changes to the land and beasts were no worse than what dragons had wrought – the only difference was that dragons had forgotten. The kar, the ancient white-haired creature, had opened his eyes to a darker past beyond the ability of even an Elder to recall. Dragons had done great harm in those forgotten days and had inflicted worse since.

"It is not too late," Sovereign said, his voice almost charming. *"End this bloodshed, Honored Elder. Join us."*

The Elder drew up his courage, his magic, his spirit, and his will. When next he spoke, it was with the full capacity of his authority, with an unwavering certainty that Sovereign could not hope to assuage.

"We were wrong," the Life Elder declared. *"These sins I cannot make amends for in full, but I shall fight until the bitter end to try. Even unto death, if that would undo it."*

Sovereign roared. His power swelled.

Even as they readied for the last fight, an icy breeze brushed against the Elder's flank. Triumphant, he bared his teeth.

Sovereign was finished. Ice was on her way.

Out of the north, a cold presence raced closer, greater than any he had felt in centuries.

He only hoped the world could forgive him.

And with the icy wind at his back, the Life Elder loosened his jaw, unleashed the last dregs of his power, and lunged at his foe.

20

DARK TUNNELS, DARKER TIDINGS

Holt and Ash chased the scourge down the highway, and it helped a great deal that the scourge seemed uninterested in them. Ghoul and bug alike ran wild, likely due to the loss of their regional control orb, and the majority seemed happiest to run away.

Ash's core shrunk to a crescent moon, and their bond became dangerously taut. It had been a long time since Holt had to be wary of Fraying his bond, but he was still only a Champion, and drawing on more than three-quarters of the core in too short a time would overburden their connection.

At length, Holt's bloodthirst began to ebb. Carving through scourge was satisfying, but it could not alleviate the grief in his heart. They were tired, worn, and they slowed. Once their blood cooled, their wounds returned with a stinging vengeance. Holt used his nose to locate Aberanth's healing balm amongst their gear. The pungent, bitter herbs of the paste smelled like flowers compared to the scourge's stench. Holt rubbed a generous amount onto the gash in Ash's side, which bubbled and hissed, then gently applied some over his hands and experienced the cool tingly sensation of the paste as it worked. Just under half of the tub remained when Holt wrapped it up again and packed it away.

Feeling a little better, they got moving again, and Ash took the lead.

At one point, they hung back to allow a column of ghouls to exit a winding pathway ahead. Ash reckoned the smaller tunnel had been blocked off, hence why they were moving up to the highway. They came across several sudden changes in the network, including one small fissure directly overhead opening to the surface. Birdsong flitted down to the depths to cheer them, and sweet fresh air momentarily relieved their noses.

If the Hive Mind's cave-in had rippled throughout the regional network, there was a chance of other openings. Holt clung to this thought like a lifeline on stormy waters.

Holt sustained himself on rations and his remaining jerky, but Ash had long since run out of meaningful food. His stomach was a hollow ache, but he did not complain. All they could do was march on.

Eventually, their route led them to a narrow tunnel leading off the highway. Ash spent a good while sniffing and whacking his tail to help determine its shape.

"It opens to the surface," he concluded. *"Scourge have been running up it."*

They discussed their options. The ceiling was low, and it might become hard to move once inside, but their other choice – to keep marching on in the hope of finding another exit – hardly seemed like an option.

Holt unstrapped some equipment from Ash's back and shouldered the burden himself. His pots and pans and sleeping kit were thankfully not heavy, just cumbersome in a fight. He couldn't easily sheath his sword with it all on his back, but he figured he'd be better off keeping it drawn.

Mustering his courage, Ash growled, then crouched and crawled into the tight tunnel. Progress was slow, and Holt took up the rear, fending off ghouls and the occasional flayer that followed them in.

At an especially narrow point, Ash became stuck and let out a pitiful sound, reminding Holt of the mewling he'd made as a tiny hatchling. The mere thought of Ash being trapped in this place, unable to move, to breathe, to be left to starve or gnawed away by scourge without hope of defense – it made Holt's heart seize. He wanted to retch again. Somehow, he swallowed the impulse back down. The worst thing he could do now was to fall to pieces.

"We'll get through this."

Ash slumped and lay still. *"I don't know if I can."* He said it so meekly that Holt struggled to retain his optimistic façade.

"Come on," Holt urged in a strained and rising voice. "There's got to be a way. There's always a way. Right? That's what Rake told us."

Ash struggled. *"It's my back. A ridge is caught."*

Holt spared a thought for the darkness behind them. He heard nothing coming, smelled nothing other than the lingering rot. Deciding he had time, Holt set his packs down and sheathed his sword. Less encumbered, he climbed up onto Ash's back, lying flat under the low roof of the passage.

Ending his sense-sharing, he raised his blindfold and cast a wisp of white light from his palm. The sudden light made his eyes sting, but he blinked through it and saw where Ash's bone ridge and the tunnel scraped together.

A grim certainty fell over Holt, weighing him down like a rain-soaked cloak, but there was only one way to deal with an unpleasant task: get it done and don't dwell on it.

"You trust me, right?"

"You know I do."

Holt shimmied until he could tease his sword out, then, still on his stomach, he wriggled into position. He gulped.

"Never had to do something like this." He breathed hard. "Hold still."

He cut. Though his motion was stunted, the dragon steel did its work and sliced through Ash's bone ridge. Ash groaned, then squirmed and mercifully passed under the rock without another of his bones catching.

They were able to move on, but the ordeal was far from over.

Due to the confines and the effort, Ash's heart began to race.

Claustrophobic and with no hope of going back the way they'd come, their only hope lay ahead.

"My legs don't want to move anymore," Ash said as he crawled on, inch by inch. Holt attempted to draw as much of the discomfort across the bond as he could, just as Ash had drawn out his grief for Rake. In dragging Ash's pain into himself, Holt's joints felt crushed and constrained. A heavy boot seemed to press on the back of his neck, his breaths became shallow, and every movement took intense effort.

He swallowed a salty Grounding elixir, chewed a piece of dust-covered jerky of the same type, and Grounded his body. With new strength, he took on more of Ash's pain and only stopped because he needed to remain able to fight the scourge that still crept up behind them.

"I won't use any magic," Holt said. "Use whatever you have left for yourself. We'll get through this."

Ash had been Grounding his mote channels too, but though cycling was an efficient use of magic, it was nothing on infusing muscle and bone with raw power. Ash didn't need telling twice. Pumping magic into his body greased their way for what felt like hours, but with the crescent moon ever shrinking, Holt worried even this would not be enough.

By some miracle, just as Ash almost gave out, they both smelled fresh air. Tasting freedom, Ash drained his core faster and scrambled on, yowling and clawing his way to the opening. Holt ran up behind him.

The sunlight felt like fire on his face, the wind freezing, but no air had ever tasted so clean and wonderous, not even when they had emerged from the tunnels of Ahar.

Holt cut the sense-sharing, and after days spent joined so close to Ash, the world around him felt dull and washed out by comparison. Removing the blindfold at least brought some much-appreciated color back to his perception.

They were in a nondescript piece of country. There were pockets of woodland, low green hills – nothing sufficiently remarkable to make locating themselves simple. But it was the

surface. It was blue sky, not blackness; a breeze, not dead stillness; the smell of grass and flowers, not sickly rot.

Ash dragged himself onto the soft, dew-laden grass and
rolled over it like a dog on a new blanket. He rumbled deeply in
bliss until, with a long groan of relief, he lay splay-limbed and
belly-down in the meadow.

Holt stretched, enjoying every luxurious movement. He
placed his packs and gear onto the long grass by Ash's tail, then
crouched down by the dragon's snout and rubbed him.

"It's over. You did so well."

Ash's chest rose and fell softly. Exhaustion crossed the
dragon bond, and Holt longed for the cool embrace of sleep as
well, but right in front of the collapsed tunnel wasn't the place
for it. They'd have to move, but a short rest seemed in order.

The first thing Holt did was to check Ash's injury. Thankfully
the cut Holt had made to the spine ridge was clean, leaving a
smooth stump at the middle of the dragon's back. Allowing Ash
to rest, he checked on their equipment.

Brode's sword was untarnished, though he expected nothing
less from thick dragon steel. The many layers he'd placed around
the recipe book had also kept it safe, leaving nothing worse than
scuffs on the leather cover. Though happy the book was in one
piece, Holt knew with every fiber of his being that he'd trade it
for Rake without a second thought. He'd be willing to trade a lot
more to get Rake back.

He had to push thoughts of Rake away and tried to count his
blessings instead: he and Ash were alive and would recover,
another scourge orb had been taken out, and their mission, despite
its high price, had been a success. Or so he chose to consider it.

The sun had not yet reached its zenith, giving him a rough
and ready indication of east, south, north, and west. He faced
west but couldn't see any sign of the mountains of the Red
Range. If they had emerged somewhere in Risalia or Brenin, they
were deep inside those kingdoms.

"Can you get up?"

Wearily and with great effort, Ash rose unsteadily to his feet, then to his full height. His knees wobbled from cramping, and he yowled as he lifted his stiff neck. His wings unfurled slowly, and he wailed twice more before they reached their full span.

"I need a little time," Ash said. A pang of hunger roiled audibly from his stomach. He sniffed heartily until he picked up the trail of some game. An echo of the creature's meat, musk, and fur reached Holt across the bond.

"A boar?" Holt asked.

Ash answered by moving off along the scent trail. Holt hastened to repack his things, then followed his dragon.

The sun had dipped past the point of midday by the time they came upon the hog. It was resting in the shade of a large beech tree and didn't stand a chance as Ash fell upon it. Holt chose not to watch what happened next and wandered off so as not to hear it either.

He found a cool spot behind another beech tree, dumped his gear, then sat with his back against the trunk. He rummaged for his rations and found his last hard tac and oat cakes crushed to dust. Sighing, he gathered the crumbs and palmed them without pleasure into his mouth. To help it down, he took alternating bites of his remaining Lifting and Sinking jerky, the taste of wine and the tang of vinegar helping to break up the otherwise bone-dry meal. He'd have to make more anyway.

As his teeth ground down oats and tough meat, he considered deeply whether anything might be made of their near defeat. Alas, no meaningful revelation announced itself. At least, nothing in the spiritual sense. What did seem obvious was that he and Ash wouldn't be suitable for further missions against control orbs. The Hive Mind was willing to collapse its own positions to bury them. Talia would have to handle the rest on her own while they…

Well, he wasn't sure what he and Ash would do just yet. Seek the Elders? Return to Aberanth? It only seemed right that someone should tell him about—

Don't think about it, he scolded himself.

With meditative concentration, he pushed everything from his mind, focusing only on the stale food in his mouth.

By the time he centered himself, Ash had padded over to find him. Flecks of blood were still smeared around the dragon's mouth.

"Feel better?"

"Much," Ash said, sounding like himself again. He licked his lips, cleaning the blood. *"I hate flying on a full stomach, but I know we shouldn't linger."*

"No. We shouldn't."

Once again, Holt strapped their gear onto Ash, then climbed onto his back. They melded senses, this time so Ash could see through Holt's eyes, and took off to chase the sinking sun.

They flew through the night, bathing in moonlight, which felt as restorative as Aberanth's healing balms. As the dawn rose at their backs, the blue-gray outline of mountains rose on the horizon ahead of them, stretching endlessly from north to south. That had to be the Red Range.

As they approached, Ash dipped lower, and from on high, they beheld massing armies. On the largest banners, Holt thought he discerned a black bird on a white field. Risalia's flag was a crowned black eagle.

So they were still on the Risalian side of the Red Range, and these were forces of Archduke Conrad. There was other heraldry besides, including a flag of a horse on a red field surrounded by some pattern of yellow leaves Holt didn't recognize.

"They've spotted us," Ash said. *"They're calling for ballistae."*

"Let them panic," Holt replied. They were well out of reach of any bolt or arrow.

Talia may not have wanted to burden them with details of what she faced, but with mercenaries in Brenin and armies camped at the edge of the Red Range, Holt was getting a good sense of her troubles. Worryingly, he saw two extremely large Risalian trebuchets under construction.

As the morning brightened, they passed over a huge valley amid the peaks. Two wide roads fed into the valley, one running in from Risalia and one from Brenin; each was guarded by gatehouses and towers where they met the dale. A mighty fortress stood dark and imposing where all the roads met.

Holt realized he was gazing down upon the Toll Pass. This was the site for which two wars had been fought in his lifetime, which Feorlen currently held, which the Risalians wanted back, and where Osric had slain his brother.

"It seems a grim place," Ash said as they passed over the gate-house on the Risalian side. *"Why do people fight so hard over it?"*

Holt cast his mind back two years to what folk had said during the war. Being on the west coast of Feorlen, life at the Crag had barely been affected by the war. Some of the garrison had marched off and the price of some foodstuffs and materials had risen a little, but if not for that, he wouldn't have known a war was raging in the Red Range. All they heard came from the king's messengers.

"They told us that Archduke Conrad attacked northern forts unprovoked and sent ships to seize Port Bolca. They said King Godric was fighting to keep Feorlen strong and free."

In truth, Holt had known little and cared less about these places, yet he'd felt stirred by the messengers all the same. His daydreams had briefly switched from dragon riding to wearing a full knight's harness and marching against the evil Risalians.

But that was when he'd been a boy. Now he'd seen the worst of the scourge, he found it hard to understand why humans would ever turn against each other.

"To be free is worth fighting for," Ash said approvingly.

Holt agreed, though he held his tongue. Something about it didn't sit well with him now. No Risalian army had ever threatened his home or even marched into Feorlen during his lifetime. Everyone said the Risalians had been choking Feorlen's coffers for years, but that didn't mean much to a pot boy with barely two silvers to rub together.

As he spoke, they flew over the main fortress, and Holt saw trains of wagons and caravans queued up before the massive gates.

"Maybe it was always about gold."

"The men who died here wanted gold?" Ash asked.

"The king's messengers never mentioned gold..." Holt said, trying

to remember the details, but on that, he was sure. They never once spoke about gold.

Ash hummed in dissatisfaction. *"The whole thing sounds confusing."*

"Yeh," Holt said. *"Yeh, it is."*

If the Risalians were so terrible, had been so terrible for as long as folk claimed, then why had Talia's uncle not brought Brenin into that war to help?

It seemed to Holt now a confusing, muddled mess. Much like most things.

They left the Toll Pass behind and entered Feorlen, speeding toward Sidastra. Twilight lay over the lake and islands as they came into sight of the hundred isles. Respecting Talia's desire for them not to fly over the city, they touched down miles away from the eastern shore of Lake Luriel and waited.

A Low Champion and a High Ascendant came to meet them. The Champion was a mystic rider wearing violet brigandine and sported a long trail of coarse brown hair. Unusually for a rider, he bore a spear upon his back. Holt was immediately put in mind of Rake, and the raw wound felt rubbed with salt. The High Ascendant he recognized, for she had escorted him into the city the first time. She was a fire rider, though nothing in her appearance suggested this, barring her red armor. Her features and hair were so pale she ought to have been an ice rider.

Wary, they remained mounted, and the Low Champion addressed them first.

"Holt the Nameless?"

Holt nodded curtly. "And this is Ash."

Ash puffed up his chest and shook his wings in greeting.

The two riders gave faint inclines of their heads.

"I am Alvah," the Ascendant said in a Coedhen accent, which reminded Holt of Silas Silverstrike. "And this is my dragon, Nani."

"My name is Ensel," the Champion said, clearly from Risalia. "My dragon's is Valtin. I welcome you, High Champions, and bid you be at peace in these tragic times."

"We wish to report on our mission," Holt said. "May we

return with you to your island under cover of night?"

The riders looked at each other, then at their dragons, and Holt guessed that some private debate was taking place.

Then Ensel said, "You'd better come now."

That took Holt aback.

They all kicked off into flight. Their two escorts did not spare any haste as they soared for the rider's isle, where there seemed a heightened sense of tension. Dragons growled or roared, and there were now more riders on the island since they'd left. Holt and Ash landed on the outskirts by their huts and shelter and found them untouched.

Shortly after arriving, Holt felt the presence of an Exalted Champion coming their way. This was the strongest rider he'd felt among the New Order. To his surprise and relief, it turned out to be Ethel.

She arrived alone, seemingly confident in her new level of power, and looked taller at a distance. Her hair was styled differently, with three braids weaving into a thick central tail, and her pale armor bore signs of damage. Only when she drew close and Holt had to look down to meet her eyes did he remember how short she really was.

Both Holt and Ash bowed to her.

"Stand," Ethel said. "Are you hurt?"

"Not badly. We're glad to see you again. We had no idea you had joined Talia."

"Adaskar questioned my loyalties one too many times." Ethel paused, then barreled into a flurry of questions. "What happened? What did you see out there? Did you see any emeralds?"

"Emeralds? No. Should we have? We saw Risalian armies massing before the Red Range on our flight back."

"Never mind Risalia," Ethel said, looking fast between them. "I thought you'd... Well, maybe you wouldn't know, but everyone should have felt it."

"Felt what?"

Ethel's voice was high and hesitant. "The Life Elder. He's dead."

21

REMEMBRANCE

The Life Elder was dead.

The bottom of Holt's stomach had fallen out at the news and had yet to return. Ethel had questioned them for what felt like hours, though perhaps that was only due to his exhaustion. When she abated, she said she would return come the morning.

Holt slinked into his hut with the cruck frame ceiling. Rather than strain his tired eyes with light, he lowered his blindfold and shared senses with Ash. Growls across the island returned to him, and now he understood them to be born of grief and fear.

The mustiness from a thick layer of dust confirmed everything as untouched. He'd left elixir crates here and was pleased with himself for the forethought. Otherwise, they might all have been crushed during the cave-in.

Partly in a daze, he stripped off his filthy clothes and sighed as the cool night air nipped at his sweat-crusted skin. The straw mattress felt soft as a cloud.

"She never even asked about Rake," Holt noted to Ash. Holt thought it a terribly sad thing. Ethel had no connection to the half-dragon, but already it was as if he'd never existed. Given his reclusiveness, he and Ash would be part of the handful who would remember him. *"He didn't get a chance to save Elya."*

They shared a moment of quiet grief across the bond, then

their energies at last gave out and they drifted into a grateful slumber.

When Holt woke, it was from a dreamless sleep. Ethel kept to her word and returned. To his surprise, she hauled a laden cart with her. Three chests were on it, along with food. Someone had thoughtfully prepared two legs of venison for Ash, which raised Holt's estimation of the New Order. Ethel handed him a large bowl of oats softened overnight in milk and cream, and he was hungry enough to eat as quickly as Ash.

Midway through a thick mouthful, he remembered his manners and said, "Thank you."

Ethel smiled wanly. "Don't thank me yet."

Holt chewed faster, then, before taking another spoonful, he prompted her, "You had more to ask us?"

She bit her lip, then said, "These questions are more personal. First, I wondered whether you came across Orvel again in your travels?"

Holt spooned more creamy oats into his mouth to buy himself time.

Ethel's expression stiffened. She pressed her lips together, evidently waiting to hear the worst.

Holt felt he could delay no longer. He swallowed and said, "We ran into him at Windshear Hold. Did Talia tell you of our plans there?"

Ethel nodded.

"Well, those plans didn't exactly work out either. That's a long story, but Orvel was there. He was working with Thrall, and he killed hatchlings right in front of me – ones Ash and I were trying to save. We fought. I won."

Holt said it all in a matter-of-fact tone, as though he were a pot boy relaying a rider's food order to his father in the kitchens again.

"That's a shame," Ethel said. "A shame on all fronts. I understand you had to kill him, but seeing as he's part of the reason

Adaskar threw accusations at me, I'd have liked to bring him in one day."

"Gea is still alive," Ash said. *"Farsa and Hava were to take her back to Oak Hall. Could be she told the riders the truth."*

"If she did, it hasn't changed Adaskar's mind."

"Did you know Orvel well?" Holt asked.

"I served at Sable Spire for a long time, but I wouldn't say I knew him well, no. He kept to himself toward the end as younger and younger riders advanced past him. I wish Orvel was a unique case, but it happens more often than the riders care to admit," Ethel said, sounding sad. "At least your advancement is proof that good hearts and hard work do pay off."

"As does your own advancement," Holt said. "I'm only now beginning to understand how hard it will be to progress to Exalted Champion."

Ethel nodded. "Took me decades, then suddenly, all at once, things became clearer."

The notion of decades didn't sit well with Holt, but he and Ash had progressed faster than they'd had a right to already. Maybe he should adjust his expectations, but then again, Rake hadn't been clear on how long it should take them. He would have thought he had more time.

Distracted, it took him a while to register that Ethel's icy gaze had fallen on the hilt above his right shoulder.

"A sword of your own, congratulations," she said, albeit a little woodenly. "Did you – did you find Erdra's grave?"

"We did."

After Holt told her of the events of Red Rock, Ethel sagged.

"I'm glad he's resting with her. It can't have been easy for you carrying his sword around either, not least because it's not right for your magic."

"We kept hold of it, actually," Holt said. He nodded toward their mound of equipment beside Ash.

"Oh – you didn't leave it there?"

"I was going to, then Rake—" The words caught in his throat. "Then Rake… called me a fool and told me to keep it. He was right."

"Fussy beggars do not eat," Ash said in a poor imitation of Rake's growly tone.

Ethel appeared a bit lost, her eyes far away.

Holt finished his oats, then placed the bowl and spoon back onto the cart. "Thank you again for this and, you know, saving our lives before."

This seemed to bring Ethel back to the present. She smiled softly. "I'm sorry I couldn't do more." She lunged past Holt for the three chests, lifted them all at once, and set them down. "Please allow the Flight Commander to deliver gifts to you from the Red Queen... unofficially, of course."

She tapped a crate with one foot and dangled a key.

His brigandine armor. Holt had all but forgotten about it. He took the key, dropped to his knees, unlocked the chest, and, despite the dire circumstances, felt a jolt of excitement when he beheld the armor within. White cloth thick as a heavy doublet riveted by gilded white studs to the hidden leather and steel plates beneath. The gambeson was black, like Talia's, and Holt thought that would make the white armor more striking.

"Try it on," Ash said.

Holt picked up the trunk of the harness and got to his feet. He raised it against his torso to check the size and was about to put it on over his shirt before remembering he was both filthy and not wearing any padding.

"I should clean up first."

Ethel plainly agreed, though she tactfully said nothing. Instead, she lifted the lid of the second crate. Inside were fresh linen shirts, smallclothes, black trousers, and white boots. There was also a bar of hardened lye soap, several jars of salty pastes, and even hazel twigs to clean his teeth.

"You'll feel better," Ethel assured him. "Then you can think about your next move."

"Right," Holt said warily.

Their next mission, their next move, seemed an amorphous, distant thing.

Ash grumbled and stretched out languidly, sharing in his listlessness. Holt scratched the dragon down his neck, then untied Ash's blindfold. "This thing could use a wash as well."

"You smell like the heaps outside of the palace kitchens."

"You aren't looking so pearly white yourself."

Ash huffed and, with a sizeable thud, rolled over to show Holt his back. With a shrug, Holt folded Ash's blindfold, then laid it atop the chest of clean clothes and soaps to take with him.

"I wouldn't bother with that ragged thing," Ethel said as she unlocked the third and final chest to reveal a mass of folded black cloth. "Talia thought you could use a new one, Ash."

Ash rolled back over, throwing up clouds of dry dust. His snout pointed toward Ethel, but his eyes stared off into nothingness, lost in their own icy hue.

"This is great," Holt said as he bent to take the new blindfold.

Ethel warded him off. "Maybe bathe first."

Deciding that was fair, Holt took the chest of clean clothes and soaps and headed for a still-crumbled section of the island's wall, passing through it and heading for the shore not far beyond.

Lake Luriel's surface shimmered under a light breeze. On the northern side of the outmost island, there was no one to watch him, save for passing boats, and those were few and far off that morning. Stripping, he stepped into the lake. The sheer sudden cold forced the air from his chest. Drawing fast breaths, he Floated his mote channels out of instinct to protect his body and found that helped against the cold.

Now that he had a chance to really look at himself, he found bruises everywhere; black and blue, purple and yellow, and some a mottled red, though none appeared as livid as the remnants of the burn he'd received from Dahaka. The bruises would heal soon enough, but that burn seemed stubborn – even for his Champion's body.

At least the cold water didn't aggravate it, and once he'd acclimatized to its temperature, he stepped deeper into the water. He'd never learned to swim, but he paddled and treaded water for a time, enjoying the reflected warmth of the sun upon his face.

As Holt waded back to the shore, he noticed how nut-brown and weathered his forearms and hands were compared to his milky torso. Next, he withdrew the lye soap from the chest and lathered it onto himself. It took three return trips to remove the disturbingly stubborn volume of blood and grime he'd accumulated on his skin.

One of the jars of paste smelled strongly of lime and salt. He used this paste to clean his hair, and the water ran dark brown through his fingers. He dried himself off and enjoyed the feeling of putting on clean new clothes. Noting there was no new bandanna or blindfold for him, he washed his own as best he could.

Finally, he chewed the end of one of the hazel twigs to expose the stem and the moist, soft bristles within. This would suffice to clean his teeth on its own, but it would leave an unpleasant residue of bark. Holt searched the other jars for...

Yes, there it was. A dry mix of salt, crushed mint, and vinegar. He coated the hazel twig brush in the minty paste, then scrubbed his teeth good and hard. When the first twig was ruined, he chewed off the end of the second and repeated. Once he'd rinsed out his mouth, he felt like a new man.

A man, he reminded himself. *Not a boy.*

He returned to find Ash sitting up, head resting on his two front talons. Without his blindfold on, his unfocused crystal blue eyes made him appear younger again.

Ethel sat by him, gently patting his snout.

"You smell like the dew on crisp grass," Ash said. *"That's a lot nicer."*

"You should dip into the lake before we go," Holt said.

"Go where?"

Holt wasn't sure. To give himself time to think, he gathered Ash's new blindfold and brought it to the dragon. The material was thick, sturdy, and onyx black. Ethel took the other end and helped wrap it over Ash's eyes.

"Ash said you suffered a great loss."

"We did," Holt said.

Rake grinned at him in his mind's eye. Once more, he resisted sinking into mourning, focusing on pulling his end of the material taut.

"It would be nice to have a place to visit like with Master Brode," Ash said.

Just then, Ethel did something quite unexpected. She sniffed and allowed a brave tear to fall.

Holt tied a strong knot in the bandanna, then stepped around his dragon to admire the effect. Ash once again looked older, more dangerous.

Ethel wiped her eye with one finger. "I'm sorry," she said, visibly trying to pull herself together. "I'd never act like this in front of the others."

For once, Holt didn't mind the implication that he and Ash were different or somehow didn't count. There was something to be shared here, and Holt's mental barriers began to crack.

"I had no idea you and Brode were so close."

Ethel spoke more to the ground as she said, "Maybe more than we ought to have been." She sighed. "That was so very long ago. It feels like a completely different world now. Or maybe that's just because of all this." She gestured vaguely around her.

"We've missed him too," Ash said. *"Although I'm not sure he'd approve of what we've been up to."*

Holt couldn't help but chuckle. He could picture Brode's lined face turning beet red at the thought of scourge tunnels, potions, dragon exiles, and even more new hatchlings. Brode and Rake would probably have killed each other after a few nights on the road.

Ethel chuckled too, maybe because Holt had started it, maybe from nerves. Either way, she rightened herself and regained her bearing.

"Maybe we can add your master's name to the wall. It's not much, but he did die in service to Feorlen."

"What wall?" Holt asked.

"We're adding memorials to the wall of this island as part of its reconstruction. The names of all those who fell in the last incursion here. A way for the riders who will defend this city in the future to understand the scale of what they fight for."

"All the names?"

"Every one."

"My father's name, too?" he blurted.

Ethel got up, suddenly bright with purpose. "I'll show you."

She led Holt back through the streets, and they passed through the shadow of the New Order's rising tower and headed to the east side of the island.

Sure enough, engraved upon the repaired wall were a few lines to mark the incursion of the previous year and how Talia Agravain had repelled the swarm with the help of the Emerald Flight. Ealdor Harroway was noted as Master of War and commander of the city's defenses who bravely fell defending Sidastra and the realm.

Then the names of those taken by the scourge began. They ran in alphabetical order, so Holt did not have to go far until he found the C's and then the Cooks. Seven Cooks had been lost, and there, in the middle, was Jonah Cook:

Jonah Cook – Fulfilled his role of Master of the Kitchens of the Order Hall of the Crag for eleven years, passed in his thirty-ninth year. May his sacrifice be remembered.

All the engravings seemed to end that way.

Holt touched his father's name with his fingertips. He felt... oddly content. There was a place he could visit now, if he wanted, like the cliff of the Crag for his mother, or Brode and Erdra's cairn.

"We'll make something for Rake one day," Ash said.

"I'd like that."

He withdrew his hand from the wall. "This is a good idea. It would have been nice to have something like this back home."

By home, he meant the Crag, but it felt bizarre to reference the town as such. Not much time had passed, but he was a world and a whole life away from it now. It didn't feel like home anymore.

Nowhere did.

His soul twitched, spasmed like a growing pain.

Oblivious to his discomfort, Ethel said, "Outside the city, it might not be practical. Here, there are plenty of walls on which to carve names. As for what happens when that space runs out, well, that's another problem. For now, we have this one. Our intention is for citizens to visit the island so they may pay their respects to those they've lost and feel closer to the riders. The riders will know the people they are defending better. Lesson one is hard and there for a reason, but secluding riders in remote Order Halls creates a disconnect that can be worse. I know it did for me, and Talia said much the same. For the people, it can lead to mistrust, so if we can avoid that in the future, it will be worth a lot."

Holt nodded. "I hope it works."

Ethel smiled. "Shall we add your master's name?"

"Oh, I think Rake would hate being lumped in with everyone else."

"Most certainly," Ash added.

"Nonetheless, the offer remains open." Ethel clasped her hands behind her back and straightened, taking on the role of Flight Commander. "You and Ash may stay until you recover. The Red Queen is with the West Warden in his new grove in the Withering Woods, trying to see what can be salvaged from this mess. All she asked was that, if you returned, you leave word on where you're heading next."

Holt gazed at his toes. The enormity of their losses was sinking into his bones.

"I'm not sure what more we can do."

Ethel bit her lip, then gestured for them to walk, and they started to retrace their steps.

"We can't help much on our own," Ash said, *"but we can try to bring the other Elders into the fight like the Life Elder wanted. Whether we're ready or not."*

Holt agreed. It was the last desperate thing they could try.

"Storm or Fire?" he asked Ash. Those had been their options before.

"It needs to count. If Fire joins the fight, surely the others will follow."

The Fire Elder led the Order, and Talia and Pyra were of the flames. Rake had said the Storm Elder valued power above all, which they still lacked. All things considered, the Fire Elder may be their last and only hope.

"Any idea where the Fire Flight is?" Holt asked, hoping Ash had some blood memory to help them.

"South," Ash said, somewhat unhelpfully. *"The Warden might know."*

The West Warden seemed one of the few who might.

With a decision came a burst of clarity and motivation, and Holt suddenly asked Ethel, "Will you come with me for a moment? There's something I'd like to give you."

Ethel frowned but followed, and they returned at a run this time. Holt found what he was looking for right away. He gripped the hilt and pulled it free from its wrappings.

When she saw what it was, Ethel's eyes widened, and what color was in her face drained.

"Are – are you sure?"

Holt presented her with Brode's sword. Now he'd not worn it for a while, he'd forgotten how monstrously broad and thick it was.

"As serious as a summons," Holt said. "I kept it out of necessity, but I have no right to it. Brode meant a lot to us, but that doesn't mean we did to him. I hope we did... but we didn't know him for very long. You did. You should take it. The blades of fallen riders are returned to high command, right?"

She looked upon the sword as though it were Brode's own body. She nodded in a distracted manner. "They're sent to Falcaer to hang in honor. We've started our own hall here... Do you mean it?"

Holt thrust the green blade into her hands, and Ethel took it as though it were made of porcelain.

"I'll take good care of it."

"As for a message for Talia, there's no need to wait," Holt

said. "We'll fly for the Withering Woods as soon as we're ready. We need to see the Warden as well."

"In that case, I wish you luck."

"May the songs guide you, blind ones," said Strang, Ethel's dragon.

Ethel left them, and with fresh fire in his heart, Holt made ready. He lacked the time and tools to repair the damage to his baldric belt and pouches, but he restocked where he could, then packed everything else up. All their supplies and gear this time – including the fallen star. He didn't imagine they would be returning for a long time, if at all.

Lastly, he put on his armor. He struggled at first, so he tried to recall how Farsa had fastened her brigandine on, though she'd made it look effortless. He managed it in the end. White pauldrons, trunk, vambraces, and gauntlets over a black gambeson. Holt had dreamed of a moment like this for most of his life. With his own armor and sword, he felt... proud.

They left Sidastra that very night and began retracing their flight from the previous spring when they'd flown from the edge of the woods to the city. The Withering Woods spanned many leagues, dominating central Feorlen, but the emeralds weren't being careful now, and they were easy to find and follow.

Half a day's flight from the chasm at the heart of the woods, they felt the presence of the West Warden. When they touched down in the grove, the grief of the emeralds was palpable. Trees that should have been bursting with new buds lay bare, and fallen petals littered the forest floor. Pools of water smelled stagnant, and there was an unnatural stillness in the air. Those emeralds present were lethargic. Dozens lay flat and defeated with injuries or drained cores.

A purple dragon stood out starkly amid all the greens and browns. Out of respect for the emeralds, Holt and Ash approached Pyra somberly.

"Little ones," she said, then she took Holt aback by insisting on nuzzling into him. *"We weren't expecting you."*

"We have to speak with the Warden," Holt said. "Where is he?"

She indicated with her snout across the grove. *"Talia is with him."*

At first, Holt didn't recognize the West Warden. He'd never seen the great dragon sitting, never mind lying down. The dark pine hue of his scales seemed grayed out as though from severe sickness.

Holt patted Pyra's neck, then he left the dragons to catch up and went over to Talia. She was pacing before the West Warden, gesticulating with strong hands as though to rouse him.

When she turned and saw him coming, they both broke into a wordless run. She threw herself into a fierce hug, but this time it was Holt who pulled back.

Her green eyes took him in. "Don't you look dashing?"

"It fits perfectly," he said, a little awkward. "Thank you."

She shook him. "Oh, never mind how the damn armor fits. We're so relieved you made it." She beamed, then looked around. "Where's Rake?"

Holt gulped.

Talia's face fell.

Holt tried to speak. "Rake... He didn't..."

Talia raised a hand to his mouth. She opened hers, said nothing, then pulled him into a bear hug again. Holt tried to be tough, but he couldn't. He gulped more air, then heaved, and more tears fell.

"I know what it's like," Talia said. "You don't have to be strong."

"I'm so scared."

"Me too," she said, squeezing him tighter. Holt took comfort from that for a moment more, but then he pulled away again.

He looked at her – properly so, for the first time. While still striking, she looked worse for wear. Her red lips were cracked and chafed, her green eyes puffy around the edges. A tension ran out from them, creasing her skin like so many waving rivers, and her temples were crinkled below her hairline. Her rosy cheeks seemed ruddy now, as though fire might have scorched them. Minor things, in truth, but he'd never noticed them before.

"What happened?" she asked.

Holt told her of their disastrous mission.

"I never even considered something like that might happen," she said when he'd finished. "I shouldn't have asked you to go."

"Attacking us would be one thing, but collapsing the chamber – we couldn't have anticipated that."

"At least you and Ash escaped. At least there's that."

"And the scourge should be pushed even further from Feorlen. That's something too."

Talia nodded noncommittally.

"What happened with the Life Elder?" Holt went on. "Was it Thrall?"

"We think so," Talia said. "I mean, we don't really know, but who else could it have been? No emeralds from the Northern Grove have come. Maybe none of them survived. It's so confusing. When we returned from the Morass, the emeralds seemed in high spirits, then a few days passed, they grew tense, then went wild – as mad as the scourge when their queens are destroyed – and then... despondent. All we could get out of them was news of the Elder. Many flew off, and we don't know where. Maybe if I wasn't so distracted..." Her voice stuck again. "I don't know what to do," she added, sounding sad and lost.

"Ash and I will go and bring back help," Holt said, as though it were that simple. "We were supposed to go to the other Elders. Maybe we should always have stuck to that, but what's done is done. We'll find the Fire Flight. If we can convince the Fire Elder to help against Thrall, that will fix everything. He has to, right? Why would any of them just let Thrall kill one of their own?"

He was trying to convince himself as much as Talia.

The Warden rumbled loudly, miserably, drawing their attention. *"Beware of hope. Hope withers. The rot has set in."*

Holt stepped forward, unsure what he could do to comfort such a dragon.

"Please," he begged, "What's the worst he can do? Turn me and Ash away? Kill us? Not much will change from that."

"In the days of strife," the Warden began cryptically, *"the Elder of Flames left in a fury… he won't be easily swayed."*

The West Warden slumped lower to the ground, then rolled onto his side, exposing the lighter scales of his belly. Holt had seen beaten dogs with more spirit.

"Please, Honored Warden, your Elder sent us on a task we were poorly equipped for. If you have any notion of where the Fire Flight is, it would be invaluable. I don't know how we'll find them on our own."

The West Warden sighed long and hard. *"Last I knew, their domain was around the mountain of flames on the southern islands."*

"That sounds like the volcanic islands in the Scalding Sea," Talia said.

The Warden droned on as though Talia had not spoken. *"Fire will not be as accepting of Ash's blindness as we were."*

Which wasn't very much at first, Holt thought.

But instead, he said, "We're used to that."

"Maybe it's too dangerous," Talia said. "You don't have Rake this time."

"We have to try!"

"Invoke my name," the Warden said sadly. *"Tell them you are flying on behalf of the Emerald Warden of the West, that I seek the guidance of the Honored Elder of Fire in the wake of our great loss."* A piece of the Warden's spirit floated out of him like a finger checking the direction of the wind. *"Ash,"* he called. *"Come."*

Ash came as instructed, and that piece of the Warden's spirit wove around Ash, then sank into him. Holt's sense for spiritual matters was hardly proficient, but it seemed as though the Warden's will had coiled around Ash's soul, like a slip of paper tied to the leg of a messenger bird.

Talia looked confused. "What just happened?"

"The Warden lent his spirit to Ash," Holt said. "The Fire Flight will know we speak the truth."

She bit her lip, then said, "You two really have progressed far."

"Helps when it's all we have to do," Holt said. "You know, what with not having our own kingdom to look after."

Despite his forced jovial tone, Talia's expression turned grim. Her skin paled, making her scorched cheeks seem blotchy, the lines on her face turned to chasms, and her puffy eyes seemed to gray out.

"Sorry," Holt said in alarm, "I didn't mean to—"

"It's nothing you said." She cleared her throat. "Doesn't matter. Nothing does unless you can get the Elder's help. Focus on that."

Holt took her gently by the shoulder. "We saw the mercenaries in Brenin on our way back the first time, and we've seen that huge army digging in near the Toll Pass. We know something happened during your wedding to make Pyra fly off – you mentioned the Morass? Pyra said you don't want to burden us, but you might as well tell us, or Ash and I will just assume something is way worse than it probably is."

She nodded, still looking utterly lost.

"Fynn's gone. Nobody knows where he is."

Holt's ready reply caught in his throat. He hadn't been expecting that.

22

THE COUNCIL OF FOUR

Wynedd had received the communication late in the night. Paragon Neveh was on her way. The Paragons should assemble.

Dread and excitement buffeted Adaskar.

Upon her return, all shall change.

And so, the Paragons waited within the inner sanctum.

Adaskar sat upon his burning coals, breathing deeply to fill his lungs with soft, sweet smoke.

Vald floated cross-legged on a cloud of his own making, surrounded by steel globes upon black plinths. Silver-blue lightning effervesced around each globe or leaped crackling between them, emitting the smell of scorched metal and burnt soap. Vald's eyes were closed, his attention remained solely focused on himself, but Adaskar kept watch over the elder Paragon.

Eso sat cross-legged between his amethysts, his staff held across his knees. Though still sitting upright, he had drifted into a bond-slumber hours ago. His shoulders were slumped, and his head hung to one side, his eyes still open but rolled back to reveal the whites. From time to time, a pink mist leaked from the corners of those white eyes, catching between the amethysts and clogging the air around him.

Adaskar reached out to Azarin. *"Does Wynedd sleep peacefully?"*

"So far as I can tell."

Eso started muttering. Gathering pace, he became incoherent, then louder, until his head snapped back and he wailed at the ceiling. His lidless eyes flashed pink, and his staff fell from his grip with a heavy clang as an amethyst exploded.

Adaskar was on his feet and moving before the gem shards hit the floor. He Lifted his mote channels to protect his mind and stepped through the purple haze to shake Eso by the shoulders.

"Peace, Eso. Awake. Remember who you are. A rider. A man. Do not let the dragon take over!"

Thick mystic energy coiled around them both. Adaskar snarled at it, though fire was ill-suited to disperse it.

"Vald?!"

A moment later, a strong wind lifted the mystic energy in a whirl of air, carrying it high above their heads. Keeping one hand on Eso's shoulder, Adaskar cycled fire to his other hand, picked up the staff, shoved it into Eso's open palms, and closed his fingers around it. He pulled Eso in close and cradled his head.

"Peace," Adaskar whispered into his ear. "Peace."

With a jerk and a groan, Eso awoke. Quiet now, he gently pulled back from Adaskar; thankfully, his eyes were his own again.

"Did I frighten you?"

"Not at all," Adaskar said. "What did you see? Was it Neveh?"

Eso seemed to gaze into another world before he met Adaskar's eyes. "Nothing made sense. The songs are distorted. Something terrible has happened."

Across their dragon bond, Azarin snarled.

"You're awake now," Adaskar said. He gave Eso an affectionate squeeze, then stood and made for his own niche.

Vald had already returned to his cloud – if he'd even got down from it in the first place.

Walking back to his alcove, eyes still fixed on Vald, Adaskar announced, "We ought to make greater efforts to find Kalanta." His bare feet reached the coals, and he sighed inwardly. "Neveh, we know, is secure. What of our emerald sister?"

Eso cleared his throat. "I would be happy to try to speak with her again... once I've rested."

"I would not have you strain yourself."

Lightning crackled around Vald, and then he deigned to open his eyes. "I should think four Paragons is sufficient to determine your motion."

Four Paragons would be enough, but four voices did not hold the power of five – *the five*. Even one missing voice would sow doubts, and from them, great thickets of dissent might grow.

"You don't seem concerned for our sister's safety," Adaskar said.

"I trust Kalanta can take care of herself," Vald said. "Do not try to pretend that it's her safety that matters to you."

"It matters a great deal," Eso said sternly, strength returning to his voice.

"To *you*, yes," said Vald.

Eso made a disapproving sound, the sound of every disappointed grandfather to a wayward grandchild. "You are mighty, Vald, but you are yet to learn wisdom."

Vald scoffed. "What of our brother of fire? Do you think his actions wise?"

"Young Master Rostam has shown great restraint in these matters," Eso said, sounding now like the approving grandfather. Adaskar didn't mind it when Eso used his first name, for he used it affectionately, whereas Vald used it to remind him he'd once had authority over him. Vald flashed Adaskar an incredulous look, but Eso wasn't finished. "To seek the guidance of the whole council despite his strong instincts shows great consideration."

Vald laughed – short, sharp, and derisive.

Fire seared the back of Adaskar's throat. "Do you have an accusation to make?"

"Meeting the Archon of Athra is no sin, of course. You are the *head* of the Order. Yet, as I understand it, any meeting with a head of state must be done in the plain hearing of witnesses, recorded for posterity, enshrined in a ghost orb. Or have you changed these traditions?"

Adaskar blew smoke.

"Do you have an orb for us to review?"

"Not on this occasion."

Eso faced him. Even across the sanctum, Adaskar saw the long bristles of his beard twitch. "Is this true, Rostam?"

How did he find out? A senatorial family? One believing itself still indebted to him after his heroics defending Athra long ago?

Eso's gaze became pleading.

"It is true," Adaskar said. "I met with the Archo—"

"For what purpose?" Vald asked.

Adaskar considered evading, flirting with the notion to obfuscate, but he'd never mastered those seductive ways of speech. Nor had it ever suited his tastes.

"The Archon is as troubled by the actions of Agravain and Skadi as we are. I met him to discuss matters of security and to suggest suitable measures. As head of the Order, it's my right in a crisis."

"Crisis?" Vald asked. "Empress Skadi has done nothing to concern us as riders. Do not conflate the girl's rebellion with it. These matters must be seen as separate."

"And how do you propose we do that? Talia is both a rogue and a queen. Any action done to the rider is done to the monarch, no matter how many words we spin. This is unprecedented," Adaskar hissed through another gush of acrid smoke. "And it must be brought to an end."

"By any means?"

"Assent to my motion, and we'll cut out the rot before it spreads."

"And if we do not, you'll take action regardless? I dread to think what you promised the Archon, what he agreed to."

Adaskar opened his mouth to argue, but a groan from Eso silenced him. The old man's utterance was not from a waking nightmare this time.

"Such maneuverings are beneath us," Eso said, then, even worse, he added softly, "You did this while I was trapped in a slumber?"

Adaskar felt something he hadn't suffered from in a long

time, strong enough to punch through Azarin's fires. Shame. In answer to Eso's question, he could only nod.

"What have you done?" Eso asked.

He told them. In explicit detail. When he'd finished, the sanctum remained quiet; not even a crackle of static came from Vald's corner.

At length, Eso spoke gravely. "Our coffers were stretched thin already. To lose years of the tithes from such rich cities—"

"What's worse is losing Feorlen, Brenin, and the Skarl Empire forever," Adaskar said.

"You saw to that, Rostam," Vald said. "The girl wounded your pride, and you've acted rashly. Escalation won't help. Re-deploy our riders. Let her have her rump of a kingdom, and when the scourge inevitably rises there again, let her weakness be her own downfall. She has not a single Lord or Lady in her ranks and won't by natural advancement any time soon. In the meantime, build Falcaer's strength. Focus inward on our own power and demonstrate we do not fear this misguided break-away. That she swayed those she did is another sign of failure – our recruits must be better inspired."

Adaskar's flicker of shame burned out. How he loathed to hear such condescending words, easy words.

"If you are so dissatisfied, then stay and assist me rather than fly to the reaches of the world to brood and advance on your own."

Vald ignored him. "You're obsessed with the girl. Will you allow your obsession to start a great war?"

"Vote in favor, and it won't come to that."

Eso rose. He clunked the butt of his staff against the floor, and it rang out with unnatural volume. Amethysts and quartz sang in ethereal voices, and a question was asked in the spiritual tongue.

'Who is the true enemy?'

Adaskar met the check easily.

'Chaos,' he answered.

"One says the enemy is 'chaos'," Eso said, his voice dominant now, reminding them why he was a Paragon. "The other answers, 'death'. Almost the same, yet entirely different." He turned his judging pink eyes on Adaskar. "Rostam, without assurances from you, the Archon would have more doubts and risks to weigh, enough perhaps to hold him to peace. Mayhaps the Agravain girl is not worth the high price you seem willing to pay."

"Chaos is a disease," Adaskar said. "It will get worse before it gets better."

Eso tutted, then faced Vald. "Death. Death is too great a foe, even for us. Fight the sun or the moon, if you will. Fight the passage of time. Death will claim everything."

Vald met the gaze evenly, and his own eyes sparked blue. "Every obstacle we've overcome was once thought impossible. The Elders do not wither. To breach the next boundary – who knows what lies beyond. Immortality? Victory? The only way to know is to explore past the horizon. I respect you, Eso, and all you've done for Falcaer and the world, but this is my calling."

"You're not the first to tell me this dream. I would rather die than have your ashes run through these old fingers. Now come together, the pair of you. Vald, what's done is done. Rostam cannot take it back. Let us weigh what we can do now to prevent worse occurring. Rostam, dear boy, do not take Vald's long absences from our halls as a slight. We each have our paths. It once took riders willing to brave the edges of Champion and then Lord to show us what was possible. The two of you must unite now against the *true enemy*. We must see beyond small troubles in the present and consider the fut—"

He ceased mid-speech, his gaze drifting to the ceiling.

Adaskar tensed in anticipation. Eso's range of magical detection was the greatest of them.

"Ice returns," Eso said.

Adaskar's bond with Azarin thrummed fast, and his heart drummed to match it.

Upon her return, all shall change.

It felt naïve to hope Eso's words were merely wind. Something terrible had occurred. He could feel it in the air, hear it, as though the songs of fate were revealing themselves to him.

Upon her return, all shall change.

The three Paragons fell silent, gathering themselves.

Adaskar tracked her every movement. Neveh and Nilak were approaching fast for their type. They landed in Falcaer, and she moved to the sanctum with haste.

The door opened with a blast of numbing cold. Where Neveh's presence met Adaskar's, steam hissed in midair before the auras evened out.

Her ebony complexion, bronze eyes, and single strand of crystal blue through her dark hair remained unaltered by her time in the wilderness. Adaskar narrowed his eyes. Something about her seemed *off*. He thought she might be thinner than before. The whites of her eyes also seemed grayer.

Then he sensed a dip in the strength of Nilak's core. Nothing that couldn't be replenished, but enough to show she'd been in a fight. A real fight that had taxed her.

But the tangible change was in her spirit. It fluttered. He focused deeply on its rhythm, then changed his mind. Not a fluttering of excitement, but a tremor. Something had shaken Neveh to her soul, though she was doing all she could to hide that in her bearing.

She moved to the center of the inner sanctum and dipped her head lightly to Vald, to Eso, and, finally, to Adaskar.

"Revered brothers, it is well you are here, for we have no time to spare."

There was no apology for her lateness. But then again, Adaskar expected nothing less from Neveh.

He stood upon his coals and said, "Foremost, we are pleased to see you unharmed. Share your burden so the council may assist you."

She dipped her head again, then moved to her alcove on Adaskar's right, where fountains fed a shallow pool of water. The running water slowed as she drew close and had frozen solid by the time she removed her boots and stepped barefoot onto the ice.

Looking at Kalanta's alcove, she asked, "Is our revered sister due to join us?"

"Kalanta's whereabouts are unknown," Adaskar said.

"We hoped you might have word of her," Eso said.

"I haven't seen her since our last meeting."

Eso frowned, then nodded resignedly.

"You have tidings for us?" Vald asked curtly.

"Brothers, there is no simple way to say this, so I shall be blunt. The Life Elder has perished in the Spine. This event I bore witness to with my own eyes."

Spiritual power radiated from her as she spoke, touching all their souls to confirm her words beyond doubt. Nilak did the same for the dragons in the grounds.

None of the Paragons needed their dragon bonds to hear the roars of disbelief from Azarin, Raiden'ra, and Wynedd. All of Falcaer shook under their bellows. Adaskar's golden bond rocked from Azarin's calamitous shock.

Upon her return, all shall change.

Adaskar couldn't be sure what he'd expected to hear. That she'd decided to join Talia? That Kalanta was dead? That a new chasm had erupted in the White Wilderness, tearing the world from Smidgar to Windshear, bringing forth an apocalypse?

Nothing in his darkest nightmares could have prepared him for the reality.

The death of an Elder.

Why do these woes come in my time?

The riders had to be united now, without delay, if they were to stand against the harrowing chaos to come.

"How?" Adaskar asked. It was all he could think of saying. "How?" he asked again, his tone biting now.

Neveh hesitated, her spirit quivering. "It's a tale I still hardly believe."

Yet it was a tale she told well. Neveh had met with the Ice Elder, which alone would have been monumental but now seemed a minor note in her story. Ice had been approached by a mystic dragon of immense power claiming to hold sway over the scourge. This dragon called himself Sovereign.

Adaskar twinged at the mention of the name.

Neveh went on. Sovereign had demanded that the Ice Elder

join him in wiping out all human life. Ice, naturally, had refused. Fearful, the Elder had pulled her dragons back to the utter north and raised a blizzard to protect her borders.

Some six months ago, the Life Elder had arrived in the northern Spine and reached out to his sister for assistance. She agreed to aid her brother on the condition that he push back the blight from her borders. This he achieved, and so after the great blizzard had been lowered, the Ice Elder finally granted Neveh an audience, during which she had learned of the plan to confront Sovereign. The mystic dragon was elusive but, in time, an opportunity would emerge, and then they would strike.

"I volunteered to fight," Neveh told them. As she went on, a brittle quality much like ice entered her voice. "By the time we arrived, the Life Elder and Sovereign were locked in a fierce battle, but we were too late to... Sovereign gouged his talons into the Life Elder and threw him down upon the valley floor."

Vald seemed enraptured by her every word. "This mystic defeated an Elder?"

Eso cut in before Neveh could answer. "Did you apprehend this dragon?"

"Sovereign's forces returned to the valley. Nilak and I fought hard to resist his domination." Her cheek began to twitch. "Greatly outnumbered, we fled."

"There is no shame in fleeing a fight you cannot win," Eso said.

Adaskar grunted at that and scrutinized Neveh again. Much like with Farsa, he could tell. He could always tell when something eluded him.

"But it is true?" Vald urged. "There is a mystic dragon out there, mightier than an Elder and in control of the scourge?"

His tone was one of hunger rather than worry. Were Adaskar not so shaken by the news, he would have been disgusted.

The girl was right. She was right. Farsa was right.

There was a lie, though. Somewhere within this disaster, there were still lies. He could feel it, as sure as he felt it from Farsa, as sure as the fires rising in him. But the Paragons were talking fast, Azarin and the dragons were awash with heightened emotions, their spirits raging in reaction to the news, and Adaskar couldn't sift through it all.

"I did not believe at first," Neveh said. "But seeing those scourge-risen dragons flying to Sovereign like an honor guard made it plain."

"This cannot be," Eso said. "Cannot be. Cannot be." He breathed hard, closed his eyes, then planted his staff before him in a two-handed grip. Amethysts leaked with arcane energy, and a wall of transparent power rose to seal him in his alcove.

Adaskar watched until he was satisfied this was a controlled containment and not a slumber from Wynedd. Eso then lifted gently off his feet. Weightless and deprived of sensory information, his mind could expand and process thoroughly what was happening. On occasion, it allowed him to glimpse the songs of fate directly.

Vald and Neveh continued speaking as though nothing was amiss.

"How has your Elder responded?" Vald asked.

"I do not know. I flew straight here from the battle."

Adaskar grew hot. This was fast getting out of hand.

Upon her return, all shall change.

Something in him snapped. "You have broken the Pact. Your actions might have doomed us, Neveh."

"My Elder invited me into her domain. *She* requested *my* aid." She looked at them, beseeching. "None here swore to the Pact. Those who founded the Order may have, but not us. Why should we be bound to promises made millennia ago? It's absurd. Do the Skarls feel bound by treaties signed with Aldunei? The world changes, adapts, advances, yet we who guard it remain frozen in place."

"Were it only that we were one united front," Adaskar said.

"Not this again…" Vald said.

Out in the grounds of Falcaer, Raiden'ra roared with impatience.

Neveh looked enquiringly between them, and Adaskar briefly explained Talia's rebellion, ending on an ominous note.

"It's only a matter of time before the Elders of Fire and Storm come forth. The girl and her rogues are actively opening tunnels. Does anyone think the recent collapse of the central Risalian network is a mere coincidence? Scourge are pouring out in all directions, threatening innocent lives. Is this the radical change you desire? Remember our oaths!"

From the hot coals, he raised fire to dance around him. Azarin crossed their bond to become a part of him, setting a blaze behind his eyes. When next Adaskar spoke, the strength of Azarin's voice wove into his own.

"I pledge myself to the Order that stands against chaos. I am the light that guides through the dark. I am the shelter in the storm. I am the first strike and the last shield." He skipped ahead to the pertinent part. "Where others stray, I shall obey. *Obey*," he repeated, and here Azarin faded from his voice. "To be rigid is our duty. To be the anchor. The last, unbreakable shield. Stand with me. Together we can restore the world to rights."

The sanctum fell quiet.

Vald and Adaskar stared at one another.

In Eso's alcove, the barrier dimmed, then dropped. He landed lightly on his feet and opened his shining eyes.

"If this dragon controls the scourge, he has made himself its dam. This is the answer to the riddles of the scourge's low activity these long years, barring the small rising in Feorlen. To kill him would risk a sudden surge we are not prepared for. Any action we take must be thoroughly considered."

"I agree, dear Eso," Neveh said quickly. "My Elder was also concerned by this."

Adaskar blew smoke and narrowed his eyes. Rarely was Neveh one to agree on anything, even something small. If the council declared something to be white, Neveh would argue it to be black.

Lies, lies, and more lies.

"An Elder has been slain," Vald said. "And power abhors a void. We must gather ourselves for that storm. If the Elders seek to punish us for Neveh's actions, then Sovereign gains. Should they slay Sovereign in revenge, the scourge are unleashed. Are we to sit idle until the blow comes or be left to mop up the mess ourselves? I say we should be proactive."

"Before we can face the world," Adaskar asserted, "our own house must be put in order."

He was growing weary of the endless debate. It would get them nowhere. Events had conspired to hurtle forward faster than he'd ever expected. A unanimous assent from the full council had been a long shot at best. Even were Kalanta here, she couldn't change Vald's and Neveh's minds.

It was time for each to declare their hand, for each to act as they saw fit.

"Revered brothers, sister, as Paragon of Fire, head of the Riders of Falcaer, I call for the arrest of Talia Agravain and the dissolution of her splinter sect by means of direct intervention from the council. I await your will." As he ended the official motion, he reached out spiritually to ask, 'Will you assent?'

Neveh responded first. 'Nae.' Though her soul still quivered, her response was strong as ever.

"I believe the council should focus its efforts on neutralizing Sovereign," she said. "We do not need the return of these Champions and Ascendants to do so."

Adaskar had expected nothing less.

Eso replied second. 'Nae.'

That came as a serious blow.

"Given all that has unfolded, these young rogues are far from the gravest threat we face. Let us bring this unfortunate chapter to a swift close without bloodshed. Offer them a way to return to the fold – get our house in order, as you say, Rostam – then refocus on other concerns. If they choose to remain apart, I'm certain they will come to their senses in time."

Vald voted last. 'Nae,' he replied, and his will was the strongest of the three.

"Rostam, you have lost perspective. The balance of the world shifts bloodily, and still you obsess over one girl who dared defy you. I find myself both ashamed and inspired by her. She fights the scourge, not us."

Vald dispersed his cloud, dropped to the floor, and walked

across the sanctum toward Adaskar. Stopping just short of the dancing flames, he extended his hand.

"Let us work together and break through the next boundary. With such strength, we need not fear the Elders, nor this Sovereign. We'll secure the riders, our world, our Order."

Adaskar looked with longing at Vald's open palm. A small part of him yearned to grasp those blackened fingers, but he knew his own will. His bond, spirit, and mind were aligned, and with a heavy heart, he said, "If you cannot condemn rogues and chaos-bringers, then you're no better than one."

"Rostam—" Eso began, sounding wounded, but Vald threw up his free hand and clenched the one that had been extended in friendship.

"Save your breath, dear Eso. Our noble leader's motion has failed to pass. He won't act because of it. I respect tradition and procedure, too, though not enough to destroy our future. Forgive me if I do not sit and wait for the end to come."

With that, he turned on his heel and left the sanctum.

Adaskar watched him go and kept staring ahead long after Vald had left. A sinking feeling dragged him down, and dry tears burned in the corners of his eyes, desperate to fall, but his fires had destroyed his ability to cry long ago. He was glad of it now, for he would despair if the others saw him weep.

"Your motion failed to pass."

Adaskar's attention was jostled back to the room by Neveh's blunt words. She'd left her alcove and stood now where Vald had stood.

"Will you join me in dealing with Sovereign?"

Adaskar cleared his throat. "On this, I believe Eso to be right. If he is the heavy door keeping the fire at bay, we run a great risk in seeking to open it."

"I have a plan."

"Does it involve the Elders?" Her insolent expression told him it did. "Then no, Neveh. I can't condone it. Nor can I guarantee your protection should the Fire Elder demand an account of these events and your part in them."

For a moment, it seemed like she would reach for her sword.

"I don't appreciate threats. Should I succeed, think better of me." She looked imploringly at Eso. "Dear Eso, come with me. Your presence would go a long way toward our success."

Eso's lower lip trembled, yet he looked stiffly ahead. "My place is here."

Neveh cast her gaze to the floor, then she, too, swept out of the sanctum.

Adaskar noted the presence of Raiden'ra and Nilak flying from Falcaer, the former to the west and the latter to the north.

"I hate to see you all like this," Eso said.

"They have revealed their true selves, that is all."

"What now?"

"The council rejected my motion. I shall accept its will. For now, we must ensure the Order does not splinter further. I fear Vald's ambition is as insatiable as a dragon's core."

23

NO CHOICE AT ALL

It had been a long time since Osric had fallen asleep to the sound of a grazing horse. Merchant's horse tearing at the grass took him back to those camp nights with his Gray Cloaks when things had been more certain. With the horse and his dragon's soft presence like a cushion, he slept better than he had in months. Being out on the road on a mission suited him best; a general would send others, but he was only a soldier again.

Their journey east from Faywallow went well, all things considered, even if their pace was slow. His main regret was in needing to reveal the dragon. Word of a one-handed man with a black dragon spreading through the Frontier would be dangerous.

In the meantime, having the guise of a mercenary escort helped assuage suspicions in a lonely wanderer, allowing him to quietly inquire with Merchant's customers as to whether they knew a woman called Petrissa. Most gave him no hope, but Merchant would collect his coins, hand over the salted trotters, and they would move on to the next settlement.

Only once did someone say they knew a Petrissa, but she turned out to be too young. On this occasion, Osric drew more dark looks than he had since Faywallow, and Merchant hurried them out of town with a severe expression.

The next day, Merchant invited Osric to sit on the driver's

seat alongside him, and after Osric declined, he insisted. Osric sat down, and they continued for what felt like an hour in silence, though Osric had the impression that Merchant was working himself up to say something. At length, he did.

"I've been thinking," Merchant began, as though the thought had only just occurred to him. "We've got a long way to go, so it might be best if you don't spend time speaking to folk along the way."

"I'm to remain silent?"

"You'll be all the more menacing for it."

Osric turned in his seat to face the man, but Merchant's eyes were fixed firmly on the road.

"This is why I've come here," Osric said.

"I'm aware. I'm just worried it might lead to some delays or trouble."

"Why would it?"

"You don't seem an unworldly or foolish man, Soldier. It's the Frontier. We're always at the knife's edge of a scrap here, and acting odd can bring that down on you."

"Perhaps you could inquire on my behalf. You'll know how not to appear *odd*."

Merchant hesitated. For the first time, his hands trembled on the reins.

"Why not?" Osric asked.

"Blight take me," Merchant blustered. "Because those thugs who wanted to beat on you back at Faywallow were Crows, that's why. Don't need that kind of attention coming our way."

Crows. Osric found the term distantly familiar and thought it might be the name of one of the criminal factions of the Frontier that were little better than large gangs, although keeping track of Frontier politics was like waging war without reconnaissance.

"How did you know they were Crows?"

"The question is, how didn't you know?" Merchant said. "What are you doing coming into the Frontier without knowing that?"

"I came for—"

"Petrissa, yes, your dear mother," Merchant said brusquely,

meeting Osric's eye. "I know that, Soldier. I was being rhetorical." He said all this in the manner of a beleaguered, frustrated officer dressing down a recruit. Indeed, he did it so well that Osric raised his brow in bemusement and noted it as further evidence of what he suspected Merchant to have been before he peddled trotters.

Merchant cleared his throat with a gruff cough, and the redness in his face and neck began to settle.

"Look," he began in a conciliatory tone, "I'm just surprised, that's all. You're clearly capable of handling any number of Crows, so being careful isn't an issue for you, but the rest of us are still just bags of blood that leak when pricked. All I'm asking is for you to keep a low profile."

"You're asking for a lot. What if someone along the way knows where she is or what happened to her?"

Merchant gave a pained sigh. "If I'm right," he said, sounding deeply resigned, "and if she is who I think she is, then trust me, you don't want to be asking too loudly after her in Crow territory."

Quite unexpectedly, Osric laughed. He couldn't help it. The thought that Petrissa could have left such a trail of turbulence in her wake, even in the Frontier, was almost poetic. He could only imagine what she'd done to turn one of the major factions of the region against her.

"What's so funny?" Merchant asked.

Osric settled himself and ignored the question. "If I can't look for her in Crow territory, then whose territory can I?"

"Good try, Soldier, but why would I reveal that when I still need you?"

"Territory is too broad to go on. And judging from what you've said, it sounds like we'd be heading that way anyway."

Merchant sucked in a breath through his teeth, then said, "Once we're into lands controlled by the Hounds, things should be safer."

"Hounds..." Osric said, once again feeling a familiar twinge at the back of his mind. A kernel of knowledge came to him, though this one had been recent, from the mouth of the lanky thug in Faywallow. "Any chance someone called 'Jackal' has something to do with the Hounds?"

"You could say so," Merchant said, though he did so warily. "The Jackal heads up the Hounds; the Vulture heads up the Crows. Bit of an uneasy peace between them since they stamped out the other gangs."

They both turned to look at the road. Osric, for his part, felt the quiet sense of satisfaction that came with the advancement toward a goal. Short of Merchant lying about all of it, this was his first piece of concrete information that Petrissa was still alive. Hard to think the Crows would have such an issue with a dead woman.

He felt the dragon squirming, uncomfortable inside his crushed shadow.

"I'll go back to walking," he told her, and then, for Merchant's benefit, he said, "I'll stay quiet, though I'd be pleased if we omitted a stop or two along the way."

"Hmm," Merchant said stiffly. At length, he added, "Alright. We can skip Hobb Burrow. Folk there are tight-fisted anyway."

A few days and two stops later, Merchant kept his word and passed Hobb Burrow by. They kept moving almost that whole day, stopping only for the sake of the horse, who Merchant refused to overwork and whom he dotingly fed pails of oats and barley, stroking her neck and speaking softly to her.

On one occasion, Osric couldn't help but overhear him.

"Such a good girl, Belle. Just a little farther today, I think. Can you manage?"

Belle nickered and sniffed despondently at her empty pail. Merchant rifled through his supplies for more oats and almost despaired before he found a last sack. He filled the horse's pail a third of the way, then caught Osric staring at him.

"We'll need to make a stop, Soldier. Need to resupply for Belle."

Osric inclined his head. He felt somewhat chagrinned to have been caught studying the man, for he was not the type to pry, and as he wished for Merchant to ask him little, he ought to repay the courtesy in kind. Yet he had another habit of needing to understand those he traveled with – not intimately, but enough that he knew what they were capable of. It was no different with Merchant.

It had only taken until breakfast on the first morning for Osric to realize that the red coat Merchant wore was of Athran make. More than that, it wasn't just any coat but the jacket of an equestrian. At some point, Merchant must have been a man of some status within the city, and if not of high-born rank, then at least part of the heavy, most prestigious cavalry.

He should have noticed it at once, but the man's jacket was so frayed, so sloppily repaired and faded, that Osric forgave himself the oversight. Other than the coat, nothing else of Merchant's attire spoke of his past; certainly not the beard, for equestrians were clean-shaven as a rule. He could have stolen the coat, Osric supposed, or perhaps killed a true Athran and taken it, but his way with his horse was almost that of a parent to a child. Moreover, Osric had felt drawn to him and granted him undue trust from the off, which he could only explain – other than as his desperation – as having found a kindred spirit.

His notion as to Merchant's background only grew more certain as their journey continued. Trepidation reached them on the tracks and crossroads, from fellow travelers or freely from the mouths of locals when Merchant stopped to hawk his baskets. News of attacks, tales of ruined towns where the people vanished without a trace.

With fears of Thrall and the hatchlings at the forefront of his mind, Osric implored his companion one night to omit more stops on their route.

"There are powers lurking in the Frontier you cannot imagine," he explained. "You commissioned me to keep you safe, but I must confess I cannot guard you against this power if it comes. I saw the town of Silt Grave destroyed and emptied of its people, all without a drop of blood on the ground."

Merchant chewed his mouthful of pork pensively while their campfire spat and the water in their cook pot simmered. After he swallowed, Merchant pointed his half-eaten trotter at Osric and said, "I knew you were a worldly man. No doubt you showing up has something to do with such trouble, but I did seek your protection, and so I shall take the advice. We'll carry on straight to Blackhollow, which is at the very edge of Crow territory. From there, we can enter Hound lands and be safe, or safer at least."

"This danger won't care whether the land belongs to the Crows or the Hounds."

"This is where you need to trust me again," Merchant said, waving his trotter. When Osric offered no rebuttal, he smiled and took another bite of his meal.

Osric attended to his own trotter. They weren't so bad once softened in the pot, but he was getting sick to death of them. Such a reaction struck him as peculiar – he wasn't one to complain about such things – and he thought it might be his dragon's influence.

Despite her initial enthusiasm, she had sent a sense of revulsion across their bond upon finally trying a trotter and during every meal since. This night was no exception, and she sat nosing her two trotters back and forth with the deepest despair in her purple eyes.

"Eat up," Osric told her. *"Our companion has been kind enough to give you extra."*

She stuck out her tongue, gingerly licked one of the feet, then turned aside with a squeaky rumble. Thoughts of juicy deer and the warm, earthy stews from Ash's human rose in her and crossed their bond.

"We don't have time to hunt," Osric said. *"And if you're spotted, we'll be in greater danger. This is what we have. You can't be fussy."*

She cooed, and Osric gained another impression of Ash conveying love or hatred for meals without being told to be silent.

"You're allowed to dislike it, but you must still eat it. Ash had to eat some disgusting fish while he and Holt were stuck underground. Do you remember that?"

She did, and so she grudgingly ate her food.

Osric nibbled at his dinner again until he'd gnawed all the meat down to the bone.

. . .

At long last, Merchant announced they were nearing Blackhollow, their final stop before leaving Crow territory. Now they were deep into the Frontier, not even a vague blue outline of the Eastern Fang could be seen behind them.

The track wound down to a lowland, and with each passing hour, the few trees that clung to life turned ever stranger, blackened with shriveled brown leaves as though burned. These dark trees multiplied as they drew closer to the town, and the day was growing long by the time they reached the gates.

Blackhollow was more heavily guarded than anywhere else on their journey had been, at least in terms of manpower. Osric wondered whether word of attacks had placed the Frontier on high alert. If the guards were members of the Crows, they were a higher tier of criminal than the thugs back at Faywallow. These had commanding voices, strong spears, broad shields, and faces veiled under black hoods.

Merchant paid a toll, and after the guards briefly inspected the wagon, finding only salted pig feet, they waved them on through. Inside the town were more burnt trees, growing here and there at the edge of the paths, at crossroads, and in crooked alleyways.

Three gatehouses, Osric noted. *Too many for this place. Wooden walls won't stop juggernauts. More ballistae, that's good, but the low elevation leaves them at a disadvantage. At least the streets have a better layout. A shield wall might be formed here,* he considered at several points, *but there's not enough real soldiers for that.*

Merchant drove Belle to the only inn with a functioning stable and tasked Osric with guarding the horse and wagon while he inquired about a room.

Even here in the inn's yard, a black tree stood tall. Curious, Osric went to examine it, wondering why the people hadn't cut down all the dead trees and how they weren't hollowed out from rot. He found the bark coarse and firm to the touch with the right amount of give, not brittle as fire damage would leave it, and the brown leaves, while curled and crumpled, were soft, flexible, and waxy between his fingers. The tree was very much alive.

He was still inspecting the tree when he heard the now-familiar gait of Merchant's footsteps behind him.

"Something wrong?" Merchant asked.

"I've never seen trees like this."

"It's just how they grow here. Might be this area around Blackhollow wasn't as well cleansed by Kosora and her emeralds back in the day."

Osric supposed so. Centuries ago, Paragon Kosora had led every emerald rider in the Order on a crusade to turn back the spread of the Dead Lands by reseeding the lands east of the Spine. Kosora expended all her power in the process, as well as many of her highest Lords and Ladies, crippling the strength of the emerald riders for a generation. Still, the encroachment of the Dead Lands was stopped and even rolled back a little. Sadly, despite such heroic efforts, the land never fully recovered, and it became the Fallow Frontier.

"I've got good news and bad news," Merchant said.

Osric turned and waited for him to go on.

"Good news is there's a warm room spare for me and a stall in the stables for Belle. Bad news is I've got a lot more stock left over, given our hastier journey. Can't traipse it all through the inn, and I'm not risking it in storage, so you'll be sleeping with the wagon tonight."

"No matter," Osric said. He might have insisted they move on, but night was already pressing in, and Belle had walked since dawn that morning. "I advise we leave at first light. If you tell me your room, I can rouse you."

Merchant did, made to head back inside, then turned back as an afterthought. He rummaged in his red coat and pulled out a small coin purse, which he tossed to Osric.

"They do decent mutton here," Merchant said. "Not as exotic-tasting as Karacatus' fare back at the Pig, but maybe she'll find that more to her liking."

Osric weighed the pouch in his hand. This would buy a lot more than mutton. Business had gone well for Merchant, despite missing a few stops along the road. Too well, frankly.

"This is too much," he said. Having asked for no payment, he hated to take anything he hadn't earned.

"Keep it," Merchant said with a dismissive wave. "We were fortunate on the road, but I've never felt more secure at market than with you growling at anyone who got too close. Rest well, Soldier."

Osric first secured the canvas over the wagon, then called one of the innkeeper's underlings for a brazier and food – and lots of it. The lad looked horrified, perhaps wondering how Osric would eat it all, but he dutifully ran off without comment.

Later that night, Osric sat eating a leg of mutton by the brazier, having positioned it such that the firelight would cast a shadow under the wagon where the dragon could safely lurk. He intended to keep the fire going all night, and while he would manage to stay awake, he missed the Lord's stamina he'd become accustomed to when bonded to Thrall. The decline to a lesser rider's body felt like he'd aged two-score years overnight.

Between tending to the brazier, he did what meditation he could, first Cleansing her little core before starting to Forge the blurry black motes. When he took breaks to assuage the pain, he noticed large night patrols pass by, more men in black hoods. He took these for members of the Crows, but there were others with them, locals perhaps pressganged into a watch. Blackhollow was on heightened alert, and thus so was he.

Years of instinct honed on campaigns told him something wasn't right. There was a tension in the air, as though the dark trees strained to reveal something to him.

All of this meant that when the first call echoed through the streets, when the first bell rang, Osric was awake, on his feet, and had Vengeance in his hand before the shrill shriek of a stinger reached him.

Blackhollow was under attack.

"Stay where you are," he urged her, then, leaving her in the shadow, he sprinted inside the inn, took the stairs to the bed chambers, and cut through the lock on Merchant's door with a swing of his axe.

He'd drawn a great breath to bellow and wake his client, but to his surprise, he found Merchant already awake, sitting on the edge of his bed and pulling on his shirt. Before either of them could speak, a bellowing seemed to shake the whole inn, and it was no scourge cry.

"Dragons?" Merchant said, seeming relieved.

"These aren't riders. Remember that danger I spoke of?"

Merchant set his jaw and continued his frantic dressing. "Fetch Belle and get her saddled."

Osric flew back down the stairs, out of the inn, and rushed for the stables. He kicked the doors open, bolted for Belle's stall, broke that lock as well, then grabbed her bridle from the hook outside her stall. Belle and her stablemates issued loud, high-pitched whinnies, some rearing back as the buzzes, roars, thwacks, thumps, thuds, and scrapes from outside grew louder.

Osric didn't have the gentleness to settle her at the best of times, and certainly not now. Only his rider's strength managed to tame her, and given the time it took to lead her back to the wagon, he was relieved to find Merchant already there, bent over his supplies and looking for something.

"What are you doing?"

"Need something," Merchant said as he tossed out baskets of trotters with abandon.

Osric bristled. "Whatever it is, leave it. You've made good gold."

"You don't understand," Merchant said through hard breaths. "Here," he snarled, standing and throwing the saddle to Osric, who caught it. He'd only half strapped it onto Belle when the sound of wood clanking against the ground made him turn. Merchant seemed to be lifting up boards from the wagon.

Fearing his client had gone mad with panic, Osric leaped onto the wagon, intending to wrestle his charge back to the ground. Salt lay everywhere, trotters scattered, and there was a newly exposed compartment filled with little jars. Jars with a bruised paste – with prepared marrow.

Osric didn't care about the drug, but he did care about the deceit.

"You lied to me."

Merchant ignored the accusation and started shoving jars into a saddle bag. "Do you need your information or not?"

Osric did, so he returned to Belle to secure the saddle.

The fighting grew louder from the west and north. People were screaming now, and scourge shrilled gleefully between baleful deep roars. Something extremely heavy caused tremors in the ground as it pounded about, smashing through brick and wood.

Yet Blackhollow was not without defenses. Bells clanged across the town. More black-hooded Crows rushed past, their ranks tight, shields raised, and spears held high. Others wielded crossbows, then the locals came out with knives, axes, scythes, or pitchforks, the women too with clubs, kitchen pans, and a few with bows.

A whistling bolt rushed out of sight, and a stinger crashed down.

Osric finished with Belle's saddle, and Merchant mounted her from the other side as Osric backed away to look for his dragon.

"Come out. You've got to run beside me. I can't carry you and fight."

She slithered out from under the wagon, tail shaking.

Osric dropped to her level. *"This is a time to be brave. Use your magic like you did on that rider we fought."*

She nodded, though her tail continued to tremble.

The ring of drawn steel made Osric whirl about, but it turned out to be Merchant, holding a sword aloft, a sudden fire in his eyes.

"The east gate," he said, then he pressed into Belle's flanks with his heels, leaned forward, and with a snort, she charged ahead.

"Come on," Osric called to the dragon as he set off after his client. He heard her scampering behind him but powered on ahead, fast now, catching up to Belle, then overtaking her as the increasingly crowded press slowed her pace.

He tried to clear the way, roaring to part the crowd, cut down shambling ghouls, and caught a hapless Wyrm Cloak unawares, but soon the clog of the panic and fight brought them to a crawl.

Belle's terrified cries marked the progress of his client when he lost sight of Merchant.

Osric felt the dragon slither and writhe, knowing where she was like an extension of his own body. A burst of fuzzy black blew a ghoul clean off its feet, and pride burned inside him.

He drew some of her shadowy power across their bond and began cycling it down the worn-out channels of his right arm. A fight was no time to ponder over the pain nor question his worthiness of power. A fight was about life or death.

He tried to form a basic ability upon his stump, but the channels there were damaged and lacked the nuanced weavings of a hand. The dark magic left his stump as a spray of shadow, achieving little and allowing his targeted ghoul a chance to catch a townsperson in its bony fingers.

Cursing, he fought on, wielding Vengeance with his left hand and swinging his useless right arm like a club. Brawn, skill, and luck would decide this, just as it ought to.

Merchant rode and fought from horseback as though born to do so, handling a steed clearly untrained for battle with astonishing skill. Perhaps the black dragon gave Belle some courage as they shouldered through the throng side by side.

A small flayer burst out from an alleyway. Osric yelled as he dropped to avoid its scything arms, cut through its leg, and rose again to bring his axe down hard through its crunchy torso. Stone cracked where he struck through to the road, and the flayer's arms thrashed as it died, catching his right arm.

With a snarl, he backed away, a thin slice along his forearm oozing blood. The burn of it took him to that heightened state that only battle could bring him to, where the world around him seemed to slow and his axes ran red. When the monster came out.

Osric spotted a fallen black-hooded Crow, leaped to the dead man's side, stepped on the lip of his fallen shield to raise it, then rammed his stump through the open arm strap. He raised the shield. Its light weight felt less secure on his forearm than the metal gate hinge, but it was better than nothing.

He put the shield to work, deflecting a halberd thrust from a

Wyrm Cloak and pushing the weapon aside, then moved in, cleaving with his axe. The cultist's shock that Osric could cut through the heavy hide of his cloak was etched onto his face as he died.

Osric roared again, harder now, breaths rasping in his chest, blood thundering between his ears.

Then panic. He felt the dragon straying too far from him, her heart racing hard enough to break a rib.

"Come to me," he said, spinning to find her. Merchant raced past him, taking advantage of a gap in the throng, yelling his own battle cry as the dragon lurched out from a shadow and headed toward Osric.

Then came an explosion of wood and stone. The sound caught up with Osric a moment later. The inn had to have been some distance behind them, but now it rained upon Blackhollow in pieces.

A hideous, deep roar cut across the town.

Over their bond, a chilling fear swelled in the black dragon, a shared terror of the hatchlings of Windshear Hold.

Then Osric saw him. The stocky ginger bruiser climbed the mound of rubble that had been the inn and bellowed to mark his conquest of the town. To call him a hatchling anymore was nonsense. He'd grown larger than Ash in a shorter space of time, his muscles rippling under taut auburn scales. He raised his neck high to roar again when a ballista bolt tore across his throat, spraying a fountain of dark blood.

Osric almost failed to handle an approaching ghoul out of shock. After dispatching the enemy, he looked up to see the ginger terror wobble on the ruins, swaying. But then, somehow, impossibly, his throat resealed, the scales reformed – good as new. He turned his attention to the ballista team and leaped, covering the vast distance in a single bound and landing in a thunderous crash that shook the earth.

His dragon's heart still pumped furiously, but her breath had stilled; for a moment, she forgot how to breathe, then she dived inside his shadow.

Osric returned to the flight, to the escape, the dragon now a dead weight at his side.

"Get out," he urged her, legs pumping hard to catch up to Merchant.

He shouldn't have left them alone even for a second. His instincts screamed at him that something was amiss. Then he realized what. Belle moved awkwardly, her steps slow, then she jerked to a halt, fell, and threw Merchant from her back. He landed better than most, scrambled up, and retrieved his sword just as Osric reached him.

"Keep moving," Osric said.

"No," Merchant said hoarsely.

Osric meant to grab him, but his dragon's weight made him miscalculate, and Merchant proved more agile than he'd expected, displaying a burst of strength and speed as he cut his way back to Belle's side.

Osric growled, lurched after him, grabbed the man by the scruff of the neck, and hauled him up, kicking and screaming,

"She's not dead! Her leg is fine. She can move."

Still holding him, Osric glanced at the horse. No leg appeared broken and there was no serious wound, yet her eyes blinked slowly, and she seemed to slip in and out of consciousness.

"You're strong, Soldier," Merchant cried. "Pick her up. Pick her up!"

As more ghouls closed in, Osric let the man go to fight them. In a quick moment after the fray, Osric bent down to Belle's side and saw the slender cut there, no more than a light graze but the smell… the smell he recognized. Wyrm Cloak poison.

Merchant knelt beside him and ran his blood-covered hands through Belle's coat as though searching for an arrow to pull out, mumbling incoherently.

"She's poisoned," Osric said. "This numbing agent can daze dragons. Her heart will seize."

Merchant tried to speak, but only spittle flew. His neck and face went purple, and he strained on the second attempt to say, "No."

"I'm sorry," Osric grunted. "Get up," he added, rising and hauling Merchant bodily to his feet again.

A red mist rose between them. Startled, Osric looked down and saw the blood on Merchant's hands bubbling and lifting away, dissipating upward upon the air. Osric followed it.

Hovering over the town was the rusty-scaled dragon, beating its wings, secure above the fighting, rivers of red mist flowing toward it.

Merchant groaned.

Osric tore his gaze from the blood dragon, shook Merchant, and dredged up the volume and tone from his days as a general.

"We cannot stay. Move it, soldier!"

The bark of such a command seemed to stir old instincts in Merchant. He gathered himself, looked at his horse, then back at Osric with watery eyes. Before turning away, he managed to say, "Please."

Osric knelt and put the poor horse out of her misery.

Better by dragon steel than by tooth or claw.

He cut the saddle bag from Belle, and Merchant seized it from him.

"It's not far now," Merchant called, a fury in him now as they fought their way to the east gate. Even a black-hooded Crow got in their way, perhaps mistaking Osric's gray cloak for a cultist one. Merchant showed no qualms about killing the man, moving on without a second thought.

They made it within sight of the east gate. It lay open and people were rushing for the escape, stampeding over anyone who fell in their way. Osric picked up what pace he could, lugging his terrified dragon along as she wriggled about in his ever-shifting shadow.

A brilliant light flashed in his periphery: yellow and radiant. More flashes came, and his dragon stopped squirming.

Her fear vanished, replaced by the rapturous joy of anticipation. Her brother was here, close by, and she had to find him.

"Not now," Osric insisted, but too late. She slid out of his shadow, then charged off down a street that curved off the main road.

A thought reached him over their bond, not quite in words but in sense and feel. She believed her brother would come with them; it was his chance to escape as well.

Osric came to a halt, and Merchant carried on, oblivious, toward the gate. Either Osric's cries didn't reach him, or he didn't heed the warning.

A choice, then. Fulfill the mission or keep her safe.

Put like that, it was no choice at all.

Osric tore after her, his sudden unencumbered speed making him feel lighter than ever on his feet. Somehow, amid the crushing chaos, no one seemed to notice that a small black dragon was weaving her way against the tide, squeaking her high roars in an effort to gain her brother's attention.

She managed to get quite far before Osric caught up to her. One-armed, he tried to turn her back around, then another flash burst farther down the road, around the bend. Even indirectly, the dazzling light made his eyes water.

Then he came. The golden hatchling, regal in his bearing, graceful in his movements, perfectly proportioned, every scale glistening. Even his roar sounded pleasing – like a symphony of deep, rich horns – as he advanced upon a tight knot of Crows with long spears.

His sister still roared for him, rearing back, flapping her wings, anything to get his attention. She got it. The golden dragon came to a halt, and when he snaked his head to face her, his noble countenance dropped to one of awed shock, and his jaw hung open.

In that moment of hesitation, the Crows did all that men in their desperate situation could. They thrust their spears at him and fired heavy crossbow bolts into his hide. One spear actually managed to draw blood that ran red and incongruous down his chest.

Osric couldn't help but be impressed at the strength of any normal man who could pierce dragon scales, young dragon or otherwise. Whoever the man was, he'd be dead in moments.

"Please," Osric pleaded with his dragon. *"We must go. This is not the place."*

But she wouldn't go. Not now. Not now her brother was hurt. He needed help.

Her twin's shock at seeing her vanished. He gripped the shaft of the offending spear between his teeth, ripped it free, then rounded on his assailants and gathered a light that would put Holt's abilities to shame.

Osric closed his eyes and used every ounce of strength to turn her head away from the blast. The screams were hideous. When Osric opened his eyes, he saw many of the Crows falling to their knees or running wild, clawing at their eyes. The golden dragon laughed, a smooth rumbling, raised a taloned foot, and swatted a blinded foe.

The black dragon fell quiet at once. Osric feared her heart broken and too stricken to move, but the stillness emanating from her was a seething one. It was also one of disbelief, but she was more ready to run than ever he'd felt.

They fled, and she now dashed ahead of him. Back at the east gate, the fleeing tide had been blocked by two Wyrm Cloaks cutting down any who tried to run past them.

Osric and his dragon pushed through, and she unleashed a coiled ball of her black breath without hesitation, launching it at the closest cultist. The Wyrm Cloak saw the attack, tried to raise his cloak in time to block it, but failed, and her magic struck him full in the chest. The man stumbled back a pace but was otherwise unharmed.

Considering her attack had interfered with a Champion at Silt Grave, that didn't seem right to Osric, but he had no time to ponder it. Cold dragon steel would make up for magic's uncertainty.

The cultist saw him and tried to fumble with something in the lining of his cloak, but he was much too slow. Osric rammed his shield into the man's throat, enjoyed the choked gag of a crushed windpipe, then split the man from shoulder to waist, driving his axe through dragon-hide cloak and all.

A woman's battle cry morphed into an unnaturally deep tone. The second cultist.

Osric turned and blocked her sword with his axe, but it was

all he could do to hold her in place. Her eyes bulged, and a trickle of blood rolled down her chin. The blood elixir began to take its full effect on her, and she grew, first taller, then thicker and stronger as her dragon-hide cloak struggled to contain her.

She brought her free arm down, and Osric met the swelling hand with his shield. Meaty fingers crept over the edge, then started to curl in, breaking the wood. Osric pulled his arm free of the shield's strap just in time before she crushed it to splinters.

Now without any defense, he faced the massive cultist. Osric spun his axe up and considered his last hope to be throwing it into her grotesque body. She bellowed like a juggernaut, then the very world around her seemed to rip apart – dark tears formed in the air, void of light, void of anything – and a shadow fell across her body. A moment later, she gasped, swayed, collapsed. A round exit hole burned in her side where the magic had passed right through her cloak.

Behind the cultist, within the shadow of the gatehouse, the black dragon seemed to float unsupported, her hind legs, body, and tail submerged in shadow, but her head was exposed, and a fuzzy smoke trailed from her mouth. Seeing and sensing he wasn't injured, she emerged and bolted out of Blackhollow.

Wordless, Osric followed her.

There was still danger outside the town walls, just less of it. No Wyrm Cloaks, but wayward ghouls fell upon tired or injured victims. Osric killed each one he came across as he called and searched for Merchant.

They found him someway from Blackhollow, doubled over with his hands pressed against his belly and blood seeping between his fingers.

The black dragon made it clear she would stand guard, and for once, Osric trusted her to do just that while he bent to Merchant's side.

"I didn't see you fall behind," Merchant struggled to say. "When I did, I... thought... dead."

"Hush," Osric said. He parted Merchant's icy hands to inspect the wound. He could honestly say he'd seen worse in his time and only cursed that he lacked proper field treatments.

The sleeves of Merchant's shirt were of decent linen, so he tore those, padded them up, and pressed them against the man's belly. Merchant groaned and managed to place a hand on top of Osric's. His face was ashen and gleaming with sweat.

"I can hold it," Merchant said, and with his free hand, he brought the saddle bag onto his torso. Through it all, he had clung onto it.

"This will hurt," Osric said as he scooped Merchant up and started running, running east, with a dying man between his arms and a black dragon at his side. She ran the whole way. Not once did she yearn to hide in his shadow.

24

IN SEARCH OF ANSWERS

Daylight glittered, and he tasted fresh air. Rake staggered out of the fissure in the rock, stumbled, caught a foot on his cloak, fell, and rolled, though luckily not far. He came to a halt on hard earth and rested on his side.

Much of his power had been spent, and he'd regained little enough to begin with.

He coughed, trying to shift the dust coating the back of his throat. The convulsion sent a shuddering pain down the back of his head.

He was parched. Very likely lost.

But he was alive.

And what a rush it had been.

Right, where are we, Elya?

A bird cheeped not far away. Another answered. Water burbled close by, and a cool breeze tickled the end of his snout. He sniffed and was relieved to find the scent of cool grass rather than the rot of the tunnels.

With an effort, he pushed himself up. Glass tinkled from inside his cloak, and he closed his eyes at the thought of the lost elixirs. Sitting upright, his tail sat limp between his legs, not even threatening a twitch of its usual energy.

He found his polearm lying beside him. It must have fallen from his grip during his fall. Around half a foot of the shaft had broken off from the bottom and much of the wood was scratched, but otherwise, it was miraculously intact. Either Aberanth was an even greater worker of marvels than they knew, or Rake had more luck than seemed fair. More likely than not, it was both.

Rake tried to gauge his surroundings. This shallow ravine must have been an old chasm. Since it had been sealed, a thin stream had wound its way through the center of it, taking the gentle incline to its journey's end. The rock, the trees, the birdsong, and the strength of the sun and the wind could have placed him anywhere west of Athra and north of Brenin. Risalia seemed most likely, but at present, he had no idea where he was. Nor could he entirely recall how he'd managed to escape the chamber in the first place.

The last thing he truly remembered was seeing Holt go through one of the tunnel archways. All else was a blur, save for maintaining a Barrier overhead to shield him from the cave-in and Blinking through gaps before they closed. His mote channels still ached from the use of it. And after all that, just darkness. Endless darkness.

How he'd longed for Holt and Ash by his side as he'd struggled blindly through it. Where were they now?

With another effort, Rake got to his feet. His legs shook, but he used his talons to brace himself against the earth. The soft breeze in the ravine cut right through his cloak, then he discovered rips in the fabric and such a layer of dust and dirt that he might never beat it out.

He expected a pulse from Elya. She had ever abhorred tattiness on clothing.

No pulse came.

Rake gulped and clutched at his chest. Without Holt around, he felt easier about doing so.

You're not dead. You are NOT dead.

No taps, no twinge, no nothing.

Whatever happened to you, I promise Thrall will pay for it.

His fury at the dragon burned fresh life into him. Rake twisted this way then that, his polearm raised, as though Thrall might be behind a turning of the ravine. Growling, Rake looked back to see where he'd emerged.

The fissure in the ravine wall had been just wide enough for him to slip free. Humans or ghouls could pass through it, but nothing larger. He'd come across many cracks in the rock like this, as though the underground passages had suffered the same as his ripped cloak. The whole world had seemed to shake as he'd stumbled blindly. He remembered that now, too.

For a moment, the voice of the creature returned to him. He winced, then clenched his jaw and involuntarily curled his tail. Just the memory of that voice felt like nails scratching along his spine. During his tenure as a rider, he'd heard the legends of whispers in the deep places, but he'd never imagined a voice could contain such hunger.

His own stomach curdled and tightened. He hadn't felt so hungry since his confinement at Windshear Hold.

Unable to fight back the desire for food and water, Rake set off, following the trickling stream in the hope it would lead to a source of water. It was almost nightfall when his wandering paid off and the stream joined a larger river.

Rake bent by its bank, then lowered his whole head and drank from the crystal blue waters, scooping it up with his tongue as much as he gulped it down. He emerged a few moments later, gasping as the icy touch of the water settled his gut and cleared his head.

A little chagrined, he cupped his hands to take his next drink – he wasn't such a beast yet as to drink like one.

Food was another matter. He'd come across no signs of a deer, rabbit, or any other woodland creature. Given his heavy steps and lack of care, he'd likely scared everything off.

A bird squawked. Rake craned his neck to search for it in the dense branches of the spruce trees. More birds cawed and rustled, thinking themselves secure in their high nests.

Rake considered it, then decided no. Birds were very rarely worth the effort of catching. There was little meat to them, and they tasted foul to him; tough, bitter, and stringy. His chief desire was for one of Holt's stews.

The thought of Holt, then of Ash, twisted his guts again, and he dipped his whole head back into the icy river. When he emerged, he sat dripping for a time until a need for action came over him. He took off his cloak to wash it and began by emptying its pockets. As expected, he found smashed glass where he'd been storing his elixirs, but his pieces of flint to start fires with were still with him. He beat the cloak in the air like a bed sheet, letting the glass fly free from the open pockets, then washed the material.

By the time he'd hung his cloak over two spruce branches and started a small fire, the stars were beginning to stir in the night sky. Rake lay down and gazed at them. The whole world might have changed beyond recognition during his life, but the stars had not.

Reading the stars, he discovered he'd gone farther north than he'd realized and didn't think he could still be in Risalia. Fornheim seemed more likely now.

Could Holt and Ash have emerged close by too? They could be anywhere. Rake didn't contemplate them being dead, not least because it would do no good to despair like that. If they were dead, then there was nothing to be done. If they were trapped underground, he'd never find them. Besides, he'd seen them get out of the chamber. The rest would be easy for them. So, they were alive. They *had* to be alive. And if they made it out, he was certain they'd return to Sidastra. Holt could be counted on to report back to Talia.

Feeling parched again, Rake crawled to the river and drank his fill. Once back by his little fire and settled under his cloak, he soon fell asleep.

Yet his rest wasn't peaceful. The voice of the Hive Mind seemed ever just behind him, biting at his tail, and try as he might, Rake couldn't outpace it. Going deeper and deeper underground, he was unable to flee, and the world shook and collapsed around him.

He woke feeling no better for the sleep. His eyes felt coarse and heavy inside his skull, though his hanging cloak blocked the worst of the morning sun, for which he was grateful.

He lay there, his thoughts consumed by the Hive Mind.

Back when Rake had trained to advance through the early ranks, the riders had still fought in tunnels close to the surface, but they were always ordered to hold back, to go only so far.

The reasons given seemed straightforward. A rider could only delve so far before losing their connection to their dragon, but even with restraints in place, Rake had known some who dared to delve deeper, seeking glory, sometimes never to return or, if they did, to return changed. A prolonged darkening of the bond served to explain this change, which was why Rake had put Holt and Ash into the tunnels under Ahar together. Perhaps they had come closer to doom down there than any of them would care to know.

The creature's existence answered why the Paragons had ceased such training, but it raised far more questions. Just what exactly was it? Did the Paragons understand what they faced? Rake didn't think so, for even as an Exalted Mystic Lord, he hadn't been made privy to knowledge of the creature. Was it a secret kept only by the Paragons? If so, for how long? Moreover, how had it purposefully collapsed that chamber?

Never in Rake's long life had any scourge shown a hint of magic beyond their own crude forms of death and decay. What the Hive Mind had done carried the distinct impression of power over the rock and earth: of emerald magic.

Everyone – from Paragon to Elder – had overlooked the true nature of the threat from below for too long. Everyone, including Rake, had allowed themselves to be willfully blind.

That couldn't continue a day longer.

They had to know what they faced.

Rake pushed himself up and faced northeast. The last they knew of the Life Elder, he was somewhere in the Spine. He would want to know of the creature's power, and if anyone had insight, it would be him.

A part of him protested at the notion. What about Holt and Ash?

Rake pondered it, then, making his decision, he stood, picked his cloak off the branches, wrapped it around himself, hefted his polearm, and began heading north.

Holt and Ash wouldn't need him to report to Talia. And though it might be a touch cruel to leave them thinking he was dead, it might be beneficial in its own way. They needed space to grow on their own. If he were around, they would remain dependent on him, and there was nothing he could do to guide Holt's spiritual development or the next revelations of ranking.

Besides, he added for his own reassurance, if they sought the Fire Elder or Storm Elder as per their great quest, Rake would only slow them down. Especially if they sought Fire. That would demand they find a ship for Rake, which seemed a needless complication.

Yes, he decided, picking up his pace. Holt and Ash were better alone for a time. And if they couldn't develop on their own, they would never make it far enough to help him anyway.

After a day of travel, Rake came across the first signs of civilization; a series of compact farms with wide pastures and a walled town beyond. The walls were thicker than most, and even this small settlement had strong square towers, which told him he was already in Fornheim.

To his delight, one of the farms kept a flock of sheep.

Rake stole a ewe in the night.

He still had his flint, and a few scrapes of his talons would spark a fire, but finding firewood would take time. Then the cooking would take time. And he was starving.

After finishing, he washed his face, picked the wool from his teeth, then moved quickly on. He never liked to linger after such a meal. Even hundreds of years hadn't fully adjusted him to his dragon aspects. Fresh blood tasted too strong for his liking, yet his body warmed in satisfaction upon receiving it.

Sometimes he'd done it so Elya could experience something of the sensation, yet even that was taken from him now.

Being close to a settlement, he found a road and followed it, keeping to the wilds but never straying too far. The road slanted eastward, and before long, he received final confirmation of where he was. What must have been the westernmost slopes of the Spine began to dominate the landscape, yet one rose above all the rest.

The Western Fang, a mountain rising from mountains, its peak beyond sight.

Built into its base was a fortress lacking any comparison. Vardguard was its name. In its prime, it had kept watch on the borders between the old Skarl Empire and the Aldunei Republic, throwing back legion after legion, never once falling to assault or siege.

Though Rake skirted the Fang and the fortress from leagues away, both anchored his journey for days until he reached the northern side of the Fang and Vardguard at last disappeared behind a keen edge of a lower mountain. From there, Rake struck east as directly as he could, ascending higher and higher as he made his way into the Spine.

The moment he set foot into the range, a feeling of unease came over him. It wasn't magical or spiritual, nothing he could measure, but it was there, like the unsettling nerves of being watched.

A world of evergreens below snowcapped summits greeted him. Two sorts of mountains seemed to exist in the Spine: those so pristine in appearance they seemed sculpted and painted by hand, and those seemingly dragged in protest from the earth, all rugged black rock that seemed to repel the snow no matter how high they rose.

His breathing was labored at first, but within a day, his lungs adjusted to the thinner air. Few realized how elevated the range was from a map. Another thing the maps never truly captured was how wide the span of the mountains was. To look at most maps, one might think someone could stand on a middling summit and behold both Frost Fangs at once. While a beautiful thought, from no such place could it be done. The Spine was much too large for that.

With more water and better sleep, Rake began running again. When he took rest, he spent time Cleansing his core, but without companions, there was precious little in the way of mystic motes to Forge in the wilderness. The ambient hum generated by the minds of birds, small mammals, and beasts was poor fare, yet Rake had learned to make the most of it.

Something was a lot better than nothing.

He was ready to turn due north and head for the Northern Grove of the Emerald Flight when a core entered his magical perceptions. The rider was still far away and would not sense Rake, so he paid them little mind, except to assume he was closer to the Order Hall of Sky Spear than he'd thought.

As he traveled, he took the opportunity to face south when he saw a gap between the distant, descending peaks. Perhaps he was imagining it, but he swore the thin blue outline of the impossibly tall tower was there. Sky Spear guarded the south of the Spine, while White Watch guarded the far north, where the living lands met the White Wilderness. Of the two, Sky Spear was many times larger.

Rake moved on, keeping to his course and going deeper into the center of the range. Two days later, the uneasy feeling within the Spine intensified. His sixth sense filled with the echoes of magic ringing down from the north. He picked up his pace, and now something like grief carried on the wailing air: it tasted of death and was laden with the bitter smell of smoke.

The feeling grew and grew until it became a weight in Rake's perceptions.

The world was screaming.

Something terrible had happened.

Rake came upon a charred and ruined valley. In his shock, he almost lost his grip on his polearm.

The forests were gone, either burnt, flattened, or a ruin of splintered trunks. An unnatural line of battered, leafless trees lay in a great circle at the valley's heart. Not a scrap of land was unscathed, and there were dozens of dragon bodies in all colors.

It could only have been a battle, and the Emerald Flight had been involved. That there was emerald power here was unmistakable. Even a Fire Novice could have felt it. But there was something else, even above the usual hum of scourge magic, that chilled him.

As he sensed no other cores, Rake moved into the valley to

investigate. Most of the bodies he took for dragons turned out to be scourge-risen ones. A second death was final. They were unsightly, but they could do no more damage now.

Thrall must have sent those; such a force of scourge-risen dragons must have accounted for the bulk of his strength. Precious few dragon corpses were ever left unattended to, so Thrall must have gathered these carefully over decades, perhaps longer. Throwing them into a battle was no small decision. Could it have been a final, desperate stand?

Even Rake's optimism couldn't stretch that far. The unease he'd felt – even as a mystic – since entering the Spine, the pain of the world, did not speak of good news.

Indeed, the more he checked the bodies, the more he began to fear. Only a small number were regular emeralds, and those were broken or maimed beyond hope of rising again. Those bodies had torn tails, shredded wings, broken necks, or missing heads. On all sides, chipped talons and teeth were scattered, marking such a dragon-on-dragon battle as Rake had never heard of before.

Yet there were no signs of burned bodies, nor burial sites in the emerald tradition –no mounds of earth and no new saplings. Those members of the Emerald Flight who had fallen here were simply gone, as though they had gotten up and moved of their own accord.

As Rake neared the strange, massive ring of broken trees, the weight of magical power became immense. Spiritual power wove around it, wills of such strength that their echoes retained their potency long after the battle had ended.

The Elder was here, Rake thought grimly.

The longer he bathed in the remnants of his power, the more he began to recognize the Elder's notes – and those of Thrall.

Morbid curiosity brought him to the center of the great circle, where he imagined the Life Elder and his Wardens standing firm until the bitter end.

Just past the center, the ground turned so cold that his foot seemed to burn. He gasped, stepped back, then lowered himself to a squat and found the grass in the offending area gripped by frost. Here, too, the magical power was enormous. Rake Floated his mote channels, then, very carefully, pressed a finger onto the freezing soil.

The punch of cold seemed to snap the bones at the back of his head. A high, cracking, ethereal drone rang between his ears, setting his teeth on edge.

He pulled away from the remnant ice magic, his head spinning with new questions. Had one or more Ice Wardens also fought here? If so, why was their power only imparted into such a small area? Had they, too, been killed and risen again?

He started running again, returning to his northern route, intending to leave this valley of death as quickly as he could. Somehow, the timing of this battle alongside his own misfortune underground seemed too close for coincidence.

The Life Elder and his surviving emeralds would have returned to their grove in the wake of the battle. The Elder would have answers.

25

FREYA'S TALE

Talia stared at the lockbox on her desk and swore it stared back in challenge.

"We found it atop his bed in plain view—" The pause in Eadwulf's speech remained, but this time he did not look sideways for his brother. "We searched his chambers... but found nothing else of note."

Talia pulled the lockbox closer to her. "And as for investigating where he is?"

"The trail goes cold at Port Bolca... Witness accounts are conflicting."

"Keep searching."

Eadwulf bowed, then turned with a swirl of his red cloak and left.

Now alone in her office, Talia took out the household keys Fynn had given her during their sword rites. There were three on the oversized ring, and the smallest fitted snugly into the lock and turned with a click. Scraps of paper and parchment were piled inside. The top one bore a message in Fynn's hand.

You go to fight where you must, and I do the same. I'm sorry.

. . .

She wanted to feel angry with him, but it did not rise in her.

Talia let the paper fall to the desk and lifted the next sheet. This one had torn edges and was written in a hand she didn't recognize. At first glance, it seemed to be gibberish, but then she realized it was in Skarl. Talia cursed. Her attempts to learn the language had been slow going. Frowning, she tried to read what she could.

They... cracked... assures – no, not assures but something like that – taken...

Damnit!

Frustrated, she dropped the paper back into the chest and locked it again.

Within the hour, the Mistress of Coin was sitting opposite her, scribbling out a translation. Talia paced then near enough snatched the translation out of Elvina's hand when she finished it.

They broke the rebels and are heading for us. He promised we won't be taken alive. I love you, I love you, I love you. Farewell.

Talia's mouth turned dry.

Pyra took notice. Warm, reassuring fire crossed the bond.

"I'm scared, girl," Talia told her.

She felt Elvina studying her reaction. As usual, Elvina's gown was crisp, her golden hair straight and perfect, her skin radiant. Everything about her was immaculate.

"Are you okay, Talia?"

Dazed, Talia returned to her desk and leaned over the stack. Were they all from Freya? Had Fynn made copies of his replies? Should she take Pyra and fly after him now, or would she find some plan within the correspondence?

"Talia?"

"I need to read them all," she said stiffly.

She met Elvina's piercing blue eyes and was glad they no longer made her self-conscious. Perhaps it was their familial resemblance to Drefan's. A jolt of old prejudice and rivalry shot through her then. She missed a Harroway? What a blighted thought.

"Can I trust in your discretion?"

Elvina dipped her quill into the ink well. "The contents won't leave this room."

"Good," Talia said, already heading for the door. "I must speak with the Flight Commander. And Elvina," she added, looking back. "Thank you."

Talia found Ethel in the mess of the New Order's tower. Ethel stood upon a slab of ice high off the ground, hanging Ramos's red blade upon the wall. When she hopped down, she didn't seem surprised to find Talia there.

"What's wrong?"

"Do I always bring such gloom?"

"You're a queen, Talia. I wouldn't expect happy news as Flight Commander." She picked up Isak's blue sword and sighed. "It shouldn't matter, but it's always worse when it's one of your own. He asked to be sent on patrol through the empire because he missed the snows… but I wanted him closer to train him."

With a sad shake of her head, she went to hang Isak's sword on the Ascendant row, then jumped back down.

"So, what's wrong?"

"It's the King. I think he's got himself into danger. As it could impact the Skarl alliance, I thought the Order ought to know."

"Are you alright?" Ethel asked, more kindly than a Flight Commander might.

Talia looked at a spot just over Ethel's shoulder. "I'm fine. I shouldn't jump to conclusions yet. Whatever happens, I can always reforge the alliance with a second marriage, so you needn't worry."

Ethel gave her a pitiful look. "You don't have to be the Red Queen when it's just the two of us."

"I didn't think you'd care for the fate of a king, being a rider and all."

"I care about you." She bit her lip, then busied herself by picking up another of the fallen swords, this one plain steel. It had belonged to the Novice, Cynnflaed.

"May I?" Talia asked. When Ethel laid the cold sword into Talia's open hands, she saw again the flayer ripping into Cynnflaed across the bog. "I saw it happen, but there was nothing I could have done."

"I was the one who called the Novices to fight." There was ice in Ethel's voice again. "You two were of an age. Did you know her?"

"Not well."

Cynnflaed had been from the Hiott family in the East Weald near the land border with Brenin. Talia recalled a visit from the Hiotts during her youth when she hadn't treated Cynnflaed well, all from simple jealousy. As a third daughter, Cynnflaed was to be a rider, and no one tried to stop her.

"I think we might have been related," Ethel said. "Though it's hard to keep track after so long."

Talia supposed she could ask Ealdor Hubbard to inspect the family trees. Ethel had come from the Cawthorne family, wedged in the forested lands between the Hiotts and the Horndowns.

"Lesson one," Ethel said.

"Lesson one," Talia repeated.

Ethel conjured stairs for Talia, and she went to hang Cynnflaed's blade on the wall. Alongside the dragon steel swords, it looked like a child's weapon. Talia drew in sharp breaths from the cold underfoot before jumping down.

There was a final green blade to hang: thick, broad, with a slanted tip. Brode's sword. Talia's jaw dropped.

"Courtesy of Holt," Ethel said. "If you don't mind, I'd like to be the one to hang it."

"Of course."

Talia waited while Ethel placed Brode's sword in pride of place. A worthy honor for Brode's role in Feorlen's survival. Holt had taken Brode's death a lot harder than her at the time, but now she realized she missed the old grouch more than she'd thought.

The feeling was strong enough to cross her bond.

"Master Brode would be proud of us."

"You think? After becoming what he feared?"

"We fight the scourge and save lives. He cared about that most of all."

Ethel dropped down. "If that's all, Red Queen?"

Talia turned to leave, then stopped. "May I ask the Flight Commander for advice? As a rider."

Ethel nodded.

"In the Morass, Pyra and I both felt… weaker. I'm a Champion now, and Pyra's core is richer than ever, but I didn't feel half as strong as when we fought in the tunnels under the Withering Woods. We've been trying to control the anger of our fire since then, but I fear that's holding us back."

Ethel considered her words carefully. "Perhaps it only feels that way now you're not letting the fire rule you."

"It's not just in my head," Talia said in a rush. "I'm sure that hybrid scourge with the core wasn't stronger than an Ascendant, but I struggled to keep up with it, even while Grounding, and it pulled me clean off my feet and met my abilities head-on. I try to maintain my training. I do. But it can be hard—"

Ethel raised her hand. "Magic and advancement should be the concern of riders with only one thing in mind. You have half a hundred at once. But I know you won't take that for an answer."

A practiced touch then inspected Talia's bond. She held her breath, waiting for the ill pronouncement.

"I sense nothing wrong," Ethel said. "In fact, your bond feels sturdier than when I met you."

"Bonds are one thing, magical power another. Strang's core is more than four times the density of Pyra's."

"Strang and I have had more than four times as long to build that core. I'm afraid I can't offer deeper insights into fire. You'll harness the rage in time. Others do. There's no rush. That could damage your mote channels or cripple your soul."

Rushing hasn't hurt Holt and Ash, she thought. Across their bond, Pyra snarled. Fire entered Talia, and she cycled it to her head to burn off on her circlet.

Talia stiffened. "A final question, if I may? What helped you with your spirit? You were a High Champion for a long time."

"Ah, if there were easy answers, we'd all become Lords and Ladies. I think how you act matters as much as how you think. If you do something you know in your heart isn't true to yourself, you may as well tie an anchor around your neck. I always felt the riders should be doing more than we were, so when Adaskar questioned my loyalties one too many times and you offered a new path, I felt more aligned than I had in decades. All the thinking in the world won't help if you act spuriously."

Talia inclined her head. "Thank you, Commander. I will meditate on this."

By the time Talia returned to her office, it was well into the night. Even so, she found Elvina still there, rubbing at her eyes by candlelight. Talia insisted she rest and start afresh on the morrow. Then, by that same candlelight, Talia selected the first of Freya's letters and began to read.

'The songbird weeps.' Really? That's the gloomiest code phrase we have. Please tell me you haven't become a blubbering mess now I'm not around?

Talia reached for the second.

You can still take a teasing, that's good. Fine, I admit I wept a little, but no one here will ever see that. Not even the great Tubbs, as I call him. A more stuck-in-the-past, gray-bearded old goat I've never met. Well, his face is goatish, but his body is swinish. He's fat, in case that wasn't clear.

Talia snickered, which somehow felt wrong in the circumstances. But then, why not laugh? Freya had made light of a bad situation.

The rest of the letters carried on in a similar manner. Fynn's replies were missing, but reading between the lines, Talia gathered that a network of singers, bards, and likely some unsavory figures ran the messages between them. Given the difficulty and distances to overcome, the letters were infrequent and quite short.

Their brevity must have been hard on Fynn. Talia only had to imagine how it would feel to hear from Pyra once a month and then only briefly, and her heart hurt just thinking about it.

I still sing, though I keep it low. I don't like the idea of them hearing me. My voice lured a prince through the palace halls once, but I think I'd only attract roaches in this drafty castle. Sometimes I take to the shore and sing to the sea. The guards don't stick so close there. Sometimes that helps.

Talia re-read this letter several times, moved by the first chink in Freya's otherwise high-spirited armor. A pressure mounted behind her eyes. Reading by candlelight could strain even a rider's eyes.

As Elvina still had most of the stack to work on, Talia left the tale there for now.

The following days came with some good news. First, Turro and a contingent of younger emeralds arrived on the shores of Lake Luriel. Though the West Warden was struck down with grief and their flight was in disarray, they still wished to assist the New Order.

Next came envoys from Laone with full pomp and ceremony. They knelt and offered Talia gifts of lilies – yellow, pink, red, orange, and many the purest white of her uncle's sigil. With the scourge in the Morass neutralized, the southern barons were rallying to King Roland's banner. His intention was to muster forces and march against the Stricken Souls raiding down the Versand.

Less pleasing was the news that pirates still plagued their trading fleets.

"The odds aren't natural," Elvina commented as she selected another letter. "These so-called pirates have a diet of only Brenin, Feorlen, and Skarl ships."

"In normal times," Talia said, "one would appeal to Mithras to guard the Stretched Sea. I fear they won't consider this an issue."

Elvina tsked. "Some oily-haired port master in Mithras is likely counting our coins right now."

"At least the land routes with Brenin will pick up," Talia said, determined to find a positive. With the King missing and a fallen Elder, she had to cling to anything positive as an escape. Perhaps that was why she found herself drawn to Freya's letters. They were an escape, of sorts, and a window into Fynn as much as Freya.

Sidastra, is it? You poor thing! How will you sleep somewhere so warm? At least we'll be closer with you there than in Smidgar. I've never met a Feorlen – what are they like?

Letters from Fynn's early days in Feorlen didn't mention Talia at all, not even by a veiled name or a pointedly written 'her.' Whether it was because Freya didn't want to know or Fynn didn't want to tell, Talia was glad to be left out of it, though the subject came perilously close to being breached in one letter dated in the late fall of the previous year.

No. No, no, no, a hundred times over. You will tell me everything about the wedding, Fynn Skadison. We never had a proper one, and I should like to picture myself there with you. I need some cheer. They are grim here. All Jarl Tubbs bleats about is how your mother wronged him. The fact his side lost the war doesn't seem to penetrate his thick skull.

· · ·

Even her High Council meetings became dominated by news of Stroef. During one urgent meeting, the Mistress of Embassy stood stern-faced as she announced, "The Blood Bards have laid siege to Stroef rather than assault it."

Ealdor Horndown slammed his bear-like hand upon the table. "So much for the ferocity of the Skarl warbands. What's caused this delay?"

"I don't know." Ida pursed her lips as if a foul smell lingered under her nose. "Oddvar was evasive."

"To be evasive is half his role," said Ealdor Hubbard. "Like as not, the Skarls are embarrassed that their bold predictions did not come to fruition. A siege will drag this conflict on far longer." He wheezed, then cleared his throat. "If the Skarls cannot be counted on, mayhaps it's time to consider reopening negotiations with Archduke Conrad."

Ida's expression turned grim. "All diplomatic channels have gone cold. Given our Master of War reports giant trebuchets are being built, I fear we're past the point of talking."

"So," Horndown boomed, "we're just to sit around and be choked by land and sea?"

"What we mustn't do is give Conrad any excuse," Elvina said.

On and on they spoke, though Talia found the words became a babble as her mind became consumed by thoughts of Fjarrhaf, of Stroef, imaging dark walls and dark minds within. Of Freya. Of Fynn.

Elvina caught her eye, and they exchanged a knowing look.

Something had to give. The contours of an idea made themselves known to her, then Talia stood, pushing her chair back with a scraping screech, and the High Council fell silent.

"There is something that might be done," Talia said, "though it will take a great deal of tact. And no small measure of luck."

When Talia entered the mess hall of the New Order again, she found the riders presiding over the crumbs of their dinner. An empty Lords table served as a stark reminder of their vulnerability, and Novices sat shoulder to shoulder with Champions.

The hanging weapons reminded them of their losses, but some good had come of the Morass fight. One Novice had become an Ascendant. That was Ulf, a mystic rider from Upsar, where the Reaving River emptied into the Bitter Bay. Yax, a rider from Lakara, had also stepped up from Emerald Ascendant to Champion.

"Champion Talia," Ethel called as she approached. "We would be pleased for you to join us. Do you require food?"

"Thank you, but I'm not hungry."

Alvah and Kamal greeted her with eager smiles. They shuffled apart to create a spot for her on the bench, and Talia sat down between them. Kamal looked like a younger version of Adaskar, though his voice was not yet warped by smoke.

"We've just agreed," Ethel began, "that Champion Oline will lead a squadron of emerald riders and dragons to the region close to the Roaring Fjord to scout for old tunnel locations."

"A fine idea," Talia said. Oline had served at the Roaring Fjord for seventeen years and would know the area well, and as an earth rider, she was well equipped to locate long-lost chasms and ways into the depths.

Champion Druss caught her eye. Blue power crackled at his fingertips as he tapped the table. "Might we expect assistance from your friends?" he asked roughly.

That took Talia aback. She looked up and down the table, meeting as many eyes as she could before addressing them.

"So, the New Order suddenly cares about Holt and Ash?"

"Our fates were not so entwined with their deeds before," said Galasso. His bond with Liliane still felt strained from the fighting.

"They always have been," Talia said. "Everyone would do well to reflect on that. Thanks to the bravery of one pot boy and a blind dragon, we may all yet live. As it happens, they are going to seek the Elder of Fire."

The New Order muttered excitably. To her left, Alvah squeaked, and on her right, Kamal gasped.

Ensel sucked air through his teeth. "I've yet to meet a fire dragon who would be pleased to meet a cripple."

Across her dragon bond, Pyra growled. Outside, she roared loudly enough for it to be heard as a deep hum inside the hall.

"Ash bears a spiritual tag from the West Warden himself," Talia said. "That will make the Fire Flight at least stop and think."

Yax uttered a pained groan. "The Warden wrapped a piece of his own spirit around them? Them and their cold light?"

"None here should deign to question a Warden's decision," Ethel said with a hard frown, and Yax slumped on the bench. "With the Life Elder gone, we cannot overlook any aid, so let us hope for their success. But this was not why you've come, Talia. What would you have of the New Order?"

Now came the hard part.

"Advice, if you'll allow me to ask. The rebellion in Fjarhaff will drag out for far longer than expected."

Einar sat upright and seemed to drink in her every word.

"With Skadi so distracted, our enemies may perceive weakness in Feorlen and act on it. Even now, the Archduke builds great trebuchets outside the Toll Pass."

Champions Druss and Ensel both moved to speak, but it was Ensel who won the race.

"You must avert this war."

His eyes were alight with anxiety, and Talia wondered if his familial lands were close to the border.

"The Mistress of Embassy despairs at any attempts of diplomacy."

Druss beat Ensel to it this time. With a flick of his wrist, he said, "Send more troops to the fortress. Make it plain it can't be taken."

Talia screwed up her courage. Druss had presented an opening, and she took it.

"I have no more soldiers to spare." Then, standing and placing one foot on the tabletop, she went on. "But I could go."

A tense silence followed. The riders fell still, not even making a rustle, until Ensel's clenched fist hit the table, throwing up violet sparks. Words, however, eluded him.

Oline recovered first. "Champion Talia surely means that her presence will make her enemies think twice."

Ensel found his voice. "And what if they call your bluff?"

The question was unanswerable.

Shadows seemed to fall over the face of every rider.

Talia hung her head. "If I am not to go, I do not know what options remain. If Feorlen falls…"

She left the rest unsaid, but the inference was plain.

The New Order would fall with it.

"There must be something you can do," said Yax.

"Like what?" Alvah said, her sing-song voice still light despite the dour mood of the hall. "She can't conjure weapons, soldiers, and supplies out of thin air."

"Lakara has not declared against her. Seek aid from there."

"It is not your place to suggest such a thing, Champion Yax," Ethel said. The Flight Commander had grown tense; all this talk of war strategy and politics toed a dangerous line.

"For victuals and other supplies, Commander," Yax said. "I did not intend to suggest anything untoward."

"Send word to Ahar as well," suggested Kamal.

Talia pressed forward with her line of attack. "Even if we had the time for such voyages, we do not have the safety of the seas. Ships of the alliance are being hunted by pirates, and there is little we can do to counter them at present. Unless," she added with sudden haste and inspiration, and she made a point of catching Einar's eye, "our storm riders could lend their aid?"

A good deal of murmuring ensued.

Einar blinked, seemingly confused as to why Talia would direct this request at him. As he was of Skarl origins, she assumed he would be the easiest of the storm riders to sway. Lucia and Druss were Athran, after all.

"You would have us destroy these pirates for you?" Einar asked.

"I would never ask that, but might the winds be turned in favor of our ships? To speed them to safety or keep the pirates at bay?"

"Talia," Ethel said. "Einar has already been assigned to Oline's squadron to scout for tunnels."

"Even were I not," Einar said, "I would not do this. It would be an abuse of the gifts our dragons grant us. Others may twist the words of their oath further, but I hold to the meaning of their spirit. We are not to be involved in such matters."

A dead weight sank through Talia from head to stomach.

Druss stood slowly, strands of lightning crackling along the ends of his hair.

Talia braced herself for his denouncement.

"Champion Talia does not ask us to take lives but to save them," he said, his tone that of someone trying to convince themselves as much as anyone else. "Defending life is core to our oath. War will steal that as much as any incursion. Our way here cannot continue if this city and kingdom fall. Yes," he concluded, as though shocked at his own decision. "I will aid your ships."

Lucia spoke next in a firmer voice, "If Druss flies, I will too."

Talia's palms were clammy. She couldn't believe it. The Athrans would help her where the Skarl would not?

"If the Flight Commander agrees?" Druss asked.

All eyes turned to Ethel.

She set her jaw, swallowed hard, then spoke in a higher voice than usual. "As the Paragons hold votes on great matters, so too shall we. All those in favor of Druss and Lucia flying to keep civilian ships safe from harm, raise your hands."

Einar did not raise his. A few Ascendants and a Novice abstained as well, yet many more raised theirs in favor. Some slowly at first, then others joined after they observed others in agreement. Even Ensel raised his.

Talia's heart raced.

Then Ethel raised her hand too.

"The vote passes." Einar opened his mouth, but Ethel headed him off. "You have your own orders, Ascendant."

Einar bristled but sat back down.

Talia smiled, her stiff cheeks protesting from lack of use.

"Thank you," she said to Druss and Lucia. "Thank you all. Feorlen owes you an unpayable debt."

Ensel folded his arms. "I trust this means you won't go to the Toll Pass?"

A squirm ran through Talia. "If our supply lines ease, we should last until Brenin can reinforce us in the Pass. There should be no need for me to go."

"It is decided, then," Ethel said in a tone that made it clear the meeting was over. "Dismissed!" Then, in a low voice, she added, "Champion Talia, a word, please."

Talia remained behind. Once she and Ethel were alone, the Flight Commander said, "You never intended to go to the Toll Pass, did you?"

Bearing in mind the need to think and act authentically, Talia said, "Not right now."

"Hmm."

Talia braced, ready for the scolding.

"I'd say you're learning to be a real queen."

"Thank you, Flight Commander."

"I'm not sure I intended it as a compliment. Go. You still have a missing king to find."

Something fouls the air here. Jarl Tubbs and his sounder of swine have been concealed behind locked doors, not drinking for once but just talking. They summon maps, old records, and the quartermaster. I appreciate being left alone, but all the same, it worries me.

Talia put the letter down, then immediately picked up the next one, dated from sometime around the new year.

Crates upon crates have appeared. They took them to the armory. The cooks told the maids, who then told me that the deep larders are now bursting with stock.

. . .

Several letters later, the inevitable news came.

They did it. They actually DID IT. They're in open revolt, and they've actually declared THRALLDOM BE RESTORED! He told me that, as his lady, I was entitled to my pick. I said I'd sooner bathe in pig blood.

Talia questioned Elvina as to the formatting of her translation, thinking something amiss.

"I wanted to convey her emotions," Elvina replied. She handed the original to Talia. "See the ink splotches? See how heavy and thick the writing gets? Could be her hand was shaking."

From then on, Talia compared Elvina's versions to the originals. In one letter, Freya had pierced the parchment as though stabbing every period into place.

He took my threat to heart, though as I'm his lady, he could not BEFOUL his own status by having me do it. Between watching a girl drown in blood or make her my... I can barely say it, never mind write it... it was no choice. I hate it. I HATE HIM. But the girl reminds me of Margret from the foundling house; they both have that same mousey look. I know you have issues with your mother, but she can't come fast enough as far as I'm concerned.

The writing grew worse, the quillwork frantic. Freya wrote of wanting to help her slave girl – whom she named Mouse – to escape.

I did it! I got Mouse out with some silver in tow. But Sigmar punished me. This wasn't the first time, but it hurt worse than usual. I'm sorry. I know telling you this will only cause you pain... but I miss you more than ever now. It's fine. It's fine. It was worth it.

One night, Talia returned to her office and caught her mother reading the letters.

"What do you think you're doing?"

Her mother jumped, tried and failed to feign innocence, then adopted a bemused expression.

"I am your mother," she said, as though that would absolve her.

"Those are private."

"But you can read them?"

"He left them for me to read."

Felice frowned, and her face grew uncharacteristically red. "And you're honoring that wish? His squeaking lute can break for all his honor is worth. Especially after he left and"—she waved a hand over the letters—"all of this."

With a rider's speed, Talia reached the desk, gathered the letters, and tucked them away.

"I knew what I was getting into. I'll honor his wishes because he's still my... *husband.* Vows were sworn. Only a fool would treat that as nothing."

Her soul quickened, then fell still just as fast. What had even happened?

After Felice left, Talia returned to the final set of translations. Her interest wasn't just in Fynn anymore. Having read letter after letter, Talia felt like she'd come to know Freya as well.

It all came back to the final, short message. The very first she had tried to read.

They broke the rebels and are heading for us. He promised we won't be taken alive. I love you, I love you, I love you. Farewell.

.   .   .

Talia set the letter down. She reached for her cup of spiced nairn root tea and found it cold. Disgusted, she sank deeper into her red chair as a crimson evening gripped the sky outside. Fynn must have received Freya's final letter before the wedding. Anything might have happened by now.

Sigmar might be dead.

Fynn and Freya might be dead.

No.

She shook that thought from her mind. Freya had helped Mouse to escape. She and Fynn had exchanged messages, maybe for years. Whatever their method, there had to be a secure and secret way in and out of Stroef. Perhaps they were already on a boat and crossing the strait right now.

No.

She caught herself again. *The Blood Bards are holding back for a reason.* Fynn had to be alive, at least as a hostage.

I must go.

The thought came easily to her, even if the how remained shrouded. Yet this felt right. Her soul began to spin. She found herself on her feet, breathing fast, feeling light enough to float. She owed Fynn – exactly what for, she could not surmise, but she owed him this much.

Suddenly, a twisting pain seized her chest. Talia gasped and folded in on herself.

"What is it?" Pyra asked. *"Who should I burn?"*

"No one," Talia said, yet even telepathically, she sounded winded.

The pain eased, and Talia righted herself with a groan. What had caused that? She wasn't lying to herself – she would go to Fynn. No doubt.

No pain this time.

Huffing, Talia hastened to gather her sword and armor. Oline's emerald squadron was due to leave for the Empire at first light, and Talia intended to join them.

26

UNITY OR STRIFE

Great currents in the high winds beckoned them back, speeding them on all the faster until Vald and Raiden'ra landed at the edge of the Storm Peaks.

Between the bristling gray teeth of the mountains, a storm gathered as if to end the world. Black, granite, and even silver-blue clouds formed thick as oil, roiling in many viscous layers beyond the edge of sight. Lightning coiled within the darkness, and thunder rolled like the drums of war.

So dense was the magic and so strong the collective will behind it that Raiden'ra could clearly hear music, and Vald heard it through him. It sounded like the roars and rumbles of a thousand great drakes, all aged and proud, harmonized in their bellowing. It was music of immense power, music to frighten the very mountains to bow down: the song of the Storm Flight.

The storm riders who had journeyed with them stood in awe. Some stepped back. Some wept. Vald could feel their lesser souls tremble, their bonds strain. Even the Storm Lords were not immune, though they hid it better than the rest.

Against such might, Raiden'ra stepped forth alone and called out to the heart of the storm. Shortly after, Raiden'ra told their fellow riders.

"He comes. Brace your spirits, for the humbling you'll feel his presence may overwhelm you."

And come he did.

The first winds that heralded his approach caused weaker Ascendants to cry out. Later, the mighty winds brought Champions to their knees. Even from afar, the spiritual pressure weighed heavily on Vald, though he was satisfied when his own soul rose to meet the challenge and he remained tall and straight, even as a Low Lady gasped and collapsed to one knee.

The Elder of Storms came alone, swooping over the mountains to land before the Paragon. His every silvery-gray scale gleamed as if hand-forged by the artisan smith of Falcaer, so seamlessly woven that in places his body was as smooth and reflective as a clean mirror. His eyes were silver as pure starlight, giving him the impression of existing beyond the physical.

And perhaps he did. Vald had considered that the first time he and Raiden'ra had met the Elder of Storms, that perhaps beyond the final boundary, there was, in fact, another, then another, ever advancing until one became power itself and joined to the world song.

Vald stepped forth, inclined his head, then reverently dropped to one knee. Unlike the others, he did so of his own volition. Raiden'ra joined him and lowered his neck to the ground.

"Revered Elder," said Raiden'ra, *"we are grateful for your swift reply."*

The Elder of Storms sniffed. *"Never have I allowed so many riders to enter my domain."* His voice struggled to cope with his own power, leaving his speech a low rasp with an ethereal echo, a voice to send shivers through bone.

"We come humbly, only to speak. The great disturbances in the world threaten to split the Order into pieces."

"My brother has been slain. Why should your quarrels matter to me?"

Vald kept his head bowed. Better to let his dragon do the talking.

"These squabbles matter not to you, revered Elder, though we bear tidings of what happened to your brother."

Raiden'ra then retold all that Neveh had said during the council, and everything else besides.

The Elder snarled. *"Why tell me of your sister's crimes freely?"*

Vald felt his dragon hesitate.

"Go on," he encouraged privately.

"Revered Elder, we know there must be a response to this affront. To punish our Order for Neveh's involvement would be within your rights, but to do so would only benefit our mutual enemy. Yet to destroy Sovereign too soon could unleash the scourge in a manner we aren't prepared for, especially in a crisis. My rider and I come humbly to beg you to communicate your intentions to us, not to work so close as to endanger the Pact, but so the Order might coordinate our efforts with yours."

The Elder of Storms stood silent for a long time. Even the great storm quietened into nothingness, and Vald's breath rang in his ears.

"You may rise, Raiden'ra."

Vald's shock was second only to his dragon's. For the Elder to allow Raiden'ra to stand before him was a privilege never granted before. Vald remained on his knee. He was but the human. Still, after the shock passed, a surge of pride arose within him and washed over their dragon bond.

Privately, Vald said, *"We have come so far."*

Raiden'ra growled appreciatively and slowly rose to his full stature.

At length, the Elder said, *"Your Order has failed."*

"Yes, Elder."

The Elder snorted and bared his teeth on one side.

It was years beyond count since Vald had last felt afraid. The feeling of a hammering heart felt as unnatural now as being apart from his dragon. Their previous fleeting dealings with the Elder had been to seek permission to train within the peaks. Now, they placed finger and talon over the edge of the Pact.

"To think my sister feared what your kind might become, yet you two, at least, I find… impressive." Another long, interminable silence followed, and then, low, almost cruelly, *"To whom are these riders loyal?"*

"To myself and my rider as the Paragon of Storms."

"And to you alone?"

A spiritual check followed the Elder's words, sweeping over

Vald's head and leaving a prickle of static running down the back of his neck.

Thankfully, Raiden'ra's spirit rose to meet the check.

"Good," said the Elder. *"Then swear yourself to me, swear that your power is mine own, and there will be no fear of reprisal. If there is to be chaos, I would gather one great storm to sweep the world and cleanse it."*

For the first time, Raiden'ra faltered. *"What of the Pact?"*

"What of it? Your riders are sworn to you, and you shall be sworn to me. All this power will be mine, not the Order's. The Pact may still stand."

Vald's cheek twitched. Talks and assurances were one thing, another oath of fealty quite another. Yet he heard his words to Adaskar, mentally replaying them now as though his conscience were throwing them back at him. He'd scoffed at care and caution. Better to be proactive than sit idle and let the Elders determine all.

Vald reached over his bond. *"This way, at least, we might have a say in events. We can keep the bulk of the Order safe."*

"We've come too far to think of turning back."

That was true enough. They hadn't traveled half the world with loyal riders for nothing.

"Revered Elder, we swear our allegiance and our strength to you."

A thick strand of spiritual power unwound from Raiden'ra's soul. Vald felt it hot over his head like tethered lightning.

The Storm Elder's eyes flashed as if with white fire. *"And you, human?"*

Vald swore and joined the soul oath.

"Rise, Paragon."

Vald stood and raised his head to meet the Elder's gaze.

"Select your swiftest flyers. News of my sister's troubles concerns me. I would know of her intentions, and those of the others. Storm Riders and Flight will travel together to show our new power. And may all show the wisdom of the Paragon of Storms."

∼

Adaskar swept his gaze over neat rows of men and women in gray and blue armor, over the riders of storm and ice. Both barracks had been emptied, and they stood before him upon the vast, enclosed fields where the legions of Aldunei had once drilled and trained.

Cycling power to his throat, Adaskar projected his voice.

"Paragon Eso and I are here to lay uncertainties to rest. The Paragons of Falcaer held council on the calamity which has befallen the world. All was laid bare. Paragon Vald failed to condemn the actions of rogue riders and departed from us in strife."

He was certain Vald had gone beyond what was permissible with the Elder of Storms as well, but he hadn't condemned Farsa without sufficient evidence, so he wouldn't falsely accuse his old master either.

"Worse," he continued, "Paragon Neveh openly boasted of breaking the Pact in pledging her sword to the service of the Elder of Ice and flying to do battle at her bidding. This, Paragon Eso and I condemn with all our might."

"No Paragon flies above the Order," Eso called, enhancing his voice as well.

Adaskar reached the end of the front line. It was too short a line. The storm riders were depleted compared to their comrades in blue. He turned on his heel and marched back the way he'd come.

"Paragons Vald and Neveh are wayward, and we hope they will return and atone. Mark this day; these are dark times for the Order. Treachery abounds. Stay vigilant. Do not lower your guard in thinking traitors lie only in Feorlen. There will still be rogues among us, loyal to a mystic dragon as much an enemy to us as the scourge itself."

Better to be direct and watch for anyone squirming. In this, Azarin acted as his eyes and ears.

A few concern me, Azarin said.

Adaskar stepped into the ranks. He slowed his pace, holding the gazes of humans and dragons alike.

"Even in the ranks of emerald and fire, they will skulk. But they will be found. Such treachery, such abuse of the powers granted to us, has never worked to bring this Order down. For too long have we stood, the last shield against the chaos – riders of Falcaer!"

Some cheers followed this, some roars, and each one Adaskar appreciated more than he could ever let them see.

"When the first swarms overran the fledging cities of man and choked the life from the forests, who rose to the challenge?"

"We did!" came a collective reply, including dragon growls.

"We did," Adaskar echoed. "When Aldunei crumbled and all seemed lost, who brought the dawn?"

"We did!"

"We did! For we are the inheritors of those great men and women and their great purpose. We of noble blood who *know* better, who understand the *honor*, the *purpose*, the *responsibility*. We will always best those who are false, those who would wield their powers as swords rather than shields. I know we will succeed again, because I trust in all of you who are dutiful and loyal. Together we shall bring this chaos to heel as our forebears did before us. And when a grateful world asks how we made it through, we shall smile, and we shall say, it was only our duty – riders of Falcaer!"

This cheer was the heartiest yet and stoked the fires in Adaskar's soul.

"You did well," Azarin said, and Adaskar treasured the rare, open compliment.

"Steel your hearts and your souls," Adaskar called with an air of finality. "Back to your duties now. Dismissed!"

As the assembled ranks turned and filed off, dragons included, Adaskar made for Eso. Along the way, he reached out to Azarin and said, *"Check on Wynedd. I would speak with Eso a little longer if I can."*

Azarin took off as Adaskar arrived by Eso's side, offering him an arm. Sometimes Wynedd's nightmares could leave the old Paragon unsteady on his feet. Already leaning on his staff, Eso smiled and looped his arm through Adaskar's.

"Can you manage the heat?" Adaskar asked in a low voice.

Eso bristled; his beard seemed to shake from indignity. "Dear boy, I could handle worse even before Vald reached Champion. I value your care, but I will not suffer being patronized."

Adaskar considered removing his arm, but he valued the closeness with the old Paragon as much as anything else. Who else in the world could he seek small comfort from? Everyone else was an infant to him.

They made their way to the fire barracks.

When Adaskar had been a boy, he'd imagined this place to be full of great braziers burning night and day, with sand on the floor and a searing presence as hot as the desert bordering his homeland. Each room was indeed hot and bone dry, maintained by a sophisticated expansion of the Alduneian pipes under the floors and inside the walls; not magical but mechanical.

Young Rostam had sought magic and wonder, yet now he was as close to magic as a man might reach, he appreciated the efficiency and ingenuity of his forebears. Why expend magical power when other means would do? They had chosen practicality over fantasy, restraint over extravagance.

Everything the Order should be.

Adaskar led Eso to the campaign room, where incursions were being mapped and prepared by the Paragon of Fire. The world lay before him upon great carved tables, with every Order Hall enlarged and their garrisons well marked. The Roaring Fjord, Claw Point, and Sable Spire were empty now, the Crag removed altogether. Falcaer looked overstuffed by comparison, as did Sky Spear, Oak Hall, and especially Drakburg. The recent tremors and openings in Risalia had demanded extra deployment.

Eso slid his arm out of Adaskar's and leaned over the western side of the world table.

"A sorry thing to see."

Even as he spoke, a Fire Champion came and removed several storm tokens from Falcaer, doubtless for the small group that had left the fortress that morning. The Champion picked up more tokens from other halls, including two ice, one mystic, and one fire, and deposited the tokens into a box to one side of the map.

Eso followed the Champion, his expression growing graver with every token removed. His fingers twitched, and he began tugging and twisting at the loose cloth of his robes.

"They lurk everywhere," Eso fretted. "How has this happened? Two more cuts and we'll bleed out."

"Possibly four," Adaskar said.

Eso's heavy white brows rose halfway up his forehead.

Adaskar pressed the matter. Eso had to hear it.

"Kalanta is still unaccounted for."

"Kalanta would never—"

"Her silence cannot mean good news. Either she's struck out on her own like Vald and Neveh, or she's—"

"I would know if she has come to harm."

Adaskar decided to bite his retort and let it slide. They hadn't felt the death of an Elder, why would a Paragon weigh on the world any more than that?

"We should ground them," Eso went on, a higher note entering his voice. "All of them. Everywhere. Stop them from leaving until we can grapple with what is happening."

"Let the traitors reveal themselves, I say."

Eso opened his mouth, choked on his words, closed his mouth, and then gripped his staff with both hands. His knuckles turned white. He seemed truly old, in a very human way.

"And then what, Rostam?"

"And then, one by one, we defeat each threat. We are bleeding riders, it's true, but we'll remain the strongest force. Altogether, we are more powerful than a single Wild Flight. Vald, Neveh, this Sovereign – they aren't working together, and that shall be our salvation. Three splinters will not reduce the entire trunk."

"Three?" Eso said. "Does that include the girl, or have you forgotten her?"

Adaskar grunted and passed smoke from his nose. In the moment, he had indeed forgotten Talia.

"Of course not," he lied.

A crooked, grandfatherly smile played at the corner of Eso's lips. He seemed to be working up to saying something when a High Lord entered the campaign room.

The newcomer was a giant of a man who stretched his brigandine at the chest and shoulders, his eyes a blaze of orange. Dowid hailed from a margrave military family in the Risalian capital of Wismar. He was less esteemed in rank than a proper duke, but Dowid had proven himself and risen exceptionally high for one of his birth. He arrived before the Paragons and bowed. Next to him, Eso seemed an old twig.

"Revered Paragons, I have completed the assignment." Dowid proffered a sealed parchment to Adaskar. "I can return later if convenient."

"I'll take it now." When Adaskar had finished reading, tickling nerves burned low in his stomach. "How soon could this restructure be implemented?"

"For halls within the belt, four days. Alamut and Squall Rock may take a week. Angkor would take longer, of course, but if whoever is sent goes without rest, we could see the change within ten days, if pushed. If you trust Commander Goldmane at White Watch—"

"Beyond all doubt," Adaskar said.

"Then we need not consider White Watch further," Dowid said.

"Very good."

Adaskar handed the sheet to Eso.

The old man's face turned sour as he read.

Adaskar dismissed Dowid so the discussion might continue in private.

Still with a look of distaste, Eso said, "A commander reshuffle might be prudent. Harsh, but prudent."

Adaskar was surprised he was so open to the idea.

"But," Eso continued, "I fear it would risk pushing more riders into Vald's or Neveh's hands. Or worse, Sovereign's."

Adaskar shrugged. "Another avenue for traitors to reveal themselves. Those truly loyal will not turn their cloak so easily."

"We spoke of unity today," Eso said, "but replacing every

Flight Commander of Storm, Ice, and Emerald, is not showing a united front, and we'll only invite new jealousies and bitterness. We've got our fill of those already."

Adaskar thought of Farsa and her conflict with Dahaka, one born of bitterness at a past decision. Orvel, formerly of Sable Spire, had been a resentful man too, he had been informed. Had Silas been as well?

Of the three, Adaskar only knew Silas well. He'd fought beside him. Bled beside him. Had Silas lived, he would have been Vald's natural successor. Surely Silas and Clesh had had nothing to be bitter about, yet they too had turned, though it still seemed unbelievable to Adaskar.

He was about to continue when more fire riders entered. More interruptions. Adaskar rounded on them, blew smoke, and told them to leave. They scurried off, but Eso also seemed in a mind to go as he turned, clunking his dragon steel staff on the hot floor.

"If you aren't going to heed my advice, Rostam, I'm sure I can find other tasks to fulfill."

"Speak plainly, then."

"I know you, dear boy. Single-minded, sometimes to a fault, but always on what's most important. You were obsessed with Agravain for months, and that's how I know you had all but forgotten her now. Considering the truth of this Sovereign and of Vald's departure, she is no threat. The time has come to offer her a way out."

"She's always had a way out."

Talia could arrive right now, bend the knee, and let her bond be broken.

Eso bristled again. "Can any rider be expected to subject themselves to such a fate? If we wish for a peaceful solution, she must be offered a golden bridge to retreat over."

Adaskar found himself stepping around to the Feorlen side of the world table. Such a small realm had become such a large thorn in his side. He met Eso's eyes and searched them for his predilection for woe, nerves, and despondency. This time he saw the stern rider he'd known as a young man.

"Why the sudden interest in sparing her?" Adaskar asked.

"If we reconcile with her, mayhaps a compromise can be found with Vald, too. Blight raise me, I would do anything to prevent the Order from tearing down the middle. The only fight we need to wage is against this Sovereign. Better to do that with our full power and crush him like the bugs he controls. How will Vald or Neveh or anyone lure riders away if we show we can change—"

A surge of Azarin's fire burned through Adaskar so quickly he almost belched flames. Instead, he gritted his teeth, winced, and turned from Eso as though he'd presented a dish of boiled vethrax for dinner.

Change... Even Eso was beset by the impulse. Too easily were the hard-earned lessons of the past dismissed. Too easily were their forebears disrespected. Adaskar would have given much to be alive in the time of Kosora the Kind, who led her emerald siblings to reseed the lands east of the Spine, or Galain the Gallant, the greatest Fire Paragon who had reigned for over one hundred and fifty stable years.

Any time but his own tumultuous present.

A lump of smoke formed in his throat, constricting his voice. "And who can guarantee that any of these changes will have the desired effect? All could just as easily become worse." He swallowed the smoke back down, and his stomach knotted as though from a bad meal.

"Rostam, what good is clinging to every ornament of the house if you're left standing in the rubble?"

Adaskar sighed and allowed his shoulders to sag by a fraction, then Azarin's voice crossed their bond.

"We burn fierce and bright. We do not extinguish."

Eso broke eye contact, his face taking on the tell-tale look of a rider communicating with their dragon. If Wynedd had woken, Eso had a duty to attend.

"Please do not exhaust yourself," Adaskar said. "Word of our fugitives can still reach every Order Hall by conventional means."

"You serve Falcaer to your utmost, and so do I. Please,

Rostam, think on what I say. There is a reason we are a council of five, not one. My desires are the same as yours. I'd rather this ended and all returned to as it was, as though none of this ever happened... but it has, and I at least am not prepared to let the house fall to ruin."

Leaning on his staff, Eso left, and Adaskar called in the waiting riders. Many came and went, relaying reports and intelligence: scouting parties had been sent to look for Kalanta and a team of fire riders to the Spine to burn any bodies that might remain from the great battle. Tokens on the table were shuffled and scourge sightings read out and marked, many from the northern fringes of the Fae Forest, while there were rumors of trouble in the Frontier. Minor engagements were noted, the progress on tithe shipments tracked.

Adaskar listened well and answered dutifully, and then it struck him that he ought not to be listening and answering alone. Vald, Neveh, Eso, and Kalanta ought to have been here with him, of course, yet the days of the Paragons working in harmony were long past. But that did not mean he had to stand alone. Fire did not need to burn apart.

He found himself leaning upon the world table, his elbows resting somewhere in the Sunset Sea. For the first time, too, he noticed how Falcaer had been made to appear at the center of the world.

Interrupting one of his Champions, he noted this observation aloud.

Bewildered, it took the Champion a moment to respond. "I had not noticed, Revered Paragon."

"Well, it's wrong. Geographically, it is wrong. And in spirit, it is wrong. Do you not think?"

The riders present looked first taken aback, then between each other, and then back to Adaskar before one found the courage to answer.

"The map has served us well for centuries."

Adaskar grunted. "The world does not revolve around us; we exist to serve the world."

He grunted again. Then, before fully thinking it through, he

moved around the table to within reach of Alamut and snapped
the wooden piece clean in two.

"It is broken now." And then, to no one in particular, he said,
"We shall fashion a new one. A better one. Fetch me the artisan
smith and the remaining highest-ranking Lords of ice, mystic,
storm, and emerald to join me in the courtyard of the inner sanctum. Now!"

His fire riders bowed, then dashed off.

Azarin's burning presence crossed the bond. *"Are you sure?"*

"I am."

*"If we buckle by one step, they'll expect us to take more. If we will not
stand firm, who will?"*

"We will stand where it matters. This is a gesture."

Across the bond, Azarin snorted.

"Do you trust me?"

When Azarin replied, he did so in Ahari. *"Dooset daram."*

"I love you too."

Thus emboldened, Adaskar set to work.

Although the circumstances were grave, Neveh rejoiced to be
back at the roof of the world where oceans were locked beneath
frigid sheets. Her heart beating, she took her first step onto the
ice, then lowered herself flat and placed her ear to its chill
surface. She closed her eyes, tasted salt in the air.

A fracture broke within the depths, releasing an exquisite,
haunting echo. For miles around, the ice cracked, and the
supernal notes formed music. It reverberated through her skull,
down her spine; her whole body eased, as did her trembling
spirit.

Then a wind too frigid even for her swept over them.

Nilak rumbled high and worried. *"We are not welcome."*

The growing wind drowned out the song of ice, and with a
sigh, Neveh opened her eyes and stood. Buffeted by the freezing
winds, she began Sinking her mote channels to leech the cold

into herself, into her soul, and pushed the excess over to Nilak's core.

Her dragon continued to rumble. *"This is punishment for our failure."* Nilak pulled his wings tighter against his body. *"I cannot fly against this."*

"Then we go on foot."

Neveh took another step, then another, pushing against the north wind. Nilak followed, his talons scraping on the ice.

They trod on. For how long remained a mystery, for the low-hanging sun never set. Its weak, watery light was broken only by clouds. With unyielding effort, they came to the end of the frozen ocean, where the land reformed.

Rock and ice seemed woven together here, impossible to tell which came first. All was black stone, pale frost, sapphire ice, and milky light that held no warmth.

It was harsh, freezing, and desolate.

Neveh knew nowhere more beautiful.

A crowning glacier rose above all, the open nest of the Ice Elder. When Neveh and Nilak reached the glacier's base, Nilak bowed, but Neveh remained standing, looked up, and waited. No bowing. No more throwing herself before another's feet. There was too much at stake to show weakness, and they had suffered to walk here already.

"You risk much in returning. Were my brothers to discover your presence, it would bring great danger to—"

"Elder," Neveh cut in, unwilling to speak in long, winding words. *"The Paragon of Storms knows of our alliance already. There is every chance he'll take this knowledge to his own Elder. The council has long suspected them of having dealings with each other. The time to worry about the Pact is over."*

From the crowning glacier came a roar as though a thousand notes of splitting ice sang as one. The Elder took flight. Briefly, she seemed a huge black figure against a low yellow sun, then she descended fast to land before them.

Seeing the Elder again, Neveh considered that there was a beauty even greater than the icy desolation of the flight's home. Each scale on the Elder's body seemed a jewel forged within the heart of winter, and her eyes were so blue and so deep that no sea of the world could hope to fill them.

"I think I know my brother of storms better than you."

"Nilak and I went to fight for *you.*" Here, Neveh's voice showed the first hint of weakness as the tremor in her soul shook again. "For *you*... all we ask now is for help in finishing the work you started."

Nilak growled and flexed his talons through the snow.

The Elder cocked her head. *"Failure is an ill smell on you, child. I fear your anger is not at me, but at yourself."*

Neveh's trembling soul began to shake. Nilak did all he could to steady her over their bond, but matters of the spirit were not so easily fixed.

For a moment, Neveh returned to the battle in the valley – all of it a blur, save the stark shock in the Life Elder's eye and his pink tongue drooping to the blistered earth.

To Neveh's great relief, Nilak interceded on her behalf. *"Your parting words rang in our minds, Elder. Fear of what might happen should the mystic be slain. When the time came... when we—"*

"I choked." Neveh placed a hand on Nilak's leg to let him know it was alright. "It was my decision at the critical moment. If there is to be blame, let it fall on me."

The Ice Elder cocked her head the other way. *"So affected by a throw-away concern at the end of a hasty and heated plea? I thought riders to be stronger-willed than that."* She lowered her long neck, as though the weight of the world were upon it. *"I swore to my brother that Ice would aid him... Your failure is mine own, child. And now we pay the price for it."*

"Elder, your caution was reasonable and your love for your flight commendable, but now is no time to wallow. Let us fly together. Let us find Sovereign, and this time, I won't make the same mistake. He will be weakened now. Whatever happens with the scourge, the Order will meet it in force. With you by our side, we'll surely prevail as we always have."

"I fear to leave my domain. My brothers... you do not understand."

"Then explain," Neveh said. Understanding the Pact had been why she'd risked coming in the first place and offered her sword to earn answers. Alas, she'd failed to earn them, but she would not stoop to begging.

Ice swished her tail. *"You did fly in my name,"* she said, her every word carefully chosen. *"If there is to be chaos, who better to turn to than our own? Hmm. I may come to regret it, but these are dangerous times for the world, and I would not have you act in ignorance. So... Very well, you asked me why the Pact was formed."*

Neveh's heart skipped a beat. She closed her eyes to turn her world inward and listened intently to every word the Elder said.

"After the first great swarms were defeated, my brother of storms became wary that the new riders might grow in power to rival his own. This he would not abide. My brother of fire, so proud and headstrong, feared that dragons would be sullied by humans. None of us had forgotten our hatred of your kind, but whereas Life and Mystic and I had lost our appetite for conflict, Fire and Storm remained agitated. To avert another crisis, I beseeched them that cool minds ought to prevail. The scourge had been pushed back, but we could still feel its presence. These new riders had vowed to guard the world. Better, I argued, to create clear boundaries and ensure no Flight nor Elder would work with or against them, thus keeping the balance of power in check. I flew between my siblings and the first riders, and so an agreement was reached and made binding by soul oaths."

She shuddered, as though her freezing power had finally got the better of her.

"By these oaths, I thought us all kept safe, and so we were, but the millennia have worn such oaths thin. If I could resist their pressure to summon you, then Storm and Fire certainly can. Do you see?" Her eyes went wide and pleading. *"I did all I could to safeguard the world and keep the peace. If my brothers learn that I broke the Pact, they will maintain no need to uphold it themselves. The consequences will be... unthinkable."*

Neveh kept her eyes closed for some time, digesting all the Elder had told her. So, the Pact was all that kept the Fire and Storm Elders from destroying the Order? An agreement into which they may have entered reluctantly.

And this was what Adaskar clung to? To think that the Order had not worked with Wild Flights against the scourge all these years to protect a deal formed to combat greed and hate was sickening. Never again would she feel guilty for breaking it.

Nilak still held reservations.

"Revered Elder," he said, *"we are greatly honored you have revealed this ancient lore to us. And we thank you for the wisdom you showed all those years ago. But perhaps the danger is not so great as you perceive? The Life Elder broke the Pact in working with the girl in Feorlen. For almost a year, he worked alongside rogue riders and a human queen, and your brothers did not come."*

Ice snarled. *"And you think his death will go without remark?"* She scratched at the snow. *"Your pardon, Paragons. I am... afraid."*

The Elder's home at the roof of the world made more sense to Neveh now. The other flights, remote and insular as they were, still roamed within the boundaries of the maps.

Neveh risked taking a step toward the Elder, her palms up, as if she were approaching a stricken animal.

"Work with us, and you won't have to face these things alone. That should always have been the point of the riders—"

She gasped, clutching her sternum. Her shaking soul had become gripped by discomfort, a tangled feeling of wrongness.

Nilak rumbled in concern and brought his snout level with her to lean on.

The Elder seemed to behold Neveh for the first time. She slowly blinked her great, deep eyes and said, *"Won't you stay with me a while? I would see you healed. I would offer you and Nilak training. Let us take a measure of events here, together, and once you're whole, we may decide what is best."*

Still with a hand over her chest, Neveh sighed. Every fiber of her being fought against the invitation. A lifetime of going against the grain was a hard habit to break.

Then she was taken back to the valley.

The Life Elder's disbelief drained from his eyes into a gray, colorless, lifeless nothing. His tail shuddered and curled as his last breath rattled. Blood dripped from the talons of the dark mystic, who laughed as he flew away.

Neveh blinked fast, as if the memory were a piece of grit in her eye she could wash out. The wrongness in her soul thumped harder.

Nilak reached over their bond. *"Just this once, perhaps you should acquiesce."*

Neveh nodded. She got down on one knee and bowed.

27

DYING LIGHT

"It's too late," Merchant rasped. He said it repeatedly as he drifted in and out of consciousness.

Osric walked on leaden legs, having run, then walked, then run, then walked some more, carrying his injured client every step of the way. East they'd gone, putting as much distance as he could between them and Blackhollow, fighting a weariness he'd not felt for an age. When bonded to Thrall, he'd all but forgotten exhaustion, but whatever rank of rider he was now, it wasn't one that could go on endlessly.

His dragon felt the strain, too. She'd stayed by his side the whole way and now walked slow, head down, tongue drooping, but still determinedly putting one foot in front of the other.

"It's done…"

Merchant's skin was now chalk-white, his breaths ragged.

Osric spotted an unusual clutch of trees, perhaps some final, northernmost gasp of the Fae Forest, a blip of proud nature in the otherwise bleak Frontier. It offered shade, rest, and perhaps something to eat.

He headed for the trees.

Light filtered through the full green canopies, turning dim at the woodland floor. The black dragon slumped down and rolled around on cool earth with a shuddering sigh, and once again, Osric wondered how much of his own relief was genuinely his.

Farther on, they discovered a small lake that seemed a guarded, secret place. The summer air was dry and pleasant here, and the faint sound of lapping water was inviting, drawing them closer to the lakeshore.

Gently, Osric sat Merchant down, propping him up against a thick tree trunk so as to look out across the still water. Reeds in the shallows swayed, their stems rustling in the gentle breeze, whispering to them. A strange feeling crept over Osric, and he began to wonder whether the lake had always been waiting for them, biding its time until it could welcome them with open arms into its peaceful embrace.

"There are worse places for it," Merchant said.

Osric grunted but said nothing. He reached for the inadequate bandages on Merchant's belly, intending to take another look at the wound, but something in his client's eyes made him stop. He'd done all he could, which wasn't much at all. Osric suspected the bowel had been nicked, leading to this agonizingly slow death. Some boiled wine may have helped, but they had no wine. The only thing in the saddle bags was marrow paste.

"I ought not to tell you what you seek," Merchant said. "You failed to keep me safe."

Osric knelt on one knee, aware the man was entirely at his mercy. A dark if prudent thought crossed his mind: he could press on that wound, and Merchant would sing like a songbird. On a few campaigns, he'd given such orders to extract vital intelligence even if he hadn't done the pressing himself. That the thought occurred to him was proof enough of the dangers in him growing powerful again, but in this instance, it was only a passing one, not an urge – as it once would have been.

With a nod to his dragon, Osric said, "I'd fail a thousand times over if it kept her safe."

Merchant smiled crookedly. "Just so." He coughed, and blood dribbled down his chin. Osric found a clean section of his gray cloak and wiped the blood away. "Thank you," Merchant wheezed, then he sagged and fixed his eyes upon the lake. "Had a little girl once myself. Bit smaller than yours, mind."

"What was her name?"

"Isabel." He sounded painted, as though the hurt were still fresh.

"What took her from you?" Osric asked, thinking of the blight.

"Pox."

"I'm sorry."

Merchant made a pained laugh, as if he might scare death off with his indifference. "Something gets us all. After she went was the first time I took…"

His voice trailed off as his gaze shifted to the saddle bag.

Osric felt sorry for the man, truly, deeply, in a way he hadn't thought himself capable of. Once, he'd have dismissed a marrow habit as weakness, but that was before he'd accepted his own failings. Once, he would have asserted that such toxins made men into monsters, but he'd been a monster without them. Monstrous men didn't need a substance to be so, but good men, perhaps as Merchant had once been, sometimes needed the drug when life's demons grew too great.

Osric could envision Merchant's fall. A fine officer in the Athran heavy cavalry, a beacon of the city struck down by tragedy and in need of an escape. Then, the habit was discovered, and he was disgraced, discharged, and sent staggering into the Frontier, where all the refuse washed up.

His eyes still on the saddle bag, Merchant asked, "Could you help me?" His arms and legs twitched, unable to move, and his fingers curled stiffly like early rigor mortis.

Osric pulled out one of the little jars with the purple pulp, then he frowned. They didn't have a pipe or a cup to make a tea with it.

"I'll take it raw," Merchant said.

Osric's frown deepened.

"You've never taken it?"

Osric shook his head.

"Rub a bit of it on my… my gums." Merchant seemed half a ghost already. "I'll tell you, then… I'll tell you…"

"A fair exchange." Osric opened the jar and ran a finger

through the paste to gather a small lump on his fingertip. "Tell me now. You may not be able to after."

"Petrissa Vogt also had another name in her time," said Merchant, fighting for every breath. "Agravain, am I right?"

Osric's heart thumped. He did know who she was.

"Tell me where she is."

"She's in Redbarrow. She's long been the partner of the Jackal."

The leader of the Hounds?

Somehow, that didn't shock him. In fact, it seemed quite fitting. Petrissa had always flitted from risk to danger, seeking thrilling fulfillment ever out of reach. A man like the Jackal seemed the ultimate end of a course such as that.

Osric thanked Merchant, then applied the paste to his gums. The man's eyes glazed over, and his twitching limbs fell still.

Osric considered the jar of marrow. What was he to do with the stuff out in the wilderness? Nothing good, at any rate. He was prepared to give the toxin to a dying man to ease his passing, but he stood firm in his belief that it could do no good in the long run. Better to empty the jars and give it to the grass.

To that end, he tipped the jar, but as the sludge-like paste slid toward the rim of the glass, Merchant suddenly reached up with some last ounce of strength to take his arm.

"Don't," he rasped. His nails dug into Osric's skin. "Keep it. Take it with you. The Jackal… wants it. It'll help… trust me…"

More trust was required, but this time Osric found he did trust the man – and fully.

He resealed the jar.

Merchant smiled, then, at last, he allowed himself to relax and sink into the numbing of the marrow. His arms fell back to his side, heavy as stone. He sighed and gazed out across the water again.

Osric took up a seat beside him, his back against the tree, and joined in quietly taking in the lapping waters, the faint twittering from across the shore, and the pleasant warmth of the sunlight between the branches. They sat for some time,

Merchant's breath becoming lighter and shallower until, as though the whispering reeds called to him, he passed with a final, almost happy sigh, and his head slumped onto Osric's shoulder.

Osric swallowed hard but did not stir for some time.

He wasn't sure what to do. Bodies must be burned, but a fire that size would produce too much smoke and guarantee they'd be discovered. There was another way to ensure a person could not rise again, though most found it distasteful compared to a cleansing pyre.

Well, there was no one here but him and the dragon. Osric had done much worse, and she'd seen worse besides.

First, he gently lowered Merchant's body onto the grass, then removed his red Athran riding jacket. Next, he started digging into the earth as best he could with his axe and hand. He wasn't long into his task when the black dragon came to join him and silently started scooping out earth with her front feet.

"Thank you."

She cooed, then kept digging. Rider and dragon dug, covering themselves in mud, until Osric became sticky with sweat, his lips turned dry and salty, and the skin beneath his savage beard itched fiercely. Wiping his brow, he jumped up out of the grave and readied himself for the final task. Taking Vengeance in a hard grip, he held the beard of the axe over Merchant's neck.

"You can look away," he told her, but rather than avert her eyes, she came closer and placed one of her wings at his back. Osric passed his appreciation across their bond. Her being there made the grizzly task easier.

Without a head, even a ghoul cannot move. Osric wrapped Merchant's head in his old cavalry jacket, then placed both it and the rest of his body gently into the grave and began to refill it. The dragon helped a lot with this, shoving great mounds of soil back into the hole with her legs, wings, and tail, then Osric used his hands to pat the mound of earth down, making it smooth, more respectful.

With the task complete, he stood for a while over the grave, shoulders hunched, sweating everywhere, his hands, arms, neck, and face covered in dirt.

Unbidden, his thoughts turned to Redbarrow.

Merchant had been heading that way the whole time, east into the lands controlled by the Hounds, which he'd felt confident would be safer for them. Safer for him, at any rate. Whoever the Athran had become in the Frontier, it was plain he had ties to the Hounds, but Osric didn't enjoy the benefit of those connections.

The question was whether to press on or not.

His soul hurt as much as his aching body. Barbs from his bond with Thrall still seemed lodged within him. Could any meeting with his mother hope to heal such damage? It was just as likely she'd inflict fresh injuries.

In a dark moment, he eyed the jar of marrow lying beside the saddle bag. For the very first time, he understood the yearning to take it. What a cruel, violent, capricious world. How unjust, how pointless it all was. He understood why men and women might don a cloak of dragon hide, why many would be happy to bring it all to an end and make the pain go away.

Then he felt his dragon's heartbeat over their bond. Osric growled, then shook the notion of marrow from his mind. He'd press on regardless. Turning back now was unthinkable. Not after they'd come this far and had a real lead on the trail.

A dip in the lake would do him good, he decided, so he stripped off his crusty clothes and waded out into the crisp waters. As he cleaned himself, his body seemed to awaken again, pulsing with fresh hurts, including the stinging cut down his right forearm and a reprisal of the phantom pain from his missing hand. Still, the water brought a clarity to it all, and removing the dirt and sweat felt like a small accomplishment.

When he emerged from the lake, he searched for the dragon, but while he sensed she was nearby, he couldn't see her. Perhaps she'd curled up into a nice shadow. She'd been especially quiet since they'd reached the lake, and Osric thought she may have wished for some privacy. He imagined she may need it after encountering her brother; he'd always needed time alone after being with Godric.

He was patting himself dry with the cleaner sections of his cloak when she came bounding back into view from between the trees with a brace of rabbits between her teeth.

"You caught those on your own?" he asked, taken aback and feeling more impressed than the feat might have deserved. She was a dragon, after all.

She dropped the rabbits at his feet, then turned and bounded back off into the woodland. Osric only realized how empty his stomach was now food was within reach. He dressed, then busied himself with preparing a small fire and a simple spit, and she returned in good time carrying another two rabbits, big, wild beasts compared to the smaller breeds rabbit ranchers raised in towns.

Saliva drooled from her mouth, and Osric gained a strong impression over their bond of how incredible the rabbits smelled to her, an intensity of flavor and desire that Osric had never felt for any food. No doubt that had helped her in sniffing them out, though it was strange it had happened now. She'd been around rabbit half a dozen times at least over the winter; Holt had even made a rabbit stew after they left Aberanth's glade, but she'd never reacted like this before. She was so eager that Osric's own mouth began to salivate, anticipating that first sweet bite.

Her stomach audibly howled.

"Just eat them. No need to wait for me."

She licked her lips, then wolfed down two of the big rabbits, then a third for good measure. Osric tasted an echo of the blood in her mouth upon his own tongue, and such a satisfaction bloomed from her side as he'd never felt before. It turned their bond searing hot, and as Osric looked inward, he found the orbit of her core positively swimming with shadowy motes. In the real world, the crisscrossing shadows of branches and tree trunks shimmered around her, bending unnaturally closer to her.

"But you ate rabbit before?"

Magic, he thought distastefully. He wasn't the best person to try and puzzle this out; he'd just work on the new facts. Rabbit was her meat type, and a creature that burrowed and hid in the dark did seem a good fit for her.

His own meat required more time on the spit. Knowing this would be the ideal time to Forge while her core drew in more raw motes, Osric crossed his legs, closed his eyes, and tried to match his heart to the beat of their bond. Given her excitement, the bond was beating rather fast, making it difficult for him to raise his heart rate through breathing alone. For a brief time, he managed it, but every pulse felt like someone was beating his broken soul like a drum.

With a gasp, he stopped. "I'm sorry. I know I'm supposed to be helping you, but—"

She nuzzled into him, contented. He smiled and stroked her snout and neck, then the tantalizing smell of the rabbit let him know it was ready to eat.

The meat tasted far better than he'd been expecting, and this time he welcomed this facet of his new bond without hesitation. By the time he finished, his stomach felt full and groaned with delight, and a powerful urge to sleep came over him despite the light of the afternoon.

He doused the little fire with water, then lay down by its warm remains and pulled his gray cloak over himself. The inviting darkness of sleep came quickly for him, and in the moments right before he fell asleep, he saw the dragon's core more clearly than ever through his bond.

The swirl of raw shadow motes had subsided, and whereas he'd only previously discerned a tangled ball of darkness, now there appeared two small figures, both vaguely dragon-like in outline: one dark, the other bright but faint.

When Osric woke, it took him a while to open his heavy eyes. There was dew on the grass around him, and the watery beads were tinged with a pink light through the branches. It must be dawn. He'd slept for a long time.

His soldiering instincts twinged. Something was amiss, or some danger neared. He pushed himself up, looking for the dragon, and once again could not find her. This time she felt more distant, her core across the water.

That was when he realized it wasn't her core at all. She must have been inside a shadow with her core veiled from broad detection, yet close enough to this other dragon for him to have confused them.

Quiet as he could, axe in hand, Osric crept down to the shore and took shelter behind a broad trunk before peering across the lake. The golden dragon stood on the far bank, drinking deep from the calm waters.

Osric's heart began to pound. The black dragon was much too close to her brother for comfort, and Osric could sense her anticipation. She wouldn't be deterred.

Like a specter, she slipped out of her shadow and crawled around the shore toward her twin. He didn't react at first and continued drinking, only rising once his sister was almost right beside him. She leaped back as he turned to face her, her head low and his held high. Her heart thundered, and Osric felt it inside his own chest, pounding against his ribs.

Things remained calm, save for a bit of growling, a little rumbling, a swish of the tail, and a playful nip. For a moment, Osric thought things might be going well, then the mood changed swiftly as a sudden rain in spring.

The golden dragon stood to his full height, his manner imperious, dwarfing his much smaller sister. She backed away, wings shivering, and he laughed high in his throat, ending on a long, dismissive roar before he took off and climbed high out of the woodland to head west.

The force of her grief almost knocked Osric to the ground. He felt the air leave his chest and slumped against the trunk before managing to master himself.

"I'm coming!"

Leaping out from behind his tree, he started running along the shore, intending to join her on the other side of the lake. A high-pitched roar shook the air, causing the water to ripple. She roared again, a more resonant, older cry than he'd ever heard her make, then she stretched her wings to their full span, beat them, and rose into the air.

She flew. For the very first time, she flew, heading across the lake to meet him. Her landing was ungraceful, nearly tripping over her own feet as she stumbled to a stop.

But she had flown.

Osric needed no bond to know she was in distress. She almost bowled him over in her need to reach him, and he wished he had his right hand back just to hold her tighter.

"It'll be alright."

The words sounded hollow, but he didn't know what else to say.

Over their bond, the river of her emotions became a flood, so much so that he couldn't pick any of them out. They were so strong he wanted to weep, scream, laugh, and rage all at once.

Then, just as quickly, they melted away, fading to nothing, and despite her being in his arms, she seemed more distant than ever. It felt... it felt as if she were dying, though their bond, if anything, was strengthening, burning outward, and her core changed. Of the two dragon figures that had been there before, the bright one faded out entirely, leaving the dark one all alone.

Osric's own memories of Godric swelled to haunt him again. All the hurt, the loss, the confusion – it wasn't how brothers were meant to be. The regret rang worst of all.

"Take it from me," he whispered in her ear, "it will be better to reconcile with him if you can. Family is... hard to replace."

She snarled, then pushed back and stared at him earnestly. He gazed back into those purple eyes and thought he might drown in them.

Her core altered again. Where the bright dragon had been, a new figure took its place, the shadowy outline of a man.

"You're my family. I know that now."

Her voice was beautiful to him but fragile. Hearing it for the first time, Osric understood himself to be in shock. He couldn't recall the last time he'd been so, not even when he'd cut off his hand. It was a struggle to think as much to speak, and when he managed words, they came out choked.

"Are you sure you want me? You don't know half the things I've done."

She rumbled, nudged him, and met him right in the eye again. She looked at him across their bond too, taking in all of him, or what was left of him.

Then, her eyes open in every respect, she said, *"Try me."*

28

THE OUTCAST

When Rake reached the outer edges of the Northern Grove, he feared at first that he'd mistaken its location. Northern flowers – pink moss, creamy rock cress, spindly blue catchfly, yellow winter poppy, and purple fraga – ought to be perennial inside the grove. Bees should have been buzzing at their honey-making, the air fragrant and sweet, the chill kept at bay.

Yet rather than a garden paradise at its summer height, Rake found the grove plagued by an early winter. No field of flowers greeted him, the bees were silent, and the wind whipped in.

The grove distorted an outsider's ability to sense those dragons within it, much like Aberanth's grotto, only on a grander scale, but painful distant growls confirmed Rake was in the right place. Things were far worse than he'd let himself believe, not least because no emerald came to challenge his approach until he was deep inside the grove. And then his challenger was not the Elder, not a Warden, not even a Lord, but a dragon closer to a mere Champion.

"I have heard of a half-breed warrior from my kin," this dragon said. She didn't seem willing to place any weight on one of her front legs, so she didn't bow to him. Her scales were also pitted with half-healing cuts. *"You may pass, soul-cursed."*

"How gracious of you," Rake said, with only an edge of insincerity. "I would speak with your Elder. Is he here?"

The dragon's reaction was all Rake needed to understand.

"Ah… the North Warden, then?"

The emerald stepped back. *"You will see."*

Rake ran on.

At the heart of the grove, he found the emeralds surrounding the shores of a great pond, its waters dark and murky when they should have been clear, teal, and brimming with waterlilies.

Many dragons lay on their sides, breathing low; some were sleeping, but many lay listless with vacant eyes. The North Warden was nowhere to be seen, nor could Rake sense a dragon of such power present. A few of those emeralds still on their feet snarled at him, but they lacked any ferocity. Those with palpable spiritual energy wavered even at rest, their morale deadly low.

Such dismay ranked amongst the sorriest sights Rake had ever seen.

To him, there was one positive. Mystic motes from the thoughts of the flight lay over the grove like a dusting of snow. Having been alone for a time, such a bounty of motes produced by so many differing thoughts seemed a feast. Were it not rude in the extreme, he would have Forged these and regained his strength quicker.

Instead, he approached any emerald who seemed alert enough to talk, but, one after the other, they shied away or shunned him until he started to lose patience.

"I only wish to talk," he told the grove at large. "I promise just talking to me won't curse your own soul!"

He waited. And waited. Then, just before he was ready to become a lot less understanding, one emerald did reach out to him.

"I shall speak with you, Rake."

Her voice caught him off-guard. He recognized that voice, every word as impeccable as though they were uttered by a thoroughbred equestrian of Athra. Deep down, there was an underlying haughtiness, too, though humbled by a fall from grace. Her name was on the tip of his tongue, but it eluded him.

"I'm by the cherry blossom," she said.

Rake turned in search of the tree. He almost missed it, for it was on the far side of the grove's pond, and its branches only held onto a few of its fluffy pink petals.

Even as he rounded the pond, the voice still eluded him. The emerald beneath the cherry blossom was no more distinctive than any other, with bright verdant scales, a slender female frame, and fine bone ridges.

She lay slumped, though, unlike the rest of the flight, she was removed and isolated. It appeared to require effort for her to lift her head as he approached. A chunk of one ear was missing, and the ragged, blackened damage had spread down to the eye on that side, such that the eye was closed and oozing yellow pus.

The dragon flashed her teeth awkwardly, as though she were trying to snarl but had forgotten how.

"I did not think to be pleased to see you again… but of late, there has been nothing but surprises."

Still at a loss, Rake said, "More surprises than we have scales, to be sure, although it's never a surprise to be pleased to see me."

The emerald narrowed her one good eye. *"You wanted to kill me last time."*

Rake suppressed a grin. "There are so many whom I've wanted to kill. I wouldn't take it personally"—and that was when it finally clicked into place for him, so he said, just a little too late to be entirely natural—"Gea!"

It flooded back to him now. Gea had been bonded to Orvel, the rider Holt had killed at Windshear. Rake had suggested they kill her to prevent her seeking revenge.

"What brings you here, Gea?" he added nonchalantly. "I thought we packed you off to Oak Hall with Farsa and Hava?"

Gea growled, but the little fire in her didn't last long. *"Lady Farsa and Lady Hava were concerned riders loyal to Thrall would come for me before all could be accounted for. I confessed all I knew to them, then swore a soul oath to seek redemption with my flight."*

"Hmm. Seems as though you paid your share of blood," Rake said, pointing to her eye. "How did that happen? The breath of a scourge-risen dragon?"

"A talon. It caught me in midair. But I don't have the blight," she added fiercely. *"It's just not healing properly. That's all."*

Rake raised his hands. "I believe you. I don't think your flight would let a dragon with a bad case of the blight enter their grove."

"My flight?" she scoffed, then she lowered her head and clawed at the ground.

More pink blossoms fluttered down from the dying branches, and wherever they landed, Gea reverently changed where she gouged the soil to avoid crushing them.

"Serves me well, this eye, does it not? Brought down by a blind hatchling, and now I'm half-blind too."

Rake didn't see any gain from pursuing her dark thoughts down whatever crooked paths she'd built in her grief. What he needed was information.

"What happened in that battle?"

Gea told him all she knew, describing the fight in vivid detail. The great clash in the skies. How the Emerald Flight woke the forest to uproot and join them. How the Elder shielded them from Thrall's domination until the North Warden fell, how the dead were beyond count, and how the Elder bade them leave for a last duel between himself and Thrall.

"He lost," she concluded without emotion.

Rake supposed she didn't know him like her wild kin did. They looked to their Elders like children to parents, but dragons of the Order knew of bonds far stronger.

"Alas, it seems so."

Rake thought it a shame that none of the emeralds witnessed the end. He would have welcomed any insight as to how Thrall had won that encounter. Thrall had been weakened after the failed Feorlen incursion. Surely one year couldn't have been enough to regain enough power to match an Elder head-on, even accounting for his despicable methods of Forging.

But it would do no good to ponder endlessly on it with what little he had.

Thrall had won.

The Elder was dead.

Rake sagged. "It seems I've traveled north in vain. To speak to even a Warden would have served—"

He cut himself off there, looking around in want of an answer. Maybe he should just start telling the whole flight about his misadventure. It couldn't do any harm, even if they were unlikely to have any insights into the Hive's use of emerald power.

"Did the Elder ever mention anything about a creature in the depths of the world? Something to do with the scourge?"

"There was talk among the flight of a powerful presence gaining in strength, though it sounded like the scourge as a whole to me rather than one creature. Such rumors were dismissed in the Order long ago, were they not?"

"Well, they're true. From what I gather, the Paragons are aware of it but do nothing."

Gea snorted, then spat into a patch of her clawed earth. *"That, I admit, has surprised me. If it's true… how dare they… how dare they keep such a thing from us."* She remembered how to snarl then, but the agitation seemed to pain her wounded eye, so she settled on a whimper. *"They care not. The great lords of the Order gave Orvel no aid when he needed it. No guidance…"*

Her voice cracked, and she fell quiet again. Rake cocked his head and stroked his chin. He couldn't figure her out, and this irked him.

"You don't seem insane, you know."

"Am I to thank you for that?"

"Meaning, you don't strike me as the type who would merrily join Thrall in his genocidal vision. Was it your rider who turned?"

For a moment, he thought she might attack him. Instead, she sniffed and spoke softly.

"Neither of us meant it. As the years wore on and we didn't advance, Orvel, he… he was angry at first, then sad, then just bitter. Nothing I did helped. I think that bitterness seeped across our bond into me after so many years of it. He should never have agreed to smuggle out that blighted egg," she added hurriedly. *"He didn't even know what he was getting caught up in. After we got caught, we decided to escape Mistress Ethel and*

Master Strang rather than be brought in. A bit of freedom sounded all well to the good. One of Thrall's riders found us, and they managed to convince Orvel that this mighty 'Sovereign' could assist his development. It was a lie! Orvel wanted to leave the moment we got to Windshear, but it was too late by then."

"Any chance you recall the name of this rider?"

"They never gave theirs. We didn't know them."

"Shame," Rake said. "They sound like one of those people I'd like to kill."

Those words hung heavy between them until they stretched into another silence. Rake filled it by checking the dirt under his talon nails and caught his reflection in the glassy surface of his orange blade. He looked leaner, though not in a way to please him or any admirer. It made him look older.

"How do you know it's true?" Gea asked. *"About the creature?"*

"Several reasons, but chiefly because I had a recent and most unpleasant run-in with it. Or a part of it. It thinks and it speaks, though not half so eloquently as me."

"What happened?"

"It *really* wanted to kill me," he said, unable to resist the dramatic flair. "Tried to bring half of Risalia down upon my head. I barely escaped with my life."

He opted to leave Holt and Ash out of the story. He saw no reason to provoke Gea to further pain and upset right now.

Ugh, what's becoming of me? The boy is turning me too soft.

"The magic it employed to collapse the tunnels felt too close to emerald for comfort. I've never known the scourge to wield such magic before. Hence me wishing to bring this to the Elder's attention."

As Rake finished speaking, he realized it was an awful lot for Gea to take in. Anticipating she would be overwhelmed in her present condition, Rake was about to take his leave when she spoke again.

"Paragon Kalanta was working with the Elder for months. Perhaps she is still around."

Rake raised his scaly brow. "The Emerald Paragon was here?"

"The flight was pushing back the blight from the borders of the White

Wilderness. Other emeralds mentioned it was part of a deal the Elder had with his sister—"

"Speak plain. Do you know this or not?"

Once again, Gea seemed ready to strike him, but she only slumped further down. *"I don't... I'm not part of the... It's just what I heard."*

Rake twisted the shaft of his polearm in his grip. "Did Kalanta fight in the battle?"

Gea shook her head. *"She did not come. I don't think the Elder had seen her for some time."*

More troubling news, and more mysteries.

He grunted. "Do you know anything else? A Paragon and an Elder working together would have been the event of the century in normal times."

"Not much. Paragon Kalanta and Mistress Tanyksha were already here in the mountains when the Elder arrived with the bulk of the flight. I wasn't there for that, but I think it was Kalanta who came to the Elder first."

Rake motioned her on with his hand. "Yes, yes, got anything solid I can use?"

"I told you they were trying to purge the blight from the north. It was long, grueling work. The only thing of note is the unusual creature they met— and no, I wasn't there. I just heard of it."

"Creature?" Rake said, his mind immediately jumping to the Hive Mind. "What creature? And don't say you don't know."

"I— ooh, curse you, Rake."

"Too late, I'm already cursed. The creature?"

Gea picked her words with care. *"Only Kalanta, Tanyksha, and the Elder met with it. We know it only as the white ape."*

Rake recited it back to the sky. "The white ape," he said, as if announcing its presence at court. "It must be a very special ape to gain an audience with Paragons and an Elder at the same time! What could such a meeting entail? Could Kalanta have returned there? Though she is more likely to have gone to White Watch... What news from the riders there and at Sky Spear during all of this?"

"The riders have not interfered. The Pact will have kept them away,

but I don't think the Elder would have welcomed any of them if they'd tried to come. He trusted no rider other than those loyal to the rogues in the west."

Rake smirked.

"What?" Gea snapped.

"You spit at the thought of the dreaded Order and the Paragons, but you're still calling Miss Agravain's faction a group of scoundrels and rogues. You know, maybe I ought to call her Mrs. Agravain now. Or is it different when one is a monarch in Feorlen? I've quite forgotten the etiquette."

Gea was staring at him, her nostrils flaring.

"What?" he asked innocently.

"Are you always like this?"

"When I'm in a good mood."

"The world seems to be ending, and you're in a good mood?"

"Really, Gea, I'm not sure my mood matters to the world. I swear, if my being glum would fix things, I'd become miserable in an instant."

Rake bounced on the balls of his feet. Despite the setbacks, despite the losses, he had always liked a good mystery, and it turned out the Spine was full of them.

"Where can I find this white ape?"

From across the pond, members of the flight started growling.

"Keep your voice down," Gea beseeched him. *"The Elder forbade any of the flight from visiting the creature again."*

"Fortunately for me, I'm not a member of your flight. You can tell me."

"I can't, Rake."

Rake held back his retort. He cocked his head the other way this time and studied her again.

Despite his flawless logic, her hesitancy was understandable. As a former member of the Order, Gea would have struggled to integrate into a Wild Flight in the best of times. Not just because of the wariness and deep prejudices, but also because of the daily routine.

Rake had discussed it with Eidolan at length: a dragon goes

from the Order with a clear command structure, focused duties, defined missions, and objectives to almost no structure, vague goals – if any – and long periods of rest and idleness.

No doubt the Life Elder's change of heart on humans and the Order made things a bit easier, and while he'd been campaigning against Thrall and the scourge, there would have been much to do.

But the Life Elder was no longer here, and the flight appeared lost.

Gea would only make life here harder for herself if she went against one of his last commands regarding the white ape.

She lay low, breathing faster. Her wounded eye no doubt pained her, and her soul must have been torturously dark, cold, and empty, even worse than his own. Eidolan had described the loss of the bond many times. Rake considered it a pain he would dearly wish upon his very worst enemies, but no one lesser. Had they killed her at Windshear, it might have been a kindness.

But Rake found himself feeling something he rarely felt. He pitied Gea. He pitied her so much that a lump formed in his throat. This he blamed on Holt as well.

That boy will be the death of me.

He cleared his throat. "For outcasts like us, nothing will ever be easy." Then, without fully thinking it through, he rambled on. "You should come with me!"

Immediately, he regretted it. Wincing internally, he scrambled to think of a way to play it off in jest, but Gea perked up and said all too quickly, *"Do you mean that?"*

And all too easily, Rake said, "Yes. I could use a guide. After I'm done here, there's much to do elsewhere. Many minds make for quick work and so forth. Though if you leave with me and break your Elder's wish, I do not think they'll take you back."

Gea got to her feet, rumbling in a manner that almost sounded happy. *"My soul oath with Mistress Hava was to find a new purpose in my flight. The Elder's death has destroyed the flight as it was... Yes, I feel I can come. It would be good to have a true mission again."*

"Hmm," Rake said. There seemed no way of backing out of it

now. "If I am to take you under my non-existent wing, then you must refer to me as *Master* Rake from now on."

She snarled again through gritted teeth. *"Very well, Master Rake."*

This pleased him. Perhaps there would be more fun in this than he thought.

"Then it's settled. You can lead the way."

29

LESSONS IN HUMILITY

South was not a simple journey. Between the southern coast of Feorlen and the volcanic isles lay a great stretch of sea few captains would ever sail directly. To avoid the risk of such a vast flight over open waters, Holt and Ash took the longer route, following the Feorlen coast eastward until before crossing into Brenin. They continued down Brenin's coast until they came to the mouth of the Stretched Sea and struck out over open waters where the distance between the continents was shortest.

There was a need for care here beyond simply making it back to land. The coasts of the Stretched Sea – from Brenin to Ahar – were under the control of Mithras, forming part of its vast commonwealth of ports and coastal settlements. Holt and Ash stayed high above the southern continent until they were far inland.

These lands were as distant and mythical to Holt's under-standing as Ahar, and if the maps were to be believed, the south stretched on and on, as vast as the lands on the northern side of the Stretched Sea and then more. Despite its size, the south was sparsely populated, filled instead with enormous barriers to human habitation.

Not far from the ports of the Mithran Commonwealth, the fertile land of wheat and olives gave way to scrub before drying into the Searing Sands. This desert stretched from west to east as far as Ahar, cutting the peoples of north and south off from each other. Once past the desert harshness, a traveler would need still to trudge for endless leagues before seeing the first greenery of the Jade Jungle. Reaching Lakara in the heart of the jungle on foot would require endurance even riders lacked.

Given all this, the only sane way for anyone to make the journey was to sail across the Scalding Sea, hugging the coastline. Holt and Ash did the same in the air, avoiding the worst of the desert heat by traveling at night and taking shelter in coastal caves and coves during the day.

Though the journey was long, it granted time for Holt to reflect upon his soul and spirit, to Cleanse and Forge, and to simply be together with Ash. They shared in the joy of long uninterrupted flights, the tingle of moon and starlight on their faces, the intensity of staring down upon the world and seeing no one, no human nor dragon, before the horizon on all sides.

Such isolation struck Holt deeply. In some ways, it was a relief. The world was enormous beyond anything he'd reckoned, larger than he could wrap his head around. And he and Ash were but ants within it.

The Life Elder's task had conferred great expectations on them – dragons and riders sometimes told them they were special. Holt risked believing it at times, but out here, so far from everything, it was a notion he could not take so seriously. They could fall out of the skies right now, make a small plop into the roaring ocean, and the world would carry on.

Proof of their fallibility came readily in hungry bellies, and hunting out here was no simple thing. Ash recognized none of the scents in these foreign lands. Strange creatures roamed the scrubland: swift cackling dogs, giant turtles with shells hard as granite, great cats with bristle-like fur, and bizarre black horses with white stripes. All looked ragged, lean, and none too appealing to Holt's tastes.

One morning, as they descended to find a place to rest, they spotted a group of animals resembling deer nibbling amongst the bushes. They were larger with redder coats and pointed horns too large for their heads. They did not scatter on first seeing Ash – perhaps they were unused to dragons – but an instinct eventually kicked in, and they bolted as though harnessing the winds. The relief of their breathtaking speed was short-lived as Ash's stamina won out, allowing him to catch one of the red deer that fell behind the herd. Holt urged Ash to fly as fast as he could back to the cooler coast as the heat of midday approached.

Later, under shelter from the sun, Holt examined the beast. It was so much like a deer, with similar smooth skin and bony legs, that he was hopeful it would provide lunar-boosting effects. The desert deer, as he thought of it, had tall horns instead of antlers – ridged, twisting, and spiraling. While he shared senses with Ash, Holt found its scent warm, earthy, herby, and oily. When using just his own nose, though, Holt thought its aroma was closer to a filthy wet dog that had rolled in a mucker's heap. Ash still thought it smelled fine, so Holt held his breath and proceeded to treat the carcass.

Its meat was extremely lean, making Holt unenthusiastic about cooking it in his pan without good oil or in his pot without a trustworthy water source. He resorted to roasting it on a spit and seasoning it with salt.

The result was far from unpleasant. It tasted mildly gamey and had a fine grainy texture not dissimilar from venison, though it certainly suffered from dryness. They could do a lot worse, and he was glad to have found some source of food. Unfortunately, while Ash chomped down the desert deer happily enough, it lacked the addictive quality Ash found in actual deer, nor did it have any magical impact. Whatever the desert deer was, it must be fundamentally different.

This came as a blow. What jerky Holt had left upon leaving Sidastra had already been close to spoiling, and on such a lengthy journey as this, and in this heat, it had turned fast. Unless they found deer – which Holt doubted – he would lack the benefit he got from the treated meat.

Their journey south remained much the same until they came upon the delta of the Green Way, where they turned west-ward over the Scalding Sea. For two days and two nights, they flew without rest before spotting the outer islands of the volcanic archipelago. Here, the humid forests of the mainland continued, though conditions were a little cooler and drier thanks to the sea wind. From specks of land to great islands, all seemed untouched by human hands.

When they sensed a group of young cores, as weak as Novices, Holt assumed they had entered the outskirts of the Fire Flight's domain. These young drakes kept themselves hidden and let them pass without question. Two islands farther on, fire dragons of Ascendant rank could be felt. These were bolder than their younger kin, sitting on perches of black rock or flying up to get a look at them at a safe distance.

Holt and Ash kept themselves braced for a fight, assuming they would be challenged sooner rather than later. The spiritual tag left by the West Warden gave them some confidence, but Holt thought the Fire Flight was the most likely to strike first and ask questions later.

When first they saw rising smoke, they thought nothing of it. This was the domain of fire, after all. Then Ash's sensitive ears picked up roaring and a howling wind, though the weather was calm where they flew. And he heard the boom of thunder.

Racing toward the source, Holt soon noticed the distant and shadowed outlines of wings, of dragons diving, spinning, and launching jets of flame against blue forks of lightning.

Storm dragons were here. And they were evidently unwelcome.

There were five. Four were scattered within the Low to High Champion range. The fifth surprised Holt the most. It was a storm rider, an Exalted Champion, launching torrents of crackling power, which were met with bouts of molten, heavy flames from an equally strong fire dragon. The two sides were evenly matched, though Holt thought the storm dragons would win out, for the rider would have deeper reserves of magic.

As he and Ash closed in on the battle, a bombardment of telepathic communications hit them.

"Who goes there?"

"Flee, storm rider, before you burn."

"I shall charr those white scales black."

One strong female voice carried above the others, ringing as though carried on the wind. *"Declare yourselves. Do you fly for Falcaer or for Vald and the Elder of Storms?"*

"We fly for ourselves," Ash replied.

"Does Adaskar hope to trick us?" the female storm dragon asked. *"Prove your loyalty and join us, or be struck into the sea."*

The Exalted Champion stood on his dragon's back and thrust high with his long spear, puncturing the belly of a fire drake and spilling black blood.

All the while, Ash glided closer to the fight.

"Aid us," came a voice of crackling wood, *"and the Fire Flight shall reward you!"*

"We should help them," Ash said privately.

"We don't even know why they're fighting!" Holt replied. *"Ash, we've never fought other riders in the air before."*

"We're here to convince the Fire Elder to help us! How will we manage that if we let his dragons die?"

Holt thought this perilous. He'd rather not get involved, not least as he was painfully aware of their lack of experience in aerial combat, and the shortcoming of his lunar powers in this situation. A Flare during the day held less danger, a Consecration required the ground and wouldn't harm the storm dragons anyway, and Eclipse was a non-starter in daylight.

But Ash was right. For better or worse, Holt made his choice.

He drew his blade, the steel a white shard under the hot sun.

A flurry of instincts crossed their bond as they considered their best approach. Ash began Grounding his mote channels to help him fly better, and at these speeds, Holt didn't risk fumbling with vials of elixir. He wouldn't have time.

Close by, a fire and a storm dragon clawed at each other, spraying blood and chipped scales. They broke apart, the fire dragon falling, the storm dragon swerving toward them. Holt took aim with his sword, braced his free hand on Ash's ridge, and blasted a Lunar Shock through the steel. The dense light struck the storm dragon's tail, and the concussive force bent it back at an odd angle, sending the dragon into an erratic flight pattern.

Another storm dragon came right at them. Ash twisted and turned, just missing a fire dragon that came hurtling in close, before breaking free of the crush.

Holt glanced over his shoulder; the storm dragon roared in displeasure and seemed intent on chasing them, its talons open like an owl aiming for a mouse, gaining on them with every second. The first dragon Holt had injured joined the pursuit.

His mind filled with thoughts of land where the storm dragons didn't have a clear advantage, and Ash immediately turned for the island.

Unable to do much facing forward, a mad idea came to Holt, and he shared an impression of it with Ash. *"Can you manage?"*

"Do it."

Holt braced his hand on the bone ridge in front of him, then, with a burst of magic pumped directly into his muscles, he used the bone like a column to swing himself around before clamping his legs hard into place so that he faced Ash's tail.

They cut their sense-sharing. Holt looking behind Ash would only confuse him, and the smoke from the burning palm trees would help guide Ash to shore.

Their pursuers gained on them, but Holt stared the dragons down.

A lance of lightning flashed, and Holt deflected it with his sword out of sheer instinct, not consciously registering the path of the attack. He Floated his mote channels, and blocked another hit, and another, blasting out lesser Shocks with his free hand whenever he dared let go of Ash's ridge.

"Incoming!"

Ash dove again as a fire dragon raced overhead, spewing fire as it collided with the storm dragon with the injured tail. Their second pursuer spun about to help its comrade, then another fire dragon swooped in to join the mid-air brawl.

Holt gasped in relief, then he felt the presence of the Exalted Champion rushing in from the side. Ash banked hard, and it was all Holt could do to stay seated. He righted himself as Ash leveled out then renewed his dive for land.

In hot pursuit, the enemy rider weaved his spear through the air as though writing out runes. A net of crackling power wrapped itself around Holt and Ash, and tightened. Bound like trussed chickens, their trajectory down became a deadweight drop.

A spiritual weight pressed upon them, woven through the netting, though not so focused as to check their morale. Holt fought back, his soul spinning to fortify his will, and he pulled on an excessive amount of magic from Ash's core to join the power he already Floated. The crush of the cage lessened just enough so that he could raise his blade an inch and make a jerked cut at a strand of the netting, yelling so hard from the effort that his voice buckled in a pained crack.

Excitement for the kill blazed in the storm dragon's yellow eyes.

Holt cut another strand, Ash bit through several, then Holt had a better idea. Still Floating his excessive magic, he grasped more of the netting, gathering the coils in his fist, intending to cut through the knot of electric rope in one go – but then static danced up his arm, causing his left side to seize and spasm. His jaw locked under the pulsing current, then his whole body refused to move.

He couldn't move, couldn't breathe.

The storm dragon opened her talons.

Ash bit through more coils of the rope, enough that its pressure lifted.

"Hold on, boy!"

Holt lunged and took hold of Ash's ridge just in time before Ash tucked his wings and began spinning. Holt's world spiraled. Upside down, blood rushed to his head, and the writhing ocean took the place of the sky before he shut his eyes.

Only their bond gave Holt any sense of what was happening. Ash had turned around so he faced their enemy, then his whole body vibrated as he unleashed a mighty moonbeam. The force of it rang through Holt's bones. He couldn't help but scream, even as a surge of glee pulsed across the bond.

"Got her!"

There was a lurch and a jarring stop as Ash flipped back the right way. Holt's head swam, but he was happy to be sitting upright again. He opened his eyes.

The storm dragon writhed and screeched – a sound of panic, not anger. A moment later, Holt realized the dragon was rider-less, and he spotted the rider falling fast, spear spinning away over the ocean. Champion or not, they were high enough for the man's body to break on hitting the water.

"Catch him," Holt said, repositioning himself to face forward again. They melded senses as Ash turned hard and dove. He plucked the rider out of the air moments before he hit the water, then made for the shore. No sooner had they reached the sands than Ash yowled and dropped his charge.

"He shocked me!"

Holt glanced back. The Champion had missed the soft wet sands and plummeted onto the hard, dry section of the beach, rolling uncontrollably across the shore.

Holt wanted to call 'We were trying to save you!' but his jaw remained stiff and unyielding.

Ash turned, flying low, and Holt jumped down and onto the beach. Unlike the storm rider, he landed gracefully, and he started running, sword in hand.

Bolts of lightning struck the beach indiscriminately, kicking up sand, each one thundering with the storm dragon's panic. Still Grounding his body, Holt weaved between them, intending to end this fast.

The rider had struggled to all fours, one hand groping for his absent spear. He looked up, one eye closed, blood dripping from his mouth as Holt reached him and threw his entire momentum and strength into a kick at the man's side. The rider went spin-ning and hit his head twice before coming to a halt.

The lightning stopped, leaving a heavy smell of ozone in the air.

Striding toward him, Holt sent out a spiritual invitation and fought against his lock jaw, bones clicking as he called, "Yield!"

In his haste, Holt's invitation was as crude as a slap across the face, and, far from helping the situation, the shaking rider got back to his feet and limped forward.

His dragon landed behind him, snarling, but her core was ragged after what must have been a long fight with the fire dragons. She took in the state of her rider, then of Holt, then the zeal in her yellow eyes dimmed. She growled low, causing her rider to turn to her. He nodded, then the Exalted Champion's exhausted eyes met Holt's.

"I yield," he sighed.

"I yield," echoed the dragon bitterly. Spiritual energy lanced between her and Ash, twisting around their souls and cementing the surrender. Rumbling, she lowered her snout. *"I did not sense the Warden's tag from afar. Forgive our aggression, blind one."*

Holt winced as he drew breath. Another ache, like a sharp growing pain, ailed his chest. Odd as it was to contemplate, his soul felt tender and strained. He must have pulled some spiritual muscle in his hasty, inept use of it.

He looked up at the sky, where the fire and storm dragons continued battling.

"What are you doing here?" Holt asked the rider. "I didn't think the riders were allowed to work with a Wild Flight?"

Still on one knee, the rider said, "Times change. Why are you here, rogue?"

"Answer me first."

The man wheezed and looked at his empty hands, perhaps wondering where his spear had gone.

"We came to parley with the Elder of Fire—"

He cut off abruptly, then looked over his shoulder. Seconds later, Holt felt it too. An immense power. A fire dragon at the level of a Warden.

The Exalted Champion's dragon mewled and nudged him. A moment later, she began shaking and lowered herself flat on the sand. It was pitiful to see, and Holt found it hard to watch.

"You should leave," Holt advised.

"We cannot," said the Champion, as resignedly as if he were

marching to his grave.

Holt wanted to urge them anyway, but the seething voice of a female dragon entered his mind, drowning all else.

"None shall leave. All here will answer to the Warden of Wrath."

Holt's spent soul buckled at once under the spiritual pressure, and his morale plummeted. The best he could manage was to take an instinctive step back as he felt Ash beating a path across the shore to join them.

"Don't worry," Ash said, sounding far braver than Holt felt. *"We have the West Warden's support. We helped the fire dragons."*

Holt nodded and placed a hand on Ash's side for comfort.

Above the island, the Warden of Wrath blazed into view. She looked three times the size of Ash and the whole of her great body seemed to smolder, like she had been plucked hot from the forge. Her belly was a weaker red, like iron cooling on an anvil, the ridges of her wings were black, and the membrane rippled yellow and orange. Where she flew, a trail of smoke billowed in her wake.

The fire dragons broke away from their skirmish, leaving the storm dragons divided. Two headed for the island but two turned tail, despite the Warden's warning.

"Fools," the Exalted Champion said. His dragon yowled in dismay.

Though the storm dragons commanded the winds, the Warden of Wrath sailed effortlessly across the skies, her sheer power driving her forward to catch her prey and belch an inferno to engulf them.

Holt's stomach clenched, twisted, then backflipped. He found himself unable to look away as the storm dragons emerged from the fires like two burnt birds, wings still flapping, then slowing, until both fell limp and charred from the sky. Standing on the beach, Holt couldn't hear them plunge into the sea, and he doubted even Ash heard it over the wailing of the storm dragons.

"She didn't even give them a chance," Ash said.

Holt gulped. No amount of Floating, jerky, or elixirs could possibly save them from such flames.

The surviving storm dragons and the single rider huddled together farther down the beach. All of them bore wounds, sporting burns, cuts, and limps. There was a pleasant cooling wind rolling off the waves, but when the Warden landed, steam hissing under her feet, that same wind blew with an uncomfortable heat that made Holt want to rip his armor off.

No one moved. Not an inch.

The Warden of Wrath looked first at Holt and Ash. Her eyes were unexpectedly blue – blue for the hottest part of the flame. Under those eyes, they wilted. Ash threw himself flat to the sand, and Holt dropped to one knee and bowed his head, unable to hold her gaze.

"*Stay,*" she commanded, then stomped off toward the storm dragons. Only when Wrath came to a halt did Holt risk looking up again.

The three surviving storm dragons were flat on their bellies. Holt couldn't hear whatever words passed between them. Instead, his attention was drawn to where the Warden had landed. Where her talons had touched down, the sand had taken on a bubbling, semi-liquid state. When this began to cool, small crystalline lumps formed. Wrath must have regulated her body's temperature afterward, for the rest of the beach lay unaffected.

As they waited and sweated, Holt fought to steady his racing heart. Across the dragon bond, Ash reached out to him, just as an adult reaches for the hand of a frightened child. Without words, they held onto each other, heart and soul, ready for whatever might come.

At last, after what felt like an eternity, the storm dragons departed. Bobbing and bowing, they backed away, then took off at top speed. Once they became thimble-sized in the distance, the Warden of Wrath slithered around smoothly, blue eyes still burning, smoke whirling, and advanced upon Holt and Ash.

Holt dropped his gaze again.

"*You two are a long way from Angkor.*"

"Honored Warden," Holt began, thankful for Ash's support in keeping the fear from his voice, "we are not a part of that Order Hall."

"Be silent, human."

Hot smoke brushed the back of his neck.

"What Holt says is true, Honored Warden," Ash said. *"We are not part of the Order. We swore no oath."*

"Is that so?" Wrath asked. At the same time, a raking presence passed over their souls and bond. She snarled. *"So, this helps to explain it. The Life Elder falls, and my Elder ponders how and why. Yet here you are, a blind whelp tagged with emerald power. A curse upon it, no doubt. What other unworthy snakes do the soft greens harbor?"*

"My eyes had nothing to do with the Life Elder's death," Ash said, somehow summoning boldness. *"Your own power is vast, Honored Warden. My presence does not weaken you, nor any emerald."*

Wrath bit the air over their heads.

"Careful with your tone, cripple. Now, tell me who you are and why you are here."

"My name is Ash, and this is my rider, Holt. We have come to humbly seek an audience with your Revered Elder to ask for his aid. We believe the Life Elder was killed by a mystic dragon called Thrall, who has gained control of the scourge."

Wrath beat her tail upon the beach. She sniffed hard, ending in a great snort. *"What is your magic, blind one?"*

"My core is formed by the power of the moon and the stars, Honored Warden."

She did not reply but growled and paced around them.

Every nerve in Holt's body screamed at him.

"Your tales sound more like hissing lies to me. I'd leave your husks here for the tide, but"—she added with all the disgust of one tasting bile—*"my Elder tells me no. He will grant you an audience. Be thankful and grateful in his presence. Betray the trust of the Fire Flight, and you will answer to me."*

"We understand," Ash said.

"And you, human? Speak now."

Holt raised his head to look at her, aware of the copious amount of sweat pouring from him. "I understand."

She threw her head back and roared, ending with a great column of flames.

"Follow me."

. . .

The Warden of Wrath led them south, where the islands clustered closer together. The Fire Flight did not hide here and unleashed fiery breaths like salutes to the Warden as they flew. A red and black mountain, as colossal as one of the Frost Fangs, dominated the area. Its slopes gently disappeared into the jungle, which descended in green shelves toward white sands.

"Behold the mountain of fire," Wrath declared. *"Domain of my Elder, most noble and ancient of all our kin."*

Holt's eyes widened as he tried to take it all in. Geysers across the mountain's vast body emitted steam, thick white smoke rose steadily from its peak, and all the land around it groaned as though this king of mountains spoke to its scorching denizens. Midway up the slopes was a cave whose mouth yawned as widely as a dragon's. The magic radiating from it could be none other than the Elder's.

The Warden of Wrath guided them to land outside the cave's mouth. Holt jumped down, felt the heat rising through his boots, and drew his first breath upon the volcanic slope.

He choked and spluttered. The air was thick with a strong, stinging odor. His Champion's body adjusted to it, though the rancorous taste of the gas remained. It would surely be lethal to normal humans, and Holt had no wish to linger. Even Ash spat and wheezed.

"I'm beginning to hate this part of the world," Ash said privately.

"It does make wintering in a freezing forest seem relaxing."

Wrath padded up to the lip of the mountain's mouth. *"Inside,"* she said before entering without so much as a backward glance.

Holt peered into the looming passage. *"Rake was right. We should have become stronger before coming here."*

"We'll be all the stronger for it when we leave."

Holt smiled and patted his dragon's side. Ash had said, 'when we leave,' not 'if we leave.' He loved that, even here, Ash's optimism could not be burnt away.

Side by side, they entered the nest of the Elder of Fire.

30

THE KING OF FIRE

The passage ran deep into the volcano, lit by thin flames issuing from crevices in the rock. Much of the rock was red, rough, and raw, unfurnished by magic, claw, or tool. How it had been made, Holt had no notion, but he didn't think it had occurred naturally.

The heat was extraordinary, the air suffocating. Encased in armor, Holt felt like he was cooking alive in his own pot. He had to stop to strip off his brigandine and gambeson and pack them away, opting not to carry his sword either as a gesture of good faith. That was how he hoped the Elder would see it, at least.

Yet it wasn't long before his open shirt began to be soaked with sweat, and he longed for the bitingly cold waters of Lake Luriel.

Ash, who by some miracle wasn't panting, suggested, *"Float your mote channels. It will help."*

Holt did so, raising his energy flow to create a second skin and dampen the temperature.

"Thanks for the reminder."

Alas, it wasn't enough, and the Elder's aura grew stronger with every step. Holt drank an elixir to aid his Floating, and as his cycling intensified, luminous veins of flowing white light became visible under his skin. The Warden of Wrath paused to give him a disgusted look but refrained from comment.

Eventually, a red glow at the bottom of a slope suggested a lit chamber. Ash entered first, Holt following behind. What he saw, what he felt, caused his jaw to drop.

Cavernous was not the right word for it. This chamber in the heart of the mountain was palatial, many times the size of Sidastra's throne room. By comparison, it made that hall of mortals and men seem but a mouse hole.

A strange type of stone wove throughout the black rock of the mountain; a bright, striking red stone that put Holt in mind of slabs of raw beef. There were outcrops of the strange rock stacked shelf-like up the cavern walls, upon which fire dragons nested, their eyes like countless embers amid smoke and steam.

A ruddy glow emanated from a smoldering dais made of the same crimson stone at the center of the chamber. There was no mistaking which dragon sat upon it as a king sits upon his throne.

The Elder of Fire was larger even than his Warden of Wrath. Rage, vigor, and dignity exuded from his scales, rippling red to black like brutal oil fires. Holt recalled the inferno that had engulfed the West Quarter of Sidastra and judged the Elder more terrifying by far. Burning black were his talons, his spine ridges, and the bones of his wings. Only the scales at his throat were lighter, shining like blood-soaked rubies.

And whether the sweltering warmth came from the searing dais or the aura of the Fire Elder, Holt feared to linger in its presence. Even with the elixir's help, Floating his mote channels only blunted the heat to something hardly bearable.

Wrath padded into the smokey gloom and went to stand behind her Elder while Holt knelt and faced the black floor and Ash prostrated himself.

After a tense silence, Holt felt he ought to say something.

"Revered Elder, we are grateful for this aud—"

A dragon snarled, cutting Holt off before a brusque male voice entered his mind. *"You dare speak first, soft skin?"*

"Settle, Pride," came another male voice, and Holt knew it to be the Elder's. It was plain and austere, a voice of utter confidence that needed no menace to instill obedience. *"Were I so easily offended, I would inform them myself."*

"Yes, my Elder," the dragon said. The Elder had called him 'Pride' – was he another Warden? Holt found it hard to tell with the Elder's power dominating the chamber like a sun blinding the eye.

All the dragons within the chamber began to growl. Holt felt dozens of clumsy inspections of his dragon bond, each taking longer than a practiced rider or dragon of the Order. Soon the chamber erupted in fits of squawking and gargled cries. Whether the fire dragons were irate or laughing was hard to say, but it was undoubtedly unsettling.

"That is no way to treat guests," the Elder said, broadcasting his thoughts for the benefit of Holt and Ash. *"Blind is the white one, but he bears the mark of a Warden of the Emerald Flight. Consider what feats they must have accomplished to earn it."*

The noise in the chamber fell to a quiet rumble.

"Better," said the Fire Elder. *"These emissaries aided our brethren against insolent storm dragons ravaging our islands. A time of war and blood, a time of chaos, is upon us. We shall not take such actions as theirs for granted."*

A sense of relief flowed over the bond from Ash. *"This is going well."*

Holt, still facing the floor, considered it might be going too well. Then again, perhaps the Fire Elder had been misjudged? The Life Elder had treated them well, and the Mystic Elder, while not helpful, hadn't been aggressive. Perhaps the Elders truly were a breed apart.

"Now, young ones," the Elder said. *"What do you know of my brother's demise?"*

"I'll speak, if that's alright?" Ash asked privately. *"I've heard how you speak to nobles when you need to keep them sweet."*

Holt considered that a good idea while in dragon territory.

"Go for it," Holt replied over their bond.

"Revered Elder, Honored Wardens, mighty dragons of fire," Ash said to the chamber. *"We are grateful for this audience. My name is Ash, and this is my rider, Holt. We are allies of the Emerald Flight, or at least to those who remained steadfast to the Life Elder."*

A small smile tugged at the corner of Holt's mouth. Ash really had picked up a knack for this.

"Our knowledge of his passing is limited," Ash continued, *"though the honored West Warden believes his Elder perished in battle against a formidable mystic dragon called Thrall. We know of this mystic. Thrall has gained control of all the scourge and brought dragons from all flights under his wings."*

The chamber seemed stunned into silence.

Wrath broke it. *"Do you see now, my Elder, how they weave lies within lies? Such wild claims."*

"A thousand apologies if my words were…"

Sensing Ash was struggling, Holt supplied a word across their bond.

"…ambiguous. These events are complex, and explaining them can be troublesome, but we swear to the truth of our words. We tell no lies."

"Good work," Holt muttered privately.

Wrath growled.

"Your words were understood," said the Elder. *"Though we shall require more explanation. How exactly did this mystic achieve control of the scourge?"*

"Thrall can subjugate the minds of his victims," Ash said. *"And we are sure that one great mind directs the scourge to act. A Hive Mind. It is as though the scourge has an Elder of its own."*

Holt felt the Elder lean toward them above his head, as if listening intently.

Ash carried on, more confident now. *"The Hive Mind threatened us during a recent mission under the earth. It tried to kill us, for my light is harmful to the blight. Our friends Pyra and Talia may know better, Revered Elder, for it was they who discovered this creature."*

"Creature?" the Elder said. Both Wardens, one on either side of the Elder, also stepped forward and leaned in. No further claims of lies were thrown at Ash, however, so he continued.

"The Life Elder told us that he long fought against the blight without hope, but now we know more of the enemy, his sacrifice need not be in vain. He spoke of the scourge as his worst regret. He hoped…"

Ash hesitated again. Holt reckoned they would either leave with the Elder as an ally or be reduced to cinders where they knelt, so a bit of boldness was needed. He sent encouragement over their bond and felt Ash rally.

"...*He hoped his brothers and sisters would share in that regret. And join him.*"

"*He said that, did he?*" The Elder of Fire snorted, and smoke engulfed Holt's head. "*It was the blight we created. The scourge came later. That it went awry must have been his error, and I made my ire clear at the time. It was always his failure,*" the Elder concluded, though not in anger, nor bitterness, just firm certainty. "*But why you two? Why should the West Warden dispatch you instead of his own?*"

"*Before he died,*" Ash said, "*the Life Elder assigned us to visit his brothers and sisters and beg their assistance in the coming fight. Thrall's aim is to wield the scourge like his own breath and kill humankind... fulfilling its purpose. The Life Elder judged that wrong. He judged that humans and dragons should stand united to defeat our common enemy. He judged that the bond Holt and I share would show the Revered Elders how close we can be.*"

The Elder rumbled in a manner Holt took as a derisive titter. "*My brother took unfortunate actions, and he has paid the price. As for your closeness, my brother ought to have remembered my will on the matter of these bonds upon their inception. I would not have my flight's esteem sullied. We dragons should not despoil our souls with lesser creatures. My sister of Ice alone understood this. Not even my brother of Storms truly cared for the integrity of our race, fearing only for his own power and whether riders might threaten it.*" The Elder ended on a biting note, becoming angrier than he'd been so far, and his ire only grew as he continued. "*And now he cavorts with riders, seeking to destroy me!*"

The old burn at Holt's side throbbed horribly.

"*And yet,*" the Elder continued, chewing each word, "*I grieve for the death of my brother. Whatever his violations and misadventures, this mystic has no right to strike a blow against one of the five. To toy with the balance of the world. Such a thing cannot stand. The world descends into ruin, but we, the Fire Flight, shall restore it!*"

He rose upon his smoldering dais and roared.

Holt was thankful he wasn't sense-sharing with Ash, for the bellow of the Elder was already deafening. The Fire Flight roared in reply, many breathing jets of fire that cast the high chamber into revealing light and threw writhing shadows upon the walls.

The Elder stretched his wings, and this signaled a call for calm. When the chamber quietened and darkened, Ash took a bold step forward.

"Revered Elder, it gives us immense pleasure and relief to hear your words. By your leave, we would fly to the West Warden at once with the news that your great flight will soon join the fight against Thrall."

"Do not presume," snapped Pride.

This time, the Elder did not admonish him.

"There is one matter I would have settled first," said the Elder, sounding strangely breathless. *"A matter in which you, young ones, may prove yourselves as valuable and worthy friends to fire."*

Haven't we demonstrated that already? Holt thought.

Ash rightly continued with caution. *"If there is any way we can be of service, Revered Elder, you need only ask."*

"Far to the east," the Elder began, his voice recovering its even confidence, *"there is a wicked creature, part fire and part beast, that we call the Parasite. When young members of my flight discovered it, the Parasite assaulted them, draining their cores until they were left as withered husks, consuming them like so much meat and leaving them for the vultures. Drake after drake flew to best it, but few ever returned, and those that did bore crippled cores."*

The dragons in the chamber gave a collective shudder.

"I flew to avenge my flight myself, but the leeching scum stole much of my power before retreating into its lair." The Elder's even tone faltered again, and fury crept in with every word. *"Its body was of living flame; it slipped between crevices in the rock, and I could not follow. Craven. False. A disgrace to its very element. Wicked, wicked…"*

He growled, biting at the air before gathering himself. When next he spoke, his voice had altered again, calmer now but aching with yearning.

"Before it fled, I felt its heart and soul. Denser than the magma beneath our home. Purest flame. Stolen from us, no doubt, but it was there, like hoarded nuts in a squirrel's cache. Delicious."

Once more, the Elder snapped at the air, and this time his wings shook as if he were wringing out his desire.

"Fell this Parasite for me, young ones. Bring me its inner fire, and I shall return to my full strength. Then I shall vanquish all our adversaries: this mystic, the scourge, the very blight – all shall be cleansed in bright flame!"

The dragons roared again, triumphant, as though they'd already won the war and saved the world.

Holt glanced at Ash, his every muscle tense. Over their bond, he said, *"If this Parasite is so strong, we can't be sure of defeating it."*

"We came for the Elder. Unless we get his help, Thrall wins."

Holt wasn't so sure. *"He seems powerful enough. How much more can it grow from this Parasite thing?"*

Their debate descended into quicker thoughts and feelings. Power on the scale of Elders was hard to understand. They never would have imagined the Life Elder falling, but he had.

After a few moments, Ash spoke to the chamber again. *"Revered Elder, your might cannot be contested. Why delay your great victory? My rider and I will take time in this task, and there is always the risk that we may fail."*

The Elder slammed one of his great black feet into the ground, shaking the chamber, then stepped closer. With every small movement, the oily fire of his body heaved, streaking black through the searing red, until, with a slight scrape of talon against stone, he halted right above them.

His aura once more seemed as blinding as the sun, though now Holt risked feeling it more closely. He thought he sensed the damage – as though the sun was falling into twilight, as though a black spot smeared its otherwise perfect surface.

"What has been stolen from me would not be gathered by a score of your kind over their lifetimes."

By 'your kind,' Holt assumed the Elder meant riders.

"Your lives are a worthy risk, but for me to fly early, without my full strength? That I cannot abide. Would you rather see the conflict end swiftly or crawl on, long and brutal, taking lives beyond count before all is restored to how it ought to be?"

Holt hung his head. The Elder's words made him ashamed.

"Do this," the Elder continued, *"and victory shall be assured."*

Holt found he and Ash were of one mind then.

"We would be privileged to bring you this gift," Ash said. He pressed his neck firmly against the ground, then dragged himself back to a respectful distance.

Holt, however, remained where he was. Something in his bearing or spirit must have stirred, for Pride rumbled in amusement.

"I think the soft skin has something to say."

The stinging, noxious fumes of the volcano were thick at the back of Holt's throat, and it was all he could do not to splutter as he said, "I do."

The Elder was using them, and in a manner no better than a capricious ealdor might send a servant into danger. He had no regard for their lives, only the opportunity to gain for himself. Why shouldn't they receive something in return? He decided to imitate Rake and ask for a favor.

"Boy, are you sure?" Ash asked privately.

"It's time to be bold," Holt replied before speaking to the chamber at large.

"This quest will be dangerous. Ash and I have fought for you already and will gladly do so again. And while it will be the highest honor of our short lives to serve you and your flight and to sow the seeds of our enemy's destruction, it might be that we, too, can benefit from this undertaking. If it pleases you to agree, Revered Elder, I ask for a boon in return for our success."

Wrath smashed her tail against the chamber floor. *"What winding words you squeak with. Speak plainly!"*

Holt ignored her and raised his eyes to meet the Elder's. Everything inside him wanted to scream; the fires in the Elder's eyes raged enough to swallow the world, and his soul would burn if he held them for long. But, somehow, he spoke.

"We are the Sons of Night. And from the night, a gift fell to us. A white steel from the beyond, sent by the stars themselves. But I cannot fashion it into a sword with mortal hands. No flame we can create is hot enough, not even from a lesser fire dragon. Yet your power, Revered Elder, surely could, else nothing can. I seek your blessing to forge a sword unlike any other, a great weapon to wield against the scourge. With your power restored, and this weapon, the Hive Mind will wither beneath both flame and light."

The Elder rumbled, but it was Pride who stalked forward until the ruddy light of the dais revealed him. Unlike Wrath or the Elder, he was thick-set with muscle; even his snout, jaw, and nostrils were broader than other dragons, colored by a red so pure no painter could have matched its tone.

"You have a high opinion of yourself, hatchling," Pride said. *"I admire that."*

"Agreed," said the Elder. *"As Valor would admire their courage, were she here."*

Wrath snorted but held her tongue.

The Elder ignored her. *"Were your eyes whole, Ash, I'm certain you would have been a member of my flight. You have that spark within you, and your human has taken it on. But, of course, light comes from fire. Yes. Yessss. How resplendent we shall be when the battle is joined! Verily, I shall grant you this boon. All I ask,"* he ended lustily, *"is for the Parasite's heart."*

A clear exchange. Another mission, then a vast upgrade to his and Ash's capabilities before the final confrontation. Holt felt better about that.

"Then we have an agreement," Holt said, relieved to have reached the end of the conversation.

A throbbing picked up at the back of his head. The heat was bad enough, but talking in such a careful, precise manner was no easy thing, never mind with a burning throat and searing skin on top.

"We do," Ash confirmed. *"Do you have guidance for us as to the whereabouts of the Parasite?"*

"One of my own shall accompany you as guide and protector," the Elder said.

Wrath stepped forward, baring her teeth.

This time, Holt and Ash sent comfort to each other at the same time, resulting in a clash of emotions over the bridge of the bond, leaving neither better off for it.

"Let us not waste more time," Wrath said. *"We have a long way to fly."*

31

THE WHITE APE

Gea turned out to be a quiet travel companion, which Rake favored. It allowed him time to think upon recent events, and she provided a superior source of mystic motes over the birds and beasts.

Raw mystic motes could not be tasted in so crude a sense, though there were differences in how they were Forged. Motes produced by happy thoughts brimmed with energy and were thus harder to hammer into his core. Motes born from grief contained less power but were far easier to Forge. Even among a small group, thoughts swirled freely and in such variety that they blended together. When traveling with a single companion for a long time, though, Rake became intimately aware of how that person or dragon felt. He supposed it was somewhat intrusive, but it was too useful to ignore, and besides, he couldn't help it, just as he couldn't help using his nose to smell.

As dusk settled one evening, Gea went hunting while Rake settled to Cleanse his core. After a while, sharp-edged thoughts flitted into his awareness, savagely brutal and primitive. He opened his eyes and caught a fleeting movement between the trees.

Pairs of yellow eyes stared back from the dark undergrowth. A pack of mountain lynxes was circling him. Then there was the sound of wings beating above, and the yellow eyes turned and fled.

Gea dropped a young musk ox from her talons, then landed beside her catch.

"You scared them off."

"What?"

"Lynxes. A pack of them was trying to decide if I was worth eating."

"Were they?" she said, entirely bored. *"The Emerald Flight has been here in greater numbers than usual. Maybe the lynxes are getting desperate for food."*

"My sympathies to them." He eyed Gea's kill. A young musk ox it might have been, but it still had hair thick as rope all over its body – brown, tough, and horrible to fight through.

Gea ripped into the beast and heartily chewed.

"Do you want some, Master Rake?"

Rake sniffed. The heavy oils in that coarse fur made it smell even worse than it looked.

"I'll pass. I don't need much."

Gea swallowed her first mouthful, then tore another chunk off the ox.

"Older dragons in the Order say that too. Are you old?"

"Very."

He closed his eyes again, intending to return to his Cleansing. Alas, Gea chewed loudly, smacking her lips and thumping her tail as she did so.

"Where did you come from?"

Rake grunted and opened his eyes. "I was once a rider. Something went *wrong*, and my dragon and I fused together."

"What went wrong?"

"If I knew that, I'd know how to fix it."

Rake always had a sense of déjà vu whenever he had to explain this.

"My apologies, Master Rake. I should not have interrupted your meditations. Forgive me… it's worrying how quickly I'm forgetting such things without Orvel. My own core feels groggy, my magic weaker."

Rake appraised her core. It felt cleaner than that of most wild dragons, though the lack of a rider to Cleanse it was starting to take its toll.

"Your body isn't used to removing the toxins all on its own. I know a dragon who was in the Order during the time of the fall of Aldunei. From what I gather, you'll feel groggy, almost with a permanent headache for some years, but in time, you'll adjust."

"How old is he?"

"Over seven hundred."

Gea raised her head from her meal. Her good eye widened, and she seemed to stare past Rake as blood and tufts of fur dropped from her chin.

"I shouldn't want to live that long like... this."

"Most don't."

There were no words that would ease her. Her rider had been ripped from her in the worst way possible. There was a chasm between losing a bond-partner in battle and for them to drift quietly in their sleep beside you as Gideon had for Eidolan. Nor had Orvel died fighting the scourge as he should, but rather at the dead end of a dark path.

Rake feared Gea would never truly find peace because of it.

Not like us, he said to Elya. *We'll hold each other again.*

As he didn't follow up, Gea returned to her meal, and Rake left her to it. He closed his eyes but only pretended to meditate. Amid the many things vying for his attention, he found himself wondering, much to his consternation, about Gea and her bond with Orvel.

Rake's obsession with the advancement process had taken him to the heights of Exalted Lord – he might have become Paragon had Paragon Tollost passed – and that same fascination that had drawn him immediately to Holt and Ash wouldn't remain quiet where his new companion was concerned either.

Eventually, he managed to still his inquisitiveness enough to finish Cleansing his core and Forge what mystic motes he could before they ventured on again at dawn.

On his own, Rake would have taken a more direct route north, but with Gea and her detectable core with him, he advised they take a detour to the west and give White Watch and its patrol routes as wide a berth as possible.

Gea remained quiet for the most part, but Rake found his curiosity about her did not abate.

Developing a bond from Novice to Lord was not only a matter of a closeness forged in or out of combat. For those like Rake who studied advancement closely, something else was considered vital for each major, transformative leap in the bond. A shared revelation between rider and dragon that could not be faked; it had to be genuine, deep at the subconscious level.

Only Thrall was unique in this regard, as his influence over his servant riders brought them into a false sort of alignment. For everyone else, these insights were a requirement and not something that could be taught. Explaining this to younger pairs would likely hold them back as they spun in mental circles, trying to reach the place that could only arise organically, if it did at all.

Gea and Orvel's case was not uncommon. Not every Champion could achieve Lordship. However, there was rarely a clear and obvious reason. A young rider telling their struggles to a Lord or Lady was like a patient telling a physician they had a sore head.

It could be anything.

After traveling west for a time and feeling safe from White Watch, they turned north again. Down from the true heights of the mountain range, the valleys and passes were shallower, and they came upon one with a wide and roaring river.

Gea came to a sudden halt. She lifted her ears and sniffed at the air.

"Humans."

"Let's hope they aren't Wyrm Cloaks."

They approached cautiously. From afar, Rake counted at least fifty. All were men, but none wore a cloak of dragon hide. Indeed, their clothing and armor were as varied as their number. Some wore mail, some heavy leather, some fur-lined apparel, and others lighter jerkins. Three wore pieces of plate armor, though none were in full harness. Their weaponry varied just as much, and there were no horses to bear them or their loads.

"They must be part of the Eternals."

"Have you had dealings with their kind before?"

"A few times. There was a period when I despaired so badly of my condition that I thought to join them until the end."

"What stopped you?"

"I came to my senses. Despair is pointless. We cannot know what the future holds, so we cannot say with certainty that it is lost. There is always hope, even if only a little. The Eternals act nobly in seeking out scourge to fight, but their outlook is nihilistic. I won't ever give up. Not on her."

Gea rumbled. Her tail brushed across the ground, and she blinked her good eye slowly. Rake seemed to have struck a nerve, but that hadn't been his intention. As she seemed lost in thought, he studied the Eternals again and frowned.

"I wonder where they're going."

After an overly long pause, Gea's rumbling peaked, then she cleared her throat. *"They will struggle to find prey now. These lands have been thoroughly cleansed."*

Rake searched for any magical hint of the scourge and found nothing in range.

"I can smell lynx close by, though," Gea said, sounding concerned.

"They'll never attack such a large group."

"It won't hurt to be careful. I'll scare them off."

She took off. Flying low over the forested slopes, she roared and snarled. The Eternals looked up, then, seeing it was a clearly living dragon, they returned to their morning meal. Shortly after, they packed up their camp and headed east, seemingly intent on moving deeper into the range.

Rake and Gea reunited at the other end of the valley before continuing their own journey north. Rake was in good spirits, but Gea continued her grumbling and took to the skies ahead of him far more than before.

While Rake didn't mind her being quiet, he found her passive aggression irksome, and so, running between the trees, he reached out to her and asked, *"Have I offended you?"*

Gea soared overheard a few times, and when he emerged into a clearing, she swooped so close as to nearly knock him over before finally answering.

"My scales are not so thin. I've just been thinking on your stance of never giving up... It's admirable, but I'm not sure it's good for everyone."

Alas, Rake thought, *she's one of 'those' types.*

"Can't say I can see it that way," Rake said. *"What's a dragon to do when things get hard, just stop? Sit down? Where will that get you?"*

"There are choices between flying at top speed and lying down."

"I've never been comfortable with a middling option," Rake said, tearing through the woodlands of the Spine. *"If you're not striving for something, working for something, what's the point?"*

"Comfort?" Gea offered. *"Rest? Time with those we love?"* Her voice faltered. *"With Orvel gone, I'm seeing things from a new perspective. I wish we hadn't spent so many years being bitter. We could have enjoyed them, found joy in our duties, and made friends in the Spire. Instead..."*

But here she trailed off again, sadder than ever. She didn't pick the conversation back up, and Rake didn't prompt her. He'd come across plenty like her before, folk who had given in, and once they slumped down, no amount of kicking could make them stand again.

I won't give up, he promised Elya. *Not ever.*

They continued north, roaming so far that Rake was sure they would have walked off the edge of any map. Each day the snowline on the mountains crept lower.

Eventually, a day came when the mountains dropped away to the tundra of the White Wilderness and the rest of the world lay in their wake. Amid these final peaks rose a set of the very highest. Where normally snow coated the mountainsides, what little of the rock could be seen here appeared like black dusting upon a white summit. It took a climb just to reach the base of these summits, and when they made it, Gea announced that she would go no farther.

"You'll find them up there."

Rake glanced up at the vast heights that awaited him.

"Would you be so kind as to give me a lift?"

Gea rumbled. She placed a tentative foot forward, then uttered a shuddering growl and backed away. *"The Elder's command remains strong. No emerald is to disturb them."*

"So be it." He spun his polearm around in thought, then, deciding, laid it down at Gea's feet. "You'll have the privilege of taking care of this for me."

Arriving unarmed seemed the smarter way to gain this ape's trust. If the Elder and Paragons had made a promise to the creature, that suggested it was intelligent and could converse.

Gea looked from Rake to the polearm, then back to him. *"You trust me with it?"*

"Sure," he said as he wrapped his cloak tighter around himself. "Besides, what are you going to do? Fly off with it, then spend an eternity alone, looking over your wings for me?" That sounded harsh, so he added, "We outcasts have to stick together. For better or worse, you're one of us now."

Gea uttered a sound somewhere between a growl and a lost mewl and averted her good eye.

"Thank you, Master Rake."

She picked up the weapon between her teeth and padded to the relative shelter under the enormous spruce trees, which were unlike any Rake had seen before. They must have been well over one hundred feet in height and had large yellow coned flowers among their slender green needles.

He tied his cloak at his collar and midriff. It did little to combat the cold, but he soon warmed up as he ascended, and his heart got to thumping. Where he could walk, the incline was steep, and where he was forced to scale the rock face, there were few handholds. Three gaps he traversed by using Blink, and once he came close to using Kickback to reach a ledge before something close to common sense prevailed.

Night fell before he reached his goal, and the effect of such a rapid climb started to take its toll on even his body. His head ached, dizziness came over him, and he felt bone tired. He took shelter inside a cleft in the rock, curling up into a ball and wrap-

ping his tail around himself as he fought back the desire to be
sick.

When he woke, he felt little better, but at least it was
daylight. Things started to ease later that morning. This group of
mountains created their own steep dell between them. Rake was
able to get inside it, so he could walk the remainder of the
journey.

Floating his mote channels helped against the cold, but the
thin air remained the greater enemy. His breathing became
unstable, alternating from shallow and rapid to deep and slow
without much warning. Centuries of Cleansing and Forging
helped him to regulate that to an extent, but he'd climbed too
fast, and his body would need longer to adjust than he had.

Not having days to spare, he trudged on.

Trees didn't grow here, only low thorny bushes, leaving
ancient boulders the size of young dragons to break up the white
landscape. The snow seemed untrampled by anything, white ape
or otherwise. Had Gea not been affected by the bounds of her
Elder's magical promise, Rake would have feared she'd brought
him to the wrong location.

What creature could live in so high and so remote a place?

Soon after, he beheld an end to the dell where the ascent
ended in a lip of grassy land with thick bushes rising like a
green crown. Strangely, their branches were unburdened by any
snow.

That's odd, isn't it, he said to Elya.

When Rake's foot met this grass, he found both it and the air
here far warmer than just a few yards down the slope. He crested
the ridge and found himself within a basin between the mountaintops, where there lay hidden a remarkably lush, flowering
glade. Long pathways ran between each strip of flowers, as
neatly arranged as any well-tilled field on the Athran plains.

Rake approached the field of flowers and found a patch of
grass flattened by a large footprint. Given its size, the white ape
must be even larger than himself.

Rake almost regretted leaving his polearm behind. The
impossible environment spoke of some magical interference.

Even if the white ape had no core, it clearly had some power of its own.

At the end of the field of flowers, he spotted a series of caves. Not wishing to cause alarm, Rake walked slowly down one of the paths toward them. There was a heavy, unusual scent here, like celery mixed with parsnips, which he assumed came from the odd flowers. Some rose as high as his waist, with gray petals and purple pistils at their hearts.

And the closer he came to the caves, the warmer the air grew. Soon, he was hastening to untie the knots of his cloak and reckoned his erratic breathing came as much from the sudden warmth as from the thin air.

Outside the caves were piles of long gnarled branches from the thick bushes, their leaves and needles scraped off and their bark gnawed. A ring of giant flat stones conjured an image of a campfire circle, and their size put Rake in mind of large abominations.

"Hello," he tried to say, but he found his voice breathy and lacking in power. He tried announcing himself again to the same effect, then drew deeper breaths to fill his lungs but to little benefit. No one deep in those caves would hear him like this.

Rather than start poking into the caves unannounced and provoke the creature, he tried speaking telepathically, casting his message out broadly in an unencumbered voice.

"I come unarmed and mean you no harm. I'd like to talk."

Despite knowing that the Elder and the Paragons must have communicated with the ape, hearing a telepathic response still came as a shock.

"Who you? What you?"

The ape's voice was low, its pace ponderous and stilted as though every word took a great deal of thought.

"Why, I am Rake! And what I am is quite extraordinary."

"You have tail. You have scale skin," the creature pronounced, and Rake turned fast about him, trying to spot the ape, for it must have a line of sight on him. *"What you?"* it asked again.

"I am part man, part dragon, if you care to know. Come outside and you'll see."

"Dragon?!" The creature sounded angry.

"Just half a dragon."

"No dragon. No dragon. No dragon!"

Rake tensed. This was far from a smooth introduction.

"I'm not a dragon. Not really. I have no wings." He shrugged out of his cloak and let it fall to reveal his lack of wings.

A grumbling reverberated inside the cave network. Just how large was this creature?

Rake kept turning, more slowly now, with his hands up.

"You only one?" Quite perplexed, Rake stopped turning. Before he could decipher the creature's meaning, the ape asked again, much more forcefully, *"You only one?"*

While fierce, Rake thought he detected fear in its voice as well. He took a guess at the creature's meaning.

"I'm here alone. No one else. No dragon, I promise you."

"If talk, you go?"

"Answer some questions, and I'll leave at once."

"Then I come."

The rumbling from within the caves fell quiet. Then, from inside the largest one, a hulking frame came into view and stepped heavily out into the glade.

Rake held his ground, but it was no small feat. The 'white' aspect of the creature's name was accurate, for it seemed a living mound of snowy fur, growing thick as ship rigging from the back of its head. Leathery, pink skin was visible on its feet, black-nailed hands, and scrunched face, where a dark nose stuck out as though tipped by a lump of coal.

The suggestion of an 'ape,' however, could not be further from the truth. It walked on two legs, reaching at least nine feet in height, and swung its heavy arms by its side as it lumbered outside.

It stopped just outside of its cave and scratched its portly belly.

"You small."

Rake bristled. *"To you, I am. Are you satisfied that I'm not a dragon?"*

"You like one, but not big one. Kar pleased." It scratched itself

more vigorously with one hand and beat its chest with the other. *"Kar unfriend to dragons."*

"Is that your name? Kar?"

"Kar," the creature repeated. *"Kar. Kar. Saumen kar. We few. I am Chief."*

So, there was more than one of these 'kars.' Rake flicked his gaze around the caves, hoping to get a glimpse of the others.

The Chief uttered something between a groan and an excited gasp. He stopped scratching and thumping himself and leaned forward, hands on his furry knees, to gaze at Rake as though debating the merits of picking him up and throwing him from the mountaintops. A waft of the kar's heavy scent reached Rake, and he almost gagged; it made the odor of musk ox seem a delicate perfume by comparison.

"Grass dragons send you?"

It took Rake a moment to process the Chief's meaning.

"Ah, do you mean the Life Elder – big green fellow – and the Emerald Paragon?"

The Chief furrowed his white brow as though Rake were being obtuse and nodded. *"Grass dragons. Grassssss dragons,"* he droned. *"One had little human. Both strong – stronngggg as hills."*

"They did not send me, great chieftain. I've come on my own. I'd like to know what you and the grass dragons discussed."

The Chief made his strange gasping grunt again, which Rake took for assent. Rake also noticed then just how oversized the kar's eyes were, even for its massive head. They were more in the proportions of a younger, more helpless creature, which made the white enormity more endearing and less threatening.

"You say you don't like dragons," Rake began. *"Why, then, did you meet with these two?"*

"Kar had no choice. Grass dragon tribe filled the sky and found kar."

Rake's best guess was that with the whole Emerald Flight out in force, as well as a Paragon, this little garden paradise would inevitably have been spotted, even if it couldn't be discerned magically. Though there was an undeniable power of sorts to the glade, or more likely to the kar. Perhaps with so much magic awash throughout the Spine, even as far north as this, this small, otherwise undetectable area stood out like his own veiled core would if other magic washed thickly around it.

Rake was so full of questions it was hard to know where to begin, but his initial desire to find any information on Paragon Kalanta eventually won out.

"Have you seen Paragon Kalanta since then? She was the little human."

"I no see. No kar see." The Chief closed his huge eyes to demonstrate.

"That's a pity," Rake said aloud. Then, returning to telepathy, he asked, *"What did you talk about?"*

"Much things. They asked things like you. Asked where kar came from. I tell that kar hide here since before sickness came to the below ground. Kar have tales. Cold dragons hunt kar, so kar hide."

It took Rake more than a moment this time to process the Chief's words, for an awful lot had been packed into them. It sounded as though the kars had lived here since before the scourge, driven into hiding by the Ice Flight, of all things.

"Why would the cold dragons hunt you?"

"Tales say cold dragons eat kar and bring rot to the big roots."

The latter part regarding roots had Rake stumped. Fortunately, or perhaps unfortunately, there was no mistaking the meaning of the former. Such imagery was gruesomely clear, but it also made little sense. The oceans of the freezing north couldn't have been so depleted as to force the Ice Flight onto these kar, could they?

Holt would have an opinion on this, Rake thought. *Food lore is his specialty.*

Then, almost as if Holt was suddenly there and blathering excitedly on the subject, the line of reasoning came to Rake.

Dragon meat types are such because they enhance the pull of motes of the dragon's magic. Fish draw the cold toward ice dragons. Why eat fish at all? Harder to catch slippery things than something on land. Why hunt these hairy kars? Because they're large and slow… or because they also do something to stir the magic of the Ice Flight?

Rake examined the Chief using his sixth sense. There was something at work here. The fact the creature could use telepathy, how the glade should not have existed at all, how the air had grown even warmer in the Chief's proximity.

A theory finally sprung to Rake's mind. The kar didn't have a core, yet it drew the cold into itself. All the kars together must have allowed their glade to exist as it did. And if they were pulling in motes of ice and cold, that would make them a juicy target for ice dragons.

A fine enough theory, but not one he was willing to run by the Chief. The kar's knowledge on the matter seemed limited to ice dragons, bad; emeralds, not quite so bad.

"You done asking?"

Rake realized he'd been quiet a little too long. *"Almost,"* he said by way of delaying, though he struggled to think what more he might get out of the kar.

He'd hoped for information on Kalanta, but that had proven fruitless. The kar's existence was remarkable and made for a head-spinning volume of questions and implications, but in terms of fighting Thrall or understanding the Hive Mind, he feared the creature would be as helpful as a blunt blade.

Lacking a specific line of questioning, Rake said, *"What else did the grass dragons ask you?"*

"Much things. Much things," said the Chief, showing his first hint of annoyance. He shuffled his massive feet and scratched again. *"They asked kar why we here so high many times. Kar explain until kar tired, made grass dragon chief sad."*

The Life Elder was saddened by something he heard from this creature?
"What made the chief dragon sad?"

"Kar no know. All kar know is tales. Kar come from the snow lands to warm caves under rocks. That before darkness come below ground, before big bugs come to low caves. High caves safer. No voice can reach the sky."

A jolt shot through Rake. *"What do you mean by that? What voice?"*

But he already knew the answer.

"Soft voice. Cruel voice. It no reach kar up high."

The recent jolt through Rake's body turned into a colder, prickling sensation that ran up his tail and spine. *"And this made the dragon chief sad?"*

The Chief gave his assenting grunt.

Rake scratched his chin and tapped his foot. The perplexing layers continued piling up. The Life Elder had known of the Hive Mind by the time he'd met with the kar. Why would news of it make him sad? Whatever had occurred, he had to assume that Paragon Kalanta had discussed it with him. Not that this assumption did much to help him.

There was something at work here. Rake felt he was on a trail shrouded by mist.

"Did the dragon chief tell you what makes that cruel voice?"

For the first time, the Chief perked up. He raised his thick brow and sniffed heartily, and his ears emerged from beneath their blanket of fur. Rake took his silence as a no.

"It's the chief of the big bugs," Rake said, tapping his head in the hope the kar would understand.

"Chief of bugs," the kar repeated, much as Rake had repeated 'the white ape' upon first hearing it. *"Kar stamp on bugs. Kar stamp on chief bug if it come up high."*

"I don't think you need to fear the chief bug up here in your high caves. It's very mighty. Mightier than many hills. Mightier than the dragon chief."

This time, the kar gasped.

"Oh yes," Rake said, starting to feel a way into one of his usual grooves. *"The chief bug almost killed me. It created an earthquake to bring a cave down on top of me."*

The Chief scrunched his face. *"What that?"*

"An earthquake?"

The Chief grunted.

"The ground shook. The stone shook." Rake went to the large flat stones nearby and began to rock them back and forth.

"Ah," said the Chief. *"Big shakes."*

"Very big shakes," Rake confirmed.

"Chief bug make big shakes. Kar sad to hear. Kar felt shakes. Kar caves growled. Mountains growl from hunger. Kar not sleep."

This took Rake aback. Could the tremors caused by the collapsing chamber in Risalia have reverberated this far north?

"You felt the mountains shake? When was this?"

"Some sleeps ago." The Chief raised one of his thick arms and pointed past Rake. *"Rumbles loud that way."*

Rake turned and thought the kar was pointing roughly to the southeast. Whatever the Chief referred to couldn't have been the same event as what happened in Risalia. Southeast of here were the Dead Lands or the edges of the Fallow Frontier. The only place of note for hundreds of leagues in that direction was the Order Hall of White Watch.

"White Watch," he muttered to himself.

Ever since he'd entered the Spine, he felt as though for every answer he got, he received two more questions.

The Chief blew out his huge cheeks. *"That is all Kar said to grass dragons. You done asking?"*

Rake smiled listlessly and nodded. *"Yes, Honored Chieftain. I believe I am."*

"Then you go?"

"I shall go."

"You make promise." The Chief thumped his chest with one hand, then the other. *"Make promise to Kar not to return, then share big root."*

Again with this root, Rake thought, bewildered.

His next thought was to make a soul oath to the Chief, but though the kar was magical in a way, its lack of a core meant it lacked a soul large and spiritually powerful enough to make such binding agreements. The Life Elder must have made a separate demand over his flight to try and fulfill the kar's wishes.

It would only be a promise of words and character, but Rake would honor it like a soul oath. This Chief and his tribe were clearly afraid of dragons and the scourge. Despite its size, it seemed a peaceful creature; the field of well-cultivated flowers didn't speak of a warrior people.

Rake made a bow. *"I give you my word, Honored Chieftain, that I shall not return to your glade and high caves. I thank you for talking with me."*

At once, the Chief stretched to his full height and let out an echoing growl through the glade, which continued ringing long after the kar ran out of breath. When he settled again and began scratching his belly, Rake became aware of movement all around the glade. Out of many caves and crevices – some he hadn't noticed before – more kars appeared.

Few were of the Chief's impressive height, but those he thought to be adults were no shorter than seven and a half feet. The children, for children they must be, were around six foot tall, though one small infant was carried in its mother's arms. Or he assumed it to be the mother. Between the females and males, there was little difference at a glance, save that the females lacked the coal tips of their noses, their faces were less scrunched, and their hair perhaps a touch finer. More kars came; it seemed the whole tribe was coming out.

The Chief suddenly lurched forward, and Rake almost used Kickback out of instinct.

"You come," the Chief said, throwing an arm around Rake as though they were old friends. Rake walked with the chieftain, though the strength of the kar would have dragged him along whether he wished to go with him or not.

They arrived at the field of tall flowers. The Chief let Rake go, bade him stay put, then started inspecting each long stem with a delicacy that Aberanth would have admired.

Three female kars bustled over, carrying baskets woven from the thorny mountain bushes. They also inspected the stems of the flowers, though they seemed much less fussy than their Chief, for they soon pointed at one and made sounds somewhere between grunts and hooting.

One produced a very flat piece of rock from the basket, fell to her knees, and started to dig with it, using the flat rock like an extremely short spade. After a few moments, one of her companions also knelt, then reached into the freshly dug ground and pulled out what looked like the profane offspring of a turnip and a monstrously large carrot, its flesh a mottled white not unlike the kars' own fur. The female kar broke off the long stem, placed both vegetable and flower into the basket, then the trio moved off in search of another.

Rake's astonishment only increased as the Chief dug up a

vegetable of his own and presented it to Rake with a frightening smile of slab-cut teeth.

"Big root," the Chief declared. *"You give promise to kar, and kar give food."*

Afraid he would be expected to eat the dirt-covered vegetable on the spot, Rake was delighted when the Chief lumbered back toward the caves.

"Come."

Rake followed.

Back by the caves, the Chief made a great ceremony out of handing over his 'big root' to a tribe member, who went about cleaning it using a smooth oval stone.

As he waited, Rake stood in awe of the whole tribe and its veritable industry. Female kars sat weaving baskets, others used oval stones to scrape the thorns off large branches, children collected leaves, while other younger members of the tribe counted out the neatly picked flowers like merchants stacking coins. The males rolled boulders to reveal the entrances to more caves, and out of one came the unmistakable bleating of goats. Sure enough, a kar emerged from it at the head of a herd of mountain goats, their shaggy bodies as white as those of their kar masters.

Most of the males were busily hunched over smaller rocks, using crude stone tools to work them. Much chinking and tapping arose from this open-air workshop, and one kar raised up his work and blew with great gusto into its hollowed-out center, releasing a cloud of dust. It looked very much like a lumpy bowl. The kars' use for a bowl soon became clear when Rake noticed a kar child milking one of the mountain goats.

To Rake, the most curious element wasn't their tools or behavior but the mystic motes now swirling thickly in the air. These were thoughts unlike Rake had ever encountered, and given a mix of mystic motes led to the healthiest and strongest cores, he was sorely tempted to ask permission to stay a while and Forge them.

Before he could dare, the Chief was ushering him closer again. The 'big root' was now cleaned of dirt, and another kar was carefully cutting it into what would be mouthfuls for it but looked jaw-breaking even to Rake.

"*Eat,*" the Chief said, ushering him closer. "*Eat. Grow strong.*"

This is the downside to being polite, Rake thought. The last time he ate something other than meat or marrow had been when Osric had fed him bread as a prisoner at Windshear. He'd thrown up after that, and his guts had cramped in fiery pain. Vegetables were more palatable for dragons, so he trusted he could handle whatever this was.

Better to do it fast, he decided, then popped a large chunk into his mouth. He bit down, and it broke apart with a satisfying crunch, releasing water that was sweet and lightly spiced. Taste-wise, it was far from terrible, though its texture was exactly what he might expect from eating a raw turnip.

After forcing down one mouthful, he hoped that would be the end, but he saw a bowl of milk heading his way and resigned himself to his fate. At least this wasn't a raw vegetable. In fact, it turned out to be creamy and quite delicious, although he did find a hair in it.

The Chief bellowed his greatest grunting-gasp of approval yet, and when he spoke, he sounded elated. "*Kar feed you. Promise is made. You go.*"

Rake bowed again. "*I am in your debt, Honored Chieftain. You owe me nothing more. Thank you for your food and for your information. May the big bugs and the cruel voice never find you.*"

He took his leave, panting as he left the glade and the full force of the mountain cold enveloped him. The journey back down took just as long as the climb, meaning that when Rake at last reached Gea under the spruce trees and prodded her awake, he'd decided on his next move.

"*Did you meet it?*" Gea asked while she yawned.

"I did," Rake said, quite pleased to have his voice restored.

"*What happened?*"

"We should get going," he said, already walking.

Gea rumbled and scrambled to catch up. "*Get going to where?*"

"To White Watch, of course. You'll be as eager as I am once you know everything. Keep up! I'll tell you about it on the way."

32

LEADER OF THE PACK

"Are you sure you want me?" Osric had asked her. "You don't know half the things I've done."

She'd met his eyes and said, "Try me."

He'd told her everything. How he'd burned a Mithran colony and the scourge inside it rather than risk his men in saving it. How he'd left prisoners to starve in the wastes between Ahar and the desert so his men had food to fight and win. How he'd taken the head of a traitor, a man he'd known for years, without so much as a thought. All this and more, including the ill deeds he'd committed when bonded to Thrall, and he made sure to tell her that Thrall hadn't forced him to do *all* those things. Worst of all, how he'd killed his own brother and why he'd wanted to. Who could come back from that?

She'd listened quietly there by the lake and remained quiet for most of that day. When she departed to hunt for more rabbits, he feared she might abandon him after all, but in the end, she returned and laid a catch at his feet.

"I'll take you anyway," she'd told him.

Osric knew it was a moment he'd remember vividly for the rest of his life, and he often recalled it while they journeyed east through the Frontier and dreamed about it at night.

"I'll take you anyway."

I mustn't let her down. That was his guiding thought now. *I must never let her down.*

As for her own woes, she'd not wished to relive them then, for the pain was still so fresh. As for whether her brother would come for them again, she was confident that he, at least, would not.

"He will not besmirch his own golden soul by harming his egg mate, but he warned us to flee these lands if we wish to remain free."

Together they had agreed that, in the end, should Thrall succeed, nowhere would be safe, and so they would move on, warned though they'd been.

Redbarrow was their goal. Merchant had been right in thinking these eastern lands controlled by the Hounds would be safer; there were more travelers on the roads, and armed men wearing brown neckerchiefs kept something like law and order. There was no talk of settlements under assault, no refugees fleeing the butchery of Thrall's minions. It all seemed normal, or as normal as such lands could be.

Merchant had also been right to insist Osric bring the marrow with him. Anytime he stopped to ask the way to Redbarrow, he only needed to flash the jars in the saddle bag and have the dragon show herself. After that, every member of the Hounds couldn't jump quick enough to assist him, and by such means they reached their destination in swift measure.

An oval hill stood alone upon a flat plain, as though a piece of the foothills leading to the distant Grim Gorge had sprouted here in error. The town of Redbarrow had been built upon it, a well-defended location in the Frontier, with stone walls covering the hill's base in a semi-circle, leaving natural rock and steep terrain to guard its flanks.

The gates themselves were the sturdiest Osric had seen in the Frontier, reinforced on the outside with heavy panels of iron. *That would give a juggernaut some pause but perhaps not our ginger friend. Stone walls are a plus, but they are thin: a determined catapult barrage could reduce them.* Although he recognized the chances of warfare in the Frontier extending as far as catapults or trebuchets to be fanciful.

Dogs barked on the other side of the heavy doors. When they opened, half a dozen men wearing brown neckerchiefs came out to meet them. They were all armed with what looked like iron-tipped spears and iron swords and wore a hodge-podge of iron plate or chainmail; only one man wore steel, and he seemed the leader. Three of the men held no weapons but kept tight hold of the chains of burly hounds, vicious and large enough to make chew toys out of men. They snarled and barked, then fell into whimpers the moment they beheld the black dragon.

She rumbled to herself, thinking on what Ash had told her.

"Become the hunter, not the prey."

The Hound wearing the steel bowed his head, then spoke. "You'll be wanting a word with our gaffer, then?"

Osric did a double take. Was this assumed of anyone who trudged through the wastes of the Frontier to reach Redbarrow, or was the assumption that someone with a dragon was evidently hoping to speak to the person in charge?

"If you mean the Jackal, then yes, I do."

"Aye, sir," said the Hound. He hesitated, then, with another bob, he added, "We wasn't expectin' you so soon, see. The gaffer's been working to get what you need, sir, proper hard he has."

Osric grunted. Quite clearly, they thought Osric to be someone else, but he saw no reason to deviate from his preferred blunt, direct communication.

"Take me to the Jackal," he said, unslinging the saddle bag from his shoulder. "I have something he wishes." And here he opened the bag. As soon as he did, one of the bolder dogs snuffled and barked, its eyes fixed on the jars of marrow.

The Hound in steel peered inside the bag. First his eyes popped, then his face became a picture of shock, then alarm, then deepest fear.

"You've brought some yerself? Why would— oh, but that ain't for me to be askin'. Pardons, sir. Our gaffer will be right happy to receive you," he added, offering the dragon a bow now as well. "Please, come," he added, ushering them through the gates.

Osric and his dragon quietly followed.

"Who does he think we are?" she asked.

"Doesn't matter. Quicker we meet this Jackal, the better."

Once through the gates and inside Redbarrow, Osric made his customary inspection of the defenses. Not good. Not good at all. The town had started well, first making use of the hill, then stone walls, a proper gatehouse, and gates reinforced with iron.

The streets, however, were a disaster. Squashed in, with dozens of winding routes weaving in all directions, it was as useful as a leaky bucket. He got a sense of a town that had long since outgrown its original confines, but rather than leave the safety of the walls, the townsfolk had built layer upon layer until every nook and cranny was filled.

From all sides came the ringing blows of hammer on metal, the fiery whoomph of great furnaces, and an acrid smell of burning coal and hot ash.

The steel-clad Hound wiped at his brow, pointed to the top of the hill, and said nervously, "I'll take you to the Den, sir."

Osric grunted again and gestured for the man to go on, inwardly thankful to have a guide through this maze. At length, they began to ascend the hill by means of a switchback road weaving around the outer edge all the way to the top. Townsfolk, Hound members, actual hounds, and mules drawing heavy wagons all gave them a wide berth as they climbed.

The relative prosperity of Redbarrow gave it one more advantage, which was ample coverage and good placement of its ballista positions. There were far more than at Blackhollow, and Osric spied good stocks of bolts at the ones they passed.

Halfway to the top, an unusually wide path branched off the main road, leading to an adit with a strong archway cut into the side of the hill. Men in helmets with pickaxes were coming and going out of the mine, their faces and clothes covered in soot.

Onward and up they went until the steel-clad Hound brought them to the largest hall on the hilltop, announcing it to be the 'Den.' There was nothing ostentatious about the inside; indeed, it reminded Osric of the halls of lesser jarls in the Empire. The walls and floor were unadorned rough stone, the tables against the wall plain, and the chairs equally plain and functional, all dimly lit by a few hanging oil lamps and a low burning fire pit.

Grim men with dark beards looked up from their drinking, dicing, and pipe smoking to give them dour looks through squinted eyes. Osric's first thought as to their smoke was of marrow, though the scent in the air was bitter and herbaceous, not the burning tang of marrow.

When they reached the center of the hall, the grim-faced men stood in force, and Osric got the hint that he should remain where he was. No one spoke, and they had only the crackle of the fire pit and the exhales of the smokers to break the silence.

Then, at last, a tall man entered, flanked by two enormous dogs. His ancestry was unknowable, his fawn complexion with warm undertones unidentifiable. It was far from the pasty pale of the Skarls, nor hard brown like a Lakaran man, but nor could you easily place him from Mithras or Ahar.

Even his hair was unusual, red at its roots and coarse black through the upper tips, with tufts of gray throughout. His ears were uncommonly large and prominent, which, combined with his long nose and cunning eyes, made him seem as much a fox as a man.

As he drew closer, his heavily lined face marked him as old, even though he strode with the energy of a younger man.

"He must be a hard one," Osric noted across his bond, *"to remain at the top in a place like this."*

The Jackal, for this could only be the Jackal, sat on a high-backed chair as if holding court. The 'throne' had huge armrests carved in the form of hunting hounds, and the real dogs went to sit upon their haunches, one on either side, growling lowly, unperturbed even by the dragon's presence.

The Jackal thrummed his fingers upon the wooden hounds, studying Osric with his foxlike eyes. Most folk would have been intimidated by such a hall and such a man, but Osric found it overdone.

The Jackal rapped his fingers against his chair twice more,

then suddenly ceased, licked his lips, and said, "It's usually you lot what kick things off."

"My lot? Who do you think I am, exactly?"

The Jackal clicked his tongue, rapped his knuckles again, then leaned forward. "Listen 'ere, I don't like tricks. Me and the lads 'av done our bit and done it best we can in lean times. You cloaked lot are demandin' more marrow than I can manage, and now you're bringing some yerself. I don't like it, see," he added with another rap of his knuckles, another lick of his lips. His dogs growled. "What you mean by it, eh?"

Cloaked lot, Osric thought. So, that was it. The Hounds thought him a Wyrm Cloak. What they thought of the dragon, who could say, but a dragon was a dragon and never to be taken lightly.

"There's been some misunderstanding with your gatemen," Osric said. "I am no Wyrm Cloak, nor do I serve their master."

Mutters whipped up among the grim-faced men.

"Show us that cloak, then," said the Jackal.

Osric raised his gray cloak, opened it on his right side, and let the material hang over his stump. "It's only wool and linen," he said, fingering the cloth between thumb and forefinger.

The Jackal leaned forward, squinted, issued a "heh," laughed a breathy laugh, then sat back on his 'throne' more at ease. He looked over to a dark corner of the hall and called, "You'll 'ave to get your head knocked, Grimbol, might be that'll fix your eyes! So," he added, facing Osric again, "what's that tongue of yours, then? Feorlen?"

Osric inclined his head.

"You a rider?"

"More of a soldier."

The Jackal gave the black dragon a wary look. "Don't know many soldiers wi' dragons." He suddenly lost patience, banged his fist, and, as if on cue, his dogs snarled. "Who are ya then?!"

For once, Osric hesitated on whether being direct was the best course. These Hounds clearly had dealings with the Wyrm Cloaks, and his name might be of great interest to them. Then again, the golden dragon knew they were in the Frontier, and whatever his own dragon might think, Osric knew they were on borrowed time.

Besides, he decided, the Jackal hadn't exactly been pleased to receive a Wyrm Cloak, so whatever their dealings were, it didn't seem to be a happy relationship. That gave him some comfort.

"My name is Osric Agravain, former General to the Gray Cloaks."

Another round of murmurs from the grim men, this time louder.

"Agravain?" the Jackal said with a tone like a cracking whip. "Agravain?"

"I've brought this marrow as a dying wish from a friend." Osric opened the saddle bag and placed it on the ground as if in tribute. "I knew him only as a merchant, but I'm sure he was once a member of the Athran cavalry."

"That's right," said the Jackal, needlessly loud. "A great smuggler. And a gifted rider n'all." He started tapping again. "What's become of his fine horse, eh? Did you bring 'er too?"

"Alas not. She fell at Blackhollow. The town was attacked by Wyrm Cloaks, scourge, and dragons."

"Pity," the Jackal threw out. "You're a loyal bugger to carry a dead man's burden. Could use a bit more o' that 'round 'ere, if ya ask me."

Some appreciative laughter and jeers shot between the Jackal's men.

Osric pressed on. "I've been looking for my mother, Petrissa Vogt. I believe she is—"

The Jackal jumped to his feet and pointed a long finger at him while his dogs braced on all fours, baring their teeth.

"Enough muckin' about. Tell us who you really are!"

"At last," Osric said to his dragon. *"Confirmation."*

She shared in his nerves and excitement.

"My name is Osric Agravain. Bring Petrissa to settle it, and we can move on."

"You're bold for a crippled soldier."

The Jackal nodded to his men. No weapons were drawn, but Osric felt them press in from all sides of the hall. He trusted humans wouldn't be so foolish as to attack a dragon, but then she was only small, they were outnumbered, he couldn't use her magic, and all one of them had to do was plant a knife in him.

As he reached for his axe, their dragon bond stirred, thumping hard and flaring pain through Osric's chest. The dragon took a step forward, snapped at the air, and growled. At once, the great hunting dogs came to their senses, quieted, and lay down.

"He traded that hand for me."

The Jackal pulled back in alarm, looking as if he'd seen a wraith pass through the hall. His men mumbled fretfully and stepped away, back to where they'd started.

Osric let go of his axe. "First time hearing a dragon speak is a remarkable thing. Now, bring Petrissa."

The Jackal beckoned one of his men to his side and spoke low in his ear, then the man darted off and disappeared through a door at the back of the hall. Osric and the dragon remained in the center of the hall while the Jackal stood before his throne, his dogs prone on the floor, with his men whispering around them. Things stayed like that until the door at the back of the hall reopened and Petrissa Vogt entered.

Had Osric not been expecting to see her, he might not have recognized her. He remembered her as being tall for a woman, full-bodied, her chestnut hair flowing thick down her back. She was different now. She'd shrunk, she'd thinned, and her hair fell only to her ears with just as much white and gray as brown. She walked differently, too, and held herself differently, but it was undoubtedly her.

Osric became aware of how wild and matted his beard was, of how dry his mouth had turned. His next breath caught in his throat.

"Is it her?" his dragon asked.

"It's her."

Petrissa swept toward the Jackal, smiling bewilderedly as though this were some game for her to figure out.

"My darling, whatever is the matter?" Her Risalian accent

was watery thin after so long from her homeland, but a trace of it remained.

The Jackal took her hand as lightly as if he were picking up a precious gem and gently kissed it. "There's someone 'ere for ya, luv."

It was then she finally looked to the center of the dim hall. She froze. Osric supposed he must have seemed like a specter to her, come to haunt her.

"Hello, mother. I know I must look different." He held up his stump and stroked at his feral beard. "But, under it all, it is me."

Petrissa's expression remained blank.

"He claims to be yer son," the Jackal continued, "but we know yer boy was done in by the Risalians years ago. Tell me ya don't know 'im, and I'll 'ave the lads chuck the lyin' cur out."

Petrissa opened her mouth, uttered a gasp, and closed it again. It appeared she'd forgotten how to speak, perhaps even how to think or breathe.

Doors banged open from behind Osric. Shards of daylight cut through the gloom, and three men wearing brown neckerchiefs rushed into the hall. The trio drew up beside Osric, panting like men who'd just run for their lives, then looked quickly from Osric to the Jackal and back again, their panic mingling with confusion.

"What now?" the Jackal shouted.

"Sorry, gaffer," said one of the breathless Hounds, "but more o' the cloaked fellas 'ave arrived. We told 'em you were already dealin' wiv'—"

"No, send 'em up."

"They're already comin'," said another, bent over double as he fought for breath. "We legged it on ahead."

"This ain't what I had in mind for the day." The Jackal's fear was plain now. "Listen up, you dogs, I reckon we're in for a spot of bother. Gus, Mick, Rono," he added, pointing at people around the edge of the hall. "Round up more o' the lads and wait outside."

People were running. The Hounds became agitated.

"Time to hide again," Osric told his dragon, and while she

slithered into his murky shadow, she did so reluctantly this time. Osric tried to slip back toward the edge of the hall, hoping he might be able to avoid the Wyrm Cloaks as part of the crowd.

"Oi, soldier!" the Jackal called. "Stay right there. We're gonna settle this good and proper."

Petrissa remained still, showing no signs of acknowledgment.

Osric pulled up his hood, rounded his shoulders, and generally tried to look unimportant in the dark hall as the Hounds shuffled closer together, forming flimsy ranks.

Not long after this, the Wyrm Cloaks arrived, striding into the Den unannounced, the butts of their halberds clanking against the stone floor with every step.

Keeping his head down and his body turned away, Osric glanced sidelong at the pair. One wore a cloak of blue scales, the other purple. Their hoods were down, but at this angle, Osric couldn't discern much about them beyond one having olive skin and thick, dark locks, the other pale skin with a straw-like mop of hair.

"Welcome, fellas," said the Jackal in a strained manner. Before he could say, more the olive-skinned cultist spoke.

"We heard a strange tale from your gatemen." His Alduneian Common was good enough but slow and laced with his Ahari background. "They said you were already in audience with one of our brothers. Imagine our surprise."

"Sounds like a lesson in not takin' every gateman at 'is word," said the Jackal. "Let's get right to business, shall we. I've got the payment."

One of the Hounds hurried out of the crowd, holding the saddle bag full of marrow jars.

The straw-haired cultist took the bag, opened it, silently inspected the contents, closed it, then turned to his companion and gave a small shake of his head.

"This payment was overdue," said the Ahari. "Our master requires more."

The Jackal clicked his tongue again. "There's more trouble in the Frontier nowadays. Makes gettin' ahold o' the plant or paste 'arder, even more so in such quantities. My own turf's dry o' the stuff now, so I'll need more time to—"

"Our master does not have all the time in the world."

That made Osric wonder. What fresh terror was the dragon brewing, and what was pressing him?

The cultist continued. "If you can no longer be of use—"

"I've got pounds of those 'erbs you needed from Coedhen," interrupted the Jackal. "Piles o' the stuff, and iron, plenty more iron – as much as you like."

"It's the marrow we're short on," the cultist said condescendingly, turning to face all in the hall. "And we demand more." He started stepping past the ranks of the Hounds. "Turn out your shacks. Pull up the weeds and find a stray strand of the leaf."

He took a pipe from one man, but after checking its contents and finding no marrow, he dropped the pipe and trod on it with a crack. He was heading perilously close to Osric now, and there was no way of moving out of the way without drawing attention.

The inevitable occurred.

The cultist reached him and took him by the arm. "Look at the state of this one! Your men aren't better than unwashed beggars." He shook Osric. "Got some hidden in that cloak?"

Osric tried to resist turning, but the cultist seemed determined to look into his eyes as though Osric might be hiding some marrow in them.

He might not recognize me.

The cultist's gasp put an end to that happy thought.

"Is it? Can it be?" He stepped away and took his halberd in both hands. "Obis, come and have a look at this. Face me, damn you!" he shouted harshly at Osric.

The Hounds behind Osric pushed him forward like a lamb to the slaughter.

The straw-haired cultist, Obis, squinted at him, then his eyes went wide, and he too leveled his halberd and nodded to his companion.

"General Agravain?" said the Ahari. "Or do my eyes deceive me?"

"That's 'is name," one of the Hounds called.

"That's right, said it 'imself, he did."

Osric maintained a stern, uninterested expression but inwardly, and to his dragon, he sighed.

"Looks like a fight," he told her as the argument unfolded. *"When it's time, you'll take the blond one."*

"Put yer weapons down," the Jackal called.

"You don't command us, you old mongrel," the Ahari said.

"Whatever happens, don't let them drink their potions."

"Sovereign and the Speaker will punish you for keeping such company."

"The vagrant arrived jus' before the two o' ya. He's nothin' to us."

"Now, repeat it back to me so I know you understand."

"Hand him over, and we can overlook your late payment."

Osric could feel her heart hammering across their bond – how exactly her heart hammered while melded into a shadow, he could not say, but it did. Despite it, she felt ready and repeated her orders as requested.

"Take the yellow hair one down; don't let them drink."

There had been times in Osric's career when he would have given much to have his soldiers repeat orders so succinctly.

"Take the cripple," Jackal said. "Take 'im and leave."

The cultists advanced, and Osric reached for his axe.

"Stop!" Petrissa cried. "Stop this!"

A shiver ran up Osric's spine. He'd almost forgotten that voice.

"What's up, luv?" the Jackal said in a cracked voice.

"He's my son," she said, breathlessly, though she'd only been standing. "He's my son."

A tense moment seemed to stretch to an eternity, then reality caught back up at blinding speed.

The Jackal turned from Petrissa and spread his arms to the hall. "You 'eard 'er, lads. Change o' plan. Our friend and 'is dragon are not to be 'armed."

His two dogs regained their feet and started barking. The Hounds drew or hefted what weapons they had; one just raised his ale mug and bared his horrible brown teeth.

For the first time, the two Wyrm Cloaks seemed unsure. They drew a step closer to each other.

"This will be the end of Redbarrow," the Ahari called. "The master will not accept any slights to his faithful."

Osric barked a laugh. "Now that's just a lie."

Both men took another step back and began to reach inside their cloaks.

"Now," Osric growled over the bond.

He felt coiled like a tight spring and was about to leap forth when the dragon sprang from his shadow, vibrating with power, her talons coated in a dark miasma of her magic.

Much like back at Blackhollow, rips in the fabric of the world tore open around her target, closed, then exploded out just as she struck, blowing the man off his feet and sending him spinning across the hall to crash onto one of the long tables. His halberd clattered to the floor where he'd stood only a moment before.

Osric leaped as well, feeling sluggish compared to the speed she'd just displayed. He grabbed the hand of the Ahari reaching into his cloak, kicked him in the shin, then twisted his elbow around as he fell to his knees, pinning him.

The cultist yelped but still clutched a vial of blood.

Osric squeezed, and the Wyrm Cloak let go of the vial, which shattered on the floor. Just to be sure, Osric broke the man's hand.

As the cultist screamed in pain, Osric felt awash with satisfaction, though it quickly soured. He reached over his bond to say, *"That was a bit of my old aggression. I'm sorry."*

"They deserve worse."

Osric glanced at the dragon's would-be opponent. The straw-haired Wyrm Cloak was out cold, blood dribbling from his ear, one leg clearly broken. Very fine work.

The Hounds descended on the Wyrm Cloaks and dragged them off.

"Lock 'em up," the Jackal ordered. "Take their kit and lock 'em up."

Amid the ensuing commotion, Osric stood firm like a ship's

keel in stormy waters. The Wyrm Cloak had been right on one point, though. Redbarrow was doomed. It was only a matter of time until their disappearance was noted and other cultists sent to search for them. Perhaps if that search party was small, they could be dealt with, but eventually, Redbarrow would face Thrall's forces. And it would be destroyed.

"You should leave this place immediately," Osric said, loud enough for his voice to carry throughout the Jackal's Den.

The Jackal looked livid. "You brought this upon us!"

"I've crossed the Frontier to be here. Towns are being attacked throughout the Crow's territory. Silt Grave was barren, its people dead or taken. Our friend, the Athran, died at Black-hollow during an attack by Wyrm Cloaks, scourge, and even dragons. There will be no negotiation. Sovereign wants all of humanity wiped out." Osric deliberately used the name 'Sovereign' as that would be how the Jackal knew Thrall. "You were only left alone for as long as it was easier to receive useful tribute from you."

"You know a lot about Sovereign for one who claims to be 'is enemy."

"I was once his rider – and his slave." Osric looked from the Jackal to Petrissa. Despite her outburst to save him, she seemed to have returned to stone again. "Mother, there is little love lost between us, but please hear me. You must go. This is a fight you cannot win."

Petrissa met his gaze and another jolt shot up Osric's back, but once again, she struggled for words and fidgeted with her hands.

The Jackal slumped back into his throne, and his trusted dogs placed their heads on his lap.

"This is our 'ome," he said simply. "Our 'ome…"

Petrissa suddenly burst into tears and fled from the hall.

Osric started after her.

"'Old it!" the Jackal called, pinching the bridge of his nose, his great ears twitching. "Give 'er some time, lad, for pity's sake. We'll find you a room."

.   .   .

Osric was shown to a squat shack near the entrance to the Redbarrow mine, complete with a narrow straw bed and discarded equipment. Given the lack of space, the dragon melded into the shadows, and presently her head protruded from one cast upon the wall by the setting sun through the tiny window. It gave her the appearance of having been hunted and mounted there like a trophy.

"They could have been well on their way to the forest by now," Osric said.

"Why don't they go?"

"Because this is all they know. Most folk here will have barely strayed half a day from the town walls."

"They were hatched here?"

"Probably most of them were."

She seemed to consider it.

"I don't understand. Where you hatch doesn't matter."

"To me and you, it doesn't, but we aren't like most folk. Or dragons," he added. "People become attached to their homes."

She considered again, then shook her head. *"Wood and stone matters not. It's your flight that matters. Where they fly, that is home."*

Wise words for one so young.

Osric had heard enough of Ash and Holt's adventures to learn of dragons developing rapidly when circumstances pressured them. She'd been in danger before, but something about seeing her brother at Blackhollow and then meeting him had provided impetus that actual battle had not.

"Thanks for speaking up for me to the Jackal and his men. It meant a lot."

"Of course, we are flight."

Through the bond, Osric saw their shadows standing by each other.

He smiled. "You seem less frightened."

"No, I'm still scared. Almost all the time."

"I think those dogs will have nightmares of you."

She rumbled appreciatively, and Osric wondered whether she might choose her name soon. Until she did, he felt like there was a final, thin barrier between them.

"Your brother, had he chosen a name?"

"Sol... He mocked me for not having one yet, said he'd chosen his first among the favored five." Her bitterness was clear, her sadness deep, and her frustration at everything strongest of all. *"With your brother, did you hate him as much as you loved him?"*

A phantom ache from his missing hand coursed through Osric, and he gritted his teeth against it.

"For years I did, then the love died."

"Did that make it easier?"

"Worse."

She snorted wispy smoke, then retracted fully into the shadow upon the wall.

Osric got up. He wasn't sure what he intended to do other than to try and offer her some form of comfort, but before he could do anything, she reached out quietly again to say, *"People are coming."*

Listening now, Osric heard approaching feet crunching over the gravel outside, and he opened the door to meet them. It was his mother escorted by four men wearing brown neckerchiefs. His stomach knotted, and his mouth and throat went bone dry again.

"Hello," she said.

Osric swallowed. "Mother," he acknowledged, somehow finding that title for her *wrong*. He was beset suddenly by dark recollections from his youngest days of her closing doors on him as strange men lurked behind her. He remembered none of their faces – they were just shadows to him – but he clearly remembered Petrissa's looks of impatience, of frustration. She never gave those to Godric.

"May we speak?" she asked.

"Yes," he croaked. It was why he'd come all this way, after all.

Petrissa bade her escorts wait outside, then joined Osric inside the shack. Osric closed the door behind his mother, feeling the tiny space now positively claustrophobic.

What sort of warrior am I, really? Unafraid of fights, even yearning for them, but terrified of being alone with my own mother. He and the black dragon were more alike than they appeared. *Always afraid, just of different things.*

They stood awkwardly, Osric not offering her a seat, she not taking one.

"I won't trouble you to ask how you found me," Petrissa said. "You were always resourceful. Very capable, from what I've gathered of your deeds."

Osric wasn't prepared to accept that at face value. He wasn't prepared to believe she cared at all.

"There will be time for us to discuss... everything," Petrissa went on, making her best attempt at sounding conciliatory. "I'm not... I'm not like I was. I regret a lot of things, b-but the reason I'm here is to ask for your help."

"My help?" he asked, incredulous. "You... want *my* help?"

"To defend Redbarrow."

"Redbarrow is already lost. Everyone must flee if they want a chance at living. There's a good chance you can get far away before Thrall finds out."

"Thrall?"

"That's Sovereign's true name."

She pressed her lips into a fine line, brought her hands together, then began rubbing a slow thumb against her palm.

"They don't wish to go."

"Then you must convince them," Osric said, not harsh, not angry, just firm.

"You were never one to shy from a fight."

Osric rasped a breath. "There's a difference between a brawl in the palace yards and this. You do not know this enemy as I do. It's time to run. I didn't think that would be hard for you."

She took that barb with grace. "This place, these people, I can't run from them, not as I used to." With a sudden movement, she reached for his hand; he whipped it away, and she took that gracefully too. Not meeting his eye, she said, "They don't know where else to go, what else to do. They're tough men, fighters, survivors."

"They're all going to die."

From the look in her eye, she'd already accepted that, and yet she would stay anyway. The most bitter part of him said that was only because she was old now. Two and sixty. Who would take her all wrinkled and gray?

Fresh phantom pain pulsed from his missing hand. He was lost on what to do. More than twenty years they'd been apart; he'd come all this way, and now there was no time.

The black dragon sensed his turmoil. She sent him comfort, then her head re-emerged from the shadow upon the wall, causing Petrissa to jump in fright and place a hand over her heart.

Osric met his dragon's purple eyes, so large, so round, wet and blinking at him.

"She's your flight, and she's asking for help."

Oh, he thought, *if only you knew everything.*

Osric made a mental note to tell her when there was time.

'I'll take you anyway,' she'd told him by the lake. 'I'll take you anyway.'

Petrissa seemed to screw up her courage for another attempt. "If scourge are involved in these attacks, then riders will come."

"In better times, the Order would come, but the Order is torn on many fronts. You cannot hope for riders to swoop down from bright skies like in the songs."

"We'd have you, at least."

"I'm no true rider. One proper rider might be of help, one with mastery of their powers."

His thought was of Holt and Ash. They had strength now. Even they might have balanced the odds here.

"It's a leader we need, not one warrior. The Jackal is good at playing against the Crows and their ilk, but he's never led more than a dozen men in a brawl and never something like a battle. For that, there are few more experienced than you."

That's just the thing, mother, I can't be trusted with power.

He breathed deeply, trying to reason out the impossible position.

"You protect now," his dragon said. *"Let us stay."*

A soldier defends…

"If we do, we'll both die as well."

"What do we have to lose?"

More wise words, he thought. In his heart, this had always been the only choice. To leave now would be pointless; the wounds in his soul would remain, and he'd be unable to develop his or her magic, meaning he couldn't protect her from Thrall.

"Nothing," he said aloud.

Petrissa looked taken aback but pleased.

"So be it," Osric said. "We'll stay."

33

AN OLD SWINE AND THE SILVER SOW

Sunset bruised the sky. Atop a cliff two days' ride south of Stroef, Oline's emerald squadron took some much-needed rest. Their westward route that followed the Feorlen coast before striking north over the strait to the Empire's underbelly had been a hard one with little rest.

Now settling down for the night, Florry, their Emerald Ascendant, and Pello, their Emerald Novice, took tutelage from Oline while the wild emeralds guided their dragons. Even Oline's dragon, Harvron – brown of belly with a mossy green back – paid rapt attention to the insights of the Wild Flight. As one, each dragon pressed a foot into the soft grass, listening to the world in a way others could not.

Talia tried to focus on Cleansing, but the fierce winds of Fjar-rhaf made it hard to concentrate. Einar and Skree had stilled the winds when they'd stopped before, but not tonight.

Einar sat further away on the cliff's edge overlooking the roiling blue-gray waters of the vast Bitter Bay. As Pyra was already asleep, Talia decided to join him. When he did not protest, she sat beside him and allowed her feet to dangle against the cliff face. She felt the difference sitting by the wind rider at once, for the howl of the air was quieter beside him.

"Aren't you tired?" Einar asked.

"I am, but worries will keep one awake."

"True enough."

Close by, Skree sat curled up and watchful. Her scales were the pale gray of a whiff of cloud, and her wide eyes were dark as iron and full of judgment, a look Talia had grown used to.

"What I do as Queen does not reflect on any rider. My kingdom is in danger, and so I must relieve it. My husband is in danger, and so I must save him."

Einar picked up a loose stone, then threw it down toward the sea. "It's not that I don't sympathize. In truth, I wish the jarls here hadn't sought fresh conflict with Skadi. We've been down that road before, and it only leads to misery." He scowled, then sniffed, clearly annoyed at himself.

"We?" Talia asked. "You're of Fjarhaff?"

Einar grimaced. "From the western reaches. I visited Stroef a couple of times in my youth. Not the grandest of places, though the beer is good."

"Does hatred for Skadi run so deep?"

"There's no love for the empress, at least amongst the older families, and Jarl Sigmar has a strong pull over them. I always thought the scourge to be a worse threat than rule from Smidgar, but I don't like to speak on such things." He shifted and cleared his throat. "Else I would have remained a minor jarling and never taken the oath."

"Maybe the oath isn't perfect if it prevents us even from speaking."

"Maybe," he said coldly. "Or maybe it holds wisdom we would do well not to dismiss."

Sensing it best to depart, Talia stood and excused herself. Away from Skree, the chill from the whipping air returned. Talia found relief in lying beside Pyra, who brought her warm wing over her like a blanket.

Two days of flying later, under a watery morning light, they came within view of the coastal town and castle of Stroef. Dark, brown, and gray, with worn old walls, Stroef looked as severe as the harsh waters of the Bitter Bay.

Once, it may have been little more than a motte and bailey. A resemblance of that layout remained, with the town sprawling in a semi-circle around a manmade hill with steep embankments. Upon the hill's flattened top was another ring wall and a strong, if small, castle. Ballistae dotted the fortifications, though Talia couldn't say when the town had last found itself in the path of a swarm.

North of Stroef, another force had made camp to choke the main gates, flying pink banners incongruous with the grizzled defenders. Yet the ongoing siege raised Talia's spirits.

Fynn must still be alive.

"Reach out to the emeralds," Talia said to Pyra. *"We could use their help."*

Pyra touched down well out of range of Stroef's ballistae. The wild emeralds landed around them and dipped their snouts, asking how they might aid the Red Banes.

Midway through their explanation, Harvron roared irritably and landed, sending a dull tremor through the earth. He snarled, and the wild emeralds seemed torn on who to listen to now.

Talia jumped down from Pyra to stand before a confused Oline.

"We only seek information," Talia said. "What harm can it do to listen to the stones and see if I'm right?"

Two of the wild emeralds began listening to the earth anyway.

Oline bit her lip as Harvron rustled and clawed at the soil.

Pello and Florry touched down next.

"What's going on?" Florry asked, the lilt of Coedhen strong in her voice.

"Pyra and I are hoping to ascertain whether there is a passage leading out of Stroef."

"Might we assist?" Pello asked, his Brenin accent more nasal than most.

"Not as a Novice," Oline said.

"We would welcome any aid," said a female emerald, *"for we are sparse here, and there is much rock to listen to."*

Florry and her dragon both stooped to the earth, then the third wild emerald added its power to the task.

Harvron snarled, then huffed moss-colored smoke. *"If they're going to do it anyway, it might as well be done right."*

With that, he muscled his way to the front of the group, pressed both his front feet deep into the ground, and lowered one ear to the earth.

Talia then became very aware that Einar and Skree were hovering over the rest of the squadron.

"Champion Oline," Einar called. "Why do we delay?"

Oline raised a finger to quiet him, then she sank to her knees, pressed a hand to the earth, and closed her eyes.

Skree snorted, and a ferocious wind whipped around Talia and Pyra. Talia raised her arms and began Floating her mote channels to shield herself.

"Champion Talia," Einar said, his voice straining between deference for her rank and his own distaste. "We did not leave Falcaer to be assets in your personal wars."

Pyra flashed her fangs, *"Pay more respect, Ascendants."*

Skree hissed. *"As you did to the Paragons?"*

Pyra thumped her tail, throwing up dirt, but restrained herself from going further.

"A glimpse of wisdom," said Skree. *"Your bond might be of Champions, but Einar has been Forging my core thrice your years. I'll match my wind to your flames any day."*

"Enough," Oline said, rising with dirt clenched in her fist. "Harvron and I could crush you both. The Red Queen's business is her own."

Seething, Einar and Skree reluctantly bowed their heads, and the winds around Talia dissipated.

"There's a passage," Oline said to Talia. "It leads from inside the town down to the eastern shore. There's a blockage, but I'm afraid we can't be more exact than that. Whatever it is, it isn't made of stone."

Wooden boards, an iron gate – so long as it wasn't stone, Talia could break it with enough force.

She looked up at the wind riders. "I'm going to try and resolve this peacefully. If things go wrong, I'll avoid unnecessary bloodshed."

Einar's face darkened to a storm cloud. "Tell yourself whatever you like."

With that, Skree beat her wings and rose until they were but small specks beneath the clouds.

Oline looked stern, then, with a heavy frown, she mounted Harvron without another word and called for the squadron to follow her. Casting many glances behind, the rest of the emeralds took off after their Champion and headed north for the Roaring Fjord. Carried on a shrill wind, Einar and Skree shot after them at great speed.

"I don't hold out much hope for a lack of bloodshed," Pyra admitted. *"All those warriors didn't come here to talk."*

"If Sigmar has any sense, he'll take my deal."

Pyra rumbled. *"I don't suppose I can convince you to change your mind on this plan?"*

"Would you expect me to?"

"I'd rather be with you, that's all."

"Me too."

"Fynn better be in one piece."

"Ah, so you do care about him?"

Pyra grumbled. *"You care for him. That means I do too."*

Minutes later, they were touching down in front of Skadi's besieging forces. Now she was closer, Talia discerned the strange flags comprised ruby red lutes upon pink fields. A band of warriors met her, their experience shown in their armor being of higher quality and their beards being longer than the younger men in the camp.

At the mention of 'Agravain,' they managed to twig who she was, or at least that she wasn't about to bathe them in fire. A squirrely-looking boy with straw hair was ushered forward. He wiped his nose on the back of his sleeve and seemed more curious about Talia than afraid as he dropped to one knee.

"My name be Hinrik, special rider," he said in broken Common. "Egil Skeelsson, leader of the Blood Bards, will be with you soon. I shall tell of your words to him, if it please you."

"It would please me, Hinrik. You may rise."

Even as the boy got to his feet, she noticed a tall, willowy-framed man garbed in red hurrying toward her with yet more fierce warriors.

Once he drew closer, she realized that tall didn't do Egil Skeelsson justice. He was six foot six at least, long of limb, and as slender as a steel blade. His short beard revealed a cruel twist to his smile, and the same menace glinted in his eye.

Talia strained to look up at him, and were she not a rider, she would have taken a step back. He addressed her in a rough voice seasoned by years of campaigning, and, once finished, Henrik interpreted. His young voice was a perfect contrast to that of the leader of the Blood Bards.

"My men say to me your name is Agravain." Even as Henrik said her name, his face screwed up with dawning recognition.

Talia thought this a brusque greeting, but she set it aside. "I am Talia Agravain, Red Queen of Feorlen."

Egil smiled, showing bright, inflamed gums. He gave a swift bow, then thrust out his hand, which Talia shook. Egil babbled something, plainly delighted.

"Your uncle's deeds inspire us," Henrik translated. "I wish I could have been in that tent when the drugars attacked the empress to test myself against them. Killing one is to earn glory. Osric slaughtered three! Where does he serve now?"

"I'm afraid I don't know," Talia said, then brought the topic to what mattered. "I've come for King Fynn. Is there word of him?"

Egil's disturbing red smile faded. When he spoke, it was with a fraction of the energy he'd reserved for Osric.

"Yes, we have word of the prince," Henrik said. "Jarl Sigmar" —and here he paused as Egil spat upon the ground—"brought him to the ramparts. If we attack, the prince will be slain. Orders from Smidgar we await."

All that was as expected, though Talia still frowned. "Do you have supplies to maintain a siege? Stroef is well provisioned."

Henrik seemed to have difficulty in translating this, but a bit of miming on his part seemed to get it across. Realizing she was currently at the mercy of a young boy's translation, Talia vowed to redouble her efforts to learn the Skarl language, whether she got Fynn out or not.

After a long exchange, Egil scratched his beard, shrugged, then rattled out some low words.

"Sigmar is an extreme…" Henrik started, and though he evidently knew that wasn't quite right, he kept going. "He knows he's done for. I am… scared for the prince's life but there is… small we can do."

"Empress Skadi won't like that."

Egil shrugged.

"I know," Henrik said, growing wary of the translation. "A shame, it is. I met the prince once in the Silver Hall – I liked very much his music, but my empress will not blame me for the prince blundered into a trap. Egil Skeelsson will not cause harm by attacking, but when Sigmar kills him, then I shall avenge my prince, and the skalds shall sing of it from here to Upsar and all along the Reaving River!"

This proclaimed, Egil's fellow Blood Bards cheered and punched their fists in the air.

He speaks as though Fynn's death is inevitable.

"Hasn't Sigmar demanded a ransom or terms?"

Henrik translated the question, and Egil shook his head.

"Sigmar won't talk," Henrik explained as Egil spat again at the name of their foe.

"Perhaps he will talk to me," Talia said.

Egil considered this, chewing his nails as he did so. With a sucking sound, he ceased, then spoke gruffly.

"He might, special rider," Henrik said. "I am not fool enough to try and stop you."

Talia smiled. "Then raise the flags to call for a negotiation."

Henrik opened his mouth, then looked stumped. Gingerly, he asked, "Pardon, special rider, I don't know what that word means."

"I want to talk with the enemy."

Henrik asked, and Egil nodded brusquely, then turned to bark the orders. White flags bearing Skarl runes were quickly hoisted over the Blood Bard camp.

Midday had passed by the time the town gates opened and the delegation from Stroef came forth.

Talia went to meet them with Henrik and Egil Skeelsson in tow. Talia explained who she was and that she was there to talk with Sigmar and offer terms. The Stroef negotiator made a good show of offering resistance, but Talia saw the gleam of hope in his eye.

In the end, the talks occurred in much the same way as Talia had imagined. Pyra growled and flashed her teeth, and Talia made a show of calming and reassuring her for the benefit of the Stroef negotiators. When they departed, Talia hoped they did so with a sense of victory.

Back at the Blood Bard encampment, Egil Skeelsson spoke bluntly.

"You realize this is a perfect trap? I told you Sigmar is an extreme... person," Henrik said, screwing up his face.

"An extremist," Talia offered. "I thank you for your counsel, Egil, but I'll be prepared."

Then, seeming to contradict herself, she unbuckled her baldric belt, then packed it and her sword away with the gear on Pyra's back. She tried to pull Pyra's neck down to meet her head to snout, but the dragon jerked away.

"Come on, girl, we agreed to this."

After mentally tussling some more, Pyra resignedly brought her head down to Talia's level. Fear and worry welled in the amber of Pyra's eyes; their golden hue shimmered, and her pupils dilated as though to swallow Talia whole. Their bond burned. There had once been a time when Pyra would never have revealed a modicum of fear to her, and Talia treasured it.

"Fire riders are known for their anger, but also for their bravery," Talia said. *"You'll be brave for me, right?"*

A shudder ran through Pyra. *"I will."*

Talia stroked her snout, and as she brushed the scales, she reached for her bond, for Pyra's bonfire core, and drew fire across the connection.

Core-forged fire swam into her mote channels. Talia kept pulling, filling herself up like a waterskin. Once full, she started cycling in a broad fashion. This general flow of energy wouldn't dissipate into a technique, an ability, or her muscles as long as she kept cycling. Round and round the core-forged fire flowed, quickening her breath, swirling around her crown of dragon steel as a hinge point, until her breathing settled.

"This is harder than I thought."

Pyra rumbled. *"Not for my rider."*

Even under the gray skies of Stroef, Talia now felt much too hot in her brigandine.

"If all goes well," Talia said, her voice a touch strained, *"I'll see you before a full day has passed."*

Rather than linger, Pyra backed away, growling as she did so, then took off, heading north on the trail of Oline and the squadron. A condition of the talks was that Pyra would fly out of sight of the town, which the negotiator felt would suffice to prevent Talia having access to her powers.

Had the castle not been so elevated, Pyra may have found a nook on the coast or elsewhere to hide – out of sight, but not out of range. As it was, by the time Pyra vanished from sight, their bond had dimmed to a red stutter.

A sudden, sickening chill gripped Talia's soul, and she teetered on the edge of losing the rhythm of her cycling. Taking shallow breaths and with a final shuddering sigh, she held on by the tips of her spiritual fingers. Pyra's presence across their darkened bond was now like a smudge on a far-off window.

Already she felt worn but, lacking her dragon and her blade, Talia marched toward the gates of Stroef. Guards fell in around her as the doors swung open on creaking hinges. The faces of the guards and the townsfolk were indistinct; the entire town became a haze to her, just one brown-gray fog of wood and stone.

The fire swirling inside her did nothing to warm the cold burrowing into her soul. Everything was mixed and warped. She heard with her nose and smelt with her ears. Hushed voices blew around her, and the wind murmured in low tones. Was that malt she smelled or rotten eggs?

Only what lay right in front of her remained clear enough to see.

A pair of feet dangled in the air. Confused, Talia looked up, then wished she hadn't. Three bodies, their faces bloated and blue, hung high in the town square.

Her escorts led her to the stairs leading up the castle's embankment, through the gatehouse on the hill, under the portcullis, and into the inner yard. Once she was finally inside the long hall of Jarl Sigmar and able to stand still, her body began to readjust to Pyra's absence. Her perceptions returned to normal, save for the need for labored breaths.

Across the hall, an old man rose from his great chair and approached. His breaths were heavy and wet, and he thumped his cane on the fur-laden floor with each step. The guards around Talia melted away to stand in neat rows along the walls, leaving jarl and queen together in the middle of the hall. And a poor hall it was, now that she took it in. It was dark and stuffy, the air stale and made stifling by too many fires, permeated by a smell of must and age and decay; an outdated place even in an empire as old as the Skarls'.

"I thought you would like it hot," Jarl Sigmar said.

Talia thought that a strange comment to make, and only then noticed the warm trickle moving down her temple and neck.

"Riders are still people. People sweat."

"People, yes." Sigmar huffed a laugh. "Not empresses, I'm told. Not queens. Some queens are so superior they do not even know their neighbors' tongues, so you'll understand my *disbelief* in seeing you nervous in my hall," he ended with relish.

Beholding Sigmar now, Talia would never have guessed he had once been a great warrior. Though tall, he was shrunken from a stoop of his neck. His gray beard grew scraggily with jutting white hairs, his broad shoulders rounded inward, and a swollen belly stretched his tunic tight, though the material flapped loose over a sunken chest. His legs bore signs of wastage from the sickness that had confined him to bed at the height of the civil war, two sticks struggling to hold up his bloated weight. Were he a better man in a better place, Talia would have felt guilty for finding him revolting, yet in these circumstances, she thought Tubs was too kind a name for such a swine.

Given the effort of cycling against the bond's chill, Talia cut to the heart of the matter.

"I've come to make you an offer."

Sigmar entered a wheezing fit. Fighting for air, he rapped his cane against the floor, then on the long table, and emerged from the fit redder in his blotchy face.

"Have it out then," he said.

"First, I demand to see Fynn is unharmed."

Sigmar uttered a noise somewhere between a growl and a bark and waved an impatient hand. Somewhere up the hall, a door banged.

"Is this the measure of the prince of the *virtuous saviors?*" Sigmar asked, quiet at first but growing louder as he worked himself up. "For a prince of the empire to come skulking into the home of a jarl and steal his bride in the night? Hmm? Is this the measure of the morally superior *line of the boar?* The silver sow herself had thralls as a girl. I remember – I was there! But maybe I should thank Skadi's little piglet," he said, spittle flying. "His trespass finally pushed my wife to show her contempt for me publicly. Caught in the arms of another man, now I can be rid of the harlot by rights and seek a more loyal wife."

Talia almost lost the rhythm of her cycling. She held on, but her mote channels began to prickle.

"You're deluded if you think you'll live to marry again," Talia said. "Skadi intends to burn Stroef to the ground. She tires of these uprisings, but I will offer you a chance to save yourself and your people."

"Will you? The silver sow won't like that."

"Your rebellion will still end, and her son will be saved. She'll accept that."

Before Sigmar could respond, a side door opened. Fynn was shoved inside, bound by shackles. Black-eyed, his cheek and lip swollen, his hair untied and matted, and his clothes torn, dirty, and bloodstained. At least he was in one piece.

Talia met his eyes, and it seemed to take him a while to realize who she was. Then he mouthed silently, 'I'm sorry.'

With cycling consuming her focus and her bond dark, Talia only felt numb. She might have been furious at him; she might have been desperately relieved.

"There he is," Sigmar said. "Not unharmed, but alive."

Just then, coarse pain burned around Talia's stomach. Her mote channels there were beginning to chafe, and maintaining her cycling grew harder with each breath. She nudged the energy flow toward her circlet, hoping it would take the edge off, but she pushed too hard, felt the sparking heat lick across her brow—

That same instant, Fynn burst into song, though his voice was dry and hoarse.

All turned to look at him.

Talia withdrew the energy from around her crown, and its small flame withered.

"Shut him up," Sigmar called, and one of Fynn's guards slammed a gauntleted fist into his stomach. Fynn crumpled, making a pained wheeze.

The guard raised his foot.

Talia stepped forward, declaring, "Lay another hand on my husband and I'll rip off the offending limb."

The guard wisely lowered his foot.

Sigmar laughed. The sound was horrible, choking, and wet.

Talia felt taken aback by the strength of her own words. In that moment, she'd have followed through on the threat.

Still laughing, Sigmar said, "You have a way with women, my prince, that I shall grant you. I wonder how well things will go for you down there with them both together."

"Jarl Sigmar," Talia said, her voice dangerous. "Listen to my offer. Surrender to me. Release King Fynn and Freya into my care and have your men lay down their arms. In exchange, I'll grant you safe harborage in Feorlen with all the protection of one befitting your rank or provide you with safe passage and coin to go wherever you wish, so long as it is not in the empire."

"And once I release my hostages and have my men throw

their weapons over the walls, what's to stop the bloody bards from attacking?"

"I'll ensure that won't happen."

Sigmar blustered and hacked.

"You'll just have to trust me. The alternative is to be starved out or killed." Talia turned and appealed to the men around the hall. "Will you let your people suffer needlessly, Jarl Sigmar?"

"My people would rather die free than under the hoof of the sow."

The guards lining the hall did not flinch. *Hardliners*, Talia thought, *or else they're insane*. Hoping Sigmar would fold had always been a long shot. She made sure her expression showed her fury while inwardly feeling thankful the audience was ending.

"I reject your offer," said Sigmar, "but I'll thank you for presenting yourself so willingly."

Talia feigned shock. "This won't work. You can't win."

"Enough!" A vein in Sigmar's neck bulged, and he banged his cane on the table again, hard enough to crack the wood. "Skadi thirsts for blood, but not so much as to kill her own son. Nor you. Now, you can go below willingly, or..."

His voice trailed off as he waved his arm, backing away as his guards swooped in like wraiths to seize her.

Many hands gripped her.

Talia let them. Then, she tried one last threat.

"If I don't leave by morning, my dragon will return for me no matter what lies in her way. She'll burn Stroef down herself."

For the first time, Sigmar frowned. His ugly smile became a sneer. He hobbled closer, his narrowed eyes intent on reading Talia. With a final thud of his cane, he seemed to find what he was looking for.

"A word of advice. Do not threaten what you're unwilling to do."

He swiped at the air again and Talia was led off, dragged along by the small army surrounding her. In the jostle of bodies, she lost sight of Fynn as she and her escort entered the dank stairwells of Stroef castle.

Maintaining her cycling was all that mattered now.

One guard gripping her bare skin yelped and let go, yelling something in Skarl she didn't catch. Down they went until the only light was a shard of gray from the fading day. The swarm of guards crammed themselves inside a dungeon far too small for so many to stand in. Her escorts seemed to be working up to something, for the chatter increased, then peaked, then a rough hand raked through her hair and fingernails scraped her scalp to seize her crown.

A heartbeat passed, then a guard howled. His comrades laughed as the circlet struck the floor. Next came a searing hiss punctured by another scream. This time, the guards fell quiet. Two burns seemed to have cooled their courage. Then, together, they shoved her past black bars and into the cell, slamming the door with a deep clang.

Breathing hard, Talia turned to face them in the gloom. The guards stood in a wide berth around her fallen crown. Two men sobbed over their steaming hands. They decided wisely to leave it there and departed, taking their oily torch light with them.

Talia first checked on the bars. As expected, they were heavy iron and embedded into the stone of the ceiling and floor. Brute strength would not avail her.

Then she heard shallow breathing. Turning in the near-dark, Talia discovered she wasn't alone. A skinny girl of a height stood with her hands clasped under the shard of dying daylight. Her hair was long and blonde but now frayed at the ends, and she wore a shabby blue frock.

She said something in Skarl that Talia's distracted mind thought meant 'a pleasure to be meeting you,' which she knew wasn't right, but she got the gist.

Her stomach sore, her head beginning to pound, and her mote channels rubbing raw, Talia frowned and asked, "Freya? Is that you?"

The girl said something Talia didn't catch, then, with an energy that belied the circumstance, the girl leaped forward and hugged Talia as though they were old friends. Talia's first reaction was one of bemused shock, then one of panic that her body would be too hot to touch.

"Careful! You need to step back."

Luckily, Freya was only in contact with the brigandine.

Fynn appeared between the bars of the adjacent cell. He muttered something in Skarl, and Freya let go and backed away toward Fynn, placing her snowy hand into his.

Deep inside, the ache around Talia's soul grew worse.

Pyra's smudge seemed more distant than before.

"I'm sorry they hurt you," Talia said.

Fynn groaned, and his breath rattled. "They've done worse." He coughed, then seemed to force a bright tone to his voice. "Talia Agravain, this is Freya... just Freya. I'm afraid her Common is as good as your Skarl." He repeated the introductions to Freya, and then he croaked, "You shouldn't have come."

"Well, I have. Tell me what happened."

"Got a ship from Port Bolca. Landed a day south. Came up the coast. Met my contact on the shore. Snuck in. Made it to the castle yard, but then I was noticed and taken for questioning. I didn't feel like talking. After a while, they took me to Sigmar. Freya came to the long hall to see what was going on and stopped them."

Freya's icy eyes shifted between them. She babbled something and touched Fynn's face as gently as if he were a kitten.

Through a wince of pain, Fynn chortled. "She says I deserved a good kicking, but only she's allowed to do that."

Despite herself, Talia laughed too, though given her strain and nerves, it emerged somewhat strangled. "I'll ask her for permission to kick you myself once we're back home."

"I deserve that."

Freya interjected, perhaps wondering what they were saying. Fynn spoke quickly to her, and then she nodded. What vitality she'd had upon meeting Talia visibly died on her face. She shook her head, her eyes growing distant, and with another soft exchange and a squeeze of Fynn's hand, she fell quiet again.

"She blames herself for what happened, but it's my fault. I came here and caused this. When Freya found them battering me, she told them who I was so they'd spare me, but then we had to tell Sigmar everything. I wasn't going to keep silent and watch them hurt her in return. I had to…" His speech faltered, and he looked away. "I had to give up the poor brewers. You probably saw them hanging on your way in."

"Sigmar killed them, not you."

He sniffed. "That f-family hadn't used those thrall-runs in decades before I started sending l-letters."

Freya sniffed too, reaching silently through the bars to run her hand gently through Fynn's hair.

"What about your contact?" Talia asked.

"He was to wait for us down the coast with a ship. Probably long gone by now."

The constant cycling was starting to make Talia dizzy. Fighting through, she pressed on to ask, "If I get us out, can you guide us back to the passage?"

"I think so."

Fynn asked Freya something. She nodded earnestly, then spoke in an anxious rush. Fynn replied to her, then he translated.

"We heard Sigmar order his four best killers to watch the brewery. I told her they won't be an issue for you."

Talia nodded, already dismissing the information. She could handle four men.

"Unless you have a better idea," Talia said, "we've got to try."

"We're ready when you are," said Fynn, who now sounded on death's door.

"You two need to rest. I'll hold out as long as I can, but we're leaving tonight."

She backed away to the cell wall under the narrow window and sat with her back against the slimy, cold stone. Fynn and Freya slid to the floor, entwined imperfectly between the bars. Fynn's breath rattled, and Freya stroked his hair and hummed what sounded like a lullaby.

As the fire weaved inside her, Talia struggled to discern the feeling of seeing the two of them together after all this time. Whatever that distant feeling was, it felt *unsettling*. Its genuineness, its realness, was a thousand-fold truer than anything she and Fynn had mimicked in public. Now she feared no one could have believed their act; only the naïve and unworldly could ever have mistaken it for the real thing.

She wondered if this was how people saw a rider with their dragon. She found it hard to recall such times. Her life before Pyra seemed separate from her life since bonding.

Talia closed her eyes, leaving Fynn and Freya with some privacy and grateful, at last, to focus only on the fire in her channels. As her world turned inward, she focused on the smudge of Pyra in her soul. Another smaller spot, little better than a blotch of watery ink, appeared beside it. It carried that weird, unsettling echo and scent, and it did not fade.

34

BLOOD AND BEER

Talia cycled long enough, deep enough, that she forgot both where she was and her purpose. Nothing existed but the fire in her mote channels, the chafing pain, the knots in her stomach, the smudges in her soul.

Something shook her.

The feeling was distant, as though her body were far, far away. It grew insistent, and then came a voice. Talia felt herself lift from the depths of her inner world, flying through the darkened soul-void back to her body.

A hand was on her shoulder. Freya's soft voice beseeched her to wake.

Talia opened her eyes, blinking heavy lids to find her surroundings not much brighter than the darkness of her soul. The shard of gray light had been replaced by a thinner strand of silver.

"I was worried you'd fallen asleep," Fynn said from the blackness.

"Almost did. Did you two manage to rest?"

"A little."

Freya spoke, her tone clearly concerned, and Talia intuited her meaning.

"No, I can't hold on any longer." She got up and crept in the dark to the lock on the cell door. "I don't think I have enough magic in me for both cells. Does Freya know where the keys are kept?"

Fynn asked, and Freya responded.

"She does."

Relieved, Talia cycled the magic to her palm, then concentrated it onto one fingertip. She brought that scorching finger to the sliver of exposed bolt between the lock and bars.

"Close your eyes," she said, doing so herself before pushing all the fire she possessed into the metal. There was a loud sizzle, a smell akin to burning oil, then Talia gasped and fell against the bars, feeling as though many arrows had been yanked from her.

"Talia?" Fynn said with concern, followed by Freya's light touch upon her back.

Breathing hard, Talia righted herself, groaned, then breathily said, "I'm fine."

She shook and groaned again. Her respect for the Lords and Ladies who could cycle like that indefinitely swelled to new heights. She felt for the bolt in the lock. It had twisted and thinned but hadn't wholly broken.

With Fynn's help, Talia got Freya to grab hold of the bar connected to the lock and pull on it. Talia then kicked the door above the lock. A deep gong pierced the still night, and the cells rattled. She cursed, but it had to be done. Twice, thrice, four times. On the fifth attempt, the damaged bolt snapped with a crack, and the door squealed as it swung open.

They rushed out. Fynn stood by his own cell door to see them off, and Freya went to kiss him between the bars.

"Come on," Talia urged, pulling her away. "We're coming right back."

Feeling their way into a low-ceilinged corridor, they stuck close to the wall and crept toward the reddish hue at the far end. The light turned out to be from a low brazier down a turning of the hallway with three identical doors. Freya tugged on Talia's arm and pointed to the second one.

Inside, they found one guard barely awake. Talia grabbed him from behind, placed her right arm around his neck and her left hand over his mouth, and squeezed the sides of his neck. He ceased squirming after a moment, and she lowered him gently to the floor. She checked he was breathing on the back of her hand, then snatched the keys and left.

On their way back, Talia initially thought it strange that every other cell was empty. Then again, Sigmar's policy appeared to be to hang those he might otherwise have imprisoned. What were valueless prisoners other than mouths to feed and willing enemies from within?

Talia made it back to Fynn ahead of Freya, trying every key in the lock until one clicked. She wrenched the door open, and as Fynn stumbled out, Freya arrived to catch him.

As they spoke in rushed Skarl, Fynn's words sounded first reassuring, then playful. He brought her chin up and kissed her again.

Talia looked away. She remembered her crown was on the floor and went to retrieve it. Placing it back on her head, she asked, "Everyone alright?"

"We will be," Fynn said. "Let's go."

The trio stuck close together as they made their way out of the dungeons. Oily torches granted light to help them navigate through the bowels of Stroef castle. Freya led them past washrooms, servants' quarters, and the cold kitchens, then out into the bailey. A cloudy, black night and winds whistling over the hill helped them cover their movements. Every lookout would be keeping their focus on Skadi's forces, or so they hoped.

Quiet as three mice, Freya led them to skirt the bailey yard and reach the base of the castle's ring wall. With their backs against stone, Talia looked up. She didn't think anyone looking down would be able to see them, and the wind should have covered the sound of their footsteps. Still, whenever a torch bobbed past on the rampart, they froze in place, holding their breath until the danger passed.

At length, they reached an indentation in the wall's base, and Fynn translated Freya's comment that it led into another guardhouse, where a postern door led out onto the escarpment.

Talia went first, leaving the wind and night behind as she walked a short way under the body of the wall. Light and alluring warmth spilled out from behind a squat wooden door. Drawing a deep breath, she wrenched the door open.

No fewer than six men were eating, drinking from horns, and playing dice inside. The moment it took for them to notice Talia seemed to last an age, then she leaped in, seized a sitting guard by the scruff of his neck, and slammed him onto the tabletop. Dice scattered, beer flew, and horns and tankards clattered to the floor. As the guard slumped, Talia drew his sword and went to work.

Magic or no, Talia was proud of her swordcraft, and it didn't take much for a rider to handle five ill-trained guards. It gave her no pleasure or satisfaction to bring her training and enhanced body to bear upon mere mortals. With every kill, she chose to believe they were part of Sigmar's diehard followers: doomed either way. She wasn't Talia the Fire Champion here, she was Talia the Red Queen, and sometimes a queen's work was bloody.

Against her final opponent, she clashed her sword against his and snapped both low-quality blades. The man fell to the ground, begging for his life, and Fynn and Freya assisted in binding and gagging him.

Talia tossed the hilt of the broken sword away, then took the belt and scabbard from another guard and strapped it to her waist. Fynn, too, retrieved a belt and scabbard.

"You know how to use that?" Talia asked.

"Not as well as a lute." He strapped it on anyway. With his face so well beaten, he at least looked the part.

Freya didn't take a sword. Instead, she glanced from the blood on the floor to Talia and back.

Talia looked down at herself. There was blood on her hands, darker flecks showing on the outer layer of her red brigandine.

Freya paled further, from white to colorless, but her expression turned grim and determined. Pointing to the door, she spoke firmly.

Fynn explained the gist. "At the bottom of the hill, we can get into the town."

Leaving the warmth and light of the guardhouse, they emerged on the outside of the castle's ring wall. The flattened hilltop was still wide enough here for at least three men to stand abreast. Talia assumed its purpose was for sallies should any attacker manage to make it up the causeway of the escarpment.

Night greeted them again with harsh wind and a roar from the sea. Beneath the immediate grassy ledge, the world seemed to drop away sharply as the steep scarp ran sheer-faced into the blackness.

"Follow my lead," Talia said.

She carefully maneuvered herself down over the edge, crab-walking slowly forward with her hands and feet. She charted an angled course to help fight the downward tug of the world and threw frequent looks over her shoulder to make sure Fynn and Freya were handling the incline. They were making their way down inch by inch, though their pace slowed, and Talia soon found herself at the bottom while they were barely halfway down, appearing as two hunched dark blobs on the scarp.

Back on flat ground, Talia stood and checked the vicinity was clear. The closest guards were high up and far off on the northern walls overlooking Skadi's forces.

A squeak of fright from above was cut off by a gasp, followed by light thuds.

Talia cricked her neck as she turned in haste. One of the two dark blobs was now tumbling down the scarp, rolling faster with each second. Talia rushed into position, braced her feet, opened her arms, and caught the body before it crashed.

The impact sent Talia onto her back, driving the wind from her, and together they slid along the earth before coming to a halt. Talia's instinct was to cover her charge's mouth to prevent them from screaming, which she did, then followed up by softly saying, "I've got you. I've got you."

As she said this, she realized the locks of hair in her face couldn't be Fynn's.

Freya shook. They were so close that Talia could feel her racing heart even through her armor. Talia's mind managed to dredge up enough knowledge of Skarl to ask clumsily, "Are you well?"

Freya nodded, and Talia took her hand from Freya's mouth.

She lifted her arm, intending to give Freya space, but Freya grabbed Talia's arm and pulled it back down as though it were a shield.

Unsure of what to say, Talia opted to say nothing. She lay with Freya cradled against her, shaking, and tightened her hold.

Recalling Freya's early letters to Fynn, it broke Talia's heart to see her reduced to this. The bright, good-humored Freya had worn away during those letters, banished by an empress who wanted her not just gone but punished, sent to marry a man as repugnant as Sigmar. Once proud, she was now weeping and curled up in the arms of a perfect stranger, who happened to be the wife of the man she loved.

Few deserved such torment.

Talia held her, and to her great relief, Freya's breathing calmed. Her heart slowed. The shaking ceased. An image of Freya smiling happily again in the palace gardens of Sidastra rushed to the front of Talia's thoughts, and she longed to see that day.

Fynn's dark outline finally made it to the base of the hill and crawled forward to them. He reached with both arms for Freya, and Talia could hear him fighting the sickening grip of relief in his voice.

Talia rolled over and away, then got to her feet. Dirt caked the back of her neck and weighed down her hair.

From the east, a faint lip of blue rimmed the sky. Dawn was approaching. Their cover of night would soon run out, but Talia gave her charges a moment together.

They were on their knees, holding each other, Freya's head laid on Fynn's shoulder. Then Freya cupped Fynn's face and, as she spoke, she made furtive glances at Talia.

A sudden heat prickled at Talia's neck that had nothing to do with magic.

"Is everything alright?" she found herself asking stupidly again.

Sniffing, Fynn said, "It is. I'll tell you why later."

The heat in Talia's neck and face grew hotter. "Is she hurt?"

Fynn asked. Freya shook her head, then, reluctantly parting from Fynn, she pointed to somewhere in the dark.

With Freya's help, they left the basin of the hill and made it into the town of Stroef. The streets on the south side were empty, save for scurrying rats and stalking cats. Twice their footsteps roused dogs to piercing barks, forcing them to run before their owners burst onto the street.

They took cover behind the corner of a cooper's workshop, and Fynn peered around it carefully to ensure the coast was clear. Smiling, he pulled back and ushered Talia closer.

"That's it," Fynn said, pointing toward the building adjacent to the cooper's, though the brewery was so large that its front door seemed streets away across the square. Its doors lay suspiciously open.

"Well, we know it's guarded," Talia said.

Fynn nodded, then his eyes caught sight of something in the square that made him shrink back.

The bodies of the brewers still hung there, black silhouettes under the first pale wisps of dawn. Two crows perched on rotting shoulders, picking at the carrion. Freya muttered something, her voice deep with suppressed rage.

"She says that Sigmar deserves everything that's coming to him."

Talia wholeheartedly agreed, though she felt uneasy about the inevitable assault on the town once Fynn was safe.

"What of the rest of the people?" Talia asked. "They can't all can be like him."

Freya answered, and her voice softened a little.

"There are good people here," Fynn said. "She's hopeful for them. Most folk should surrender once the walls are breached. My mother's forces are brutal, but they aren't butchers. They're here for Sigmar. I'll do what I can to steady their hands as well—"

Freya spoke over him, her voice hardening again.

"But there are plenty who she won't weep for," Fynn continued. "And there are some she'd like to take an axe to herself."

Freya motioned by gripping an invisible axe shaft and swinging.

"It's a complicated place," Fynn said, now speaking for himself, "in a complicated region. The real shame is it couldn't have changed peacefully."

His words rang in Talia's ears. She thought of the trebuchets outside the Toll Pass, of Paragon Adaskar looming over her. Few things changed easily, and if some dug in to maintain the status quo, Talia had to be one of those willing to fight for change.

A vision of the future unfurled before her in frightening detail.

A vision of fire and blood.

Yet, for now, there was the mission at hand.

Talia reached up for her blade before remembering it was gone and all she had was the flimsy sword from the guard. She drew it anyway. Then, with Fynn and Freya close behind, they darted for the brewery and slipped inside as a cockerel crowed.

Inside, great kettles and treatment vats sat cold with moisture pooling on their outer surfaces. Talia splashed through a puddle, releasing a sour smell of bad yeast and a putrid scent like rotten eggs. They all gagged and coughed, and Talia wondered whether Sigmar's so-called killers would even be here. Who could withstand the smell?

Fynn led them through to the back and downstairs into what some would call a cellar, though to do so would be an understatement. Sunken deep, it was almost a small valley in its own right, with hills of keg and mountains of barrels stacked high under round windows through which the budding dawn crept in.

At least the stench wasn't so foul down here. Fynn remembered the way, leading them through the passageways between the walls of kegs and down what appeared to be a dead end, where they discovered Sigmar's men hadn't been entirely without industry.

A section of the barrel wall here had been dismantled. Iron rings, rivets, and broken barrels lay strewn about, and wheelbarrows, pickaxes, and hammers lay abandoned around the site.

Among the debris was evidence of a ripped-up trap door, since replaced by crudely cut planks.

Talia spotted a crowbar, picked it up, and handed it to Fynn. "You heave, I'll pull."

She sheathed her sword as Fynn angled the crowbar, rammed its teeth under a plank, then, with a hard grunt, pushed down. Talia got a grip on the wood, then tugged at it, ripping it up from the floor. Nails flew and tinkled across the ground. The removal of two more planks revealed a passageway leading down. There were no steps, but at least there was an ancient-looking wooden handrail.

Something whistled, then a blow hit Talia's side with the force of an arrow, expelling the air from her lungs. Though she felt sore, there was no sharp, burning sensation of pierced flesh. Her brigandine had done its job.

A tiny axe clattered at her feet.

Another whistling ring.

Freya yelped as another axe flashed past Talia and thunked into the keg wall above the passageway.

Talia lunged for Freya, pulled her back, turned her around, and shoved her and Fynn into cover so they were out of the enemy's line of sight, all as another axe cut the air.

"Keep low," she hissed, pressing her back against cover.

Fynn's brow glistened with sweat. He handed Freya the crowbar and clumsily drew his sword, holding it in both hands.

Not enough of the passage had been uncovered for them to slip into it. Talia would have to fight. She drew her weapon, peered around their cover, saw four black-clad figures, then pulled back again as quickly as a cat.

Talia searched for anything she might use as a shield.

The wheelbarrow.

She was about to make a break for it when she heard the whistling and pulled back. The throwing axe punctured a keg at the edge of the work site and beer glugged from the wound, releasing a smell of malt and crusty bread.

How had the guards managed to get close enough for an ambush without her hearing?

As though hearing her thoughts, Fynn panted, "Drugars!"

Fear jolted her heart. Drugars. Four of them. And she had two vulnerable people to keep alive – all without her blade and her magic.

Another exploratory axe sailed past, then came the trill of drawn steel.

Talia reached deep into her darkened soul for the blurry smudge of Pyra at the back of the void, pleading, begging her to hear and come back.

"I need you, I need you, I need you…"

But it was impossible to know if anything made it through; it was like trying to hold water between her open fingers.

She had no time. The drugars were closing in. She looked again at the wheelbarrow, a thick-set, heavy old thing, its wood chipped from toil.

Knowing it would be better to take the fight to the assassins and away from Fynn and Freya, Talia dove in a swift, lunging roll. She arrived at the wheelbarrow on one knee, clenched her left fist, punched through the nose of the tray, grabbed the wheel, then pushed herself to her feet, raising her makeshift shield to catch two axes that slammed into the underside of the tray.

Talia advanced at a half-crouch, barrow raised and sword ready to meet the drugars. Clad in charcoal leather and cloth from head to toe, their faces were hidden, and their footsteps made no sound. They all wielded a short blade in each hand, and there was enough space for two to face her at once.

She met the closest one head-on, blocking one blow with her barrow and the other with her sword, the steel clashing with such force that it disarmed him and sent his arm wide. She kicked his knee and bones crunched, but though the drugar went down, he uttered no shriek of pain. Instead, he slashed with his remaining sword even as he fell.

Surprised, Talia leaped backward, but a thin line of searing pain exploded from her unarmored calf.

Instinctively she reached for Pyra, and the pain fueled her voice.

"I need you!"

This time the smudge squirmed, but the reality was more pressing.

Talia backed away from the wild cuts of her crippled foe, then turned to intercept the second assassin trying to flank her.

Wheelbarrow raised, she rammed into him, pushing him back so that his body curled around the body of a large keg. More snapping bones and more silence from her foe. Talia thrust with her sword, piercing leather, then flesh, then wood. A copper tang of blood bloomed, and the drugar ceased struggling.

More pain exploded from her hip. A black axe had found its mark.

Gasping, she ripped her sword free, blood and beer running from its tip, then wrenched the throwing axe from her hip. Both her legs throbbed in protest as she staggered and raised her barrow to catch another axe.

The drugar with the crushed knee crawled forward, sloshing through dark beer, but Talia couldn't finish him, for his two comrades pushed ahead to shield him. They advanced on her, angled such that whichever one she chose to fight, the other would have her.

Snarling, Talia took another unsteady step back. She couldn't retreat beyond this point. Any farther and the drugars would see Fynn and Freya.

Heat blazed in her soul. Pyra's presence grew from a droplet to a hot pool, though it was still too faint to draw magic across.

A desperate idea sprang to mind. Talia spun – hip and leg pulsing – and launched the wheelbarrow toward the drugar on her left. The assassin sidestepped with astounding agility – the barrow crashed into the keg wall – but in his haste, he slipped on the blood and beer underfoot.

Seeing him go down, Talia focused on the assassin to her right. She pressed the attack, but the drugar turned, jumped, ran two long strides up the keg wall, and flipped backward overhead. Talia had known riders less agile, and only her enhanced speed allowed her to turn in time to block both his strikes with her lone sword.

As the drugar pulled back for another exchange, Talia's right side trembled. Her hip felt on fire. The pain from her left calf was less, though still there. As a rider, she could push through pain, but her body worked like any other – cut enough of her strings and she would crumple.

Leaning on her left side, Talia could meet one blade but not the other. Using her left arm, she tried to swipe at her foe, but she might as well have tried to grasp a fly out of the air.

With her arm raised, she was exposed, and the drugar punished her for it. The tip of his second sword found the weak spot under her left armpit; cold steel bit into her, and for a racing moment, her vision flashed—

Pyra bellowed. The gray human town rushed to meet her, its wooden buildings stacked like so much kindling. Good for burning. She would burn the world to save Talia.

—Talia regained herself as the freezing steel pushed in deeper.

Screaming, she brought her left arm down as hard as she could, knocking the drugar's arm down and the blade from his hand. The sword slipped from her and hit the ground.

And then, Fynn came out swinging, catching the drugar full in the back. The assassin contorted, and his cowl slipped to reveal a rictus expression. Rigid, he fell forward, and Talia finished him.

Freya yelled something, though Talia didn't understand her. Then she noticed the assassin who had slipped on the blood and beer now knelt on one knee; his arm was outstretched, and something flashed in the space between him and Fynn.

Freya lurched into the path of the thrown axe. Her voice cut off with a rattle of wind as though she'd been punched in the throat.

The pain in Talia's arm, chest, hip, and calf vanished. Her scream emerged more as a roar, as if she might reverse time if she screamed hard enough. And she made for the kneeling assassin. He tried to raise his sword, but Talia swung harder, swung faster, taking his arm off, then she switched to a reverse grip and cut across his neck.

From behind, Fynn's howl pierced her very soul. His grief poured out as hard as any rider who had lost their dragon, as if even now his soul were darkening, crumpling, his non-existent mote channels turning black and foul.

The pain in Talia's body returned in full force. She slumped forward. Neither side wished to take her full weight. Blood seeped from her hip and poured from under her arm. She rasped, each breath sending daggers through her chest.

Underfoot, beer and ale rose as a brown tide, streaked with long ribbons of bright blood. One drugar remained, the one with the crushed knee. He crawled along. Talia wasn't sure whether to be impressed or disgusted – what training could teach this? To not care for the odds, to forget they were only human?

Fynn fell upon the assassin, kicking, hacking, stamping. Even after plunging his blade into the drugar's back, he didn't stop.

Talia limped over to him.

"Fynn!"

She grabbed him, and in his primal state, he almost took a swipe at her. His eyes were red, swollen things. He stumbled back to Freya and fell to her side.

Talia swayed, blinking against her darkening vision. Dimly, she knew they had to keep moving. More guards would surely come.

Then, all at once, her wits returned. Fire returned to her soul. The dragon bond opened in full, and she could see Pyra's bonfire core again. Like someone dying of thirst, she subconsciously pulled magic across the bond. The pain from her wounds dimmed, and she stood straighter before the flood of panic from Pyra hit her with full force. She cycled it up to her dragon steel crown, desperate to—

Pyra flew low over the gray town; barely able to feel Talia's weak presence underground. Her rider was hurt. Bleeding. Dying. She might be dead already. They would pay. All of them. A bolt cut the air not far from her. They would pay for that as well.

—Talia's brow burned. Even for her, the flames were uncomfortable, but the cycling allowed Talia to exist somewhere between her thoughts and Pyra's. She was faintly aware of Fynn howling. He sat cradling Freya, his body bent over hers, his face red, mouth open in shock and loss, his fingertips hovering over her skin, unable, it seemed, to touch her.

Never had Talia witnessed grief this raw, and though terrible, something about it punched through Pyra's panic and fury to wake her.

Talia snapped back to her senses, head still ablaze, but she only had her own panic to contend with now.

Fynn still howled, and now Pyra's roaring mixed with his, rumbling into the cellar from the world beyond like thunder. A menacing red light flickered through the windows above.

"Pyra! Pyra, stop!"

No response. Their bond was wide open, yet Pyra could not or did not hear her.

Talia pulled more magic across the bond and infused it straight into her body. This was no time for efficient cycling techniques.

She hauled Fynn to his feet, then lifted Freya and threw her over her right shoulder.

"To the passage. Go!"

Fynn didn't seem to understand. She shoved him, and his blank eyes finally woke up. He staggered toward the trap door, but Talia got there first. She burned the remaining planks to soot, then descended into the tunnel, followed by Fynn.

The passage fell away into the earth, though not so far as for Talia to lose her connection to Pyra. Fynn's breathing grew heavier with each step. When light glimmered at the tunnel's distant end, Talia urged him on.

They entered the shelter of a large, open cave, hidden within a cove on the shore. Talia's feet sank into soft sand and the salt wind nipped at her skin and wounds, but she kept heading toward the sea. One foot went before the other, faster now, leaving Fynn behind. The sea might wash it all away. Such dark waters had never looked so inviting.

Pyra landed hard, sending torrents of sand billowing. As if waking from a fever dream, she finally spoke.

"W-what have I done?"

Talia wished for nothing more than to go to her dragon, but her legs no longer responded to her will. She felt rooted to the spot. The sand seemed to have clamped onto her boots and would not let go.

And she still had Freya.

Fynn caught up to them. Without a word, he sank to his knees, his face vacant, his eyes lost. Talia placed Freya into his arms. There was no dignity in her passing. Her skin was white, her lips already paling, her golden hair befouled by sticky beer, and the front of her frock was drenched in blood from a wound above her heart.

Relieved of her burden, Talia stumbled to Pyra. Leaning on her dragon, she looked back up at Stroef. The walls and rooftops on the eastern side were little more than black outlines against an inferno. Fire clawed skyward, hungry to devour. Cries and screaming mingled with thousands of hoarser calls from the north. Skadi's forces were charging in.

"I burned the gates," Pyra said, as though recalling a nightmare. *"Talia… Talia, say something."*

Talia opened her mouth but choked. She could barely stand, barely think straight.

Never. Never, ever, ever had she envisioned being a rider would lead to harm.

Wyrm Cloaks, of course. Enemy soldiers and assassins trying to kill her, a horrible necessity. For civilians to burn in their homes, no matter their views, no matter their innocence or guilt in any matter… never.

"I… I don't know what happened," Pyra said, as meek as Talia had ever heard her.

Talia's insides might have turned to cold slime. Feeling like she would be sick, she wrenched her eyes away from Stroef and toward the ocean.

Pyra roared a long, trembling, mournful roar.

"I could return, Sink my channels, and try to draw some of it back in."

Talia faced the town again. The fires were spreading fast. The distant sounds of battle now mingled with the fury of the flames.

At last, Talia managed to say, *"We can't go back."*

Another presence rushed out of the north.

Skree and Einar pulled up hard and glided at extreme speed over Skadi's forces, then over the fires of Stroef. They looped around the edges of the town, and as they flew, the wind blew fiercely, buffeting the flames and suffocating them under the rising gale.

Talia dropped to her knees in relief. Pyra's legs also buckled, and she fell forward, joining Talia upon the sand.

"Skree won't respond to me," Pyra said.

The wind riders swooped over the warring town twice more before turning and heading for the shore. They stopped to hover high above, and Talia had to crane her neck to see them.

Einar and Skree continued to hover. To Talia, it felt like an age.

Eventually, Skree's voice entered their minds. *"Adaskar was right."*

Without another word, the pair shot eastward over the Bitter Bay.

Not knowing what else to do, Talia crawled over to Fynn on her hands and knees. She didn't deserve any comfort for a catastrophe such as this, yet still he opened one arm and allowed her in.

They held each other, and Pyra came to snake her head around them as the battle raged and the red dawn lit the Bitter Bay on fire.

35

A TUG OF PUPPETEERS

Rake wove between the trees, fighting to maintain a good pace through the dense forests of the eastern Spine. Leaves trembled and fell from their branches as Gea swooped low over the tree-tops, circling in loops so as not to get too far ahead of him.

A break in the trees didn't offer easier ground to cover. Ahead of Rake now lay a swathe of gorse whose pretty flowers disguised its prickly nature.

"It will take you too long to go around it," Gea said. *"Best to cut through where you are."*

Rake hefted his polearm and started hacking at the gorse. When Gea flew by on another pass, she worked her magic, and chunks of the thicket moved of their own accord, thinning out to make his passage easier.

"I'm trying to understand all of this," Gea said, mainly to herself, though she clearly intended Rake to hear her. Presently he was too busy shredding thistles and nettles to acknowledge her, but for now, she didn't seem to require his input. *"You and Holt encountered this Hive Mind in an underground chamber under Risalia, and it tried to kill you by collapsing the chamber on your head using magic eerily close to emerald power. The saumen kars are also aware of this creature, which is why they climbed so high to escape it."*

"And to get away from ice dragons," Rake reminded her as he

leaped over a stretch of low gorse. *"A past you have in common with them."*

"You're the pinnacle of wit, Master Rake."

The next time she flew over, the gorse grew thicker and thornier. Rake supposed he deserved that.

"You interrupted my train of thought… Oh, yes. So, the kars climbed high to escape the Hive Mind, then, recently, they too felt tremors in the earth, emanating east of the Spine. We still have no idea where Paragon Kalanta is or where she was during the battle. A powerful ice dragon was there, though it must have arrived after the Emerald Flight fled, but we have no idea who it was or what happened to them either."

When Gea laid it out like that, Rake had to admit it did sound rather vague. He hacked some more, and sliced gorse flew around him. A piece of thorny thistle lodged into his mouth, and he spat it back out.

"Everything you said sounds about right."

"Forgive me," said Gea, *"but I'm not sure how that makes any more sense of our current course. Why should we go to White Watch merely on the chance we'll discover something?"*

"Don't you think it's bizarre, verging on ominous, that the riders there have been so quiet?"

"Not if they have held to the Pact."

"Come now, Gea," Rake said with a mental tut. *"You know as well as I that Wild Flights are monitored, especially if they move en masse, and the emeralds were most certainly doing that."*

He reached another patch of gorse where the thicket grew low with a clear stretch of land beyond it. Rake trotted back, then made a running jump as far as he could before he Blinked the remainder, emerged beyond the sea of thorns, and dropped in a roll to safety on the other side. In a moment, he was back on his feet.

"The Paragons don't like to be taken by surprise," he said.

Gea came to land by him. *"I'll take your word for it. I wasn't aware of any squadrons shadowing the Emerald Flight as they flew west into Feorlen last year, but then we never ranked so high in the Order as you did to be privy to such matters."*

Rake frowned, judged her to be within reach of his polearm,

and so bonked her on the snout with the butt of his weapon. Gea snorted, rumbled irritably, and snapped her teeth as though meaning to catch the pole, but he yanked it back too quickly.

"What was that for?"

"For your whining," he said aloud. "What good has it done you, I ask? What good did it do for your rider?"

She huffed pale green smoke, narrowed her one good eye, but held back whatever retort he saw brewing behind it.

"White Watch intrigues me," Rake went on, in a manner to assuage debate. "And unless the answers to all the riddles have been drawn out on the tundra of the wilderness, then there's nothing left to learn in the north. We'd be heading south wherever we were going. White Watch is only a short detour."

They continued south, returning to a section of the Spine that would at least appear on most maps, and while the terrain remained difficult, it was better than the alternative. East of the Spine lay the Dead Lands, and there they would find no food nor a drop of clean water. Where the Dead Lands met the living lay the Fallow Frontier, lands which were only half alive at best. For now, Rake was happy enough that the chill of the far north had reduced from a deep bite to just a nip at his heels.

At length, they reached the vicinity of White Watch. Rake remained vigilant for the first hint of a rider entering his detection, but it was a group of Eternal warriors who they came across first. They observed them from the vantage of a high ledge. The men were encamped without any fire, clearly bearing signs of hastily bandaged wounds.

"Is it the same group?" Gea asked.

"Hard to say," Rake said. He counted them. Just over thirty. If it was the same group they'd seen heading east, their numbers had greatly diminished. "They must have run into a tough scuffle, but I thought these lands were clear of scourge."

"They were… but the scourge are never truly gone."

"True enough. Yet we're so close to White Watch, there shouldn't be scourge regardless of the Emerald Flight's actions. Still think nothing is wrong with the Order Hall?"

Gea rolled her good eye and snarled. *"Let's go ask them, shall we?"*

And so Rake and Gea moved as quietly as they could, not wishing to alarm the men. Rake called out to them at a good distance to announce their coming.

At once, the Eternals gathered into a huddled, defensive knot and replied with a chorus of rattling weapons and fearful shouting. Rake dropped his polearm and approached slowly with his palms open and up.

"Steady there, Eternals. Since when have I or a dragon ever attacked you? I've had dealings with your kind before. Surely one of you knows who I am?"

The Eternals muttered among themselves, then, at length, one of their number stepped bravely out. His height was impressive for a human, well over six feet. He had close-cropped black hair and a large black beard and wore a fur-lined, sleeveless jerkin. Dirt, blood, and sweat helped contour the muscles on his beefy arms.

He half-turned to his fellow warriors and called to them, "It's t' Wanderer! Like from old Yarwick's stories. Neither dragon nor man, sharp o' tongue and sharp o' claw – where he walks, even t' scourge fear t' tread!"

His accent sounded Feorlen – from where exactly was hard to place, but he was plainly not noble.

Rake couldn't help but place a hand over his heart and say, "Oh stop, you do so flatter me," as though the packed Eternals were chanting his name on parade and were not, in fact, staring at him with either abject fear or bewilderment.

"'Ave ye come to help us, Wanderer? We were attacked by a rider, no less."

"Well, that is rather alarming! Do tell me more."

"They came wi' no word or warnin' for t' slaughter, an' their magic seemed more like the black arts o' the scourge than any rider power."

"A risen rider can't perform blight magic like that," Gea said, though she said it privately to Rake.

"Why don't you tell them that yourself?"

"They are lowborn," Gea said. *"They aren't riders."*

Rake mentally rolled his eyes. He sometimes forgot that facet of the Order. *"Hate to remind you, but you aren't part of the Order anymore. You're just a dirty malcontent like me and Holt and the rest of us. Stop being so proud and speak to the man."*

Gea huffed, but she did as she was told and projected her thoughts broadly.

"You are mistaken, commoner," she said without tact. *"A risen dragon might take on the magic of the scourge in their cores, but a risen rider will gain no such power. The bond is lost on death, and no human has magic of their own."*

The leading Eternal dipped his head to Gea. "We speak as plain as our eyes saw. We don't know all the ways o' dragons and riders, to be sure, but we know the plague oughtn't to get a hold o' them as it will for most men. This dragon had blue skin, but that were already turning sickly, reekin' o' the scourge 'n all, and we know that stink as well as any."

Rake sensed no bravado or exaggeration in the man, and judging by the way his comrades looked at him, he was clearly admired in the ranks.

"What's your name?"

"Alsthan, Lord Wanderer. Jus' that, no role name since joining."

Rake chuckled. "Call me Rake. My emerald companion is Gea."

"Greetings, humans," she said, her tone condescending.

Rake went on. "Tell me, young master Alsthan, where were you when this happened?"

Alsthan pointed to the southeast. "Not far thataway. We set out cos of rumors and reports what reached us west o' t' mountains 'bout a strange sort of chasm. A deep 'ole, the scouts said, close to White Watch. Them emeralds did fair good in scrubbin' the scourge out the mountains, so we decided to come for lack o' scourge to fight. We expected riders would 'ave it sorted, but sometimes they let us help out 'round the edges, if ye take me meanin'."

"I take it very well," said Rake. "And this scourge hole, so to speak, is where you were attacked?"

"Jus' so. Strange for a chasm. We found no hint o' t' scourge anywhere, not even the green light or sick fog common in such places. The 'ole just went deep beyond sight or 'earin' of a dropped stone. We camped there a few days, but before we could decide what to do, that blighted rider fell upon us."

"Hmm. Thank you, Alsthan," Rake said, thumbing the blade of his polearm in thought.

Gea spoke privately to him. *"You want to go, don't you."*

"How can we not after that? I fear your Life Elder missed something vital by leaving White Watch be."

Then, speaking aloud for the benefit of the Eternals, he asked, "Was it just the one rider?"

There was a general murmuring and nodding of agreement from the warriors.

"That could mean anything," Gea hissed to him. *"One Ascendant or one Exalted Lord."*

"Only one way to find out," Rake told her, and then aloud, he informed the Eternals, "Gea and I would like to investigate this matter. Is anyone brave enough to lead us back there?"

The warriors muttered and debated again, though it wasn't long before Alsthan answered on the group's behalf.

"We'll all come, if it pleases you. Our brothers lie fallen, and we'd rather spare 'em from risin' again if we can."

Rake beamed and clenched his fist in the air. "I expected nothing less from Eternals." And, as a bonus, thirty additional minds would give him ample new mystic motes to Forge while they journeyed with them. "Lead on, Alsthan. Lead on."

When Alsthan said they were close to the site, Rake climbed a tall alder tree to gain a vantage over the descending hillside. He hadn't anticipated anything shocking him as much as the saumen kars' existence – not for a long time, at least.

Yet this 'chasm' made his jaw drop. It seemed wrought by an

immense drill that had bored deep into the land, leaving a gaping maw wide enough for a scourge queen to soar through. Yet no queen or scourge of any kind were present, nor putrid light or pungent mist. It was as if a tunnel leading to the world's core had simply been revealed.

Bodies of the fallen Eternals lay strewn on the maw's western side in a trail of carnage, meaning there was still a chance to burn them. And there, on the far side of the maw, sat the blighted rider and dragon. The dragon had once been an ice dragon, just as Alsthan had described; where its scales had once been a steely blue, they were now webbed in dark, blight-infested lines. From all appearances, it looked like the rider was sitting by a campfire, perhaps preparing a meal, as if nothing were amiss.

"What rank are they?" Gea asked.

Rake gently inspected their bond and core strength so as not to arouse their notice. "They feel like Exalted Champions to me. Nothing to worry about then." He scrambled back down the alder, dropping the last twenty feet to land in a crouch before Gea and the Eternals. After a pained grunt, he said, "Seems the poor fellows need to be put down, but I'd like to get them to talk first and try to glean something from this mess."

Gea gave him a perplexed look, while the Eternals nodded grimly.

Rake managed to take four long strides before Gea growled and hastened out to block his path.

"Are you mad?"

"A lot of people ask me that. It's starting to wear thin." He tried to shove her snout aside, but she snarled, pushed back, and moved to block him. "Get out of my way."

"I was there when you single-handedly came for Thrall, remember? The way you overcame two dragons and our riders, then General Agravain, then almost killed Thrall, all so fast – well, I'd never witnessed anything like it. Few Exalted Lords could have managed it. The way you moved, the confidence and precision, each ability perfectly made and timed."

"Is there a point to this? Even I can only take so much fawning."

"I can't feel your core, but it's plain you're not what you were. You don't walk with the same grace and power, never mind anything else. Thrall nearly broke you. He would have, had Holt and your friends not come to save you. You're lucky to have them. Don't let their efforts be for… be for naught," she ended in a cracked voice.

Rake looked up at her again, but she couldn't quite meet his eye. Once again, he found he pitied her and wondered when she had last been able to call another rider, a dragon, anyone, a true friend.

"Don't look at me so."

"Don't look at me so, *Master Rake.*"

Despite his taunting, her challenge struck him. Were he to be honest, he'd have to admit he wasn't in fit shape to face off against an Exalted Champion without thought. Not anymore. The fight with Sigfrid at Silt Grave had tested him far too much for his liking, and he'd blown much of his recovered core strength in escaping the cave-in.

He looked inward to the tattered remnant of his once marvelous core and the emptiness of his soul, now little better than a tinkle of water at the bottom of a dark, deep well. Sagging, he realized he'd taken his power to challenge any Lord or Lady for granted. Those days would come again, but not if he continued to drain his magic almost as fast as he could Forge it.

Resigning himself, he said, "Fine, you're right."

"Good," Gea said, suppressing exasperation. *"Now, let's do something Orvel and I should have done long ago – adopt a wiser strategy. Do you think our new friends would mind acting as bait?"*

"Oh, if we ask nicely," Rake said, then he called, "Oh, Alsthan! Come here, will you? We could use your assistance."

The Eternals proved obliging and brave once more in agreeing to Gea's plan. The chance for victory over a blighted rider and dragon would likely be the pinnacle of their fight against the scourge.

Everyone got into position, and then they sprung their trap.

Alsthan led his fellow Eternals out of the woods, screaming

at the top of their lungs. The blighted rider headed for them immediately, running fast while his dragon took flight and followed. The Eternals turned around at once to make for the trees again, as though their charge had been a hot-blooded mistake.

Rake tensed as he watched the rider close the gap, gripped his polearm tight, and started Floating his mote channels.

As he'd anticipated, the dragon landed to block the Eternals' retreat, getting between them and the woodland. Even at a short distance, the dragon reeked of the blight; it made Rake's nose itch.

He took off at a run as fast as his strong body and long strides could allow, knowing he had to reach the blighted dragon before it started bathing the humans in its foul breath.

Rake's veiled core often offered him the advantage of the first move in a fight, and he'd always aimed to make the most of it. As the dragon reared back and black light gathered at its jaw, Rake channeled magic down to coat the tip of his orange sword, then thrust, adding a touch of spirit to will the Soul Blade forward. A shining orange projection of the attack appeared, solidified, then rushed forward like a spear of fire, striking the blighted dragon on its wing and skewering through its leathery membrane.

Had the dragon known Rake was there, had it thought to Float its own mote channels to ward magical attacks, it wouldn't have been so easy. Yet it hadn't, and now it howled and thrashed around, unable to fly.

"Now," Rake said, stretching his thoughts westward to where Gea lay in wait, all while he kept running in. As his enemy flailed, Rake got under its front leg and cut it below the knee joint, then—

He turned to meet the enemy rider's blade – but only just in time. His instincts had almost failed him there. With three quick strokes, the rider made it inside his dead zone. Rake brought his polearm to his chest, turned, and slammed his foot down in a Kickback, flipping up and over his opponent's head.

He landed, but the rider was already running for him,

throwing black scourge flames at him. Rake deflected each one with his orange blade, reducing the flames to sparks, which fell as black ice to the ground. A shard hit Rake, and while his Floating protected him, he could feel the true power of the Ice Champion buried under the scourge's influence. It shouldn't have been possible.

The rider's dragon tried to start forward, but as Gea roared into view, it became entangled by lashing vines, thick as tree trunks, strong as spider's silk.

Rake took advantage of the rider's distraction to angle himself and then Blink the remaining distance between them. He re-emerged on the rider's side, lowered himself, and spun with his tail held taut, sweeping the rider's legs out from under him.

Gea's vines were already grabbing the rider when Rake threw his weight on top of him to pin him down. He slammed his tail onto the rider's arm again and again until the man let go of his blade. Rake flicked the weapon out of reach and called for the Eternals. Alsthan and several of his strongest men came running, and together, they heaved the ice rider's sword away.

Gea's vines tightened, and the rider's squirming became weaker.

Rake sat astride the man, brought his glassy blade to the man's neck, and yelled, "Yield!" Spittle flew as he fought for breath while the spiritual ribbon wove toward the dragon for acceptance. "Yield or I'll cut his throat!"

A string of spirit looped around Rake's, and the dragon accepted. Both opponents ceased fighting, and Rake felt a compulsion to ease the pressure he exerted on the rider. He was still panting, his side burned from a deep stitch, and his soul felt dry and squeezed.

Curse her, but Gea had been right. Holt had been right.

Gea landed close by but kept herself braced low to the ground as she worked to keep the vines in place. Her core burned but had plenty of power left in it.

"Can you still speak?" Rake demanded of the blighted pair.

It was the rider who answered.

"Why would you ask such a thing?" he said, revealing a mouth of horrors – blackened gums and a green-tinged tongue.

"Why?" Rake spat in complete consternation. "Maybe it's the blight coursing through your veins. Did you consider that?"

"There's no blight in us, fool. It can't linger long inside healthy riders."

"This fool just trounced you, so I'd watch your disgusting tongue. You're so infected with the blight I could smell it a mile off. You're supposed to be ice riders, yet your aura isn't remotely cold. Tell me what happened to you, and we might be able to help."

The rider laughed. It was a crooked, shrill sort of laugh, a sound no human should make.

Rake's impatience got the better of him. "Were you stationed at White Watch?"

"Yes," the man rasped.

"Why didn't they help you?"

"There's nothing to help, fool. Those loyal to Sovereign have nothing to fear of what's to come."

"Nothing...." the ice dragon said, almost in ecstasy.

Rake snarled. He dearly wished to break the man's arm or leg, or anything really, but the acceptance of a yield held power over the victor too.

"Five riders are stationed at White Watch," Rake said. "How many have sworn to Sovereign?"

"Threeee. The others are dead." His eyes seemed to roll toward the maw of the scourge cavity.

Gea shuddered but maintained her vines.

While this helped to explain the absence of the White Watch riders, it didn't explain why they hadn't been summoned to the pivotal fight against the Life Elder. Nor did it seem likely that they could have gone unnoticed for so long.

"Has Falcaer sent no one seeking a report? To make a change of rotation?"

The rider started to twist and turn, trying to fight against the vines, and said nothing.

Rake began pressing his weight onto the man's left arm with

his right foot, slowly, until he yelled in pain. Rake's soul blazed with fresh pain as he pushed at the boundaries of the yield.

"Speak!"

The rider spat. "Commander Goldmane has Paragon Adaskar's trust – he has worse to worry about now."

"Rake," Gea said with concern. *"If Thrall has influence over these riders, they might already be on their way. We should go."*

"He isn't in direct control. He can't hear and see everything his minions do all the time. This man's mind is still his own – well, almost."

Whether Thrall was to blame or the blight, some cruel experiment was being played out on the pair and probably on the other two pairs left at White Watch.

It was time to address the obvious.

"What is this giant hole for? Why are you guarding it?"

The rider squirmed, then he screwed up his face and closed his eyes as he fought some inner battle.

"No," he squawked. "Shan't say. Mustn't say."

"Stop this!" his dragon cried, sounding normal again and frightened.

Rake brought his sword back down to the rider's throat. "You can answer me then."

"The deep chasm was made f-for—"

But then the dragon's voice cut off with a horrible crack. He writhed, his rider writhed, and Gea roared from the strain of holding them. Then it ended, and they fell still. Far too still. Both the rider's and the dragon's eyes rolled back, leaving only whites.

Then the rider spoke in a manner Rake had hoped never to hear again.

"I have information for thee." The Hive Mind used the man's physical voice, warping it horribly, adding an unnatural volume and body.

Rake barely resisted killing the rider and ending things right there. "I really don't care what you have to say."

"It regardeth our enemy and his intent. Thou must stop him."

Rake scoffed. This thing was more brazen than him at his worst moments. "You tried to kill me, Holt, and Ash, and you think I'll help you?"

"The boy and the blind defiler still doth live."

Rake's heart stopped. He wanted to believe it, but what trust could be placed in this *thing?*

"Rake?" Gea asked, afraid. Her shuddering continued. *"Is this the beast below?"*

He heard her, but he was too caught off-guard by the news of Holt and Ash to reply.

The Hive seized the chance of Rake's silence to carry on.

"There is no time. He hath the intent to move against another Elder. When once he doth succeed, he shall become unstoppable—"

The Hive cut off in a wet rasp, then the body of both rider and dragon writhed and thrashed again. Their eyes rolled back down, only now they were shining black.

"Be still," the rider said, his voice changed again, now full of might and laced with hate. "Ah, Rake," Thrall said, "what a pleasure to find you here."

Unbidden, Rake returned to Windshear, to the cold floor of that hatchery, to the whimpering pup curled up as his last, painful memory with Elya played out over and over and over.

In panicked haste, he raised a barrier of mystic energy between the two halves of his mind. Should Thrall attempt to dominate him, the dragon would first enter the left half of his mind, leaving his right free and his own, at least for a while.

Thrall seemed unconcerned. "How is your soul?"

In that moment, it hurt worse than ever. Elya seemed to have washed from his mind – could he even recall the true color of her eyes?

"Gea," Rake said, distraught at how his voice shook. "Come to me."

He wanted to place the protection in her own mind and couldn't do such delicate work at a distance.

The rider's black eyes snapped to Gea. "You as well? This will be swee—"

Much like the Hive Mind's had, Thrall's voice cut short, and the blighted rider thrashed again.

"Gea, come here!" Rake said, even as he left the rider and moved to her. Fumbling, he managed to place a mystic barrier in her mind. All the while, the rider and dragon jerked in agonizing movements, uttering half-formed words, some in the Hive Mind's voice, others in Thrall's.

Rake hefted his polearm and readied himself to Blink back to the rider and end it, but Gea's vines wrapped around the man's throat and twisted. Bones cracked, then the rider lay still, and Rake felt the restraints of the yield lift from his shoulders.

The rider's dragon seemed uncaring.

Rake changed the direction of his Blink, and as he zipped to reach the blighted ice dragon, Thrall's voice reached them telepathically.

"I shall find you—"

This time, the voice ceased due to Rake piercing the dragon through the heart. He thought it a mercy – instant and without pain. He twisted his polearm and pulled it free, causing a mixture of normal red and scourge blood to spill from the wound.

For a moment, he stood there, watchful, to ensure both voices were truly gone. Then, swallowing hard, he stepped heavily back to Gea.

"Are you alright?"

"I think so." She looked down at her talons and moved them over the grass as though numb and unsure. *"What did you do to me?"*

"Protection against Thrall. It will fade soon. Next time, if I'm not able to help, find the one thing about you which is unbreakably true. Hold onto that. He'll find it harder to take you."

"You can't give him a moment's chance," she said, looking down at the limp body of the rider.

A part of Rake wanted to say, 'Well, maybe everyone else can't,' but that part of him seemed very small indeed right then. He placed a hand on Gea's back.

"You're right. You can't allow him a second. Thank you for acting so quickly. I was… lost in bad memories for a moment."

Gea rumbled appreciatively, then she crept gingerly to the rider's body and sniffed it. *"Which one of them was really in control?"*

"Of all the riddles, that might be the most important question of all."

Rake trod carefully back to the rider's body and leaned over it. The loss was tragic. Who knew if the pair had genuinely gone over to Thrall or not. Were Holt and Ash here, they might have been able to burn the blight out of them.

Just the thought of them alive burned off some of his own trepidation. The Hive Mind was treacherous, but Rake chose to believe Holt and Ash were alive. That belief restored fresh life to his body and soothed the smoldering in his core and soul.

Rake became dimly aware of Alsthan's voice calling him.

"Lord Wanderer? Lord Wanderer!"

Alsthan and a dozen of the Eternals were cautiously approaching.

Rake threw out a hand. "Stay back, the blight is strong in them."

The Eternals stopped.

"What were all o' that?" Alsthan asked.

Rake sighed. "We haven't the time to explain it. Be thankful for that, for you'll sleep better not knowing."

"As you like. We're 'appy as is to 'ave avenged our brothers, though it's a bit of a worry if riders are runnin' foul o' the blight now. What use can men be if the enemy's growin' so strong?"

His question seemed to be rhetorical, for he awaited no answer, and he and his men moved at once for the closest dead Eternal.

Gea clawed at the ground. *"We cannot linger here. Thrall knows where we are."*

"Agreed," Rake replied privately. Though his breath hadn't fully recovered from the short but intense fight, he hefted his polearm, began Grounding his mote channels, and cricked his neck, which helped to clear his head. *"Best warn this lot."*

With that, he caught up to Alsthan. "My young friends, I

implore you not to linger here. Gea and I have drawn the enemy's eye, and though we'll try to draw the danger off, there is every chance others will come."

"Our thanks, Lord Wanderer. We'll leave soon as we've burned t' bodies."

"Where will you go?"

"Back to our bases on west side o' the Spine. Eastern bases 'ave gone quiet lately, an' I fear they've been caught up in these troubles. Those of us left need fair warnin'. No one signed up for this. Even those willin' to fight t' death want to know we can make some small difference in a fair fight."

Rake leaned in. "If you're seeking a fight elsewhere, I know the queen of your homeland is in a spot of bother with her neighbors. I'm sure she'd find good use for a seasoned warrior and leader like yourself."

"You flatter me, lord, but I 'ave to say no. I came to fight t' scourge until I die doin' so. We all did. We all wanna do our bit to keep others safe, no matter who or where they're from. I shan't find such honor fightin' other men for rulers I've never met or broken bread with."

"I admire your commitment. The world is blessed to have you fighting for it, even if many will be ignorant of that fortune. Farewell, and good luck to you. May your arms swing true, and your legs never tire!"

The Eternals raised their weapons in salute of him, with cries of 'Wanderers! Wanderers!'

Gea fell in beside him. *"Don't look so pleased with yourself."*

Rake smirked. *"They're calling 'wanderers,' not 'wanderer'. They cheer for you as well."*

Gea sniffed and averted her eyes, though a rumble of pleasure rose in her throat.

"Try to keep up," Rake said.

Then he started to run, not at his fullest pace, but enough to put the scourge pit far behind him before long. Gea flew and kept close.

"We're heading for the Dead Lands?" she asked.

"Just cutting across the corner of it, then we'll enter the Frontier."

"Surely that is toward the danger if you suspect Thrall is there?

"It is, but I don't see another way. I wouldn't trust the Hive Mind one jot, but the fact Thrall came to stop it means its warning was genuine. Thrall means to move against another Elder, and if he succeeds, it will 'make him unstoppable'," he ended, using the Hive's own words. "Have you worked it out?"

It took her a moment, but then Gea roared, and Rake took that for a yes.

"We'd have to cross the whole of the Frontier," she said in alarm. "If Thrall sends forces after us, we'll never make it."

"He will," Rake said. "He won't risk us living if he can help it."

What felt like a long minute stretched on in tense silence. Every stride Rake took and every beat of Gea's wings made the silence harder and harder to break.

Eventually, Rake said, "You can fly on ahead of me."

"Why would I do that?"

"Because then you can alert the Elder. Because I'm the juicier prize. Because... oh, I don't know, you can save yourself."

Another painful stretch of silence followed, save for the sounds of pounding feet and wings beating the air.

At length, Gea said, "I'm not leaving you alone. Outcasts have to stick together."

Rake gave her an exaggerated nod by way of avoiding an answer. He didn't much want her to hear the relief he felt at knowing he wouldn't be making such a crossing alone.

Yes, he thought to himself. *Yes, we must stick together.*

And so he ran, letting the movement be the meditation to distract from the aches deep in his chest. The Fallow Frontier and a world of danger awaited them.

36

TO THE EDGE OF THE WORLD

Never again would Holt think of Rake as a harsh taskmaster. Compared to the Warden of Wrath, Rake had been a gentle hand. She led them with little rest back to the mainland, avoiding the delta of the Green Way in favor of striking north-ward to where the jungle skirted the arid scrubland. Once there, they turned east again and followed the jungle's border like a riverway, where yellow grass grew from flatlands pale and dry as parchment.

Used to traveling by night, Holt now baked under the summer sun. He Floated his mote channels at all times to protect his skin and wrapped his spare shirt around his head. When night came, Wrath drove them on, allowing them little sleep and giving Holt no chance to Cleanse or Forge.

One morning, Wrath rudely awoke them with a fierce roar.

Holt blinked against the burning light and clutched his head.

Ash stirred sluggishly. He lifted the wing covering his head, yowled, and quickly covered himself again.

"*Get up,*" Wrath said irritably. "*Vengeance awaits.*"

Ash's stomach grumbled, and Holt felt a tightening in his own guts.

"Aren't you hungry, Honored Warden?"

She didn't appear to hear him.

"*Might we go on a hunt, Honored Warden?*" Ash asked groggily.

"The Parasite must be punished."

"We can't fight if we're exhausted when we arrive."

Wrath paced about, glaring at them and swiping at the dry earth, throwing up dirt and dust. *"Hatchlings and their stomachs,"* she muttered. *"So be it. What do you eat?"*

"The animal I like best roams in the north. Here, I shan't be fussy."

She rumbled. *"My flight enjoys the taste of antelope. We shall find some for you."*

Ash thanked her, then shared his hope with Holt that 'antelope' wasn't disgusting.

Wrath led them on a hunt, finding a herd of the red deer they had hunted on their journey south nibbling at thorny bushes in the shade of a gnarled tree. Their collective heavy scent – warm, earthy, herby, and oily – was almost overpowering.

Wrath dove for the herd, causing the red deer – no, the antelope – to spring into leaping bounds before beginning a mad dash for survival. The herd split into three groups heading in different directions – a smart move, for the dragons picked the slowest group and tailed it.

Ash fell upon a slower beast at the back of the pack, but Wrath carried on. She ignored the laggards, her wings casting the herd into shadow as she blazed ahead, trailing smoke, then fell upon the leader, driving the beast hard to the ground with a roar of triumph. As though synchronized, the antelope sprang aside to avoid her, forming two new groups that headed in opposite directions.

Wrath started on her meal. Between raw mouthfuls, she charred the carcass by blowing on it with uneven bouts of fire. Through Ash, Holt could smell the mix of scorched blood, bone, and hide.

Ash brought their antelope back into the shade of the crooked tree, and Holt was in the middle of preparing a small fire and a roasting spit when the Warden landed hard beside them.

"What are you doing?" she asked, licking blood from her lips and fangs.

"Holt needs to cook his meat," Ash said. *"He can't eat it raw."*

Wrath frowned.

"Also," Ash went on, *"the way Holt prepares food makes it far tastier. It can even help draw magic into my core."*

Wrath swished her tail but said nothing.

Holt finished setting up his fire and spit, then moved to dress the antelope. After skinning the beast, he considered how large a haunch he would need. Still kneeling, he glanced at Wrath. He assumed that if the fire dragons hunted antelope, then something about the meat helped to attract fire motes to them, as beef did in the north.

"It would be a privilege to prepare food for you, Honored Warden. Before I bonded with Ash, I labored in the kitchens of an Order Hall, helping to make the meals of many noble dragons. The fire dragons especially enjoyed spices in their meals. I'm certain I could locate some during our journey."

Wrath gazed at him intently. *"Why do you speak like that?"*

"Apologies, Honored Warden, but I am unsure what you mean."

"You're doing it again. Hatchlings on our outer islands speak bolder than you. Are all humans this meek? And are all dragons in the order tainted by it?" she added, flicking her eyes toward Ash.

"The dragon flows into the human. Not the other way around."

"I'm not so sure."

"Think what you will. But I can speak plainly if you desire."

"I don't care. Just speak in a manner true to you. Pride liked your flattery and nice words, but I resent falseness."

"Easily done then," Holt said, dropping the pretense. "I won't speak so fancy if there's no need. But same question. Would you like me to cook you some antelope?"

Wrath snorted smoke. *"No."*

"Suit yourself."

Holt carved two haunches: one for his spit, the other to salt and save for later.

"Don't worry about cooking it all," Ash said, padding over. *"We don't have time for that. Plus, I'm starving."*

Holt left him to it. As he cooked his portion, Wrath paced

back and forth under the blazing sun, though her steps were soft. Holt's impression was that she simply found it hard to stay still.

Ash yawned, stretched out languidly, and watched Wrath's endless trudging.

"Honored Warden, why did you hunt the fastest of the pack?"

"Because the prey sought to outrun me."

To Ash, Holt said privately, *"I'm glad she's on our side."*

He was under no illusions, however. Wrath was on their side as long as they stuck to the Elder's task, and she was here to ensure that was what they did.

"We should start thinking of a plan to defeat the Parasite," Ash said. *"How have these creatures been beaten in the past?"*

"There is only one," Wrath said. *"It's an abomination of our element. A distortion of the Fire Song. Could be that the blight made it."*

Holt wasn't convinced. Fire was second only to light when combating the blight, so the idea that the blight created a firey monster was shaky at best.

"Or maybe rider magic created it," she said. *"You are leeches of a kind."*

"That's not true," Ash said.

"Your human draws upon YOUR power."

"His name is Holt," Ash said, his frustration emerging. *"He has shown you the respect you demand. Show him the same in return."*

"You're amusing when roused."

"Your Elder doesn't mind if a human brings him this Parasite's heart. You don't think your Elder is wrong, do you?"

Wrath slowed her pace to a more dangerous crawl, her wings twitching.

"Careful, runt. You amuse me, but do not test me." She shook her head. *"I can't comprehend why you would bind yourself to a lesser creature."*

"Dragons are made stronger by bonds. Holt can draw upon my core, but he also strips it of impurities and pushes more magic into it."

Wrath laughed and returned to her more relaxed pace. *"My own core is vast, and I have never had a rider. To rely on another is no way for a true dragon."*

Holt, who had been pressing the meat with his forefinger to check its tenderness, stopped and looked up at that. "Your Elder seeks the power of another."

"I said nothing ill of my Elder," she said, though for the first time, her voice contained a hint of nerves.

"I didn't say that you did."

She snorted smoke and turned away. *"Eat up... Holt,"* she added, sounding somewhat pained.

Holt turned the spit and lightly pressed a finger into the thickest part of the meat. Were it beef, he'd consider it between medium and well done. He'd prefer to take strange food further to be safe, but he had a High Champion's body and didn't think a bit of rare game would kill him. Not even that revolting eyeless fish from the underground lake had managed to finish him off as a starving Ascendant.

He removed the haunch from the fire, cut a strip of meat away, and tested it. Much like before, it was lean, gamey, and somewhere between veal and beef in flavor. Altogether, it wasn't bad. He might even risk cooking it less in future. That first taste also sent his mouth and stomach into a frenzy, and he devoured the rest almost as fast as a dragon.

The following days passed much the same, though, for whatever reason, Wrath allowed them more sleep than before. Despite her declared dislike of riders, she also asked more questions on the nature of bonds and more practical questions about the Order.

One evening under the moon, she unleashed a stream of inquiries. How many Order Halls were there? How many riders? How many of each type?

Holt had to remind her that he and Ash were not members of the Order, and this pleased Wrath, who growled appreciatively.

"To strive alone is a noble thing." She seemed to ponder this revelation, tilting her head to behold the moon. *"Perform your duties,"* she ordered before settling to sleep.

Each night after this, she allowed Holt time to Cleanse and Forge.

One night, midway through an especially difficult Cleansing

session, Holt opened his eyes to find Wrath staring at him. Not entirely comfortable, he pressed on into Forging, and after pushing a fistful of lunar motes into Ash's core, he felt Wrath's inelegant presence inspect their bond. She said nothing, though she rumbled in a manner Holt took to be one of reluctant admiration, albeit far from approval.

Despite his discomfort at having Wrath watching him, Holt enjoyed these sessions. Though a chill gripped the scrublands by night, Wrath's aura balanced things to a pleasant temperature. No campfire meant no light, and that meant nothing interfered with the soothing silver light of the moon and stars.

I'm becoming an odd creature, Holt thought. *Relieved at sunset and fearful of the dawn.*

Holt had been humbled by the endlessness of the world when flying south, and this feeling only magnified as they flew east. Ever east. After days and days of flying, still the Jade Jungle stretched to his right and the scrubland to his left. The days began to blur into one, not least because every sporadic meal was the same thing.

"Please cook it this time," Ash said on their fifth hunt. *"I'm sick of it raw."*

They had found their dinner close to the jungle, where some of the trunks were so massive as to make Wrath seem small. Under the shelter of the heavy canopy, where the air was hot, damp, and deathly calm, stocky trees still thrived despite the lack of light.

As Holt slowly roasted their antelope, Wrath paced again.

"This takes too long."

"You could help," Holt said, expecting nothing but scorn. But, to his great surprise, she growled and brought her own kill over to join him.

Holt was so stunned he stammered. "D-d'you mean, you'll help?"

"If it speeds things along," Wrath said. *"And as we're doing it... I shall try mine bathed in fire as well."*

Anticipation shot across Holt's dragon bond. Both he and Ash shared a cautious hope that the Warden was softening.

Holt guided her, and she breathed gently over the antelope with remarkable control, sizzling the meat while not burning the skewer. When they were ready, Wrath lunged and tore half her meat away in one bite. She licked her lips, then lowered her head, snorted, then turned away as though disgusted with herself, and stomped off.

"The draw of heat is stronger."

A sense of excitement shot through Holt that he hadn't felt since assisting Aberanth with his experiments. The confirmation that antelope improved the pull of a fire core raised a host of new questions.

Holt was so amazed that he struggled to speak. "I'm... glad to hear it."

"You see, there are benefits to having a rider," Ash said.

"For you, perhaps. I can roast my own meat."

Holt jumped in, speaking fast now. "It goes beyond just cooking it. Adding spices to beef increases the benefits for fire dragons in the Order. We could try spicing your antelope."

He couldn't prevent his imagination from running through the possibilities. If Wrath tried a spiced haunch, loved it, and understood the benefits of it, she might begin to appreciate all the other benefits of a bond as well – how humans brought a lot to help their dragon, that the partnership was mutual and real.

And if they could change the attitude of a Warden, then she might help sway the Fire Elder, and surely every wild dragon would see what the Life Elder had done. After Thrall and the scourge were defeated, what new friendships between humans and dragons might form?

They might fulfill the Life Elder's task after all.

Ash felt excited too, though even he tried to cool things down. *"That's a lot to place on a meal, boy."*

"I'll think about it," Wrath said, scathing as ever. She looked to the east, then raised her snout as though to sniff the non-existent breeze. *"We're almost halfway."*

"Almost?!" Ash gasped.

Holt sighed, trying and failing to grasp the distance. He had a sudden mental image of heading toward the world's end, to where the singers said the land finally met the sky and led to the stars.

So, onward they traveled.

On, and on, and on.

Finally, Wrath changed her bearings, turning to the southeast. Dense jungle stretched in all directions until the land rolled distantly upward toward hazy mountains.

"Be vigilant," Wrath told them. *"The rider nest of Angkor lies south of here."*

"Does the blight affect these lands?" Ash asked.

"It is rare, but when the plague comes, it rages like wildfire."

"The Hive Mind must find it hard to control the scourge this far away."

"Where is this creature you speak of?" Wrath asked.

The question took both Holt and Ash by surprise.

"We don't know," Holt said.

"How are we to kill it if we do not know where it is?"

In truth, Holt hadn't thought deeply about where the Hive Mind might be. His thoughts naturally turned to the Great Chasm, which seemed the most obvious place. The riders surely would have encountered it by now if that were true, but for all they knew, it could move.

"Thrall must know," Holt said. *"Maybe you'll pry it from him yourself, Warden."*

"The dragon who controls minds?" Wrath asked. *"Trust a mystic to wield such a power. Tricksters and riddlers all. Reducing him to ashes will be glorious."*

They approached the mountains now where the jungle heaved over sheer misty slopes, up and up, so that the canopies appeared like wilted spinach in a steaming pan. As the mist cleared, Holt saw stone structures with great ramps leading to wide flat tops, leaving him with nothing but questions about their purpose and who made them.

Passing through these green mountains, the dense jungle gave way to a land of rivers and crashing waterfalls, where teal waters sparkled white under the sun. The mere sight elated

Holt. Fresh water would be easy to find here, and those crystal waters looked inviting after the sticky jungle.

Wrath took them to the bank of a fast-flowing river where fat fish rode the currents. They were red with white stripes, yellow tails, and bulbous heads.

"Eat if you're hungry," she said.

Holt looked from Ash to the river and back to Ash. "Can you even sense the fish in the water?"

Holt looked around as though a fisherman might magically appear to assist them.

"I could try scooping my feet through," Ash said.

"I don't think they're close enough to the surface for that."

"Hmm," Ash mused, padding off down the riverbank. *"There might be a way..."*

Wrath seemed entirely unbothered. *"If you can't manage, we'll move on."*

"Is there nothing else we could hunt?"

"Not until we pass the Caged Sea."

Holt was about to ask what and where that was when Ash yammered excitably and said, *"Come, boy. The river becomes shallow this way."*

Ash pointed his snout toward the spot a hundred feet down the river. Here, the banks were lower, and the stones and silt on the riverbed were raised. Were he not a rider, Holt would never have waded into water with fish this gruesome, but of the things he was prepared to do for Ash, this was the least of them.

He took off his boots, sat, and dipped a foot into the river. When the fish ignored him, he assumed they wouldn't attack. He stripped off to his smallclothes, taking only his sword, and waded out until the water lapped at his ribcage. The fish parted around him like a rock, but after three failed attempts, he managed to perfectly time a sword thrust and speared two fish. Their weight dragged on him as he returned to the riverbank, then he drew on some magic and leaped straight out of the water to deposit the fat fish on the grass.

Ash sniffed, and Wrath glared at him.

"Having your core tended to is one thing, but don't allow yourself to

be cared for like a hatchling. What would you have done were Holt not here?"

Still sniffing the fish, Ash said, *"I hope to never know a day when Holt is not with me."*

"Same here," Holt said. He wondered why Wrath found this so hard to understand. "Don't fire dragons care for one another?"

"We care, and because we care, we let our young struggle and learn. What good would it do my flight if I tended to their every little need? How would they grow resilient?"

"It's just a couple of fish."

Wrath snorted. *"You clean his core of impurities so his body does not adapt to the struggle, you pack strength into his core while he sleeps, clean his kills and cook his meat; you guide him with your eyes, even speak for him on occasion. Perhaps my notion of which one of you is the slave was wrong."*

She stomped toward them. Holt instinctively backed away, but she only lowered her snout over the two fish, breathed lightly, then pulled back, leaving their scales crisped.

"Shouldn't you let us struggle?"

"You take too long."

Ash merrily ate a fish.

Still dripping, Holt rummaged for his cook's knife, then cut a chunk of the second fish away and popped it into his mouth. A sharp, chemical taste washed over his tongue.

He gagged, then chewed fast in the hope the taste would become bearable – it didn't. He spat the fish out. "Ugh. How can you stand that?"

"It's not the best, but I'm hungry."

"Have mine if you like."

As Ash ate, a clump of bushes caught Holt's eye. They grew a lipstick-shaped fruit, some red, some yellow, some purple. Holt recognized chili peppers when he saw them.

"Yes!" he cheered, returning to their bags for a clean cloth.

Not knowing how hot the peppers would be, he wrapped up several of the different colors.

"These will be perfect to spice your antelope," he told Wrath, ignoring her narrowed eyes.

Fully dry now, he put his clothes back on, then scouted the area for anything else useful. Another riverside bush grew fruit with red-green skin that looked like miniature apples and were sour enough to make his eyes water. Tall trees with fan-like stems grew bushels of berries that tasted tart and coarse, as if caught somewhere between a blackberry and unsweetened chocolate. Farther from the riverbank, long vines held a dark yellow fruit. Each one was the size of Holt's hand, and when he cut one open, he found a juicy, gelatinous center filled with plump black seeds. It was easily the tastiest of the bunch, sweet with a chewy texture like pudding.

After this, Wrath led them ever eastward to the Caged Sea, an inland ocean fed by the countless rivers of these lands. Rather than striking out over open water, Wrath turned north to follow the coast.

Signs of a civilization stood at the water's edge, where great huts rose from the water upon wooden columns, connected to the land by long bridges. Fleets of shallow boats traversed the sea or bobbed in the jetties. The people were tiny from up here, pointing up to them, many scarpering toward their huts.

Wrath laughed heartily.

"They rarely behold the majesty of fire. The emeralds have a grove somewhere in these lands, but who would fear them?"

Holt and Ash quietly agreed to fly higher so as not to add to the people's anxiety. Wrath roared her displeasure, though she beat her wings to join them shortly after.

They followed the coast of the Caged Sea for a day and a half, wherein the most notable event was Holt finding small wild onions with purple tips. Assuming them to be some form of shallot, he took them, nursing his ambitions to spice a haunch of antelope before they faced the Parasite.

"We are close now," Wrath said as they flew over the rivers which fed the Caged Sea from the east, their roots stretching far into the distance. Whether it was because Holt was growing accustomed to the climate or because the land held some innate

quality, he felt at peace here. Beauty lay in everything, from the neat clumps of verdant foliage to the icy hue of the shining rivers and the golden riverbeds.

The antelope here were larger than their western kin, more brown than red, and with no less than four horns that curved out and up as though each were crowned. Their scent was much lighter on the nose.

Catching one, hunger overshadowed Holt's thoughts, so he ate his fill quickly without attempting to use his spices. Once satiated, he noticed his all-purpose skinning and cooking knife was looking worse for wear. Skinning the latest antelope had been tough. Even with his enhanced strength, he'd felt like he'd been ripping with brute force rather than carefully cutting.

He realized he'd had this with him since leaving the Crag, along with his black iron pot and pan. His tools had gone through everything he had, but unlike him, they hadn't benefitted from magical transformations. The knife was only made of iron and wasn't designed to endure all it had been through.

He washed the knife of blood and fur, then grabbed some drier-looking sediment from the bank and gently rubbed it across the knife's surface. It was a far cry from the pristine sand Aberanth had at his lab, but it helped somewhat with removing the rust. He took the chance to clean his pan too, using ashes from the fire to mop up the oils before rinsing it in the river.

The next day, Holt was better prepared to plead his case to spice their meat. Even if Wrath refused, he would do it for himself just for the sake of variety.

"It's not much farther," Wrath said, though she'd been saying that for days.

Holt, who'd been lugging a large four-horned antelope over his shoulders, dropped it before the dragons and blew out hard.

"Might not be another chance if the Parasite kills us."

He said it in jest, but he supposed it was perfectly true.

Wrath grunted, blew smoke, stamped, then, as though it pained her, she nodded. Holt beamed. He'd had a feeling that deep down – really deep down – Wrath was curious to try his cooking.

Their catch this night seemed absurdly large, and Holt had the sense to cut and salt several steaks for himself in case hunting got scarce closer to the Parasite's lair.

As Wrath braised the antelope with her powers, Holt worked fast to prepare a spicy paste, using one of the beef recipes in his cookbook as a guide.

To check how spicy the chilies were, he cut the tops off one of each color, tapped a finger to the membrane under the head, then dabbed it on his tongue. The reds were mild, the yellows medium, the purples searing.

"Phwoar!" He gasped, then coughed as tears distorted his vision.

Ash sniffed, then yowled. *"Those things burn my nose."*

Wrath chortled – a sound like heavy wagons trundling over cobbles. Her blue eyes burned, and Holt decided this was no time to hold back. He chopped the purple chilies as finely as his worn knife allowed, using the flat underside of his frying pan as a board. He scraped the flesh and seeds into Aberanth's mortar, then chopped in his shallots. To have a hope of making a paste, he uncorked his precious supply of olive oil and poured in three hearty glugs. Finally, to aid in the grinding, he added two generous pinches of salt. Garlic would have been a welcome addition, as well as some sweet peppers to help mash it all together. The thought gave him a spurt of inspiration, and he added the gelatinous innards of the yellow fruit he'd picked. Not ideal, perhaps, but it would provide a needed balance of sweetness and body.

Wielding the pestle like a mace, Holt ground the ingredients down into an extremely smooth paste. Another benefit of his strength he'd not considered before. He committed the sin of not tasting the food he was preparing, but he wished to keep his tongue intact, and he was hardly cooking for the Archon of Athra. This was all to test whether spiced antelope increased the pull of Wrath's core, and he was assured the paste would be plenty spicy.

Wrath still breathed lightly over the meat, as delicately as if she were trying to mist patterns onto cold glass, turning it golden brown all over.

"Let me rub on the paste."

And he did so, cycling magic around his hands to help blunt the heat until half of the antelope was coated purple.

"Give it one more light touch."

Wrath obliged him, and the paste sizzled tantalizingly. Holt held his breath so as not to accidentally inhale a deadly whiff and backed away as Wrath lunged at her dinner. Teeth tore into moist meat. There was loud chewing, then a growl, growing swiftly to a thunderous roar.

Holt studied their fire. The flickering flames titled toward Wrath, then one of the strands stretched out toward her, dispersing into embers and then to nothingness as it reached her scales.

Wrath bristled and shook out her wings. Gripped by some mania, she looked everywhere but at Holt, and then, as quickly as it began, it ended, and she settled into a braced stance, as though ready for a fight. Her quickened breath threatened to blow their little fire out.

"This… this is what dragons in the Order experience daily?"

"Not quite so dramatic as that, but then your core is very large. But you see? Riders can add so much to a dragon's life. And we do so gladly. There's even more we can do too."

Holt hurried into telling her about jerky and the uses of cycling elixirs, both of which could benefit dragons as well. He would have shown her jerky if he had any left, but the elixirs were still good.

"Would you like to try one?"

"I saw what those did to you," she hissed, then narrowed her eyes. *"You discovered all these… things… on your own?"*

"Oh, no. Well, the jerky I did, sort of. Though I had help from Ab— a friend of ours. He's a genius."

"A human did this?"

"Our friend is a dragon," Ash said happily.

"That makes far more sense. A fire dragon?"

"He's an emerald."

Wrath snorted. *"I should have known. Always meddling."* She fell quiet, dangerously so, and started pacing as she had not done since their first hunt. Back and forth, back and forth, with much grunting and swishing of her tail.

Holt wasn't sure what to make of it, and Ash sensed his trepidation. *"We've done all we can to show her the benefits. Let's eat. She isn't going to burn us to a crisp. Not before we kill the Parasite, anyway."*

While Wrath paced, Holt started working on his and Ash's dinner. After cleaning out the mortar, he made a second, milder paste using a few yellow chilies, shallots, oil, salt, and fruit.

When their meal was ready, Holt found that experiencing a taste other than lean game for the first time in weeks reawakened a piece of his soul. A tightness in his chest unwound, as did a tension in his jaw. The spice was there, mild, layered, and balanced by the tang of shallot and sweet gooey fruit. It was easy to forget how much a fine meal could lift one's spirits.

Throughout, Wrath's pacing did not abate.

Concerned now, and emboldened by the spice in his stomach, Holt asked, "Is something wrong?"

"To see the flames drawn toward me like that... it reeks of the Parasite."

The warmth in Holt's stomach cooled and plunged. Wrath's reaction was far from what he'd hoped for.

"All the food and potions do is enhance the natural effect of a core."

"Humans have four limbs. Should we work to add a fifth?"

"That's unfair, Honored Warden," Ash said. *"Holt isn't saying we should grow a second tail, just that we make what we already have the best it can be."*

"Where would that end?" Wrath demanded. *"For all we know, practices such as these created the Parasite."*

This rapidly approached the issue Holt had spotted at the beginning of their journey.

"Your Elder seeks the Parasite's power for his own. If you think that's wrong, you should say so. We could go back."

She stopped pacing. *"My Elder is just and strong. What he decides* is not for me to question. *The leech must die. And we're too close now to turn back.*"

It took another half day of flying before Wrath descended to the shore of a lake at the foot of a mountain. Pointing her snout up, she bared her teeth.

"The Parasite's lair."

Holt followed her line of sight. High above, frothy water poured from the mouth of a cave into an unseen pool, then down in a flight of waterfalls until the cascade ended in the clear lake. A bright rainbow arched over the highest waterfall, a bizarrely cheerful gateway to the lair of such a malevolent creature.

Ash walked along the shore, sniffing and orientating himself. He must not have smelled or heard anything distinctive, for Holt would have gained an impression of it even when not sense-sharing.

Holt followed, getting to grips with their immediate surroundings and checking for fruit-bearing trees. It was a few minutes before he realized Wrath wasn't following. Holt turned to find her standing stock still where she'd landed.

"I will go no closer." Indeed, she even backed away. *"I won't give the Parasite one drop of my power."*

"So, what's the plan?"

"You will enter its lair and destroy it."

Holt was increasingly regretting to agree to this, though recalling the situation and their tenuous safety in the stifling heart of the mountain, he forgave himself. There had been little choice.

"We'll wait for nightfall. We're strongest then. Who knows, maybe the Parasite will be asleep."

With it being just past midday, they had time to kill. Now they were within sight of the creature's lair, Holt took the precaution of putting on his gambeson and brigandine, and restocked his baldric belt with elixirs. He found relief from the heat within an open, rocky shelter behind the waterfall. The light spray of water was refreshing, and it felt reassuring to have solid stone at his back. He placed their supplies and equipment there and Cleansed throughout the afternoon until dusk.

The waiting was awful. Most perilous situations came on suddenly, leaving little time to worry, and once a battle began, all thoughts condensed into the moment. In the tunnels under Ahar, there had been no time to think, only push on. And when Rake had been with them, Holt had never really been afraid. Now they faced a creature which the whole Fire Flight feared, which even an Elder felt unable to master.

Ingrained instinct and a need for some habitual ritual led Holt to setting up a fire near where Wrath had retreated farther down the shore. Prior to embarking on something dangerous, a little routine and comfort was a welcome distraction. There was no magical benefit from their salted antelope, but having something in his stomach was preferable to fighting on an empty one.

"Do you mind if I focus on mine tonight?" he asked Ash over their bond.

"Not at all."

Holt gave him an appreciative scratch along his neck, then tossed his dragon two of the larger steaks. For his own, he set his frying pan over the fire to warm.

Wrath fidgeted. Every now and then, she'd look in alarm toward a snapping branch, a rustle in the undergrowth, the loud croak of a frog, or the shrill squawk of some bird.

That a Warden was this wary ought to have terrified Holt, but he told himself the Parasite couldn't drain lunar magic, so they didn't have to fear it as she did.

Instead, he focused on the rumble of the waterfall, the spit and sizzle of the oil in his pan, the Warden's heavy breaths, the soft sand beneath him, and the heady smell of the hot forest, the way its scents seemed to sit on his shoulder and seep into all his senses. All of it meditative in its way.

The pan began to smoke. Holt placed in his steak away from him to avoid the eruption of hot oil. Flames under the pan surged up the handle, reaching as far as his hand. He cursed and let go. Fat and oil must have spilled over the edge.

The flames continued to drift toward him, which was odd because Wrath was on the opposite side of the fire. One strand trailed out as far as Holt's chest.

Over the dragon bond, he felt Ash grow alert. His sensitive scales felt what Holt did not yet register – a cooling of the air.

Wrath scurried backward, throwing up sand.

Red light shone from behind Holt, casting his silhouette in a long shadow.

His free hand went for his sword.

He drew, turned, pulled magic across the bond, Floated his mote channels, and cycled the excess to his blade. White steel fought against the red light, turning the sand pink.

What seemed like a blazing spirit rushed toward them, gliding low over the shore quick as an arrow, yet silent and scentless. Ash twisted his head this way and that, unable to locate it, and then the fire emerged right in front of him.

Two wings unfolded, a short body, a fan-like tail, two legs with taloned feet, and a beak of golden flames. Ethereal and flowing, the creature seemed drawn by quick brushstrokes of living fire, a fire that emitted no smoke.

The air turned chill.

Wrath's roar sounded distant.

The Parasite's intent seemed bent toward Ash. As it descended, it turned corporeal, the living flames thickening until a creature part eagle and part pheasant pressed deeply into the sand.

Ash twitched as he finally located it, but the Parasite screeched shrilly and lunged at him. Blood flew. Ash snarled, flailing his claws and backing away, disorientated and confused.

With one hand gripping his sword and the other his frying pan, Holt screamed in fury and leaped in. He slashed, trailing silver light. White steel sliced through the Parasite's tail, cutting off a long red feather.

The firebird squawked and turned on him. Its eyes narrowed, eyes whose whites were a fiery orange and whose pupils were slits of black. A cry rushed from its golden beak, carrying a staggering heat and weight. Holt raised both arms to shield his face.

Despite his Floating, his skin prickled wherever the hot air touched him.

The Parasite screeched again, but this time it sounded frightened. Holt lowered his arms to find it hopping back along the shore, its body hunched and guarded, and its furious gaze enraptured by Holt.

No, not Holt. What he held.

The bird was looking at his frying pan.

Feeling rather stupid, Holt raised his pan and brandished it as he advanced. The bird shrieked, reared back, and beat its wings. A gust of hot air blew up sand, forcing Holt to shield himself again. By the time he recovered, the creature had retaken its ethereal fire form and was flying back up the mountainside, screeching all the way.

Ash sent a moonbeam after it. The solid light hit the beast clean in its side but passed straight through without harming it. The Parasite dwindled, then disappeared into its cave.

Light from Holt's sword dominated the night again.

His first thought was of Ash's wounds, and he went to his dragon.

"It got you good," he said, inspecting the deep cuts running across Ash's chest and over the top of his leg joint. Seeing Ash bleed, seeing the red flow over the pristine white, never sat well with Holt, and it only sharpened his desire to take the Parasite down.

"It's not so… bad," Ash said bravely. "Just… stings." He started licking the wound. Across their bond, Holt tasted a tang of copper.

Holt's mind caught up to his own pains. His knuckles, the backs of his fingers, and his collar were hot and stinging, his skin red from the creature's breath. Luckily his gauntlets had protected most of his hands, and his armor had saved the rest of him.

Inspecting his hands, he was taken by surprise again to see he still held his frying pan. The antelope steak lay in the shallows of the lake, doubtless hurled aside when he'd turned to meet the creature. He spared a moment to mark the loss of his dinner, then he noted the lack of firelight. Their campfire lay extinguished, faint smoke trailing up from the blackened wood. The Parasite had consumed it.

"*Did you slay it?*" Wrath asked eagerly. Judging by the position of her core, she had flown about a mile and half away.

"*It fled into its lair,*" Holt said.

"*You must pursue it!*"

"*Ash is hurt. We need a moment to stop and think. I'm not sure we can even hurt it in its fire form.*"

Wrath's roars rang as tremors between the trees.

"*The leech took a bite of me. You aren't leaving here until you try.*"

She flared her core, as if Holt needed any reminder of her power. It made him think about the Parasite's might, which only raised more questions. The firebird didn't have a core, at least not one that Holt could feel.

"*Did you feel a core in it?*" he asked Ash.

"*Nothing.*"

Holt frowned. A lack of a tangible core didn't mean one wasn't there. Rake's core had been imperceptible, after all.

He went back over the encounter, focusing on what they knew for sure. It could be harmed, at least when it was in its physical form. And, somehow, Holt had managed to frighten it into fleeing.

He looked at his frying pan again. In the white light, the oil dripping from its rim shone ghostly pale. It seemed ridiculous to Holt that the firebird had feared the black iron, but given the circumstances, he was willing to experiment.

No matter what Wrath thought.

37

ONE OF A KIND

With the dual threats of Wrath behind them and the Parasite ahead, Holt knew which one he'd rather face.

They set about preparing. Firstly, Holt put down his pan, sheathed his sword, and went to soak his burnt fingers in the lake. As the stinging from his hands eased, the pain from his collar nipped all the worse – though compared to Dahaka's burning power, this was nothing.

While he bathed his fingers, he dreamed about becoming a Lord, when his skin would turn tough as dragon hide and minor injuries like these would become a thing of memory.

After treating his hands, he redrew and lit his sword to search for the tail feather he'd cut from the firebird, hoping it might offer some insight. Alas, all he found was a clump of hot soot and cinders.

"What is this thing?"

"Its claws are as sharp as your dragon steel," Ash said. *"Sharper than a flayer's arm."*

The three nasty cuts across Ash's chest and upper leg no longer bled, but streaks of dried blood remained on his scales. Ash took some tentative steps, wobbled, and seemed unwilling to place his weight on his right side.

"I can't fight like this."

Holt brought out Aberanth's balm. There wasn't a lot left in the small pot, and Ash's wounds were large. He used it all, spreading it as evenly as he could across the gashes.

Ash winced.

"Give it a moment," Holt said warily. He didn't like the idea of taking that *thing* on without his dragon.

Ash stiffened his jaw as he hobbled along, but it was obvious he couldn't fight effectively. The wounds weren't severe, but they were fresh. If they had time—

Holt pushed that thought aside. Wrath wasn't giving them time. He could feel her prowling a mile out, her fury still palpable.

There was only one thing for it.

"Can you fly?"

Ash beat his wings. *"I can fly."*

"Okay then," Holt said, trying to psych himself up. There was little left to do but make the attempt, so he checked his elixirs were secure, then, acting quickly so as not to overthink it, he picked up his frying pan.

It can't hurt, he told himself, tying it onto his belt at his hip. A frying pan on one side and his beleaguered knife upon the other. Truly he was a Cook ready for war.

Avoiding Ash's injured side, Holt climbed onto his back. With a groan, Ash took off and made the short journey up the waterfall stairway, touching down on the overhang outside the beast's lair. Holt slid down carefully, then approached the mouth of the cave.

Not far inside, the pillars of rock clamped like teeth to block the way. What gaps remained were narrow, little more than crevices.

The only sound coming from the cave was the flowing water. The only smell was damp stone. Even when using his sixth sense, Holt could only grasp the vague notion of *something*, the quiet notes of a song that faded the moment he tried to hear them.

He peered through the narrow crack. A faint glow of red light emanated from somewhere out of sight. The Parasite must be in its fire form.

Holt pulled back and spoke telepathically. *"Can you hear it?"*

"No," Ash said, frustrated. *"It's hard to picture what's inside with so much rock in the way… I think there's a short passage leading to a cave. There's a hiss of steam too, and bubbling water."*

Holt tried to formulate some semblance of a strategy, though his options seemed limited. With Ash stuck outside and the bird seemingly silent in its fire form, Holt wouldn't be able to fight blind, so he couldn't make use of Flare. Considering his minor burns, Floating seemed sensible, but he worried that he over-relied on that technique. Rake had wanted him to be more aggressive, and the Parasite had certainly been that. Grounding his body and doubling down on that physical boost by using Consecration seemed his best bet to gain the upper hand.

"Is this the only way in and out?" Holt asked.

Ash took a moment to check. *"I can't hear any other openings."*

"Think you can stand guard in case it tries to escape?"

"I can try… but if it comes out in its fire form, I won't be able to tell."

"What if you share my eyes? You might at least have warning if the thing tries to flee."

"It's better than nothing."

They melded senses. In a small way, Holt was pleased he could offer something to Ash for a change. Other than flying, they had come to rely on Ash's hearing in almost every situation.

"Show me the moon."

Holt looked skyward, lingering on the silver light shrouded by clouds. It seemed small tonight and distant, as though their journey had led them further from it as well as the rest of the world. Ash, through Holt, drank it in, and a sense of gratitude welled over the bond.

"I wish the clouds would pass, but I feel better knowing it's at my back." Ash limped into position. *"If the bird comes at me as fire, what can I do? My moonbeam passed right through it."*

Holt lowered his gaze from the moon and looked at Ash. He placed a hand on his dragon's snout and said, *"Magic might go through it, but it can't pass through you. Ground your channels. Don't let it pass."*

Ash sniffed and pressed his snout into Holt's hand. *"You shouldn't have to face it alone."*

He scratched Ash's chin and smiled. *"I'm never alone."*

A quiver shot through his soul.

Of all the times, he thought, wishing he could consider it more deeply.

Instead, he made his final preparations by Grounding his body, readied two elixirs, then chided himself and took out a third. This was no time for caution. One after the other, he downed the potions and gagged from the saltiness. His stomach clenched, tremors running through his muscles.

For a moment, he regretted the overdose, fearing he'd gone too far. Then, all at once, the enhancement came. A flood of motes cycled through his channels with minimal effort. All soreness and weariness snapped away, leaving him supremely confident in his body, in feeling he could scale this mountain with a single leap or knock out Wrath with a single punch. White and silver creases shone from his skin, largely hidden by his armor and clothes but visible at his neck and palms.

He unsheathed his sword. He 'unsheathed' his frying pan. White dragon steel in one hand and coarse, black iron in the other. He felt like an idiot as he crept forward. For once, he was glad Rake wasn't here to witness this, else he'd never hear the end of it.

"Maybe you could cook it some vegetables," Ash teased. *"The taste might kill it."*

Holt imagined the fiery bird fussing over a cluster of mushrooms like Aberanth and he exhaled a short, breathy laugh. His knot of nerves loosened. Ash always knew how to help him.

He squeezed through the crevice and entered the Parasite's den.

With each quiet step down the short passage, he reminded himself that the creature had fled from him once already. This time he was ready, fully cycling and forewarned with some knowledge of it.

He directed a portion of his energy flow to his sword, casting soft light to see by. His dragon bond beat steadily, warming from the steady pull of magic.

All too soon, the passage ended, and he edged into the cave. A dampness lay in the air and gleamed upon rocks close to a small pool. The rocks were the same raw meat red as those in the chamber of the Fire Elder. Steam rose from the water, just enough to create a crimson mist where it met the glow of the creature.

The Parasite stood in repose in its fiery form. Much like Ash and his blindfold, without visible eyes, the beast looked more ominous for it. It wasn't a living creature at all but some corruption of magic, as the Elder had warned.

A fuzzy pop, snap, and sputter entered his mind, like a dragon's telepathy, but rough and wordless.

Holt only had a moment to fear he'd been wrong not to protect his mind from attack when the Parasite morphed into its physical form. Part eagle, part pheasant, the bird stood at a towering nine feet with crimson feathers. Without its red aura, the cave turned dark, save for the dim radius around Holt's blade and the parasite's blood-orange eyes.

It screeched, then charged at startling speed and a heavy weight that shook the cave floor before it lunged with open talons. Unable to press down a Consecration in time, Holt slid sideways, but the bird clawed after him. A pressure buckled his left arm and caused him to stagger; a shrieking scrape of talons on steel. Holt slashed, bought himself a moment's reprieve, then back-stepped and found himself against the cave wall. He still had a grip on his pan, but it had been a close thing.

The creature landed with a slam, then spread and beat its wings. Holt spun around, ducked his head, and tucked his arms under his chest. His armored back bore the hot gust like a turtle's shell.

Attack, he thought. *Press the attack.*

The moment the hot gust abated, Holt unfurled, jumped, kicked off the cavern wall into a leaping turn, and thrust his sword toward the bird. The Parasite shielded itself with heavy wings, but the dragon steel cut deep into the wall of feathers.

Screeching and with the strength of a dragon, the bird opened its wings so fast it ripped Holt's sword out of his grip. Horrified, Holt watched as the sword seemed to tumble in slow motion to land by the hot pool, and its light extinguished.

At least the beast had injured itself. The bird's wing looked ripped in two like a cloven hoof, and a line of ashes lay on the stone underneath it. Yet even now its feathers were reforming.

It could regenerate.

Holt's heart thundered. Over the bond, Ash implored him to fall back.

The bird gave him a baleful stare and cried, sizzling spittle flying from its open beak.

White light still shone on his right hand where he'd been sending magic to his sword, so Holt brightened it, tightened his grip on the panhandle, and raised it in awkward guard.

The bird's eyes narrowed, then it fizzled and transformed again. Moments later, a trail of fire moved toward the exit.

Ash saw it all through Holt's eyes and braced.

Holt made a dash for his sword; two steps in and Ash's deep roar drowned out the bird's shrill tones. Danger gonged from across the bond, leading Holt to skid to a halt just in time to pivot and turn, swinging his frying pan hard even as the bird whooshed red and burning back into the chamber. It tried to swerve aside, but Holt's blow slammed into its flaming wing. The force he'd thrown behind the swing turned him right around, but his Grounded body found its footing and stayed upright.

The Parasite was in its physical form again, a stooping figure in the darkness which hobbled away. Taking the opportunity, Holt rushed to send magic to his legs and laid down a Consecration. Webbed lines of light erupted beneath him. A rush of new strength filled his body, swelling the benefits of his elixir-enhanced Grounding. The silver light also brightened the cave, throwing the bird into sharper relief.

It was hunched over his sword, holding one wing low and limp by its side. Smoke rose from a blackened area of scorched feathers on its injured wing, and this time it wasn't healing itself.

The pop, snap, and crackling in Holt's head spiked in volume, so sudden and so loud he winced and gritted his teeth, but still he took a determined step forward. He even drew his cook's knife in his right hand. If the pan damaged the creature, why not it?

Squawking, the firebird rushed him for a second time, but its limp wing weighed it down, leaving it off-balance. Holt exploited that weakness. Upon Consecrated ground, his body responded well. He dodged the bird's snapping beak, then rammed his knife into its side. Hissing smoke and bright, shining blood spilled from the wound. A screech from the beast threatened to burst his eardrums.

Holt pulled his knife free, stepped back, then thrust again, only to find the knife a ruin of melted iron. Holt registered this, then noted the creature's blood flowing in thick beads over his skin like gelatin. So strange.

Momentarily distracted, he almost took the great golden beak square in the chest, but he evaded it at the last moment. Weaving aside, he brought his pan up to strike, dropped the useless hilt of his knife, and gathered power for a Lunar Shock.

The Parasite shrank away from him, still smoking from its three wounds.

Holt sensed victory. But just before he released his Shock, the fiery noises in his mind twisted into something he understood.

"*Cease. Cease!*" came an old, pressing, and aggressive male voice.

Holt jerked to a standstill. The Lunar Shock in his hand remained bold and bright, and the bird raised its good wing to shield its eyes.

"*Did you hear that?*" he asked Ash.

"*I did. Holt, there are no dragons out here.*"

The dizzying realization struck them both.

"You can speak?" Holt asked the bird.

"*I can think, which is more than the pair of you did when you arrived with that devourer. Cease, I say. You have bested me.*"

Holt didn't move an inch. It would be too simple a trick for the Parasite to feign surrender, only to strike when he lowered his guard.

"Swear you won't attack us."

"You demand I swear? You entered my nest. You struck at me with your cold light, your long white claw and freezing metal."

Holt glanced at his frying pan in astonishment. "This really hurt you so much?"

"It burns. It burns. It burns." The bird shivered. *"Do not use it again. I shan't fight you. I shan't."*

In a display not unlike a dragon, the great bird lowered its head and wings to the cavern floor.

"There's no lie in its heart," Ash said. *"Now the fight is over, I can hear that much."*

Holt accepted Ash's assessment. He lowered his pan and dimmed his Shock but kept enough light to see by as his Consecration had worn out.

"You're the one who attacked us first earlier."

"I emerged to chase off the devourer. You were with her. You were a threat."

Holt breathed hard, but the bird had a point.

"We've come to collect something. An essence of power the Fire Elder wants. If you can give us that, then there's no need to fight."

"Then you come to thieve. Who are you, thieves?"

Holt noted the evasion but decided humoring the creature could do little harm. He had his... frying pan, after all.

"My name is Holt Cook. My dragon, Ash, is outside. You gouged a chunk out of his hide."

"Which can be forgiven," Ash said. *"So long as we get what we came for."*

"More threats. Threats from such young ones, no better than fresh embers from the ashes. What a pitiful end this will be. Seasons beyond count I have waited. All for naught. Oh, what an end."

The Parasite looked sharply around its cavern again, as if suddenly remembering where it was and what was happening.

"Why would the devourers send you?"

"We're friends of the Fire Flight, and the Fire Elder claims you stole his power."

The bird squawked wickedly, then worked itself into such a state that its voice descended into wheezes.

"You have been led astray. The heat of the world belongs to no one being, or at least that was once true… long ago. Thief, they call me?" He squawked again and clawed at the stones. *"They are the thieves. Liars. Devourers, one and all. Him too,"* the bird said, flicking his orange eyes toward the exit, toward Ash. *"Oh yes. Not of heat, no, but of something. He'll gobble and gobble until there is nothing left!"*

"If you mean my magic," Ash said in a tone Holt thought exceptionally calm given the circumstances, *"it is of the moon and stars. I cannot devour the moon."*

The bird spat more sizzling spit. *"Just you see. Even all the stars won't be enough for you one day."*

Holt brandished his frying pan, and the bird shrank back and lowered its beak.

"Ash has a kinder heart than anyone. Insult me all you like, but if you want me to remain peaceful, you'll be nice to him." The firebird trembled before the pan, and Holt felt an ill-tasting mix of pity and guilt. "Look, the last thing either of us wants to do is kill anyone without need. The fire dragons – the devourers, as you call them – call you the Parasite. It didn't make us think too kindly of you, I'll admit, but you do drain fire. You inhaled our campfire and some of the Warden's power. She fled so you wouldn't drain more from her core."

The bird ruffled its feathers, making it appear to swell in size. *"They are the ones who stole our essence. Stole our home. So long… so long ago… Do they even remember?"*

"Are you saying they were more of your kind once?" Ash asked.

The bird cocked its head unnaturally. Holt felt something imperceptible pass between it and Ash.

Did the bird have a spirit of its own?

Ash must have felt the same thing, for he added, *"I am the only one of my kind too."*

"Truly?" asked the bird, without quite as much bite this time. *"You are a strange pairing. None of the others I see are your color. Red,*

green, blue, gray, some violet, but none are white. None." The bird cocked its head the other way, seeming contemplative. It sighed, then took a single hopping step forward. *"The difference between the devourers and I is that I can control my hunger."*

Steam rising from the hot pool was suddenly pulled toward the bird and curled around it.

"You pull in heat, not just fire?"

The bird gave him a withering look. *"What is fire if not heat?"* He turned for the exit again. *"Did they hunt your kind as well, white one?"*

"No. I am the only one of my kind to have hatched."

"Might others hatch?"

"It's possible."

The bird leaned forward, a keen and knowing glint in its warm eyes. *"Then make sure they do. Make sure. If phoenixes could arise from shells like your kind, I would have made sure we weren't wiped out."*

"What's a phoenix?"

"I am," said the bird proudly. *"Born of fire and smoke. More ancient than the flying reptiles... yet gone now like so many others. Devoured. And gone."*

Holt shared an uneasy feeling across his bond. The bird – the phoenix, as it had called itself – seemed half mad, but if what it said was even remotely true—

"Are you saying the fire dragons... hunted all of your kind?"

"Are all you pink apes so slow? Yes, they hunted us. For our fires. For our essence. They took it all, until they formed songs of their own. Long, long ago... Before I saw the first of your kind come down from the trees."

The phoenix's agitation eased, its feathers smoothed out, but its energy did so with it, and its good wing drooped.

"I've lived too long now. My memories of the primal days are clouded. Much is lost to me; even how I came to find this warm cave far from home. There were once others like me who escaped. They tried to return to our old nests at the mountain of fire – a last chance to renew themselves. I called them fools, told them to wait. They flew anyway."

The old phoenix let out a rattling sigh.

"Fools. Heh! I should have flown with them and got it over with. I thought myself clever... All I gained was solitude. And ever since the

devourers found me here, they've never ceased hunting me, as of old. Only now they have power they fear to lose, so they send the small, the weak, and the young into my cave."

"The Elder said younger drakes sent here were left crippled or killed outright."

"What would you have me do? Lay down and di— heh heh heh..." The phoenix's mad guffaw degenerated into a real hacking, dry squawk.

Holt's uneasiness turned into disgust. Not for the bird, but for the situation he and Ash found themselves tangled in. They had been used for a terrible purpose, manipulated as neatly as Thrall himself would have done. Weren't fire dragons meant to abhor such subterfuge?

Holt kept a wary gaze upon the phoenix as it swayed and tittered to itself, then asked Ash, *"What should we do?"*

Ash felt as lost as he did. *"I don't know. I don't want to kill him... poor old thing. He's the last of its kind."*

Holt bit his lip. His grip on his frying pan grew slick from a cold sweat. *"If we leave, Wrath won't be happy. She'll either force us to come back in, or..."*

"Maybe she doesn't know? Maybe we can reason with her?"

"Deciding what you should do?" the phoenix asked with some-thing like relish. *"Slay me, take my heart, and save your own feathers, or else leave and face the devourer's flames?"*

"Something like that." Holt crouched to meet the bird's eye, hoping to show it he genuinely meant to find a peaceful solution. "Is there any way we can get what they want without your death?"

"Can anything be eaten without destroying it?"

"What about some of your feathers?" Holt asked, desperate now. He knew it wouldn't work. One of Ash's claws didn't contain his power.

As the dark necessity dawned on him, the pan grew heavier in his hand.

The bird croaked more laughter. *"I trust she will be displeased if you fail?"*

"To put it mildly."

"*Good. Good.*" It sounded giddy. "*And the great one, he shall be enraged, yes?*"

"Yes…"

More scratchy laughter, more wheezing. The phoenix stood again to its full height. Holt jumped up and back, ready to fight, but the bird shook its great head in an exasperated manner.

"*I know what you must do, but do allow me to sit comfortably in my nest.*"

It thrust its beak toward the back of the cave, where Holt noticed a stack of palm leaves, twigs, and other jungle detritus ringed by a collection of crimson stones for the first time. He stepped aside and let the phoenix limp past him, its broken wing hanging awkwardly at its side.

Holt went for his sword, picked it up, and rechanneled the motes running to his hand into the dragon steel. His blade took the dim motes and made them brighter. His heart thundered again, though for very different reasons than the fight. The old phoenix seemed to be giving up, accepting Holt's grizzly task as inevitable.

The phoenix made a meal of bedding down, pulling a few leaves toward it and rearranging some twigs before it finally sat.

"*That's better.*"

"*Please,*" Ash said, "*let us go to the Warden and plead your case. Perhaps she'll listen.*"

"*Cease this pretense at worry for my being. You'll do what you must to spare yourselves – heh heh heh – but I won't give you that. Not I! You shall not have my heart. I would ask you to remember me, the last of my kind, but I doubt you'll live much longer yourselves, heh heh. Oh, that gives me some pleasure at the end. A curse on you, a pall on the devourers. May doom consume them and this whole world. Enjoy your deaths!*"

Still croaking with wicked laughter, the phoenix caught fire, as suddenly and fiercely as though it were covered in oil.

"What?" Holt cried dumbstruck. "No!"

He started forward, but the intensity of the heat warded him off. He switched cycling to Floating and raised his arms to shield his face, but too soon the squawking became gargled, then cut off. As fast as the inferno had come on, it ended.

Despite the fire, no smoke clung to the roof of the cave, and none of the leaves and twigs of the nest were burnt black. But the bird was gone. Reduced to nothing but a heap of dark ashes.

Holt stepped slowly to the ashes and dropped to his knees. Dazed, confused, and panic-stricken, he reached for the cinders of the once mighty bird, and the moment he touched them, despite his Floating, he yelped and pulled back from their fierce heat.

He felt Ash frozen in shock, too stunned to say or do anything.

From far away, Wrath's roar seemed to shake the mountain.

38

A LAST CHANCE

Holt and Ash stood with bowed heads outside the lair of the phoenix. A pale streak of pink and blue crossed the eastern sky as the moon faded fast, abandoning them to the Warden of Wrath. She hovered just beyond the edge of the waterfall, beating heavy wings, spewing smoke with every breath.

Holt kept his gaze down, expecting a fiery end to come. After hearing of the phoenix's self-combustion and Holt's failure, Wrath had fallen into a silence far more dangerous than rage.

"I can still sense it," she said at last.

"It's nothing but ashes."

"Then bring those to me!"

Holt turned slowly, fearing this would only delay the inevitable. He returned to the cavern. With the phoenix gone, the cave was already warmer, the air stickier from the steaming pool. The handle of his destroyed cooking knife remained where he'd dropped it, and he left it there.

He didn't have much to carry the ashes with other than his bare hands or his frying pan. At least they'd cooled enough to touch. He sprinkled a pinch of the soot into his pan to check for adverse effects. When nothing happened, he scooped up a larger pile and took it out for Wrath's inspection.

Standing on the precipice of the waterfall, Holt raised the pan toward her. She sniffed it and closed her eyes, listening intently for something Holt and Ash could not hear.

"The essence is still within. Dispersed and weak as a frail mystic, but it remains."

A pulse of tentative hope passed between Holt and Ash.

"Can you draw in the power, Honored Warden?" Ash asked.

Wordless, she stared at the ashes as though to frighten them into giving up their secrets. At length, she grew frustrated, and whether she intended to or not, her heaving breaths led to her snorting the soot up her nose. At once she snorted and spat. Holt backed away, intending to stand beside Ash if the end came.

Wrath righted herself, spewed more clouds of black smoke, and spoke with pure venom, *"How could you let this happen?"*

Her aura intensified. The cool waters flowing out of the phoenix's lair began to simmer.

Holt reached Ash, and that gave him some relief and courage.

"The phoenix reduced itself. We had no warning."

Wrath snarled. *"What kind of coward takes its own life?"*

"One trying to end things on their own terms. He was no wild, unthinking beast. He was intelligent. And he had nothing but hatred for you and your flight."

"Then the feeling was mutual."

"Seems he had good reasons."

"Are you swayed by every passing breeze? Did you not consider that the Parasite could have LIED?"

Her aura, already sweltering, flared hotter. Holt Floated his mote channels but feared his body would sweat until he shriveled like a raisin.

"I sensed no lie in the phoenix," Ash said boldly.

"Then your senses are not as keen as you think. Its words have no bearing on reality. I would recall a flock of these leeches, don't you think?"

"No one could invent such a story in the moment. What are you not telling us, Wrath?"

Holt knew his error the moment the disrespectful tone left his lips. Spiritual energy whipped him, its power coiled thick as rigging on a war galley. A crushing mental pressure pressed on him and he felt winded, though no air left his lungs. Carried with the weight was the unspoken challenge, 'Do you think Fire would lie?'

Holt gathered his spirit to respond, yet, on this matter, he was conflicted, his will brittle. Wrath's certainty shattered his feeble resistance, and he emerged from the exchange upon bended knee.

The phoenix's ashes from his pan lay strewn across the stone, some already blowing away in the wind. He glanced at Ash and saw him lying down. The movement must have torn at the gashes on Ash's chest, for a fresh trickle of blood ran down his front.

"What does it all mean?" Ash asked privately.

Holt came up wanting. Something was missing in all of this. The Fire Flight and the phoenix could not both be correct.

"The Parasite told lies," Wrath insisted, *"and it worked – your minds were addled, so you let it destroy itself rather than ensure the power of my Elder be restored. I spoke against using such ill-begotten allies as you. Such folly – such a waste!"*

Wrath's aura thrashed now, intensifying to a point Holt hadn't felt since she'd driven off the storm dragons. She opened her jaws.

"Your Elder sent us on this mission," Ash said. *"Don't we have his protection?"*

"You failed my Elder. He will not name you a friend of the flight for that. Failure gets you nothing." Still furious, Wrath's voice dropped to something softer, drier, shuddering. *"Failure means punishment."*

Flames gathered at her mouth.

The change in her voice clicked into meaning for Holt. She was afraid, just like them.

Holt threw up his hands. "Wait! What if we could work the ashes into something usable?"

Wrath's gathering breath didn't stop, but it did slow.

"You've seen what we can do with potions and food. It could work."

Wrath closed her mouth. *"And how would you do that?"*

Before Holt could reply, Ash sensed his intention. Over the dragon bond, Holt felt doubt skittering throughout Ash's soul.

"I feel the same," Holt said privately. *"But what else can we do?"*

"We've been saying that for a while now. It isn't our right to bring anyone to Aberanth's grotto."

"I know… but I fear it's this or our deaths, and he wouldn't want that."

"Stop playing for time," Wrath demanded. *"Answer me!"*

Holt performed the spiritual equivalent of squeezing Ash's hand. Ash squeezed back.

"It would be beyond our knowledge, but maybe not our friend's. The emerald we told you about who created the potions."

"The so-called genius?"

"Surely it's better than giving up?"

"Better for whom? I grow weary of this venture. Too much time has been wasted already. There is a fight at hand."

"And what will you tell your Elder if you return empty-handed? Could you swear to him that you exhausted every option?" Wrath roared at that, but Holt pressed on. At this point, he had little to lose. "You don't want the phoenix to have its victory, do you?"

Wrath fell quiet again. Holt held his breath, but when the pressure of her aura lifted, he knew he'd won her around.

"I shall allow your friend a chance."

Holt bowed. "Thank you, Honored Warden. I know it's our best chance to fulfill your Elder's wishes."

The spiritual pressure on him fully eased, allowing him to rise.

"Make sure you bring it all," Wrath said.

Shaking a little, Holt nodded before he and Ash flew down to retrieve their gear from the rock shelter behind the waterfall. He took off his asphyxiating armor, noting the damage to his left vambrace where the phoenix's talons had scratched through to the steel plates.

Given the wounds the phoenix had inflicted on Ash, Holt considered himself deeply lucky still to have his arm. His right gauntlet ought to have been covered by the phoenix's blood, but there were no stains on the material. He only realized then that there was no trace of blood on his right hand either, despite the eruption from the wound his knife had made in the bird's side.

A little dazed from the events and the pressure exerted by Wrath, he thought he must be misremembering the fight. He had been moving extremely fast, so the blood mustn't have touched him. Whatever had happened, it hardly mattered now.

His frying pan also bore damage from the fight. The base and one side of the pan were worn to a rusty orange as though from long neglect. In places, the iron blistered and peeled like burnt skin. A fondness for his trusty pan bloomed. It had served him very well indeed, going well beyond the call of duty.

Hoping never to have to fight such a strange, magical creature again, Holt packed his battered pan away, then repacked his armor, though he kept his belts and pouches out, removing all content he deemed non-vital. Although it pained him, he threw away the last of his fruit and chilies. Every inch of space, every scrap of cloth, every usable pouch was emptied and made ready and taken back to the phoenix's lair.

Only then did he remember the pillars of stone blocking the way like clenched teeth. He'd never get his boxes in and out of there.

"Uh, Honored Warden? Could you help us with something?"

Wrath listened to his request in silence, then, without a word, she gathered power. Holt and Ash hastened aside as Wrath swooped forward and rammed the stone teeth at full force. Once the last piece of rock fell still, Holt crept back around to find the entrance wide open, the rubble blown all the way up the length of the passage beyond.

He grabbed his gear and entered. The mound of ash was impressive. They filled every container and pouch he had, but it still wasn't enough. Resigned, he uncorked and poured away his remaining elixirs, even those in storage. The result was another box he could fill, as well as a lot of newly emptied vials. By the time he was done, there was little more than dust left on the leaves and the bright red stones ringing the nest.

Holt picked one of the stones up, wondering if there was any worth in scraping the ashes off. He decided not but was struck by the strange quality of the rock. They seemed more like lumps of ore, streaked through with a glassy substance like scarlet quartz. Now he had time to take the cave in, he noticed a size-able natural deposit of the ore by the hot pool as well as other little pockets of it throughout the cavern.

Maybe it reminded the phoenix of home.

When he emerged, the bright face of the sun seemed to mock him with its radiant confidence, and he shrank under it. Tired and deeply anxious about what would follow, he realized he hadn't the faintest idea how to get to Aberanth's glade from here. He wasn't even sure where 'here' was.

"Do you know how to get to the Fae Forest?" he asked Wrath.

"I don't know the names your kind have given to every wood."

"The emeralds have a grove there," Ash said. "Where the East Warden makes his nest."

"Ah, then yes."

"If you can get us to the forest, we'll manage the rest."

"Then keep up. This time we shan't be stopping so often."

39

DISENCHANTMENT AND DISAPPOINTMENT

Neveh walked barefoot around her spherical quarters in the Ice Elder's domain, running her hand over ridges of sapphire ice that gleamed like diamonds under the permanent pale sun. Nilak was out with the Elder and her Wardens, happier than he'd been in a long time.

Waiting went against every bone in Neveh's body, but she could admit that her recovery had been necessary. Her soul had been in turmoil, and she would have been good for nothing with a crippled spirit. There was still a crack, running like a white vein beneath sheets of ice. It troubled her, but perhaps it would always remain, as scar does to flesh.

Her contemplations were interrupted by a gust of storm on the magical landscape. The next thing she knew, Nilak was returning at speed with no fewer than two Wardens.

"Stay in the nest," he told her. *"We are not to emerge."*

Neveh frowned, then ran for her armor and sword. The tapping of her feet was soon drowned out by the beating of wings as Nilak arrived in their nest, and the two Wardens touched down above so that their shadows spread over the frosted floor.

As Neveh pulled on her boots, Nilak asked, *"What are you doing?"*

"Dressing."

"But we are to remain here."

She pulled her gray gambeson over her head.

"Elder's orders."

"We aren't a member of her flight. She cannot order us to do anything."

From above came two low growls. The Wardens bared their teeth at her, but Neveh smirked, waved, then began attaching her vambraces. She was tightening the straps on her pauldrons when storm wielders came close enough to be tangible.

There were riders in the group. Riders.

A stab of cold fury cut through her. Seeking alliances with the Wild Flights had been her idea, and now Vald had done it? He and the Storm Elder had broken the Pact.

She snorted. It was rich enough to turn her stomach. But at least her own Elder could no longer feel queasy about the notion.

The two Wardens snarled louder.

"Sheathe your fangs," Neveh called to them. She strapped on her baldric belt and considered whether two Wardens could contain her and Nilak.

Here, at the roof of the world, his core had swollen to new heights. A lifetime spent scrounging on the smallest scraps of cold had made Forging here feel like breathing through both lungs for the first time.

No, she considered, two Wardens couldn't contain them, but that wasn't why they were perched above them. Other Lord-level drakes and many others besides flew close over their nest. They were here to cloud and muffle the radiance of Nilak's power from the storm party.

Neveh held the gaze of the Wardens until her restless energy overcame her. She huffed, scuffed the ice with the heel of her boot, and began to pace.

"I understand it's hard for you to take instructions," Nilak said reproachfully.

Neveh gave him a mocking scowl. "It's worked for us, having my own mind."

"All except for—"

"Yes," she said, a little tart. "Except for that. I know sometimes you go along with my will just to keep the peace, but I could feel your heart in that moment as well."

"I never said it was wholly your fault. We are equals."

Neveh felt a stirring in her heart and soul.

Privately, she said, *"You're the only one I've ever wanted to change my mind for."*

"I know."

There arose within her a great desire to head out there and see what was going on, like a tremendous itch she could not reach.

"Doing nothing is hard…" she said, drawing out the word.

Nilak rumbled with amusement. *"I know it is."*

Somehow, she contained her impulse to disobey.

The meeting with the storm party was brief. They must have traveled exceedingly far and drawn heartily on their cores to prevent themselves from freezing, and for what?

"They are gone now," the Ice Elder said. *"Come, child."*

Nilak took flight, and within a minute, they'd landed in the Elder's palatial nest – a wide, shallow basin ringed with unnatural pillars of spiked ice, each precisely placed with no uneven gaps.

Neveh stayed on Nilak's back to take advantage of the extra height.

"We need not fear your brother's position now," she said. "It's clear he has made common cause with Vald."

"You won't feel the same after hearing what they wanted."

That itch she couldn't reach grew worse. She threw her arms wide to invite the Elder to tell her the latest excuse.

"They advised I take heed of Storm's wishes, especially given my 'interference' in the matter of our brother's death. I wish you had held your tongue in your councils."

"Keeping secrets is for rogues and traitors."

Neveh regretted her choice of words at once. The crack in her soul throbbed anew, and as the pain coursed through her, she knew she could stand this inaction no longer.

"They seemed to leave peaceably. What did you tell them?"

"*I told them the truth – that at the time of my brother's demise, I was here, safeguarding my flight and domain. As for vengeance, if Storm wishes to take action, that is his business.*"

Neveh had to fight to keep the disgust from her face.

"So, you still intend to do nothing? Your own brother has taken up my idea. If he and Vald intend to move against Sovereign, then we should be there too."

"*They demanded I swear loyalty to my own brother. His lust for power knows no bounds. You would not accept such terms, Paragon.*"

"No," Neveh admitted. "I would not."

"*Stay with me, I implore you. Ice should stick with Ice, as Storm is Storm. Here we can outlast any conflict.*"

Neveh was ready to decline and do so firmly, but Nilak hastened to answer on their behalf.

"*Elder, that cannot be our way. Above all, we swore an oath to defend the living, to defeat the scourge. To do that, we must defeat this mystic. We would prefer you by our side to ensure our victory, but we will go either way. We must.*"

A wave of affection and love bloomed in Neveh for her dragon, so strong it threatened to melt the ice underfoot.

The Elder of Ice tilted her head one way and then the other. She narrowed her eyes to slits and spoke bitterly, "*Go then… as you must.*"

Neveh turned her back on the Elder. The cracking in her soul halted.

Shortly after, as they flew south again with cold winds pressing at their backs, Nilak asked, "*Where to now?*"

"She isn't the only Elder left in the world. We must try another."

Within a jagged valley under the eye of the storm, the court gathered, with dragons perched all around. On the small stretch of flat where the slopes met, Vald and Raiden'ra stood in the esteemed position just behind the Elder.

The first of their delegations had returned and now bowed before them and the court. This group had been sent to the mystics but had been unable to find the Elder or the flight at all.

"Only the weak are so cowardly as to hide," Storm proclaimed. *"My diminished sister is no matter now."*

The next time the court assembled, it was for the group returning from the roof of the world.

"Your sister of Ice bade us fly home," the lead dragon said. *"She and the Paragon are aligned and have sworn to join their power with your mystic sister's."*

If true, Vald thought, this helped to explain the Mystic Elder's evasiveness.

The Storm Elder reacted by showing a hint of fang. *"Which of my sisters leads this alliance?"*

"Our feeling was your mystic sister, but Ice spoke with much anger and confusion. In her fury, she let slip that her own Paragon was present when your brother perished."

"This we know."

"I beg your pardon, Your Reverence, but your sister's words suggested a more direct involvement than merely witnessing it."

Raiden'ra hissed, and a howling gale erupted between the peaks of the court.

Storm showed more fang.

"Did you see Neveh?" Vald asked, placing his voice upon the winds for all to hear.

The delegation said they hadn't felt the presence of a Paragon. She may have already gone to the Mystic Elder to discuss terms.

Storm thanked the delegation and dismissed them. Afterward, when only the Elder and his Wardens remained, Vald spoke openly.

"Something strikes me as amiss."

"It seems plain to me. You said Neveh has long sought alliances with Wild Flights. Now she has sewn two together... in a bloc against me."

That had almost sounded like fear, a tone Vald expected from Eso's worried mouth but not from the most powerful being in the world.

"She lacks patience for negotiations."

"*Given the circumstances,*" Raiden'ra said, "*is it so unusual she might change her ways?*" Their dragon bond flared as Raiden'ra followed up with private words. "*We did.*"

"*Whatever the truth is, we have been refused,*" said the Storm Elder, and his tone made it clear the matter was resolved.

The Elder brooded for long days after this news. During that time, the gathering storm blackened, casting the mountains under a shroud of eternal night.

Vald found the Elder's reaction bewildering. One day, as he and Raiden'ra flew within the eyewall of the storm, where the wind was fiercest to Forge and lightning fell like rain, Vald let his concerns be known.

"*This jostling worries me.*"

"*How so?*"

Over their bond, Raiden'ra's voice came clear and strong, even above the raging winds.

"*The scourge seems only a secondary consideration to the Elders. They care more for their own status and protecting themselves and their domains. There's no drive toward the ultimate victory.*"

"*We have quarreled with other Paragons our whole life. Why should the Elders not disagree as well?*"

Vald wanted to say, 'Because they are Elders.' Strange to think he was still capable of such young and fanciful notions.

"*A reckoning will come,*" Raiden'ra said. "*The strength of each side's conviction will be tested, and when all is settled, there will be one great flight. These squabbles diminish us and allow death to spread.*"

The dragon tucked his wings and dove, spinning with the wild wind. Lightning struck them only to be absorbed by their perfect Sinking techniques. Such maneuvers usually brought Vald joy, but this time, he remained tense.

"*At what cost will this great flight come?*"

"*At the cost of the stubborn and the foolish. Why should Storm ever buckle and concede? We are the mightiest, our Elder the greatest power in existence. He is the natural leader of the Elders and thus of the world.*"

Despite the buffeting rain and wind strong enough to uproot trees, Vald nodded slowly. It was how the dragons worked. It was how the Order worked too. Power was all that mattered when determining position. A prodigious young pairing that reached Lord could be set in charge of old Champions twice their age. Only the Paragons squabbled with each other, despite the evident disparities in power between them. He and Raiden'ra were already the strongest in the Order – a fact no rider could doubt – yet the others questioned them.

The Storm Elder knew better.

Unchallengeable power and firmer action would be needed.

Vald turned inward. The screaming wind, the lashing rain, the deafening thunder, and the blinding lightning disappeared. His swollen soul spun fast, their tornado bond-bridge whirled.

Might makes right. When I advance, I will make them follow me.

Then everything froze.

It was as though the Ice Elder herself had cursed him.

The tornado bond-bridge ceased spinning. Vald's soul ground to a halt. He lost his own heartbeat, his own name. There was only a long, low note, itself trapped, suspended, the first drawn breath before the first thunder to break the sky.

Then, all at once, his bond grew taut, and his soul spun so fast its gray light became a solid orb. A coil of Raiden'ra's silver-blue power balled up in the bond-bridge and began to roll. When it reached Vald, the magic became trapped within the vortex of his soul. Vald felt the sear as though his flesh were branded. He wanted to scream, though whether in anguish or delight, he could not say.

He opened his eyes. Falling. He was falling through lightning and hail, through a world as dark as the void.

Raiden'ra's magic began to sink in. Vald gasped, though no air entered his lungs. Not through his mouth, he realized. His soul had gasped, his very being inhaling, breathing in motes of the storm raging around him.

Now he knew his scream would be one of delight.

He'd done it.

He'd done it!

At this moment of triumph, all froze again. His bond-bridge shuddered, undulated, then shook so violently it would surely snap. The branding power was searing through his soul-wall – it would consume him.

Raiden'ra's voice reached him. *"Expel it!"*

Vald gasped for real this time. Still plummeting through the air, he drove his mote channels into Floating, pushing any magic within him up and out. His spinning soul slowed, and its solid surface became porous again. Raiden'ra's coiled power entered his channels as painfully as a bone catching in his throat, and then, with a final effort, it dispersed into a thousand motes and joined the rest of the magic forming his second skin.

Raiden'ra's talons wrapped around him. Vald felt weightless, and for the first time since reaching the level of Ascendant, he blacked out.

Ever since the riders had moved to Falcaer, the Paragons had maintained the old villa they used as the sanctum. It would forever be the constant, beating heart of the Order. A great mosaic in one of the courtyards had recently been earmarked for restoration: a chipped image of a golden legionary shield trimmed with laurel leaves.

But rather than restore it, Adaskar had decided to make a change.

Ascendants and Champions of all types now traipsed across the mosaic, carrying strips of shaped dragon steel. Even Novices assisted by constructing the wooden frame of the new world table. As he watched the mosaic be destroyed, Adaskar could feel a phantom clout around his ear from Aodhan.

Just this, he assured his predecessor. *Just as much as is enough, and no more than is necessary.*

Gnarled posts holding floating light stood between the court-yard's columns. Of late, the lights throughout Falcaer had glowed a vigilant orange or a dispirited brown, but here, the glow was warm and yellow.

Fire Lords bent their power to weld pieces together under the calculating eyes of Ice Ladies, while Emerald Lords spoke to the earth beneath the mosaic to grasp the legs of the huge table and keep it steady. Though the remaining storm riders at Falcaer were wary and wayward since Vald's departure, even they assisted in keeping the weather at bay to allow the work to carry on day and night.

Already the mountains of the Spine could be discerned, as well as the skeleton of Sky Spear's great tower. A hundred shades of dragon steel, each piece hand-forged by Ascendants. Adaskar intended that every rider should contribute in time so that the new world table would belong to all, allowing them to draw up their plans together.

Adaskar headed for the Artisan Smith leading the project, stepping over piles of steel and weaving between Ascendants who sprang back out of his path.

"Mr. Smith," he said with a smoky hiss.

The artisan froze as though caught naked. He beheld Adaskar with wide eyes, seemingly thinking it was a mystery why the leading Paragon should be walking through the sanctum.

"Lord Adaskar has come," the smith said. "Will he be pleased or wrothful?"

Adaskar was used to the smith's eccentric manner, but even so, his muttered fears took him aback.

"I came to say what a wonderful job you're doing here."

"My Lord, it is delicate work; each piece requires exacting—" The smith cut himself off, looked around as though waiting for someone to explain, then blinked. "You are pleased, Lord?"

The artisan's assistants held their breath, and the bustle of work fell quiet. The courtyard seemed to draw a collective breath. Adaskar felt many eyes upon him, but he held the artisan's gaze and gave him the respect he deserved.

"The thought of its first use fills me with great anticipation." Inspired, a sudden good mood upon him, Adaskar magnified his voice. "I can impart judgment on a great many matters, but in metalwork, you are a paragon of your craft."

Adaskar proffered his hand. The artisan looked unsure, hesitated, then clasped his nut-brown hand into Adaskar's darker one. Pale green flashed from the gnarled posts.

The artisan beamed. "We are pleased to work on something new. Very pleased."

Adaskar smiled and found his cheeks were stiff, then he returned to his coals in the inner sanctum.

"Leave these doors open," he told the Low Lords on duty, one of each type.

No sooner had he settled cross-legged onto the spitting coals than Azarin reached out with news. One of the traitors had been found and brought back.

"And who achieved this feat?"

Azarin tsked a laugh. *"Exalted Champions Sigfrid and Ruateng."*

"Is that so?"

Adaskar put his boots back on, then made for the exit. Eso and Wynedd still slept, and he saw no reason to disturb them.

Sigfrid, it turned out, had taken his prisoner directly to the cells. Adaskar found them outside the non-descript building, little more than a cover for the stairs that wound deep underground.

A young woman in maroon brigandine knelt on both knees, head bowed, a dark curtain of hair covering her face. Sigfrid had slung her sword over his shoulder and held his own long icy blade at her back. The spiritual tension of a yield linked them. Nearby, Ruateng stood imperiously over a smaller dragon, his cobalt scales glistening where her maroon ones appeared washed out.

Azarin landed hard behind Adaskar.

"Do not think your treatment will be better for your type, traitors."

The rogues said nothing. The girl – for she seemed only a girl to Adaskar, a High Ascendant at best – kept her eyes fixed on the ground.

"Where did you find them?"

"Out beyond the Brown Wash, Paragon." Doubtless, Sigfrid had returned there in the hope of picking up on the trail of the blind dragon. "We recognized their names from the list Paragons Eso and Wynedd sent out."

Adaskar stepped forward to stand before her. "Your name?"

"Gryta," she said in the tough manner of Fornheim.

Azarin stamped forward too. *"And yours?"*

"Bresa," the maroon dragon said, trying and failing to maintain a scolding tone.

"And whom did you abandon Falcaer for, Gryta?"

Still with her head down and her face hidden, she said, "We were in service to the great dragon, Sovereign. He who will rid this world of the scourge."

"Look at me."

She raised her head and shook the hair from her face. She had a strong nose and jaw but couldn't have been a day past her mid-twenties.

"Will you talk willingly?"

Gryta glanced at her dragon, then bit her lip. "For Bresa's sake."

"A shred of good sense remains," said Azarin.

Adaskar caught Sigfrid's eye and saw a longing for forgiveness in them. His deed did not make up for the loss of the boy. Adaskar's first instinct, fueled by Azarin's backing, was to be truthful in that... but he resisted. In his earnest desire to press the Order to be the best it could, perhaps he had been too harsh at times. The artisan had feared rebuke almost as a matter of course.

"You've done well, Sigfrid. A good step in earning back favor."

Sigfrid strained to suppress a smile, nodded, then stood taller.

Adaskar looked upon the girl again. "Release her," he ordered, and the spiritual tie between them dropped at once. "On your feet, Gryta. You shall come with me."

Azarin remained to watch Bresa while Adaskar led Gryta away from the cell block, past the Fire Barracks, and toward the Ice Barracks. She groaned as her fate dawned on her.

"Speak quickly," Adaskar said, "and we won't have to stay for long."

Gryta panted as he nudged her over the threshold. Ascendants weren't proficient in cycling, but he Floated his mote channels to ward off the snap of cold, and ice riders backed away under the heat of his presence. Adaskar took Gryta to an empty meditation room, shoved her inside, and closed the door behind them.

Frost covered the floor, and each of his steps sent up clouds of hissing steam as they ducked low-hanging icicles. He sat Gryta down on a frozen bench and let her cool there for a while. Finally, he asked her to tell him everything.

Where was Sovereign now?

In the Frontier, though she didn't know exactly where. He didn't allow every rider to come close, especially those who had arrived recently and unannounced.

What was she doing when Sigfrid caught her?

Gryta had been sent out along with others to scout the Frontier for signs of a one-handed man wielding a blood-red axe with a black dragon companion. Sovereign desired this man be returned before him, maimed if needed, but still alive.

The description matched one of the cook boy's companions, as Sigfrid had reported. The other Agravain. Adaskar noted it, then moved on.

How had she been recruited?

Not directly. A Storm Champion had brought her into the fold during her recent rotation at Squall Rock.

"I shall need the name."

She gave it willingly. Arms and legs tucked in as tight as she could, her shuddering grew worse. He only needed a little more from her, though it was the most important part.

"Why do it? What possible reason did you have?"

"T-to d-destroy the... the scourge," she managed through chattering teeth. "Sovereign will use his c-control to end it once we're all g-gone."

"Once who is gone?"

"Mankind."

"You're a human. What of you?"

"Riders who join him will b-be spared for t-their dragon's sake."

"Will you renounce this evil now?"

She shook her head.

Adaskar shook his in turn. Fury would have been appropriate, but he was too much at a loss.

"You swore to defend."

"At least this way the c-cycle will end."

Adaskar sat on the frozen bench beside her. Water pooled beneath him. He looked Gryta over and tried again to guess her age. Whether old or young, her rank told him that she was no veteran of a score of risings or incursions. Not like himself, or Vald, or any High Lord who had suffered the loss of friends and comrades and long outlived their original families.

"You're too young to be so cynical."

"I've seen enough. H-heard enough. I would rather it be over sooner than live a century longer... j-just waiting for death on the battlefield. All for nothing. Wh-what point is there in that?"

Adaskar leaned in. In his dismay, he spoke in a low whisper.

"That, child, is the entire point. You are – you *were* – the last shield. Every life saved because of you is a blessing; every child born because of you is a blessing; every happy moment and loving union made because of you are blessings. But somehow, you have dismissed all of that. Why? Because none of them thanked you personally? Because you could not see the fruits of your labor firsthand? Because no one hailed you as a hero and smothered you in fame and honors? How selfish you are to rob all those blessings from the world."

He understood then how this issue was at the heart of his current woes. All of them – Vald, Neveh, Kalanta, even Talia – held in their hearts a desire to defeat the scourge for good. Their motivations were pure. Who wouldn't wish to end the scourge? But they were all of them naïve. All wrong.

"You cannot defeat death, Gryta. You can only keep it at bay."

She made a jerky, defeated nod. Her lips were turning blue.

Something dangerously close to pity threatened to flicker inside him. "I think that's enough."

As Adaskar got to his feet, he offered Gryta his hand. She took it, and, summoning a touch of spirit along with his fires, he willed her to be warm. Her next shudder was one of relief, and with hobbled steps, she allowed herself to be taken from the icy chamber, then from the barracks.

He walked her to the fire barracks and summoned High Lord Dowid to see her confined under strict guard. Bresa would be grounded in the nests of the barracks with her privileges to beef revoked.

"Until a council of Paragons can decide your fate," he warned.

Head bowed, she said weakly, "Yes, Master Adaskar."

He pulled Dowid in closer and spoke quietly. "More patrols are to sweep the Frontier." The fire riders sent to burn the fallen in the Spine had reported there had been no bodies to deal with. This Sovereign had been at large for long enough; he had to be located and subdued, if not destroyed outright. "Prepare three squadrons. I shall ready their orders upon my return."

Dowid placed a fist over his chest, inclined his head, then led Gryta inside the barracks.

Adaskar called for Azarin, hoping a long flight would help clear his head.

Minutes later, they were flying north over flat country. Azarin didn't say a word.

"You disapprove," Adaskar noted.

Azarin tilted his head up, snorted, then looked ahead again. "Are you going soft?"

"Anything is possible."

Azarin grunted. "You had every right to pronounce judgment without the others."

"I could have... though what happens should more be brought back? There aren't enough cells for them all, and I require assistance if I am to break a bond."

"Then what is to be done?"

"I don't know." It gave him no pleasure to admit it. "That so many are persuaded by these wretched views means that we – that I – have failed. Yes... I have failed."

"We have failed," Azarin insisted. "All you do, we do together. The triumphs and the stumbles."

Adaskar reached down and patted his dragon's molten-red scales.

Unprompted, Azarin stretched his wings, then banked to the right. When he leveled out, they faced south, where the Great Chasm cut the world like the edge of night.

"We should inspect the activity," Azarin said.

Adaskar thought that to be a prudent distraction. Even before they crossed the boundary and flew under the wound in the sky, the presence of the enemy loomed in their minds. In the recent turmoil, even basic duties such as dampening activity here had been neglected. Fewer groups of Novices and Ascendants had been dispatched to harden themselves in battle, and more low-level froth of the scourge had undoubtedly emerged from the pitted depths.

For that was the nature of the chasm, as it was with the scourge. You could sweep them clean off the face of the world, you could delve into a few tunnels with fire and lightning or collapse the rock and stone upon them, yet more always came.

"Where did this notion come from?" Azarin asked. *"That the enemy could be defeated for good?"*

As they flew high above the screeching and scuttling, the Paragons ruminated together. Perhaps it was the efficiency with which the chasm had been cleansed in recent centuries, or perhaps it was how quickly other small openings in the world were located and sealed; either way, the Order's proficient strategies, honed over centuries, may have created a false confidence.

Azarin grumbled at these dark thoughts. *"What are we to do? Allow things to decay so that the younger riders will understand what they face?"*

"We need not go that far."

Adaskar considered the first lesson: you cannot save them all. A necessary lesson, grim and wise, yet it did not run deep enough.

"I say we need a new first lesson," said Adaskar. *"You are fighting a war you can never win."*

The wording could be worked on, but he liked the notion.

"Another change," Azarin said with a sigh. Then, after a moment's thought, he growled, *"But a good one, Rostam."*

With a burst of speed, Azarin beat his wings, climbed higher, looped, then swerved down to face west and headed for home. They discussed the new lesson and increasingly found it to their liking. All their woes might have been averted had the others accepted this harsh truth.

Vald sought power to defeat death itself; Neveh demanded new alliances and strategies; and Kalanta wished to confront the darkness directly – as did Talia, although she at least had the sense to prune only a few thorns off the monstrosity.

In comparison to his fellow Paragons – in comparison to Sovereign's desires – were Talia's actions quite so terrible?

Adaskar's soul grew taut. Perhaps it was the cloying air above the chasm, seeping into him, that conjured such ideas. Azarin felt his turmoil and rumbled both in his throat and in his soul. The vibrations crossed the golden bridge of their bond.

"Perhaps," Azarin said, *"pruning the thorns would be another… prudent measure as part of the containment."*

"Yes," Adaskar said, glad it had been Azarin who'd prompted the idea. *"Yes, provided riders swear not to delve too deep and expose themselves to the corruption."*

"I am certain the dragons will aid you in that. None of us would wish to see our riders taken by the whispers."

"Yes," Adaskar said again. He repeated it, over and over, and patted Azarin to reassure himself as much as his dragon. As with the world table, the decision felt… pleasing, once made, even if it did seem as though his conscience were being stretched upon the rack.

"We'll make terms. Bring her back to the fold. Re-open the halls in Brenin, Feorlen, and the Skarl Empire. One united Order again."

So it was that Paragon Adaskar returned to Falcaer in better spirits than he had been in weeks and Azarin's scales glowed like actual lava. They were just about to descend when a telepathic call begged them to listen. The female dragon sounded worn.

"Revered Paragons, please, we beg your audience the moment we land."

From the northwest came the glint of pale scales, a storm dragon gliding fast, like a swift-moving cloud.

"*Declare yourselves,*" Azarin said.

"*I am Skree, Revered One, and my rider is Einar. We beg your forgiveness… and bring dire news from across the Bitter Bay.*"

When Vald woke, he felt as if his whole being had been shattered and then hammered back together with rusted nails. Opening his eyes, he found he lay upon a soft conjured cloud encircled by Raiden'ra's tail.

As Vald sat up, Raiden'ra rumbled deeply and gave him a look as if he were rousing from an indulgent nap.

Vald clutched at his sternum. "How long?"

"*Five days.*"

Five days. One for each stage of advancement, including the one he'd all but tasted.

"*We can discuss what triggered it later,*" Raiden'ra said. "*The delegation from the Fire Flight is here.*"

Vald coughed and swallowed to wet his throat. "Then we should be there."

When they arrived at the court of storms, the Elder greeted them with the merest of nods. It seemed like that was all the praise or sympathy they would receive.

The group sent to the Scalding Sea had returned, fewer in number than those who had been sent. Two dragons had been burned to cinders by a Warden. The rider had even yielded to a young Champion with a strange white dragon.

"*One of Adaskar's?*" the Elder asked.

The question prompted something in Vald and made him consider the issue. Why did he know something about a white dragon and a young boy? His Lords might have briefed him on it when he'd returned to Falcaer, though it had seemed trivial to him at the time.

"*The role-breaker and the blind cripple from Feorlen,*" Raiden'ra said. He snorted silver smoke. His electric blue eyes bulged, and he stalked around the failed Exalted Champion and his dragon, examining them from all angles as though wondering where he might hurt them most. *"Pathetic."*

The Champion flinched. His dragon pressed herself flat to the ground and wailed.

"Answer my question," demanded the Elder.

"The blind dragon is not one of Adaskar's," said Vald. "He would never ally himself to chaos-bringers such as them. Whatever their business with the Fire Flight, it was not by Adaskar's will. That much I assure and would swear to."

The Storm Elder grunted. *"Still care for your pupil's reputation?"*

"It is the truth."

Storm clenched his teeth, a sound like scraping steel. *"Would he seek his Elder? As you have and Neveh have?"*

"Never."

"Even if the alternative was doom?"

Vald hesitated. The instinct to defend Rostam's honor was still strong in him, but the frightful truth was that Rostam would rather face doom than change. Even when Vald had taught him swordcraft, Rostam would question him for breaking explicit forms and guards.

Unbidden, Vald's lip curled boldly up his cheek, a memory of simpler times coming to him, when even Azarin and Raiden'ra would nip each other in affection. An apparition of a far younger Adaskar seemed to appear before him, smiling instead of frowning.

Why could you not follow me? Vald asked it.

Before Adaskar could answer, the Elder lowered his head through the specter, breaking it into wisps of smoke.

"Paragon?!"

Vald set his jaw. "Even to his doom."

"Could you convince him to join us?"

That took Vald aback. "That will never happen."

"Such a shame," Storm said with tremendous bite. He prowled forward to address his court. *"A blind Champion is irrelevant. My brother of Fire has declared open war against me. My sisters plot together, and as it stands, we must consider the Order hostile."*

Vald felt the spirits of the riders grow tense.

"It seems the whole world resists the natural lead of their superiors," said the Storm Elder.

At this, there was a rumbling approval from the Wardens. Farther back in the court, the weaker dragons remained quiet.

"Will this deter us? Is thunder cowed by the caw of crows?"

More growling from the storm Wardens and Lords, accompanied by a few roars and one streak of forked, silver lightning that threw the court into stark relief and shadowed every face and snout.

"Any who dare oppose us will fall, be they dragon or rider!"

The Elder finished his speech by lifting his neck high and roaring to the gathering blackness.

Vald stepped back, Raiden'ra stepped forward, and they met, eyes level with one another. What passed between them occurred quicker than thought.

All should have bowed to Storm – it was his right – but he threatened the riders now, and most were only following oaths and orders of their own. To slaughter riders had never once crossed their minds, nor could it now. No matter Storm's power, they would not be a part of that.

The solution came to them both as a deadened weight, crushing Vald's shoulders and turning Raiden'ra's wings to stone.

"I'll do it," Vald assured his dragon privately. Then, speaking for all to hear, he said in a magnified voice, "There is another way."

The court of storms fell silent. Even the world-ending blackness that blotted the sky fell quiet.

The Elder held his head imperiously high. *"And what way is this?"*

"This flight is the mightiest, of that there is no mistake, but even the mighty can fall if outnumbered. We riders know that best of all. How much is each of us worth? Several drakes? Some of us are worth far more. The Order of Falcaer combined can best the strength of any one Wild Flight... even that of storms."

Disgruntled mutters arose from the court.

Falling to one knee, Vald pressed on. "Revered Elder, I have sworn my sword to you, and the swords of all those here are bound to me. Let me go further in your name. Let Raiden'ra and I bring the whole Order under new leadership and thus guarantee the loyalty of the most powerful faction in the world."

Storm brought his snout over Vald's head, then lowered it gently to be level with him, as though he intended to whisper.

"That is a most enticing offer. But how can it be done?"

Raiden'ra stamped and slammed his tail. *"By breaking the last boundary! Then all will fall in line."*

"Can it be done?" Storm asked, and Vald had the impression that the court had vanished and only he and the Elder remained.

"It can." For the first time, it felt good to say it with the benefit of experience. "It will be done."

40
———

A NEW HOME

After such a long journey, Aberanth's glade had never seemed more inviting. Ash touched down in the thick summer grass, and Holt slid off his back. The Fae Forest had once felt claustrophobic and oppressing, yet compared to the humidity of the jungle, the forest's air was light, fresh, and seemed to dance just beyond the tip of his nose.

Were it not for Wrath, he might have relaxed, but she circled above.

"*Hurry,*" Ash said, but Holt was already scanning the forest floor for the trap door. With the glade overgrown, it took him longer than usual to find it.

Using his feet, he hammered out a pattern of knocks to signal who was there. And again. And again.

"*Holt? Ash?*"

"Aberanth, open up. We need to talk with you!"

"*Yes, I concluded as much from your frantic knocking. By thunder, boy, what's the matter? Are you hurt? What's going on?*"

"*We can explain best above ground,*" Ash said.

"*Hmph, yes, yes, yes, I'm coming.*"

Holt stepped off the trap door. Aberanth couldn't be too deep underground if he was speaking with them.

Sure enough, within moments, the trap door swung up, and Aberanth came charging out into the glade. Mouse-like, the muddy emerald sniffed frantically at the air, and his oversized eyes twitched between them. Ash bounded up, heading right for Aberanth.

Aberanth yapped and tried to back away. *"Careful, Ash. I'm only little."*

"So am I," Ash said, lowering his snout. Aberanth hesitated, then, with a flick of his neck, he touched his nose to Ash's and withdrew as quick as if he were touching a hot flame.

Aberanth backed away some more, then gave them an appraising look. *"You both look thin. Ash, your chest, your back – is that a missing ridge?! What's going on? Where's Rake?"*

Their silence spoke volumes.

"He's… He's hiding, isn't he?" Aberanth asked. *"Trying to take me by surprise. Come on out, Rake! I've had my fill of frights for the day."*

Holt gulped, struggling to form words.

"He fell behind," Ash said. *"We were underground again, and there was a cave-in. Master Rake… didn't make it."*

Since meeting the little emerald, Holt had never known Aberanth not to have a ready reply. But nothing came now.

"Listen," Holt croaked. "We'll tell you everything, but that's not why we're here. We need your help. We don't have much time to explain, but there's a Fire Warden flying over us. She'll come down soon."

Aberanth's huge eyes went wide and vacant.

"Aberanth? Did you hear me?"

Aberanth shook his head, then strained his neck to look skyward. Wrath was still too high for Holt to sense magically, but the day was clear, and she must have been visible. Aberanth yelped and clawed at the earth.

"W-who is that?"

"She's a Fire Warden. The Warden of Wrath."

"And you brought her… here?"

"We didn't have a choice. Please. You're the only one who can help us."

"If we succeed, the Fire Elder will help kill Thrall," Ash said.

Aberanth was only half paying attention. He reared up,

roaring in fright, and backed up toward the entrance to his grotto.

"*She's coming,*" Ash said.

Holt looked to the sky. Sure enough, Wrath descended fast, trailing smoke. Her aura and spirit hit Holt again like a tidal wave.

"*The heat,*" Aberanth wailed, shortly before the Warden landed.

Too big to fit neatly in the glade, she flattened four trees and smashed the trunks of many more with her swinging tail as she pressed heavily forward. Delicate wildflowers wilted before her.

"*I waited long enough. Will your friend assist or not?*"

Aberanth seemed frozen in place.

"Float your mote channels," Holt said. "It helps."

The only sign of life in Aberanth was his eyes, twitching between Holt and Ash again.

Holt gave him a pleading look and silently mouthed, 'Please.'

"*Well,*" Aberanth muttered at last, "*it's all rather terrifying. Hmph. But Rake… yes, even Rake would have struggled to defy such a dragon. Yes,*" he ended, fighting to assert himself. Trembling snout to tail, he padded up to face his latest guest. "*Honored Warden, I should be delighted to assist you in this matter.*"

Wrath's gaze took a few seconds to fall. Her burning blue eyes took Aberanth in, and she flashed her teeth.

"*Oh, there you are,*" she said, her voice tart with a cruel relish. "*I almost didn't see you there behind the grass. What in the world are you? A mole with wings? I thought Ash to be small, but you…*" She descended into rumbles of amusement before recovering. "*What other oddities will we rely on next? Pride would have a fit if he knew the lengths we were going to.*"

"Good thing you aren't your brother then," Holt said.

"*A good thing for you.*" She returned her attention to Aberanth. "*Now, what should I call you, little mole?*"

"*My name is Aberanth, and you can call me just that, if it pleases you.*"

"*It would please me to bring my Elder what he demands. Have Holt and Ash explained the task?*"

"We can head below and start working right away," Holt said. "I'll explain everything."

"*Yes… yes! Below. I shall start at once, Honored Warden,*" Aberanth said, bowing very low.

"*Spare your false flattery. Holt can explain that to you as well.*"

"*False?*" Aberanth squeaked. "*Not I, Honored Warden. Never false. I'm a dragon of mind and logic, and you are truly the mightiest I have ever met. Deserving of all deference.*"

Wrath hissed smoke but did not appear unpleased to hear it. "*Begin.*"

And with that simple order, she curled up at the edge of the glade, uncaring for the carnage she'd wrought in the trees behind her.

Still shaking, Aberanth headed for the trap door, then turned to check Holt was following.

"You go on. I need to collect a few things."

Nodding, Aberanth scurried into the tunnel. Holt took their gear from Ash to free him of their burden, then grabbed one of the crates filled with the phoenix's remains.

"*Will you be okay up here?*" he asked Ash privately.

"*I'll be fine, boy. I doubt she'll have much to say.*"

Ash sounded flat now, as he had been since leaving the phoenix's lair. Something weighed on him. Holt could feel as much over their bond, but the arduously long flights hadn't granted a chance to broach it.

Ash nudged him. "*Go on.*" He sniffed furtively. "*I might try going on a hunt.*"

Holt wasn't sure when they'd last eaten. Some days ago, or so it seemed.

"*Bring something back for me if you can,*" Holt said, then he entered the passage.

By the time he reached the glittering fireflies, Wrath's aura no longer affected him, which was enough of a relief that it balanced out the discomfort of the weakening connection to Ash underground.

So it was with a smile that he stepped into the grotto proper, back into the cozy presence of the beech tree and its soft glowing roots and branches. At least one pot bubbled away with a thick, gray mixture Holt didn't recognize.

Aberanth was nowhere to be seen. Holt called for him.

"I'm in the shroomery."

Holt set the crate of phoenix ash down on a workbench and picked his way carefully through the lab. He found Aberanth snout deep in a pile of wide, flat-capped yellow mushrooms.

"I know this must be a lot to take in."

"I half-dreaded you'd all return battered and bruised one day, but that's the risk I run offering safe harbor to lunatics like you and… Rake." He chomped some more, then emerged from the pile with a long-stemmed snow puff mushroom dangling from his mouth. *"Anxiety makes me hungry – are you hungry?"*

"I am, but maybe not for mushrooms."

"I have eggs. Forty-three, to be exact."

Holt's spirits soared. He'd all but forgotten about the hen they'd left behind. "You kept the chicken?"

"I took her cage up to the woods one day," Aberanth said sheepishly. *"But I discovered I didn't want to part with her. She's been good company. I've called her Gallus."*

Holt cleared his throat with a small cough. "Uh, Gallus?"

"Yes, Gallus. From the name given to the species by learned humans from the Aldunei Republic. Gallus gallus domesticus. I have a volume of their classifications around here somewhere."

He trotted past Holt and back into the lab. Holt followed, watching as Aberanth raised vines to help him shift boxes and equipment around, evidently searching for something.

Fearing Aberanth would present him with this tome from Aldunei, Holt hastened to say, "So where are these eggs?"

"There we are," Aberanth said absentmindedly, withdrawing a book from under black slabs of bark notes. *"What were you saying? Oh, over here."* He led Holt to a workbench on the other side of the beech tree and delicately pulled out a large basket in which he had stacked each of his forty-three eggs in exacting, neat rows. *"You can cook and talk at the same time. Good to be efficient. Hmph. Yes. I shall take notes."*

Holt debated returning to the surface for his pot but opted

for one of the smallest black pots Aberanth had, which weren't much different from cooking ones. Aberanth used charcoal rather than open fires, and some were usually already hot for experiments.

As he cooked, he told Aberanth of everything: of how they'd come upon evidence of Thrall's five hatchlings at Silt Grave, of Osric and Soot parting on their own journey, of events in Sidastra – Talia's wedding and making his sword – and of the mission to take out the control orb under western Risalia. After detailing the encounter with the Hive Mind and escaping the collapsing chamber, he focused on eating and allowed Aberanth a chance to catch up on taking notes.

"So you didn't actually see Rake's body?"

Holt paused in spooning scrambled egg into his mouth. "No," he said thickly. He swallowed hard. "He must have been crushed."

"That's only an assumption," Aberanth said, seeming to poke out each word.

Holt gave him a pitiful look. "I didn't want to believe it either—"

"I'm just saying we don't know for a fact." Then, crestfallen, Aberanth said, *"What came next? How did you escape?"*

It took Holt less time than he anticipated to run through the rest of their adventures, leading to this very moment. Once he trimmed out all the traveling, there wasn't as much to it as he'd thought. Aberanth spent more time asking for every minute detail of the phoenix: its appearance, how it moved, its powers of regeneration, the bizarre interaction with his knife and pan, the fact it bled, even how it made its nest. Aberanth checked the details again and again until Holt's head hurt from straining to remember.

Feeling Aberanth desired greater clarity, he said, "I'm sorry I can't be more accurate – it all happened so fast."

"Mhm. Shame." Aberanth looked up from his notes and gazed at the crate of ashes. *"How much is there?"*

"Three more full crates, all my intact pouches and bags, every scrap of cloth I could bundle up, and loads of vials I filled too."

Aberanth crept over to the crate and gingerly lifted the lid. He sniffed deep, then replaced the lid with a harrumph.

"Just to make sure I understand," Aberanth said, slowly. *"The Warden of Wrath requires that I, somehow, process these remains into a viable, physically digestible, magically enhancing substance so as to return power stolen from the Fire Elder to him?"*

"That's the gist."

"I see." Aberanth lifted the lid and sniffed again at the dark contents. *"Yes, there's something to them."*

He fell quiet, and his little tail tapped a quick beat against the leg of a workbench. Holt braced for him to reject the idea as impossible, to sigh and doom-monger, so when Aberanth yipped loudly, cheerfully, and bounced around, Holt dropped his spoon.

"How exciting! What unique properties and potential. And to think the work might serve an Elder. Hmph! Hmph! I can picture the indignation on the East Warden's face at the mere thought, and that's worth a lot, let me tell you."

Holt beamed. "Do you think you can do it?"

"Not a clue, Master Cook. Not a clue," Aberanth said delightedly. *"But that is largely the joy in the work. The exploration. The anticipation. Although less… pressing circumstances would be preferable."*

"Well, let's get to it then. I'm here to help in any way I can."

"I should damn well hope, so what with you causing this and all." Aberanth began pacing around the beech tree, growling to himself. *"Where to begin?"*

"Maybe make an elixir using the ashes and see what happens?"

"Oh, just to see what happens? What an inspired idea. I'll just whip that up then and we'll be done by breakfast. Hmph, really. I can't use such potent materials carelessly."

"It was only a suggestion."

"I suppose you'll want more cycling elixirs as well?" Aberanth said as he disappeared around the beech tree on his marching route. Before waiting for Holt to answer, he barreled on. *"I just hope my supplies will last. I'll start fresh batches. It'll give me time to think and conduct some basic tests."* He rounded the tree again. *"Hmph. That scabbard isn't suitable for you either."*

"We tried modifying Brode's."

"I'll make you a better one. And more balm too, yes."

"Are you sure? I don't want to give you a mountain of work."

Aberanth rounded the tree for a third time.

"I'll let you know what's mountainous. Besides, there's plenty to do around here. You can attend to your old duties and take over the shroomery. I trust you recall what to do? Oh, and Gallus. Don't you forget to feed Gallus!"

Holt took to life at the lab again like putting on an old glove. He assisted Aberanth in the lab as directed, cleaning and organizing the place; he washed his clothes and did what he could to repair the vambrace ripped by the phoenix; and in the shroomery, he cut stems and replanted each variety to spawn and grow among sawdust, soil, and moss. At night, he tended to Ash's core, and in the mornings, he drilled with his sword while Ash hunted, practicing sending Shocks through the blade to get used to the blowback.

He hadn't forgotten about the meteorite or their bargain with the Fire Elder, though he was trying not to let his imagination run away with him. Moreover, it hardly mattered unless they could restore the Elder's power in the first place. If they did, he intended to ask Aberanth if he had any smithing insights that might be of use.

Ash brought deer from the woods, allowing Holt to hang new strips of meat to dry and take some scraps down to feed Gallus.

Aberanth had given the chicken the run of a small alcove off the lab, where she walked free from her cage and rummaged the earth for worms and other insects.

Wrath brooded quietly for the most part, offering little other than biting requests for updates and telling them to hurry up.

Aberanth worked diligently, and while brewing fresh cycling elixirs, he ran the phoenix ashes through dozens of tests.

"I've scattered them over hot coals, boiled them, baked them in hot sand, all to little effect, I'm afraid," he rattled off one evening. *"Not to worry! These things take time. Here's my latest."* He directed Holt's

attention to one of several bubbling alembics. A gray liquid lay in the receiving chamber. *"I mixed ashes with a lukewarm solution and distilled it. Take the distillation up to the Warden to test, please."*

Holt's stomach knotted at thought. "T-to Wrath?"

"Well, I do hope there isn't another Warden in my glade."

Holt didn't relish the thought of asking her to drink this, but he drained the gray liquid from the alembic into a glass jar anyway. Just before he stepped into the firefly tunnel, Aberanth called after him.

"And don't forget to set up a fire beside her!"

Back in the glade, Holt lit a small fire near Wrath, who sat there primly, though with an irate expression. After much coaxing and pleading, she eventually consented. Holt poured the mixture into her open mouth. Her hot breath smelled of burnt hair and the greasy smoke released from a dirty oven.

"Nothing is happening."

Trying not to gag from the smell, Holt coughed lightly and asked, "There aren't any immediate side effects though? That's a positive thing. It's a first step."

She growled. *"Work faster."*

Holt sighed, then went over to Ash, who was curled up tight upon the grass.

"How you doing? You hungry?"

"Don't fret about me, boy. Go back to Aberanth. He needs you more right now."

Ash still sounded flat, but he'd probably been dozing; indeed, he soon closed his eyes again and settled his head onto his front feet.

Holt returned to Aberanth, but the little brown emerald was in no way perturbed by the lack of results. He made some notes, padded in circles around the beech tree, then sprang into fresh action, directing Holt to assist him.

Hours later, they had produced two new elixirs. Each contained the same base formula as the cycling elixirs, with the addition of the distilled solution in one and a direct pinch of the ashes in the other.

"Take them up," Aberanth said, a little nervous this time.

Holt did.

Grumbling, the Warden of Wrath drank the distilled elixir. Nothing happened. She drank the elixir with the pinch of unaltered ashes. Her grumbling turned to a gruff clearing of her throat, then a tense silence.

Tendrils from the campfire fluttered.

"That's better. My core spins faster, as it did when eating your spiced meat."

Holt smiled. A little of his tension eased.

"But it's hardly enough," she snapped. *"I cannot return to my Elder with this."*

The tension returned with a vengeance.

"We'll keep working on it. But this is good news. Means we're on the right path."

She sneered, then flicked her head to dismiss him.

As before, Holt went to Ash, who was worrying at a large leg bone.

"Great news, isn't it?"

"It is," Ash said, without enthusiasm. He dropped his bone. *"If you're going back below, I'll head into the woods for a bit."*

He slinked off toward the trees without waiting for a reply.

"You going on a hunt? I could come with you?"

"Just a walk, boy."

"Is everything alright?" Holt asked privately.

"I'm just enjoying the forest before we fly back to the hot lands. Go help Aberanth."

Holt wanted to go after him, but he couldn't begrudge Ash some time alone if he wanted it.

"He's been slinking off a lot while you're with the mole," Wrath said.

Holt looked over his shoulder to find one of Wrath's burning blue eyes fixed on him. Was she bored and hoping he would react? He threw her a look of disgust, to which she snorted.

A day and a night later, which included one trip into the forest to collect herbs for more base elixir formula, Aberanth took their new concoction off the heat to let it cool.

"This one has quadruple the concentration of a regular elixir, and I added more phoenix ash in proportion. Let's see how she handles it."

Holt took the vial. It was still warm to the touch.

Before he left, he heard a clatter. Aberanth had knocked over some of his instruments and looked dizzy as he inspected the mess. He was blinking fast, his big eyes bloodshot and swollen.

"You should rest."

"Poppycock!" He yawned, then started to pad off. *"Well, maybe just a short nap…"*

His hopes high, Holt took the enhanced elixir up to Wrath. She drank it, but when the campfire merely flicked lazily toward her, Holt's hopes plunged to his boots.

"This won't do."

Holt rubbed his eyes. "We'll try again."

"Try harder."

There was no point in arguing. The only question was whether he should return to the lab to make Wrath think they were still working. He intended to give Aberanth a chance to sleep.

A bruised sunset dimmed over the glade. Ash wasn't there, though judging from their bond, the dragon wasn't far away.

"Are you in the woods again?" Holt asked.

"Yes. I smelled a rabbit, but it got away. Are you going back below?"

"Maybe. Probably should."

"Then I'll stay out here."

Holt decided enough was enough. *"I'll come find you."*

Their bond grew warmer as he drew closer to Ash, and he found the dragon milling aimlessly by two fallen trees.

"What's going on?"

"I'm waiting."

Holt spotted the opening to a burrow, but he knew as well as Ash that its inhabitants wouldn't come out with a dragon wandering outside.

"What's bothering you?"

"You've got enough to worry about with helping Aberanth."

"You wouldn't accept it if I tried shrugging you off like that. Now tell me."

Ash grumbled. *"It's what the phoenix said. It won't leave me alone. He seemed a bit mad, but I didn't sense a lie… His heart was beating fast, so maybe I missed it… but if it's true, it changes so much about dragons. It makes me feel guilty and ashamed."*

"For what?" Holt said with genuine surprise. "You aren't responsible for what the phoenix suffered."

"But dragons are."

"Maybe it was just something the Fire Flight did."

"If fire dragons took their power that way, what of the others? Were there other beings like the phoenix?

"I've never heard of other creatures like that."

Of course, given how little Holt had known of the world beyond the Crag and given that he had never heard of a phoenix until recently, his reassurance meant little. Other such ancient beasts could easily have existed – they may even still be out there in hiding.

"I know I'm putting a lot of weight on the words of one half-mad bird," Ash said, *"and it's hard to put my thoughts into words… I wasn't hatched to a Wild Flight, but my blood memories give me a sense of what it would be like to be part of one. A sense of pride. Dragons seemed a noble race, part of the songs of the world, keepers of something ancient and pure, and I was happy to be one… but if the phoenix is right, then dragons aren't great at all. We took that greatness from others. If that's true, how can I be proud to be a dragon now?"*

Holt bit his lip. This was no small matter, and he picked his words carefully.

"Whatever their sins, they aren't yours."

"Wrath doesn't care at all," Ash said sadly.

"You've spoken to her about this?" Holt said, surprised and a smidge hurt that Ash had gone to her first.

"She just insists the phoenix lied. I asked her what she would think if he was telling the truth. She said only the toughest and greatest survive; that if other races have failed, that's because they were weak, and if any aroused the wrath of the Fire Flight, they deserved to face the consequences."

Consequences.

The word weighed heavily on Holt. Saving Ash had saved a

kingdom, but it had also got him banished and hunted and led to Thrall hatching more dragons with new powers to twist to his own ends. It had led to Rake's death. His choice had led to good, but plenty of ill, too, some of which might not yet have come to pass.

Consequences.

"Well," Holt said, his voice low and serious, "we think differently from Wrath. No shock there. Maybe she doesn't care, or maybe she's just ignoring it, but that's not who we are. If what the phoenix said is true, then it's better we face that dark truth head-on and never forget it. Maybe we can try to help, but we can't do anything about it if you're too busy flogging yourself."

Ash rumbled high in his throat and lowered his snout for Holt to stroke.

"If there are other such creatures out there, we would help them, right?"

"That's what we do, isn't it? As long as they don't try to kill us on sight," he added with a chuckle. Ash's rumble turned into laughter. Their bond glowed, and Ash's side felt lighter than it had since meeting the phoenix.

"Once this is over, I'd like to find those who really need our help again. Saving folk from the scourge, trying to rescue hatchlings, even if that didn't go so well, that all feels right. Helping an Elder regain power only strengthens the mighty."

"In a way, I'm glad the phoenix reduced itself... Would you have killed it?"

Holt thought back to the moment, but he knew what he'd find. His pan in hand; the phoenix sitting in its nest, already defeated; Wrath outside the cave, the fear of her as weighty as her spirit. Holt knew the truth, and he had to honor that for the integrity of his soul.

"I would have – to keep you safe from Wrath."

A deep understanding crossed the dragon bond.

"I would have done the same for you. I'd choose it every time for you. Is that wrong?"

Holt frowned. It was a fiendishly difficult question.

"I think almost everyone would choose it to save their family.

If that's a sin, then we're all immoral. I'd choose it every time for you too."

His soul quickened, spinning like a Lunar Shock in his hand, then expanded. His next breath came easier, as though his lungs had opened alongside his spirit.

And then, and he couldn't say why, his treacherous mind drifted to thoughts of Talia and Fynn, but not in the way he might have before. Her chance at a new family was something he could never have. Rake had told him that, and, as ever, he'd been right. That stable life wasn't possible for him anymore. He was an outcast, free yet alone. Save for Ash.

Ash is the only family I will ever have.

This he knew must be true. When he'd reflected along similar lines in Sidastra, he'd not gone far enough. Not having a home was one thing, but this went deeper.

He looked inward, anticipating the response from his soul to the hard truth bravely borne. Instead, his breath caught in his throat. His chest tightened as though he had a stitch, and the spinning growth of his soul ground to a halt, even reversing by a fraction.

There could only be one conclusion. Holt was wrong. Somehow, he was lying to himself, and he didn't even understand in what way or why.

"What's wrong?" Ash asked.

"Now I understand why so many riders struggle to make it to Lord."

When Holt returned to the lab, Aberanth was awake, sitting cat-like with his feet beneath him, his head bent over an open book and reading it so closely his snout touched the paper.

"Ah, there you are," he said as though Holt were late. *"What are our results?"*

"Not great, I'm afraid."

"Yes, I thought as much. Hmph. But I've had an idea!" He got up, closing the book using branching vines. *"I'm almost embarrassed to voice it, but as our current route of inquiry is proving ineffective, we need*

to change it. Attempting the same thing over and over in the hopes of different results is true folly. If a quadruple-strength elixir isn't meaningfully different, then one of ten times won't be. Our supply of ash is also finite."

"Are you sure? It did work, a little."

"We aren't even close to matching the intensity of the phoenix's nature. Ridiculous as I find it, I've gone back to the more outlandish theories of human alchemists. The most, erm, 'ambitious' of your kind believe they can turn lead into gold on the baseless assumption that all substances have a spiritual quality that can be taken to higher levels. Damned nonsense.

"But it got me thinking… What if I'm approaching this from the wrong direction? The phoenix was a living, breath— well, maybe not breathing, but certainly living, magical, and spiritual being. That may account for the strange feel of its ashes, as though something in them yearns to be alive again.

"I can't very well create the creature in a glass vial," he said, snorting at the very thought. *"But I – well, that is to say, we – might be able to create conditions such that the spirit within the ashes… believes itself alive again… and thus we might reawaken its power."*

Holt could not honestly say he followed.

Aberanth sent the book toward him on walking vines. *"Have a read for yourself if you like."*

Holt took the book in his open hands without thinking. The title read, *A Treatise on Higher Forms of Alloys.* He opened a random page and found screeds of impenetrably tiny writing.

"Erm, I'm not sure I have time to take it all in."

"Hmph. Well, quite. Do you think me mad?"

"I think if anyone can figure this out, it's you. Just tell me what we need to do."

"I suggest we need three components. The first is easy. Heat was part of the phoenix's being, which is easily added. The second is something which resembles what the phoenix was. The third. Hmph. The third is the trickiest. A substance which will represent life itself."

"Water gives life," Holt said, though the pitying look Aberanth gave him made it clear that water would be much too easy.

"I can't rule it out, of course. Water, soil, food… If only we knew what

the phoenix ate." He lowered his tone to a more conspiratorial one. *"There is also flesh, bone, and… blood."*

Memories of Wyrm Cloaks swigging dark vials reared in Holt's mind, as did Osric's reports of their Blood Alchemist mixing rider and dragon blood.

"Blood?" Holt repeated.

"Yes," Aberanth squawked. *"If the phoenix had a physical form and bled, I don't see why not. Ideally, we'd use a sample from its own species, but, seeing as we don't have access to that…"*

Holt's stomach felt like a sudden lead weight. Were his blood or Ash's required, he doubted Aberanth would be trembling.

"You need Wrath's… blood?"

"Well, let's not jump to conclusions," Aberanth yammered. *"I hope it isn't necessary. I'd rather eat moss for a year than stoop to the ways of Wyrm Cloaks, but they've demonstrated the efficacy of dragon blood in no uncertain terms."*

More than ever now, Holt wished the Fire Elder hadn't sent them on this task.

"Let's hope something else works then. What should I do?"

"You can start by scouring the forest floor for bird feathers."

Before heading up to the surface, Holt knew of one bird close to hand. He found Gallus enjoying her favorite pastime: scratching and pecking at the soil. It wasn't the time of year for her feathers to molt, but he found a couple that had fallen early or else been rubbed free when she'd rummaged close to the hard earth wall.

When he returned to the surface, he recruited Ash for the feather hunt. His expert nose led them to find after find. Holt put on his own blindfold and slowly began to pick out the scent of feathers within the woodland. What surprised him was how sweet the feathers were once he became attuned to them, odors he didn't think his human nose could have picked up. With Ash's assistance, he found some feathers smelling of a strange mix of lavender, honey, and dust and others that smelled like orange peel or a musty apple cider.

After filling a small basket with feathers, Holt returned to the lab and laid them out on a workbench. Short black feathers, long black ones, tawny ones with stripes, whites with red-tipped plumes, buttery yellows, green-blues, and mottled grays. Aberanth scrutinized them in a manner that reminded Holt of his father inspecting plated food before it was sent to the Commander's table.

"A fine haul, Master Cook. And you even arranged them in neat, orderly groups. I'm so proud."

"The best Cooks are neat and orderly. You've seen recipes from my book. The instructions can be quite precise."

"Says the boy I see lobbing ingredients into pots and pans with nary a measuring spoon in sight."

Holt smiled. "Guilty as charged. It's good to follow recipes closely when learning, but once you've done it a lot, it's better to go by feeling. Or so my father did. It's one part alchemy, one part art. Especially when you're making up a new recipe."

Aberanth tsked. *"Speak to Eidolan of art if you will. Hmph. Though perhaps his input would be of value here. I'm treading perilously close to the field of art with this project."* He shuddered, then picked up one of the short black feathers with his vines and took it to a mortar and pestle.

They made potions – or 'fire brews,' as Holt came to think of them – with leaves, with soil, and with water to represent life. Only the water one held any promise. Holt knew Aberanth was playing for time, hoping not to have to resort to blood, but they didn't have all the time in the world.

"Maybe we should try cracking in an egg?" Holt suggested. It seemed as good as anything to represent life.

Aberanth scoffed, then cocked his head and fell quiet. *"You know, that's just crazy enough to work."*

They tried Holt's idea.

Wrath drank the eggy fire brew, and while it spiked activity in her core better than the elixir, they were still a long way from replicating the inexorable pull on fire that the phoenix had.

"Alas," Aberanth said upon hearing the news. *"But it shows we're on the right lines of inquiry."*

He returned to work, jovially taking notes, even humming.

Try as he might, Holt couldn't match Aberanth's mood. He

wondered if the emerald was putting it on, because with each trip up to Wrath, his own nerves frayed a little more.

As he selected another feather to grind in the mortar, he found himself asking, "How can you stay so cheerful when we keep failing?"

"It's a matter of mindset. If I thought of every unsuccessful attempt as a failure, I'd wear out. Instead, I try to see each failure as learning 'what not to do,' and so I succeed in advancing my knowledge regardless of the outcome." He threw Holt a quick and nervous look. *"Besides, there's no point in despairing when giving up isn't an option. I won't let you and Ash get hurt – not if I can help it."*

Touched in a way he'd not expected, Holt ceased pounding with the pestle. Even more unexpectedly, his soul stirred.

"Aberanth?" he asked softly, then again when the dragon didn't look at him. "Aberanth?"

The emerald looked up from his work, not quite meeting Holt's eye.

"I should have said it already, but just in case we don't succeed, thank you. Thank you so much for this, for everything. And… and I'm sorry we brought her here."

Aberanth fidgeted, rumbled, and fluttered one wing as though to wave Holt off. *"It's quite alright, Holt. Hmph. Yes, it is. I'm glad to at least try and give you both a chance. I'd…"*

But here he seized up in embarrassment and fixed his eyes on the equipment before him.

Holt's soul pressed him. He moved around the workbench and knelt by the little emerald.

"What is it? I can't be as scary as the Warden."

With some effort, Aberanth put down the mortar and looked at him. This time he met Holt's eye and did not look away.

"I'd let this whole glade burn if I thought it would keep you both safe."

Two strong emotions vied for supremacy in Holt. One, profoundly moving. The other, a spike of fear. He pictured the glade burning and the fires rushing down through the firefly tunnels to scorch the lab, burn the beech tree and the mushrooms, and choke every nook with smoke. It was fear for Aberanth as well as the place, a type of fear he hadn't felt since the Crag had come under attack and he'd seen his home engulfed in the black fires of the scourge.

His soul quickened, spinning faster.

I'm not alone. Not just Ash, but Aberanth, Rake, Eidolan – they're my family too.

Beneath his sternum, a hardened fist seemed to shake.

This is my home now.

As though his spirit had long been waiting for it, his soul expanded, swelling as fast as a river fed by a burst dam. Out and out, until he breathed easier than ever before. A fog lifted in his mind, dead wood burned away. His confidence grew with it, and he felt more settled in himself, surer, his will hardening from bronze to iron.

Joy surged through him. Holt threw himself forward and took Aberanth in a fierce embrace.

"Oh, I say!" Aberanth tried to wriggle free, but Holt was too strong for him, so the dragon settled with a growling groan.

"Better get used to it. You don't need to be so guarded around us. We've been through too much for that."

"Hmph," Aberanth said, plainly uncomfortable but no longer wriggling. He raised one of his bark-skin wings to pat Holt on the back. *"There, there."*

From anyone else, it would have been patronizing, but for Aberanth, it was akin to a declaration of love.

Holt squeezed harder.

"Holt," Aberanth squeaked.

"Yeh?"

"You're crushing me."

41

OUTLANDISH DRAGON ALCHEMY

"It has to be done," Aberanth said, talking more to himself as he paced around the beech tree.

A flare of Wrath's power managed to find its way underground, hitting Holt's skin like a drop of boiling water.

"I'm losing my patience."

Holt put the pestle and mortar down and pushed them away to join the remnants of a half dozen failed experiments. He wiped his brow, then blinked rapidly, trying to keep his eyes open.

His eyes were hurting now, for while the glowing roots cooled and brightened with the daily cycle, they never fully darkened in the main lab.

Aberanth kept looping around the beech tree, muttering, *"Has to be done. Can't see another way."*

Holt looked despondently at the cluttered worktops and had to agree. Each fire brew came closer to the mark, but they seemed doomed toward a direction neither of them wished to pursue.

"You can try my blood if you like."

Aberanth sighed sadly. *"Whatever this phoenix was, it was more magical than mortal. Human blood won't work."*

"Osric said the Blood Alchemist at Windshear took rider blood for their potions."

"We're running out of time. What's more likely to work?"

Resignedly, Holt took the clay bowl Aberanth offered him and went up to ask Wrath for a donation.

Her scowl could have melted the Frost Fangs.

On one knee, his neck bent, Holt waited with bated breath. Birds had long since fled Wrath's presence, and any nearby wildflowers had wilted. The only smell remaining was that of scorched grass under her great body. Holt clung to the fact that since her Elder had demanded this be done, she would do it in the end.

Though he waited a long time.

"Meddling like this caused the scourge."

"What we're doing can't create anything like that."

Her hot, sour breath swept over the back of his neck. *"My Elder had assurances on the plague as well."*

"We've tried everything else. If your Elder fears his brother's intentio—"

Wrath bit the air. *"My Elder fears nothing!"*

Now that's a lie, Holt thought. *And I thought fire never lied…*

"If he wasn't concerned, he wouldn't have sent us on this impossible quest. Don't you want your Elder's power restored?"

Wrath hesitated. She tried to cover it up with a snarl, but Holt had felt it. Perhaps he should have been more surprised, but he wasn't.

She doesn't want this, or at least not in this way. This is taking and relying on another's strength, which she despises.

"The honor of fire will prevail above all, no matter what. It was Storm who insisted on the Pact, and my Elder's love for him and his siblings led him to accept it – he would have ignored your kind elsewise. Storm breaking reveals his true intentions. He and his ilk are liars, and I do not believe that falseness can ever prevail, for in the heat of war, what bonds of trust can there be between liars?"

For what felt the dozenth time, Holt asked her, "Would you have us give up on this mission?"

A snarling fit came over her, and she slammed her tail through two trunks, breaking them with terrible cracks.

"She's torn in two," Ash said privately.

Holt winced as Wrath thrashed around the glade, and, most unexpectedly, he felt sympathy for her. She must have been just as frightened as they were at the thought of failure – and all for something she felt to be wrong.

Wrath sniffed, slammed her tail into the earth a final time, then, slowly, she settled back down, almost defeated.

Ash bravely soldiered on. *"Holt and I chose to seek your aid, not Storm, not Ice. If we succeed, your Elder can make everything right."*

After another long pause and a pained groan, she relented. *"I will give of my blood,"* she seethed. *"For my Elder's sake."*

His heart thrumming and his soul braced, Holt rose and went to retrieve his sword. It felt much too small for the task, like wielding a butter knife to carve an ox. Wrath's smoldering glare did nothing to ease him. Drawing up before her, he made sure the clay bowl was at hand, then gripped the hilt firmly in both hands.

"Be steady. One slip, and I'll swallow you whole."

Carefully, almost delicately, he pressed the tip of the white steel into Wrath's hide. He parted her scales, stopping the moment thick dark blood welled at the wound, steaming in the air as it dripped into the bowl. The ceramic grew warm in his hands.

By the time Aberanth had finished brewing, his eyes were puffy and bloodshot again. Holt imagined he must look little better from the stress of it.

This was their final attempt.

Of substances that might instill life into the potion, they lacked access to anything greater than the blood of a Fire Warden.

This time, Holt thought the fire brew looked much more the part. The vial was far larger than a standard elixir, and inside it, a dark red and black storm raged around a tiny golden sun.

Holt took it to the glade. Once more, he prepared the camp-fire. Wrath lit it for him, then got into her now-familiar position for Holt to pour the potion into her mouth. She drew back at once, groaning in evident discomfort.

Ash came to stand reassuringly close, and Holt reached out across their bond to steady his nerves.

This had to work. There was no other way.

In the magical landscape, Wrath's great core pulsed, and she stretched out trembling limbs to claw the earth while the flames from their small fire were visibly drawn toward her, stretching abnormally long before dispersing into motes of heat. Yet just as her pain and the pull of fire seemed to peak, the pulses of power ceased.

Holt stood silent and still. Wrath breathed hard as though winded.

"It seems a painful price to pay, but my Elder is far stronger than I. He will handle what I cannot… and if not, we'll all face the consequences."

Holt checked the campfire. It burned low, drained but not quite extinguished. The true phoenix had eaten the fire whole in a moment.

His mouth dry, Holt said, "We could try to improve the potion."

Wrath's growl rattled. *"You said my blood would be the best chance. What more can be done?"*

"I don't know."

"You two are honest at least, I grant you that," she said bitterly. *"You will prepare another, and we shall take it to my Elder."*

Holt nodded, his entire body stiff as a board, and his legs felt numb as he turned to head back to the grotto's entrance. On the way, he stopped by Ash to lean into his dragon, throwing one arm over his neck. He patted Ash and ran a gentle hand over the wounds on his chest. The gashes the phoenix had raked were healing well, mere pink lines with scales regrowing over them.

"Is it the best Aberanth can do?" Ash asked.

"I don't see what else can be done."

"Then it will be enough. And when Thrall is defeated and the scourge burned clean from the world, we'll know it was worth it."

Holt nodded, then, with a nuzzle from Ash and a fierce hug, he headed back underground.

Aberanth came scrambling up the firefly tunnel to meet him. *"Did it work?"*

"Well enough," Holt said, then pushed past him into the lab. Their tidiness had declined over the course of their efforts, and Holt had never seen the lab in such a state of disarray. "I'll help you clean up before we go." He started right away, grabbing alembics, vials, beakers, and bowls for the wash basin.

Aberanth padded back in, his head low. *"Doesn't sound like it worked."*

"It enhanced the pull of her core," Holt said as he stacked the washing up, "Just not as much as the actual phoenix. It sucked our campfire dry when it attacked us, but who's to say we could ever get the power to revive in full. That was always wishful thinking with just its ashes." His words tumbled out now. "It killed itself on purpose, it didn't want us to succeed, it wanted to take us down with it – where's the soap?" he asked, flustered, before remembering and going to fetch it.

Throughout all this, he was painfully aware of Aberanth's wide, worried eyes.

"It's alright," he said, trying to reassure the dragon as much as himself. "We've done all we can. The Elder will... understand that. There's plenty of heat in a volcano he can draw upon."

Without a word, Aberanth wandered off.

Holt busied himself with adding lye soap to the water and placing the dirty equipment in the sink to soak.

Aberanth reappeared, bringing with him a stack of bark slabs. *"Let me review the details again, ensure there's nothing we've overlooked."*

"Sure."

He had his way of coping, and Aberanth had his.

They retraced Holt and Ash's encounter with the phoenix in full, then went through Aberanth's questions again.

"It definitely bled?" Aberanth asked.

"Yes," Holt said firmly. It had most certainly bled.

"Good, good. Then we weren't wildly off the mark there. Hmph, nothing more expansive here though... what was its blood like?"

Holt lowered his arm deeper into the basin, searching for the next bowl. He tried to recall the creature's blood, but the details were hazy. In his mind, it was... well, it was blood.

"I dunno." This exercise seemed futile to him. They couldn't make it work, and that was that.

With a scrape of bark, Aberanth shifted his notes. *"Hmm, here you mention that your gauntlet wasn't stained by its blood."*

"Well, it mustn't have touched me, otherwise it would have stained the cloth."

"A logical assumption, to be sure. Unless..."

Holt's searching fingers found another bowl. He took hold of it and pulled it out of the soapy water. "Unless what?"

"Unless its blood was materially different to other creatures." Aberanth sounded excited again, on the cusp of something. *"Think back, Holt. Think!"*

Holt frowned and closed his eyes, trying to put himself back in the fight with the phoenix. Everything had been so quick, but he tried to retrace his steps through each part.

"I stabbed it with my knife. Blood sprayed out. Some was on my hand, or I thought so. It was"—he recalled a bright red sheen —"shiny, almost metallic. And it moved funny," he added, the thought popping into his mind.

"What precisely do you mean by 'funny'?"

"It sort of... rolled in big globs," Holt said, feeling foolish. "But it can't have," he added with a dismissive wave that sent water and soap flying. "It couldn't have touched me."

But Aberanth no longer seemed to be paying him any attention. The little emerald scratched out fresh runes, then laid the slabs out around himself and stared transfixed at them, as though willing them to release their secrets.

"Heaviness to its steps... hot pools... a metallic sheen... its nest... red ore, you said, not red stone – wait!" His voice almost cracked. *"Wait there!"*

Aberanth abandoned his notes and scurried hither and thither across the lab, from bench to bench, pulling out boxes, baskets, and crates. He darted into alcove storerooms to the sound of thuds and crashes, then he skittered back through the lab, heading for other stores. Already messy, the lab descended into mayhem.

Holt felt awful. He had never seen Aberanth so frazzled. The stress must have broken him.

"I know it's here… I know it's here…"

"Aberanth," Holt called, trying to get in the dragon's way, but Aberanth slithered around the beech tree, evading Holt's grasp and disappearing into another branching tunnel.

"I know it. I know it. I know—" There came another thud. Then a high roar of sheer delight. *"Yes! Yes! I knew it. I have it!"*

Moments later, Aberanth came charging back into the lab, knocking into a workbench as he wove toward Holt. Between his teeth, he carried a chunk of red stone.

"Is this what you saw?"

Aberanth dropped the rock at Holt's feet.

He picked it up and found it wasn't rock but the same reddish ore from the phoenix's nest. Holt stared at it in amazement, then at Aberanth. The little emerald was panting, his eyes bugging out of their sockets, larger than Holt had ever seen them.

"This is it," Holt said, his voice thick with shock. "H-how did you? What—"

"That," Aberanth said with glee, *"is indeed ore, Master Cook. Your instincts were well served on that front, though I'd say its color is vermillion, to be precise. It's called cinnabar, and it's quite rare here in the Aldunei Belt because it comes from areas of volcanic activity."*

Holt blinked hard and observed the cinnabar again. Turning it over in his hand, he said, "I still don't understand how this helps."

Aberanth laughed, not at him but in deep relief, as though the seriousness of the situation had been revealed as some elaborate prank, as though their fates and possibly that of the world didn't really depend on it.

"Cinnabar is greatly prized as a source of mercury, which human alchemists believe holds the key to many of their crackpot theories. You might have heard of it as 'quicksilver'."

The term was familiar to Holt. The apothecary at the Crag used to bemoan the difficulty of acquiring it.

Aberanth seemed to be anticipating Holt joining him in the revelation. When he didn't jump for joy, Aberanth rumbled and carried on, almost stumbling over his words.

"Quicksilver is fast-moving and forms into thick beads. It's heavy, which accounts for the weight you describe in the bird, though it isn't a good conductor of heat. Hmph!" he added with undue anger. *"It might conduct nerve signals well enough. Might be the phoenix had a partly organic, partly magical variant in its veins. Fascinating. Hmph. Yes, fascinating."*

Holt was lost. "Sorry, Aberanth. I might be being stupid, but—"

"Oh, come on, Holt! Don't you see? The phoenix's blood was quicksilver or some magically adapted variation of it. Though it moves like water, it's really a metal, and it doesn't like to separate from itself. That's why it slid off your skin and the treated leather on your gauntlet. Skin and leather aren't porous enough to have beads of it seep in… though I'd maybe give your glove another hard shake to be on the safe side."

Holt turned his right hand over, suddenly expecting to see something wrong. "Is it poisonous?"

"Very," Aberanth said merrily. *"But you're a rider. A tiny amount on your clothes wouldn't hurt you. Well, probably not."*

He picked up the cinnabar between his teeth, took it over to a workbench, then stopped and gazed at the mess.

"I'll shift that stuff."

Before Holt could act, Aberanth raised thick vines and swept the worktop of its contents; glass shattered, metal clanged, and papers hissed and flapped in all directions.

"No time to lose. You can make your rider strength useful here. Get a hammer and a large mortar and pestle."

Holt left his dishes and picked through the debris of the lab to an alcove where Aberanth kept heavier human tools. Saws, hammers, strong tongs, and other smithing equipment mostly collected dust here. Holt grabbed a hammer, washed out the largest mortar he could find, and returned as instructed.

"Crush the ore into as fine a powder as you can."

Holt began hammering. Aberanth's energy was infectious and revitalized Holt's spirits.

"Aberanth," he called over the noise. "You know you're a genius, right?"

"Let's see if it works first, shall we?"

Cinnabar was hardly dragon steel, so it crumbled under Holt's High Champion strength. He added the pieces into the mortar and pounded them until the powdery remains were to Aberanth's satisfaction.

Then the dragon took over, placing the crushed ore into an alembic, this one open to the air – Aberanth insisted that was important. While Aberanth worked, Holt used his newfound energy to start tidying up the lab. It was halfway to looking respectable when Aberanth called Holt over to see the fruits of their efforts.

Liquid silver filled a bulb-shaped vial.

"Is that enough?"

"We shall find out."

Fortunately, when the new fire brew was complete, it looked obvious, even to Holt's untrained eye, that this version was the best one by far. Mixed and simmered with the strong elixir base, the feather of a hawk, and a dollop of phoenix ashes, the quicksilver swelled in volume and took on a burning orange hue akin to the phoenix's eyes.

Aberanth bottled and corked it, and in the open space beneath the cork, a heatless fire burned, much like the phoenix's ethereal form. Whenever Aberanth tilted the bottle, the contents flowed frenetically and released the same cold flames wherever new space opened. The lively liquid metal had become living fire.

Holt was pleased now to repeat himself. "Aberanth, you're a genius."

Aberanth rose to his full height, stretching his neck so he almost came up to Holt's eye level. He spread his lips in a wide, toothless smile. *"I just hope it works. Take it up now. I'll clean things up here."*

Holt emerged onto the surface to find Ash brooding over the

fallen star, his snout inches over it, as though waiting for it to hatch.

Wrath stirred at once. She sniffed like a starved hatchling smelling their preferred meat for the first time and crawled forward on her belly before scrambling upright to meet him. She drew so close, her blue eyes fixed on the potion in Holt's hand, her mouth open; Holt feared she'd rip his arm off to get at the vial.

"That's it..." she said, caught somewhere between desire and disbelief. Then she snorted, gave a great shake of her head, wings, and tail, and backed off, bowing her head as though buffeted by a storm. *"It reeks of the Parasite. I... I do not want this thing,"* she added, but her tone spoke otherwise. Before Holt could say anything, she backed farther away, tail swinging, and would have knocked more trees over had there been any left nearby. *"We shall take it to my Elder at once."*

"Do you not wish to test it first to make sure—"

"Yesss," she hissed, before digging her feet into the soil and twisting her neck away in revulsion. *"No. I mustn't. I do not want... We shall take it to my Elder."*

Holt inclined his head. "We'll make ready at once."

He ran over to Ash. "Hear anything different from it?" he asked, nodding at the white steel.

"Same as before. It feels like... like the ore is trying to speak to me."

Given all they'd been through, Holt didn't find this weird at all. He tried listening again, but since it had first crashed down, he'd struggled to hear the music again.

Ash seemed to emerge from a dream. *"Wait, you did it! It worked?"*

"Aberanth did it. We owe him big time; a hundred supply runs might never make up for this."

"We'll come back and try," Ash said. *"Once it's all over. We can come home."*

"We'll come home," Holt said, enjoying a tingling through both his bond and soul.

He kept those thoughts close to his heart as he prepared to leave. Departing this time felt torturous, but go they must.

As before, Aberanth had a parting gift.

"A scabbard?" Holt said. He'd all but forgotten.

The sheathe was the perfect fit for his sword, shining wood with carvings along its length on both sides depicting a full lunar cycle.

"Aberanth, it's— when did you find the time?"

Holt swore the dragon blushed.

"I slept even less than you did. Often do. Might be why I'm so small, heh." Aberanth ended on a strained laugh that put Holt eerily in mind of the phoenix.

"Thank you. Truly. There's no way we can ever repay you. Which is why I feel awful to ask for a final—"

"Hammer and tongs?" Aberanth said brightly. *"Already packed them along with some books on smithing and the new batch of elixirs. I couldn't make as many as last time, and without Rake, I figured... Anyway, you should have enough for your belts. I've given you my last tub of balm, too. Use it wisely, as it's hard to make."* He stopped, raised a scaly brow, and looked concerned. *"You're going to hug me again, aren't you?"*

Holt fell to his knees and opened his arms.

"Oh, very well," Aberanth said and walked willingly into Holt's embrace.

This time, when Holt tightened his arms and thanked him again, Aberanth wrapped his wings around Holt and squeezed back.

"Stay safe, Holt. You too, Ash."

"We will," Holt murmured into the dragon's ear. "With luck, when we come back, this will all be over. And I might have a new sword to show you."

"I look forward to it. Very much so."

42

A SEA OF BLACK AND GOLD

In the pre-dawn dark, Drefan Harroway walked the curtain walls of the Risalian gatehouse, exchanging words with the men he found on duty. They were on high alert, for a dragon rider had been seen landing in the distant Risalian encampment the day before. That had been a first, and Drefan disliked any strange occurrences in war, especially after a long stalemate.

For weeks now, they'd lived under the threat of destruction from the monstrous trebuchets. Even in the morning gloom, Drefan could pick out their vast silhouettes like two mechanical hillocks over three hundred feet in height. He'd asked his siege corps to estimate the cost of building one of their own, but five master carpenters and fifty lesser carpenters and laborers would take three months to complete such a task. A crippling cost. And the Risalians had constructed two. He'd barked a laugh at that and remarked that the Mithrans and Athrans must have more gold than capable soldiers.

Given their dread dominance of the landscape, Drefan found it hard to look away, managing only when word came to him that a messenger from the Brenin gate awaited him below.

Drefan left the ramparts and hurried down to the bailey behind the walls. A barrack house, stables, and a workshop supporting mangonels were squeezed into the narrow pass here. If the enemy made it through, they would then contend with a series of earthwork defenses to slow their advance into the Toll Pass proper, where the main fortress blocked the junction at which the three lesser valleys met.

A lone brazier stood at the bailey's heart, and the new Knight Commander of the garrison was speaking to a cloaked messenger by its low light. When Drefan approached, the messenger saluted and handed over a small, hastily written note from the Knight Commander of the Brenin gatehouse. Drefan read the message twice, thanked the courier, and bade him take a rest after his hard ride. He then handed the note to Edgar, the Knight Commander on the Risalian side.

With one cheek and side of his neck ravaged by pox, none would have called Edgar comely. Reading by the brazier's red light, his expression first curdled, then turned thoroughly grim.

"What're they playin' at?" His lowborn speech had never truly left him, as was the case for many who rose through the army's ranks. "Bivouacs sounds like they mean to attack us, but they can't 'ave the equipment."

His shrewd gray eyes scanned the note again as though expecting to find a hidden answer.

Drefan recalled prior intelligence gathered on the Frayed Banners and Stricken Souls. "They'll have ladders with them already. That's how they sacked Evoire."

Edgar shook his head. "Ladders on their own ain't gonna help 'em much against a garrisoned gatehouse. What's the use?"

Drefan agreed it was strange. Assaulting one of the fortified gatehouses into the Toll Pass would exact a tremendous price for no obvious treasure. He blew on his hands, then raised them over the brazier.

"I'll take reinforcements with me." He was due to inspect the Brenin gate later that day at any rate.

Already more life stirred in the bailey. In the blue world before dawn's true break, smoke curled up from the barrack kitchens, birds twittered high on the slopes between the trees, and his own retinue was already heading for the stables. Then a knight already in full harness emerged from the barracks: Ulrich.

This is early for him. His shoulder must have been playing up badly.

All of Edgar's chattering concerns about the Brenin gate faded as Ulrich approached. The knight had thick, floppy gold hair, a trim figure, though far from skinny, eyes dark like two inkwells, and a wolfish grin reserved just for Drefan.

Ulrich paid the Master of War and the Knight Commander a disciplined smile and a firm salute.

"You're risin' early this morn', Knight Captain."

"I slept finely, sirs. More soundly than I have in weeks, as though some spell of a mystic rider bedded me down." He threw Drefan a look, and despite the chill of the morning, Drefan felt a new warmth that had nothing to do with the brazier.

"It pleases my heart to hear it, Knight Captain."

Oblivious to the exchange, Edgar rubbed at the back of his neck and said, "Ack, for a sound night's sleep. Could be doin' wi' some o' that magic meself."

Drefan suppressed a laugh.

"All the same," Edgar went on, "watch yerself, Knight Captain. It's not on to be so familiar around our Master of War."

"There's no trouble, Edgar. Ulrich is a knight from my family lands. We've known each other since we were lads. I'd also be dead if it weren't for him."

"Aye? Is that so?"

"The Master of War exaggerates. I took a blow on my back in his stead."

"Which would have killed me."

Ulrich shrugged, then winced and raised an arm to his left shoulder. "Damned Risalian had quite the strength, I'll grant him."

"Least it weren't on yer sword arm," Edgar said. He scratched his chin. "Now would that have been at, oh, where was it, don't tell me... Fort Dittan?"

Drefan inclined his head. "I'm impressed, Knight Commander."

"I'm impressed such a harebrained sally actually cleared the enemy off – eh, sir."

"There were losses," Drefan added, somberly. "We may have pushed farther than we needed to." He glanced toward the walls of the gatehouse. "I'm not infallible." At these words, a phantom itch from the missing part of his ear returned with a vengeance.

As the dawn burst pink and orange, the warm scent of baking bread wafted up from the kitchens. Men and horses emerged from the stables, all garbed, saddled, and ready for a long ride.

"Won't you stay and break your fast, Ealdor?" Ulrich asked.

"I cannot. Duty calls at the Brenin gate. I shall eat a late meal there."

"Quite right, quite right," Edgar said as he snapped his feet to attention. "Good morning, Ealdor, and goodbye."

"My thanks to you, Knight Commander. I shall just say my farewells to Ulrich, then I'll be on my way."

With a gruff salute, Edgar departed, leaving Drefan and Ulrich alone with the brazier between them. Leaving was painful every time, but Drefan couldn't afford a leisurely departure. As Master of War, he had virtually no privacy anymore, but since visiting the Risalian gatehouse with a smaller retinue wouldn't raise much suspicion, they'd mutually agreed that Ulrich should be deployed here. To be caught wouldn't be disastrous – it was the army, after all – but it was worth maintaining professional credibility, though Drefan knew he valued that more than Ulrich.

Calmly and casually, Drefan stepped around the brazier until he was close enough to murmur, "I really must go. The mercenaries—"

"You don't have to explain. I trust you."

Drefan gave a toothless smile and offered his hand. "I look forward to my next inspection, Knight Captain."

Ulrich took his hand in a shake more tender than firm. Drefan gently rubbed his thumb against Ulrich's own and held his inky eyes for a heart-thudding moment.

Then they parted.

Drefan strode toward his retinue without daring to look back. On horseback, he'd traveled an arrow's shot from the bailey – almost to the earthwork defenses – when echoing shouts from behind made him stop. Then came the distant sound of deep, hard-struck Risalian drums.

Turning in the saddle, Drefan saw the men below the gate

burst into sprints for the barracks and the siege corps. Soldiers along the ramparts hastened inside the gatehouse or one of the two flanking towers. A Feorlen horn blared, and answering blows soon rang out up the valley heading back to the main fortress.

Drefan raised himself up on his stirrups.

Finally, a fight!

His very next thought was one of concern, swiftly descending to anxiety. Drefan searched for Ulrich, but the assembling garrison drowned the yard, and no one man could be picked out from the rest. The mangonel crews loaded stones. Men of his retinue asked for orders, then fell quiet as two dark lumps hurtled from beyond the walls.

Time stood still.

Stone broke upon stone with a force to break the entire valley, then a large swathe of the ramparts cracked and seemed to melt away.

Though not wholly destroyed, the wall became a mound of debris that the Risalian foot might scale. Drefan looked on in stunned horror. Weakened as the walls still were from the last war, such destructive force still took his breath away.

The soldier in him yearned to draw his sword and ride to battle, but the Ealdor and Master of War thankfully had control. He sent a rider back with orders for Knight Commander Edgar to hold out for reinforcements and to fall back to the earthworks, if needs be.

One last time he searched for some sign of Ulrich, but the garrison ranks were too dense, Drefan was too far away, and he could no longer dwell on his own concerns.

A war had started.

Turning about, he led his retinue at a galloping pace back to the great fortress.

General Edric – a weatherworn soldier with a white beard – met him on the way in. The Feorlen horns had done their work, and reinforcements were already assembling.

As they discussed the situation, a thunderous crack traveled up from the Risalian pass, then word came down from the observation deck that one of the gatehouse towers had collapsed.

Fear knotted in Drefan. Those trebuchets were proving themselves worth every coin.

Taking what men were ready, he and General Edric left the fortress with all haste. At the crossroads, they were met with riders from both outer garrisons.

The Brenin gate had also come under assault. Despite losses, the mercenaries had proved more tenacious than anyone expected and had already gained a foothold inside one of the towers via the ramparts. Now they pressured the gatehouse from within.

"Are we sure these are mercenaries?" Edric asked in his crisp city voice. "What kind of coin could turn them from easy looting to bloodying themselves like this?"

"The same sort that built those trebuchets," Drefan said. The knot of fear in him rose to his chest and clenched at his heart. He'd told Talia he relished the chance to face the world and win, but he'd misunderstood the challenge. Inside the Toll Pass, he could master men and horses, but a tidal wave of gold was another matter.

Word from the Risalian gate was even worse. The defenses had deteriorated quicker than anticipated. Four smaller trebuchets had been wheeled forward behind the advancing infantry, and with one wall and tower already reduced, the defenders were hard-pressed to repel their crews with arrows. Worse, one of the Feorlen mangonels had been struck and broken, crippling the garrison further.

General Edric ground his teeth.

"What would you advise, General?"

"I'm almost more concerned by the Brenin gate. When an enemy maneuvers so wildly, it either means they've lost their minds, or they're a genius, or they know something you don't. I incline to the latter."

Drefan agreed with the sentiment. Knowing the reputation of the Stricken Souls and the Frayed Banners, he doubted they'd turned suddenly insane.

"Can we hold the Risalian gate?" he asked.

"The land rises half a mile back from the gatehouse," Edric said, "so we can blunt the range of their siege engines there but not negate them entirely. There would be a bloody price to pay to keep the ground, a high one and needless when we have the fortress on our side. With both gates under attack, I would send men only to assist in a retreat and fall back from both valleys. Can't keep one without the other. Of course, as you're present, the decision lies with you, Ealdor."

Drefan looked down the Risalian pass. The land ran northward before bending east and out of sight. He felt a great pull to return. What a dreadful decision to have to make, yet it was a clear one. His duty was to the tens of thousands, not the one. He couldn't risk himself as he'd done in the last war.

With a heavy heart, he said, "Our minds are aligned, General. See to the retreat from both gates. I must send word to Sidastra at once."

He left General Edric to oversee the work and rode back inside the main fortress. The elevation of the fortress would give the Risalian trebuchets a far harder task. Their forces were larger and better provisioned than when King Godric left himself overexposed during the last war, and with many winding routes for sorties, Drefan was confident they could hold the pass as long as morale held.

Yet, in the end, something new would be needed to tilt the battle in Feorlen's favor.

If the Skarls didn't come, or if King Roland of Brenin failed to stir, they would lose. Even if it took a year and crippled the coffers of the Free Cities, enough weapons could break the power of even this great fortress.

As Drefan ascended to the higher levels of the fortress, he wondered when he'd grown afraid. At Fort Dittan, he hadn't been afraid. While holding Fort Bracken in his father's lands against the scourge, he hadn't been afraid.

Climbing endless stairs to the observation deck, his heart raced. Ulrich's golden locks and dark eyes filled his mind. He told himself Ulrich was capable, far better with a sword than he and clad in the best steel the Harroway smiths could forge.

Drefan emerged onto the crescent and sheltered balcony of the upper fortress, granting a commanding view of the Toll Pass. From this vantage, the land seemed to drop away, leaving both outer gatehouses visible to the naked eye.

Horns rang in a constant triple-blasted drone, sounding the Feorlen retreat.

Half the Risalian gatehouse was now little more than a mound of rubble, over which the Risalians swarmed like black ants. Much of the garrison could be seen retreating up the pass, heading for the safety of Edric's fresher troops.

Yet upon the remaining ramparts of the gatehouse and the tower top, a swirl of Feorlen yellow and gray remained fighting, cut off and trapped. A white flag waved from the tower, yet still steel flashed under the morning sun.

Drefan gripped the balustrade until his forearms ached.

Staff and officers around him fell silent as they too watched the unfolding horror. Down at the gatehouse, the Feorlens kept waving the white cloth, but the Risalians didn't abate. Black eagle banners billowed in the pass now, and from over the mound of the collapsed walls marched Athran banners, many golden horses upon many red fields. Bite by bite, the horses and the eagles ate away at the Feorlen yellow until even the white flag fell and drowned in the sea of black and gold.

43

REPENTANCE

Talia and Pyra stood on the eastern shores of Lake Luriel. Silhouettes of the New Order's island and tower rose as dark ghosts from the pebbled waters. Misery was the day. The grief of Stroef had followed Talia home, engulfing Sidastra in days of slanted rain under a sky like mottled seal skin. Misery scented the air, damp and chill, and the water tasted bitter on her lips. Misery was in their hearts; for Pyra, visions of the burning buildings and the echoing screams; for Talia, the losses, yes, but one loss in particular.

The New Order flew out to witness them, appearing like winged shadows amid the rain. Under such bleak light it was hard to tell them apart, but Talia felt three Champions, five Ascendants, and three Novices.

Fewer than there ought to be.

"May we be forgiven," Talia said over their bond.

Pyra growled mournfully, tucked in her wings, then, with Talia on her back, she slid into the water. Her next breath came sharp and short. The cold constricted their very bond, but despite its grip, Pyra beat her limbs and started to swim. Nothing about it was graceful. Her tail dragged like a dead weight, yet, stroke by struggled stroke, Pyra inched toward the island of the New Order.

Above them, the riders hovered and watched. Even the wild emeralds who nested near the city came, adding to the passing shadows behind the curtain of rain.

Talia wondered if Turro was up there. She wondered whether he still respected them.

After what felt like hours, Pyra dragged herself onto shore, crawled up the wet sand, and slumped onto her belly. She wouldn't use magic to burn off the icy water, for that would defeat the point of the endeavor.

The New Order descended to join them. The Champions landed on the beach and the Ascendants on the grassy mound overlooking the shore, while the Novices remained hovering in the air.

Talia slid down from Pyra and took tentative steps toward the Champions: to Yax, Galasso, and Ethel. It was hard to say which chill was worst, that of the lake or that of Strang and Liliane's combined aura. The slanting rain turned to hail as it neared them.

Twenty paces from the Champions, Talia came to a halt. No one spoke. Aside from beating wings, only the pit-pat of the endless rain sounded between them. She shivered.

Wordless, Talia unfastened the straps of her baldric belt, then shrugged it off and threw her scabbard down at Ethel's feet. Next, she loosened her pauldrons, untied her vambraces, and peeled off the brigandine trunk from her chest and back. Off came her gambeson and her boots so that her bare feet sunk into the sodden sand. She took another step toward the Champions. By the time she was ten paces shy, her crimson shirt was already soaked through and clinging to her skin. Inside the aura of two Ice Champions, and not cycling to fight it, her next breath steamed.

Slowly, Talia reached up to the dragon-steel circlet on her head. The steel was cold to the touch. Gripping it with numb fingers, Talia took it from her brow, bent one knee, and laid her crown upon the sand

"Honored Riders, a great tragedy has occurred, one for which

I hold grave remorse. Civilians in the town of Stroef were… *burned.* Their lives were lost because of me."

Pyra uttered a low wail. *"It was I who lost control. It was my fire."*

Talia stiffened her jaw. "It may have been Pyra's magic, but responsibility for us being there lies with me."

"And why were you there?" Ethel asked, projecting her voice.

"I went in my role as a queen. I went to ensure the king consort was brought back safely so that my alliances would hold…"

It was all she could do not to wince, for pain twisted through her soul and chest. For a moment, all Talia felt was the rain splattering against her cheek.

"I – we – deeply regret it and can only hope that in the years ahead, we shall save far more lives than we stole that day. We are sorry."

The silence that greeted her plea dragged on for a worrisome time. Talia remained on her knee, shivering, not daring to move.

At length, the icy aura of Strang and Liliane eased, and Ethel stepped forward. "The New Order has heard your confession, Champion Talia. We shall consider it, as will those riders abroad upon their return. For now, rise."

Talia did, and whether from the cold or the quiver through her soul, her legs shook as she stood. Pyra picked herself up and came to join her.

Ethel dismissed the riders, then asked Talia and Pyra to meet her by the shacks where Holt and Ash had stayed before she mounted Strang and took flight.

Talia gathered her armor, clothes, and sword and followed on barefoot. Pyra padded heavily behind her, splashing through every puddle on the dirt roads. Their destination lay on the other side of the island, and by the time they got there, the rain had finally abated. A lightness returned to the air, though not yet to their hearts.

Ethel and Strang awaited them under the simple pavilion that had served as Ash's shelter.

"You didn't have to walk."

"We wanted to," Talia said.

Pyra rumbled. *"We needed to."*

"'*Tis heartening to hear genuine shame from a daughter of fire,*" said Strang.

"Your penitence will go some way to persuading those undecided," Ethel said, though she sounded none too optimistic about it.

"Who has left?" Talia asked. "With the weather and the cold, I found it hard to tell."

"Ensel took off last night."

Talia made a pained expression. The loss of a Champion came as a heavy blow, although as Ensel was Risalian, it didn't come as a great shock. Their lone Ice Ascendant and another Novice had also departed before dawn.

"I've recalled Druss and Lucia from their mission in the Stretched Sea," Ethel went on. "Oline and the emeralds will take longer to return. Unless they fly by Stroef itself, they won't know of events until they return from the Empire. What they will decide is anyone's guess."

"And you, Commander?"

Ethel averted her eyes. "It's a mess, Talia. A real mess. Truth is, I don't know what to think or feel. I can't recall a time when a rider accidentally killed people directly like this, or if they did, they were traitors, or mad, or blight-corrupted. Not the sole person an entire Order depends on... Oh, what a mess."

She seemed to consider, then sniffed, straightened, and met Talia's eye again.

"I've had to condemn innocents to die in my time. Fight in enough incursions and I fear it's inevitable; one village, one town, one fort or another. Hard choices, awful choices, but as riders, we do that sometimes. The only way I've reconciled that is knowing – hoping – that we would save far more in the end. In saving two kingdoms, you've already saved more lives than the rest of us combined. Weighing the scales, can any of us really condemn you? No, but it still feels..."

"Horrible."

Ethel nodded. "We all need time to process. Others may yet leave, and if they choose to, I will not stop them."

"We understand."

"*It was an accident,*" Strang said, "*though one which must never happen again.*"

Pyra ruffled her wings and pressed her neck low. "*Never. Never again.*"

"*What caused such a loss of control?*"

"*Our bond was closed over from the distance between us. I felt so little from Talia, and then a fear reached me from her side, all raw and confusing, then came the pain, blurred and unfocused and burning. It felt like… like Talia was dying… After that, I don't remember much until we reunited on the beach.*"

"To be so overcome is not something I've heard of before," Ethel said. "Especially as you have both been wary of fury overtaking you."

"*It wasn't anger, Commander… it was something else. The memory of it frightens me. Rage, I am accustomed to, and even fueled by it, I have never lost myself entirely. But in me then was such a blaze as I've never felt before, and my breath seared inside my throat.*"

Strang hummed as he mused over the matter. "*I wish I could counsel you daughters of fire, but ice has no insight into such things. We must hope an experienced fire rider joins us in time to guide you.*"

"Alas," Ethel said, "I fear all of those are too loyal to Adaskar."

The mention of Adaskar seemed to draw the air in close. The harsh reality was that they only remained here by his grace, and courtesy of Einar, word of Stroef would have long since reached him.

Ethel must have read Talia's thoughts on her face. "Until he comes, we keep going. I trust that not all of what happened was in vain. With Fynn back, is your alliance secure?"

"Stronger than ever, I think," Talia said grimly. "Stroef was brought to Skadi's heel far quicker than expected, and with fewer losses on her side than there might have been…"

She felt transported back to the gray dawn following the storming of Stroef. Jarl Sigmar had held out inside his castle, but a fearful and divided garrison mutinied in the night. Despite Sigmar's assertions that his men were loyal to the death, he'd been slain by some of them. Not all had been as insane as she'd supposed.

"There are still some rebel holdouts around Brekka, but the war is all but over. Skadi can look again toward Feorlen's plight."

Ethel nodded. "And what of the King's thoughts on all of this?"

"He's been quiet. Since we returned, he's been held up in his chambers. We haven't spoken." She cast her eyes to the soft mud squelching between her toes.

"A mess on all counts," Ethel said. She fidgeted with the straps of her baldric and the buckle of her belt. "We must await Druss and Oline's return before we know the extent of the reaction. I'll try my best for you. I told you I've never felt more aligned since coming here, fighting the scourge in new ways, better ways, with the Emerald Flight to help. Whether we like it or not, if we're to last, we need you. And we may need to accept you're different from us. I treat you differently already, even if I try to pretend otherwise. In the Morass, I sent you to the safe side of the hill even though a Fire Champion should have been placed where the fighting was thickest."

She reached up to take Talia by the shoulder. Given her stature, it wasn't as impressive a move as it might have been, but her spiritual pressure more than made up for it. Though taller, Talia wilted.

"You two must figure this out," Ethel said. "We cannot let this fall apart."

The days that followed were dour yet busy. Talia found herself back in the throng of queenship, where ravenous demands ate away at any time in which she might reflect.

Fynn kept to his chambers. He ate and drank little but played his pipe and flute well into the small hours of the night. On occasion, Talia passed his door, trying to summon the courage to enter, but she never did. The understanding that had formed between them seemed lost. She felt like she'd be walking in upon a stranger in grief. What could be said?

Freya's body had, of course, been burned outside the walls of Stroef. There had been no long journey back to the north lest the blight thread its tendrils into her. Fynn had been unable to set the fire himself, so Pyra had done it.

One day, a small piece of positive news wound its way up from the kitchens. Upon returning, Talia had at last commissioned cycling jerky to be made as per Holt's notes, and now the first batches were ready to be tested. Sure enough, each flavored piece aided a different cycling technique. Talia took them to the New Order, and Alvah, Sokeh, and Kamal came eagerly to try. These three at least seemed softer toward her.

Upon hearing the results and testing the additional power of the fire riders' cycling, Ethel commissioned more to be prepared as well as meat for all other types to be tested.

A day later, Druss and Lucia returned from assisting civilian ships in the Stretched Sea in high spirits. With their control over the wind – Lucia more so than Druss – they had spared many ships from being boarded and blown many of the so-called pirates off course. Knowing what an impact they were having seemed to brighten their eyes. And as a Lightning Champion, Druss became especially enamored with the chicken jerky.

Talia made efforts to visit Turro and his emeralds. Each time she did, she found Yax and his dragon there, talking long and deeply with his wild kindred. Talia made sure to apologize to them as well, for they had joined their honor to hers, and she had sullied that. Turro assured her that he and his dragons were here for the long haul. Their Elder and their Warden had regrets far greater than hers.

Then, a little over a week after her atonement, Oline, Florry, Pello, and their squadron of wild emeralds returned with maps marked with likely areas of old sealed tunnels near the Roaring Fjord.

"While we were there," Oline said, "a black sky covered all the distant Storm Peaks. An unnatural, endless storm."

Speculation was all the New Order had, but it seemed clear

that the Storm Flight had expended a deal of power for some purpose. For Talia, it was a humbling story. She still feared and assumed that Adaskar brooded on them, but on the grand scale of the world, they were likely but a minor rising against the looming incursions on other fronts. It was a faint hope, perhaps, but hope nonetheless.

Then word arrived from her Master of War. The Risalians and Athrans had smashed their way into the Toll Pass. Both gatehouses had fallen. The war Talia had hoped to avoid had come. She should have known the good news couldn't last.

Talia's first instinct was to reach across her bond to Pyra. *"I can't help but think we caused this."*

"That may well be so," Pyra said, sounding a bit more like her old self. *"But your enemies would have seized on any excuse. Now or a year from now, this fight had to come. They won't give up. Will we?"*

Talia knew what she had to do. She knew her duty.

Before summoning her High Council, before going to the New Order, before anything else at all, she found herself hurrying through the palace to Fynn's chambers. She dismissed Eadwulf and her Queen's Guard keeping watch on his door and entered alone.

If Talia's situation was a mess, Fynn's rooms seemed equal to it. Furniture lay upturned. Dishes sat in stacks on the floor, on the dressers, even at the end of his bed. Books lay half opened and sprawled, and sheets upon sheets of music were strewn everywhere. All this under the heavy gloom of drawn curtains and thick, musty air.

Among the devastation, Fynn sat slumped against the back of an armchair, his clothes crumpled and dirty, his beard as unkempt as it had been in his cell, and his hair untied and shaggy. His fingers tried to strum his lute but met only air.

She dropped to his level. "Fynn?"

He seemed to wake from a deep dream.

"Hello, Talia."

But almost at once, he was drifting off again.

"Can I help you up?"

He didn't answer. Talia picked him up anyway and helped him into the armchair.

"I didn't come sooner because I didn't know if you were ready to see me. Or if you wanted to. Maybe you were mad at me for failing her."

Still he said nothing.

Talia opened the curtains. Dust glittered within the rays of fading yellow light. She opened the windows, then returned to Fynn, who was watching her with glassy eyes.

"The war's started. I need to go. Fynn… I need—"

Talia cut herself off and started pacing, searching for the right words. But what was it she wanted to say?

"Before I accepted the crown, Holt told me something that made me rather proud. He said that he thought I would be a good queen because I would be able… able to make the hard decisions. It feels awful to have let him down. To have let everyone down."

As she paced, she noticed one pile of papers remained neatly stacked and orderly inside a lockbox. Freya's letters.

"None of my ealdors have been angry, at least not to my face, but I can tell. I've suppressed anger enough times to see it in others. I know they want to tell me you're as much to blame. I want you to know, Fynn, that I'm not mad at you. I understand why you went because I've been where you were… and though I resisted it, I did regret it. I always wondered 'what if' – well, now I've had a taste of it.

"People like us aren't free to follow our hearts. We have duties – not just to those we love but to everyone who depends on us. Brode chided Holt about this once. I think I forgot that lesson. I've tried hard since the tunnels last year not to risk the lives of my people, but risking myself is no better.

"I understand why you went for Freya, but you shouldn't have gone. You had a duty here, to me, to this kingdom, to your own people, and even to Brenin – to help me, so I can help the New Order fight the scourge. Far more depends on that. You've been careless in the past because you think your family doesn't mind what becomes of you, but you're not disposable, Fynn. Not to me. So you aren't to millions. I need you back," she ended, rather abruptly and rather dryly.

Fynn fixed his eyes downward on nothing.

"My wants feel turned to ash," he said. "Gone. Is this... is this how it feels for a rider to lose their dragon? I wish the blight would sweep over me and take this pain away, to make everything go dark and quiet."

Talia's breath felt stolen away. "Did you even hear me?"

Are you still there?

Fynn gulped. Blinking slowly, he finally met her eye. "I heard," he said softly, and as he spoke, his fingers strummed sad notes as if by impulse. "The war has begun. You need to go to the Toll Pass. We've both been selfish and must think of the greater world and all those who depend on us. You're not mad at me, but I still think you ought to be. You wonder if I'm mad at you for failing? ... Never."

He seemed to wake up then, sitting upright and reaching for her hand.

"No truer friend have I ever had. I say that with no poetic liberty."

Moved in ways she could not articulate, Talia bent and kissed him on the brow. She pulled back almost apologetically and said, "I might not come back from this. If I don't, just know... know that I'm sorry."

By the time she set out for the New Order, night had fallen. She went with a stiff resolve. Seeing Fynn brought so low seemed worse than anything the riders could throw at her.

Talia clung to her duty as she and Pyra made their way back to the island of the New Order. She kept that clear, burning need in her heart as Pyra reached out to them all to come, wild emeralds and all.

Riders emerged from barracks, from the training grounds behind the tower, and from great high-roofed nests. The humans gathered in the courtyard before the tower, and the dragons squeezed in where they could or in the wider streets. Some smaller wild drakes perched on rooftops while others hovered and watched. Alvah, Sokeh, and Kamal provided firelight, and Talia kept a low flame in her open palm as well. Faces and snouts came alive with dancing shadows.

"The war has started," Talia told them, her voice stilted with nerves. "And I must go to prevent this kingdom from falling. At my coronation, I swore vows to defend Feorlen and its people. I feel twisted in knots by oaths and promises. To fulfill one, I must break another.

"You knew what I was when you came here. You knew I was a queen and that, at times, queens must go to war and send men to their deaths. That whether by my hand or my words or my mistakes, people would die. You knew this, and yet you still came. I have never asked you to raise steel or magic against unbonded humans, and I never will. All I ask is that you don't abandon all we're trying to build here when I fight for my people and for us."

A tense silence followed.

The first to speak was a Mystic Ascendant called Ulf, who was Skarl but from the north near Smidgar.

"Do you think some dried meat makes up for what happened?"

Pyra growled. *"You're still here, aren't you?"*

There was murmuring and rumbling at that, but Talia and Pyra had to assume that those left were either accepting of them or were at least still open to having their faith renewed.

Yax folded his muscled arms and nodded. "We have all flown and fought and bled beside the wild emeralds. For that, we're all oath-breakers already."

Perhaps fearing herself outdone by a subordinate, Oline spoke next, her voice stony. "Harvron and I let you know there was a way out of Stroef…"

But then she trailed off, leaving the guilt unsaid.

Harvron was by Oline's side. His brown belly and mossy green back were muddied under the firelight. *"I should like to learn from the West Warden. Our own Paragon would not allow it… but she rarely offered guidance at all."*

Next came Lucia. In her neutral Athran accent, she spoke in a nervous hurry. "I cannot speak for Masters Druss and Barack, but Amon and I were moved by our mission to the Stretched Sea. One night as we lodged in port, sailors we'd saved found us and wouldn't listen as we tried to turn down their offer of drinks. They weren't as frightened or deferential as usual. We'd saved them, and they were thankful. And we got to know them and know what a difference we made. We've saved people from the scourge, of course, but we always fly away right after and never feel the impact. I say if we can help more, then why not? It's not in the literal words of the oath, but it's surely in its spirit. The New Order offers a chance for this."

After hearing such enthusiasm, Talia looked hopefully to Druss, but unlike his younger fellow Athran, he remained tense with his brow furrowed.

"You may not ask us to fight your war," he said, his husky voice throatier than ever, "but what will you ask of us when other riders come to stop you?"

"*We were prepared to stand by her last year,*" said Strang, "*against Adaskar and five Lords. If we were prepared to fight and die then, why not now?*"

"That was different," said Galasso. "The risk was low with the West Warden close by. Adaskar would never have risked open war with a Wild Flight, but with the Elder dead—"

"Does your courage only survive your most powerful defender?" said Yax in his most sonorous tone yet.

"*Be mindful when speaking to your superior,*" hissed Liliane, Galasso's dragon.

Hugon, the Mystic Ascendant from Brenin, walked out of the circle of riders, a finger raised as though addressing a class of Novices. "The question comes down to whether Talia and Flight Commander Ethel's vision is worth fighting for. If it was then, it is even more so now. I say we stand with them again."

As the chatter and growling of debate grew louder, Turro spoke.

"*May I be permitted to address the New Order?*"

"Of course," Ethel called up into the night. "You're as much a part of our ranks as any rider."

A section of riders parted in a shuffle, and Turro touched down within the courtyard. Under the red light from the fire riders, the scars across his wing and body seemed to radiate a painful heat.

"Once, every emerald of your order tried to heal the lands east of the Spine and only managed to keep it barely alive. Since removing the influences of the deep, the land of Feorlen – from root to hill – shows signs of healing. There is a chance, then, for all the world to heal, but not if things drag on as they have. My flight sister fell in the tunnels last year, and I would not see her sacrifice or any other be in vain. Where the Red Bane of the scourge flies, we shall fly with her."

Enthusiasm from the emerald rumbled through the very ground.

Emboldened, Pyra let out a strong roar, and Talia felt their bond warm from joy for the first time since Stroef. Feeling emboldened as well, Talia launched into an impassioned speech.

"I've been struck by how steeped in the violence of change Fjarhaff has become. Old ways were clung onto there at the cost of countless lives. I thought that, here, we might be allowed to carve out a new way. I thought I could avert a war altogether if our enemies saw we were strong. But I see now how naïve that was. The old ways and old powers aren't just going to sit and watch us grow; they'll fight us, wherever we go. I realize that's inevitable now.

"We know this is the better way. We've done more to combat the scourge as two dozen than the whole order has achieved in centuries. Even so, they're going to fight us. They will fight to hold onto what they know, and so we must be willing to fight even harder! Else what's the point? If we don't, then we never believed in it at all."

The emeralds roared, as did Hugon's dragon, Enhadyr, and Lucia's dragon, Amon.

Speaking with her bright, lyrical voice, Alvah exclaimed, "We stand with the Red Queen!"

It was plain she spoke not just for herself and Nani but for all the fire riders. Sokeh beamed, and Kamal, grim-faced as ever, nodded. His uncanniness to Adaskar, especially in the firelight at night, still left Talia a little unnerved.

Druss finally motioned to speak. While Ethel was of the highest rank due to her spiritual advancement, Druss's dragon, Barak, was arguably more magically powerful than Strang. That power would lend great weight to their choice.

"My relations seem determined for bloodshed. Oath or no, it gives me no pleasure to think of Athrans dying, or anyone else. I asked what we will do when other riders come to make sure every one of you understands what we're choosing. The Order will intervene if Talia goes to war, and our blades will not clash against chitin or rotted ghouls but against dragon steel and dragon scales."

Hesitation crept over the gathering like a rain cloud over a summer fayre. Talia felt the mood balancing on a knife's edge, which could cut deep either way with just a slight tilt.

Druss had more to say. "I believe the scourge should be fought above all. That's why I came. Lucia did not claim to speak for me, but the joy she felt in saving lives touched Barak and me as well." He pressed a hand firmly over his heart. "If other riders fight us for that, then they are not true riders in my eyes. My conscience will be clear."

As Druss finished, he raised his hand, and Barak raised his dark snout. Strands of pale lightning coiled upward from hand and snout as though trying to return to the skies. The crack of power dampened, but Talia's spirits soared.

Through the cheering, Galasso pushed his way forward to find her. "I hope you did not think my words cynical," he said, fighting to be heard over the whoops and growls. "The loss of the Elder is a huge blow, naturally, but that does not mean we should give up his cause."

Liliane reached out as well. *"My wings still ail me, but I would never have flown again had you not arrived in the Morass with help when you did. We're pleased to repay that debt."*

Suddenly, the cheering hushed. Ethel and Strang made their

way through the throng. The Flight Commander held something purple in her hands.

"You left this on the shore," she said, handing Talia back her crown. "I trust you'll be needing it back, Red Queen."

The steel started to warm again in Talia's hands, and she placed it back on her head and set it aflame. Amidst fresh celebrations, she bent her thoughts eastward. To the Toll Pass, where her father had died. To the war she'd always had to fight.

44

FRIENDS OF FIRE

Their return to the volcanic islands of the Fire Flight passed quicker than the outward journey. The success of their mission filled them with anticipation of what would come next.

A return to the fray with reinforcements out of Thrall's nightmares.

The beginning of the end.

As for whether the fire brew would work, Holt had little doubt. The attention of every fire dragon they passed confirmed it. Every drake, from those taking their first flight to those that might be deemed Lords in the Order, tailed them as they soared over the islands.

Wrath led them to the great volcano, to the maw that led into the heart of the mountain. She hurried into the wide tunnel, keeping her distance from them as she had throughout the journey. Holt checked the potion was secure on his baldric belt, then, Floating as efficiently as he could, he followed Wrath inside.

Now he recognized the red ore as cinnabar and carried the words of the phoenix in with him. In the mists of time, phoenixes had once called this place their home, long before dragons took it from them. Perhaps the phoenixes had taken it from other beings before them. It reminded Holt of Feorlen and its disputed history. The Skarls had settled and claimed it before the Alduneians came, but even the Skarls must have taken it from a people long since forgotten.

When they reached the inner chamber, Holt and Ash strode in with their heads held high. At once, the nesting flight rattled and growled, and their agitation made the sweltering air even hotter.

Holt and Ash knelt.

"My Warden informed me of your difficulties," said the Elder of Fire in his level, assertive voice. *"I commend your ingenuity. Present it."*

Holt felt countless red eyes leering at him as he pulled the potion free from his belt. The fiery quicksilver still burned, its deep orange unaffected by the red hue of the chamber.

"Revered Elder, we hope this can restore that which was taken from you."

Hunger shone in the Elder's eyes. He stepped forward.

"Stop!" Wrath rushed to stand between Holt and the Elder. *"My Elder, I beg of you, do not do this. Do not contaminate your core and soul with the Parasite's nature."*

"Move aside."

Wrath did not. *"Do you trust these two over me? They had the temerity to enter our domain uninvited, to make demands of us! Of you! They should have been burned like any impurity!"*

Holt tensed, as did Ash. All their efforts to demonstrate the benefits of a bond, of friendship, had been for naught.

"The leech stole from me, from us," the Elder snarled, and an aspect of his rage entered his voice. *"Would you let that go without punishment?"*

A wayward piece of spiritual pressure struck Holt, and even that small piece almost skewered him – and he hadn't been the intended target. Wrath trembled from tail to snout but held her own.

"These methods… are unnatural," she said. *"Even your sister did not foresee the ruinous outcomes of tampering with the natural world before."*

"I recall perfectly."

"Then please, my Elder, do not do this." Wrath's voice contained a hint of hope. *"Dragons in the Order claim their riders make them*

stronger, but those dragons come to rely on them. Strip away their humans and what are they but hollow shells, unable to last on their own. We who toil for centuries are strong. Fire is pure; we must stay pure. Do not rely on this concoction made by freaks and fueled by a creature we hated."

"Weakened as I am, how are we to achieve our goals?"

"Together, my Elder. With me, Pride, Vigor, and Ardor by your side, who could oppose us? Not the broken emeralds, not the weak-willed mystics, not the sly drakes of ice, not the squabbling storms who vie against each other. Who would dare stand before the full might of fire?!"

The rumblings in the chamber grew. Some dragons even roared in agreement with Wrath, but most awaited the Elder's say.

"I admire your courage," the Elder said, his voice unwavering. *"You are not wrong. Compared to fire, all else is flawed. Where my brother was soft of heart, I will make the hard choices. Where my brother is greedy, I seek only what was taken from me. Where my sister only talks, I shall act. And where my sister doubts and dithers, I am strong of mind and will. That is why we shall succeed where they would fail. My dear Wrath, I do this because I must, and I shall go no further than that."*

The Elder stood to his full and terrifying height. Holt braced, anticipating the roar. When it came, his ears stabbed with pain, then rang shrilly, then everything became muffled. Everything save the Elder's voice.

"Fire shall set this world to rights!"

Holt was partly glad his hearing was dampened, for it was clear the dragons were riled up and bellowing their approval.

Ash checked in with him over their bond, and Holt let him know he was fine. His hearing wasn't gone, just temporarily rattled, as though he'd taken a blow to the head. He was more interested in what Wrath might do next.

She twisted her neck around to give Holt and Ash a contemptuous look. Holt considered options to evade a breath and readied his spirit to try and form a defense if needed. Her objections had been swept away and her anger would be worse than ever, but she only snarled and slinked back into the darkness of the chamber.

The Elder rushed forward again, and the vibrations rattled

Holt's jaw. He raised the phoenix potion high, then it left his hand seemingly of its own accord. Drawn by an invisible force, it shot toward the Elder's open mouth, and he swallowed it whole, glass and all.

At once, the oppressive heat in the air lessened. Holt no longer had to Float to bear the chamber. The Elder reared back, exposing his belly and throat, where, under the thin ruby scales, ethereal flowing veins of golden fire appeared.

To Holt's astonishment, he felt a shiver through his bones. His next breath steamed, catching the red light of the dais, and his hearing returned as the Elder landed back on his front feet with a thunderous boom. The Elder stooped and lowered his head. The chamber fell silent, and Holt feared something had gone wrong.

"The pull is beyond anything I imagined." The Elder flexed his talons, issuing a blood-curdling scrape along the stones. He fought through whatever ailed him and rose, speaking firmly again. *"Wardens, go now to every corner of our domain and summon the flight."*

Then he stomped forward without a word of warning.

Holt and Ash threw themselves aside as the Elder rushed past and into the cinnabar passage. They followed him outside, where the Elder stretched his wings and bellowed as though to shake the islands awake, then took off, rising high toward the volcano's peak.

Fire dragons stampeded out of the cinnabar tunnel, then flew to join their Elder and the rest of their kin in an encircling flight at the volcano's summit. Only the Wardens did not join. Wrath and Pride flew in different directions, off to gather dragons from abroad.

Holt and Ash flew up to see what was happening. Between the gaps of the soaring dragons, they saw the Elder land on the gaseous, smoking top of the mountain where a lake of black-red lava raged. Thick trails of power streamed away from the lava, breaking down to clay and then to red dust as the motes neared him.

"He'll drain the mountain dry," Ash said in awe.

"Thrall won't stand a chance."

They descended to the sandy shores where, far from the Elder, the heat of the island returned, though the breeze off the water took the edge off.

During their return journey, they'd discussed how best to attempt forging the fallen star into Holt's existing sword without the usual equipment. The manuals supplied by Aberanth, with pages noted for Holt's attention, had been invaluable.

Before finding a spot to settle down, they searched for a suitable boulder to function as an anvil. The best they found was a large craggy rock with one smooth side. It was much too large for Holt to stand at, so Ash helped to dig a hole in the ground, which they then slotted the boulder into, leaving the flat side up. They dug out another hole, this one to act as a mold for the metals to mix.

Holt unpacked all he would need. His hammer, the tongs, and, of course, the white steel. He set the ore down in front of Ash for him to ponder one last time, then Holt lowered his bandanna, sat cross-legged by Ash and the star, and began his meditations.

As he Cleansed and Forged for unbroken hours, he entered a dream-like state in which time melted away. Ash's dragon song stirred loud and clear.

Bright, springy notes rang from a harp complimenting the growing confidence of the flute, which rose and fell in an assured rhythm. Layered deep behind these, a rich cello bound everything together. A princely song for the young stag coming into his own, carrying scars with him, mementos of lessons well learned.

When Holt emerged from the trance and raised his bandanna, he found the world caught in the grip of dusk. A red sky blazed in the west. The volcano no longer groaned, and no smoke or gas issued from the summit. The fire dragons were dispersing, and out from the swirling flight the Elder blazed forth, his swollen core evident even at this distance.

He flew directly for them. When he landed, Holt's burgeoning soul trembled, and he Floated his channels to bear the Elder's aura. Undoubtedly, the potion had worked. The Elder's core had been restored, perhaps even beyond its original strength. He felt mightier than the Life Elder had been, though Holt didn't trust his perceptions to fully comprehend; he might as well try to guess how much water was in the ocean.

"You did well, blind ones. I hold our bargain fulfilled and name you Friends of Fire."

"We are honored to have been of service," Ash said. *"Now we humbly request you fulfill our request."*

He looked between them. *"You spoke of a weapon. Explain your requirements, and if it is within my power to do so, I shall assist."*

Ash nosed the fallen star, rolling it forward, and described what they needed to do.

The Elder inclined his head. *"Proceed."*

Holt hurried to the beach and brought back dry sand to line the mold they'd dug in the ground. This mimicked adding sand and glass to a crucible to bind and remove slag in the ore. As the metals were already of dragon-steel quality, he didn't think there would be any impurities, but the sand was right there, and it was a simple precaution to take.

With hammer, tongs, sword, and ore, Holt readied himself. Darkness descended over the island, and a thin crescent of shadow darkened the moon's outer edge this night. A shame it wouldn't be full for their labors, but with the dragon song still echoing in Holt's mind, he knew he wouldn't struggle.

"Close your eyes," Ash told him. *"Let the song guide us."*

Holt lowered his bandanna and melded his senses with Ash. Lapping waves, growling dragons, the thud of the Elder's great heart, the smells of earth and sand, sweat and smoke – all slowly faded as he focused on the feel of the leather on the grip of his sword. He peeled the leather away so that only the dragon steel would enter the mold, then placed both the sword and the star into the mold.

Holt stepped back. The Elder approached and held his snout above the pit for a long time. His power radiated, and slowly, very slowly, the dragon steel and the white ore melted down.

While the molten metals mixed, Holt fully sank into Ash's

dragon song, leaving only the wrought iron tongs in his left hand and the wooden haft of the hammer in his right as links to the real world. Moon and starlight caressed his skin, cooling him against the Elder's aura, and even the smell of the molten metal dulled as he lost himself in the music of the night song.

When the new metal had cooled and solidified into a billet, Holt picked it up with the tongs and sat it upon their makeshift anvil.

"Keep it hot enough to work but no more," Ash said, and again the Elder obliged.

Holt began. The billet bowed to his hammer more willingly than simple steel ever had. Inspired by Aberanth's insight that the fire brew needed to be treated as a living thing, something with a spirit of its own, Holt summoned his growing spiritual power and asked metal if it was willing to work with them. Into a bar he forged it, then the steel answered and sought instruction.

'*What are we to be?*'

In the wordless tongue of spirit, Holt and Ash replied together, 'A sword.'

Still blind to the physical world, Holt's grasp on reality gave way completely.

He stood now inside the nightscape of Ash's core where his mind's eye beheld that which his true eyes never could. Overhead and underfoot shone an endless starry night. The moon hung huge, full, and silver as the stars rotated and constellations flashed one by one. A squat hut with a broken roof; a flying dragon and rider above treetops; a tower struck by lightning; a boy holding a man between his arms; two clashing figures over a crumpled body; a branching tree enclosed by a bright circle.

Together, Holt and Ash wove their wills into one, and to it the metal bowed. Holt hammered, and the blade took shape. No folding this time. The lunar steel was already perfect, accepting their magic as willingly as Ash had once accepted Holt on a cold, straw-strewn floor. Within the nightscape the blade took form, white as cream, smooth as porcelain, radiant as the stars, and when the ghost-blade rose to join the constellations, Holt knew the real sword to be done.

The nightscape faded, and the real world returned. Once again, Holt felt the iron tongs in his left hand and the wood of the hammer in his right, and the Elder's breath smelled of heavy coal smoke. His mouth was bone dry, though otherwise Holt felt renewed, as though he too had been reforged by the song of night.

Holt lifted his bandanna. The new sword glowed red hot. Lying beside the blade was a spare piece of flattened-out lunar steel. Holt was considering what to do with it when the Elder asked, *"Is it complete?"*

"Almost."

Gripping the blade with the tongs, Holt headed for the beach and then the water's edge. An unnatural calm gripped the ocean. Reflecting the moon, the water's flat, glassy surface held the silvery gloss of quicksilver.

Wading out until the water came to his knees, Holt waited for the water to turn still again, staring at the horizon until all he could hear was the hiss of the hot metal. Then he plunged the blade down, quenching the sword in the moon-bathed sea.

Steam plumed, thick as the gas from the volcano's summit. Like before, the steam carried an echo of the night song with it, wisping up and up to return to the stars.

Holt drew the sword from the water and raised it to catch in the moonlight. The lunar steel, his spirit blade, seemed darker than before, a coarser gray, yet running luminous up the groove were starburst patterns glowing white and silver. Under the tip of the blade was, unmistakably, a clear crescent moon as though etched there by a master craftsman. Holt turned the sword and found the same etchings on the other side.

A fire rose in his chest, though this was his dragon bond, white-hot from their accomplishment and burning with delight.

"I can hear its magic," Ash said.

Holt heard it too. The same qualities of the fallen star were now firmly fused into the existing dragon steel, creating an aura of lunar energy around the metal.

He tried Sinking his channels to create an Eclipse. As before, the lunar light caught in the blade, bringing the starburst patterns to a dazzling gleam and rendering the technique useless. But Holt wasn't worried by that now. In the sword's creation, the night song had guided him, letting him know the new steel could adapt and help him solve such problems if he worked with it.

Reaching out with his spirit, he willed the sword to 'go dark.'

Nothing happened. The sword resisted, but it gave him a mental prod. The idea was right, but the words were wrong. A verse of the night song returned, reminding him that the metal was of the moon and stars.

Holt reached out to the blade again and willed it to 'wane.'

At once, the flow of lunar motes into his body dried up as the sword drew them instead. Holt ceased Sinking his mote channels, and still the miasma of darkness remained. Not only could he use Eclipse again, but he didn't need to cycle to achieve it. Shrouded in darkness, he could take advantage of other techniques while he fought his enemies.

Holt reached out to the sword again and found it eager to listen.

'Wax,' he willed it.

Currents of magic shifted in reverse. The starburst patterns lit so brightly Holt was forced to look away. It wasn't quite a Flare, not exactly, but he challenged anyone to fight him while his sword shone in their eyes.

There was one final touch to add. Holt returned to the shore and the stone anvil and laid the sword atop it. At the center of the crossguard was a clean rounded groove. Holt withdrew the opal from a pouch at his belt. Holding it between thumb and forefinger, he turned it over: on one side was a brilliant rainbow of light trapped in creamy stone, while the other was coarse and dark gray, much like the grainy edges of his new blade.

He felt a tug between the opal and the hilt. Holt placed it into the groove. White light threw the night briefly into relief, forcing even the Elder to turn aside, growling.

Holt took the sword in hand again. He could hardly believe it was real. It felt as though the sword had emerged from him, straight from a waking dream. The lunar steel felt as natural in his hand as his own skin, blurring where his arm ended and the sword began. His confidence surged as though, merely by holding it, all his shortcomings in swordcraft would be overcome.

"An impressive creation," said the Elder.

"I still need to sharpen it, but I'd say it's complete."

Ash rumbled proudly. *"We hold our bargain fulfilled, Revered Elder."*

They hadn't made an official soul oath, but even so, knots of spiritual energy emerged, loosened, then faded away.

"May it serve you well in the battles to come."

The Elder withdrew.

"Elder?" Holt said. "If we are to wait upon your full flight arriving, might we be so bold as to request a little more of your time?" He looked to the remaining lunar steel upon the stone anvil. He knew just what to make with it. "It would be a shame to waste it. I promise it won't take long."

The Elder snorted and curled his lip to flash his fangs at them. *"You really ought to have fire coursing through your souls to be this daring. Very well, blind ones. I shall humor you one more time."*

Holt held to his promise. It took far less time to create a cook's knife from the remaining steel. Dawn seemed close at hand when he took it to the sea, the moon already fading, but even so, the knife glittered lightly in starburst patterns when he held it high.

Widest across the heel, the knife was long and broad, with a straight spine and a tapered cutting edge. As with his new sword, he felt no need to add anything to the grip. It felt perfect in his hand, as though every cut of meat would be expertly made, every vegetable diced or sliced to match the skill of the most talented cooks. A fine replacement for the knife the phoenix had melted.

As Holt strode back onto dry sand, a collective roar rang to the south. The Elder of Fire turned and bellowed in reply as the first distant wave of dragons arrived.

"Ardor returns," he told them.

From this distance, Holt couldn't discern much of the new Warden beyond its size, which was comparable to that of Wrath and Pride.

The Elder stretched his wings, clearly meaning to take off.

"You have our gratitude, Elder, as you soon will from the whole world," Holt said. "This chaos needs to end."

"Agreed. Ready yourselves, blind ones. As soon as the flight is gathered, we fly to war."

45

PROGRESS, INSIGHT, AND ADVANCEMENT

The Grim Gorge wasn't so bleak as Neveh had imagined. Flying in from the north, the mountains seemed to lean away on either side as if they'd seen too much, but besides their dour character, there was much verdant grass, trees lush with early copper of the turning season, and many streams running like white threads.

Idyllic and false.

A haze lay over the gorge. To Neveh's eye, it seemed to shimmer like the steamy air of the Jade Jungle.

"The mystics have set veils against intruders," Nilak said. He began to summon his spirit, and Neveh did the same. Mixing spirit and magic, they challenged the shrouds to reveal their truth. As the first veil fell, so did the others, the haze washing away to reveal the Mystic Flight.

Flocks of plump sheep milled on the valley floor. Large nests ringed by trees, boulders, or within the shelter of open caves popped into view. The pinks, lilacs, and mauves, as well as the other odd colors – ivories, cyans, and olives – made each dragon easy to spot against the landscape.

The arrival of Paragons gained a swift reaction from the Mystic Elder, who came at once to meet them. Her scales were an unexpected flaxen yellow, yet Neveh felt a further surprise in the feel of the Elder's core.

"Is she well?" Nilak wondered.

Neveh couldn't imagine an Elder being sick, and yet the Mystic Elder didn't feel as hale and powerful as Ice. There was a frailty there, hard to define but brittle under a spiritual touch.

"Sovereign will still be weakened," Neveh said. *"Her strength added to ours will be more than enough to crush him."*

They met upon the valley floor, far from the sheep herds. The Elder landed light upon the ground, barely making any indent into the earth, and brought her striking violet eyes to bear upon them.

Nilak bowed and pressed his neck low, but Neveh stood tall and stepped forward.

"I am Neveh, and my dragon is Nilak. We are the Paragons of Ice, and we come on a matter of urgent need and haste."

"You were not supposed to come."

The Elder's voice was dreamlike and floaty. She sounded like Eso or Wynedd during one of their strange turns.

"Not supposed to?"

"My foresight fails me now. My brother should never have perished."

Neveh's cold heart skipped several beats.

"You come about Thrall."

It was a statement, not a question.

Nilak raised his neck and rumbled in surprise.

Neveh frowned. "We do not come about a slave, Elder, but a dragon, a mystic no less, who controls the scourge and slayed your brother. His name is Sovereign."

"Thrall is the name his rider forced upon him. What he might have chosen for himself in better circumstances, we can never know."

"You know of this dragon already?"

Neveh felt foolish as soon as she asked the question. These great mystics seemed to know far more than they should, for all the good it did them.

"Why have you done nothing?"

Her accusation came out blunt and harsh, but justly so in Neveh's opinion. For too long the Elders had been the eternal powers in their realms, leading, Neveh believed, to their atrophy and idleness.

"You are not the first to ask that of me, child. I have tried to guide the songs of fate before and always to disaster. Foresight is more a curse than a blessing. To see all ends is not to know the path by which one reaches them. But now I cannot see, and so I feel... free."

Hope arose in Neveh. For a moment, even the bothersome warmth of the sun felt pleasant on her face.

"You will aid us then?"

The Elder started as though becoming aware of them for the first time.

"First, we must take counsel. There is one among my flight who had recent dealings with Thrall. I shall summon him."

Neveh grew eager. Anyone with direct experience with the enemy would be invaluable.

While they waited for this dragon, Neveh sat cross-legged and Cleansed Nilak's core, but the sun dipped deep into the afternoon sky before the mystic drew close. Sensing his approach, Neveh opened her eyes and beheld a lavender dragon flying up from the south of the gorge. A brave bird flew strangely close to his side. As he was still some way off, she closed her eyes again and managed three more purifying huffs before he arrived.

His scales appeared washed out, his wings were thin and leathery, his back ridges were worn and rounded, and he hung his head in a stoop. Curiously, he wrapped his tail around a small boulder. To her consternation, Neveh found herself fixated by this. Something about it seemed *off*, though she could not think why it bothered her so beyond the oddity of the behavior. Was he doing it to support himself? Just how old *was* he?

Nilak awoke from his slumber, and his eyes widened as he took this dragon in.

The Elder made the introductions. The old dragon was called Eidolan, formerly of the Order.

"How long ago was that?"

"Many lives of riders," Eidolan said. *"If it pleases the Paragons to know, I am seven hundred and seven years old."*

Neveh's brow rose. Such an advanced age was impressive. Only Elders seemed unaffected by time – even Wardens were rumored to age and pass eventually. He must have lost his rider well over five centuries ago, making his age all the more impressive. Such pain was said to be unbearable, and she wondered why Eidolan had borne it for so long.

While she turned these thoughts around, Nilak answered on their behalf. *"Thank you for joining us. In times such as these, even Paragons are grateful for the wisdom and insight of one so venerable."*

"My Elder tells me you wish to know of Thrall."

"Please," Neveh said, "tell us all you know."

To his credit, the old dragon did not so much as hesitate. He regaled them with a story that stretched back hundreds of years, from before the fall of Freiz when humans still inhabited this great gorge to the recent past of just a year ago.

He told them of Wyrm Cloaks, of Windshear Hold, and of a group of outcasts and rogues who had gone to kill the enemy, failed in the attempt, and were lucky to escape with their lives. Talia Agravain – the thorn in Adaskar's side – had played a part, as had a Lady of the Order, though her name Eidolan begged to keep, for he wished no ill to befall her.

To that, Neveh said, "You may keep her secret. It is to the shame of the Paragons that others were forced to fight our battles." Resentment roiled and spilled out of her then. "When this is over, I'll see that Adaskar is disgraced for this. But you, Elder," she added, her voice cold, "you have much to answer for as well."

"Ere the end, I shall."

Though glad to hear it, Neveh didn't immediately respond. A nagging doubt refused to leave her alone. Something in the world was a lie. Damned mystics – what were they trying to do to her now? Neveh drew on her spirit to guide her, and at once, the distortion became clear.

It was the boulder around which Eidolan wrapped his tail. She cast forth her spirit to reveal the gorge, yet nothing changed. The boulder remained. Only then did she understand her error. The illusion was not out in the world to be dispersed but inside her own mind. Now she noticed it, the kernel of doubt flitted inside her like a black spot darting across her vision. Lifting her mote channels to secure her mind, the trickery broke.

The boulder dissolved, revealing another small mystic dragon curled up inside Eidolan's tail. At first glance, the dragon appeared the same lavender as Eidolan, then it shimmered bluer, though its throat and belly remained pale as pink roses. Only now did Neveh feel a fledgling core, one she hadn't perceived until that moment.

How had a hatchling deceived her, even briefly?

Nilak rumbled heartily as though the whole thing were a fine jape. *"Why, hello there, little one. That was a fine trick you played on us. May we know your name?"*

Her yellow eyes widened, becoming like two round balls of butter. She chirped but said nothing.

"Begging your pardon, Revered Paragon," Eidolan said. *"But she cannot speak. At least, not in the usual manner."*

Nilak tilted his head and kept his gaze on the young dragon. Neveh felt waves of affection radiating from him.

"I'm afraid I don't understand," Nilak said.

"The dragon is mute," Neveh said. She was about to remark her surprise that the Mystic Flight had let her hatch, but something from the illusionist's story caught up with her. "She came from the egg you rescued from Windshear."

"She did, Paragon. Hatched just after the longest night last winter. As she cannot speak, I searched for a name for her. Yume is the one she took to."

"Is she... unusual?"

This time, it was the Elder who spoke. *"She is of our flight, that much is certain, and she has my blessing and care. After the deeds of the Son of Night, we should not judge those still in the shell before giving them a chance to stretch their wings."*

Neveh looked upon the little mystic named Yume. She must have been twice as big as most ponies, growing fast and certainly no shrunken thing, but her demeanor made her appear smaller than she was. Yume's eyes seemed to swirl, and Neveh felt a soft poking sensation around her mind.

Eidolan gave a sharp growl and jostled Yume, who yapped,

lowering first her eyes and then her head, averting her gaze from Neveh's presence.

"A thousand pardons, Paragon," Eidolan said. *"She was trying to speak with you. I have reminded her to be more respectful of ones so high."*

Yume mewled and pawed at the ground.

"If you'd permit her," Eidolan said, *"she would like to explain."*

"Would you willingly allow another to invade your mind?"

"What harm can a hatchling do to us?" Nilak said.

Neveh liked this little, but her curiosity got the better of her. She ceased Lifting her mote channels, and as her mental barriers lowered, she beheld a bizarre vision of many pairs of narrowed dragon eyes floating in the air. The collective gaze turned upon Yume. She shook, and a moment later, a gnarled thorn bush appeared where she had been sitting, and the judging eyes turned away.

All faded. Yume's magic left her mind.

"We might all wish for power to disappear at times," Nilak said. *"But heed the warning from your master. Others will not be as tolerant of unexpected visions, especially when your Elder is not here to vouch for you."*

Yume nodded, then curled up tighter within the comfort of Eidolan's tail.

"I praise you, Eidolan," Nilak continued, *"for lending your voice to her own. To seek change is no simple matter in our kind, whether rider or wild, as Neveh and I have sorely discovered."*

If dragons could blush, Eidolan did. The purple scales up his neck grew darker. *"You are too generous, Paragon."*

"Let us return to the matter of Sovereign – of Thrall, I mean. What a foul name... Small wonder he wishes to be known as the opposite. Before starting, can we have your assurance, Elder, that you will assist us? Let us bring an end to this dark chapter together."

"What of Ice?"

"She fears your brothers more than Thrall or the scourge."

"Is that so?" The Elder hummed and frowned. *"It is the scourge that I fear. The power in the depths has grown beyond all reckoning. Should Thrall be slain, worse horrors will be unleashed."*

Neveh's soul tightened, and her next breath felt more like a wheeze.

"Your sister raised that same challenge in passing wonder. I allowed it to get the better of me."

She regretted the admission at once. The crack in her soul threatened to sunder again, and then Neveh returned to the battlefield in the Spine.

Burning trees, scorched earth, dragon corpses dotted like an illness upon the world's flesh. The stench of death, of the scourge, the torment audible in a dreadful song she both heard and felt in her soul. All of it so vivid she thought Yume might have conjured it.

The moment of her indecision seemed to play out for eons. The Elder of Life, emboldened, rushed in for the kill, and she, usually so sure, faltered, her own Elder's misgivings loud in her mind. Neveh recalled power flowing through her body, unconscious, as if in a dream. The ice clasped around the Elder's hind legs and tail and held him fast.

Two gentle powers reached out to her. The first was Nilak, cold and pure. The second was far older, less solid, yet firm.

Neveh left the valley of the battle behind and returned to the gorge of the mystics. She found one of her arms around Nilak's snout, and the Mystic Elder was huddled in close, looking maternal.

Before she knew it, she was telling the Elder everything. As she spoke, she felt the tightness within her ease. Her purpose was to change how the Order operated. To show how backward and stubborn Adaskar and every Fire Paragon before him had been. In her panic, she had worked against herself. Talking it through now, she marveled that the crack in her soul hadn't been a chasm.

When she finished, she braced herself for the Elder's retribution.

"I see, child," was all she said. It would have been preferable had she screamed.

The Elder stepped back and stretched her neck as though to gaze beyond the world to the stars. After a long silence, she roared as though all the grief of every branching timeline flowed through her and ended with a worn, sad sigh.

"My sister has ever been the wisest of the five. Her caution is well-founded. I think it's time I told my own story and the history of the flights. It is part of the tale of Thrall, though it stretches far back before the blight and its creation."

And so, Neveh listened to another great tale, this one more terrible than the story of Thrall could ever be. A tale of destruction and misfortune.

"In the primal days, I presumed to understand the songs of fate. Since then, I have realized the folly in it. One might perch atop the highest mountain and behold their domain but never know every small movement of those who dwell below. From atop my high peak, I saw an end to the conflict between dragons and humans and impressions of what would be needed to achieve it. A mutual foe stood out in many of the strands, though its shape was obscured.

"I confided my visions to my sister. Wary she was and cautious, for she knew our siblings would not accept any plan to bring peace. It was she who suggested I present the plan as a new force meant to kill the humans on our behalf and so smuggle in my vision of fate under the hateful snouts of our siblings."

Neveh looked across her bond to Nilak. Ice hadn't mentioned any of this. Perhaps, Neveh thought, she, too, was ashamed.

The Mystic Elder continued. *"My brother of Life took to the notion of a plague, and through the haze of fate, this seemed the right path, though I could not yet determine why. But things went awry. The blight grew beyond our intent into the scourge. In time, the first riders bonded, and I began again to hope. It seemed my visions might come true after all. Alas not, for my brothers of Storm and Fire could not abide it."*

Here Neveh interrupted the tale, for Ice had told them of the Pact and how she'd averted further conflict.

"Were it that we were all so cool of thought and emotion as she," said the Mystic Elder. *"In trying to assuage my fears, she argued that my vision had indeed come true. A mutual foe had brought dragons and humans together, and now, the conflict between us was ended. She was right... to a point, although the future I had sought had not been one of an endless cycle against an enemy we could not defeat.*

"Centuries upon centuries passed, and I all but gave up on that glimmer of a peaceful future. Then the dragon Thrall came to us. I felt a tug from fate that I had all but forgotten. Yet again, I mistook the signs. By the time Thrall revealed the extent of his black heart, it was too late."

Neveh was unsure what to think of it all. For years she had wished for insights into the past, and now too many were coming at once to handle. As she considered, she bit her lip. Some new unsettled feeling cast over her mind like a shadow, though this time, it was not due to any mystic power.

As she chewed on the Elder's story, she thought perhaps it was only her disappointment at learning that no one, not even Elders, could be counted upon to make the best and right choices. It was the same feeling she'd had upon realizing that Lords and Ladies were just as afraid as Novices and that even Paragons could die.

Yes, that had to be it. Another unnerving reminder that the oldest and greatest in the world were as susceptible to error as anyone, while the consequences were all the worse for it.

Once again, the limp body of the Life Elder flashed before her, but it was patchy now and coarse. She itched to draw her sword and cleave at the memory. She ached to hear the beauty of the singing ice once more and drive away all the sorrow and mistakes.

"The past is done," Neveh said, loud and crisp. "No more woe and weeping and hiding. No more avoidance. Answer me now. Will you come with me and fight?"

"My brother worked to right the wrongs he and I inflicted on the world… It is only just I avenge him and see his work finished."

Nilak's elation roused his aura to new heights. He beat his tail and wings, and a freezing wind whipped through the trees and frosted the grass.

"Let none say again that the mystics speak much and do little," Nilak said.

The Elder inclined her head. *"All that remains is to find him."*

Neveh was delighted.

Why, then, could she still not shake that ill feeling? It seemed as though she was still missing something.

When Adaskar slept, he dreamed the same dream. Aodhan stood stern and proud at the head of the other Fire Paragons, all tall and broad, dressed in full harness, their faces unknown to him but not their names. Meigor, Flame of the East, who hailed from Freiz and would be wroth to learn of its fall; Galain the Galant, who had shepherded the Order at its peak; Quintus of Aldunei, the fifth son of a fifth son, who subdued the swarms of the Great Chasm after the republic fell, the only Paragon to survive that crisis. More were there besides. Each a shining example of superior ages. All loomed over him. He asked what he should do, why these things occurred in his time. None answered. Instead, one by one, they turned from him. Then he would wake.

Crisis after crisis sapped his ability to rest. Squadrons sent to scour the Frontier reported many of the western settlements empty and destroyed. Riders at Oak Hall were trying to locate the source of the attacks, but the enemy proved slippery. The news of Stroef had grieved him, then Einar had returned from the Toll Pass to bring the unpleasant tidings of the Risalian blundering. Then, worst of all, arrived the news from the riders of Angkor that the Fire Flight – the whole flight – was on the move.

Now he and Eso were alone with their dragons on the dry plains north of Falcaer, awaiting the arrival of the riders selected to fly west in their stead.

Azarin stood tall on his four stocky limbs, tail swishing in agitation. A rarer sight was to see Wynedd awake and outside the fortress. She sat on the scratchy grass in repose, and with her slender neck, delicate snout, and small talons, she almost looked dainty. Any sense of weakness would be dispelled by looking into her eyes: sage green with pupils dark as wine, eyes which seemed to gaze upon every version of what you were or could be.

Under such a penetrating stare, Adaskar's final barriers melted, and he was ready to admit he had been wrong.

"When I sent Einar to the Risalians, I included a direct instruction not to attack – and that you and I would come in time to deal with it ourselves. But it seems those at the frontlines were too eager. A lesser man would blame them, but I riled them up, didn't I? All but gave them the blessing of Falcaer. This... chaos is of my making, and were the Fire Flight not on the move, I'd go myself."

"As would I, dear Rostam," Eso said. "For all I feared backing Talia into a corner, I did not dream she would turn her powers onto innocents. They have committed a heinous act worthy of the very worst rogues in our history, demonstrating why no ruler should ever be a rider in the first place. Alas, in such circumstances, perhaps such tragedy was inevitable."

"Nothing is inevitable," Wynedd said.

Adaskar risked holding her gaze. "Except for death."

Something in the sage green depths of her eyes twinkled back at him.

All four waited in companionable and contemplative silence until the dragons informed them of approaching riders.

Moments later, the squadron entered Adaskar's perceptions.

Some were coming from Falcaer, some from the west from Drakburg, some from the north from Oak Hall. They were ten in number, including one Low Lady and one High Lord, and that was Dowid. A sufficient force, Adaskar hoped, to make the girl think twice before turning her fire onto Risalian and Athran soldiers.

Five pairs he knew to be loyal beyond any doubt. Included in those five were Einar and Skree, who had begged for the chance to atone for their folly. The other five still had questions surrounding them, including Farsa and Hava, summoned from their posting at Oak Hall.

All riders knelt, and all dragons lowered their necks.

"These are dark days," Adaskar called to them, "and soon we may find them equal to the hardest in our history. The rogues in Feorlen now follow a Low Champion who has burned civilians to advance the cause of her ally. Your task is to watch over the forces of Risalia and Athra who fight to unseat her. Should she dare to bring her powers to bear upon mortal men again, you will stop her."

He stepped aside, allowing Eso a chance to speak.

"The Paragons would have her and any who join her in such monstrous acts brought here for judgment. If it comes to blows, make them yield. All must learn of their crimes, and none should be made martyrs."

Altogether, the ten riders and ten dragons replied in the affirmative. Adaskar paid close attention to Farsa, but as ever, her expression was unreadable.

Eso raised his staff high, then brought it crashing down. "Then fly true."

As the squadron began readying for take-off, Azarin sent a private word to Dowid and his plum red dragon, Visaeyra. Dowid hurried over in answer. His growing spirit was quickly becoming equal to his huge frame. If he kept his head, he had the capacity to go very far indeed.

Dowid stopped five paces from Adaskar and inclined his head before receiving permission to approach. When he did, he stepped in close and spoke just above a whisper.

"Have I offended you, Master?"

"What makes you think that?"

"Every other Lord and Lady is being mustered to monitor the Fire Flight. I would sooner join them, not be sent to dispatch a Champion."

Adaskar gripped his forearm and pulled him closer. "I trust you greater than any at Falcaer, save for Eso. You misunderstand the true delicacy of this mission, which is why Azarin called you here. You'll note there is a certain Storm Lady in the ranks."

"I have. She won't be a problem."

"There are others too." And as he spoke, he slipped a small note into Dowid's hand. "Test them. If it comes to blows, do as Eso says, but do not risk needless loss. If there is any doubt as to the balance of power, fly home. Eso and I will handle them personally once the purpose of the Fire Flight is determined. No needless loss of *loyal* life – is that understood?"

It was a credit to Dowid's forthrightness that he did not hesitate, did not entertain a moment's objection or a counterproposal. He accepted the command, and Adaskar let him go.

The Paragons watched the squadron shrink into the west.

"To think," Eso said, "that I pushed you to offer her a golden bridge."

"I was ready to give it. It breaks my heart, but at least her true nature has been revealed."

Eso hummed and nodded sagely. "Your proposals need not be wholly abandoned, especially in the wake of whatever this Sovereign has wrought with the enemy. More active suppression of the dark terror might be wise. Even necessary. Kalanta will approve, I'm sure. Mayhaps it will even sate Neveh."

Adaskar doubted it would suit Neveh, not least because it wasn't her idea. She'd gnaw through that bone after a mission or two and then seek something new to pursue. But for Eso's benefit, Adaskar smiled and nodded.

"Perhaps it will, dear Eso. Perhaps it will."

Having come so close to triumph, it made matters all the worse when Vald couldn't understand the next step. Endlessly, he turned over the words he'd mused upon, examining them without risking declaration.

'Might makes right. When I advance, I will make them follow me.'

This insight, such as it was, had drawn a piece of Raiden'ra's core to him. The failure meant the insight was somehow untrue, yet it couldn't be far from the mark.

When he could make nothing more of the words, he considered the altitude at which they had flown, their speed, even his position on Raiden'ra's back. They returned to the deadly eyewall of the immense storm to fly in endless loops until even those winds broke and the skies lightened.

The Elder had called off the black storm. All dragons had been gathered, and the time to fly would soon be upon them.

"And you will deliver the Order to me," the Elder warned. *"Either advanced or as you are."*

Vald and Raiden'ra changed their approach.

"It is within you that you must search," Raiden'ra determined.

Vald returned to the spot upon which he had sworn to deliver the Order. A bright sun shone, near-blinding after so long under black clouds, and uprooting winds still howled through the court. Floating their mote channels, the Paragons sat within a quiet world of their own making.

For five days they sat there. Five days, during which their loyal riders came to meditate alongside them. Wild dragons came too – a few at first, then more, until half the court observed their painful progress toward breaking the final boundary.

Within their bubble, Vald and Raiden'ra saw their onlookers but didn't hear them. Vald wondered whether he would have even heard a dragon's roar over the thoughts tumbling inside his head.

When I advance, I will make them follow me....

Again, his soul stopped spinning, the tornado bridge between him and Raiden'ra fell still—

Vald pulled on a coil of power and cycled it, just some small thing with which to interrupt the process.

"Why did you stop?" Raiden'ra asked.

"Nothing felt different. Making the same attempt would lead to the same result."

"Last time you fell from my back. That may have interrupted the process."

Vald thought that to be a stretch. "I fell because of the pain."

He recalled it vividly. A seed of Raiden'ra's core had tried to take root in his own soul. Never had he felt pain close to it. Unimaginable. Unbearable.

"I cannot believe that's how it's supposed to feel."

Raiden'ra frowned, flared out his nostrils, and exhaled silver smoke.

Vald knew that look well, but he had never seen his dragon give it to him.

"If it were a matter of endurance, I would not have failed."

Raiden'ra flicked his tail. *"Not consciously."*

"You cannot suggest that I mean to fail?"

"I think a part of you has always feared it, feared what it would mean."

"Speak plainly, Raiden'ra. If not now, then when?"

"Very well. Then you must also not avoid the distressing truth, as you often have. I've felt your heart avoid it, even if you've been unaware."

"I am a Paragon. My alignment is second to none."

"You are stubborn, Vald. All the evidence tells us that something is amiss, else the advancement would have progressed. Are you certain you desire it?"

"I can't believe you're asking me that. Of course I do, not least to save the Order from a terrible conflict. And once we show it's possible, then others will yearn to follow, all the old barriers will fall away, and perhaps, if all goes well, I shall lead many Dragon Souls into the utter depths and so destroy our enemy for good."

"I see," Raiden'ra hissed. *"I'd sooner see the knowledge kept for our own."* He seemed to sense his poor choice of words, for he flicked his tail and added in haste, *"At least until we are so great as to never be challenged. Once we seize leadership of the Order, it will flourish either way."*

As if acknowledging what was being said, the tornado bridge of their bond swirled faster, tugging on both ends. Until now, Vald hadn't understood this difference between them. Raiden'ra was right to say he'd been avoidant.

"You wish to take leadership by force?"

"There is no other way."

Vald opened his mouth. Closed it. Another false start, and then, "Why should we have need of force when our supremacy will be plain? You said it yourself; strength is everything in the Order. Once we show ours is beyond any Paragon, then even they must fall in line, and so all others behind them."

"The Paragons would not bow willingly to an Elder."

"That's different."

"Rostam would fight to the bitter end."

"There will be no need for—"

"If we are to lead the Order, then we must needs defeat the others... and if not all, then the Paragons of Fire at least, for they have too much

pride to kneel. Then and ONLY then will our rule be unquestioned. THAT will be a clear demonstration of our supremacy."

To Vald's shame, his soul trembled. There were still times when he thought of Rostam as a young Champion struggling with his first spiritual insight. He remembered him even younger and smaller as a gangly teen, brought far from his home but already with a brow like rock. Aodhan had thought Vald's interest in a rider not of his type to be peculiar, and Vald could never have admitted to him or anyone else the reason, for they would have feared it. In Rostam, Vald thought he had found someone to walk the path with him. It was the great grief of Vald's life that, while Rostam learned of magic and swordcraft from him, Aodhan had claimed the true victory by embedding his values into the boy.

Quite unexpectedly, a tear burned in the corner of Vald's eye. As with many mortal things, he had almost forgotten the sensation. He lifted a finger and gently wiped it away.

"How long, Raiden'ra? How long have you hidden this *truth* in your heart?"

Raiden'ra rumbled lightly, and his expression softened. *"A long time, I think... but it hardened in me after the last council. They will not relinquish control. They will oppose your dream of marching into the depths, as they always have. They will cling to their power. So we must bring ours, and we will see who is right."*

"If we are to do this," Vald began, the hurt plain in his voice, "it cannot be only for us. You have told me a hard truth, so now I will tell you one. Once we prove that a rider may take a core of their own, others will follow. Whether by our guiding hand or otherwise, this new rank cannot be ours forever. Nor would we want it. What good is all the work – all the horror – if it is not used against the enemy? If we do this... then let us raise as many to join us as can be managed. Let us march in confidence against the terror beneath the earth and end it. Such a feat *will* belong to us forever. None will ever match it."

Raiden'ra's rumbling grew lusty. He huffed more silver smoke.

"This is the least I can adjust to. Your sacrifice will be the greater."

Vald wished never to think upon the matter again, but the means of alignment demanded the opposite. He closed his eyes. Looked inward. His soul quivered in anticipation, almost as if it were a being unto itself. It seemed to speak to him in its own way, letting him know it was ready.

And with that same binding tongue of will and soul, Vald and Raiden'ra together settled their last great truth.

Their souls agreed.

And the world froze.

46

THE WANT TO FORGIVE

The mine was dark, damp, and treacherous. In a larger chamber long since mined dry of its iron, Osric raised his lantern to get a sense of the space.

Long stalactites descended like razor teeth, glinting with menace under the light of flickering lanterns. Working bellows kept the air breathable, but they didn't remove the coal smell or the debris dust so much as move it around in a cold, close swirl. Water dripped mournfully, and the occasional ping of a distant pickaxe echoed up the dark shafts.

Civilians ought not to be sent into those deeper tunnels, but if it came down to the danger of the mine or the danger of a battle, Osric would send them down. Anyone still in the town when the fighting started would just be a liability.

That's why men like me are tolerated. To make the hard calls.

"We should clear these," Osric said, pointing to the stalactites, "then put up scaffolding and stack platforms to maximize the useable space."

Behind him, the mine manager grunted in acknowledgment.

"See it's done well," Osric said pointedly. "It would be a sorry thing if we won the fight only to find the women and children crushed under timber."

The manager grunted again. "It'll hold."

Outside the mine, back in the bright daylight, Osric's black dragon rejoined him happily, followed by the members of the Hounds who were making do as his field officers.

Osric greeted his dragon by rubbing her neck. *"You'd like it down there, nice and dark."* Then, speaking aloud for the benefit of the Hounds, he said, "I'll inspect progress on the gate next. Keep up."

Progress at the gatehouse at the bottom of the switchback road was good. The heavy iron being added to reinforce the doors from the inside was now fully complete on one side.

"Can the doors still be opened and closed?" Osric asked the gatekeeper.

The man wiped his brow nervously. "We've extended the winch, put more muscle behind it, and fiddled with the counterweight. They still move, but just barely… uh, sir."

"I foresee no need to open the gates in a hurry. Carry on. We need that second door secure."

It had already taken over a week for the smiths to supply sufficient iron for one door; all he could hope for was another week. And maybe another.

One week, one year, it won't really matter.

All the same, Osric had never shown dismay to his Gray Cloaks, and he wasn't about to show it here. For appearances' sake, he placed a hand on the new iron, as though giving it his blessing.

"Will it hold?" his dragon asked.

"I'm not sure even steel this thick could hold back that brute."

The gates at Silt Grave had certainly offered no resistance, smashed from the inside out. It was a tremendous tactical advantage to have what amounted to a devastating battering ram that would fly over walls to strike defenses where no one would expect.

"I'm trusting he'll go for the gates," Osric told his dragon. *"The walls are thinner than I like, but they're still stone. The gates will look weaker, like he's used to. If we have any luck, the extra iron will slow him down or, better yet, daze him. Any hindrance could make the difference between me cutting him with the numbing agent or not."*

He'd acquired vials of the poison from their Wyrm Cloak

prisoners, and they'd been a valuable source of other intelligence, like confirming that the rust-colored dragon worked a form of blood magic capable of healing even devastating wounds. Given Osric had witnessed the ginger brute taking a ballista bolt clean through the neck and live, he well believed it. Dazed, poisoned, or otherwise, it might not matter what they did to the muscled dragon so long as his healing brother was nearby.

Then there were the others to consider. The cultists claimed that the crystalline one could fade out of existence, becoming untouchable. Osric thought their understanding of the dragon's magic must be lacking, or at least he told himself this. He didn't have the faintest clue how he'd defeat a dragon that couldn't be touched. At least he could put the teal dragon with the webbed feet and gills out of his mind; the cultists had said she wasn't part of the Frontier attacks.

If they all showed up... well, at least it would be over quickly.

"Maybe he won't even come," his dragon said, her thoughts still on the ginger brute.

"Maybe," Osric said, though the prisoners had said the brute led most of the attacks. *"But if not the first attack, it'll be the second, or the third. He'll come, and we must try to be ready."*

Following that vein of thought, Osric withdrew his hand from the door, gave words of encouragement to the workers, then swept off with the black dragon, heading for the smithies.

Given the mine inside the town, Redbarrow had more blacksmiths than a settlement of its size usually would. Had there been a ready supply of charcoal, it would have been the heart of a major steel industry in the east. As it was, Redbarrow was limited to what could be traded from Coedhen, limiting the smiths to working iron: weapons, mail, and a lot of tools. Yet even iron was now being stretched with the need to reinforce the town gates.

Osric, however, had made one request of his own.

The sky darkened, threatening rain as they wove through the maze of Redbarrow's streets. When Osric reached the open-air smithy working on his commission, the sky finally burst, and the downpour fought against the clanking hammers for supremacy.

"Mr. Smith?" he called.

It took a few moments to get his attention, then the smith set his hammer and tongs down, leaving the red iron steaming on the anvil. He had the most imbalanced arms Osric had ever seen, one corded with sinewy muscle, the other almost malnourished.

"Ah, Honored Ri— Lord General... ah, sir," the smith blustered. 'Sir' seemed to be where most folk landed when addressing him, which suited Osric fine. "It's just ready it is. Sound work, I reckon, if you don't mind me ringing mi' own hammer, sir. Sound work!" he called, his voice fading as he bustled into his storehouse.

Osric stepped under the shelter of the forge's roof and waited. The iron cooling on the anvil still glowed a cherry red, its warmth a comfort against the sudden onset of the rain.

The black dragon went to stand in the downpour, her neck raised high, eyes shut, letting the water wash over her. Onlookers gave her odd looks as they shivered under shelter or gawped at her from their workshop windows.

"Isn't that a bit miserable?" Osric asked her.

"I like it."

The smith loped back out of his storehouse, lugging something wrapped in cloth with both hands, breathing hard.

"It's... heavy, sir."

"I'll judge that," Osric said, accepting the bundle. Its weight would have been impractical for a normal man, but Osric wasn't normal.

Unwrapping the cloth revealed the iron buckler within. Slightly larger than a standard buckler, the shield was unremarkable, except its wooden base was entirely encased in iron and the boss more bulbous. It was dull, gray, and heavy, but it would serve to turn all but the greatest of blows.

"It's ideal, Mr. Smith."

"Thank ye kindly. I added an extra strap while I was at it, seein' as you need it secure on your arm. Thought I'd strike while the iron was hot, if you don't mind me sayin', sir."

Osric almost cracked a smile. He placed the buckler down on

a workbench, then took off his cloak and placed it beside the shield.

A red vial rolled out from an inside pocket and fell from the worktop, and Osric moved quickly to grab it inches from the ground. The bloody contents sloshed as he placed the elixir back into the cloak's lining and made doubly sure the pocket was closed this time.

The idea of drinking the wretched things was sickening... but sometimes, needs must. He'd never liked magic, but when it came to fulfilling the mission or failing, life or death...

"My apologies, Mr. Smith," he said to excuse his delay, then he turned the buckler over and began pulling at the straps.

"Will you be needin' some help there, sir?"

"I must try myself."

Osric tightened the straps until they squeezed his forearm. It would be a disaster if it fell off during battle or someone managed to tear it off his arm.

Happy it wouldn't fall off, he raised it high and performed quick movements to check it would stay on. Despite some hard twists and fierce shakes, the shield stayed on.

"Excellent work, Mr. Smith. Thank you."

He stepped out from under cover into the rain to show his dragon. She finally averted her gaze from the dark sky and took in his new shield.

"It seems small."

"This will suit me. A buckler is lighter, better for quick movements, better to throw my weight behind in a brawl, better to smash in a cultist's face."

"Then I like it."

Osric really did smile this time. He thanked the blacksmith, then returned to the endless task of preparing Redbarrow for battle.

After barricades were built and traps set in the streets, he drilled the Hounds and assisted the Jackal in giving their new 'volunteers' a semblance of basic training. The ballista teams would have an unusual role in the coming fight, so Osric also spent time ensuring they understood it.

Everything was vital. Everything. So why did he find it so hard to apply that same need to his time with Petrissa?

She headed the civilian preparations, so he met with her almost daily, but despite needing to 'heal his soul' or 'seal his fate' or whatever magical claptrap it was, he kept sidestepping the painful topics. Their interactions remained stilted, but bit by bit, they worked toward more cordial interactions.

One evening, Osric entered what passed for a small drawing room in the Den, spotted glinting steel in her hand, and drew his axe with a growl.

"Osric!" Petrissa admonished, and he had flashbacks to his childhood. "Really? You think an old lady is going to try and kill you?"

The steel in her hand turned out to be a razor blade. A large, steaming basin sat on the table behind her, and she placed the razor down beside scissors, coarse brushes, cloth, and what looked suspiciously like soap.

"What's all this?"

"What does it look like?" She gestured to a chair. "Go on, sit. The water will get cold."

Osric sheathed his axe and instinctually touched his beard. He was so taken aback, caught so off-balance by the ambush, that he could only say, "This?"

Petrissa nodded. "I would never have known that you were standing in the hall that day without you telling us. I thought you'd deal with it yourself, but enough is enough." She patted the back of the chair.

He licked his lips, unsure why he felt so nervous.

"You'd better step out," he told his dragon, and she emerged from his shadow into the little room, knocking into the table and causing hot water from the basin to spill over its side.

Petrissa gasped, clutching a hand to her chest. "I keep forgetting she's there." She caught her breath, then adjusted the position of the chair and looked at him expectantly.

Resigned, Osric went to sit down. Discomfort swelled inside him as his mother attempted to comb the beastly beard down, then started cutting away rough chunks with her scissors. Next, she dipped the cloth in the hot water and wrapped it around his face. When she applied a lather of soap to his shortened beard, it stung his skin.

Knowing what came next, his heart began to thrum, affecting the dragon bond too.

"Don't be afraid," the black dragon told him, and she said so sincerely without a trace of jest or exasperation.

Petrissa picked up the razor. "Can this even hurt you?" But she didn't wait for a reply. "Hold still."

Her cold fingers pulled the skin on his right cheek taut. The metal gleamed in the periphery of his vision, causing his heart to bang against his ribs, and then the blade ran smoothly down his face, removing the hair in a clean stroke.

When Petrissa withdrew the razor, a weight of great relief slid through Osric, down to his toes. His racing heart began to settle, and, somehow, a question he'd been longing to ask spilled out.

"What made you leave?"

There was a slosh and a swirl of water as she cleaned the razor, then a moment of silence as she seemed to consider what to say.

"I was driven out," she said, pulling his cheek taut for another pass. "The High Council had wanted me gone for a long time. After Talia was born, Oswyn had an heir in Godric—"

At the mention of his brother's name, Osric shivered.

"Hold still," she said. "Yes, Oswyn had Godric, and Godric had Leofric and a spare in Talia. I was long past being required by then. When Hubbard spoke out against me during a High Council and Oswyn said nothing to defend me, I knew I was done for." She sighed. "I'd always taken Oswyn for granted – always thought him soft for a king, with a soft name."

His fists were hard enough.

Petrissa turned back to the basin, and Osric took the opportunity to clear his throat and work his suddenly stiff jaw.

There had been any number of scandals by the time of Talia's birth, all quietly hushed up. The High Council could have taken their pick, but Petrissa had dutifully provided them with a fresh one by bedding a Risalian Margrave stationed at the embassy in Sidastra. The then Master of State claimed she was supplying the Margrave with military secrets, a conspiracy which was, in Osric's estimation, nonsense. Spies were subtle by trade, and Petrissa was anything but that.

"For what it's worth," Osric began, "I don't think you were you passing that Margrave secrets."

"Thank you," she said, thickly. She removed another wedge of beard, then returned to the basin to clean the razor.

It was all such a peculiar feeling. They hadn't exchanged so many words with each other in twenty years, and they'd exchanged few enough in the years before she'd fled the realm. Osric had been in the Empire at the time, having escaped the city himself before his eighteenth birthday, wishing to find purpose, blood, and honor in the frigid north.

"Where did you go?"

"Back to Risalia. My brother ruled the Vogt estate as Duke at the time, but it was our mother who was truly in charge, and she turned me out at once. I tried going to old friends for help, but by then my reputation preceded me. None of my erstwhile friends were willing to let me in. Bit by bit, I drifted to the Frontier, where no one would know me, but in truth, I didn't have much choice. It was here, Ahar, or Lakara, perhaps, and I could never have borne such heat."

The razor hissed as she scraped it over his jawbone, then she stopped, bit her lip, and sounded hesitant.

"I don't expect you to take me at my word, but from the moment I met the Jackal, everything changed."

"Can't you call him by his name?" Osric asked, irritated. He grew tired of referring to the gang leader by his ridiculous title.

"I won't break that trust. Not for you, not for anyone."

Osric scoffed, but he appreciated the loyalty.

More loyalty than she ever showed to Father, or to me.

Petrissa went on, her voice softer again. "With him, everything felt different. I never once felt bored. I think I was so sick of the fawning that it was a surprise to encounter a man I couldn't shame and guilt into whatever I wanted. Tantrums, rows for little reason, he shrugged it all off," she finished quietly. "Somehow, that made me feel calm... for the first time. And in the Frontier, of all places! I'm not Petrissa Vogt, or Agravain. I'm a Jackal, too, the Lady of Redbarrow."

Despite himself, Osric believed her. Whenever he saw her and the Jackal together, he could feel a trust between them that might have been a soul bond.

"There," she said. "That's much better."

Lost in her words and sharp memories, Osric hadn't noticed the shaving. He accepted the hot cloth she offered and enveloped his face in it, as though the steam might cleanse him of his old pains.

"It feels like you're holding back," the dragon told him.

"I don't know what I'm supposed to do."

How he hated these ways of magic and souls. No straight answers, just feelings and instincts, it seemed. Far easier to hunt down one old woman in the whole Frontier than to have the first clue on what he should say or ask that could fix a lifetime's worth of hurt.

He removed the hot cloth from his newly smooth face, then lurched to his feet.

"There's so much to do," he said, averting his eyes from Petrissa. "Too much to do. I should go. Thank you, *Mother*... but I should go."

Redbarrow was close to enjoying its second gate door being reinforced with iron when more Wyrm Cloaks arrived. The Jackal and a score of Hounds stepped outside to meet them, while Osric pressed himself against the gate and listened in, his buckler and axe ready in case of trouble.

As expected, the cultists asked after their brothers, and the Jackal assured them that the marrow had been paid and the men had left weeks ago.

"Could be they was stopped on their way back," the Jackal

said. "Not just you and yer masters who want their 'ands on the paste."

The cultists wondered who these other interested parties could be.

"Ruddy Crows come in scavenging, don't they."

The cultists thought that unlikely and said so. They asked to enter the town, but the Jackal held firm. Osric felt the dragon squirm in anticipation within the shadow of the gates, but fortunately the Wyrm Cloaks chose not to start a fight they couldn't have won.

The Jackal and his men returned through the gates, though they looked pale.

"Close one that. I still reckon we shoulda taken 'em like the other two. A few broken fingers an' teeth wouldn't 'ave gone amiss, but I get it. Don't wanna make it any easier for this Thrall fella to know summin's up."

"You've shown great prudence so far."

"Oi, enough o' that. It's been no easy thing leavin' the rest of my lads stranded out there." The Jackal bristled. "D'you have any idea how hard it was to bring my turf to heel? And now it's all to be left to them cloaked lot to ravage."

"My advice is still to leave, but if you won't, you'll have to accept the losses and be grateful to anything and anyone you can spare. Treat this like a scourge rising."

"Scourge don't come 'ere much. Not enough people. All the southern cities draw 'em like flies to dung. Thought I'd made a place where folk might feel safe, y'know?"

"You don't strike me as a charitable man," Osric said.

"Ha!" the Jackal laughed. "Cutting, just like yer mother. She was always tryin' to get me hackles up in the early days," he grinned, clearly enjoying the memories.

The contrast between the Jackal and Osric's father really was remarkable. Oswyn had been good-natured and strong around everyone but Petrissa, with whom he'd been besotted, even pleading at times. Petrissa had reviled that, scorning him; Oswyn would drink, and so the cycle spun to its hideous end.

All this he understood now, better than he'd ever been able

to as a child creeping through the palace corridors. As to why Godric had avoided the poisonous consequences of this dysfunction, he was still unsure.

Perhaps because he was the heir, whereas I could be viewed like any bystander.

The arrival of the Wyrm Cloaks prompted Osric to try speaking with their prisoners again. He felt almost compelled to return; as with his mother, the same ill feeling of unfinished business hung over him.

In their cramped, damp cells, all bruised and dirty, the two men looked small without their dragon-hide cloaks. The one with the straw-colored hair, Obis, sat eerily still, his dank hair covering his face, his breath so low he might have been dead.

No real spine. No real conviction. Just lost boys and girls following a mad dragon with no clue of what they're dealing with.

The Ahari man still sat upright. His name was Omid, and he was from a village far to the east of Negine Sahra, a place few cared about. A wind rider had left them to fend for themselves against the scourge; there had been more critical locations to defend.

Such tales were not uncommon among the Wyrm Cloaks; whether from the scourge or a cruel superior's hand, each had been wounded, and none had ever recovered.

Wounds can fester, and those inside are no different.

Osric stepped inside Omid's cell to speak with him on a more even footing. He asked about Omid's past again and why he joined the Shroud. This time, the cultist ended on a darker note.

"The scourge treats us all the same. It does what it does, as the golden cats of the desert hunt the gazelle and the gazelle eats the grass. Just their nature. Only men show favor; only men choose who lives, who dies, who gets what, who is what. It's unnatural."

Bitterness. Osric knew that scent well.

"So the solution is to let the scourge consume everything?"

"If a camel falls and breaks its leg, it's kinder to cut its throat than let it writhe in suffering."

At last, Osric thought he understood the mania of the cult. None before had ever put it quite so clearly, though the Speaker had come close: 'In death, we are all equal and free,' she had told him once with a grin. The cult really worshipped death, and Thrall was death's current master. It was a long, twisted road from their origins of worshipping dragons.

They all want to put the whole world down.

In his darkest moods, Osric had harbored similar thoughts: that life was naught but brutality and pain, though his thoughts had congealed around Godric, the brother who should have defended him.

"I thought much the same, once," Osric said, "but I was wrong. You are wrong. The Speaker is wrong. There is always a chance to turn back, always a chance for meaning to return if only you'll let it. Fate was unkind to you, Omid, as it is to so many, but what you do in response is always in your power. Will you accept you were wrong?" Osric extended a hand. "It begins with that, I think. The hard road back begins with that step."

For a moment, Osric thought Omid might just take his hand. The cultist's lip trembled, then he frowned, screwed up his face, and spat on Osric's palm.

Osric clenched his fist and withdrew it as he retreated from the cell.

Not everyone is as lucky as I was. There are no helpless black dragons here for them.

Osric locked the cell door. "I pity you, Omid."

As he headed back to the hilltop outside, his dragon emerged from his shadow.

"Why speak with them so much?"

"I don't think I can truly be forgiven, but as I'm acting as if there's a chance for it then I need to treat others the same. Trouble is, they have to want to save themselves. Any of them that do, I think we should listen."

She chirruped like she was a tiny hatchling again. *"Do you think you will forgive your mother?"*

"I don't..." He choked up for a moment. "I don't want to hold onto the torment forever. It's good for nothing."

Perhaps it was with this in mind that, during his next meeting with Petrissa, he found the courage to ask the thing he'd always needed to know.

"Did I do something wrong?"

She looked confused. "Something wrong?"

"You loved Godric, never me."

"That's... I—"

"You both did."

Petrissa continued struggling for words. "I... I can't speak for Oswyn. Things were complicated, but it wasn't your fault. I should have done better. I know I should have, but—"

She gasped for breath here, and then she started to cry.

Ice skittered up Osric's spine. He'd never seen his mother cry before.

His head hammered with rushing blood as though in battle. He struggled for breath himself, his palm grew slick, and he wanted to turn, to flee. It would have been a relief for word to come of Thrall's forces on the horizon.

Facing that hopeless fight would be nothing compared to this.

Sensing something was wrong, his dragon reached out to him. *"Did you tell her about your brother?"*

How could he do it now with her in such a state? What good would hurting her do? How could that heal either of them?

Osric didn't know what to do. His mother's weeping eventually roused the Jackal from the adjacent room. Scowling at Osric, he looked more wolfish than foxlike.

Osric fled like a coward.

The next day, he tried to set the previous night's horror aside by training hard with his dragon at an old quarry near the mine. He drilled her in gathering and launching her breath again and again.

"Keep going," he said, deflecting another of her shadowy bolts with his axe. "That one had no weight behind it at all."

All four of her knees wobbled, and her pink tongue hung

from her mouth as she panted for air. *"I'm not doing it any differently."*

"It's just practice. The power of your magic is inconsistent, and that might prove fatal." He raised his axe. "Again. Don't worry, I won't let it hit me."

Her panting turned to a snarl and then a deep growl. She sent attack after attack at him, darting around as if trying to catch him unawares. Osric met each dark ball with a lazy flick of his wrist. None of them felt strong enough to tickle him, never mind blow through dragon-hide.

Her core also seemed unfazed by the drills. Both shadowy figures seemed solid and well-defined, proving she wasn't drawing on much magic at all. Perhaps it would take a real fight with real danger to scare her into it.

Osric was about to tell her to stop holding back when footsteps and men calling drew his attention.

"Word from the gate, sir!"

"That's enough," Osric called to the dragon, turning to meet the pack of Hounds rushing into the quarry.

Something rushed at Osric's back, and his every instinct screamed to move aside.

The dragon yelped and telepathically cried out to everyone, *"Look out!"*

An errant shadow ball whizzed past Osric as he jumped aside. The Hounds tried to scatter, but one froze, staring wide-eyed at the attack, which hit him square in the chest.

For a moment, time seemed to stand still.

Then Osric was running to the man's side, looking for the wreckage of a ribcage, but he found a fully intact, unscathed torso.

"Are you hurt?" Osric asked.

The Hound spluttered and wheezed. "Touch winded, but nothin' worse, I think."

How is this possible?

For Osric to find her attacks weak was one thing, but a normal, unenhanced man struck full-on by a dragon's breath couldn't have hoped to be unharmed.

"Are you wearing armor?" Osric asked, his hand grasping at the man's clothes, expecting to find heavy chainmail, hardened leather, anything.

"No, sir."

The black dragon slid from shadow to shadow and arrived at her victim's side. *I am sorry, human. I did not mean to strike you.*

The man seemed more impacted by hearing her speak to him than by her magic. "No harm done, your dragonship."

"Takes more'n that to break a Hound!" one of his companions trumpeted with a mock baying of a real dog. They all started laughing about such a close encounter.

"It's not possible," Osric muttered while the men guffawed.

She'd blown right through a dragon-hide cloak and killed a blood-swollen cultist with a single blast. And now this? There was no rhyme nor reason Osric could fathom for the inconsistency.

Is her magic weak when hitting someone in the chest?

The very notion was absurd, and it was, but the true revelation then came to him, striking like a gong across their soul bond. For a moment, he came close to feeling excited, then he recalled Hound had been trying to tell him something before he was struck.

Helping the fallen Hound to his feet, Osric asked, "Now what was that about the gates?"

The laughter of the Hounds died at once.

"Scouts report a dragon ahead of a force of scourge headin' this way, sir."

Osric's cluttered mind cleared. All thoughts of his mother, gone. Intricacies of the dragon's shadowy powers, gone. Riders talked endlessly of meditation, but Osric had found nothing so good for clarity of mind than a battle. He considered it one of life's rare pleasures.

Giving orders to the Hounds present, he dashed for one of the lookout points near the Den high on the hill, his dragon running by his side. When Osric arrived, the Jackal was already there, peering through a spyglass.

"Ain't lookin' good," the Jackal said. "I'll start clearin' the roads to evacuate into the mine." He handed the spyglass to Osric and hurried off, barking orders.

Osric extended the spyglass to its fullest, then placed one eye to the lens. Across lands of thicket, gorse, and struggling farms, he spotted a dragon flying strangely low. It was an emerald, not one of the favored five, and it didn't appear to be scourge-risen. Dragons had joined Thrall of their own free will, of course, though few had ever been emeralds.

Something moved fast on the ground below the emerald. At first, Osric thought it a Wyrm Cloak, for the figure wore a great, billowing cloak, but such a cloak was too dark to be any known sort of dragon. An orange flash drew his eye, then he saw the glassy blade.

Rake?

His dragon bond began to beat, rising to match both their hearts.

Dazed by the shock of seeing the half-dragon, Osric stood there for a while, just watching and wondering what on earth was happening. Rake wasn't moving close to his top speed, nor did his legs rise nearly as high with each of his shortened strides.

Then Osric saw the scourge; ghouls and bugs were pursuing Rake and the emerald, and the faster flayers were gaining on their prey.

"Can you speak with them?" he asked his dragon.

She screwed up her face, arched her back like a cat, her whole body vibrating from the effort, then slumped down. *"They are too far away."*

Osric looked through the spyglass again. The wisest course would be to stay holed up behind Redbarrow's stone walls, wait for Rake to come within range of his dragon's telepathy, then get him to run here to safety...

"We'll go to them," he announced, snapping the spyglass shut.

By the time he arrived at the gatehouse, those few men with hunting bows were already heading to the ramparts. No ranks of serious, skilled archers with strong longbows and keen vision here. Redbarrow's army, such as it was, was more an enthusiastic rabble. Most townsfolk hadn't held anything more deadly than a knife until weeks ago.

"Open the gates," Osric called.

"The moment you can," he added to his dragon, *"reach out to Rake or that emerald."*

She growled to acknowledge him, her heart thundering.

Osric twitched his fingers as the gates groaned open, painfully slow under their new weight, but luckily they only needed to open enough to let him and the dragon through. They burst out, running to intercept Rake and his emerald companion.

Ahead of them, a few flayers rushed out ahead of the small swarm and closed the gap on Rake and the dragon. Osric could only watch on helplessly as they were forced to draw to a halt, fight the flayers, then try to return to their previous pace. Every moment, the greater part of the small swarm gained on them.

"I have them," the black dragon said.

Osric continued sprinting, his legs pumping like a galloping horse.

This time when Rake and the emerald stopped, they whirled to face him. A moment later, they were moving again, now heading straight for him.

As they met, stingers came hurtling down from above. Vines leaped from the earth and caught one, dragging it down with a body-breaking crash. Rake stood still, awaiting the shining point of the great wasp's sting, then, at the last moment, he Blinked, vanished, and reappeared twenty feet away as the stinger splattered into the ground where he'd been standing.

"Well, this is a sight for sore eyes," Rake cried, sounding hoarse. "What screeching notes of fate bring you here, Grumps?"

"Let's have it all out behind the walls," Osric said, pointing to the town half a mile away. "Come with us!"

"Stopping wasn't really the plan," Rake said, yet his body betrayed him, his knee buckling as he tried to take another step. The emerald landed by his side, trying to help him up. Her own core felt worn thin.

Then a tremor ran underfoot. The black dragon yowled and began tugging at their bond as though to lead Osric away.

Suddenly, the distant swarm was blown apart as the ginger dragon appeared, pounding the earth at terrifying speed.

"Change of plan," Rake said. "Run!"

They ran. The black dragon's fear of the bruiser turned Osric's breath ragged as the quakes in the ground licked at their heels. They made it to the gates, mercifully still ajar. Osric, his dragon, and Rake bolted through as the emerald flew above. The moment the doors began to close, they heard the ginger brute come to a skidding stop.

Osric raced up to the gatehouse and emerged on the walls to find the great bruiser pacing out of range of any bow or ballista bolt, bellowing and slamming his tail against the earth. He snorted black and orange smoke, roared again, then turned and loped off.

The butt of a long pole clunked down beside Osric.

"Been chasing us for days, that one," Rake said.

"Once you catch your breath, do you think we could take him?"

Rake grunted and leaned on his polearm for dear life. "Give me a minute, Grumps. Just one min—"

Before Rake could finish, he collapsed on the rampart.

47

THE GREAT CHASM

Despite their long travels, Holt and Ash had yet to behold the Great Chasm, the calamity that had sundered the old republic in a single day.

Alongside the Fire Flight, they beheld it now.

The size of the chasm was the stuff of legends, but those tales did no justice to reality. From on high, the torn earth stretched from west to east and further still. Even to think of it as a single Great Chasm was false. Branching canyons and ravines cut into deep abysses as though some enormity had stabbed savagely at the world, leaving ragged wounds seeping a black-green mist. Even the sky had fled in fear, leaving a jagged window to the night beyond.

Starless. Soulless. Hopeless.

It looked like how the world would end.

And this was but a piece of it.

When the flight had reached the Stretched Sea, Holt assumed they would strike east to fly around the chasm before heading north for the Fallow Frontier, so it came as a shock when the flight veered west, hugging the sharp edges of the outer ravines.

"Where are we going?"

"I know as much as you do," said Ash.

Fire dragons roared at one another all the way back up the column.

The Warden of Wrath was one of the few who did not. She'd shadowed them during the journey, though she'd been quiet and sour the entire time. As the flight changed course, she shot them a sneer and a frown as though it was all their doing. And perhaps it was.

With little to lose, Ash asked her, *"Where are we going?"*

She snarled and turned away in disgust. *"The chasm narrows ahead. We will cross there."*

The flight sped up. Ash beat his wings harder.

The Warden of Valor flew at the head of the flight alongside the Elder. Valor had returned to the volcano at the head of the largest group of drakes. A pale orange, almost golden in places, she was easily the most pleasing to look at of all the Fire Wardens. Ardor's coloring was the most unusual of the four, being a blushing red, closer to a ruddy pink in places.

They maintained their westward route through the night. Dawn broke against their backs, and as the morning wore on, only then did the Elder adjust his bearings. The whole flight banked to the right, turning north and striking directly over the chasm.

Under the cracked sky, what light there was seemed to pass through a filter of filth. Below, where the bottom of the gorges could be glimpsed, scourge scuttled like ants. The Order allowed scourge to gather here to be used as training for Novices, Ascendants, and Low Champions, though the current build-up was more than Holt expected to see. Distractions in the Order would not have helped in that regard.

"Once Thrall is dead," Holt said to Ash, *"I suppose the Fire Flight will cleanse the Great Chasm first."*

He and Ash shared a mental image of dragons swooping through the chasm, burning all the sickly green away.

"I hope they leave some bugs for us when they do," Ash said.

Holt agreed. He was itching to test his new sword.

"I wouldn't worry about that. There will be plenty to fight below ground."

And that time would have to come, for any victory over the Hive Mind surely required a mission into the depths of the world. To wherever the Hive might be, if indeed it existed in a single location. Given the Elder and many dragons besides couldn't hope to venture underground, delving into the darkest places would be for riders.

The Fire Flight roared again and rearranged into a tighter formation. Wrath drifted closer to them, a little nearer than seemed necessary.

"Is something wrong?" Ash asked her.

"More riders," she spat. *"They're closing in."*

Given the riders kept watch over the chasm, that wasn't unexpected. Riders had been tailing the flight since they'd reached the Stretched Sea, and reports of a full Wild Flight on the move so close to Falcaer would doubtless have caused alarm.

Holt tried to search for them with his magical senses, but with so many dragons packed so close together, he didn't have a hope of picking out any individual core, save those of the Elder and the Wardens.

"They won't cause trouble," Holt said. *"Adaskar respects the Pact above all else."*

"One Elder is already dead. Nothing is certain now."

Holt's unease grew. The sooner they crossed the chasm, the better.

Before long, the dragons further tightened their formation, and a Warden shifted to guard each side. Wrath went to defend one of the flight's flanks, and Holt couldn't say he was sorry to see her go.

The riders grew in numbers and boldness, drawing close enough that Holt could sense them beyond the mass of the flight. More arrived from the west, and as the chasm abated and the Fire Flight came within sight of clean earth, a contingent approached from the north.

The Elder of Fire bellowed as mightily as he had in front of his volcano, descending just beyond the northern edge of the chasm, where he came to a halt. Hundreds of dragons beat their wings, hovering, while the Elder and his Wardens went forth to meet the delegation.

Lacking direct instruction, Holt and Ash flew below the

formation but didn't go so far as to land. At some distance from the fire dragons, he could discern the presence of the riders against the familiar, glaring power of the Elder and Wardens.

The delegation was no joke. Four Lords met the Elder on the ground, with six Exalted Champions hovering behind them. Still others must have skirted the flight at a distance. Among the Lords, there was one of each type, save for storm.

Holt and Ash couldn't overhear what the Elder or Wardens were saying, for the dragons had no reason to project their thoughts outside the group. As Ash could manage to hover in place without sight, Holt lowered his bandanna. Their sense-sharing adjusted so that Ash's ears took over, and they could just about hear what the humans were saying.

"...Falcaer would know your purpose, Revered Elder," a woman said in the lilting tongue of Coedhen. "It is the right of the Paragons to ask... These lands are under rider jurisdiction. Much harm has been done of late— no... Elder, we humbly request... What?"

Here, her voice snapped into indignation that could only be that of a fire rider.

"Submit to you? That is a gross violation of the Pact! Return to your domain at once... No – never!"

Spiritual power washed out from the Elder. Holt felt only a ripple of it, and even that was like a great oak falling on his head.

"No, *my Elder*," the Fire Lady said, strained, defeated. Her knees hit the ground. "We do not dare defy you."

There were growls of panic. A flurry of voices, sounding weak from the effort of resisting the Elder's will.

"Lady Enya, what are you saying?"

"What of our oath?"

"Elder, take your dragons and leave!"

Pride landed hard behind the riders.

Valor hissed but did not move.

Ardor looked between his fellow Wardens and his Elder and edged slightly away.

Swords rang from sheathes, a heavy war hammer was raised. Cores flared.

The Elder stomped toward the Lords. Wrath moved too, and as within the flight's domain, she moved to stand between the Elder and his desire. His snarl carried no patience. Her growls became high-pitched, and such an incongruous utterance from the Warden of Wrath struck Holt with more fear than the Elder's advance.

Wrath clawed at the ground before the Elder, mewling, and when he did not stop, she leaped toward him like a fearful dog hoping to push their master away from an unwitting fall. The Elder reared, threw her aside, and Wrath slammed into the earth, her chilling wail quickly lost in the clamor of battle.

The Warden of Pride laughed and fought the three resisting Lords at once.

Valor scowled and turned away.

Ardor hastened to Wrath's side.

Holt froze. Ash had no words, no plan. To move would be perilous. The Elder seemed the clear aggressor here, but Holt and Ash would be reduced to cinders in a moment. Holt did all he could, raising his bandanna again so they could at least fly.

The riders had the good sense not to fight to the death. They harried Pride, then mounted their dragons and fled. The Exalted Champions were already speeding westward. With luck, the Elder would bellow at their backs but then return to his original northward course – to Thrall.

So long as that happened, so long as Thrall was removed, everything else could be fixed.

The Elder bellowed after the retreating riders, spraying spittle that flashed into embers upon the ground, but he did not turn north. Rather, he stared long and hard to the west until, with a sudden, fierce movement, he spun to look up at his flight, eyes bulging, his oil-fire body blazing.

"We cannot move ahead with enemies at our backs. How is fire to save the world when it does not act as one? What is stronger? Five flights or one? One mighty flight, one world, one order. All those who would restore the world to rights will join us, and all others will only oppose us in time. These riders who claim to guard the world have let it fall to ruin. Let us see if they have the humility to admit their failings!" He rounded upon the

Fire Lady, the only rider of the delegation to have submitted to the Elder's invitation. *"Here is a noble pair who will atone."*

On bended knee, the rider drew her sword and presented it to the Elder as though to swear a fresh oath. Off to the side Wrath got to her feet, eyes raging like two blue suns, then fell upon the orange dragon with tooth, claw, and lashing flame.

The Warden was so fast and so brutal that even this Lady of the Order stood no chance. Her shrill, primal scream of loss rang only for a moment. By the time she leaped up to fight, a blue inferno had consumed her, cutting her scream short and leaving nothing but a charred body.

Holt no longer felt his own heart. He felt numb and cold all over.

"Ash... what do we do?"

Ash replied shakily. *"I... I don't know..."*

Pride lunged for Wrath now, but Valor intervened, stopping the fight. Ardor growled at Wrath, perhaps begging her to stand down, but whether because a living fury possessed her or because her blood was up, Wrath belched a screen of viscous black smoke, then took off, making straight for Holt and Ash.

As Wrath's jaws opened, her dominating spirit crushed any thought Holt had of resistance – then the Fire Elder himself flew in to shield them. Wrath came to a sudden halt, and both she and the Elder hovered in the air.

"You will not hurt them. I may have need of their talents in the future."

"It is they who have done this!" Wrath said, sounding deranged. *"They and their twisted human magics. Please, my Elder, you are not yourself!"*

"I am more myself than I have EVER been!"

A shudder ran through Holt and into Ash. It seemed to ripple through the entire Fire Flight.

"We're not friends of fire at all," Ash said privately. *"We're just here in case he needs another potion."*

Pride, Ardor, and Valor were closing in on Wrath. She threw Holt and Ash a final look of pure hatred, then swerved hard and covered herself in another great cloud of impenetrable smoke.

Even the Wardens hacked and backed away. As the smoke cleared, Wrath could be seen trailing flames as she blazed to the northeast.

"Where is she going?" Ash said fearfully.

Pride seemed intent on following her, but Valor and Ardor kept him in check. The Elder roared and brought them all to heel. It seemed he was willing to let Wrath rage elsewhere for the time being. The Fire Flight had more important matters.

"The forest," Ash said in horror. *"Holt, she's heading for the forest."*

Holt finally found his voice.

"Aberanth." He knew it in the pit of his stomach. Why else would Wrath head for the Fae Forest? *"Ash, tell the Elder – if he wants more potions, he should stop her."*

"Revered Elder, you must stop her!" Ash called. *"We fear she's going after our friend who helped create the potion!"*

The Elder turned his full attention onto them. *"Could you craft it alone?"*

Alongside this came enormous spiritual pressure, not a direct question to check their will, but enough that the truth was demanded of them.

And the truth was, Holt had watched and assisted in so many attempts that he could mimic Aberanth's final process exactly, even if he didn't fully understand it.

Under the Elder's full spiritual weight, Holt found it impossible to lie outright, and nor could Ash.

"We could make it, Elder," Ash said, voice shaking, *"if we had to."*

To Holt, he said privately. *"We have to go after her."*

Holt agreed wholeheartedly. How they would be able to help Aberanth was irrelevant. He was alone and unprepared, and he needed them to try. It was as simple as that.

Much of the Fire Flight was already flying west.

Holt's mind raced. Fighting their way free was impossible. They could never outfly Pride, never mind some of the greater fire dragons, nor shake their pursuers in the open air.

He thought his sword was *nudging* him from behind, trying to get his attention, but now was hardly the time.

The Elder's pressure lifted from them. *"Come along, blind ones."*

Inwardly gasping with relief, Holt couldn't muster an answer.

Ash managed, *"You swore to defeat Thrall and the Scourge."*

"And so I shall. Come now, don't tell me you care for the insolent riders? They would kill you on sight. Let us find out which ones are loyal to the world and which to the mystic snake and their own greed."

Holt's racing mind locked onto an answer. A desperate move, but it held more prospects than defying the Elder outright. Over the bond, he shared the idea with Ash, summoning the images, feelings, and sensations he anticipated. Ash was alarmed but then accepted it.

"You're either with us," the Elder warned, *"or you oppose us."*

Holt tightened his hold on Ash's bone ridge and pressed his legs in hard as he could.

Ash tucked his wings.

"We are loyal to the world," he said. *"Not just to you."*

Ash dove.

The ground rushed up to meet them. Ash pulled up just before impact, gliding fast under the mass of fire dragons. Tendrils of heat grazed Holt's back. They reached the precipice of the Great Chasm, gulped deep breaths, then Ash dove again, down into the black-green fog.

Holt struggled to see anything, meaning Ash couldn't either. Over the bond, Ash implored him to switch their sense-sharing. Holt closed his eyes, screwing them tightly shut. Ash's ears took over, and they carried on, down and deeper.

Holt felt lost. They'd never flown blind before. Sounds and smells rushed in too quickly for him to form a sense of what lay ahead. Distant roars rang from high above, but he lost his grasp on them.

"We're under the fog," Ash said.

Holt breathed again, but the air down here was saccharine and rancid. The stench of sickly-sweet death was choking, as though the fog were a lid keeping the worst from rising out of the chasm's pot. Stranger still, the cores of the dragons disappeared from his perceptions. Just how deep had they gone?

Ash glided low over a ravine floor. Now with a moment to spare, Holt lowered his bandanna to deepen his blindness, and his perceptions started to adjust.

A cacophony rose in the narrow pass. It was full of clicking, buzzing, and rattling bones. Scourge everywhere. Holt kept his mouth shut, resisting the urge to cry out as they hurtled along. The last thing he or Ash needed was for him to add noise of his own to the confusing rush.

Ash picked up speed, soaring over the bulk of the bugs. Screaming magical bolts shot up from casters on the ground. Ash rolled in midair to dodge but emerged too close to the gully wall. He closed his wings and met the rock face with his legs, causing Holt to lurch and almost fall.

"*Sorry, boy!*" Ash said, scrambling along before kicking off into flight again just as two more screaming bolts slammed into the rock behind them.

Holt's hazy impression of the ravine finally came into sharper focus. Three gaping tunnels to the depths. A narrow cleft ahead. And from high above, more dragons roared. Yet Holt still couldn't feel their cores. The dense fog must have blocked his sense of them.

Shrill whistles drew his attention: several stingers were plunging toward them. With the pass narrowing, Ash couldn't risk veering aside again. Holt squeezed onto Ash harder with his legs, then sent Shock after Shock at the stingers, but with the harsh angles and the jerking speed, he missed every time.

Desperate, Holt readied more Shocks, then felt another mental and spiritual tug from his sheathed sword, insistent this time. It had a solution for him, giving him the clear sense of a dazzling ray of purest moonlight.

Trusting the steel, Holt drew his sword. Taking it in both hands, he channeled power to the blade as if for an empowered Shock, except now he willed the lunar steel to release the magic as a ray.

The result was a beam of power like Ash's solid breath, shooting out for dozens of feet and holding. Holt dragged the ray through the air, slicing through each stinger as he did so, severing one right through its bulbous abdomen. The creature howled to its second death as Ash sped on, pounding with his wings before tucking them in tight – all thought bent toward navigating the cleft.

"I can make it," Ash assured him.

Holt braced.

Ash entered the fissure. The thumbs of his wings scraped against stone, then they burst into a wider canyon on the other side. Groaning, Ash unfurled his wings and began to rise. Tall columns of rock caused a ricochet of sound Holt found dizzying, but Ash weaved his way through the maze.

Thankfully, no scourge threatened them here.

Sadly, three fire dragons found them instead.

The dragons dropped below the fog, and Holt felt their presence racing after them. Yet the canyon would be dark to them, and the pillars of rock dangerous obstacles. One dragon immediately crashed into a column, and a bone-breaking crack echoed.

Ash turned around the pillars in tight circles to confuse their pursuers, striking them at their narrowest points with his hard breath. Holt assisted with rays from his sword whenever he could.

Round and round the maze they flew until their joint attack at last battered a stone column into splitting. It swayed, then fell with a yawning groan, and boom after ringing boom thundered as countless pillars knocked into each other.

Ash pulled magic directly from his core to fuel his flight as the two remaining fiery cores winked out. Beating his wings hard, Ash climbed out of the canyon, up through the green mist, back up to the surface world.

Two more cores popped into Holt's perceptions as though from nothing. The fire dragons bellowed, swerved, and headed toward them.

Ash yearned for Holt to open his eyes again, but he kept them shut.

"Stay straight ahead!" he told Ash, then sheathed his sword and raised both hands. Magic coursed down his arms and balled in his palms.

The fire dragons converged upon them, jaws wide, claws primed.

Holt released both Flares at the same time. Even with his bandanna down, he saw a dull flash through his eyelids. Their pursuers howled and flailed violently in the air; one even started falling, and the other two did not pursue them.

With no other dragons on their tail, Holt raised his blindfold and opened his eyes.

An expanse of flat, parched land stretched beneath them, only turning green again miles from the Great Chasm's edge. The Fae Forest was still well beyond the edge of sight, but Holt kept the trees, the glade, and the grotto at the forefront of his mind. Aberanth bustled into the image, smiling shyly. He shared this with Ash, and the dragon released a fretful roar before he drove on harder, faster than he'd ever flown before.

Their friend needed them.

48

THE WAR BEGINS

The dead lay on tables of stone, side by side and head to toe. The dead lay still while the living shuffled with bowed heads. The dead were many.

As Talia entered the mort house of the Toll Pass fortress, she extinguished the fire on her crown out of respect, then drifted between the undertakers who cared for the fallen.

As a girl, she'd found undertakers frightening, with their gray hoods and gray masks. Their scented candles released a pungent floral smoke that made her lightheaded before becoming a rider. She disliked the sweet aroma even more now, like sugar dunked in her nairnroot tea, but for normal humans, the candles would be a welcome relief.

The gray-hooded men and women moved like ghosts. Some carried stiff rolls of parchment, taking note of the names for the rolekeepers; others stripped the dead of valuable gear; still others washed the bodies before pulling white gowns over their heads. Undertakers were known to have stiff upper lips, working in silence. Not so the comrades of the fallen. Wherever soldiers crept to identify friends or company members, stifled sobs could be heard the length of every stone aisle.

As well as the undertakers, Talia noticed an unusual number of officers, Knight-Captains, and even Knight-Commanders assisting in performing the rites.

Amid the grim company, Talia found who she was looking for. Her Master of War stood by one of the corpses. Half of the dead soldier's face lay hidden behind hair matted with blood, dirt, and worse, his skin was blue with cold, and his torso was covered with many black bruises. Wielding a wet cloth, Drefan washed the soldier. Indeed, he seemed so absorbed in the task that he didn't react to Talia until she arrived right before him.

"Your commitment to your men is humbling."

It took Drefan a moment to register her. He looked weathered. His uniform and clothes – including the blue hawk tabard of his house – were still crisp and well-fitted, but his hair was disheveled, his face darkened by stubble, and his eyes swollen red. The ragged tissue on his left ear looked inflamed.

"Talia," he said by way of greeting, as though he'd been expecting her. "In this tragedy, I proposed all should help give dignity to the fallen. No one required that to be made an order." He wiped something dark and crusted off the soldier's chest.

Harroway's letter had detailed the Risalian and Athran attack. Upon her arrival, Talia had learned that the enemy had dragged the bodies up the valley and left them there for the Feorlens to collect. Black-clad messengers had then ridden to the fortress to declare Talia's crimes and demand justice against her.

Drefan continued to wash the soldier. When he reached the man's face, his hand trembled. The water ran red onto the stone bed. He dipped the cloth into a bowl, wrung it out, then brought it back to the soldier's head. A final pass returned the man's hair to its natural golden hue. His now-cleaned face was otherwise unharmed. He might have been sleeping.

Drefan smiled weakly. "That's better."

Plainly the soldier meant more to Drefan than a regular member of the rank and file.

"Who was he?" Talia asked.

"His name is... was... Ulrich. He came from a long line of knights from my family's lands. We trained together as boys, honed our swordcraft together, fought together. We should have..." The rest of his words died in his throat.

Talia had the feeling he'd wanted to say, 'We should have died together.'

Aware they were still in public, she asked him, "Did you love this friend?"

Drefan did not take his eyes off the fallen knight. "Very much."

What a painful decision to order the retreat rather than fight through to ensure his dear friend was safe. A sound decision, taken with the benefit of his whole army, the wider war, and all Feorlen in mind.

Talia feared she would not have made the same one.

Drefan cleaned the stone of blood and grime, washed his hands, then readied the white gown. Talia stepped in to assist, lifting Ulrich upright. Drefan said a quiet "Thank you" before pulling the gown over Ulrich's head and fitting his arms through the sleeves.

"I feel I owe you an explanation," Talia said. As she spoke, Drefan busied himself by tying the strings and laces to fit the generic gown onto Ulrich's body. When Talia finished her tale, she braced herself and said, "You succeeded where I failed."

"This doesn't feel like success." Drefan tied a knot at Ulrich's wrist, then stepped back to examine the work. "I appreciate the self-reflection, Talia, but you might be being too generous to me and too hard on yourself. You're a rider. All that power... I can only imagine what that feels like. You can dream of such feats because it's possible. Would I have gone after Fynn like that? Would I have advised it? No. But then, I'm just a man. If I were a rider, perhaps I might have thought to hold the gates on my own. It's easy to say what another person should have done, especially when you will never be in that situation yourself. As for the Risalians, they can hang their excuses. Their own crimes need answering."

He smoothed down the wrinkles of the white gown, leaving Ulrich pristine and peaceful.

"Though, if I may ask," Drefan continued, "why did you go?"

Her shoulder throbbed, and for a fleeting moment, the short sword of the Drugar seemed to pierce her again. She gritted her teeth, rolled her shoulder, then, almost dream-like, Talia fell into repeating her usual story – of saving her husband who was vital to her alliances, though this time, she managed to stop herself before the twist in her chest reached its full blaze. She still managed to give herself away with a wince.

Drefan looked concerned, and though he could not have known about souls and spiritual pain, he had the intuition to ask her, "What's the real reason?"

And perhaps because he'd bravely confided in her before or because love clearly caused him so much pain, Talia began to speak without any filter.

As she spoke, she realized the truth of why she'd gone. In the end, it came down to a sheer refusal to let one more person she cared about go without her help.

Her father.

Her brother.

Not Fynn. Not him too.

Her soul stirred. When next she breathed, her chest swelled, and a deep tension within her unwound.

Leaving Drefan to attend to Ulrich, Talia hastened out of the mort house to find Pyra, all the while keeping that bubbling sensation around her dragon bond at a low simmer. Feeling the anticipation, Pyra rushed to meet her, causing men to scatter as she bounded across the inner yard of the fortress.

As they met head to snout, Talia closed her eyes and looked inward.

It's not only anger that fuels our fires. Love burns hotter.

Love for her family. Love for her friends. Love for her people.

Pyra rumbled so hard she shook.

"That's why you lost control, girl," Talia told her. *"Because you'd thought you'd lost me."*

"No fire rider has ever mentioned such a thing."

Talia knew that better than most. Never during her late studies in the library of the Crag had she come across such writings.

"Riders swear away from love and family. We're supposed to be unfeeling so we don't compromise our decision-making. There's something

to be said for that, after what we've done... but there may be something here the Order has long missed."

Pyra snorted. *"We've done so much against the Order already... why not this?"* She laughed then, a deep, haughty laugh, making her sound more like her younger self before all the troubles of being tied to the Red Queen. *"I knew we would do great things, Talia! Yes! Let us wholly redefine what it is to wield fire until Adaskar himself comes seeking our knowledge and aid."*

She roared hard and high.

Talia opened her eyes to find them wrapped in a vortex of thin red flames, spinning higher than the fortress walls. Their bond widened and strengthened. Now the heat in Talia's channels felt less volatile than before, as if she had finally opened her ears to its voice and better understood its language.

Then Talia felt an entirely new sensation. Her soul expanded, burning outward much like her dragon bond, swelling for the first time. A new power wove vitality and resolve around the strands of flame. Its scent and taste hit the back of her throat like fresh wood smoke on a crisp winter's day.

Taken aback by its sudden appearance, a burst of her spirit pulsed outward, traveling far enough to touch some of the New Order perched within the valley. Many answering roars reverberated between the hills and mountain peaks.

Strang reached out to them. *"Well done, Red Queen. Well done inde—"* Strang's voice cut out, and one by one, the others fell quiet. *"They have come,"* he said at last.

Other riders crossed into the very edge of Talia's perceptions.

Ten pairs there were, out in the Risalian skies. And the group was mighty. Only one was an Ascendant, whose flickering aura felt familiar to them. Seven Champions there were too, most of them Exalted. The remaining two were Lords. It had been some time since Talia had felt the presence of such powerful riders. Their weight seemed to bend the world, as though all motes were drawn toward them. One of the Lords seemed distantly familiar to her as well, though she couldn't place the feeling.

Their collective strength radiated outward as though to mock the New Order. Talia's side had the numbers; eleven pairs, including herself and Pyra, and five wild emeralds. Yet they only had five Champions – Talia, Ethel, Oline, Yax, and Druss – against Adaskar's seven, while their emeralds, including Turro, were little better than High Ascendants in power. The rest of their company – Hugon, Alvah, Sokeh, Kamal, Florry, and Ulf – were still only Ascendants. Galasso remained in Sidastra, for Liliane's wing still troubled her, as did Pello and the rest of their Novices. Lucia had returned south to aid ships on the Stretched Sea.

There was no one else they could call upon or hope would arrive to assist them. And Adaskar's two Lords alone might destroy them.

Despite all their conviction, Talia wavered. Perhaps this would end quicker than she'd imagined.

No one attacked, but the Falcaer riders stayed, and they watched. The tension never left the magical landscape nor the skies, making sleep elusive for every member of the New Order at the Toll Pass.

Wherever they flew for reconnaissance, the Falcaer riders shadowed them, but they didn't engage, and so the New Order gathered a picture of the broadening conflict. They discovered that the Frayed Banners and Stricken Souls had assaulted the Brenin gatehouse because King Roland pursued them with a Brenish army. Given the damage the companies had inflicted on Brenin, Talia didn't imagine her uncle had been in a merciful mood. Throwing themselves at the gatehouse had evidently been more appealing.

The gamble had paid off, although with Roland closing in behind, it seemed whatever exorbitant amount the companies had been paid didn't stretch to defending the gatehouse to the death. Since the attack, the mercenaries had marched up the valley to the safety of Risalia, replaced by regular Risalian and Athran troops.

During a long meeting into the night, Harroway, tireless and with a new zeal, proposed a plan to retake the valley.

"With your uncle's troops in position, we need only cut the Risalian and Athrans in two at the crossroads in the valley and then retake the Brenin gatehouse. With their reinforcements, we can push the enemy out of the pass altogether."

Though prepared in short order, the attack seemed well-planned down to the last detail. The generals were confident. The only issue was timing, for the Risalians were digging in. Trenches already crisscrossed the valley with mangonels, catapults, and smaller trebuchets to defend against counterattacks. The longer they waited, the more costly retaking the valley would become until the cost would be too high. The great trebuchets could be spotted from the fortress's observation deck, slowly being disassembled piece by piece, no doubt to be rebuilt in range of the main fortress. The Risalians were even readying ballistas such as might be used against stingers.

Or dragons.

On the second night after Talia arrived in the pass, while the Risalians dug in and the watchers watched, Talia and the New Order assisted in laying the Feorlen dead upon the funeral pyres. Given the delay in collecting the bodies, many already swelled with the death bloat, but once atop wood and kindling, at a distance, the rows of white gowns appeared solemn and dignified.

Drefan conducted the rites from horseback before the assembled men and women who garrisoned the Toll Pass. By the end, his voice ran hoarse as he ordered the fires to be lit.

The fire riders assisted in this. Pyra's amber eyes were hard set as she lit the bonfire upon which Ulrich lay.

"I feel as though I've lit too many pyres of late."

Talia agreed. There were also the losses they had not been present for. The Life Elder and those of his kin who had fallen in the north. Pyra thought of Rake. There had been no funeral for him either.

Talia's thoughts turned to Holt and Ash, out there, somewhere, in the wide world.

I hope you're both safe.

After the funerals, the garrison retired for an early night without feast or song. For the dawn would bring their vengeance.

In the deep blue before first light, Talia stood on the observation deck with Ethel and Drefan. All had been agreed.

"As soon as we see smoke, we'll enter the valley," Drefan said.

Talia nodded, then checked in with Ethel. "If the watchers are waiting for cause, this will be it. I don't expect or demand any of you to come to my aid. I just hope that you will."

"Strang and I will be there." Ethel followed this up with a strand of spiritual power that wove around Talia's soul and tied an unbreakable promise. "Feorlen was and is my home as well."

There was nothing left to do or discuss. Talia untied a small pouch at her waist containing strips of beef jerky soaked in vinegar. She ate a few as she made her way to Pyra.

So it was that under the thin, watery light from the east, Talia and Pyra descended into the valley. The flames on Talia's crown burst higher and hotter than before.

Pyra took the first catapult with her talons, breaking the frame, crashed into the second, set the third on fire. Risalians and Athrans screamed in confusion; the siege teams climbed onto their machines, hoping to shield them with their bodies. Talia summoned her lashing whip and latched it directly onto wooden beams, then she channeled magic down the flaming thong to set the engines ablaze. The crews wisely fled.

The vinegary beef left a poor taste in her mouth, but it worked wonders as she Sank her mote channels. Fire crossed the bond in a smooth, controlled flow, hotter and more invigorating than ever.

For the first time since becoming a Champion, Talia felt the true strength of her new rank as she whipped one Risalian siege machine after the next, burning her enemy's ability to cause harm to her people. Love of them drove her, not mere queenly duty. Pyra was moved by Talia in turn, and when a ballista bolt whistled toward them, she incinerated it in midair.

Through the Risalian pass they flew, over the gatehouse, toward the great trebuchets with blistering speed. Fire, talon, and tail left the siege equipment as smoldering mounds of broken, charred wood.

Pyra's roar of victory had barely left her mouth when the pressure of the watchers pressed upon them. The Falcaer riders were closing in. One of the Lords flew ahead with such extreme speed they could only be a wind-rider.

"By order of Falcaer," came the familiar voice of a female dragon, *"disengage at once."*

Pyra placed the voice first. *"Mistress Hava?"*

"Disengage," Hava said, *"and follow us."*

Farsa and Hava sped into view, heading a little way to the south, where the Red Rush flowed down from the rugged mountains, and Talia and Pyra followed after them.

Pyra touched down near the banks of the river. Its own endless roar reverberated amid densely packed trees. Here they were on the other side of the Toll Pass, but the highest towers of the fortress could still be seen between the peaks and treetops. Talia could also hear the Feorlen horns, their peerless drones heralding Drefan's counterattack into the valley.

The rest of the watchers came. Now they were closer, Talia spotted Einar and Skree.

Pyra reached out to them. *"We wish we could take back what happened."*

"There is nothing left to say here, rogue."

Farsa dismounted from Hava and beckoned Talia to her.

"Kneel," Farsa said.

"I'd rather die on my feet."

Farsa cocked her head, yet somehow, her sleek black hair remained still. A pressure emanated from her. Having only just expanded her soul, Talia found it crushing. Alongside that force came a question.

'Are you sure you deserve that?'

Talia tried to answer, but her fledgling strength and the open wound of her guilt held her back. In failure, she found herself sinking to one knee, though she took comfort in how her body shook on the way down. Some part of her tried to resist.

Farsa drew her sword and held it above Talia's shoulder.

"You're a Champion now, with a little spirit in you. And so young. It seems turning rogue is the key to advancement. We should have joined Master Rake in the wilds long ago."

"And you're a Lady, congratulations."

Farsa dipped her head in acknowledgment. Her steely face gave nothing away.

Talia licked her lips. She was painfully aware of Farsa's sword above her ear. It seemed to hum.

"Is it true?" Farsa asked. "Did you burn that town to help the Empress?"

"Is that what they think? It's not true, but the town did burn, and though we never intended it, it was our fault."

The hum from Farsa's sword seemed to grow.

"All I wanted," Talia went on, "was to save my people and fight the scourge. I hoped not to have to fight anyone else... but I will if I have to."

Farsa raised her brow. "Even against a Lady and a Lord?"

Talia's soul burned gently. "If I don't, then I never truly believed in the cause."

Farsa made the smallest of smiles.

Talia risked breaking eye contact to look at the force arrayed against her. She could not win.

"Are you going to take me back to Falcaer?" Talia asked.

"Those are our orders. This is a last test of loyalty for some of us."

"What happens if you fail?"

"That will depend on the manner in which we fail."

Now it was Farsa who risked a glance to the west. The New Order were behind the mountains guarding the mouth of the river.

Farsa returned her attention to Talia. "Are the others prepared to fight with you?"

Talia gulped. "We'll find out."

"Are you prepared?" Farsa shifted her eyes subtly to her left. Over her shoulder, the High Fire Lord waited not so far away.

"I am," Talia said, even if such a fight lasted no longer than it took for Adaskar to fly from Falcaer. Her only surprise was the creeping feeling that Farsa was foolish enough to join in that same doom. "Are you?"

Farsa nodded slowly. She raised her sword like an executioner, then, with furious speed, she turned and unleashed a gale of wind. Hava beat her wings, adding to the windstorm. The sudden upsurge drove the hovering dragons back and made even those aground turn aside to avoid it – all save for two Ice and Emerald Champions, who rushed forward unfazed.

Talia jumped to her feet and drew her sword. Pyra hurried to her side.

Every core upon the magical landscape flashed, readying for battle.

All this happened within moments, then the High Lord of Fire flicked his wrist, and Farsa's storm dissipated. Swords rang from sheathes, and an Exalted Mystic Champion hefted a great mace.

Then two others broke away from the Falcaer watchers. Another ice and another emerald, both High Champions, turned tail and fled to the northeast. This divided the attention of the watchers, who were now reduced to five: the High Fire Lord; Einar and Skree; and the three Champions, two mystics and one fire, all of whom were Exalted and pushing at the boundaries of Lords.

The pause from the watchers allowed Talia, Farsa, and their two new companions to gather themselves. Talia wolfed down a piece of gingered beef and switched her cycling to Floating. No sooner had she raised her magical defenses than the High Fire Lord – a true giant of a man – cried out to his riders, "Leave them! Focus on the girl."

Talia wondered whether Adaskar had sent a man of Risalia to bring her in on purpose.

A scorching spiritual pressure surged for her even as a rushing wind rose to shield her. Farsa gasped as she vied spiritually with the High Lord, then backed off, almost stumbling as she went, her steely features breaking into a grimace.

A chill came to strengthen the struggling winds. Strang's sharp roar rang between the peaks as Ethel, Oline, Druss, Yax,

and all the others descended to assist. Hugon and Enhadyr's
Battle Song filled their hearts. For a wild moment, Talia believed
she could take a High Lord head-on, and the New Order flew at
the watchers, who awaited the incoming blow as a mountain
stands uncaring amid a storm. Even the arrival of Turro and the
wild emeralds didn't make the watchers blink. The High Lord's
dragon advanced, his heavy feet pounding into the soft earth,
issuing steam and smoke.

The two sides met.

Fire raged, ice speared, wind battered, rock and earth were
hurled, lightning forked, and arcane powers exploded. One of the
mystic watchers blurred out, then five copies of him appeared on
the battlefield, each indistinguishable from the original. One
copy engaged Talia, and every stroke of its sword felt and
sounded real.

She lost sense of the wider fight, save for her own footing
and swordwork and the sense of Pyra flying overhead. It quickly
became clear that her mystic opponent – real or not – was trying
to disarm rather than kill her.

Soon the press of battle thinned as members of the New
Order fell to their knees and the High Lord stepped away from
them, trailing strands of spiritual yields.

The New Order were herded together.

Talia glimpsed a gray-clad rider moving at great speed.
Einar's face was distorted with a zealous frenzy as he half-ran,
half-sped on conjured wind through a gap in the battle, sword
raised, his warped eyes fixed on Pyra.

Talia warned Pyra across their bond, then she was forced to
parry a blow from the mystic copy. Pyra received the warning but
could not move to meet the threat. A surge of panic threatened
to drown all else from their minds, then suddenly it broke.

A dragon screamed in tremendous pain, cutting across the
battlefield, and ended hard in a death rattle.

Talia's heart almost froze. She thought Pyra had been slain,
but then she felt the bond still hot in her chest, and the relief
almost brought her to tears.

Yet a dragon had died. As Talia's illusory foe disengaged

from the fight and moved to regroup with the rest of the Falcaer riders, the High Lord shouted orders in his amplified voice.

"Get back, Ascendant. Leave this place!"

The body of a wild emerald lay sprawled before Einar. Dark blood ran from his sword, his expression livid, perhaps furious at the emerald for getting in his way.

Talia raced to Pyra's side even as Einar rushed in, but Turro reached him first. He fell upon the wind rider from above, driving him into the dirt with chipped and bloodied talons. Turro's core shone with dazzling power, drained, and the earth dragged Einar down, hardening to stone until only the tip of his long sword remained visible.

Skree's roar of anguish confirmed the kill. She descended upon Turro with murderous intent, and two wild emeralds, Enhadyr, and Pyra came to his aid. They pinned Skree down. Held in place, her core vanished in a flash of full use. A tornado of black wind spun into being, tearing riders off their feet before Farsa tamed and dispersed it.

Drained and tormented, Skree would not settle. She would not listen. She thrashed and bit and vowed death on all of them. After her tail struck Enhadyr across his snout, spraying blood, Pyra lunged for her neck.

After Skree fell still, Talia readied herself for the full wrath of the watchers. There would be no more yielding after this. Not now the first blood had been drawn.

The Falcaer riders were still in a tight formation around the High Lord.

"No more good rider blood will be risked," he called. "Enjoy what time remains to you, traitors." With that, he and his Exalted Champions flew from the mouth of the river. No celebratory roar chased them on their way.

Talia joined Ethel and Farsa over the bodies of Einar and Skree. For some reason, everyone seemed to be waiting for her decision on what to do with them.

"We are holding to our oaths in our way, as they held to theirs," she said. "They should be burned with all honors, and

Einar's sword shall be returned to Falcaer in time to hang with all the rest."

Turro and his kin held their snouts over their fallen sister, humming a mournful lament.

Pyra approached the group with her head respectfully low. *"The blade was meant for me. I hope to prove the sacrifice worthwhile."*

Turro closed his eyes and lowered his neck in return. *"Her death was for a higher purpose, Red Bane. The oak that shall grow over her body will be tall and broad and long-living."*

The New Order parted to give the wild emeralds space. Altogether, Turro and his three kin joined in another audible song. The body of their sister began to sink into the earth as if lowered down by gentle hands, and soil and stone refilled the hole. When it was over, a small mound marked the site, covered in thick grass and speared by a young sapling reaching three feet into the sky.

It would have been a quiet, beautiful, and peaceful privilege to watch had it not been for the blaring Feorlen horns, the beating Risalian drums, and the screech of steel within the Toll Pass. From the south came the bright tones of Brenish trumpets.

Here by the river, Ethel knelt before Farsa. "We're grateful to have you join us, Honored Lady. Although I fear this venture won't be long-lived."

Farsa bade her stand. "The honor is mine. As for Adaskar, if he comes, then he comes, but do not brood over this doom. I think Adaskar will be occupied by larger matters for some time."

Talia dreaded to think what greater issues would concern the Paragon of Fire that was not Thrall or the Hive Mind. She tried, however, to take Farsa's advice and not to brood over such doom until the day should come.

49

HEALING TRUTHS

Rake looked between Osric and his dragon again, then scratched his chin.

"Run me through it once more time."

Osric huffed. "Keep up this time."

Rake raised his brow. "If I am to be used as target practice, I want to at least be sure there is some actual risk to my life... elsewise, where's the fun?"

Osric scowled but didn't answer him. Braced in front of the quarry wall, he called to his dragon, "Are you ready?"

The black dragon attempted to strike a fearsome expression. She wasn't quite as small as before, though barely so, and still very slender for a dragon. Given she still hadn't picked a name, Rake still thought of her as 'Soot.'

At least she was talking now. That was progress.

"I'm ready," Soot said.

"Then go on, try and hit me," said Osric.

Soot did, shooting shadowy ball after shadowy ball at her rider in a steady rhythm.

As Osric blocked the barrage, he explained his theory again.

"Her magic swings wildly from weak to incredibly powerful. I think it's due to whether or not the target sees it coming. If they do, it impairs her magic somehow."

When Soot's next attack came, Osric let his hand fall by his side and took the hit full in the chest as though it were no more than a leaf blown on the breeze.

Rake followed but wasn't sure this was a thorough explanation. "You also *knew* it was coming," he said. "What if she caught you by surprise?"

"That could be a factor," Osric said, "although just before you and Gea arrived, she accidentally hit one of the Hounds. The man saw it coming, but he can't have been expecting it, and he was completely fine."

Rake scratched his chin again. Admittedly, this was rather intriguing. Such a magical effect would be bizarre even by mystic standards.

He spread his arms wide. "Hit me, Soot."

She growled. *"I don't like that name."*

"Then I advise you choose one you do like. Everyone needs a name. You can't just be 'little black' foreve—"

Soot attacked. Rake saw the magic leave Soot's mouth and observed its trajectory as the orb of shadow hissed into his midriff.

"That the best you got? I've had flies land on me with more impact." He chuckled. "Okay, Grumps, I'll bite. That Champion at Silt Grave didn't see it coming, I take it?"

"I had the rider distracted. At Blackhollow, I had a cultist focused on me, and she tore right through the dragon-hide cloak like it was nothing."

"No small feat," Rake admitted.

"Moments before that, she hit a cultist, and the attack did nothing. He saw her magic coming dead on. Finally, in the Jackal's Den, she pounced from inside my shadow at one of our prisoners and sent him halfway across the hall."

"An ambush from the shadows. A sneak who can plunge her talons deep into your back." Rake smirked. "It doesn't exactly mesh with your style, does it?"

The former general, learned in the techniques of the Skarl berserker, shook his head.

"Very well," Rake said. "I'll be your test subject." He Floated his mote channels, forming a layer of magical armor over his body. "Let's trust my cycling is stronger than a dragon-hide cloak. Give it your all, Soot."

As expected, she growled again and shot another frail shadow ball at him, which puffed out to nothingness against his armor. Soot side-stepped, sending a few more attacks as she moved that Rake didn't even bother to deflect, then she slipped into the shadow of a storehouse.

Rake lost track of her, but he wasn't trying very hard to find her, just waiting, tapping his foot. Then something slammed into his lower back, forcing him to take stumbling steps to regain his balance. His Floating held, but he could feel the reverberations from the attack through his channels like a gong ringing between his ears.

Osric grunted louder than usual, which Rake took to be his form of celebration.

Soot slid out of the shadow of a miner's cottage, looking pleased with herself, then bounded over to Osric, who dropped to one knee to speak quietly to her.

Rake dusted himself off with mock exaggeration and was about to congratulate the pair of them when Gea reached out to him in a hurried manner.

"More scourge approach. Wyrm Cloaks as well, though I can't count them this far away."

Instinctively, Rake gazed to the skies above Redbarrow to try and spot the emerald, but she was out of sight.

"I take it our brutish friend remains?" Rake asked.

"He's still there, stomping back and forth."

The bruiser had remained annoyingly close to Redbarrow – too far for a swift attack to be mounted, yet too close for Rake and Gea to get away unnoticed. At least, not by daylight. It would be simple enough for Rake to slip out under cover of night undetected, but that would mean leaving Gea behind, and annoyingly, that didn't sit right with him.

A decision would have to be made soon. They'd only spent one day resting in Redbarrow, but in that time, Thrall's forces had gathered around the ginger dragon with remarkable speed.

"We've brought the enemy here early," Gea said.

"You heard Osric, another day, another week, this was always coming. Half the Frontier is in ruins." They'd both witnessed the devastation on their mad dash across the territory.

"Just the way of it, is it?"

"I suppose so," Rake said, a little lamely for his liking, but what could he say that would make her feel better? Things were just this bad, and they had a pressing matter of their own to attend to.

"Better inform Grumps," Rake said.

Still on one knee, Osric looked skyward.

"You don't have much time," Rake said.

"We've prepared as best we can." Osric got to his feet and adjusted the strap of his iron buckler. "What will you do?"

Rake hesitated, a feeling so strange he had to resist a shiver.

"I have to warn the Mystic Elder."

"Then we wish you luck."

Rake frowned, though he was unsure what bugged him so much. "You're terribly calm about all of this."

The corner of Osric's lip twitched. "Should I be running around naked, flapping my arms and screaming?"

"It's just..." Rake began, twisting the shaft of his polearm in his hands. "You'll all die."

"Most likely," Osric said, as though he couldn't care less.

Holt and Ash would be devastated if Soot died, and Rake had no trouble admitting he'd become fond of her too. Rake supposed this was his doing too. He'd been the one to tell Osric to seek a way to heal the wounds in his soul... and here he was, trying to do so like a good soldier.

Part of him wanted to stay and help. But the ruthless, logical part of him asserted that warning the Elder was far more important.

"You're welcome to stay as long as you want," Osric said. "But if this is where we part again, then—"

"Another dragon has come," Gea said, this time to all of them, including Soot. *"It looks reddish."*

"Like rust?" Soot asked.

"Yes, it could be."

"The one powered by blood," Soot said.

The healing dragon, or so Osric claimed.

The brawler and his personal physician. A deadly combination.

Yes, the defenders of Redbarrow were certainly going to die.

"An attack will be imminent," Osric said. "I'd appreciate you telling me when you're leaving by telepathy. You need not waste time trying to find me."

And with that, Osric turned on his heel.

"Wait," Rake called.

Osric halted, glanced back.

"In matters of the soul, truth is key. Truth can be healing – do you understand me?"

"I fear I do," Osric said. He inclined his head, then strode off. Soot scurried after him.

Rake very much wanted to say more, though he wasn't sure what. He remained rooted to the spot, frozen by a most irksome sense of indecision, then he sensed Gea flying closer. She swooped into view at last, then came to land by him.

"I'd like to talk."

"You know, one of the benefits of telepathy is that you don't have to be close by."

"Some things are best said face to face."

Rake read her face like an open book. He'd seen and heard enough foolish heroics in his time to know what she was going to say.

"Why do you want to stay?"

"Because you have a better chance of getting away on your own. Because the Mystic Flight will be less likely to reveal themselves if I'm with you. Because this is partly our fault, and defending a town against a scourge attack, this… this is what I know."

"What about outcasts sticking together?"

"What about doing what's right?"

"For goodness' sake, must all my companions be so high-minded?"

"Almost sounds like you care."

"I… bah," he growled, twisting his polearm as if he were wringing its neck. Holt and Ash weren't dead, they just weren't, but a part of him knew they might be. "Fine, I *care*," he said, cringing. "I love to take a risk as much as the next half-dragon, but even I don't think we should fight a hopeless battle with little commensurate gain for the odds. What's the point?"

"The point is just to do it."

"Sounds like lying down and giving up to me."

Gea flapped her wings and scowled. *"Perhaps sometimes that's what we should do."* Her voice crept higher. *"Sometimes, I wish Orvel had given up on trying to advance. Maybe he wouldn't have turned so bitter about everything. He could have accepted our place as Low Champions. Would that have been so terrible? Not every rider can make it to Paragon – it's not possible – but Champions can still do a lot of good, like defending a town from the scourge. We could have been happy helping in our own way... Instead, he's dead."*

She was plainly determined, and an internal war waged within Rake.

Well, that's her choice, the ruthless side of him said. Rake could complete the mission alone.

Did we not try that last year?, his softer side asked. Going to Windshear alone hadn't worked out.

Her, Grumps, even Soot, they don't matter in the grand scheme, the ruthless part of him said, *but—*

Rake silenced that part of himself. The thing about spending time with others is that you start to care. First, it had been Eidolan, then Aberanth, then Holt and Ash, and now this sorry lot.

Having given Holt a lecture on thinking and acting truthfully, Rake would be a poor mentor not to take his own advice.

If I go, he thought wretchedly, *I'll regret it.*

"In matters of the soul," Rake said, "truth is key. Truth can be healing. Do you understand me?"

Osric became painfully aware of his soul again. It hurt. It felt like one of the thorns from his knotted bond to Thrall remained lodged there, though he kept that hurt to himself as he inclined his head and said, "I fear I do."

Feeling there was nothing more to say, he strode off, leaving Rake to head up the hill.

"Not to the gates?" the dragon asked, hurrying along at his side.

"First to the lookout point."

He arrived, accepted the spyglass, and placed an eye against its lens. Sure enough, Gea was right. The rusty dragon flew back and forth over the gathering swarm while the ginger bruiser paced below, and there was little chance they were just here to keep an eye on Rake and Gea.

Osric folded the spyglass into itself with a snap. "Time to start the evacuation," he said, more for himself than the few Hounds present. To them, he added, "Ready yourselves for battle. I'll inform the Jackal."

After a short dash across the hilltop, he and the black dragon entered the Den. The hall was better lit than when Osric had first arrived but emptier, for the long tables had been sent down the hill to form part of the barricades. Only the Jackal's high seat with the carved dogs remained.

The Jackal was on one knee, trying to soothe his dogs as they yelped at the dragon's approach. Members of his crew stood around him, the oldest, toughest, most gnarled of the Hounds.

Osric strode right up to them and told them, "It's time."

To their credit, none of the Jackal's men looked afraid.

They should be.

The Jackal's great ears rose, looking more pointed than ever. "You heard the man. Get runnin' to it, ya slack dogs. Go, go, go!"

Osric turned to leave, but the Jackal grabbed his arm.

"She's through the back. I dunno every detail of what's been goin' on between you, but I know she'd wanna see ya before the killin' starts."

Osric hesitated. A final farewell with Petrissa loomed more terrifying than facing the ginger bruiser and his blood healer. Better to face something dreadful head-on at full tilt without overthinking it. That's why you ought to bellow and charge into a fight rather than whisper and saunter. All the same, Osric found this battle hard to charge into.

The dragon gave him a nudge across their bond. *"You have to tell her while you still can."*

Osric stiffened his lip. He adored his dragon, though it was sometimes rough having someone bonded to you who knew what you needed better than you did. There was no hiding with her.

"I'll be there with you," she said.

He smiled and breathed deep, his eyes on the back door leading out of the hall. While it could be rough having a bond such as this, her support outweighed any downside.

"I'll go," Osric said, giving the Jackal a light thump on the back as they parted.

Bells were clanging by the time he found her. The dragon's weight in his shadow felt comforting this time, though his soul continued to throb, as if something was pressing on the thorn.

"Mother…" he began, then struggled for more.

"Yes?"

"It's time. They're coming."

"I can hear the bells." She hesitated. "Thank you for helping us… I didn't deserve it, but the people here—"

"There's something I need to tell you."

Petrissa looked taken aback, then she settled and gave him an encouraging smile.

Better to charge the enemy while screaming, he thought. *Better to run in, not to overthink it.*

His dragon lent him a little courage to help him into this charge.

"It's about Godric," he said, every word a fight to get out. "About what happened to him in the war."

"Oh?" A shadow passed over her face. For the first time, Petrissa showed her age.

"The Risalians did attack him in the fortress of the Toll Pass, and they did breach the outer wall, that much is true… but he didn't die at their hands."

Osric gulped. *Better to charge in screaming.*

"I killed him." Now he'd said it, the truth poured out of him. "I flanked the Risalians, routed them, led the charge to retake the fortress, ran past all my men, up every level, killing Risalians along the way, took one of their maces, and crushed Godric's chest with it."

Petrissa's expression was blank, almost as if she hadn't heard him. The shadow lingered over her face, and she seemed to shrink and thin before his eyes.

"This..." she said, her voice trembling. "This was when you were... enslaved... by that dragon?"

"It was during that time, but... but the dragon didn't make me do it. He wanted Godric to live, and I... I defied him."

A resentment strong enough to overcome Thrall's domination.

"He would have had me kill Godric eventually," Osric said, as though that made it better. "But when it happened was my choice. I did it."

Another long, terrible silence. Then, slowly, Petrissa nodded, and she bit her lip to stop it shaking.

"Was I really so terrible to turn you into a—"

"A monster? No, not just you. No one thing made me what I am. Blame for all my actions lies solely with me." Osric gulped again. He'd charged into this battle at last, but it wasn't making the fight any easier. "I didn't want to tell you before because... despite it all, I didn't see the point in hurting you. But I've been told the truth can be healing, so—"

"I have something to tell you as well," Petrissa said, rallying herself. "I saw no reason to before, for it could only cause more pain, but if you think the truth is *healing*—"

Osric held his breath. The dragon's heart thudded over their bond.

"—then it's best you know before there's never another chance. You're not an Agravain. You're not Oswyn's son."

For a second, Osric had expected a crippling blow, something awful, something vile. But though Petrissa had struck, Osric didn't feel the hammer. He didn't feel anything.

"Are you sure?"

"I'm certain. Oswyn and I never actually spoke about it, but he knew. That's why he was... the way that he was."

"Huh," Osric said breathily. If this was shock, it felt oddly calming. His prevailing thought wasn't misery or pain; it simply made sense of a lot. It gave reason to much of his life and his father's behavior where it had once seemed arbitrary.

He was not an Agravain.

"The worst part," Petrissa went on, "is I don't know who is."

This slid off him, too, though it really shouldn't have.

He was nameless, roleless, a child born of chaos.

"It doesn't matter," Osric said. Strangest of all, he really meant it. In a way, he didn't want to know. All that mattered was that he wasn't an Agravain.

"I'm so sorry," Petrissa said.

The shock was wearing off now. Osric could feel and move his fingers again. Within his soul, one of the old thorns seemed to ease, wriggling itself free.

"Thank you for telling me." He turned to leave. "I must make ready for battle. You'll be safe as you can inside the mine."

And with that, he retreated, fleeing from the fight. Outside the Den, the black dragon emerged from his shadow to run by his side. Osric kept running, heading down the hill, until, close to the mine, where a throng of people blocked the road, he slowed, then came to a halt.

His heart pumped feverishly, far faster than such a light run should have caused. As it calmed, he noticed he could see through the dragon bond with greater clarity: the shadowy figures of her core seemed thicker, stronger somehow.

"You were right," he told her over their bond. *"That had to be done."*

"I'm glad you had the chance."

Osric grunted. *"I'm sorry you may not get the same chance with your brother."*

She shuddered from neck to tail. *"I'm not ready for that. I hope he doesn't come. I hope he's somewhere far away."*

Ahead of them, the throng of evacuees started to grind to a halt and risked a crush.

Gathering himself, Osric pushed forward to find Hounds, bark orders, and gain some semblance of control. Once lines had formed and they cleared the road for men and weapons heading to the lower levels, Osric made his way to the gates.

On the way, he assisted in other final preparations, using pulleys from the mine to help hoist heavy loads to hang over choke points in the maze of streets. Two ballista positions had been set up at ground level, hidden behind makeshift barricades, both with a line of sight to the gates. Such hopes to take down the bruiser were a long shot, but some hope was better than none. Osric had each of the crews repeat their orders to confirm they knew their business.

He paced the walls and made many more checks than a general would have to in more civilized places with armies and officers; here, he had thugs and green, unblooded men.

More like green, unblooded boys.

Gea kept a stream of updates coming on the enemy movements until, late in the afternoon, she announced the swarm was advancing on Redbarrow. From the ramparts, not much of the enemy was clear beyond it being a vaguely writhing mass.

Osric stepped onto the gatehouse ramparts to lead directly from the front. No hanging back and issuing orders here. Even if he'd been inclined to do so, logistically, the Hounds couldn't manage it. That they'd divided their fighting men into teams, placed them evenly upon the wall, and supplied each with a stack of rubble from the mine to throw was already quite the achievement.

The scourge came closer, though their shrieking wasn't yet audible. The two dragons appeared to be holding back, letting the bugs soften the defenders up.

Osric tightened the knot at his throat that kept his gray cloak in place, then reached into the pockets, lightly touching the vials to check them. The numbing agent would be vital; the blood elixirs, well, he knew they were there.

Behind him, someone thunked their spear rather loudly.

"Easy," Osric said without turning. "That's a weapon you have, not a toy."

"And yet I have so much fun with it."

Osric twisted around. "I thought you'd be long gone?"

"Being the generous sort that I am," Rake said, smiling widely, "I've decided to stay and help your doomed cause. You're most welcome."

He must have told Gea this at the same time, for she roared in delight above.

The little black dragon cocked her head and rumbled, *"You said you had to warn your Elder."*

"I'll go right after we're finished up here," Rake said.

"You're the one who said we'd all die."

"I did, didn't I? Then I thought about it and decided my own Elder is quite tough. She has four Wardens and an entire Wild Flight to assist her, whereas you lot have"—and here, Rake twirled his polearm with a flourish—"me, so I'd say your odds of survival just shot up."

If the half-dragon was fishing for applause or effusive thanks, Osric wouldn't give him the satisfaction.

"Very well," he said. "Then you'll want to know the plan."

Rake leaned forward on his polearm, expectant. "I hope it's a good one."

Osric explained his strategy, and to his surprise, Rake simply nodded and repeated it back to him without even being asked to. No quip, no jockeying to change it just for the sake of it, just acceptance. The only thing Rake did was reach out with an open hand.

"I'll be needing something venomous then."

Osric gave him a vial of the numbing agent, and Rake slipped it inside his own black cloak.

By now, the swarm's howling, shrieking, and buzzing was audible from across the fallow country. Osric stepped over to the parapet, placing his hand upon the stone.

"I feel like I could have done more."

"In life?" Rake asked, stepping beside him.

"Here," Osric growled, not taking his eyes from the scourge.

"You did a lot with what you had. Shoved a weapon into the

hands of every man who can hold one. Might be there's time to give the boys rocks and clubs too."

Osric snorted. Such things were for bards. He'd heard songs where the defenders summoned every man and boy able to bear a sword for a last glorious stand. All of it hot air. The bards knew nothing of war, else they'd know that boys only get in the way in a real fight. Boys screamed, they cried, they ran away when you needed them to stand. Boys did not defend the living. That was men, with true grit and iron in their veins. And he'd served long enough to know that not all boys were young. Some boys never gained the grit, growing larger but remaining soft. Some boys grew into old ones.

"It's more men I need. Real men, but in Redbarrow, as across the world, there's always a lack of those."

"Men like you?"

"When it's time for blood, suddenly everyone needs men like me."

Monsters like me.

His dragon passed a reproachful feeling over their bond, sharing her memory of watching him save her from the Wyrm Cloaks atop the mystic tower in Windshear Hold. Even bleeding from a fresh stump, the monster in him had taken them all down. An occasion where the monster had been more than welcome.

As the enemy closed upon Redbarrow, Osric gave himself permission to let the monster out.

50

DEFIANT

Upon a once great road in the ruins of Aldunei, with the Great Chasm and the window to the eternal night some miles east, Adaskar and Azarin stood poised against the onset of doom.

Warnings had come that the Storm Flight was heading for Falcaer as well. Against two Wild Flights, abandoning Falcaer was the right choice, if a terrible one.

Even the servants had gone with heavy hearts. The Artisan Smith lamented leaving the new world table incomplete, and Adaskar shared that sorrow. In the aftermath of the coming chaos, its completion would be healing.

It gave him hope.

Thankfully, they did not stand alone.

Thirteen High Lords and Ladies of steely spirit stood with him. He'd asked only for volunteers to face the wroth of the Fire Elder. Dowid – having just returned – had been the first to step forward, but then others followed, then more, until the response became so overwhelming that Adaskar needed to turn most down and assign them to lead the withdrawals.

To his left, an ice and two emeralds huddled with their dragons between the pillars of a once vast gymnasium. To his right, along a boulevard overrun with dark thorns, a Fire Lord and a Mystic Lady braced themselves in the crumbling colosseum. Throughout the ruins, the thirteen made ready.

Adaskar felt their collective spirit strain.

The world held its breath; the air stood still, thick with dust and scourge stench.

A beat of wings and a gruff roar. Visaeyra swooped down, and Dowid jumped from her back. While Visaeyra and Azarin greeted each other with bouts of smoke, Dowid came to Adaskar's side.

Upon one knee, head bent, he said, "The evacuation is complete, Lord Paragon. Only Paragon Eso remains."

Adaskar searched his perceptions, but even he was too far away to feel Eso in slumber. He just hoped their collective presence in the ruins would draw the Fire Flight to them instead of the fortress.

"Rise, Dowid."

The High Lord stood but kept his gaze averted.

"Look at me," Adaskar said. Hesitantly, Dowid did. The weight he carried had dimmed the orange blaze in his eyes. "You followed your orders, and I'd much rather have you here beside me for what may come."

"You're too kind, Lord Paragon." His voice grew thicker. "When you fly to deal with her, I beg that you take me with you."

"You shall have that honor."

Azarin parted from Visaeyra to grunt his assent.

"Dowid," Adaskar said, dropping the man's rank altogether, "you know I've come to rely on you."

The orange flicker returned to Dowid's eyes. "I am humbled, Lord Paragon."

"I trust you will always be honest with me."

"Yes, Lord."

"And should your heart ever feel wary, to speak up, even against my will."

"If it is your desire."

Facing the chasm and the edge of night, Adaskar asked, "Is there anything you would say to me now?"

"I would not see you so burdened, Lord. This strife is not of your making, as no chasm which opens is of your doing."

"I wonder..." Smoke curled from his lips. Azarin rumbled low, and, for a moment, the golden bridge of their bond seemed cast in shadow. "Was it always Vald's intention to break from us? Neveh went to save the Elder of Life, yet some ill befell her and lodged in her soul. Talia Agravain did not intend for fire and death, yet that is what she wrought. A lack of foresight punishes us all.

"All these unintended consequences... This is what I fought against, but there is only so long you can claim fault in all but oneself, only so long you can allow righteous pride to deafen you against any challenge. I did not cause these things, but I bear some responsibility for them. Do you understand what I'm telling you, Dowid?"

The High Lord scrunched his face in consideration.

Pressed for time, Adaskar pulled Dowid closer. "When your time comes, don't repeat my mistakes."

Before Dowid could answer, cores flooded onto the magical landscape from the east.

The Fire Flight had come.

Adaskar saw fear enter Dowid's eyes.

"Stand fast," Adaskar said. "There is always hope."

Azarin came to him, and together the Paragons walked down the old road to meet their guests.

As the flight approached, one dragon's might burned brighter and hotter than the rest. Adaskar studied that presence and compared it to Azarin's power. While the Elder's strength was remarkable, it wasn't so vast as to be unconquerable, and as the flight came into view, another spark of hope arose. Their numbers were less than reported.

Azarin sent out a final reminder of their purpose: to defend Paragons Eso and Wynedd while they slumbered and to spearhead a breakthrough to safety once they woke. Today was not the day for the Order to make its last stand.

The Fire Flight arrived and hovered over the ruins of Aldunei. A red cloak now enveloped the city even as an oppressive gray sky pushed in from the west. Yet for all their power, Adaskar found he could stand tall. Fewer wild dragons could equal a Lord of the Order, it was true, but it went deeper than that, though he could not put it into words.

Azarin tugged on their bond, sharing the same ill-defined feeling, and Adaskar instinctually placed a hand on his dragon's warm, comforting body.

"Long have I dreamed of meeting the Elder of my kin," Azarin said. *"I thought I'd be in awe, yet I find him so... real. A dragon of scales, blood, and bone like any other; mighty, yes, but graspable. I thought my kindred would be noble, bright, and pure as the blue arrow of a flame.*

"Yet I find these drakes... lesser to me. Their spirits are that of fire, but such fire as has never been buffeted by the wind or burned against the cold. It is the greatest disappointment of my life. More than ever, I am glad to have bonded with you. My bonds with Wynedd, Tanyksha, Nilak, and even Raiden'ra are greater for all the ways we have grated against each other."

Adaskar nodded. There was truth in that.

His soul quickened and burned.

Challenge from friends makes us stronger. Only enemies seek to dominate.

For the first time in years, Adaskar felt a tension in his soul ease and lithe new spiritual power stretch out.

He wished he'd realized this sooner.

He wished that none of these things had happened in his time. But they had.

The Elder descended from the red shroud to meet them upon the old road. His scales writhed as though made of living flame, silently raging from red to black. His talons, spine, and the bones of his wingtips were dark as smoke, yet his throat and belly shone like blood under a failing sun. Doubtless his aura was blistering, but Adaskar and Azarin thought it fine as a steaming bath easing old bones.

"The world already burns." The Elder's voice was as steady, confident, and assured as only an Elder's could be. *"The riders have failed to spare the world from chaos. A dragon once of your Order seized the scourge, and you did not realize. Some of your own have joined him. Others swear now to Storm, threatening the balance of power. My*

brother lies dead. All this under your watch. Repent and submit, and I shall make things right."

Despite the magnitude of their foe, Adaskar's first thought was to reflect further on his own behavior.

Is this how the others saw me when I told them to bend the knee?

In quiet agreement, Adaskar and Azarin didn't dignify the Elder's demands with a reply. As the silence stretched out, the Elder growled, and his calm confidence gave way to a livid fury.

"I speak now to your dragons. Where is your self-respect? Or are you so tamed that you let the humans speak and think on your behalf?"

Adaskar sensed the fire dragons on his side shudder. Far behind, Visaeyra thumped her tail.

Azarin gnashed his teeth.

Before the Elder could continue his censure, a male dragon of the flight spoke fiercely for all to hear.

"Elder, I can take no more. I thought we flew to avenge your revered brother and bring a great foe to heel, but this… is hatred. And hatred is cold. It ill-befits us, and I will not be party to it."

At once, a section of the flight broke apart. A great dragon pink as a dogrose led many fire dragons away. Within the press of powers, it was hard to tell at first, but Adaskar realized the retreating dragon was a Warden.

Now he focused, he realized there were only three Wardens in the sky. Where was the fourth?

The Elder did not remove his gaze from Adaskar and Azarin. If he raged against the departure, he did so without projecting it to the riders. Little physically or spiritually changed except for the Elder's eyes, which turned from scarlet to black.

Now seemed the moment to press for a different outcome.

Adaskar cycled power to his throat and called out, "Elder, you broke the spirits of Enya and Solveig, fine Ladies of Fire. Such a crime deserves an answer, but we will grant you a chance to withdraw and so uphold the Pact. Leave now, and there will be no further retribution."

The Elder's countenance turned cruel and mocking. *"You appeal to the Pact?"* he laughed. *"I see now what a meek measure it was.*

I should have acted before now, but the will of the Five maintained it. Now the Five are Four, and old agreements are broken."

Azarin roared and slammed his tail. *"You ridicule our humans at your peril. My rider alone could face even the strongest of your flight."*

Dragons of the Order roared their agreement.

Adaskar began to center himself, his body, his bond, his soul, and his channels for the coming fight.

Then, moving slowly down from the hovering flight, came another Warden. Though visibly smaller than Azarin, this dragon was stout with a crushing jaw and scales of the purest red conceivable. The Warden fixated on Adaskar and bared his teeth in something eerily close to a sly smile.

"You riders claim yourselves the stronger, yet you would presume to face my Elder two against one? Now we are equally matched."

A fair fight? It was so absurd that Adaskar almost drew his sword right then.

The Warden and Elder lowered their jaws to summon power. Many lesser dragons of the flight beat wings and backed off, creating many holes in the red shroud. They at least showed some wisdom. Drakes of Ascendant power or below caught in the crossfire of Lords, Wardens, and Paragons would not last long.

And then, as if by some miracle, another noticeable portion of the Fire Flight began to break away.

"I will not do this, Elder," came a female voice, gallant and full of mettle. *"This is no fair fight. You and Pride have let your disdain and vanity blow you off course. I shall not besmirch my honor nor those of the flight who still hold to such values."*

Leading this latest desertion was the last of the Wardens. A dragon of burnished copper with tints of gold shining even under the grim sky.

As before, if the Elder raged, then he did so only to his flight, or what was left of it. In the dark hearts of his black eyes sprang blue fire, and smoke issued between the gaps in his scales.

Adaskar reached overhead and drew forth his great, red blade. Battle seemed inevitable, but he would impart a final measure of insolence toward the Elder of Fire, this greatest of disappointments.

"You should heed your Warden – those beneath us can reveal what we fail to see."

Whatever restrained the Elder broke violently. His countenance became a horror of fire and shadow, and his spirit lashed out with such force that even the stones of the ancient road cracked.

Adaskar and Azarin summoned their defenses. The spiritual blow from the Elder almost toppled them, the check of will more a statement than a question.

'This world will be safer under my rule.'

Azarin, even more than Adaskar, did the answering. With gritted teeth, he raised one leg high, slowly, as though against the weight of the world, and then, with a mighty effort, stamped forward.

Triumphant.

Courageous.

Defiant.

"You underestimate our will, Elder."

Adaskar's pride in his dragon burned off the last of the Elder's pressure. With a heaving combined effort, they threw him off and cast their protection wide to the thirteen who defied the Elder alongside them. Stabilizing, the riders rallied and their dragons roared.

Adaskar looked between the Elder and the Warden – the one named Pride.

"How shall we divide this labor?" he asked Azarin.

Azarin gave a gruff snort and nodded toward Pride. *"You take the little one."*

Adaskar smiled. Despite it all, there was something pure about a worthy fight.

51

MONSTERS

Rake Blinked. He zipped along the thin rampart, swept his polearm around, knocked three ghouls bodily from the wall, then slammed his weapon down, cutting off a flayer's arm as it scrambled for purchase on the parapet. The few Hounds he saved looked at him gormlessly.

"Eyes on the bugs," he told them, then he was off again, darting to relieve other beleaguered positions.

The screaming, the shrieking, the ringing of iron and steel, the snapping of chitinous exoskeletons, all a cacophony; the mix of blood, of bile, of sickly death a harsh mix in his nose. A stinger scuttling along the rampart spewed its sour breath over him as he ran it through with his polearm, then he heaved and swung, flinging its body off his weapon and back over the wall.

His ribs began to ache, his sides split, his breath heaved.

Rake blamed his recent run across the Frontier. He blamed his lack of time to meditate. He blamed a lot of things.

Rake spat and carried on, trying to reserve his core for the opportune moment.

A flayer got away from him, leaping down from the rampart and into the town. Rake cycled magic down his arm, intending to catch the flayer with a Soul Blade, when thick vines burst from the ground at its feet, clamped its thin limbs in place, then twisted hard, breaking its body.

"*Good work,*" he said to Gea.

"*I wish I could do more,*" she said, hunkered down somewhere within the labyrinthine streets.

A heavy thrum overhead made Rake look up. Carriers flew over the walls.

Rake dropped his gaze back to the rampart and wheeled about. He'd run halfway down the western wall and ought not to neglect the eastern side any longer. As he neared the gatehouse, a bunch of men, some with neckerchiefs, most not, were rushing for the doorway to the stairs leading down. Rake Blinked into their path, blocking them.

"Not running, are we?"

He marshaled them back to their position at the parapet, pushing a couple more along with his tail.

"If the bugs don't get you, I will."

He spared a moment to check on Thrall's dragons, but they were still waiting, just as Osric had predicted.

They'd better get on with it. The longer this dragged on, the more likely these thugs and conscripted townsfolk would break.

A mighty crash echoed from somewhere inside the town.

"*The carriers are dropping onto ballista positions,*" Gea said.

Then came more great bangs of smashed stone and breaking wood.

"*Osric's ordered the ballista crews to flee,*" she said. "*Get ready.*"

Making it seem like their air defenses had been destroyed or abandoned would be crucial in drawing the bruiser and the healer into Osric's trap.

More heavy bangs sounded, though this time from below. Juggernauts and abominations pounded at the gates so violently, so powerfully, they seemed intent on shaking the defenders from the walls. The heavy iron held up well, but it wouldn't do for their plan if the enemy managed to break in through the gate just yet.

Rake hurried onto the rampart of the gatehouse. Osric was no longer there – his dragon's core popped in and out of Rake's senses over on the eastern wall.

Cycling a deal of power onto his glassy blade, Rake reached

over the parapet and slashed wide, drawing a long Soul Blade, which formed and then rushed down. The hardened magic cut through the arm of an abomination and sliced the horn from a juggernaut but did little to the armored backs of the rest.

But Rake didn't relent. He stabbed more Soul Blades down, aiming one by one with spear-like power at the hulking bugs and giant skeletons. One... two... three... he felled a fourth before he was forced to pull back. Green-black bolts of magic exploded on the parapet where he'd stood a split second before, and Thrall's dragons roared in outrage.

That's it, come on and break yourselves.

Buzzing dampened all other sounds.

Stingers swooped for him, and though Rake dodged them, they swept other men screaming from the gatehouse or carried them in their claws or mandibles to drop them high over the town. And they kept coming.

"Get away," Rake yelled, and the poor souls fighting by him didn't need telling twice.

Soon he fought alone. Nothing new there; he'd been alone for centuries.

Suicidal carriers fell for him now, breaking themselves upon the gatehouse, some carrying ghouls that tumbled out of their backs and scrambled over each other to get to him.

The space in which to fight reduced with every dead stinger, carrier, or ghoul. Enemies crawled around him, tearing at his cloak. He became cornered, and a shadow fell over him as two final carriers dropped from above.

Rake raised a Barrier overhead with one hand while he swished and stabbed with his polearm one-handed. The bugs crashed onto his Barrier, splattering as though hitting stone. Their bodies slid off, but his ability fizzled out, and the ricochet sent Rake to one knee.

Pain exploded from that knee, his left arm went numb, and blood thundered in his ears. His soul twisting, chest burning, he struggled for breath, and his grip on his polearm slackened as more ghouls crawled toward him.

A bad way to go.

Then something strange caught his eye. The shadow of a dead carrier seemed to undulate, a lump moving like a mole tunneling close to the surface of the earth.

Soot leaped from the shadow, her body forming like living smoke, darkness wrapping her talons and tail. The ghouls she caught were blown aside like rag dolls, then Osric arrived, roaring like a madman as he hacked, cut, and slammed his iron buckler through the throng. He rushed to Rake and offered him a hand.

"You need to know your limits."

Rake snorted but accepted Osric's hand. Once back on his feet, he rolled his shoulders and cricked his neck.

"I had no limits before *he* tortured me."

Osric hacked a laugh at that. "You need to know how to take your own advice too."

Rake's twisted soul tightened further, and his very essence groaned and creaked like a piece of leather wrung by an iron grip. Scowling, he was ready to retort, but a thundering bellow distracted him.

The ginger brute was charging in, the blood healer flying directly above, high and well out of reach.

Rake smirked. "Seems I got their attention."

The great brute bellowed and started to charge. Time to see whether his scheme would work.

Incredibly, Rake was smirking. "Seems I got their attention."

Osric ignored him. "Still got your vial?"

Rake tapped his cloak.

"Then make sure you're in position."

Which position hardly mattered so long as Rake could cut the beast.

They parted, Rake heading one way and Osric the other. The black dragon bounded into Osric's shadow as he entered the gatehouse tower and took to the stairs.

"Stay hidden," he told her. *"We don't want him distracted once he lands inside. We need him to try and break the gates."*

He exited onto the street. In the short time he'd gone to assist Rake and run down from the gatehouse, the situation inside the town had seriously deteriorated. Ghouls and flayers were inside; some had been dropped in by carriers, others had crawled over and down the walls. Had these been the only threats, Redbarrow might have held, but once the gate fell – once those juggernauts, abominations, and dragons came through – it was over.

The ground quaked under the bruiser's charge, and fighting raged throughout every one of the many streets, including one of their ballista positions. The barricade there crawled with scourge, and Osric sprinted toward it. As he ran, as he fought, the tremors in the earth peaked, and he feared the dragon might try to ram the gate from the outside after all.

Then the ground fell still.

"He's flying," Rake confirmed a moment before the crash came.

Osric cleaved a flayer from the barricade, turned hard and smashed a ghoul with his buckler, then called for the ballista to be revealed. He glanced back down toward the gate to see the ginger dragon within the walls, standing assuredly inside a small crater of mud and rubble. The blood healer hovered directly overhead, entirely at ease.

Osric had hoped his foes were smart enough to learn from their fights across the Frontier. At Blackhollow, they had attacked before dealing with every ballista, running the risk of injury. Here they had cleared the way first – or thought they had, at any rate.

Osric looked away, back to the barricade, and sprang to help the survivors move the wagons and other cordons hiding the ballista. Osric strained to heave a wagon away all on his own, yelling from the effort, but his cry was drowned out by another shattering crash – this time from the gate.

"He didn't break through," Rake said.

Osric spared a glance back. The brute was backing away from

the gate, his back leg shaking, swaying his head from side to side: against double reinforced iron gates, he'd met his match. The dragon's power was truly extraordinary, for the reverberations from the blow caused more rickety buildings within Redbarrow to collapse.

Above, the core of the rusty dragon flared, and the brute began to regain his balance.

"I'm ready," Rake confirmed.

"Ready," Gea said.

Their presence lingered in his mind, awaiting an answer.

"Hold," Osric said as he yelled again, helping to shove the last pieces of the barricade aside to expose the ballista. The paltry crew scurried to prepare it.

The ginger brute still swayed a little, but with a kick with his back leg and a bullish snort, he lowered his head and charged the gate again.

Tough, Osric thought, *but not the smartest.*

BOOOOOM.

Somehow, the gates withstood the second blow. The core of the blood healer flared brighter.

"Sir! Sir!"

It was one of the ballista crew.

"The base is damaged. It's not a clean shot."

Next came Rake's impatient growl. *"Surely now?"*

"Wait," Osric said, trying to assess the problem. *"Hold on."*

The damage to the ballista's base meant it leaned to one side. Osric squatted, then lifted the base up to level the ballista out. He grunted, blew spittle from a hard breath, and the winch cranked as the crew wound it for release.

It was at times like this he wished riders could project telepathically to others, not just over their bond, but his dragon sprang to his aid.

"We're ready now," she told Rake and Gea, even as the hulking dragon rammed the gates for a third time. This time, two clangs followed the boom, then both were drowned out by tremendous slams beyond the walls of Redbarrow.

The gates had been blown open from the inside.

Swaying wildly now, the ginger brute staggered back and slumped down, his head streaming with blood and visible bone, which already shimmered as the healer worked hard overhead.

"Go!" the black dragon ordered.

Many things happened at once.

Gea launched herself from a dead end near the base of the hill, flying right for the healer, even as she conjured thick vines around the brute's legs.

Rake leaped from a rooftop and drove the blade of his polearm deep into the dragon's back.

A bolt from the second ballista team flew into the dragon's side.

Osric yelled, "Loose," and his crew released the tension in the great bowstring, air whoomphed, and the bolt shot toward the target, sticking the dragon through its leg.

The brute tried to flail, but the numbing agent from Rake's blade made him sluggish, and fresh vines lashed the dragon around his snout, exposing his neck. Rake flipped off, landed by the dragon's battered head, then opened his throat.

Scourge poured in through the shattered gates.

Rake Blinked to get out of their way.

The brute fell still.

For a giddy moment, Osric thought they'd done it.

Then the blood healer's core all but exploded in his magical senses. The rusty dragon still wrestled in the air with Gea, stubbornly unwilling to leave, simply taking cuts and bites from her as it healed not only its own wounds but all they'd done to the ginger beast.

The bruiser's shattered skull healed, his limbs snapped free of the binding vines, he gargled blood, then sprayed it out in a roar as he rose to his four feet, good as new.

A cold feeling sunk through Osric. The healer's core was guttering now, but they'd never get another chance like that.

Bellowing, the bruiser beat his wings and rose into the air.

Osric guessed at the danger.

"Tell Gea to come to the ground," he told his dragon.

She did, but it was too late. The healer kept Gea in place, and now it seemed she'd fallen into their trap. Between healer and brute, she had little chance. The one mercy was that it was quick. Blood poured, her roar died in her throat, her core vanished, then her limp body fell from the sky.

Gea collided with a distant rooftop, then slid down and out of sight.

There must have been a great noise, but Osric didn't hear it. The cold feeling inside him turned icy, numbing him. It always had on the rare occasions he'd stared defeat in its mocking face.

The Iron Beards had a saying for when the fight is lost: 'Time for every man to decide how he dies.' Better to go out on your own terms; better than your face in the mud and steel through your back.

Osric had long ago decided he'd go down fighting, roaring a battle cry loud enough to rip his voice to shreds. The monster inside him reared eagerly, the bloodlust ready to take over.

Somehow, the blood elixirs were in his hand. He hadn't even registered pulling them out of his cloak. As he considered them, Rake materialized from a Blink right in front of him and held out his own scaly hand.

"Give them to me."

Rake opened the beast's throat in a red grimace; he would have cut his whole damned head off, but the scourge were pounding in behind him, and he was forced to Blink away and duck into a side street to evade the coming tide.

When he turned to defend himself, the bruiser was already pushing to his feet. He shook as though ridding himself of rain, then launched skyward. It all happened so fast. Rake couldn't have helped even if he had the means of jumping that high – such a Blink in his current state would have been impossible.

Rake wasn't bonded to Gea, but as the brute's talons and teeth sunk into her, he felt something of it ripple over his own body.

"*Rak—*" she gasped, cutting off as the roar died in her throat, her core emptied, and she fell, dead and gone before she struck a rooftop and crashed out of sight.

Rake slammed a foot down, and the arcane blast of the Kickback dazed the scourge nearby as he leaped backward. He landed and kept backing up the road.

Something roiled inside him.

It dredged up old memories, ones he'd buried for a long time, of when he stood in the streets of his old hometown, slaying scourge in a desperate stand even as Freiz and all of the east fell to ruin. There'd been no glory in it, no purpose or chance of victory, nothing the bards could sing of. Rake had fought until everything he'd sworn to defend crumbled, until the descendants of those he'd loved and sworn to protect all lay dead, until there had been nothing and no one left to fight for.

His guard had been up for so long now he'd all but forgotten why.

But it had weakened enough now that he cared about a fallen emerald whom he'd only recently considered a comrade.

She'd made mistakes but was trying again.

Such noble drivel shouldn't have affected him, but now the roiling was insistent. That was the trouble with caring.

Enough is enough.

He knew what he had to do. Rake dashed through an alley that led into Osric's street. Osric already had the vials in hand. Rake rushed to him, Blinking the last gap, and emerged just in front of him.

"Give them to me," he said, reaching out with his hand.

Osric seemed uncharacteristically shocked. He gave Rake a look as if asking him, 'Why?'

"Because of her," Rake said with a nod to Soot. "I'm not important, but she can't lose you."

Osric looked stern, but he handed over a vial.

Rake scoffed. "All of them," he demanded as a thunderous boom announced the return of the bruiser to ground level.

Osric gave him another look as if he were mad, then handed over the rest of the blood potions. Rake unfastened his cloak, letting it fall as he began drinking the elixirs all at once.

The cloying concoctions ran heavy and metallic over his tongue, then he began to grow. His muscles bulged and hardened as he went from seven feet in height to eight, then nine, then more. His polearm seemed like a twig in his huge hands, and he stamped with a foot now big as a shield. Grounding his body, he came alive with a strength unlike anything he'd experienced before: a wildness he couldn't quantify, but he knew what he might do with it.

The blood healer still hovered, its core simmering low.

Rake dropped his polearm – he wouldn't need it – then started running, his strides like great leaps, shaking the timber frame buildings. Eyes fixed on the healer, he leaped high into the air. Even with the vast jump, he wouldn't quite make it, but he came close enough to Blink the rest, pouring much of his remaining core into it and appearing right beside the healer.

He seized the dragon in his giant hands.

The rusty dragon shrieked and thrashed about but was powerless against Rake's crushing grip. He had the healer's wings pressed in tight; it could go nowhere, and so they began to fall, tumbling over and over, biting at each other in a deathly embrace as they plummeted toward the ground.

Rake flipped them around so the healer took the brunt of the damage as they smashed through a roof, then several stories before colliding with the blood-soaked ground, sending rubble and bodies flying everywhere.

Rake's skull felt as though it had been shattered with a hammer and then nailed back together. His grip slackened. Somehow the healer's core still flashed, the last of its power waning. The rusty dragon bit into Rake's shoulder, causing him to howl and roll away, and the dragon wriggled out from under the mound of wood and bricks.

Rake pushed up onto one side, his vision a daze. The rusty dragon staggered sideways on two broken legs, bleeding from a dozen wounds, but its wings were snapping back into position, and as the last of its core winked out, the healer took off. Rake struggled to his feet, swaying, unable to do anything as he felt the healer climb higher and higher, then fly north and away from Redbarrow.

The brute. The brute still had to die.

Rake felt its presence, turned toward it, then collapsed, his blurry vision darkening as the beast issued a rattling bellow.

"Give them to me."

Osric stared at Rake. Had he not just warned him about knowing his limits?

Rake nodded to the black dragon. "I'm not important, but she can't lose you."

Osric felt like a coward, but he handed a vial over.

Rake scoffed. "All of them!" Then a thunderous boom announced the return of the bruiser to ground level.

He's even more reckless than me, Osric thought grimly, but he handed over the rest of the blood elixirs anyway. The monster inside Osric snarled, disappointed in him.

Rake swelled to a colossal size and charged off down the street.

As a general, Osric should have been up on the hill, sending messengers running between him and his subordinates, carrying orders as he directed the battle from a commanding position.

As it was, he climbed a remaining barricade and yelled to every defender he could, trying to rally something of a last stand.

Hounds and stricken townsfolk rallied to him, then came another almighty crash from somewhere near the smithies. The core of the rusty healer was all but gone – had Rake killed it?

Then he craned his neck and saw the dragon flying north, fleeing the battle. Once again, Osric wished he could send telepathy on his own.

"The half-dragon isn't answering," his dragon said.

Perhaps the madman really had gone out in a blaze worthy of the bards after all.

The monster in Osric snorted, its thirst restored. With the healer gone, the brute could be killed. He still had one vial of the numbing agent, so he braced his axe against his body with his maimed arm, then took out the vial and smashed it directly against the head of the axe. Poison shone along Vengeance's beard.

As if decreed by fate, the bruiser burst through nearby buildings at that moment, emerging onto the street where Osric was trying to rally the defenders. Then again, with the black dragon and her perceptible core at his side, perhaps it wasn't fate.

Their foe had come in behind the ballista, so there was no point in reloading it.

Men not crushed under the debris scarpered or scrambled to join Osric. A general wouldn't rush into a fight to shield his men, but he wasn't a general here, not really. Just a glorified soldier – and a soldier defends.

The bruiser's beefy neck seemed to swell with rage, and its dark oak eyes narrowed onto him. Osric had never noticed before how much those eyes were like Thrall's.

Not enough men had rallied to him. Not nearly enough.

The brute shifted his gaze to the black dragon.

Osric let the monster out. He cried, howling against the dragon's roar, and started running. The bruiser kicked through rubble in his haste to meet him.

Osric drew his arm back, then hurled Vengeance, sending the axe spinning, glints of poison flashing before it lodged into the brute's chest, biting deep. The dragon's roar became more of a rattle as it slowed, then staggered.

Its oak eyes went wide as it strained against the poison, then the brute buckled, slipping in its own blood. Snorting, it started to rise again. Perhaps its great bulk and strength were enough to burn off the poison on their own.

Behind its eyes, Osric thought he saw, thought he felt, a glimpse of Thrall—

Then the black dragon leaped from a shadow, her body wreathed in dancing darkness. She struck the brute in his side, and both were lost in a void of night and an explosion of heatless smoke.

Coughing, Osric raised his arms against the smoke and reached desperately over his bond. *"Are you there? Say something?"*

She didn't answer in words. Instead, a flurry of murderous thoughts crossed the bond; she wanted to rip, to tear, to kill. She felt every bit the monster Osric knew he was.

When the smoke cleared, he found her rearing up by the brute's exposed belly, her talons raised and teeth bared, but she howled instead, dropped to all fours, then backed away.

Osric ran to her, and she pressed tight to him, her heart pumping hard enough to burst.

The brute was dead, without a doubt. A bloodless black chasm had cut him nearly clean in two. The black dragon's core felt worryingly low. She seemed ready to pass out.

Osric only realized then that the battle around him had stopped. Two Wyrm Cloaks who had followed the bruiser turned and fled. There were still scourge fighting and shrieking – the brute wasn't their Queen, after all – but this time, when Osric called to rally the men of Redbarrow, they all came.

They pushed back toward the gates where abominations and juggernauts were shouldering each other to squeeze into the town. It would be no easy fight, and countless more would die, but then the hulking form of Rake came staggering out onto the main road, still massive, still freakishly strong. It wasn't clear whether Rake knew what he was doing, but he smashed one abomination to a pulp, then drove a stampeding juggernaut down into the mud with just his foot.

"Help me," Rake pleaded in a strangled voice.

With Rake handling the scourge, Osric drew his men up and managed to get them into a strong line.

"Go to the mine," he told his dragon. *"Bring back as much marrow as you can."*

She took off for the hill as Rake broke the strength of the swarm single-handed. Without the abominations and juggernauts, the ghouls were little threat.

Osric was in the middle of directing fighters to sweep the streets and the base of the walls when the black dragon returned, carrying a basket between her teeth. Inside the basket were jars of marrow paste – some he recognized as those he'd brought to the town – and there were many loose leaves of Kosora's Tears yet to be boiled and pulped.

"Your mother brought it out," she said.

Osric took the basket, then made his way cautiously toward Rake. The half-dragon had begun to shrink, though the process seemed sluggish. He was down on his hands and knees, hissing and arching his back like a cat.

"Give me your hand," Osric said.

With a wince and a shudder, Rake obliged, laying his palm flat. Osric upended a whole jar of marrow paste onto the stretched scales.

"Take a little at a—"

Rake licked it all with a single flick of his forked tongue.

"More," Rake growled.

So he gave him more. And more. Rake ate three whole jars and snorted a lump. Osric tensed. Just a pinch rubbed into the gums had been enough to drift Merchant into a painless death.

Eventually, he refused to give Rake more. The half-dragon tried to swipe the basket from him, but Osric remained quicker and lithely dodged Rake's large, grasping hand. But the drug was starting to work. Rake was closer to eight feet tall now, not the monstrous ten he'd been.

Once he was back to his normal size, Osric offered him a hand again.

"You're lucky."

Rake clasped his hand, and for once, he had no witty remark.

"Gea?" Rake rasped.

"We'll burn her later, together. I promise. For now, get some water and rest."

Rake nodded without protest.

Osric clapped him on the back, perhaps a little harder than necessary, then went off in search of his dragon. He could feel her presence a few streets back, over the huge mound of debris where the bruiser had fallen.

The brute lay dead on his side, tongue lolling from his mouth. The black dragon stood by his snout with a hard look in her eyes. Now the battle was over, Osric noticed the persistent burn in their bond, though it was a pleasant sort of burn. Perhaps it was relief, or perhaps it was happiness; Osric wasn't sure when he'd last felt either of those.

"You showed great restraint at the end," he told her. "I commend you. It's not easy to control blood lust like that. I've failed more than most."

Without looking away from the ginger dragon, she said, *"I remembered what you said about forgiveness... I hated this dragon even though I'd never met him. Back in the tower, I could feel the fear from all the other hatchlings. He was the worst of them... or I thought he was. I can't forgive him... but I want to let it go."*

Osric placed a hand on her back and considered the cruel dragon before them. He wasn't sorry to see this one dead. Osric recalled the wet slap of guts the brute had happily spilled from another dragon upon the hatchery floor.

His dragon's ability to let go of her hatred only impressed upon him again that he didn't deserve her.

'I'll take you anyway,' she had said.

"Why?" he croaked aloud. "After all I did, why take me?"

"Because you protected me, and I know you always will." She nodded to the brute. *"I'm glad I was able to defend you for once."*

"Is that what you think? That only I benefit from this?" He moved so that he could face her, looking into those purple eyes that had led him back through the dark. "You saved me that day at Windshear, too. You've saved me a little every day since. I need you just as much. If anything, I need you more."

Her eyes welled with affection, and their bond pushed outward, expanding visibly, and though Osric's soul still stabbed with pain, it was nothing like before. Just when he assumed the burn would fade, it kept going, then grew hotter. He felt a jolt throughout his whole body, felt the mote channels in his legs reawaken, stiff from a long slumber.

Becoming an Ascendant for the first time was an unforgettable experience, like switching from wielding a bronze dagger to a steel longsword. There was no such great transformation this second time around – for he was already enhanced – but Osric appreciated the subtler differences.

For one thing, the shadowy figures in the dragon's core were more detailed than he could have imagined. And the man now had a missing right hand.

52

CONSEQUENCES

Fire spread in the Fae Forest. Ash flew to his limits while Holt searched the edges of his sixth sense for Wrath, but he found nothing of her presence; she'd taken her vengeance and gone.

They'd known this grim reality would meet them.

Wrath was faster than them, stronger than them. They would never have been able to stop her, but it would have been better to be there for Aberanth. At least he wouldn't have faced the end alone.

Holt pictured the little emerald trembling as the blue fires engulfed him. Fear, shame, guilt – all thrashed inside him, and increasingly, something else bubbled to the surface. A cold anger: an unnatural fury that frightened him.

They reached the center of the inferno. The fires spread outward in a ravenous circle from Aberanth's glade, the black eye of the conflagration. Holt ate a piece of Floating jerky and drank an elixir to wash it down, then Ash angled down and shot through the flaming canopy, entering a nightmare.

At ground level, nothing of the moon or stars breached the choking smoke. The world seemed split between intense bright-ness and utter black; black as the charred grass, black as the silhouettes of burning trees. Flames yellow as steel drawn from the hearth licked up bark and bush, roiling to livid reds. Cracking screams of a thousand dying trees carried upon the howling wind hot as the volcanic realm, the air suffocating, acrid and clawing at his nose and throat.

"He isn't on the surface," Ash said.

Holt hacked and coughed as he leaped down from Ash's back. He found the trap door to the grotto torn off its hinges and the ground around it ravaged with deep talon marks. Eyes stinging and streaming, he lowered his bandanna, then jumped down into the tunnel.

As he left Ash behind, his ability to picture the world through sound, smell, and touch reduced until his sense of Ash dimmed and he was left with his lesser human perceptions, but his experience of walking these tunnels took him to the lab.

Smoke filled the grotto, heavy under the ceiling as it clumped beneath the ventilation shafts. Holt entered in a crouch, using a worktop as his guide.

"Abera—"

A soot-filled breath sent him into another fit of hacking coughs. Burnt bark spoke of damage to the beech tree, and the smell of burning charcoal mixed with that of wood and bitter chemicals. Glass exploded, and Holt ducked further and covered his head.

Aberanth's silence was terrifying.

Holt's senses struggled to cope. He shuffled deeper into the grotto, and his guiding left hand dropped from the worktop onto the rim of a crate, his fingers brushing over its powdery contents.

Blistering pain followed. Screaming, he whipped his hand out, his skin hissing despite his enhanced Floating. Holt lost a moment to the agony. Groaning, he pushed on, crawling along one-handed, keeping his left-hand tucked underneath him.

More glass exploded.

Shards struck his armor, a hot edge cut at his cheek. He wanted to call out for Aberanth again, but breaths were hard to come by. A new scent reached him – burnt feathers and blackened chicken.

Not scales, though, he told himself. *Not scales.*

Poor Gallus. Aberanth had been fond of her.

That was it.

Holt shifted his search, scuttling bug-like along the grotto floor toward Gallus's alcove. Just outside the nook, his scrambling hands came onto something. A tail.

The dragon's body was hot. Too hot. And sticky, though whether from blood or broiled flesh, he could not tell.

Somehow, Holt managed to get purchase under the little dragon, his burnt hand screaming at him the whole time. Breath held, he pushed down through his feet and lifted Aberanth into his arms.

Through the devastation, he fought his way back to the exit, stumbling often but never once letting go of Aberanth. Out of the grotto. Up the smokey tunnels, trying only to think about the way ahead and placing one foot after another.

Ash's presence reanimated within his soul.

His senses sharpened; the way ahead became clearer.

"Boy? Hurry. She's coming back!"

One foot after another. Back to the horror of the surface.

The moment Holt emerged, his conscious mind became aware of Wrath's approaching aura. He'd come to know the feeling of that core well.

Come to fear it.

To hate it.

Holt laid Aberanth down on dead grass. The burns ran deep beneath his scales. His chest quivered with a faint heartbeat, frail and doomed as a flower in drought.

Yet still it beat.

"Aberanth," Holt wheezed. "We'll be here with you."

Ash drew close. He raised his wings, blocking the worst of the heat, then lowered his snout under his wings to join them. Holt put his burned hand on Ash's cool nose. He sighed. Despite the imminent dread, a surreal calm fell over him.

Then Wrath crashed down through the inferno.

"If it's to be death, boy, I'd rather face her."

His sword thrummed. Better to fight, it seemed to think, than to cower.

Holt agreed. He sniffed, then reached for the hilt with his

right hand and clenched his left, numb now to the burning pain. Ash withdrew his wings, and the misery of the dying forest returned in full force.

Holt rose, unsheathed his sword, and stepped to meet the Warden of Wrath.

Her racing heart and fast, shallow breaths spoke of a perverse pleasure.

"Thank you for bringing the mole from its den."

Holt stopped between Wrath and Ash, planted his sword in front of him, and took the grip in both hands. Ash drew in behind him, reassuringly close.

The Warden's laugh was deep and cruel.

A mental weight pressed upon them. This time, Holt's soul stirred in response to bolster him. Ash's will weaved with his own, and even a measure of the sword's hardness joined to stiffen them.

This evil was their doing. So here they stood, between the Warden of Wrath and Aberanth's blistered body, unable to undo their mistakes but willing to take responsibility for them.

Willing to face the consequences.

Wrath's spiritual pressure pressed harder, and a snide question was asked of them: 'Are you willing to die for him?'

Holt and Ash replied as one. 'Yes.'

No hesitation. No doubt whatsoever.

Meeting the check of will, Wrath's spiritual pressure lifted.

She stopped laughing.

"Better you all burn. Then the filth of the Parasite can never corrupt my flight again."

Holt had no breath for speech, so Ash answered for them.

"When your Elder learns of this, he'll punish you."

"Your vile alchemy has swollen his pride… but, in time, he will return to himself. My Elder is noble. He will forgive me. I do this to help him."

Her jaw crunched as she opened it wide, then the air seemed to be sucked in as flames gathered in her throat.

Holt maintained his enhanced Floating, not that it would do much good.

He felt the heat leave Wrath's mouth.

Heard the whoomph as the flames rushed forth.

Then a chill sapped the air. Strange, Holt thought, wondering if his mind might be trying to distance itself from the coming pain.

He waited. Nothing came.

Wrath roared and bounded backward, giving a roar of shock as well as fear. Then another worldly screech like singing glass filled the burning glade.

Holt lifted his bandanna. He did not believe what he saw. Watery though his vision was, he recognized the ethereal, flowing fire, taking a willowy shape as if painted in the air. Fire which emitted no smoke.

No larger than an eaglet fresh from hatching, the phoenix unfurled its wings, its babyish features ill-proportioned. It opened its golden beak and swallowed Wrath's blue breath whole. As it ate the power, it grew. Around the glade, the raging fires began to disintegrate, turning from flame to sparkling dust.

Wrath yowled and leaped farther back, froze for a moment, then spread her wings to take flight.

The phoenix shot toward her, turning into its physical form. With real feathers and talons came its real shrill squawk. No larger than an eagle, it flew straight for Wrath's enormous wings and went to work with beak and claw. Wrath twisted hard to throw it aside, but the damage was done: she was grounded.

Thrown by Wrath, the phoenix returned to its fire form and made for the burning trees. Its sweeping route around the perimeter was marked by the fires snuffing out.

The Warden turned her gaze back onto Holt and Ash, her eyes flashing with murderous intent. As the forest darkened, her eyes were all that remained visible.

Through the parting smoke, a strand of cooling moonlight reached Holt.

He lowered his bandanna.

As the world reformed in his mind's eye, he grasped an understanding of Wrath's core for the first time. The power of Elders and Wardens was beyond his comprehension to measure, but Wrath's core had now entered the territory of a Lady, maybe an Exalted Lady, leaking magic every moment as though punctured.

Ash tugged at him over their bond, sending him an idea. They split up, Ash heading one way, Holt running for Aberanth. Playing for time and hoping the phoenix would drain Wrath dry was their best hope.

Behind, Wrath cried with fury and charged. Her sheer size and strength were still more than enough to crush them.

As Holt ran, he Grounded his body, then willed his sword to wane, drove his blade into the earth, picked Aberanth up, and ran on.

Wrath came careening into the still-expanding blackness.

"I smell you! I hear you!"

She snapped her teeth but met only air.

Holt kept to the plan. The entrance to the grotto was close by, made wider and deeper by Wrath's gouging of the earth. With Aberanth in his arms, Holt ran around the drop until it became a trench between him and Wrath. He panted and huffed deliberately hard for her benefit.

She raked at the earth and charged again.

Then Ash sprang from the darkness, throwing his full weight into her side. Wrath stumbled. Losing her balance, she swung her tail, the vertebrae crunching, and struck Ash full in his body. Holt sensed wet pops and sharp pain across their bond as Ash collapsed, but the ambush worked. Wrath's front leg fell into the deep descent of the tunnel, a trap she had helped to set. Her head hit the ground, and her momentum tilted her great body into an awkward slump.

Wrath's core was now the strength of a High Lady and dropping, though not nearly fast enough.

Holt continued running, leaving the area of his sword's Eclipse behind and entering the smokey ruins of the forest. He heard Wrath thrashing around, her roars and movements crazed. He halted. Any farther from Ash and his senses would weaken. He crouched to lay Aberanth down, his mind racing as to what he should do now.

Whoomphing blast followed whoomphing blast. Unsteady

and only halfway back to his feet, Ash peppered the Warden with bursting moonbeams.

Wrath's writhing limbs mixed with rushing bouts of fire, which vanished at once from the magical landscape. Holt had no sense of the phoenix's position. It must still be in its fire form, keeping safe until enough of the Warden's strength had been drained.

Finally, Wrath pushed herself free of the tunnel to the grotto, rearing up and back, beating her one good wing to aid her before landing hard.

Ash stood outside the Eclipse to keep himself as visible as possible.

"Run," Holt urged.

"Not this time."

Wrath gushed another stream of fire, continuous and more powerful than Holt had ever felt a fire dragon put into a single breath. Even siphoned by the phoenix, her magic blazed in Holt's sixth sense.

Ash met it with his own moonbeam.

Unsure what to do, Holt started running back.

Ash's core dwindled. Stars winked out of the nightscape, and a shadow flowed over the moon as it sped through a cycle. His moonbeam remained solid, but under the weight of Wrath's attack, it retreated inch by inch.

Wrath's core became that of a Low Lady, then wavered on the edge of Lordship.

A weak crescent moon hung against a starless night in Ash's core.

Holt's sword called to him, as if to remind him of its presence. It was still in the ground, close to where Wrath stood inside the Eclipse. And it was swollen with gathered lunar motes.

Still running, Holt reached out to his blade and willed it to wax.

Blind himself, he didn't see the flash, but Wrath's howl proved it had worked. She staggered, shaking her head, and with her breath interrupted, Ash's moonbeam struck her head-on.

The phoenix cawed. It swooped back in, doubled in size, and clawed at Wrath's eyes.

Close now, Holt drew his new cook's knife from his belt.

Wrath shook the phoenix off and wailed, a chilling, stomach-turning sound of lost hope. Ash's moonbeams continued crashing into her, and one leg buckled, her core barely that of a Champion now.

Holt finally allowed himself to yell as he swung at her throat.

Ash's breath ripped a clean hole right through her.

The once proud Warden – reduced to an Ascendant – crumpled, her presence and core dissipated, and her final breath rasped into a gargled death.

A stillness gripped the forest, cut only by breaking wood and Ash panting.

Holt gathered enough wits to wipe his knife on his trouser leg, then reached out to his sword and willed it to return to its normal state. A feeling of satisfaction met him, and the sword's thrumming presence quietened as if falling asleep.

Holt drew it from the earth, then sprinted back to Aberanth. Once at the dragon's side, he dropped his sword and fell to his knees. As gently as he could manage, he pressed his hands over the little emerald.

The scales felt raw and blistered, and while the heat of the burns had gone, the sickening smell of seared flesh, fat, and hot copper remained strong. Aberanth's blood pooled internally, his heart stuttering so weakly Holt almost missed it. He placed his hand in front of Aberanth's nostrils, and despite his increased sensitivity to touch, he barely felt the feeble breath.

Holt scrambled around in his pockets and pouches, desperate for the balm. The jar must have cracked in the fight, for cold paste squelched as he took hold of it. Yet anything would help. Anything at all.

He poured it all over Aberanth, but there wasn't enough to cover his whole body. His superior senses betrayed him, letting him hear and feel every excruciating moment of his friend's slow death.

Holt fell back onto the scorched earth. An urge overtook him, and he tore his bandanna free. With the covering off, he sighed. Merely seeing the world was like a salve on his senses. Aberanth lay quietly before him. He might have been sleeping.

Shaking, Holt burst into tears, or he tried to. His eyes stung, but his body had little water to spare. A weak, single tear managed to fall but nothing more, though he heaved and heaved as if to wet the earth back to life.

His parents. Brode. Rake. And now Aberanth.

He couldn't take anymore.

Still dry heaving, wishing for tears to cool his face, Holt slumped onto his side, howling, exhausted, struck down by grief and regret. Ash's wail echoed throughout the dead trees, long and lonesome.

Across their bond, they did not attempt to console each other but fed into each other's anguish. Holt registered an ache in his thigh and ribs, echoes of Ash's own pain. At some point, Ash limped over and gingerly laid down, curling his body and tail around them both.

Holt could not have said how long he lay there whimpering, only that he came around when the phoenix, silent in its fire form, landed before them. He stood in repose, not even half the impressive height it had been, though far larger than the fledgling that had emerged from the grotto.

A crisp pop and snap of fire entered Holt's mind. This time, it settled quickly into words he could comprehend.

"I hoped never to see you two again." Its voice was younger and brighter. *"I wanted you to fail."*

"I wish we had."

The phoenix morphed into its physical form.

Holt cast light to see by. Through force of habit, he pushed motes to his left palm, then grunted from the burnt skin there and switched hands.

The phoenix's feathers were fluffier than before, but otherwise he was a perfect replica of his previous self. Spirited as a sparrow, he hopped closer to Aberanth and lowered his golden beak over him.

"Don't touch him."

"I've never seen a dragon this small. You defended it from the devourer."

"We were too late."

Somehow, Holt found the strength to sit upright. Sniffing, he wiped his nose, smearing soot across his face. He tasted charcoal and spat. Shuddering, he brought his breath to something approaching steady, then met the phoenix's slitted eyes.

"I'm sorry we came for you. We didn't know…" But the words caught in his throat. No excuses. "We're sorry."

The phoenix cocked its head.

Holt gulped painfully hard down his bone-dry throat. "How is it that you're here? We watched you die, carried your remains."

"My kind would live forever, but decay sets in, and so we reduce to be born again from the ashes. Inside the mountain of fire, there is a great stone on which we used to do it. I remember clearly now."

"You look a lot better."

The phoenix chuckled. *"I'd long been lost to despair in that cave. Now, I can wait again."*

He looked skyward. Holt felt them too. Cores. More dragons, though these were coming from the east.

"Not more devourers," the phoenix said in relief. *"But I shan't wait to discover how wicked they are. All of them are, in their own way."*

Ash stirred. He snuffled and raised his snout a little off the ground. *"Not all dragons are like Wrath or those who hunted you. Not even all fire dragons are like that. At least, they're not now. I wish I could show you that side of us."*

"The past cannot be erased, blind one. Yet slaying a thousand of your kind would not balance our wings. I wish only to be left alone. Will you respect that wish?"

"We will."

Holt nodded.

The phoenix cawed approvingly and hopped. *"You did not mean for these things to happen, but were it not for you, I would not be here now, nor would I have had this chance for revenge. Small though it was, it tasted sweet. For that, I would have us part in peace."*

"I would like that."

"Me too."

The phoenix dipped its beak low, then transformed again. It took flight, a flash of thin, wispy flames heading to the south.

A deep ache and fatigue radiated through Holt, exacerbated by his throbbing soul and the sear of their bond. As Ash had been the one to draw greatly on his core, their bond was not close to Fraying; rather, it burned from the experience. Facing a Warden and winning would surely grow it as they recovered.

The dragons approaching from the east were now becoming easier to discern. There were five, the strongest perhaps equal to a powerful High Lord. Holt and Ash hadn't the strength to flee, so they waited.

Thankfully, it turned out to be emeralds. The strongest entered the dark of the glade beyond where Holt could see.

"Help," he croaked, his throat still raw. "Our friend's hurt. Please."

As the other emeralds circled above, magic wove throughout the desolation. Pockets of the damage were healed. Burnt trunks crumbled to dust until a kernel of the tree remained and new shoots emerged from the stumps.

His calls unanswered, Holt got to his feet. Dizzy from the effort, he raised his palm to cast his light farther and called again, "Help. Please."

Heavy feet headed their way, and soon the dragon entered Holt's weak light. This emerald was radiant, its scales akin to the gemstones of the flight's namesake.

"Our friend, he's dying. Won't you help him?"

Holt thought of the great leaves the West Warden had conjured around Brode.

The dragon shook its head. *"All is cinders and ash."* His voice was serene and beautiful, as far removed from Wrath's as it was possible to be. *"We heard the cries of the forest and flew at once. How were the fires extinguished?"*

"I made a promise. I can't tell you how."

The dragon's eyes widened as he took in Holt and Ash, seemingly for the first time. *"You are the Sons of Night. My Elder spoke of you both, though I understood you were to help convince the flights to join us, not kill their Wardens."*

"It's all gone wrong." Dry tears burned in Holt's eyes again, and he gestured with open hands toward Aberanth. "Won't you help him?"

The emerald padded to where Aberanth lay, sniffed, and listened for his song. *"I know this one. I sent him from the Eastern Grove long ago."*

Holt suddenly realized this was the East Warden. In different circumstances, he would have been shocked at the state of his core.

"His name is Aberanth. He deserved better."

The East Warden gave a low rumble.

"Please," Holt begged. "This is our fault. He doesn't deserve to pay for our mistakes."

"My strength is not what it was, but we shall try."

He stretched his neck, raising his head high, and uttered a soft call like birdsong. His fellow emeralds circled above. Aberanth's body began to bubble, and his blackened scales and the exposed white fat and bloody tissue reknitted until the third-degree wounds became second or first. Their song held for a little longer, then, abruptly, it ended.

The East Warden pulled back and rasped a breath. The circling dragons dispersed, and two landed nearby to lie down. Aberanth remained a blotchy, inflamed mess, but it was a clear improvement. Some color had returned to his brown scales, and beneath him, the forest floor turned verdant again.

"I cannot risk more," the East Warden said. *"I cannot say he will be comfortable, but he should live."*

Ash cooed. *"His heart is stronger."*

Holt gasped and fell to his hands and knees. "Thank you, Warden. Thank you."

The Warden gritted his teeth, then winced. When next he spoke, his voice had lost some of its serenity.

"My Elder died fighting for a new world. I won't give up that fight until my core is empty and my soul is crippled. Long ago, he gave me stewardship of the East. It was my duty to safeguard all emeralds in my care.

What sort they were should never have mattered. By right of my position as Warden of the Eastern Grove, I hereby welcome Aberanth back into the Emerald Flight… or what is left of it."

Holt sensed the spiritual power flow from the Warden to Aberanth to seal the pronouncement and wondered whether Aberanth would be proud or happy. Moreover, Holt wondered again why, for many, it took a calamity to usher change.

Miraculously, Aberanth's eyelids fluttered. Puffy and swollen though they were, he managed to half-open them.

Holt crawled to his side, his hand shaking as he stroked the dragon's head.

"Holt? Ash? W-what happened? The Warden—"

"She's dead… she's gone. You're going to be all right. We're going to take care of you. You're going to be all right."

53

THE FALL

Old stone rained around him. Adaskar weaved through chunks of falling ruins, trying to gain ground even as Pride toppled building after building.

A clear path suddenly opened, and Adaskar seized it. Leaping high, he channeled great plumes of pressured fire from his hands, propelling into a flight of his own making.

Pride blew a gushing jet of fire, hot enough to strip flesh from bone. Still flying, Adaskar Floated his mote channels and met the breath head-on. Soaring through the flames, he landed by Pride's front foot, drew his sword, and cut, but Pride slid aside, viper-quick despite his huge size. In dodging, Pride's tail slammed into a ruined archway, forcing Adaskar to weave through another rain of stone.

He cursed. Somewhere in the carnage, Azarin fought the Elder and needed his help. Adaskar burned to go to his dragon's aid, but Pride proved tenacious. Where magical strength was comparable, most dragon-on-dragon fights came down to tooth and claw, and this battle was no different. Gaining the chance to strike at Pride's vulnerable belly or, better still, his wings proved easier to train for than to achieve.

Ever under the surface, ever wishing to burst through, the ferocity of Adaskar's inner flames raised his blood to a boiling battle lust. He got close again, scarring Pride across his hardened chest, drew blood from a leg as they battled along the ancient road, yet always Pride slipped free, trying to bury Adaskar under what remained of Aldunei.

A piece of debris crashed onto him at last. His head burst with pain, his shoulder screamed, and he tasted blood. Pride belched more fire, and as Adaskar summoned his own in defense, a vortex of wreathing flames engulfed them both.

Then something strange occurred. The flames of battle began to lift as though the earth pushed them up and away. An amethyst mist replaced them, spreading rapidly, filling every crack and crevice in the ruins, rising until it covered Adaskar's head. The mystic power was so thick in the air Adaskar could taste it: the sensation of a wonderful dream veering into a nightmare.

Above his head, the mist solidified into a draconic rune of gleaming violet.

His heart leaped. Eso had awoken.

Knowing this technique well, Adaskar backed away into the mystic fog, putting distance between himself and Pride.

"Do not hide, soft skin."

Adaskar continued backing up, and Pride obliged by following, charging headfirst into the floating rune. Adaskar turned, leaped off the road, and slid down into what might once have been the cellar of a grand villa.

Pride didn't follow this time. Rather, he swathed the road in such flames as might have come from the volcano itself, the spreading heat uncomfortable even to Adaskar, as if Pride intended to melt the stone. And Pride kept going and going because he believed Adaskar stood in the path of the blaze.

Eso's magic showed Pride a reflection of the recent past, of Adaskar on the straight road of beaten stone, while the real Adaskar was out of harm's way but close enough that his presence would feel in the right place.

Wynedd reached out to him. *"We are ready."*

The rune's reflection ended, and Pride ceased his attack.

"Coward!" Pride bellowed.

Adaskar emerged from the cellar back onto the scorched

road. Pride rounded on him with a snarl, then Wynedd and Eso landed behind him.

Eso lifted into the air, spinning his staff. Trailing mist formed into five new runes of purple flames, tethered together so that each became the point of a pentagon. Five runes, each empowering the others, which gathered and formed a new purple sun around Eso. He thrust his staff through it, directing the power into a beam of unfathomable might.

Pride raised a defense that few could have broken – but Eso could and did. His most powerful ability smote Pride and sent him stumbling into the mountains of rubble he had created. As he slumped, a wound in his chest billowing with violet smoke, the fire in Pride's eyes went out – along with his core.

Knowing the toll such a technique would take, Adaskar dashed to Eso's side and reached him in time for the old Paragon to stumble into his arms.

Across the ruins of Aldunei, red dragons swarmed like stingers and magic collided in such bright explosions that the gray sky was lost from sight, yet the loss of the Warden sent a wave of roaring shock and grief through the ranks of the Fire Flight. Whether in fear or being freed from duress, many began to flee.

Azarin and the Elder clashed high above, but the Elder let his wroth be known.

"One Warden I can replace, but when I am finished here, nothing will remain. Only ash and scorched stone!"

Adaskar held Eso tight as the very sky trembled. Who knew what damage this much magic would work. The tormented sky now bled light of the five types as though the world had been punctured and its inner power spilled out. Ozone from the lightning burned in his nose and throat.

Adaskar craned his neck for Azarin but could not find him inside the new inferno. He reached over their bond and urged his dragon to land.

Wynedd pounded over to Eso's side. *"Rostam, we'll take you up with us."*

Just then, a dark crumpled mass hurtled down from the

inferno high above. Azarin crashed into the old senate house, throwing up a mushroom cloud of earth, rubble, and smoke.

Adaskar felt the blow as though to his own body. Golden bricks of their bond-bridge crumbled into sand. He went deaf to the world, with only a low ringing still audible between his ears.

Eso nodded and mouthed at him to go.

With a pull of magic and a mighty blast of fire from his palms, Adaskar shot high and arced forward. His only thought, his only care right then, was to reach his dragon, the panic hotter than any fire he could conjure.

He need not have feared. Even as Adaskar descended, Azarin roared, pushed up from beneath the rubble, and unfurled his wings, sending dust and debris in all directions. The panic in Adaskar's heart turned to burning pride. Azarin could take worse punishment.

He landed amid the ruins of the senate house even as the Elder's crushing spiritual pressure pushed down from overhead. The Elder descended near-vertically, his oil-fire body blacker than ever, his jaw wide and shining with molten energy.

Then another great violet rune expanded between them. The Elder's breath struck the rune, but Eso's technique held. Still the Elder came on, perhaps intending to break the rune with sheer physical force, yet four more colossal runes bloomed in the sky and clamped down upon the Elder in midair.

The runes joined. Tightened. Inside Eso's containment, the Elder writhed.

An errant bolt of pale lightning struck the runes but to no effect. From the ground came a pike of ice as broad as an oak, and it, too, shattered off the cage.

"Nothing will pass unless the seals are broken," Wynedd called. *"Save your power,"* she added, all while her own core drained at an alarming rate.

More fire dragons fled from across the city, many bleeding or flying awkwardly from injury. As the cluster of cores in Adaskar's perceptions eased, he picked out his surviving Lords and Ladies. Seven pairs were yet alive, including Dowid and

Visaeyra – her presence was away to the east, closer to the chasm.

The Mystic Paragons flew in over the rubble of the senate house. Eso stood on Wynedd's back, spinning his staff to maintain their ability.

Adaskar jumped onto Azarin's back, and they took off to join them.

"*We need to kill him,*" Azarin said, "*not hold him.*"

"*His flight already flee,*" Wynedd said, her voice straining. "*We must… we must…*"

Eso helped her, calling loudly, "If he yields to us, then the flight will be forever defeated."

"He is fire made flesh," Adaskar called back. "He's even more stubborn than me."

"That is why it will crush him all the more." Blood ran from Eso's ears and nose. He rose from Wynedd's back, floating higher until he was almost at a level with the caged Elder high above the city.

"*We must try,*" Wynedd said as she rushed to take up a position on the other side of the runic cage. Her core dwindled tangibly by the second.

Azarin beat his wings and started to ascend. To Adaskar, he said, "*Death will be too kind.*"

Trapped behind violet bars, the Elder ceased trying to break free and locked his baleful gaze upon them. Within those black and blue eyes, Adaskar found little reason left. The Elder had reverted to something primal and raw.

"*Let us try,*" Adaskar said to Azarin.

Then Adaskar, Paragon of Fire, leader of the riders of Falcaer, joined his will to his dragon, and together they made their demands in a voice that roared across the ruins of Aldunei.

"Elder, as you break the Pact, so too have you broken your flight. Your strength is diminished. Surrender to us, go back to your lands, and never again venture forth in challenge. Two Paragons you have faced here. You cannot hope to overcome the might of the Five. Be gone forever!"

Alongside his words went the spiritual check.

The Elder did not react. No roar, nor growl, nor even a scrape of his talons against his cage. A dangerous silence fell in which the dwindling sounds of battle became lost.

The world seemed to fall away, and only the Elder and the Paragons remained. The beating of Wynedd's and Azarin's wings. The whirling of Eso's staff. The labor of his breath.

Adaskar felt something run down his brow and, to his astonishment, realized it was sweat. His sword arm shook. The exertion of pressing his spirit against the Elder was the greatest task of his life. To defend a blow was one thing; to strike back in equal measure was quite another.

Wynedd's core continued to shrink.

Then the Elder met the check of will and the mix of spiritual and spoken words.

"I cannot burn out. I am THE FIRE, that which will not cease unless quenched!"

An explosion of magical power erupted from the Elder unlike anything Adaskar had perceived. Several Lords expelling all their might in a single moment could not have compared to it.

The rune cage buckled.

Eso moaned. Wynedd shrieked like a wounded animal. Her core spluttered.

"Let go!" Adaskar called, and Azarin rushed forward.

The runes broke, purple flames fell as embers, and the Elder burst free in an eruption of smoke and black flames.

Azarin raced to close to the gap, and to Wynedd's merit, she followed close behind. Adaskar could do little more on his dragon's back than Float his channels, raise his sword, and trust he'd find an opening for his steel.

Cloaked in his shadow fire, the Elder came at them head-on. Then, at the very last moment, he swerved aside. Azarin's lancing talons struck, drawing a trickle of blood from his softer belly but not gouging deep.

Behind came a crash of bodies; the breaking of bone; tearing flesh; and a wet, gargling howl.

Adaskar threw a glance over his shoulder. Wynedd and the

Elder tussled in the air, entwined like lovers, yet teeth flashed at each other's necks.

By the time Azarin turned to help, it was too late.

Wynedd's eyes rolled, and her neck slumped. Dark blood fell from her open mouth, and she fell with it.

There was no time to think before Azarin slammed into the Elder to take her place. As their talons raked at each other, Adaskar burned through his own shock to look for Eso.

He'd been floating in the air.

Sure enough, he, too, was falling.

The clawing dragons balled together, spiraling down. Adaskar flashed an image of Eso to Azarin, switched cycling to Grounding, slid down Azarin's back, his neck, then slipped free.

By chance, the thrashing dragons turned so that Adaskar passed within reach of the Elder's wing. Taking his blade in a backward grip, Adaskar cut to the side. Elder or no, dragon steel still parted membrane, sinew, and cartilage, and then Adaskar was free of the fight. He sheathed his blade, tucked his arms together, angled toward Eso, and propelled himself forward with fire from both palms.

The air screamed around him. A hundred feet from the ground, he caught Eso, braced him with one arm, then furiously blasted fire downward with his free hand to slow their descent.

The landing was clumsy. Adaskar's legs gave out from the impact, and he fell, Eso and all, hard into rubble. His vision swam, and he tasted iron in his mouth.

Then a rush of jubilant triumph surged over his dragon bond, and his world refocused.

Adaskar spat the blood from his mouth and sat up. A crash thundered somewhere out of sight, shaking the world. Debris rained around him, and he raised an arm. Old stone struck harmlessly off his Grounded, Lord's body. Far off, he saw the flames blooming high over the runes, shadow flame striving against orange-gold.

Via his dragon bond, Adaskar understood the Elder's injured wing had grounded him. The battle now raged within the ruins, but Adaskar was consumed by the soft whimpering below him.

Eso lay limp in Adaskar's arm. Blood from his ears and nose now ran in dark streams, and his neck was bruised, as though he'd been choked half to death. Adaskar pulled the old Paragon up, held him firm against his chest, and wrapped another arm around him.

Eso's voice came out as a faint shudder. "So dark..." His spirit was a ghost of what it had been.

Adaskar gulped. He felt numb. Dry tears burned in the corner of his eyes, still unable to fall. He'd witnessed many riders lose their dragon but never a Paragon. Never.

The Elder would pay for it with blood.

Approaching cores brought Adaskar back to the fight at hand. The Fire Flight descended on them, perhaps thinking them weak and defeated.

Drawing his sword, Adaskar relished proving them wrong. With his propelling flames, he cut through one in midair, landed behind the second, and pinned its tail into the earth with his biting blade. He drew deep from Azarin's core and his own spirit and formed a fire so strong it created a rushing updraft. Air from the surrounding area was sucked in to replace it, even as the howling winds from the northwest twisted the updraft around and around, forming a tornado of fire.

"To me!" he roared, cycling enough power to his throat to reach across the entire city. "To me!"

More of the Fire Flight arrived to challenge him, yet under his guiding will, the searing twister moved to meet them, scattering some, warding off others, and burning any it touched.

An Earth Lord and a Mystic Lady answered his summons, and the Fire Flight abandoned the assault, flying instead in the direction of their Elder.

Azarin still fought. His battle with the Elder could be tracked by the explosions of rubble and warring fire across the city, moving closer to the Great Chasm with every step.

"I need you," Azarin said, then his presence left Adaskar, consumed wholly by the battle.

Adaskar pulled back his will and cut his magic to the whirling fire. The tornado dissipated just as Dowid and Visaeyra landed by him. One of her eyes was closed from a deep cut along her brow and the bone of her wing-thumb had cracked, but her core remained solid.

"Go to Eso," Adaskar called. "Keep him safe. Everyone else, with me!"

Without waiting for acknowledgment, he sheathed his blade and launched himself high over the ruins, flying east to catch up to the titanic duel. A long trail of flattened ruins and crushed stone followed the path of the brawling dragons.

Countless fire dragons lay dead or dying, yet under the driving will of their Elder, those left fighting flew against the riders in a final, desperate charge.

An Earth Lord raised barriers of stone to block flames; a Mystic Lady summoned birds of arcane energy which detonated on contact; an Ice Lord extinguished their fiery breaths and cooled the air to sap their strength.

But now the shock of Wynedd's death gave way to a seething fury. Adaskar exuded a scorching will against the Fire Flight, parting the dragons as if parting a red sea.

He reached the vicinity of Azarin and the Elder's duel. Here the world was consumed by walls of black fire and columns of spinning orange flames. Even Adaskar found the smoke choking and bitter vile. Their roars put thunder to shame.

Azarin's power waned.

"I'm here," Adaskar cried across his dragon bond, thrusting himself up in a final arching flight to join the struggle. As he descended, he drew his sword, the blade gleaming like a red dawn.

Within the Elder's black eyes, that red glint sparked a panic.

With wild abandon, the Elder thrashed, almost lost his footing over the precipice of the chasm, then came down on Azarin with the last vestiges of his strength, sinking his talons deep.

Adaskar gasped, feeling as if cold knives had punctured his lungs.

Azarin staggered, then the Elder's tail slammed into him, throwing him back into the last of the standing ruins. Brick and marble collapsed onto Azarin's back leg. Blood poured from his chest, and he did not rise.

"*I'll hold him,*" Azarin said, his voice hoarse, as the Elder raised his talons for the kill.

Adaskar's scream tore his own throat. Descending fast but not fast enough, he threw his sword with all the strength in his body.

It did its job. Forced to avoid the oncoming blade, the Elder turned his attention from Azarin, who lurched up, quick as a snake, and took the base of the Elder's neck in his jaws.

Adaskar landed. Picked up his sword.

What strength remained in Azarin could not deliver a fatal bite, and the Elder threw Azarin off, then reared back, his roar half-drowned in his own smoking blood.

Adaskar leaped one last time, cutting up with his sword, up and up, until, at the top of the Elder's neck, he slashed in a wide arc, and he slashed *hard.*

The Elder staggered and swayed, his mouth open to heave in a breath he could no longer take. The blue flames in his eyes died, replaced by low candles flickering with dread. With a final effort, Adaskar drew on the reserves of his spirit and gathered it into a kick at the Elder's chest, willing his enemy, '*Down!*'

And down he went.

Over the edge of the Great Chasm the Elder fell, crashing down beneath the dense putrid fog; down, until his cries were silenced; down, until all trace of him was lost save the ringing echoes of his demise.

Standing upon the brink, Adaskar panted as the weight of his deed sank in. What remained of the Fire Flight fled in earnest, their weakened cores blinking like fireflies.

They were irrelevant now. Adaskar forgot them as he hastened to Azarin.

His dragon's majestic body lay bent and awkward. Blood oozed through the rubble piled upon his back leg. Even more pooled out thickly beneath his chest.

Adaskar dropped his sword and bent to move the bricks and marble.

"*Rostam…*"

Azarin's voice chilled Adaskar's heart.

"*Rostam…*"

Adaskar tried to draw on more magic to assist him but found only cinders. Their golden bridge seemed as ruinous as the city around them, its shine dulled to rust.

"*My body is broken.*"

Adaskar fell to his knees. He couldn't speak. Half-crawling, he managed to reach Azarin's snout and pulled himself up enough so his dragon could see him.

"You can fight it."

"*We cannot defeat… death.*"

Adaskar tried to speak, but all that came out was a blubbering sob. He fell forward, pressing himself against Azarin and rubbing his scales. All their warmth was fleeing him.

"*You must be strong.*"

That broke him. "Dooset doram, Azarin. Dooset doram."

"*I love you too.*"

Azarin's last breath stretched out into a soft sigh, almost peaceful. The remnants of their golden bridge collapsed. Adaskar's soul turned black, bleak, and bitter cold. The only heat that remained in him was in the corners of his eyes. He blinked, and tears fell down his mortal, bloodstained face.

54

HERE TO HELP

Holt cradled Aberanth's head in his lap, telling him it would be all right. The East Warden and his emeralds stayed for a time, assessing the damage to the forest, or so Holt assumed.

When the earliest pale light of dawn began shimmering through the withered trees, the emeralds gathered around Wrath's body, evenly spaced and with their necks held high. Magic bloomed in Holt's sixth sense, strong but gentle like the guiding hand of a parent to a young child. A faint, sorrowful music. As the emeralds worked, Wrath's body sank deep into the earth, out of sight, until it looked like she had never been there at all.

With little left to do, the emeralds began leaving the charred glade one by one, except for the East Warden, who trod softly back to where Holt, Ash, and Aberanth lay.

"Aberanth, if you will accept being carried, I can have drakes bring you back to the grove with us to recover."

Aberanth's eyes seemed far away. They rolled this way and that, not quite looking at either Holt or the Warden.

"Stay... stay with... Holt and Ash."

Holt sniffed. Ash made a squeaky rumble.

"Are you certain?" asked the Warden.

Holt was beyond touched, and he gladly would do all he

could for Aberanth, but he wanted to do what was right by his friend.

"The emeralds will be able to take better care of you."

"*Stay...*"

Ash's rumbling went higher.

"*If that is your will,*" the Warden said. "*Should you ever wish to return to the grove, you'll find it open to you. May you grow strong again, young dragon.*"

There seemed little more to be said. The Warden gave them a final, regretful look, then took off after the rest of his kin.

Silence at last fell in the glade. No wind, no birds, no beasts rummaging within incinerated bushes. Even their breath seemed barely audible. The loudest thing to Holt was his own heart thudding between his ears.

Everything ached, from head to toe, body and bones and soul, but of the two of them, Ash was the worst for wear, suffering sharp stabbing pains from his broken rib whenever he breathed.

"We can't stay here."

"*Where will we go?*"

"I don't know."

He got up before he was conscious of doing so. He swayed, one leg like lead and the other like jelly. Beyond the patch of healed grass where Aberanth lay, everything was black. His entire body was so thickly covered in ashes and soot Holt couldn't imagine washing the white leather and cloth clean again. He'd have to become the black rider or perhaps the gray one. What little of his left hand he could make out beneath the grime was scarlet. He tried to flex his fingers but found them numb and unyielding. It didn't hurt anymore, though he suspected the pain would return later. A trace scent of burning hair seemed to follow him, then he reached up and discovered parts of his own black hair had been singed.

As for what came next, where they might go, his mind was as blank as the barren world around him.

For lack of any ideas, he drifted back into the glade. It was hard to imagine now that he'd spent months camping here, as though such normal things were only a fantasy of his own making. Which part of the scorched earth had he knelt on tending to his pot, pan, or spit? Who could say.

He found himself drawn back to the grotto as though in search of those happier times. While the entrance had been churned up by Wrath and the fight, the descending tunnel remained largely untouched. Wisps of smoke drifted up from below.

Holt didn't like the thought of the grotto remaining exposed like this. It was Aberanth's home, and it was Holt and Ash's home as well. He didn't want his home, even the wreckage of it, left open for all manner of creatures to move into.

"Is Aberanth awake?" Holt asked Ash.

"He's sleeping now."

Then a decision would have to be made.

It was then that Holt spotted the trap door under a pile of loose dirt. He brushed the soil away to find it cracked, chunks ripped free where the hinges had been, and its handle torn away, but otherwise remarkably in one piece.

Holt took it to the mouth of the grotto's tunnel and held the door over it. It wasn't a perfect fit anymore, but maybe with a little work?

He packed earth around the narrow entrance so that the frame of the door would cover it entirely, then he set it in place and stepped back to admire the effect.

A moment later, he shook his head and was rewarded by a pulsing pain in his temple. He chided himself. What was he thinking? He must have been knocked in the head during the fight after all. How was a hunk of battered wood going to do to seal the grotto?

Seal, he thought through the punching behind his eyes. *I need to seal it.*

He moved back to the trap door again, raised his hands, drew a breath, and only then remembered that he'd never placed a spiritual seal before. How hard could it be?

'Easy,' he imagined Rake telling him, 'All just a matter of willpower.'

The memory of Rake's voice, here in the ruins of his new life, was almost too much. Rake was gone, but Holt reached for the next best thing he had. With a pinch of his spirit, he asked the blade if it could help him.

Yes.

Holt unsheathed the sword, then drew upon more of his spirit. His soul felt stiff from the battle with Wrath like a pained muscle after training. It was a good sort of ache, the feeling of being worked but not injured.

With the sword's guiding presence, Holt willed the door to remain shut, to protect his home. A spiritual check was needed for any who dared approach it, and he left what felt most fitting in the moment: 'Could you fight a Warden?' Anyone who could easily and honestly answer 'yes' to that question would be capable of breaking through his seals no matter what he left to check them.

As he did this, Holt felt the disembodied impression of his left hand moving of its own accord, his fingers flicking dexterously. When he came back to his senses, his fingers were burnt and unyielding again, but a silver mark had been left upon the door: a crescent moon, glimmering silver, though it emitted no true light at all.

That felt like the best he could do. Feeling marginally better for accomplishing something positive, he trudged back to the dragons and dropped down to check on Aberanth. The blistered scales looked sore beyond measure, but nothing in the burns appeared fatal anymore.

"I've been thinking about where to go."

Holt waited for the answer.

"Red Rock."

"Red Rock," Holt muttered. "Of course."

It was such an obvious answer he should have thought of it at once. Red Rock wasn't so far away, they'd made supply trips there over winter, and it was just the place for outcasts like them with nowhere left to go.

"How are we going to move him?"

"I've thought about that as well."

So it was that, as the morning sun rose, Holt and Ash were

ready to leave the desolation behind. Holt had managed to lay Aberanth about midway down Ash's back over the blunted space left behind from where Holt had cut one of his spine ridges. Holt had used his bundled traveling cloak, his sleeping roll, every spare garment he had, and anything else soft at all to help pad and cushion Aberanth, then secured him using the same cords he used to tie their gear onto Ash when traveling. Holt carried the remnants of his things – the smithing books Aberanth had given him, the hammer, the tongs, his pot, his damaged pan, the recipe book in his satchel. Anything he deemed non-vital, he left behind.

He kept his sword in hand, for he could not sheath and draw it readily while carrying everything else on his back.

"Ready?"

Ash grimaced, and a throb of pain from his lower rib beat harshly over their bond.

"We'll take it easy."

Their progress would have felt painfully slow in healthier times, but given their current state, Holt felt like they struck up a good pace. He walked ahead, cutting and clearing the way to make Ash's route easier. Ash's every step was as gentle as a dragon could take, and he did everything in his power not to jostle Aberanth as he drifted in and out of troubled sleep.

When they stopped at night to rest, Ash only dozed rather than risk moving in his sleep and throwing Aberanth from him, and Holt, despite his exhaustion, found he could not sleep at all. He just lay there, staring up at the canopy that blocked the stars.

No matter what he did, he couldn't shake the prickling notion that everyone who had ever scorned them, everyone who had ever warned them about breaking the rules, of not toeing the razor-thin line, had all been right. Holt and Ash had tampered in issues well above them, and for what? Falcaer may even now be burning. Thrall would be laughing, the Hive Mind elated at the feast of corpses.

They called us chaos-bringers… and look at what we've brought.

After another day of arduous progress, Aberanth seemed to come around enough to be asked to be put down, and he limped along for a few hours before he swayed from the effort. Luckily, by then, the southern border of the forest was close.

Ash was able to carry Aberanth the rest of the way, out from the trees, then up the steep rocky slope toward the hollowed-out mesa on which the people of Red Rock hid from the world.

Past pillars of red and yellow stone they trudged, beaten and filthy, winding through windswept canyons. On the final approach to the settlement, Holt immediately felt that something was wrong. He knew the sickly aura of death all too well. The stench of the blight was present, though Ash couldn't hear any buzzing wings or shambling ghouls.

As they entered the outskirts, all seemed quiet save for a single shanty home under a shelf of the ruddy rock. Holt could tell at once the blight was strong within that dwelling.

"There's seven people in there. Three of them children."

"Where's everyone else?" Holt asked grimly, fearing the whole settlement had been wiped out.

"Most of them are deeper in, past the monument to Brode and Erdra." Ash raised his ears and turned his head. *"The canyons make it harder to tell, but I think they're close to where Fiona lives."*

Holt nodded. The old woman who remembered Brode saving the settlement long, long ago was something of a town matriarch. If there had been trouble, it seemed natural that survivors would gather by her.

For now, there was an obvious task at hand. Holt approached the shack of the infected, calling out to them to try and assuage their fears.

"It's Holt," he called. "I'm here with the white dragon." The people of Red Rock had come to recognize Ash, at least. "I can help you!"

He pushed on the door, which creaked horribly. Little natural light made it inside the shack, so Holt created a gentle one from his palm.

What he saw made the bottom of his stomach fall away. The people were as sick with the blight as he'd ever seen, as sick as his father had been. Their veins were green beneath translucent skin, each one slumped or lying down, their eyes fixed far ahead and wide. The Hive Mind was perhaps already staring back at them.

Despite his aches, despite his weariness, despite everything, Holt felt a fire stir within him.

'Help the others.'

He set his baggage down, then moved to inspect the closest child, a skinny little thing, all elbows and tangled hair. The girl's chest didn't move as she breathed, her every exhale less than a whisper. He feared to move her lest he break a bone, and a new fear arose in him, one he hadn't ever needed to consider before. Would he kill her in his attempt to cure her?

The feeling was hard to place. Perhaps it was what came with being a High Champion and moving ever higher up the ladder of ascension, but the girl seemed as frail as a blade of grass between his fingers. He was a dragon compared to her.

In the past, his issue had been a lack of power to purge the blight, but now, he could not honestly attempt this without risk. Perhaps if the people weren't so far gone, but the way he pushed lunar magic into them was similar to how he channeled a Lunar Shock – a little too much, and he would surely kill them himself.

Perhaps it would be a mercy.

He groaned, struggling to clench and unclench his burned hand, knowing he could never do such a thing while there was still the slightest chance.

"You could try a Consecration," Ash suggested, sharing the memory of when Holt had used it to cure people on Sidastra's quarantine isle before the siege. Lunar power diffused through the ground would be a lot gentler than from his hands, but he had even less control of it once it left his body, and the risk remained. Still, it seemed his best option.

His sword nudged him.

Guide the magic, it suggested to him.

Holt recalled how Farsa had stepped down from Hava upon stairs of air. He couldn't create stairs out of light, but perhaps he could better control the power and positioning of his abilities using spirit. Rake had said he sometimes needed spirit to guide his Soul Blades.

Holt tapped his foot, dislodging a wisp of yellow dirt like sawdust. The ground here was rock hard, but it was still earth, not impenetrable stone.

Holt drew his sword, brought it together in both hands, and pointed the tip down. He began cycling lunar light through his channels, weaving his spirit with the motes he sent down his arms, then plunged the sword into the ground.

'Gently,' he willed. 'Cure them gently.'

The sword understood, accepting his will and his magic and adding its own guidance to the ability. A Consecration radiated out from the sword, a web of a thousand white and silver veins, throwing the shack into shadowy relief and flashing eerily in the deadened eyes of Holt's patients. As the light wove around each patient, it dimmed only to pulse every so often.

On this occasion, unlike a regular Consecration, which Holt would lay down before walking away, he stayed in place, feeding his sword a steady trickle of lunar magic. The minutes dragged on, but Holt's will remained strong, his sword a firm guiding hand, willing the magic to do as they wished.

"It's working," Ash said. "Their hearts are growing stronger."

Slowly, very slowly, the patients began to come around. One of the children was the first to blink back to life and gasped as though rising out of deep water.

The longer it went on, the more the webbed strands started to take on shapes of their own. Here and there a constellation appeared, the hut and other patterns from the nightscape of Ash's core, and new ones besides, like the outline of a long blade and a jagged rock trailing starry dots across the dark earth.

Once all his patients were awake and sitting upright, Holt cut the flow of magic to the blade and drew it from the ground. The constellations within the Consecration winked out, leaving the shack in gloom.

"If you can walk, let's head out to fresh air."

All seven followed Holt outside, and the little bony girl squeaked in fright when she saw him in the daylight. Holt looked down at himself. He was still caked in dirt, soot, and Wrath's blood.

"Sorry," Holt said. "I didn't mean to scare you."

The girl clung to a man Holt assumed to be her father.

"It's the white dragon," her father said, patting her hair. "Friends of the Green Grace."

"That's right," Holt said. "Our magic can heal the blight, and I think I've cured you. May I check each of you to make sure it's been purged?"

No one protested, so Holt went up to each of them, one by one, to listen intently for any hint of the scourge with Ash's help. Only one woman had a drop of the sickness still in her, and Holt dispelled it with a pulse of light from his hand, confident she could handle it now. Each patient bore some silver and purple markings from the lunar magic. The little girl had a silver streak that arced over one eyebrow down to the top of her cheek.

"There you are," Holt said. "Good as new, at least so far as the blight goes. I can't fix anything else."

Tears were in all their eyes, and none seemed able to find any words.

"Shall we head into town?"

The little girl's father nodded, sniffed heavily, and then they all headed deeper into Red Rock. Aberanth was still fast asleep on Ash's back.

On the way, Holt asked whether the scourge had come or just the blight. To his great sadness, he learned that scourge had recently attacked the town, several raids in quick succession.

"We weren't prepared," the girl's father said. "There's been so few attacks since the Green Grace came, and only one of note in my lifetime."

It was a worrying development. Red Rock's remoteness was its greatest defense, as the scourge were drawn toward heavily populated areas. A small, scant settlement on the fringes of the Disputed Lands shouldn't have been targeted, especially as the riders kept the Great Chasm in check.

But the Order has been distracted, it's splitting apart, and now... now who knows what's become of it?

They drew a crowd as they walked into town. They made for a curious sight. Holt looked like he'd just been through a war and back, while Ash was limping and breathing heavily with another dragon slumped over his back, all followed by seven miraculously cured, silver-marked townsfolk.

Within the center of a circle of stalls rose a thin spire of stone, such a dark yellow as to be almost gold, with a green cloth dragon wrapped around it in honor of Erdra, who had died to save them.

The Green Grace. A shame they don't have such a nice title for Brode.

Whenever Holt had come to Red Rock, there had been the tantalizing smell of tender lamb from open-air charcoal grills, but not today. There was only the haze of dry red dust and the earthy scent of sagebrush with a welcome touch of mint.

A man armed with a spear made his way through the crowd. Holt thought he might be one of Fiona's descendants, for he always wore the same ill-fitting plate armor rusting at its edges and joints, but Holt didn't know his name.

One of Holt's patients rushed to greet him. "They have cured us, Janek – look, see here," she said, rolling up the sleeves of her baggy shawl to show him. After the others displayed their own markings to him, he turned to Ash and Holt in amazement.

"You have come at a desperate time," Janek said, his tone accusing. "Since your last visit in winter, all manner of evil has befallen us."

"We're so sorry to hear that," Holt said, fearing his exhaustion made him sound insincere. "If you'll allow us to—"

"We thought you were watching over us," Janek said. "My grandmother said you would be. That's why you were coming and going."

Holt's head began pounding again. *Are we to be hated even here?*

"We were living not far from here over winter, but we had to leave. We—"

Holt stopped. He didn't have the strength to explain it all. Not now, not here in front of all of Red Rock.

"She died," Janek said, his accusation breaking into fear and grief. "You stopped coming. She died. And then the scourge came."

"Fiona passed away?" Holt asked.

Janek nodded fiercely, seemingly amazed Holt could not know. She had been Red Rock's world, a living embodiment of the Green Grace's protection.

Holt opened his mouth, then closed it again. He gazed at the faces surrounding him, hooded in shawls, dust-covered, terrified.

"We're here now," he managed to say. "We have a friend with us who's badly wounded. If you'll allow us to stay, I promise we'll fight any scourge that come. We've got..." His voice caught. "We've got nowhere else to go."

For a moment, Holt thought Janek might try to attack him, for he lowered his spear as if to thrust it forward. The man's face contorted, first in anger, then in fear, then he broke into wide-eyed relief. He dropped his spear and fell to his knees, hands up and open, his lips quivering and eyes watering.

"Thank you," Janek said, voice choked. "Thank you, Honored Rider. Thank you."

The rest of the crowd took their leader's cue, bowing or kneeling as they saw fit, a chorus of thanks and cheers for the white dragon echoing off the canyon walls.

Holt was too stunned to react at first.

Ash rumbled high in his throat.

Aberanth woke up. *"What's going on?"* he asked thickly.

Holt looked upon the man weeping in relief before him, and it made him feel oddly ashamed, oddly guilty. When they'd returned to Sidastra, he'd expected less powerful riders there to treat him with more regard. Had he wanted this from them? Would this have satisfied him?

He stepped forward and helped Janek to his feet. "Don't kneel to us."

Not after the mistakes we've made.

"We're here to help. And we're happy to do it."

55

LETTING GO

The bonfires of the dead ran the length of Redbarrow's walls, burning pile after burning pile. Rake stood just beyond the gates, looking upon Gea, her eyes closed, her expression peaceful. Given the effort required to move her body, they hadn't taken her as far out as the others, but there had been plenty of wood from the destruction to stack a dragon-sized pile for her.

Rake set the kindling alight, then stepped back and stood with his head low, his shoulders slumped. Crackling flames soon snapped at the air. At some point, Soot padded to his side, then sat quietly beside him. A little while after that, Osric also arrived.

"Rake," he said with a nod.

"Agravain."

"Not anymore."

"Oh yes," Rake said without apology.

Osric gestured to Gea. "My condolences."

Rake shrugged. "Hardly knew her. It's a shame though... a damned shame."

At least she hadn't given up to the point of not fighting.

Her wish that Orvel had abandoned his advancement still haunted Rake. What a terrible thing to wish for – to lay down, to simply stop trying.

I'll never stop trying, he promised Elya, as he'd done a thousand times before.

Some time passed in silence, and the fire kept crackling.

At length, Osric asked, "How are you recovering?"

"My head still feels like the brute kicked it in, and I'm a bit stiff." The truth was, he could hardly move his tail without wanting to gasp. "Main thing is I'm still alive."

"Hmm," Osric grunted. Somehow, it carried a wagonful of judgment.

"Let me worry about me, Grumps. I've pushed myself to the limits and beyond my whole life, long before this"—he waved a hand over himself—"ever happened."

"It's what you said up on the gatehouse that concerns me. You claimed Thrall caused your present… difficulties."

Rake gritted his teeth. "I was fine for *hundreds* of years until Thrall. Before him, I could still feel Elya in my soul."

To Rake's consternation, Osric started to laugh. It was a bit of an ugly laugh, as though he'd forgotten how to do it.

"Isn't laughing at a funeral morbid even for you?" Rake asked. When Osric didn't stop, Rake rounded on him. "What's so damned funny?"

"You. I blamed Thrall, too. For the longest time, I blamed him for everything… even the stuff before I met him. His influence made things worse, but he wasn't the cause of my woes. Blaming him makes things easy, but it doesn't do you any good. If Thrall made things worse for you, then there was something already wrong for him to stoke. You keep saying that nothing went wrong, that you did nothing wrong, yet here you still are. Freakish and soul-cursed. How has that story been working out for you all this time?"

It felt like ice water had been poured over Rake while he slept. Holt had pushed this same point, but despite all that had befallen him, the boy was still young with a brightness behind his eyes, and Rake had dismissed him. Osric was another matter altogether. If even Osric was telling him this, Osric who had been tormented by Thrall for far longer …

"You told me that truth was healing." Osric placed a fist over his heart. "You need to take your own advice."

Rake closed his eyes and looked inward. Months and months without feeling even one faint beat of Elya, not one stir of laughter, not one swoop of joy or pride.

Unbidden, the memory of Thrall's cruel voice resurfaced.

'You and Osric aren't so different. You lie to yourself.'

A twitch ran from his tail and up his spine, prickling the back of his head.

Still with his eyes shut, Rake said, "Alright, maybe... maybe I did do something wrong."

But he had no idea what it could be. He'd thought long and hard on their attempt to breach the last boundary and couldn't figure it out. If the process had started, all must have been aligned and in place. That was how every other stage of advancement worked, after all.

"Maybe it *was* my fault... somehow. I'll think on it."

And then it came. His soul *tapped*. It was the meekest feeling, like a dying breath, but it was there where there had been nothing for a long time.

Elya? Is that you?

Another light touch, like a feather tip dusting against callused skin.

Rake placed his hand over his heart. "She's there," he said thickly.

"That's good," Osric said, as if commending a report on rations.

Rake fought to steady himself. "I couldn't imagine this... everything was *perfect*... that's how we got so far in the first place."

Clearly, things hadn't been perfect.

Rake checked on Osric's own soul. There were still flutters and pangs in there, but if a soul were a heartbeat, his sounded stronger than it had months ago.

"You've done better than I thought you would," Rake admitted.

Osric grunted, then said, "You mentioned wounds. How many do you think remain?"

"That I cannot tell. These aren't visible cuts – just feelings. Only you can know what's left unresolved within you."

Osric nodded, and Soot squeaked kindly and nuzzled her rider.

The three of them stood in strangely companionable silence while Gea slowly burnt to cinders, safe forever from the clutches of the blight and the Hive Mind.

At length, Rake rolled his shoulders and smoothed down his cloak. Swathes of material had been torn away from the hem, and between this battle and his escape from the Risalian chamber, it had enough holes to negate the drag of the cloak as he ran. Such a minor benefit aside, he'd need to procure a new one.

"I must head east at what speed I can. The Mystic Elder must still be warned."

"I hope you reach her in time."

"What will you do?"

Osric shrugged. "Not sure, but now folk have tasted what's truly set against them, I don't think there'll be the same appetite to stay. I think they'll finally go."

"Well, people can be stubborn." Then, with a smirk, Rake added, "I should know."

Osric grunted a laugh. "We took one of Thrall's five down, and that's worth a lot." He offered Rake a hand. Rake took it, and this time Osric didn't see the need to squeeze quite so hard.

"Good luck to you."

"And to you, Grumps. And to you too, young one."

Soot cooed. *"We still need a rematch."*

"Well, keep working on sneaking up on people, and maybe you two can offer me something close to a good match."

With that, Rake stood tall and faced the east. His run was nothing like his full speed, perhaps not even half that, but for once, he didn't feel like killing himself in order to get the task done.

∾

The Jackal's Den was lighter than before, largely because a carrier had crashlanded in it during the battle, and now light spilled in through the gaping hole in the roof. Compared to lower Redbarrow, however, this was barely a scratch.

Osric stood at ease off to one side of the hall while the Jackal, his Hounds, and prominent townsfolk all shouted at each other. As he'd predicted, they were in favor of leaving. The only question was where they would go and how they would get there.

"Athra is strongest. We should go there."

"And drag ourselves west across the whole Frontier? Madness!"

"South. Into the forest."

"Coedhen will take us."

"We can take 'em iron."

"No city will 'ave us."

"Everywhere else is too far!"

Feeling it wasn't his place to intervene, Osric stayed quiet and listened, wondering all the while, as he'd done before, why it often took the worst-case scenario before fearful rulers or clients listened to his assessments.

When he'd led the Gray Cloaks, clients would come with gold in search of help or guidance, but frequently they didn't like his assessment. Some even seemed to think their gold was there to get their own view validated. Osric had once told the Prefect of a sea town of the Mithran Commonwealth to pack up and sail for Mithras before a swarm arrived to overrun their neglected defenses, but the Prefect had dismissed his prognosis. That town hadn't fared half as well as Redbarrow.

Throughout it all, the Jackal slumped further down his high-backed chair, and his dogs grew more agitated. Eventually, they started barking, and the Jackal had to yell to try and bring order back to the hall.

Seeing him struggle, the black dragon roared, more deeply than usual, and this at last commanded silence.

"This rabblin' is gettin' us nowhere," the Jackal said. "Goin' west is off the table. We're tryin' to flee the Frontier, not march the length of it. It'll 'ave to be south, into the forest. Wherever we go, there'll be trouble. Scum like us ain't wanted anywhere."

Some appreciative laughter accompanied this, but also some grumbling, leading the Jackal to speak louder.

"Might be our soldier 'as an idea?"

The Hounds jostled and turned to get a better look at Osric, and the Jackal waited until Osric met his eye before continuing.

"We didn't listen to ya before, and we should 'ave. So, what say ya now?"

"If you care to ask, I'd say your best hope is the Disputed Lands. You might find more welcoming people there. Only the marrow trade sets the Frontier apart. It would be a long, hard road, with no guarantee of safe harbor, and those lands can be threatened by the Great Chasm, but beggars can't be choosy, and right now, the enemy in the north squeezes harder. Going through the forest would be safer, if slower. Take all the iron and coal you can, and you'll have a better hope of bartering your way."

The Jackal seemed pleasantly taken aback. A broad smile stretched his foxlike face.

"How... *decisive.*"

Osric had always considered that better than dithering. Be efficient, be determined, be effective. Do the job and do it well.

"Whatever you decide, do it now. Every hour risks the enemy returning."

The decision was made, and the people of Redbarrow hastened to pack up what remained of their lives into every available cart. They readied every precious horse and mule and helped the wounded onto wagons with all their worldly goods packed around them. Many would leave with only the clothes on their backs.

At last, it was time, and three days after the attack on Redbarrow, Osric led the long trailing column of survivors out of the wrecked gates, past the blackened piles of the dead, before turning south and heading toward the distant Fae Forest.

The black dragon walked proudly by his side. There was a restlessness to her that hadn't been there before. He caught glimpses of her imagination running wild, envisioning aspects of her future magic now they had some understanding of it. However, he could also feel her holding back, worried about how he'd cope.

"I know I've said I hate magic, and I think I'll always be wary of it, but I'm excited to see how you'll grow."

She felt immediately better, and some of her enthusiasm spilled into him, inspiring him to draw some of her shadows across their bond. It still wasn't exactly pleasant to cycle magic through his body, but it wasn't the torture it had been. Time and training would be needed; Osric would commit to a stricter regime of meditations on the road.

He was his own worst critic, but he could admit one good thing about himself, the soldier, the general, the monster; when he decided on a thing, it got done.

Do the job and do it well.

As they marched, his mind wandered onto the question of what other wounds might have been in his soul before his ruinous bond with Thrall. Osric wasn't a wise man or a deep thinker, but even he knew the obvious. He'd known the moment Rake mentioned the subject.

He could see it all perfectly again, as though the world morphed before his eyes.

She wrapped the shawl around her head as she headed off onto the sands, her hand reaching back – did she mean for him to follow? – but he'd had to let her go. Between his own happiness and the lives of all his men, the mission, what choice had that been?

No choice at all.

Under the searing sun at the desert's edge, he'd waited for her to return, longing to see her cresting over the dunes, but she never had.

Esfir... was any of it real?

He forced the deserts back to the dark corners of his mind. Time for that later. Right now, he had a job to do.

Osric turned back to check on the column. All seemed in order, or as much order as one could expect. He and the dragon were some way ahead, while the Jackal and Petrissa headed the march proper. As he glanced at them, Osric almost caught Petrissa's eye, but they both quickly looked away.

There had been few words since the revelations prior to the battle.

The last pains had been inflicted on both sides.

What more was there to say? What more was there to do?

This time it was the black dragon who picked up on his mood. *"Do you still want to forgive her?"*

Osric pressed his lips into a hard line and knitted his brows into another. "You might ask her whether she can forgive me. She might have been neglectful and unloving, but I robbed her of her one good son... I don't see any way back from that. I don't know if there can be. I don't know if there should be."

"You saved a lot of people there."

"Can sparing blood make up for spilling it? These questions aren't for the likes of me to answer. But like you said about the brute... I want to let it go."

He turned back, and they marched on.

For the rest of that day, the sun shone hot at their backs. The black dragon slipped into Osric's shadow to cool off, and as the sun bled red into the west, he raised his arm against it, grateful when night finally fell. With the sun gone, his shadow faded, and she slid back out like oil made flesh, her individual scales almost imperceptible.

Suddenly, their bond burned fiercely.

"What's going on?"

"I think I know my name." Her voice matured a little as she spoke, making her seem less a young girl and more an adolescent. *"Only, I'm not sure whether you'd like it."*

"Does that matter? It's your name."

"Of course it matters."

"Well, go on then. Try me."

"My name," she said dramatically, *"is Nox."*

56

TO DREAM BEYOND THE DREAM

Yellow and blue filled the Toll Pass. From tabards to tents and the great banners of the Feorlen crowned swords and the Brenin white lily, while all traces of the black eagle and the golden horse had been driven out. Harroway's counterattack had succeeded, and with less bloodshed than anticipated. After the watchers of Falcaer fled, the Risalians and Athrans lost heart. Perhaps they'd feared Pyra's hungering flames would seek human flesh after gorging on the wood and metal of their siege engines.

One week on, the rapid advance was still being consolidated. Brenin troops now bolstered the ranks, and though they were less experienced than the embattled Feorlens, they were fresh and brought greater provisions to share.

King Roland, however, was not with them. Brenin's general brought tidings that His Majesty was preparing a second force with which to assault the crossing over the Red Rush. Just the threat of this would draw Risalian and Athran forces to defend the crossing, and with long-promised aid from the Skarls surely on its way, the Feorlen leadership almost dared to feel hopeful at their prospects.

However, the Master of War urged them to maintain a healthy pessimism. "Holding a fortified valley is one thing," he told a gathering of his officers, "especially against Athra's heavy horse. Pushing into Risalia for open war will be wholly different.

Even with aid from the Brenish, we'll be outnumbered until the Skarls arrive, and we have Coedhen and Mithras to consider as well. They are in tacit support of our enemy's coalition already. Should that turn into military aid, the scales will weigh heavily in their favor."

General Edric bristled his white mustache and played the notion down. The whole of the Aldunei Belt hadn't been at war since the chaos following the fall of the old republic, and before then, only when Aldunei vied for supremacy against the ancient Skarl Empire.

"We must hope that you're right, General," Talia said. "But as a rider, my instincts are to anticipate the worst. This war is becoming about far more than an old grudge or the control of trade between three nations: far more than even a rider becoming a queen. I fear it will spiral to be about everything. Should that happen, we may have to worry over the mind of the Sha of Ahar and even the Magisters of Lakara."

These issues paled in comparison to what the New Order had to consider. For now, the alliance's ships were guarded by the powers of Lucia and Druss, but if other riders came to challenge them and the Mithrans dropped the charade and deployed their entire navy, then the coasts would be lost. And while two new Champions and a Lady added power to their ranks, the New Order could only last for as long as Adaskar and Eso remained distracted.

Farsa had brought news that the Fire Flight was on the move. The last she knew of their movements, the flight had crossed the Searing Sands and turned north. Their bearing would see them fly over the eastern edge of the Great Chasm itself, though to what end no one knew.

"We know the Life Elder was also in the northern regions when he died," Talia had explained in a private meeting with Ethel and Farsa. "If Thrall is there, and Holt and Ash have succeeded, the Fire Flight might be going straight for him."

Farsa steepled her fingers at that and spoke slowly. "There were worrying reports coming out of the Frontier while I was at Oak Hall. All we can do now is wait."

And then, nine days after the retaking of the Toll Pass, Fynn arrived.

He came unexpectedly and early in the morning as part of a red company. Now assigned to his personal protection, the Queen's Guard escorted him in full force, flying a modified Feorlen banner wherein the encircling crown was purple. Eadwulf rode alongside Fynn, and the two exchanged a smirk of a secret jest as they passed through the gates.

To Talia's relief, Fynn looked better. Not quite his old self, but better. He sat upright on his horse, wearing a crimson traveling cloak like the rest of the guard. Even at a distance, it was clear his beard had been trimmed and groomed, and his golden hair had been restored to his former knot.

Given their meeting was so public, Fynn dismounted, then bowed before his wife and queen.

"Congratulations on your victory, Red Queen."

The formality made Talia wary. "You can stand up, Fynn," she said in a hushed voice, although nobody but Eadwulf was in earshot. "Why are you here?"

"I have to speak with you. Somewhere we can do so freely, if it please you."

She led him inside the fortress and climbed to the observation deck, where she ordered everyone else back inside. Eadwulf took Fynn's riding cloak from his shoulders, revealing the marriage sword dangling from his hip at an ill-fitting angle. His clothes were otherwise of his usual taste, save that he'd swapped his customary jerkin for a cheery red one instead.

"Thank you, Eadwulf," Fynn said as the Queen's Guard took their leave. Once Eadwulf was safely behind the door, Fynn added, "He's fine company that one, once you get him talking."

"You wished to speak?"

Fynn made a nervous smile, rocked on the balls of his feet, paced a little, then rocked again. He seemed to use the vista before them as an excuse to delay speaking, gazing across it before, with a sudden intake of breath, he cleared his throat and began.

"When you last came to see me, I was in a dark place. I still am. For how long... I cannot say. At the time, it felt like I was drowning, and in that struggle, I said something about my desires turning to ash. A little exuberant," he added with a sad laugh, "but after you left, I got to thinking. If my desires are ash, then I might look to those of others. You're fighting a war and other riders – all to fight the scourge in new ways. And I wondered, is that to be all there is to it?"

Talia frowned. "The aim is to defeat the scourge. I think that's lofty enough."

"But what comes after that?"

Talia blinked fast, opened her mouth, croaked half a word that died in her throat, then closed her jaw. No one had ever asked her that before. Now that she thought about it, she'd never considered it either.

The truth of why was disheartening.

"Fynn... thinking the scourge can ever be destroyed is dreaming enough."

"I once traveled the empire seeking every song of my people. Not one of the old songs ever mentioned a world without thralls. That was thought impossible until it changed. I can understand why thralldom came about. Every generation must fight with all its might lest it be the one to fail. We exert control over every minor matter so our armies, our strongholds, and our food stores are ready. The Skarls span such a huge, sparse, and harsh region that we faced those problems to an extreme. But other peoples in the world did not have thralls, and they survived incursions too.

"I traveled to Athra and Mithras, where people were said to have a say in their leaders and their laws, as the Alduneians did of old. But their peoples had scarcely more freedom than the thralls of Fjarhaff before the war. Even riders, princes, and queens have little freedom. We're all bound by our duties to the endless cycle to survive, but nothing more."

"Not if the scourge are stopped."

"If we manage the impossible, what then?" Fynn asked, his eyes widening as he opened his arms. "My mother abolished thralldom as a means to win her war. She did it with little thought; it was nigh on careless. Decades later, my people are still adapting to it. We should consider what this new world will be like, not simply blunder into it."

"And how do you envision this new world?"

Here Fynn faltered for the first time. Doubt crept across his face.

"All Freya and I wanted was to roam the world and sing and play and be together. We never truly had that chance to choose. I think a new world could allow people to shape their own lives." He bit his lip, then shrugged. "I don't know the answer to how, but it seems something worth defeating the great enemy for. It gives us a reason to, doesn't it?"

Across the dragon bond, Pyra purred.

"A new world," she said with tantalizing awe. Then she beat her wings, rising from the yard until she hovered within arm's reach of the balustrade. Her amber eyes widened to a pale gold, and she spoke to them both. *"A world free of the scourge and free from fear. Such a world could become so much more!"*

Talia went to the balustrade and, with one hand upon it, reached out to her dragon. Behind Pyra, the morning sun crested the peaks of the valley, its yellow light tinging pink off Pyra's scales before warming Talia's cheeks. From up here, looking out to the lands east of the Red Range, one could dream of a new world.

Freedom. Where a child's fate was not determined at birth, where there were no rolekeepers, and where folk might even make their voices heard as the stories of old Aldunei told.

And had she not warned Harroway and all her high officers that this war could become about everything?

Fynn's hand lightly fell upon hers. "Don't you wish you had had a choice, Talia?"

She had wished for that. Many times.

Talia met his eyes, then quickly looked back to the landscape.

"Might be your imagination is getting ahead of you, bard. But yes. Why not. Let's consider what we're really fighting for."

Pyra's purr became audible, and she leaned in so that Talia's hand could meet her snout.

"You too, Fynn."

Taken aback, Fynn reached out to her tentatively, as though afraid Pyra would pull away in mockery. She did not, and Fynn touched the tip of her nose.

"I admire your ambition."

More confident now, Fynn lightly ran his palm up her snout as far as he could reach.

"I'm honored."

Pyra sniffed, then drew back. *"I smell our food is ready."*

Then she dived back to the yard. Talia had the feeling that Pyra had just made an excuse to cover her embarrassment, although a rumbling hunger did cross their bond. It echoed inside Talia, and she found her own stomach suddenly hollow.

"Some food wouldn't go amiss, actually."

"Ah," Fynn exclaimed, rummaging at his belt. Then, as if by magic, he handed her almonds with a dark coating. "It's the last of the stash I kept aside for you," he said in answer to her stunned look.

"Thank you, Fynn."

She accepted the large handful and ate some. Spicy pleasure exploded with every bite.

"I'm glad you're back," she said. "As much as you can be. If there's anything we can do—"

"I know," he said with his old smile.

Talia ate a few more almonds. She found there was so much left unsaid, too much, but how could she ever hope to put it into words? As her treacherous mind roved over the memories of Stroef, she lingered on the moment below the castle when she'd held Freya shaking in her arms, feeling she'd failed her as much as Fynn.

"Freya said something about me," she said, almost dreamlike as she recalled the dark scene. "You said you'd tell me later. Is now the time?"

Fynn's gaze fell as he contemplated, and he tried and failed to adjust the badly askew sword at his hip.

"Not yet," he said, though he did so kindly. Then, with quick fingers, he lifted an almond from her palm and popped it into his mouth. At first, he seemed to bear it, then his face reddened, water pooled in the bottom of his eyes, and he coughed. "Your tongue must be cremated," he said through choked laughter.

Talia shoved the remainder of the almonds into her mouth and smacked her lips as she cheerfully gulped them down. Fynn stuck out his tongue in disgust and stepped away, his arms held out as though she had the blight. Smiling, Talia took a sudden step forward, and he ran in mock horror back inside the fortress.

That evening, Talia drifted to sleep easier than she had in weeks. A peaceful dark embraced her until she became aware of two figures huddled on a spit of land surrounded by a pool of pale gold water which frothed with a malty scent. Talia rushed into the pool to reach them. The water came up to her waist, and she seemed to gain no ground. Her hip and calf burned. She tried to leap but only fell headfirst into the bitter dark. A scream reached her, muffled and distorted by the water. She kicked and thrashed, and in her need, fire poured across her dragon bond, into her channels, and out through her hands and mouth. She burned all the water away. When she emerged, she found the figures were gone, and the world was on fire. Timber cracked and crashed onto stone streets; glass shattered from a hundred windows. A sulfurous stench of burning hair coated the back of her throat. Panicked, all Talia wished to do was to help, to stop the flames, her flames, but she could no longer move. The burning in her legs rose into her chest, and Pyra's presence became nothing but a wildness, unrestrained.

"Talia... Talia... Talia..." Pyra said, though her voice was much too calm. Her bond seared, and then Talia woke.

Darkness gripped her bed chamber. It had to be the middle of the night, but for some reason, her bond did burn for real.

"You must get up," Pyra said without apology. "Riders approach."

Talia leaped out of bed and scrambled for clothes and armor.

"Is it Adaskar?" she asked over her bond, even as she stretched blearily out to the extent of her magical perceptions. The strongest presence she felt was still Hava.

"No, but there are five coming. Come quickly. Mistress Hava demands all Champions join her at the river."

Talia sped through the sleepy fortress, still tightening her brigandine even as she met Pyra in the yard. Strang took off just ahead of them, and Yax was close behind on Orino. All seven Champions of the New Order touched down by the Red Rush, where they'd confronted the High Lord Dowid and his watchers. The stars above still shone in full bloom, with dawn but a distant thought.

Talia and Pyra created a small fire for them to gather around, and Farsa stepped into the firelight. She seemed about to address them when her eyes gained the faraway look of one concentrating on telepathy.

"They've just come within Hava's range. They wish to join us."

Talia's heart thudded. Could it be that their cause was finally making headway?

With bated breath, Talia took note of the bonds of the five newcomers as they landed at a safe distance downriver. They counted no Lord or Lady in their number, which was a shame, though at least one was a powerful Exalted Champion, and of fire, no less. Now they were closer, Talia felt the true extent of their cores and bonds and spirits. Each bore distressed signs and aches of recent battle.

It was the fire rider who crossed the gap between the groups to bow before Farsa and present his sword to her under the stars.

Seeming satisfied, Farsa beckoned the others to her, and so the five came to join the New Order. One even walked with a limp, and as they entered Talia and Pyra's low light, their many cuts, bruises, torn armor, and dirtied faces were thrown into relief.

They came from Drakburg, the fire rider told them. They came bearing the worst of all news. What Talia then expected to hear – whether it be that Thrall had defeated the Fire Flight or that another incursion had erupted – she could not have guessed.

The news from these riders of Drakburg would ring in her mind forever.

"Paragon Adaskar is dead."

How long he sat slumped beside Azarin's body, Adaskar did not know. It must have been little more than minutes, though, for Dowid and the others came seeking instruction.

The Storm Flight was almost upon them.

Adaskar strained, but of course, he couldn't sense them. He thought it a miracle he could sense anything at all. His insides were ice. Empty.

He was no longer the Paragon of Fire, no longer a rider. He didn't even hide the tears still flowing, ever flowing.

Adaskar told them they should leave while they had the chance and that they should leave him behind. Their protests died quickly, as the thought of moving him from Azarin's side was not to be contemplated. He asked after Eso. Dowid said Eso was with Wynedd. Adaskar nodded and said that was right.

"I hope to make you proud, Lord," Dowid said, and then the survivors of the battle left, leaving only the corpses.

Half a corpse himself, Adaskar did not move. The wind from the northwest grew stronger. Magically blind and deaf, he felt naked. Without it, nothing seemed to make sense anymore. The dragons of the Storm Flight seemed fake, as if each gray drake were an apparition.

Even when he spotted Raiden'ra, he felt nothing at all.

He no longer cared in what state Vald found him.

Vald came to him. For once, the crease on his brow and the rigidness of his face broke into plain grief. His blackened fingers trembled, and the hurt came through in this voice.

"I should have been here."

Adaskar had no reply to that. It wasn't an apology, and even if one had been offered, he wouldn't have accepted it. It was too late for that.

He squinted up at Vald. Aside from the pain in Vald's face, there was something new in his bearing. Though Adaskar could no longer feel magic or spiritual aura, *something* was different. There was something... *more*.

"You managed it?"

"I did."

Despite himself, Adaskar was impressed.

Vald gulped. "I came to do a task, but it isn't needed now." He proffered a hand. "I would still have you and Eso at my side."

Adaskar looked at the hand of his old master, then past it to where Raiden'ra stood side by side with a great dragon, one seemingly made of immaculate, reflective iron with eyes of silver jewels. Few dragons in the world could have stood by Raiden'ra with such ease, and one of them had just been slain.

Although Adaskar's magical and spiritual perceptions were gone, his natural instincts told him everything he needed to know.

"I cannot join you."

"Rostam, please. Don't make me do this."

"Make you?" At that cold rebuttal, Vald had enough grace left to be ashamed. "I swore an oath," Adaskar said, falling forward. He struggled to one knee. His hand grasped across the ground for his sword.

"Please, everything has already changed."

"Who's doing is that?"

Adaskar found the hilt, then wrapped his numb fingers around the grip.

"I swore an oath," he said, a final, rasping whisper.

He began to rise, drawing up his sword.

There came a silver flash, a deep, cold cut, then Paragon Adaskar fell into an inviting darkness and knew no more.

57

THE MOST USEFUL SERVANT

Their long search had come to an end. Now, Neveh and Nilak were on the hunt. Over the Dead Lands they flew with the Mystic Elder, three of her Wardens, ten dragons at the strength of Lord, and many Champion-powered drakes besides. Not the entire force of the Mystic Flight, but the cream of their kind.

That the great confrontation with their enemy should be fought in such desolate lands felt fitting. Beauty, Neveh thought, could be found everywhere in this wide world, even in the cracked red earth of the arid scrublands bordering the desert where the cacti grew.

The Dead Lands held nothing. The cracked earth here was ashen gray, drained of all nutrients needed for life, and so dry that the wind moved clouds of it like sand. No grass, no trees, no sound of any creature great or small; a land as lifeless as the blackened flesh of an exhumed corpse.

No distractions. And no chance of having innocents caught in the crossfire.

The fact that Thrall had chosen to emerge and make a stand here had at first aroused her suspicions. A devious foe might have taken to a populated area, where those trying to do good would hesitate to offer battle, or he might have guarded himself in a place of strength rather than come forth on such decided terms.

Nilak had offered an explanation. *"Thrall cannot know we are with them. He must think he's here to fight the Mystic Elder alone."*

This seemed reasonable. Perhaps victory against one Elder had made him overconfident; perhaps he'd forgotten he owed that fight to Neveh and her knot of uncertainty. When at last she'd detected Thrall's core at the edge of her perceptions, her own heart thumped so hard her bond grew uncomfortably hot.

Nilak roared, as did the Mystic Elder, a haunting bellow of remorse girded with new zeal. Her fellow mystics roared in reply. Their cores blazed on the magical landscape, and then the abilities of the flight took effect to prepare them.

Visions of a hundred new dragons appeared to bulk their numbers, and strange music filled the air, louder than the hundreds of beating wings. It made Neveh feel as strong as when she Grounded her body, steeling her soul.

"Guard your minds above all else," the Elder said.

Neveh and Nilak started Lifting their mote channels, shielding their minds as best they could with their frigid power. Given all that the Elder and the illusionist Eidolan had explained about Thrall's magic, Neveh was not concerned for her or Nilak's defenses, but the fight would swiftly turn ill if dragons on their side attacked each other.

Best to cut the head off the snake before the tail has a chance to rise.

Soon, Thrall's forces came into sight. A swirling black cloud of stingers and carriers seemed to blot out the sky while the rest of the swarm writhed upon the coal-dark earth. Thrall's size and blood-red scales made him easy to spot, but there were two smaller dragons as well which, at this distance, seemed like a small shining purple crystal and a glint of gold. Their cores spoke of very young drakes, lending more weight to Nilak's theory of an overconfident foe.

There were scourge-risen dragons too, a great many green, but one of their number caused her whole body to tense. The Life Elder. His scales no longer rippled but remained a dull, dead green, his eyes shone not with the season but with sickness, and the pine-needle green of his spine ridges had darkened to black. The Life Elder, risen again, now a common slave to the scourge and so to Thrall himself. In death, the Elder's magic had been reduced to a stump of its former might, but unlike the others, his living corpse still held a tangible core, one that would frighten most Lords of the Order.

Neveh looked into those sickly eyes, and despite the miles between them and her, she shivered, finding them accusing.

As the gap closed and battle drew near, Thrall spoke to them all.

"Your time is at an end, Elder. Submit to me in peace, and no mystic blood need be shed. I would spare our flight from needless harm."

The Elder hovered in the air, and her flight drew into a tight formation behind her, illusions and all. Neveh and Nilak remained a little outside the formation, magic ready, blade in hand.

If Thrall was surprised to see them, he showed no sign of it. Reaching out just to them, he said, *"It is good to see you again, Paragons. Have you come to serve me another Elder?"*

Nilak snarled. Neveh gritted her teeth.

"You are no member of my flight," the Mystic Elder said, angrier than Neveh had thought her floaty voice capable of. *"You've betrayed every kindness ever granted to you. You've raised the body of my good brother, desecrating dragons and the whole world."*

Thrall ignored her. *"I speak now to every mystic present. Fight me, and your mind will be broken, your power will become mine, and you shall be forced to submit. Join me freely, and together the Mystic Flight will become the strongest of the five."*

Nilak roared louder than any of the mystics. Rarely had Neveh felt such battle lust in her dragon.

The end had come.

Words were no longer needed.

Weaving her spiritual power with Nilak's and the cold from his core, they began channeling their most sophisticated ability.

Still airborne, plates of thick ice formed over Nilak's body, along his tail, his chest, his belly, and his neck, snapping into place over his head. The same armor encased Neveh, too, better fitting than any smith could hope to produce, more durable than steel. A frigid blue visor clamped over her face, narrowing her vision to a slit.

"*We kill him together,*" she said.

Nilak hummed in agreement.

Without final insults, the battle began. Vile bolts of scourge magic flew up from their casters upon the ground, from the mouths of the scourge-risen dragons, from the Life Elder's living corpse. The black cloud of stingers broke, and the bugs zipped toward the Mystic Flight while the coward Thrall beat his wings, pushing himself back while his minions were sent hurtling into the fight.

Nilak rushed toward the stingers, and together they froze the moisture in the air, filling the stingers' flight path with spikes and shards like so many caltrops. Buzzing mixed with shrill screams as the icy traps ravaged the swarm.

Nilak dived under the carnage, dodging the hail of bodies, broken wings, and rain of green blood to come up under the surge of stingers and raise high walls of ice to meet Thrall's ground forces. Scourge hit the walls, bunched up behind them, made themselves ripe for slaughter.

Even Paragons could not keep up such exertions forever, and they went to work with blade and claw.

This clash of armies was one of the most brutal Neveh had ever experienced. Rarely had so much magic been hurled around her. Never had such consistent pressure been applied to the defenses around her mind. Never had she fought as the sole dragon rider for such dire stakes.

Through her visor, her world was a thin, gruesome strip. Nilak tried to fly directly to Thrall, but scourge-risen dragons flew into their path, one after another, uncaring. Thrall could always raise another army in the wake of this battle.

That could not be allowed to happen.

They would not let that happen.

Foe after foe fell, each victory bringing them closer to Thrall.

Something small, shimmering like purple crystal, shot past at great speed. A shard of magic Neveh didn't recognize surged from it and struck Nilak full on his body with devastating force –

a boulder thrown from a mountaintop would have been softer. A plate of Nilak's ice armor cracked, but there was no time to repair it.

The little dragon hit hard, but Neveh could hit harder. Her lance of ice flew for it, but the dragon faded like a ghost, and the lance passed clean through it. Nilak's breath followed next and passed right through the dragon as though it wasn't there at all.

"Don't let it distract us," Neveh said, searching for Thrall in the chaos.

A glint of gold caught her eye, and then everything turned yellow, then white. Her eyes seared and tears streamed down her cheeks, dark spots flashing over a world turned white. Nilak suffered the same, and for a few moments, they hovered in the air, blinded, until they cycled magic to their eyes, dispelling the pain.

Blurry vision returned to them just in time for Neveh to see a Mystic Warden crash to the earth at Thrall's feet. His core began to pulse, almost undulating, then it seemed to grow in power as the Warden's core shrank.

Blinking heavily, Neveh feared they had made a huge mistake in meeting him here, but she had no more willing allies.

It was now, or it was never.

Nilak dove, ignoring everything sent against them, taking the attacks upon his armor, pushing through the bombardment, the teeth, the claws, almost reaching their enemy—

The Life Elder's corpse came at them, its jaws wide.

If fighting the master of the scourge in the Dead Lands was fitting, Neveh found it equally so that she should put the Life Elder down. Last time she'd made the choice to kill him but been too much the coward to do the deed herself. She owed him a second death, a definite rest, a modicum of peace.

She deflected his magic with her blade, summoned a thick lance of diamond-hard ice, reinforced with spirit, then rammed it into him, willing it to shatter his magical armor, pushing the ice deep to where his heart ought to be. The green glow in the Life Elder's eyes died; the accusation in them went dark.

Neveh clawed for breath, her bond and soul aching. Never

before had she drawn on so much power at once. She shivered, trembling all over – and not in a good way. Using spirit, she willed herself to remain seated on Nilak, screaming, even as Nilak fought to right them and look for Thrall again.

They found him far across the killing grounds, cornered by the Elder and her two remaining Wardens. Nilak roared and headed to assist.

Nothing could get in their way now.

A new presence then appeared on the magical landscape, mighty enough to shine through the stench and din of the slaughter, frigid and immense, carried upon freezing winds that ripped over the battlefield.

The Ice Elder.

Joy thundered from Nilak. *"She has come!"*

Neveh could hardly believe it. After everything Ice had said at their last meeting, she could never have expected this.

"She must have listened after all," Neveh said, letting Nilak's joy fill her and usher in a fresh push for victory. With their Elder coming, the end was all but certain.

Yet Thrall did not flee.

He must have felt Ice coming for his flank, and still he did not break from the hopeless fight.

Then Thrall laughed, a jaw-clenching rattle, as though he chewed on glass and stone, roaring across the blood-soaked battleground.

The Ice Elder descended from the north, flying right past Thrall with two Wardens supporting her. She opened her talons and gouged one Mystic Warden before swooping down upon the Mystic Elder and sinking her cold talons deep.

Neveh almost fell from Nilak in shock. For a few moments, she could neither think nor react.

Ice reached out to her. *"Thank you, child. You have been my most useful servant."*

The insult provoked Neveh into finding her voice. *"I don't serve you!"*

"You allowed my brother to die, and you've brought my sister into our clutches."

Mystic writhed, and Ice bit into her neck, not deep enough to kill, but enough to hold her in place. Blood ran hot down Mystic's flaxen scales, steaming in the aura of the Ice Elder.

Still laughing, Thrall bounded toward them like a hatchling to their first meal.

"No one," Ice said, *"has served me better."*

As the Mystic Elder squirmed feebly, Thrall loomed over her, licking his lips.

Time distorted. Everything around Neveh, every ghoul, every bug, slowed down as though pushing through thick treacle until all was almost still. Waves of mystic power burst from the Elder, her core flaring hotter than the sun of Lakara, spending her last strength in a single eruption.

Only Neveh and Nilak seemed unaffected by the distortion, and they cut forward, intending to reach the Elder and rescue her.

Ice still had the base of Mystic's neck in her jaw, but her eyes swiveled fast as though she could see this magic but could do nothing about it.

Mystic managed to twist her neck around to face the Paragons. Her violet eyes shone bright, then they rolled back.

"The true master will change," she told them, her voice harsh. *"The betrayer shall be betrayed. Death shall grip the world until balance restores it."*

The fullest force of her spiritual pressure blasted into Neveh, along with a final, quiet word from the elder, though it was no less powerful.

"Flee!"

Her core dissipated.

Neveh wanted to argue, to cry out, to fight on, but the strength in the Elder's final words burrowed into her heart. The world around her began to speed up as Nilak banked hard in a sharp turn.

For once, they were of the same mind from the outset.

Neveh looked over her shoulder to see Ice's eyes still moving quicker than the rest of her, following Neveh as she fled the battle. Then, all at once, the world returned to normal, time resumed, and the carnage returned in all its ear-splitting, bone-shaking, soul-hammering clamor.

A hundred booms of magic fought a hundred thundering roars for dominance, but Thrall's triumphant bellow won out over all else.

Neveh turned away. She did not look back, but, with building horror, she sensed Thrall's core swell, growing so fast it seemed almost to chase them as they tried to escape.

"Nilak... what have we done?"

EPILOGUE – DEFINING DESTINY

Aberanth sniffed lightly at the water in the trough, then began to drink, lapping it into his mouth with jerking flicks of his tongue, able to drink without assistance again.

Some of the tension in Holt unwound. He could feel it in his back, in his shoulders, in his heart. A slight ease, but there was still a long way to go.

"Interesting taste to this stuff," Aberanth said. *"Tingles at the back of the throat. Hmph. I wonder what its mineral content is?"*

"Folk say the stones make it rich," Holt said, recalling what Fiona had told him when he'd tried her heavy-tasting tea.

"Sodium is quite intense," Aberanth said, as though he hadn't heard Holt. *"And there's a chalkiness too."*

"I'm sure you'll figure it out in no time."

Whatever was in the waters of Red Rock, it seemed to be helping Aberanth heal through his burns. Already the pink patches on his scales were beginning to return to their old brown, and the anger of the harsher reds was cooling.

There was just one worrying thing.

"How are your vines?"

Aberanth continued licking up water as he spoke. *"Not today, Holt. Please."*

Guilt bent Holt's insides out of shape again. Ash, who was

waiting outside Aberanth's shack, supported him across their bond as though placing his wing at his back.

"I'm not a physician, but I know if you're injured, you need to move a little every day to help recover."

"This place is too rocky. Yes. Hmph. That's the real problem."

Holt picked up the jug of water he'd brought in, then set it down in front of Aberanth.

"Please try."

Aberanth snuffled, frowned at the jug, then, with a pained growl, started using his magic. Holt felt the pulses from his core, more like splutters, as he strained to cycle the magic through his body.

A single, thin, pale vine sprouted out of the dusty earth like a weed, rising slowly and lacking the dexterity with which Aberanth used to control them. The feeble vine looped through the handle of the jug, and Aberanth rasped his breath and hissed between his teeth as he began lifting it up toward the trough.

When he tried to tilt the jug to pour water, the vine shook and shuddered violently, sloshing water everywhere. The vine withered, and the jug fell. Holt caught it before it hit the floor, and Aberanth whimpered and slumped back.

Holt stood there, unable to meet Aberanth's eye. A white snout appeared at the tiny window, then the black cloth of Ash's blindfold, as though he were looking in on them.

"We understand if you can never forgive us," Ash said.

Holt nodded, his throat dry. "If we'd never come back, you might still be safe in the lab."

Though breathing hard, Aberanth's features softened. *"You had to come back. Would have been no good in letting Wrath kill you, I told you that. Maybe I should have come with you in the first place rather than staying snug in my cave.*

"But, logically speaking, things would have ended up the same – or even worse. I might have died during that chamber collapse. Assuming I survived and managed to travel all the way to the phoenix's lair, I'd have brought us back to the lab to try and save us anyway.

"I could have remained hidden for years down there but never have achieved any results. I don't need more data to know that. Safe and

sound… but alone. If it's between being alone or having you both and this danger, shocked as I am, I'll take the danger."

Holt adored the little emerald for being so kind to them; it was more than they deserved. He left Aberanth to rest. Water, food, and sleep would be the best things for him, and fortunately, the people of Red Rock had a hearty store of mushrooms that they harvested from the forest and kept dry.

Red Rock bustled again, the people more confident now Holt and Ash were here, but today Holt couldn't stomach the praise, the hopeful looks, or the gifts of food or clothing they tried to shove into his hands. Not when he knew himself to be a fraud.

None of this danger might have come were it not for us.

Sensing his want for seclusion, Ash took them far from the settlement to the top of a towering dusty-red pillar. Here, away from everything and everyone, they spent a quiet afternoon just sitting and taking in the world below. Just being together. They spoke of everything and nothing, of their close escapes, of their triumphs, and – as the ruddy sun dipped below the horizon – of their failures.

Holt flicked a stone with his foot, sending it over the edge of the pillar to crash down out of earshot.

"We got used. We were so eager to fulfill the Life Elder's task, we never really stopped to think when the Fire Elder gave us another."

To remind Holt of the situation, Ash shared the sensations of being in that chamber in the heart of the volcano, crouching in the presence of the Elder with his Wardens. The unbearable heat, the spiritual pressure crushing them, the horrible feeling of knowing there was no way to back out.

"Even if the Fire Flight understood the truth of the phoenix, they wouldn't have told us."

"You're right," Holt said, reaching to the sky with open hands as though ready to accept an answer. "But still… we made some huge mistakes. We rushed into accepting everything he told us because he was an Elder and because we were so desperate to help, to change things—"

He stopped himself from running on and on. Repeating it all

for the thousandth time now felt exhausting. Then another thought occurred to him, almost cruel, but as he considered it, he found it fair.

"I told Fynn that I had no regrets, that we'd done more good than harm. I don't think we can claim that anymore. Everyone was right about us."

"Everyone judged us without even knowing us."

"We've done the same in turn. We judged Adaskar, and he's just been trying to hold things together, as he saw it… Given what's happened, maybe he was right. Maybe Adaskar was right to try and stop us. Who on earth did we think we were?"

"The Sons of Night."

"Ash, I'm being serious."

"I know, boy. Me too. It makes sense people would think us mad because we acted mad at times – but they weren't there. They weren't in those situations. They didn't see what we did, smell it, hear it, fight it.

"I hate what's happened, but what else could we have done? Landed in Falcaer and had our bond broken? Not answered Talia's call for help? Doing nothing is no option at all. In the future, though, I say we do what we think is best. No more missions from others, no more letting anyone convince us that helping them is the right thing, not without us being absolutely certain ourselves."

Their dragon bond began to glow, and Holt felt a tingling in his chest, his soul. A warmth was spreading through him.

"Not even the Life Elder's mission?"

"Not even that. He must have misjudged his siblings to think we could have made things work. From now on, I say we set our own missions."

Holt smiled. He wholeheartedly agreed.

"We choose our own destiny now."

Holt's soul started to spin, then the dragon bond burned at the edges, threatening expansion like during their early days together. Nothing more happened, but it left Holt feeling more himself than before. There had been something almost spiritual in that decision, something he would have to ponder.

As the dying red light faded fast and the sky peeled back to reveal the cool embrace of night, Ash's ears shot up, and his tail went rigid.

"Scourge are coming."

Over their bond, Holt heard faint echoes of the shrill shrieks of scourge mingled with the bustle of life from the people of Red Rock far behind them.

Holt leaped onto Ash's back.

Although it had been long since they'd needed the guiding words for sense-sharing, Holt felt like saying them for old times' sake. Ash agreed.

"My eyes for your eyes."

"Your skin for my skin."

"My world—"

"—for your world," they said together.

The moment their senses began to weave, Holt felt a tug from the sword on his back. It wanted to join in. Holt gladly unsheathed it, the starburst patterns seeming alive with a silver fire as each of them, Holt, Ash, and the blade, gathered their spirit.

'Our wills as one.'

Holt raised his sword high, his channels brimming from cycling power, his soul bright, his dragon bond as strong as it had ever been.

Ash launched them skyward, roaring to herald the new moon, then tilted into a hurtling dive, spreading his wings and gliding through red canyons, flying fast to defend those no one else would.

AFTERWORD

Now that you've made it to the end of *Defiant*, I do hope you enjoyed the story. If you have, then I'd ask you to consider leaving a review on Amazon. Every review really does help the series out and gives Amazon a nudge to recommend it to new readers. After that, please recommend the series to any friends or family who you think would enjoy Holt and Ash's adventures. Word of mouth is still the best marketing any author can hope for.

This book was fiendishly hard to write at times, but when it was finally done, I was very happy with it. An author can work on a book forever, but there comes a point where it needs to be let loose into the world for readers to enjoy. We've got two more books to go in this series, so I've got a long road ahead. Right now, I cannot be sure when book four will be ready, but if you want to stay up to date on my progress, there are a number of places where you can do so.

I keep a progress update on my website, on my Discord server, on my subreddit, on Facebook, and via my mailing list. If you want to be sure of getting updates, I'd suggest joining my mailing list or the Discord server, as they're the most reliable. If you join either of those, you'll receive a link to a free novella about Brode and Erdra, as well as a bonus story from the world of my first series, *The Dragon's Blade*.

Lastly, many readers have emailed me asking about hardback editions and signed editions. Right now, the best way to get ahold of signed hardback editions of *Songs of Chaos* is by visiting The Broken Binding's bookstore online. I'm sure many of you have bought special editions from them already.

You can find links to all of these channels and to the signed hardbacks on my website at www.michaelrmiller.co.uk

For any Dungeons & Dragons players out there, *Songs of Chaos* has been adapted into a 5E-compatible campaign by the developer Wider Path Games. If the thought of playing as a dragon rider excites you, head over to www.widerpathgames.com, where you can pick up the game book.

Finally, if you're looking for more books from me while you wait for the next installment of *Songs*, you may wish to check out my first trilogy, *The Dragon's Blade*. It's about an arrogant dragon prince who is reborn, secretly raised by humans, and must learn to become the king his past self never was. In this series, the dragons are quite different from those in *Songs*. Here, they've taken on human form, but they're a lot stronger and faster, a bit like Captain America. Best of all, the entire trilogy is available as a combined set: that's three epic fantasy books for the price of one.

I know that was a lot to take in, so this is just a reminder that you can find all these things on my website at www.michaelrmiller.co.uk.

ACKNOWLEDGMENTS

As these books grow longer, so does the list of people I am indebted to for getting them over the line.

As always, I'm especially thankful for the developmental editing support of my friend and colleague Brook Aspden. When it comes to working through every issue, from character arcs to magic systems, I know no one better than Brook. In *Defiant*, Holt's sword would not be the same without his input.

Other mentions for their high-level feedback and ideas go to Neil Atkinson, author Phillip C. Quaintrell, and Niall Donnelly. Niall is also the moderator of my Discord server and has been invaluable in helping it run smoothly. Fresh blacksmithing consulting came from Jonathan Smidt (author of the *Dungeon Core Online* series).

Major thanks go to the copy-editor, Anthony Wright, for working an unusual schedule and battling through such a large book. Extra care was needed for those tricky accents from some of the new characters in *Defiant*, and he rose to the occasion. Any remaining errors are, of course, my own.

Thanks also to my parents and to my partner Pegah Adaskar (yes, that's where I got the name from) for reading alpha versions of Holt's chapters when they were extremely rough. My advanced reading and beta reader teams helped a lot in catching other small errors and inconsistencies, giving me insights into how the book flowed and giving me some relief that the book was actually working! A very special mention goes to Alicia White, who was truly the MVP of this process.

Randy Vargas did an absolutely stellar job with the cover art. Seriously, I have no idea how we're going to top the cover art for books 4 and 5, but if anyone can do it, it's Randy. The graphic artist and designer Bandrei was also a joy to work with again in the creation of the final cover, cover wrap and marketing images. Credit for the stunning world map goes to Soraya Corcoran.

Thanks once more to Peter Kenny for lending his incredible talents to the narration and for being such a great bloke to work with in bringing these characters to life. This time, recording took place at the Audio Always studios in Manchester, so I'd like to thank the team there for their work as well. A vital new addition to this list is my new rep at Audible, Patrick Mulligan. No amount of thanks can cover how important his work is in championing the series within Audible itself and fighting to get more exposure for the books.

Beyond the English versions of the series, I'd like to thank my foreign rights agent Helene Butler of Johnson & Alcock, who's working on getting the series translated into different languages and on finding readers all over the world.

In addition, I'd like to thank Kevin Ferrone of Wider Path Games and the team there for taking a chance on the series to adapt it into a D&D game. I hope the players are happy with it, and I hope we can update the game later on when the series is finished.

Finally, and most importantly of all, thank you for reading and listening! Authors say it all the time, but we really mean it – without you, there would be no books. The support you give in the reviews you leave, in the messages you send, and in the love for the series I see when you recommend it to others is what allows me to keep writing and to have my dream job.

My very best wishes to you all,

Michael R. Miller

ALSO BY MICHAEL R. MILLER

All my books are available in ebook, on Kindle Unlimited, in paperback and as audiobooks on Audible.

The Dragon's Blade Trilogy

An epic story of redemption, for Darnuir, an arrogant dragon prince who is reborn, secretly raised by humans, and must learn to become the king his past self never was.

1. The Reborn King

2. Two Veiled Intentions

3. The Last Guardian

The entire trilogy can also be bought in one combined ebook and audiobook bundle.

The Dragon's Blade: A Complete Epic Fantasy Series

Battle Spire

When a mysterious hacker takes control of Hundred Kingdoms, Jack Kross is trapped inside a fantasy VR world along with millions of other players. Playing the profession-based Scavenger class, and at a low level, Jack's prospects of fighting his way out are next to impossible. Crafting gear, traps and weapons, allying with a deadly dungeon master and an AI he can't fully trust, Jack is in a race against time to save not just himself but the millions of players held hostage.

Battle Spire - A Crafting LitRPG

SONGS OF CHAOS DND 5E

The developer Wider Path Games has created a way for you to role play inside the Songs of Chaos world! Take on the role of a dragon rider, battle the Scourge, and deal with sinister plots of kingdoms, dragons, Wyrm Cloaks, and more in this epic DND 5E setting!

This book contains everything players and GMs need to adventure in the Songs of Chaos world, including...

- 6 new dragon rider classes where you play the role of both dragon and dragon rider
- New Power system with more than 100 Powers to choose from
- 44 monsters that bring the world to life, including a system for turning any creature into a blight-infected monster
- A system for crafting your unique dragon rider weapon
- 14 new Special Items
- 25 engaging encounters that bring to life unique aspects of the world
- An adventure that introduces players to the Songs of Chaos RPG

You can find more information by visiting https://www.widerpathgames.com/

CPSIA information can be obtained
at www.ICGtesting.com
Printed in the USA
BVHW041631020723
666644BV00001B/1

9 781399 953122